STORIES FROM THE GREAT CHALLENGE

52 STORIES IN 52 WEEKS

MICHAEL KINGSWOOD

CONTENTS

INTRODUCTION

By way of advice, Ray Bradbury often said that a writer should write a story a week. Because it's impossible to write 52 stories without having at least one of them be good.

In the Spring of 2019, having been writing for a bit over 8 years, I decided to embark on this Great Challenge. To do so, I coordinated with a long-term professional writer that I consider a mentor, committing to sending him a story every Sunday.

Lots of people attempt this kind of challenge. Even if they don't do all fifty-two stories, it's a victory because it almost always improves their writing productivity and skill.

I crushed it.

In the year from April 2019 through April 2020 I wrote 53 fully-completed stories, with a 54th that I set aside because it was getting too long to finish in time to meet my deadline. Since then, some have been published. Some have received acknowledgement from prestigious writing contests. But most have languished on my hard drive, begging to get out into the world.

This collection is their means to escape that prison. The stories are presented in the order in which I wrote them, with two exceptions. Story #9 is a science fiction adventure entitled "Lost On

Cordant Station." It is not presented here, because it is currently under submission to a professional writing competition. In its place is another science fiction piece that I wrote later in 2020, entitled "Hermes' Kringle." The other story not presented here, story #53, has been left out for two reasons: 1) A publishing company has indicated their desire to publish it in a forthcoming fantasy publication, and 2) 52 stories is a better, more round number for the year. I trust these exceptions will not prove too obnoxious for you to overcome.

Thanks for taking the time to read my work. I very much appreciate it, and I hope you'll enjoy reading these stories as much as I enjoyed writing them.

Best Wishes,
Michael Kingswood
San Diego, California
January 2022

Enjoy the book! After you're done, please come to Michael's website and sign up for his mailing list at www.michaelkingswood.com/newsletter-signup/. Guaranteed to be spam free, he uses it to announce new releases and special promotions for his fans.

1

———

RED ORCHID

G eorge paused inside the doorway to the back patio of Gepetto's and adjusted his tie. He had selected a light blue one with silver-white polka dots, to offset the charcoal grey of his suit. It was a good look, he knew, and he knew the tie accentuated his eyes nicely. He would not normally dress up this way, but tonight he really needed to look the part. But the damn tie was tight.

Too tight, no matter how he adjusted it.

He knew it was just his nerves getting to him, but that knowledge didn't help.

Nor did it help to remind himself that he was the good guy here, blowing the whistle on some bad stuff that was going down. Whistle-blowers were celebrated, praised.

They are also crucified, said that small voice in the back of his head that he had been fighting against for weeks, the one who told him he needed to go along to get along, not risk what he had.

And maybe he was wrong, misreading things. He didn't know the full context of what was going on in his lab. Maybe...

He knew that voice was spewing bullshit. So he shoved it aside and looked around.

Gepetto's was built of brick, and the front section was two stories tall and meticulously maintained. The rear patio was a new addition, wider than the main building, with a round knee-high pool in the center, constructed from poured concrete and designed so that people could sit on the pool's lip and converse, or just watch the water spouting from the mouth of the stone trout that was breaking surface in the pool's center.

Off to the left, a white marble-topped bar dominated, with a dozen or so stools, about half of which were occupied by customers, and every sort of bottle a man could want. A slender guy with silver hair pulled back into a ponytail, in a black collared shirt with Gepetto's emblazoned on the right breast in gold, held court behind the bar.

George recognized him from somewhere, but he couldn't place where; he had never set foot in Gepetto's until tonight.

Didn't matter, he wasn't here to chat up the barkeep.

The rest of the patio was scattered with tables, ranging from settings for two to one over in the back right corner that could take eight. They were all covered in Gepetto's black and gold table cloths, with lit candles in clear glass holders in the centers, and wrought-iron chairs that looked like they would dig into a person's back and bottom.

They were mostly filled, though, and the chatter of the various conversations almost drowned out the soft music—Italian folk from the sound of it—that came from a pair of speakers on either side of the bar.

"Excuse me," came a voice from behind him, and George half-turned to see a short black-haired guy in Gepetto's staff attire with a full tray trying to get past.

"Sorry," George said and moved out of the way, stepping off the single brick stair that led from the doorway down into the patio.

The waiter swept past, and the scents of freshly-baked bread, a basil risotto—and was that veal piccata?—swept over George in the wake of his tray.

Between the step and the scents of some other person's dinner, it was like a switch threw in George's mind, and he snapped to focus.

He needed to get to it.

He swept his eyes around, scanning the various customers for his contact. Or rather, for the red orchid tucked into the hair above her left ear that she was to wear tonight, so he would know her.

He had on a similar sigil, for her benefit: a lapel button from the Boston Marathon, the one and only race of that kind he had ever run, as a bandit when he was going to college at BU.

There. The far end of the bar, last stool. A woman in a red skirt, loose for the warmth of the summer evening, and white short-sleeved, collared blouse that had the top two buttons undone. Her wavy blonde hair hung loosely past her shoulders and halfway down her back, and was held back from her face by a white hairband.

A white hairband with a red flower on the left side, just above her ear.

George drew a breath and gathered himself, then, straightening his back and pushing his shoulders back, he walked over toward her.

Wouldn't do to appear to be anything but friendly. Just a normal guy out on the town. Not at all someone out for a covert meeting that could get him fired. Or worse.

As he approached the woman, he put on a smile that he hoped was warm and open.

Stephanie was late, but Karen found she didn't mind.

They were supposed to meet up for dinner here at Gepetto's tonight, to clear the air. Karen had suggested it; hell she had almost felt like she'd begged for it. But all the same she had dreaded the meeting all day.

It wasn't every day that your best friend accuses you of trying to seduce her husband—ex-husband, Karen corrected herself, though truth be told the signatures were not yet dry on their divorce paper-work—and Karen had no idea how to react, or how to respond. She had most certainly not done that.

Never even thought of it.

But try telling Stephanie that. Their fight had been epic, all the more so since Karen couldn't understand how Stephanie would have gotten that impression and, more to the point, why she would care what her ex did, anyway.

She had made a big point about what a pussy he was, and she was so glad to be rid of him, and she was much better off. And then she goes all jealous bitch about him?

Karen lifted her glass of chardonnay to her lips and sipped, then sniffed out a snort. Stephanie probably thought Matthew would spend his life pining away after her. Instead, word was he had turned into quite the man about town.

Though how that translated into Karen trying to hook up with him, she had no idea.

"Sellers remorse," Karen murmured to herself.

She checked her watch. Half past eight, and they were supposed to meet at eight. She had given Stephanie more than enough time, and frankly Gepetto's menu was more expensive than Karen really felt like tolerating. If she wasn't going to show, there were plenty of leftovers back at her place that she could heat up, and save some money.

Karen took another look toward the doorway leading into the restaurant's main building, and did a double-take.

The guy walking over toward her section of the bar was hard to look away from. Tall, trim but not in a skinny way; he clearly worked out at least sometimes. He was clean-shaven and had sandy blond hair, and wore a well-fitted charcoal grey suit that accentuated the breadth of his shoulders nicely. The blue tie with white dots set off the tint of his eyes, making their blue all the more plain.

It registered that he was not just coming to her section of the bar —he was coming to her—at the same time as it registered that if she could tell the color of his eyes—and such beautiful baby blues!—he was already really close, and she had been staring too long, and far too obviously.

He smiled as he slid into the empty stool next to her, and a little flutter of warmth went up Karen's body.

He nodded to her. "I'm George," he said, as though he expected her to take note, and recognize him as something special.

Karen found herself nodding in return. "Karen."

"Nice to meet you, Karen."

The stool was cushioned, but barely, and the contour was off just enough that it felt awkward sitting down.

For whatever reason, that semi-uncomfortable sensation dominated George's entire consciousness for a second after the woman gave her name.

He heard himself saying rotely that it was nice to meet her, and cringed inside. That sounded dumb, considering.

It wasn't like he had never approached a woman at a bar before, but this wasn't a social call, it was business. Serious business. She didn't care if he liked meeting her or not; she was here for his information.

Although, truth to tell as he got a better look at her, he truly wouldn't mind knowing her more, and not just biblically. Her green eyes flashed with intellect and she had cute little dimples that came out when she smiled as she gave her name. To say nothing of nice boobs.

Eyes up, George. This is business.

He noticed her wine glass was about two-thirds empty at the same time as the the bartender arrived at his stool.

"Good to see you again, George," the guy said, and George cursed himself again for not remembering the guy. "What'll it be?"

George cast about, then gestured at Karen's glass. "What she's having."

The bartender gave her a look, and she said, "Chardonnay," in a tone that sounded a bit intrigued. Her right eyebrow had gone up when the bartender greeted him by name..

As the man stepped away to fill the order, George cleared his throat and said, "You've been waiting for a while," hoping that was not the case.

Karen gave a little shrug, still looking at him as though not quite able to figure him out. "Little while. I was supposed to meet someone." Her eyes flicked down as though she were annoyed, and he felt a surge of chagrin.

The guy, George, was clearly a regular here or the bartender would not have known him. Did he make it a habit of coming up to women like this here?

If he did, he seemed at ease with it, and he even managed to suss out she had been waiting on Stephanie.

"Sorry," he said. "I got caught in traffic."

The completely deadpan way he said that confirmed it. Definite player.

Some other night she might have told him to take a hike. But tonight, considering the reason she had been coming to meet Stephanie, and to be perfectly honest with herself, considering how long it had been since a guy who was worth giving the time of day to had come calling, she rather enjoyed the attention.

And though part of her said she should have found that notion off-putting—she was not there just for his amusement—instead Karen found herself even more interested in him.

The bartender brought George his wine, and George slipped him a twenty.

After getting his change and leaving a tip that was a bit bigger than completely necessary, George took a sip from this glass, pursed his lips in appreciation. A second later, he looked around quickly at the people nearby to them, then leaned in a little bit closer. "So how do we do this," he asked in a lower, almost conspiratorial, tone of voice. "Stay here, or go someplace more private?"

Karen blinked. He was getting a bit ahead of himself. But again, strangely, that just made her more intrigued. "Don't you think you should tell me something about yourself first?" She tried to make it sound teasing, but she heard a bit of a bite in her tone even as she said it.

He didn't recoil, though. Instead he cocked his head at her, and she saw confusion on his face. "I don't..." He shook his head, some of that assurance gone. So easily? That was disappointing. "I mean, you know where I work. What else matters?"

She blinked again. "I beg your pardon? Where you work?"

He was beginning to look more confused now, and he raised his left hand to tap at his lapel pin.

Karen had noted it, but hadn't really looked at it before. Boston Marathon? She frowned, shook her head. "You work for the marathon? But this is Miami. You on vacation or something?"

Now he did recoil, looking at her like she had three heads. "You *are* with the Herald." It was a statement, but it sounded like a question all the same.

Karen shook her head. "No, I'm a school teacher."

George mouthed, "What the hell," but didn't say it. Instead, his eyes flicked to her left ear, and he blinked, chagrin showing through on his face, followed by embarrassment. "That's not..." He shook his head. "Damn, I'm sorry. I was supposed to meet someone here, and I'd know her because she had a red orchid in her hair. I saw red from over there," he gestured toward the doorway, "and never looked again."

He shook his head and put on an apologetic smile.

Karen lifted her hand to the carnation she had slipped into her hair band. It was something she had been doing for years; wearing a flower to match her clothes. She'd forgotten why she started doing it, but continued because it felt like something uniquely hers about how she did herself up.

She hadn't met many other women who did the same, and could totally understand how it had confused George.

All the same, disappointment welled up within her, and embarrassment. For him and his predicament, but also for herself. She had enjoyed his come on, and now felt the fool.

Anger threatened to flare up, but she forced it down. It wasn't his fault, and it wouldn't be fair to lay into him.

Instead, she put on a reassuring smile. "Blind date?"

He gave a quick shake of his head. "No," he said and looked away from her. The first time he had truly looked fully away, his attention really elsewhere than her, since he had sat down, and Karen hated that she felt that lack. "Business," he added, and from the resigned, almost bitter way he voiced the word she got the impression it wasn't business he liked or wanted to dwell on.

He frowned and let out a sigh, then tensed, preparing to rise. "I'm sorry I disturbed you," he said. "I'll let you get back to your night."

Karen surprised herself by reaching out to lay a hand on his shoulder, stopping him from getting up.

He stopped at her touch, looking surprised as he turned his gaze back onto her.

She found herself flushing, but forced herself to say anyway, "My girlfriend stood me up, and... Well, I can't stand the idea of eating alone tonight."

Even as she said it, Karen knew it was true, and that she had been lying to herself earlier about being perfectly happy with leftovers at home, alone. Even if she couldn't make up with Stephanie—and maybe even if she could—after the emotionally draining day she'd had, she really just needed...company.

And George's promised something...she didn't know what it was.

But she really wanted him to stay, that she was certain of.

When Karen put her hand on his shoulder, George felt a rush of heat travel from where she touched him to every square inch of his body.

Her invitation redoubled that heat, and he felt sure he was flushing. "I..." He stopped, swallowed. "Are you sure? I don't want to impose."

Her fingers tightened on his shoulder and she nodded, and suddenly he saw a deep need in her eyes that reflected his own. But while his was the need to get the word out about the chicanery going on at his company, the possibly illegal and certainly dangerous things going on in the labs there, hers was....something else, but something equally real for her.

Whatever physical attraction he had felt for her—and there was enough of that—faded in the light of the sensation of mutual distress that he felt radiated from himself to her and back.

Even if she had been a land whale, he didn't think he would have wanted to say no to her request, right then.

But he did still have business to take care of.

Nodding, he said, "I'd like that. But I do need to take care of this one thing." He saw disappointment in her eyes and hurried on before she could give it voice. "Let me make one more round through, to make sure I didn't miss her. I'll come right back."

She hesitated, then nodded.

He left his wineglass on the bar, to show he would be returning. But when he turned away he had the distinct impression she thought he was shining her on.

He moved quickly through the patio, checking all the faces at the tables and the bar—and periodically glancing over to make sure Karen hadn't decided to just go—and did not see his contact anywhere. He was about to turn back to Karen, but decided he really should check the front of the restaurant, just to be safe.

He knew tomorrow he'd want to be able to say he really had put forth every effort here.

But a look through the front building was just as fruitless as his look around the patio had been. In the bar near the entrance, with its old-school mahogany finishwork and warm but dim lighting, in the main dining room, sprawling and filled with hand-carved darkly-stained tables for parties of all sizes, topped by Gepetto's tablecloths and candles, to the three private event rooms upstairs—all locked except one that was taken by a private party, or so the maitre'd said and no he couldn't go in—there was no sign of the woman from the Herald.

She must not have taken him seriously after all.

Feeling almost insulted, George headed back down the softly-lit hallway that led from the main dining room, past a connecting hallway for the bathrooms, and to the back patio.

He should have felt relief, that he didn't actually have to go through with this thing. Instead irritation that he knew would quickly turn to anger began to kindle. What was he, chopped liver, that they wouldn't even look into what he was trying to tell them? If they -

"If you're done flirting, how about we get down to business?"

The voice, low but still feminine, came from the hallway to the bathrooms just as George was walking past it.

He stopped and turned quickly, on guard.

The woman there was short, maybe five foot even, on the heavier side, and in her mid-fifties. She wore a navy blue pants suit with a white collared blouse beneath her jacket, and eyeglasses that reminded him of his High School librarian. Her hair was fully grey, and done up in a bun, and she wore a businesslike expression on her face. Her eyes shined with intellect, but he thought he saw a hint of amusement in them as well.

But what he lingered on most as he looked her over was the red orchid she had tucked behind her left ear.

He felt as though a weight had lifted, and all the doubts he had been harboring slipped away. He grinned and stepped toward her.

"Let's do this."

***

Karen highly doubted George actually meant to come back, whatever he had said. But still, she found herself hoping he would.

But after he vanished into the doorway leading back into Gepetto's main building and then didn't reappear for several long minutes, she knew for certain.

He had ditched her.

Just like Stephanie had.

Stephanie's betrayal—and her accusations were a betrayal,

whether Stephanie wanted to think so or not—had hurt. Hurt a lot. But somehow George's leaving tonight stung in a more profound way, going straight through to the core of her womanhood.

How could Stephanie actually think she could seduce her ex even if she had wanted to?

Karen shook herself. Enough of that kind of grousing. She waved the bartender, Sam, over and got the bill for her wine.

She did not spend any time on self-pity as she bent over and picked up her purse from where she had left it at the foot of her stool, fished out the money to pay for her drink, and paid Sam.

She definitely did not. She wouldn't feel that sort of thing over some random guy she'd just met and had only talked to for five minutes. That would be silly.

Looping her purse over her shoulder, Karen stepped off her stool and turned away from the bar.

George was right there.

The smile he had been wearing slipped as he looked from her to the money on the bar and to her purse.

"Leaving?" He clearly tried to hide it, but she could hear that he really didn't want her to.

She shook her head but stayed silent, not entirely trusting herself to speak. The rush of feelings when she saw he hadn't left after all— relief, annoyance with herself, anger at being annoyed, embarrassed about being angry, happiness, and lastly an odd hope—left her uncertain what she would actually say, and she had learned long ago that it was best to just shut up in those sort of situations.

His smile returned, and Karen only now saw that before, warm as his smile had seemed, it had not fully gone through to his eyes. But now, it seemed like some burden had been lifted from him, and she sensed peace flowing from him.

It felt good; it was a feeling she wanted.

"Hello Karen," George said, and held out his hand. "I'm George. I work in biotech."

Karen returned the smile and shook his hand. "It's nice to meet you, George."

2

———

DEBTS AND OBLIGATIONS

A twig snapped beneath Ben's boot and he froze in place, peering about and listening closely for signs that the unwelcome noise had alerted someone to his presence.

The pine forest around him had thinned. Where just a few dozen paces back the trees had been dense enough that he could have easily hidden from someone only a few yards away, here the trees were smaller, the trunks thinner and more widely spaced until ten or fifteen yards ahead they ceased entirely, the woods giving way to a grass-covered meadow where a lone cabin, hewn from fallen logs, stood.

Or, had stood.

Now, the breeze brought the scent of charred wood to his nose from that direction, along with another, more rank, odor that filled him with dread. The front of the cabin was blackened, the door fallen off its hinges and the lintel sagging beneath the weight of the thatched roof as the entire wall seemed to long to collapse.

A fly buzzed around his head, the only other sound besides that of his own heart and the rustling of the tree branches from that same breeze.

It was the middle of the day, and the warmth of the oncoming summer felt all the more oppressive beneath his breastplate and leathers. His shirt beneath his armor was matted to his skin, but his tongue was dry, stuck to the top of his mouth.

He should have filled his water skin from the creek he'd passed a mile back, but he had thought he could re-provision at Lewan's home, as he had so many times before.

Apparently not.

He thought of his bow, and the quiver of arrows he wore strapped to his back. But he kept the bow unstrung for travel, and by the time he would be able to ready it for use, anyone who was lurking out there could be upon him. So instead, he waited, listening and watching, with his right hand resting on the grip of his longsword.

Nothing.

He was just about to start forward again when suddenly a new sound, higher pitched and seeming to be coming from within the cabin, reached his ears.

A child. A child sobbing with fear and pain.

Biting back a curse, Ben surged forward.

He had to duck beneath the lintel to get within, then he immediately found Lewan.

He was on his back a pace inside the doorway, rent by three savage wounds in his chest, belly, and shoulder. They were not smooth, like would have come from a sword or axe, but jagged, as if whatever had struck him down had ripped at him.

It appeared Lewan had been caught unawares, because he wore only his roughly-tanned leggings and a homespun shirt, ruined now from the tears and blood. Ben knew he had a set of leathers and an old breastplate in storage here, from when Lewan had also served as one of the Jarl's rangers; had he had time he certainly would have donned them.

Ben looked down at his old comrade, his long, brown, double-braided beard lying limply atop what remained of his chest and his eyes wide in a final expression of rage and terror, and said a quick prayer for his soul. Then Ben forced his eyes away.

The child's crying had stopped; Ben had made a lot of noise coming inside. But there were only so many places to hide.

The interior was dim, despite the holes in the front wall and sagging roof that admitted the mid-day sun, and stank of blood and char and fear. What furnishings Lewan and Hilde had were upturned, their belongings strewn about. Whoever had done this had looted the place thoroughly; even Lewan's sword was gone from his hand.

Worse, Ben saw no sign of Hilde at all.

Hope flared up within him for a second as he considered that maybe she hadn't been here, that she had escaped this horror some-how. But just as quickly, Ben cast that thought away. It was too much to hope for.

A shift in the rubble in the back left corner of the cabin's single room drew Ben's attention and, moving carefully to avoid stepping on Lewan's body, he stepped over to where their eating table, upturned and leaning against a tumbled cabinet and a mound of strewn rags and bits of clothing, lay.

The rags shifted, and Ben heard a sniff from behind the table. Grasping it by a leg, Ben dragged it aside and looked behind.

Little Andros lay there, partially covered in one of Lewan's shirts and his right leg wedged beneath the fallen cabinet, his grey eyes wide with fear that gave way to recognition and then a smidgeon of hope when he saw Ben standing over him.

"Uncle Ben?" the boy said, and Ben's heart wrenched within him.

Lewan had not truly been his brother; nor had Hilde been his sister. But they had all three known each other most of their lives, and before it became clear that Hilde's heart leapt only for Lewan, Ben had fancied her.

And when he was being completely honest with himself, he admitted that one reason he still had not married was that he pined for her still. But he would never dream to impose on his friend, ruin Lewan's family. So he had left it unsaid. And now...

Sniffing, Ben forced the twisting of his heart down deep. He could grieve later; Andros needed him now.

Squatting down next to the boy, Ben nodded. "It is me, Andros," he said. "Are you hurt?"

The boy certainly looked quite the worse for wear. His shirt was torn in two places and soot smudged his cheeks. His eyes were red from crying, and his black hair was unkempt.

Ben's real concern, though, was for his leg, and Andros confirmed that fear by saying, "My leg hurts. I can't move it."

The cabinet was solid, heavy. Made from the pinewood of the surrounding forrest, probably by Lewan's own hands, it had once housed the cups, plates, bowls, and utensils that now lay strewn across the unstained planks that made up the cabin's floor. It would take a bit of effort to lift it so Andros could pull free, but it should be doable.

Ben maneuvered himself around and squatted to work his fingers beneath the cabinet's edge, then looked Andros in the eye. "This will hurt, I think. When I lift you'll need to push yourself out of the way. Can you do it?"

Andros bit his lip, but he nodded.

Ben heaved, and the cabinet lifted off Andros' leg. The boy hissed through his teeth, but pushed himself with his palms and free foot. A moment later he was clear, and Ben let the cabinet fall back to the floor.

Andros was sobbing again. It was difficult to see in the dim light, but the boy's leg looked like it was resting at a weird angle. Now that the weight of the cabinet was off it, the blood was probably flowing more freely and the boy could feel the obvious break more plainly.

Ben needed to get him outside to be sure, though.

He stepped over and offered Andros his hands. "Come. Let's get you outside."

The boy wiped his nose on the back of his hand and nodded, then took Ben's hands in his own. Ben pulled him up and a moment later, Andros was standing, weight fully on his uninjured leg as he leaned against Ben's side for support.

His breath caught in his throat then, and Ben realized he had seen the body.

"Da," Andros said, his voice breaking as fresh sobs came forth. But now he was not crying just for himself.

Surely he must have known what happened to his Da, but maybe he had held out some hope that he was mistaken.

No longer.

Ben guided the boy outside, being careful to block his view of his father's corpse as much as he could as they went. It was not sufficient, but it was the only mercy he knew to give right that moment.

Outside, he guided Andros to the corner of the cabin, away from the stink and death inside, and helped him slide down to sit on the ground, his back resting against the logs of his home and his injured leg stretched out in front of him.

It had only been a few minutes inside, but the sunlight seemed less bright, like a portion of the shadows from inside the cabin had come with them.

Ben shook his head. Imagination, and grief that he could not fully give voice to yet, were playing tricks on him.

He needed to focus. Help the boy. Find his mother.

Ben squatted down in front of Andros and looked him over. Aside from the leg, he seemed whole. Take away the way his wide eyes darted from one place to another, never settling down in one place for more than a heartbeat, and the haunted expression on his face, and he could have been a lad who had just injured himself falling out of a tree.

Take away that. Good luck with it.

"Your leg's broken. I'll need to make a splint," Ben said, and Andros' eyes stopped flitting about, coming to rest on his face. Ben leaned forward. "Where is your mother?"

Andros swallowed. Hard. Then he shook his head. "They took her."

"Who? Who did this?"

"They..." The boy shuddered. He closed his eyes for a long moment, breathing quickly. Ben was about to ask again when he spoke, slowly, distantly, with his eyes still closed. "I don't know what they were. They came at dinner time. Broke in the door. Da tried to fight them, but..." His voice broke and he trailed off for a second. Then he opened his eyes again and spoke more steadily than Ben would have given him credit for, considering what he'd been through. "Ma told me to hide. I was going for the bed, but the cabinet fell on me. I heard Da scream, saw them grab Ma... I passed out. Woke up, and you came."

"You said you didn't know *what* they were. Not who."

Andros shook his head. "Weren't people."

Ben drew back from the boy a bit, looking at him carefully.

He must have seen the doubt on Ben's face because Andros' lips compressed and his gaze sharpened as he refocused on Ben. "They had grey skin. Big pointy ears. Long arms. Big black eyes. Teeth." He shuddered again.

That made no sense. What he was describing was something out of stories; the big scary that would come get you if you didn't do as your mother told you. Not something real.

Ben frowned, considering the boy. People's minds had been known to crack if they'd gone through something horrible. He had seen it happen once, and now he was beginning to wonder whether Andros wasn't far more injured than he appeared, but in a way that could not be healed.

He was putting fanciful faces onto the men who had attacked his family, that much was certain. Ben just hoped it was only a temporary refuge from reality, and not permanent.

"You don't believe me." The boy spoke matter of factly, but his eyes were accusing.

Ben shook his head. "Of course I believe you," he lied. Straightening a bit he looked around.

All remained still and quiet, except for the buzzing flies that were beginning to congregate more heavily around the cabin.

"Did you see which way they went?"

Andros shrugged dissolutely. "Heard Ma screaming before I passed out. Came from that direction." He pointed off to his right.

Ben followed the boy's finger with his gaze and frowned. The meadow continued for a few hundred yards in that direction, then faded into forest again, the pines quickly obscuring sight as they grew more thickly than in the section of woods Ben had come through earlier, and the ground began rising more steeply as the rolling hills where Lewan set up his homestead became the Frostfang Mountains, several miles distant.

He looked up at the few clouds in the sky. It had been overcast earlier this morning, and there had been rain last night. That was probably why the cabin hadn't burned completely, and thank God it hadn't or Andros would have suffered a truly horrible end.

But the ground may have been softened enough that the raiders had left tracks.

He needed to see to Lewan's body and get Andros to town, where the healers could see to him. But if he could find the raiders' trail...

"I'm going to have a look," he said, straightening his legs fully. "Will you be alright for a few minutes?" The boy stirred, and Ben looked back to see him looking afright and opening his mouth to object. Ben added quickly, "I won't go far, and will be back before you know it." He put on a determined smile that he hoped was comforting. "I'm not leaving you."

Andros' lips quivered, but after a second he nodded.

Ben returned the nod, then hurried in the direction the boy had pointed.

He was right, there was a trail.

The grass was beaten down in several spots on the way across the meadow, and there were depressions in the soil beneath that had to be footprints, leading straight toward the woods.

Ben moved quickly, easily following the signs, but paused as he reached the first overhanging boughs of the pine trees. The grass quickly faded out, replaced by fallen needles and smaller bushes in the dimmer light beneath the forest canopy. On a patch of bare earth near the first of the tree trunks, he found another track, this one plain and obvious.

But this was not the track of a booted man. It was long and thin, with three toes, the center one longer and thicker than the outer two.

A chill went up Ben's spine, and he reached for the grip of his sword.

His mouth was already dry from the heat, but he felt it wither all the more as he began to suspect Andros' mind hadn't cracked after all.

He stopped, peering about and listening, scenting.

This far from the cabin the smell of char and death was gone, and there was only odor of dropped pine needles on the air. The tree branches above continued to sway in the breeze.

But there was something else, a subtle creaking noise from further back in the woods and uphill a ways.

Swallowing, Ben drew his sword and advanced, careful to avoid any offending twigs.

He found Hilde a hundred paces further up.

She was hanging spread eagle by her wrists, which were tied to separate boughs from two different nearby trees. Her back was to him as he approached. She was stripped to the waist, and her head drooped forward, her blonde hair falling loosely. She swung slowly back and forth, creating the creaking noise Ben had heard earlier.

"Hilde?" he said, softly, as he approached.

It was a vain hope that she still might live, but he hoped anyway. Until he rounded where she was hanging and saw the front of her.

"My God," he said.

Her chest was ripped open between her breasts. They had taken her heart.

And from the rictus of terror and pain on her face, she had been alive and awake when they'd done it.

Ben turned away, tasting bile as his stomach heaved. He pressed the fist of his left hand to his mouth to hold back throwing up, and for a moment the world swam around him.

It settled after a few moments, and when he took notice of the rest of the area, his blood went to ice.

An outcrop of rocks, half again as tall as he was and covered in moss and lichen, stood opposite where Hilde hung. A crack in their center lead into the darkness of a narrow cave. The trees seemed to ring to the crack, and there were strange glyphs, all circles and sharp angles, carved into the trunks, and into the rocks.

In the center of the ring, in front of the crack, was the stump where a great tree, twice as thick as the other pines nearby, had once stood. About knee-high, it was blackened on top, as though used for many burnings.

It was smeared in blood, and little chunks of meat.

Ben didn't need to ask what kind of meat.

There was a sense of unclean power about the place, and Ben shivered uncontrollably.

What was this place? And how had whomever used it come to be here without Lewan knowing about it?

Lewan had been a ranger like Ben, until he took an arrow to the knee. But he loved the woods so he had made his home here, and made his living as a hunter and trapper, trading the skins he took in town for items he and Hilde could not make themselves.

He knew these woods like he knew himself. He would never have settled near such a place, or allowed such a place to be made near where his family lived.

The implications of that thought struck Ben to his core. This was new, recently done. Which meant everyone else living in the valley under the Jarl's protection could be in danger as well.

Ben sheathed his sword and turned away from the crack, to Hilde. He took his knife from its sheath on his right hip, and moved to Hilde's side. He put his arm around her waist and cut first her right hand and then her left free.

Her body slid stiffly down onto him, and he lowered her gently to the ground. Then he took a moment and just looked at her face.

He had known her since he was a boy. She had brightened his life, and the lives of everyone around her. If she hadn't chosen his friend and comrade...

He put his knife away, reached out, and ran his fingers along her chin line, and realized tears were flowing down his cheeks.

"Oh, Hilde," he said, and the grief that he could not show before in front of Andros sprang up through his chest, and he hung his head, sobbing for his friend, and for his love that could have been.

A sound that wasn't a sound swept past him, and Ben jerked, his eyes snapping around to look at the crack in the rocks.

It felt like he was staring into the eyes of an enemy, but there was nothing to be seen there. All the same...

He rose, his hand going back to his sword hilt, and waited.

A sense of presence, of malice, seemed to grow all around him. He looked left and right from the corners of his eyes and saw nothing, but it seemed there must be creatures coming up on all sides.

He swallowed, and bared a couple inches of steel.

The malicious presence faded, and the sound that was not a sound echoed through the scene of atrocity again. Then it was gone completely.

Ben released his weapon, and it slid all the way home again with a soft thunk of steel contacting wood. Moving quickly, he took a moment to tie the scraps of Hilde's blouse up to cover her breasts and the horrible wound in her chest. Then he picked her up and put his back to the crack, moving as quickly as he could to get away from that place.

Ben did not begrudge Andros his tears when the boy saw his mother's body. But he did not have time to join him in his grief or offer him comfort.

Whoever it was that had taken over that section of the woods, whoever had accosted Lewan and his family the night before, had left a remnant of some sort. Ben would bet good money those people....creatures...whatever...would be back. And he and the boy needed to be far gone from here when they came.

But he couldn't just leave Lewan and Hilde to the scavengers, so he got to work.

Lewan kept a work shed at the edge of the woods behind his

cabin, and Ben was relieved to see it hadn't been looted the way the cabin had been.

Relieved, and puzzled.

But he could ponder the whys later. For now, he ladeled himself out some water from the cask Lewan always kept there and picked out a spade that Lewan had hung on the wall.

The digging was difficult, because the soil adjacent to the cabin was rocky, and he made slow progress. By the time he had a hole deep enough for Lewan and Hilde's resting place the sun was a quarter of the way from its zenith to the horizon, and his back and shoulders felt rubbery with exertion.

After he lowered the bodies into the hole, he took a few minutes to make a splint and a crude crutch from felled branches, then set about making Andros' leg as good as he could make it.

The boy winced as Ben helped him up onto his foot and crutch. Ben watched him hobble his way over to the grave site and did an inward assessment, then grimaced himself.

It was going to be a long, awkward, and uncomfortable walk back to town for the boy. But he couldn't think of a better solution, with what was available.

He joined Andros next to the grave and looked down at the two bodies. They still had some of the post-death stiffness, but their limbs had loosened enough that he had been able to maneuver them into a semblance, at least, of an embrace. They could enter eternity together, the way they had faced life.

Ben and the boy stood in silence for a time, Andros sniffing back more tears.

Unsure what to say, what if anything could help, finally Ben said, "They were my good friends. I will miss them." Then he gave the boy's shoulder a squeeze and said, "I'm sorry."

Andros placed his hand atop Ben's for a second and gave it a squeeze, then looked up at him and nodded.

Ben returned the nod, then set to filling in the grave.

After he was done, he filled his water skin from the cask in Lewan's shed, and the two of them set out for town.

Ben cast his eyes skyward as they walked into the pine forest, retracing his steps from earlier in the day.

They probably only had four or five hours until full dark, at most. It was five miles to town, through the forest and down into the valley before reaching the river that flowed past the town walls.

If it was just him, Ben could have made the journey with a couple hours to go, at least. With Andros along, injured as he was... He wouldn't give odds of them beating the darkness.

"I know it's difficult, but we need to hurry, Andros," he said. "If the creatures from last night are still around, we don't want to be caught out after dark."

The boy looked at him, and Ben could tell he noted that Ben had not called them people. Well, after that setup by the rocks, he was no longer so sure.

Andros nodded understanding, and he did put forward an effort, crutching along at a much quicker pace than Ben would have given him credit for. But he still could only go so quickly even on level terrain. And that was impossible to find out in the wild.

Still, while they made better progress than Ben had feared they would, he began to grow anxious as time wore on and they still seemed to, comparatively, crawl.

He told himself there was no reason for his concern. The raid had been fast, and deadly, and those who perpetrated it must assume their deeds would have been discovered. To come back to the same location would be insanity.

That didn't stop the nagging feeling of dread in the back of his mind. That presence back in the rocks...

"Where did you find Ma?" Andros asked. It was the first thing he had said since they set out, some time ago.

Ben looked sidelong at him, and saw the boy struggling over a root that penetrated the earth in front of him. Ben thought to help him, but he managed over it. All the same, he could tell the effort had pained Andros, and he was beginning to look as though he was tiring.

How much longer could he keep up this pace, through the pain of his leg and the crushing grief that had to be eating at him?

As long as he has to said a soft voice in Ben's head. True enough.

Andros looked back at him, an eyebrow rising expectantly, and Ben brought his thoughts back to the boy's question.

He cleared his throat as he considered how much to tell him about that gruesome place. Finally, he said, "Near an outcropping of rocks a ways up the hill on the other side of the meadow. The one with the deep crack leading into a cave?"

Andros frowned, then shook his head. "There's no cave there. The crack ends after a couple feet." He continued crutching along down the slope, silent now except for the sounds of his breathing and those of his foot and crutch disturbing the blanket of needles on the ground.

Ben stopped, watching him go on, and felt that crawling dread grow deeper.

There most definitely *had* been a cave at the end of that crack. There was no mistaking it. And that menacing presence had looked out at him from within.

But Andros had grown up in that cabin, played in the woods all around his house. He would know that place, and if he said there was no cave there...

What in God's name was going on?

Ben hurried to catch up to the boy, who had already put twenty feet between them while he was pondering. They needed to get out of these woods before nightfall. The certainty of that pulled at Ben's soul like the lead on a hunting dog.

"Push on, Andros," he said by way of encouragement. "We should be to the stream soon. We can rest for a few minutes there, but we need to keep up the pace."

Where the stream flowed, the forest parted. It was only a small parting, twenty or thirty feet at most, but after the last hour or so tramping beneath the forest canopy, to see the blue sky and the brightness of direct—or near enough—sunlight made Ben's spirits lift considerably.

The stream was only four or five feet across, but it ran swiftly through a little gulley that it had carved over countless years, creating eddies big and small as it swirled past moss-covered rocks on its way down to the valley below, where if Ben's memory served it joined with a minor tributary that then ran into the Greenflow, which flowed straight past town.

The sound of insects, always present through the woods but louder now as waterborne creatures added their buzzing to that of the flies that had seemed to follow him and Andros from the cabin, combined with that of the flowing water, gave Ben a feeling of peace that was accentuated by the scent of freshwater and the of undergrowth that fed on it.

Almost, he could forget the horror of what had occurred, a bit more than a mile to their backs.

Almost.

Ben took a moment to help Andros get seated on a small boulder that sat on the edge of the stream, and rest his injured leg on a smaller rock nearby. He gave the boy his water skin, and Andros drank deeply.

Handing it back, Andros said, "I'm hungry."

Ben's stomach growled in agreement with the boy's words, and he cursed himself for not taking the time to more thoroughly inventory the remaining contents of the cabin. It had been looted, but surely there must have been some food, even a loaf of bread, left behind.

But he hadn't looked, and so he had only the basic rations he always carried, as part of his ranger kit.

"I've got some jerky," he said, and reached into the pouch that he kept at the small of his back, where he kept his rations. He pulled out a small handful of the dried meat and passed it over to the boy, who accepted it eagerly.

Ben began gnawing on some of the jerky himself, and washed it down with a pull from his water skin.

The skin was halfway depleted, and they had a long way to go still. He turned away from Andros and bent over to fill it, but stopped when the boy spoke.

"What will become of me, when we get to town?"

Ben looked back at Andros and saw that he was looking at him with eyes that could see no hope in his future.

"Don't worry. Your father served Jarl Henri well, and the Jarl remembers that. He'll make sure the healers take good care of you."

Andros nodded, but he didn't look reassured. Swallowing, he said, "I mean..." He paused, and drew a breath. "Where will I live?"

Ben frowned. He hadn't thought of that. He'd been more focused on the immediate tasks at hand. He considered for a moment, then shrugged. "There are many families who would be honored to take you in. The Jarl will make sure you - "

"Can I live with you, Uncle Ben?"

Ben froze.

Andros was looking at him with an open expression that showed a hope that he dared not actually embrace, and Ben had no idea how to respond for a moment.

Then he shook his head. "I don't have a wife to help take care of you, Andros. I - "

"I don't care. I want to."

Ben could see that Andros meant that, but he couldn't understand why. Yes, he had been friends with Lewan, and he had known Andros for the boy's entire life. But others had -

He stopped himself in mid-thought. Actually, no. Others had *not* had the same experience with Andros. Living out away from others as they had, Lewan and his family only rarely had visitors. Ben made it a point to stop through every time he had the high elevation patrol duty, but he had no idea how many of the other rangers did the same.

Yes, it was their duty to check in on all of the Jarl's people, but there were isolated homesteads all throughout the hill lands surrounding the valley. In reality it would be nearly impossible for a patrolling ranger to check in on everyone with any regularity.

But Ben had always stopped by Lewan's place. Andros probably felt like he actually was an uncle. Or near enough to it.

Ben frowned, but found he had no argument against the earnest expression, and need, on the boy's face.

"Tell you what," he said, finally. "Let's worry about getting you to the healers and healthy for now. We can talk about what comes after later, ok?"

Andros held his gaze for a long moment, then he nodded, looking down toward the water flowing past his perch.

Ben could tell his answer wasn't at all satisfactory, but it was all he had to give right then.

He turned away from the boy and unstoppered his water skin, then bent over and lowered it into the stream to fill it.

A sound that was not a sound swept over him, and Ben stiffened.

Losing his grip on the water skin, he straightened and spun to face back the way they had come, his right hand coming to rest on the hilt of his sword.

He peered back through the trees, toward the cabin, though it was lost from view at this distance. The lengthening shadows beneath the forest's canopy suddenly seemed sinister, threatening.

Andros had noticed Ben's change in demeanor, and he straightened on his rock, his eyes widening.

"Andros," Ben said. "You said the attackers came at dinner. Was it full night?"

The boy considered for a couple heartbeats, then he shook his head. "No. It was more twilight."

Ben cursed inwardly. He was about to tell Andros it was time to go when another wave of sound that was not a sound struck him. But this time, there was a voice carried with it.

He could not hear the voice, but the words emblazoned themselves into his mind nonetheless.

Give us the boy.

Ben drew his sword and advanced two steps. The weapon was made for use with one hand, but the hilt was sized so that he could grip it with both hands if he had need to strengthen his swing.

He did so now, bringing the blade up to a high vertical guard, with his weight divided equally between his feet.

Ben moved his gaze to the left, then right, the left again, scanning the forest in front of him for movement. There was nothing. But as before, in the grove where he'd found Hilde, he sensed a presence, growing by the moment.

"Uncle Ben?" Andros' voice squeaked, pitching upward in fright.

"Show yourself!" Ben roared.

Still nothing accept for that ominous sense of presence. Of malice.

"Uncle Ben, what's wrong?"

Ben's mind raced back to the tales he'd heard as a child. The tales Andros' description of the previous night's attackers had brought back to his memory. Of the dark spirits and devils who waited to prey on the unwary, or the greedy, or the wicked.

The wicked seemed to be anyone who didn't do what their mothers told them, back in the stories of his youth. And he had scoffed at them then.

He wasn't scoffing anymore.

What had the stories said about those creatures? Their weaknesses?

He flashed to a singular fact, and he grasped onto it like a drowning man to a log.

They could not pass over flowing water.

"Andros. Go to the other side of the stream."

"Uncle Ben?"

"Do it now!"

Behind him, Ben heard Andros get up onto his crutch and struggle across the flowing water. Ben remained still, watching and listening to the woods ahead, feeling the presence back there, growing steadily.

The sound of a tumble came from behind him, and Andros let out a cry of chagrin and pain.

Ben glanced back, and saw the boy sprawled out on the far side of the stream where he had fallen.

The sound that was not a sound swept past again, and Ben felt amusement within it, and the assurance that they could not escape the presence's grasp, whatever it was.

Well. He would damn sure try.

Sheathing his sword, Ben turned and hurried back to the stream. He hopped from stone to stone across the flow, noticing with chagrin as he went that his water skin was no longer where he had dropped it; the current had swept it downstream.

He got to Andros' side and helped the boy to his foot, and his crutch.

"Are you alright?"

Andros nodded, but his eyes were frightened.

Ben didn't give him any time to ask questions. "Come. We've got to move."

The shadows were much longer now, the sky when visible through breaks in the trees turning to the pink-orange of sunset.

They were running out of time, and though they had made progress, Ben knew it wasn't enough.

He had changed tactics, choosing to follow the stream down its course to the Greenflow, rather than take the direct route through the remainder of the woods and then across the prairie lands to the bridge spanning the river just downstream of town. It added more distance to their journey, but he had reasoned if the creatures were continuing their pursuit—and he had no reason to think they were not—being near to the water might be of some aid if he and Andros had to evade them again.

Now, he was beginning to think that had been a mistake.

It was hard to estimate how far they had come in the time since crossing the stream. Two miles? Three? But their progress had slowed considerably; Andros was tiring, and finding it harder and harder to maneuver his crutch as the shadows deepened, hiding pits in the earth and tangling roots.

They were not going to make it to town before nightfall, that was certain. But if -

Andros let out a yelp and stumbled, losing grip on his crutch as he overbalanced. The yelp turned into a cry of pain when he struck the ground, his injured leg taking the brunt of the impact.

Ben rushed to his side and squatted down.

"I can't go any farther, Uncle Ben," Andros said.

Exhaustion was written all over the boy's face. And not just from the physical effort. The grief and fear of the last day had worked its foul arts on him as well, and Ben saw he was well and truly spent.

But they had to keep going.

"We can't stop here, Andros. It's not safe."

Andros shook his head, tears welling up in his eyes. "I can't."

Ben sighed and looked over his shoulder back the way they came. It was getting more difficult to see any great distance, from the loss of the light. It was nearing twilight, when the creatures had attacked yesterday, and Ben had no doubt they would be coming shortly.

Unless they truly had been stymied by the stream. But Ben would not give odds on that. For one thing, the stream did not run forever. Go far enough up into the hills and they would find its source, and skirt it.

For another, how high would that resistance stretch? Would a fallen log across the stream's gully allow the creatures passage?

For that matter, would the bridge over the Greenflow?

Regardless, he and Andros could not remain here. Even if the creatures had to go all the way to the stream's source, they would be coming. He had gained time, but not an eternity.

He looked back down at Andros and nodded. "I'll carry you then."

Andros looked to object, but Ben didn't give him time. Grasping the boy under the armpits, Ben straightened and lifted, pulling the boy up until his head was even with Ben's shoulder. Andros grunted from pain again as Ben shifted him around so that he could more effectively support the boy's weight. Then he wrapped his arms around Ben's neck and shoulders.

"This will not be comfortable," Ben said, but there was no help for it, so he set out.

The boy didn't weigh all that much, maybe forty pounds, but it wasn't long before that weight began to wear at Ben's arms and back.

Not that he wasn't used to exertion. But between digging the grave, moving the bodies, and now carrying Andros through the deepening shadows of the waning day, Ben's arms soon began quivering, his back aching from the strain of the day.

How much longer could *he* keep this up?

Suck it up, ranger, said that quiet voice in Ben's mind, echoes of his father and of the men who trained him when he first joined the Jarl's service. Echoes of Lewan, who encouraged him to not quit when the training got hardest.

Resolute, Ben focused on putting one foot in front of the other.

Ahead, it looked like the forest was thinning, and the ground began to rise. The stream, grown more broad now as it flowed downhill, bent to the right, away from that elevated place. Ben thought to continue with the stream, but there was something about that rise that triggered his memory. He had not been this way in some time, but wasn't there a rise at the edge of the woods along the bank of the Greenflow?

Perhaps they'd come farther than Ben thought.

He headed toward the rising land and thinning trees, allowing himself to indulge in a bit of hopeful thinking.

The going got more tough as the upward slope increased, but as the trees became more sparse he saw more patches of sky. The reddish-orange was fading, turning to the grey-blue of twilight. The very first, brightest stars of the night were just becoming visible.

Something tickled in the back of Ben's mind, disturbing his brief stint of enthusiasm. Something...

The hairs on his arms rose as he realized what he was feeling. The same presence as at the grove, and the stream. He stopped, looking left and right, then behind himself.

The world was a dim half-light, the shadows grown deep and

menacing as the last of the day's light drained away. He couldn't see anything, but he knew without doubt they were coming.

And just then, the sound that was not a sound echoed, and Ben's blood went to ice.

He turned a full circle, and could just barely make out the stream, now far off to his right. He thought to head in that direction.

But something passed between the trees over there.

The sound came again, noiseless and menacing, and containing a grim, resolute, and implacable malice.

"Uncle Ben," Andros said, into his ear. "There's something out there."

The boy was right. All around, back a ways in the woods but coming closer, shadows flitted from trunk to trunk, somehow clearly visible despite the growing gloom, as though they were more purely black than the mere lack of light caused by the setting sun.

They were everywhere. Except further up the rise.

Ben swallowed, forcing his growing dread down deep. "Hold on tight," he said, then turned and ran up the hill.

He could not go anywhere near as fast as normal with his burden, but Ben felt the growing certainty that even if he were able to, he could not outrun the presence that he now felt plainly, giving chase to them.

Ben's heart pounded in his ears, and his breath came in heaves. His legs burned, and his back screamed for him to lose the weight of his burden.

He ignored it, drawing on all the miseries of his ranger training, and pushed on.

They emerged from the woods near the top of the rise, and Ben for a moment felt a flash of hope. But then he reached the top, and drew up short.

This *was* the rise on the bank of the Greenflow; Ben could see the river below, and downstream to his left, maybe a mile distant, the torches of the Jarl's watchmen atop the palisade wall that ringed the town. But he had forgotten about the nearly sheer drop from the rise's top to the water, some thirty feet below.

There was no way to go forward, here.

Looking to the right, he could just spy where the stream he had been following merged with the Greenflow, a couple hundred yards away and below where they now stood.

Damn his stupidity. He should have stayed with the stream. If he had, they could be -

Andros sucked in a breath, more liked gasped, in Ben's ear. Ben turned around, and despair threatened to overwhelm him.

They were there, down in the woods and ringing his position at the top of the rise. Shadowy figures, blacker than black and emanating that malicious presence that he had felt before. But now, closer on, there was a scent about them, sickly-sweet like a body that had just begun to rot but had not completely succumbed to decay yet.

They stood there, still and watching, and Ben felt his skin crawl under their gaze.

There was a rock not far away. He bent over and set Andros down on the bare stone, freeing his arms, then took a step toward the creatures, whatever they were, and drew his blade.

"Well?" Ben said, trying to make his tone confident and fearless and not sure how well he succeeded. "Let's get to this. Face me, you devils!"

There was a stirring among the group of shadows, and then movement from directly in front of Ben and down slope, just within the trees. One of the creatures, a bit taller than the others, moved out into the open, and Ben's guts went to water.

It was just as Andros had described. Tall and lanky, rippled in muscle, with arms that stretched to just past its knees and large pointed ears that could have been horns, they rose so far on its head. Its chin was sharp and pointed, jutting out like a spear tip from the rest of its face, which was angular and chiseled. Its eyes were large, oval, and completely black, and it had a tuft of black hair atop its head. It was naked, but it needed no clothing because it was completely sexless, as far as Ben could see.

It carried a sword in its right hand. The last of the waning light seemed to flash off the blade as the creature...devil...whatever...gave it a swing, and Ben knew it was Lewan's sword the thing was wielding.

"Devil," the creature said, and it used an actual voice instead of the strange voice that was not that spoke to Ben's mind before at the stream. "Such an unimaginative term."

It moved closer, and Ben raised his sword to a high guard, moving to place himself more fully between the creature and Andros.

The creature raised its free hand, palm out toward Ben in a placating gesture. "Peace, ranger," it said. "We have no quarrel with you. We just want the boy."

The thing's voice was smooth but gravelly, like slime running across a carpenter's sanding stone. Hearing it turned Ben's stomach, and he tasted bile for a second.

He swallowed, hard. "Why? He's an innocent."

The creature shrugged. "His father made a pact with us." Its brow furrowed in a freakish imitation of amusement. "A matter of the heart that he wanted resolved in his favor. And resolve it we did," a black, wormlike tongue flicking across its lips, "for a price." The thing drew a breath. "Two nights ago he tried to renege. As a result, everything he had is forfeit. His soul, but that was forfeit already. His wife." The thing's eyes, though pupil-less, nevertheless clearly shifted from Ben to regard Andros. "His son."

"You lie."

The thing shrugged again, not responding.

"Then why did you not take Andros last night?"

"An oversight. We thought he was dead, and thus lost to us. We cannot claim a soul that is not already pledged to us unless it is taken in," the corners of its mouth turned ever so slightly upwards, "a certain way."

Ben flashed back to the scene of Hilde's death. Her heart taken out, and chopped to bits on the burned stump. His sword lowered from its guard, unbidden, as the import of the thing's words struck him to the very core of his being. Horror that he had never conceived of before, the existential dread of eternal suffering without release, welled up within him.

The thing was saying that Hilde - ?

"Your gesture at the grave site was fitting," the thing said. "They *are* together for all eternity." Its smile broadened. "With us."

"Oh God," Ben said, not realizing he was actually speaking until the words left his mouth.

"God has nothing to do with it." The mockery in the thing's voice was plain. "Stand aside, ranger, and let us claim our prize. No need for you to suffer as well."

Ben only thought he had felt grief before, at the cabin and at the place of atrocity. But even then, he had harbored some solace that though his friend and his love might have passed from this mortal realm, they lived on in the next life, in bliss eternal. If what this thing was saying was true...

"No!" he snarled, the horror and grief fusing into fury at what the twisted thing had done to his friends. "No, you shall not have him."

The thing looked at Ben for a short while, then again made another of its shrugs. "We could, perhaps, agree to a trade."

Its eyes pierced through to Ben's soul, and he knew exactly what the thing meant. "Me for him, is that what you're saying?"

"A fair deal, wouldn't you say?"

Ben snorted.

The thing looked away from him for a second, toward Andros, and its expression softened, somehow. "She would have chosen you, you know, had we not intervened. You were always first in her heart."

It was like a dagger in the chest. Ben found himself taking a half-step backwards and dropping his guard completely, the thing's words struck him so hard. "What do you say?"

The things moved forward, maintaining the distance between them. "I know all her secrets, now. She often thought of you, even while lying with your friend."

Ben's shoulders slumped. He had dreamed of being with Hilde so many times in the past, and though he had forced himself to put those desires aside for the sake of his friendship with Lewan, part of him dreamed of her still. Or had, until today. And now, to hear that she had felt the same...

He shook his head in denial.

"She no longer wishes to be with him," the thing said, and it moved closer, though Ben hardly noticed in his shock. Its tone was smoother now, like oil running down silk. "I will let you have her, the way you always wanted. And the boy will go free, to live his life in peace. Just...give yourself over."

It reached for him with its free hand, the one that had made the gesture of peace a moment ago.

It was so tempting. Visions of fantasies that he had kept close to his heart for so long swept through Ben's mind. Dancing with Hilde in the tall grass. Tickling her and kissing her. Lying with her, and making a family. All the things that could have been, and that he had longed for.

If not for this foul creature in front of him.

The temptation was strong, but it collapsed before the reality of what the thing was, and what it was really offering. What it had already done to his friends, and what it would gleefully do to him, if he let it.

"No!" he snarled again, and he swung upward with his sword.

It took the thing's arm at the wrist, and its hand went flying off into the growing night.

The devil recoiled, howling in surprise, and Ben surged forward. A backswing took the devil across its throat.

Black blood welled up from the cut, and the thing, apparently still shocked at the turn of events, raised the stump of its hand to press, futilely, against the wound.

Ben kicked it in the chest, and the thing fell backward onto the ground. Lewan's sword fell from its grasp as the devil's body slid half a dozen feet down the slope.

It spasmed for a second, then went still.

Well. That was easier than Ben thought it would be.

He moved backwards to his original spot, and flicked the black blood from his blade.

None of the other devils had moved.

"Well?" Ben called out, "Who's next? I haven't got all night."

Still they remained where they were, unmoving.

Overhead, all of the night's stars were now plainly visible. The last blue-white remnants of the day's light glimmered from the western horizon, but night had completely taken hold on the land. The moon had not yet risen, but Ben's eyes had adjusted naturally to the growing darkness, and the light of the stars was enough that he could see, dimly.

Ahead of him, and down slope, the fallen devil's body twitched, and then it sat upright. It ran its good hand across its throat, and then it rose. It hunted about in the grass of the slope for a moment, then rose and held up the hand that Ben had hewn off. Pressing it to the stump of its arm, it paused for a moment, then spread its arms wide, the fingers of both hands flexing clearly and without difficulty.

Ben watched all this, a growing numbness spreading through his body as the true enormity of his situation struck home.

The devil snarled, and Ben knew he could not win against it. Not with steel.

It advanced, and its gaze promised unimaginable torments that would surely be his. Forever.

Ben cast about, but everywhere he looked were more of the devils, moving forward now in time with their leader.

There was no escape. No way out of the trap he had run himself and Andros into.

Except one.

Slamming his sword home into its scabbard, he turned his back on the devils and sprinted toward Andros, who still sat atop his rock with an expression of utter horror on his face.

Ben didn't stop, but scooped the boy up into his arms.

And leapt off the edge of the rise.

The bottom fell out of Ben's stomach, and Andros screamed in his ear. Wind whipped past his head as he fell.

He looked down, and saw the starlight glimmering off the flowing water of the Greenflow, rushing to meet them.

At the last minute, Ben rolled his body and hugged Andros tight against him.

He hit the water with his back, and the breath rushed out of his lungs. The frigid cold of the water closed around him, and he had to restrain himself from inhaling, lest he drown.

It flashed through his head that if he had not been wearing his breastplate, the impact would have hurt like what the devil above had planned for him.

Then he struck the bottom, and he stopped being glad for that hunk of steel.

He pushed himself upward and kicked for all he was worth, his lungs burning.

Ben broke the surface, and he heard Andros gasp in a breath. He only had a second to take in his own bit of air, and then Ben sank beneath the waters again.

He released Andros, allowing the boy to float, and groped about for his knife. He needed to get his boots and his breastplate off, before it was too late.

There. The knife was free.

Moving by feel, Ben sawed at the ties on his right boot, then his left, and he kicked the heavy implements loose.

Again his feet struck the bottom, his toes oozing into the river's mud, and he pushed himself upward. The weight of his breastplate dragged at him, but he managed to kick and pull himself to the surface a second time.

He heard thrashing from off to his left, and Andros' voice calling something in a panicked tone. Then he was under again, having only time for another gasping breath.

Ben found the three straps that held his breastplate to his body on his left side, and began working them with his knife.

The first parted, and he moved on to the second, but he was beginning to lose focus. His lungs burned, and his body cried out in panic for him to take a breath, and no matter that it was only water surrounding him.

He forced the urge down, but he knew it would not be long before he would be unable to continue doing so.

He redoubled his efforts, moving the knife by feel in the blackness of the water.

The second strap parted.

He must surely take a breath now, or he would die.

The illogical thought burned through Ben's mind, and he could not force it away.

The strap. Had to get the...

It parted, and the breastplate loosened. He shrugged his way out, losing the knife in the process. But it didn't matter.

He had to get to the surface. Now.

He kicked upward. It was taking forever...

Ben broke the surface, and he let out his breath in an explosive exhalation, then heaved in a huge lungful of blessed air. Then a second.

Ah, it never felt so good, just to breathe.

But after a few seconds of bliss, the situation recalled to his mind, and he cast about in the darkness as the river's current bore him downstream.

"Andros!" he called, concern for the boy driving his earlier relief from him.

Downstream a ways, and off to the left, he heard a thrashing, then a coughing. Then, weakly, "Uncle Ben!"

He sounded weak. His broken leg had to be making it difficult to stay afloat, even if he hadn't already exerted himself past his normal limit of endurance.

"Andros!" Ben called. "Swim to me!"

He couldn't tell if the boy heard him, but it didn't matter. Ben crawled toward him, the boy's noises getting louder as he neared him.

Finally, he caught sight of the boy, just a few feet ahead.

"I'm here," Ben called, and Andros twisted around in the water, his face dipping under.

Ben reached out and grabbed hold of him, pulling him close and bearing his face clear of the choking fluid.

The boy clutched at him, and Ben almost found himself dragged under in the process. He freed his arms, and treaded water, though it was difficult with the boy's added weight on him.

"Are you alright?"

Andros shook his head, and began sobbing.

Ben couldn't blame him.

He turned to look behind them, and saw the rise they had jumped from. It was just a shadow set against other shadows in the night, and the river's current had already swept them a few hundred yards away. But he thought he saw another shadow, deeper than the blackest night, standing motionless atop the rise.

He felt the devil's gaze following them, and whatever relief he had felt in their escape fled, replaced by that existential fear he had discovered up on the rise.

Then the shadow slipped down the slope, out of sight.

They would not give up, just because he and Andros had slipped through their fingers again. They would follow, and though they could not directly cross water to get to him and the boy, they would find a way.

Probably the bridge; it crossed a good fifteen feet above the flowing water.

He didn't have a whole lot of time to come up with another plan.

"What are we going to do?" the boy said into his ear, and Ben honestly didn't have an answer.

But then he noticed that they were beginning to speed up, and he heard a low rushing sound from ahead, and he grimaced. He'd forgotten about the rapids above the city.

They were short, and not particularly difficult to navigate in a canoe. In the middle of the day.

But at night, without a boat...

He looked forward, and could see white foam a few hundred yards ahead.

He couldn't go to the left bank; the devils would be there. There was no way he could make the right bank before the rapids.

"Hold on to me," he said, kicking his feet up to the surface so he was floating on his back. "Don't let go, and keep your feet pointing downstream."

Andros seemed confused, but then he looked downstream and also saw the approaching rapids.

He screamed.

And then they were shooting through. The current jostled them, threatening to rip them apart from each other, then sucking them down a chute between unseen boulders.

He hit an eddy, and thought the worst of it was done, but then his momentum carried them through to the other side, and the current grabbed them again.

At some point, Ben got spun around, and he struck a rock on his right side.

He cried out as pain stabbed through his body, and he felt a rib give.

Then they were through, and he was panting, a mixture of pained groan and need for air driving his breaths. Andros floated next to him, sobbing again, but apparently no more injured than he already was.

Ben tried to move his arm and winced as his ribs protested the motion.

But the lights of the torches on the town's wall were drawing nearer. They needed to get to the bank before they were swept past the town, to the bridge and beyond.

Once thing was certain: their only chance of survival was inside those walls.

"Hold on tight," he said, and began crawling toward the right-hand bank.

Every movement was a lecture in pain, but slowly, seemingly inch by inch, he continued until finally, when it seemed the distance would never close, he felt mud beneath his toes and fingertips.

The bank.

Relief swept over him, and he clawed his way halfway out of the water. There he collapsed, face down in the mud, completely spent.

He wanted to just sleep, but that would only lead to their deaths. And worse than death.

So after a few minutes, Ben pushed himself up onto his hands and knees, then turned to sit on his rump. He did a quick inventory, and winced even more than he had been from the pain in his ribs.

His bow and quiver were gone. His armor was gone, and his knife. His rations and water skin were gone, and his firestarting gear. He had no boots.

But he had his sword. For all the good that would do against these devils.

He racked his brain, thinking back to all the stories he'd heard about them in his youth, and from the priests in the Temple. He had never concerned himself very much with what the priests had to say before. Yes, he believed in God—what fool didn't?—but he'd always figured God had His own concerns and didn't need Ben bothering Him with his.

Seemed a bit of a foolish way to play it, in light of today's events.

Devils couldn't pass over moving water. He thought he could reliably infer that limitation was true; he strongly suspected they would have caught him and Andros soon after their first interaction at the stream otherwise.

What else limited them?

An angel could best them, but that didn't do Ben a whole lot of good. He didn't know any angels.

They could not pass...

Ben jerked upright, and he looked at the town's palisade wall, just a couple hundred yards back from the river and downstream the same distance from where they sat, and to the place where, if it were light out, he could see the spire of the Temple's steeple, the tallest point in the town, even taller than the Jarl's palace, rising toward the sky as if trying to reach heaven itself.

They could not pass onto sanctified ground.

And a priest, or man of great faith even if not anointed, could exorcise them.

Ben grinned, feeling victory in his grasp. They just needed to get to the Temple, and the devils couldn't touch them.

He reached over and shook Andros, rousing him from where he had been dozing.

"Andros, we're almost there."

The boy looked up at him, blinking as if confused.

Ben gestured toward the palisade wall. "Town's right there. We just need to get to the temple, and we'll be safe."

Andros sat up, grunting in pain as he jarred his injured leg. But he didn't move to rise any further.

"Uncle Ben," He trailed off, looking at his feet, and the river water just past them. "My Da and Ma. It said - "

Ben cut him off, grasping his shoulder and turning it so the boy would look directly into his eyes. "Don't you believe it," he said. "Those devils serve the Father of Lies. You cannot believe anything they say. Ever." He said it as forcefully as he could short of shouting, but even as he did so, inwardly he knew he was lying to the boy.

Devils may be liars, but they had no need to lie if the truth could serve their designs. And much as he hated to think on it, Ben strongly suspected the devil had been speaking truth on that rise.

Not that it mattered. And not that Andros needed to believe it, anyway.

The boy just looked at him for a long moment. Then he nodded.

Ben got to his feet then bent over to help Andros get to his. As he rose, his splint fell to the ground, the wood forming its spine having broken at some point in the river.

Ben looked down at the tangle of cloth and broken wood, then shrugged. "We'll get you a new one in the town." Turning around he squatted down in front of the boy. "Get on my back. It will hurt, but it won't take long to get there, now."

The boy hesitated, then slipped his arms around Ben's neck. Ben looped his left arm beneath his left thigh and straightened, picking him up piggy-back, except that he let the broken leg dangle behind.

Andros hissed as the leg jangled, but he did not cry out.

Ben found he admired the lad his tolerance. His ribs had

screamed like a stuck pig when he'd lifted the boy, and it was all he could do not to drop him. But Andros bore it with a lot more resilience than Ben felt, right then. Or maybe he was just so drained from the day that he didn't really notice the pain so much.

Either way...

He got going, and quickly found himself wincing as well. Besides his rib, his left ankle felt wrong, aching as though he had turned it.

And of course, he was barefoot, and he was not used to that. Even the soft grass of the prairie land here held brambles and rocks and pits... Very quickly, his feet were seas of aches and pains.

But it didn't matter. They were almost there.

In only took a few minutes to get to the nearest corner of the palisade wall, where Ben knew there was a guard station. And sure enough, as they drew near he saw a helmeted head peering out from over the wall.

"Hello the wall," Ben called when he thought he probably would be within the circle of light cast by the various torches spaced around the wall.

The head moved, and a moment later poked out a crenellation. Ben couldn't recognize his face in the gloom, but he recognized the voice.

"Who goes there?" A second passed, then, "Is that you, Ben?"

"Aye, Toram. It's me, with Lewan's son. Need you to open the gate for us."

Toram shook his head. "Can't do it, Ben, you know that. Jarl's law: gates will remain closed from sundown to sunup."

Ben ground his teeth. "I know the bloody law. But this is a matter of life or death. We need to get to the Temple and we need the priests. Now!"

Toram pulled back inside the crenellation, and Ben heard the rumblings of a conversation. He thought he heard something about the Captain.

"Yes," Ben called up. "Call the Captain." More quietly, he said, "Get someone with a brain involved," to himself.

"Uncle Ben."

"Just a minute, Andros," Ben said as Toram stuck his head back out.

"Give me a few minutes, Ben. Need to get approval."

"Uncle Ben! The bridge!"

Ben looked downstream where, maybe a quarter of a mile past the far corner of the palisade wall, the bridge spanned the river. Watchmen manned stations on both sides, and lit lanterns every night, so the bridge was always visible from the town.

Ben couldn't see much in the way of detail, but there were shadows moving swiftly across the bridge.

And from the watch station on this side of the river, two men emerged, running for all they were worth away from their post and toward the town.

The shadows gave chase, and Ben imagined he could hear the screams of the men as the devils ran them down.

"Dammit! Toram, the bridge is overrun. Open the gate now!"

"What?"

Ben looked back toward the bridge, computing distances and time in his head, and came to a bad conclusion.

Even if the guardsmen got started opening the gate right this second, they wouldn't have it open in time for Ben and Andros to get inside before the devils got to them, or best case they wouldn't be able to make it to the Temple in time.

And even if they did, that would leave the devils to rage havoc inside the town. Ben and Andros might be safe in sanctified ground, but what about everyone else?

This wasn't going to work.

He cast around, working hard to fight off onsetting despair. Worst case, could he get back to the river and evade them there?

But to what end? They couldn't stay in the water forever, and there were no other sanctified places...

Ben spun around, looking back upstream and inland. He could just make out mounds a few hundred yards away.

The burial grounds. The priests said blessings on them every week.

"Throw me a torch!"

"What?" Toram was getting repetitive.

"Throw me a damn torch!"

A second passed, then a flaming brand came falling toward them. Ben missed catching it, and it landed in the grass at his feet. But he was able to squat down and grab it easy enough, though damn did his rib hate him for it.

"We're going to the burial grounds," Ben called up to Toram. "Get the priests, and send them to us!"

"I don't understand - "

"Send the damn priests!"

Then Ben had his back to the palisade wall, and he was running.

More like hobbling, between his feet, his ankle, and his rib. But he was moving. Fast as he could. And he didn't need to get very far. Just two hundred yards.

One hundred.

He felt the devils' presence behind them, heard the sound that was not a sound, and it carried a tinge of victory as it echoed.

Ben didn't think about it. He just ran as best he could.

And he prayed. For the first time in a long time, first time he could think of at all, if he was honest with himself. And this seemed the right time to be.

He prayed in halting words, between gasping breaths. For the strength to get there. For God to make the devils' steps stumble. For the will to, if all else failed, give Andros a merciful end, to save him from the torments the devils had planned.

The burial grounds were a series of mounds and tombs, surrounded by a simple wooden fence. There was a single entrance, on the side facing the town. It was always open, so there shouldn't be any issues getting in.

They just had to get there.

Fifty yards.

The presence was stronger now, eager, and closing in.

He heard real sounds of footfalls and rasping breathing from behind.

He didn't look back.

Twenty yards, and he could see the outline of the fence, and the entrance ahead.

"Andros, when we get there, you're going to jump off my back and get clear. Ok?"

"Ok."

Ten yards.

Ben glanced to the right, and saw one of the devils, paralleling him. To the left, and the same.

He wasn't going to make it.

Five yards.

The devils on either side turned and began veering toward him, like predators closing on prey.

Three yards.

Ben launched himself forward, diving ahead like he was going to fly through the entrance, or at least slide through it. "Andros!" he shouted as he went.

He felt the boy kick off his back, then the devil crashed into him from his right side.

Ben struck the ground and rolled onto his back, losing hold on his torch. The devil was on top of him, its lips drawing back to reveal long, razor-like teeth.

Ben punched the devil in the face with his left hand, and it recoiled. Some of its weight left him, and Ben pushed himself out from under the thing.

Or tried to. It recovered quickly, bearing down and plunging its claws into the meat of Ben's chest.

He heard himself screaming as six points of fire ignited in him, one for each of the devil's fingers. He flailed about, and his right hand came down on something hard. And warm.

The torch.

He brought it up and over, and stuck the fire into the devil's face.

It screamed, rearing backward and off of him completely, and Ben pushed himself to his feet, ignoring the fresh agony in his chest on top of all the others.

The other devil, the one from his left side, backed off as Ben waved the brand in its direction.

But there were more coming. Dozens. And Ben clearly saw the leader in their midst.

He glanced over his shoulder and saw that Andros was within the burial grounds, and had pushed himself over near to one of the mounds a few feet inside the entrance.

The devil Ben had singed came back at him, and Ben dropped back down to the ground, beneath the devil's swiping claws.

He rolled on his side twice, ignoring the screams from his ribs, then came up onto one knee, on the inside of the burial ground entrance.

He wanted to scream in triumph, but what if his memory was wrong? What if the sanctified land thing was not true?

The group of devils scraped at the dirt outside the fence, but stopped their advance. They parted as their leader came forward.

Ben rose as the devil approached and backed up, so he would be out of reach of Lewan's sword, which the devil held in his hand again. Then he grinned and spreads his hands out wide, as though showing off the burial grounds for them.

Because, well, he was.

"Sanctified land," Ben said, and couldn't hold back a smug tone as he said it.

"That means nothing," said the devil.

"Then why do you not enter?"

It did not reply, but Ben thought he could hear it grinding its teeth. If it could have seen behind itself, it would have ground them harder, because Ben saw activity around the gatehouse.

"It makes no difference," the devil said. "You can't stay in there forever."

Ben shrugged. Looking to his left, he saw a post driven into the ground with a sconce meant to hold torches. He stuck his torch into the sconce and said, "I've got no place to be." Then he took a few steps over to where Andros sat with his back to the mound and sat down next to him.

"But I've been remembering a thing or two about you lot," Ben said as he got situated. "You can't stay here forever, can you? Once you're summoned, the doorway closes after a few days, and," he snapped his fingers, "back to the Pit with you."

The devil just glowered at him.

"Unless a priest exorcises you first. Speaking of which," he gestured toward the town, where the gate was now open and a troop of men was hurrying forward, toward the burial grounds, "here they come now."

The devil looked behind itself, as did its fellows. Ben could tell the rank and file were becoming uncomfortable now. They bounced back and forth on their feet, and it looked like the only thing keeping them from running was their leader's presence.

It turned baleful eyes back on Ben. "This isn't over, human. There is always some fool who wants to make a deal, and summons us. Next time that happens, we will remember you." He shifted his gaze to Andros, re-emphasizing the threat. "Both of you."

Ben shrugged again. "When that happens, I'll look forward to seeing you again. But for now, if you don't want to go back to roasting sooner than absolutely necessary, you'll get out of my sight." He paused, the added, "Now."

The devil looked at Ben for a long few heartbeats, then turned its gaze back toward the men advancing from the town. They were approaching quickly, and Ben could see, in addition to half a dozen of the Jarl's guardsmen, a quartet of men in the white and gold raiment of the priesthood.

The devil considered for a bit, and Ben almost thought it had decided to stay and make a fight of it, to test the priests' faith maybe. But finally it turned its back on Ben and sped off to the right, into the prairie land away from the river, and the town. Its underlings followed, and just like that they were gone.

Ben let out a long sigh and slumped back against the mound.

"You did it, Uncle Ben," Andros said, his tone excited, disbelieving.

"Course...I did..." Ben tried to make it sound lighthearted, but he found he barely had the strength to speak.

The exertions of the day, the pain of his wounds—now that he could afford to listen to it—and the general stress of the entire encounter left him completely drained, and the world began to fade around him.

"Uncle Ben?" he hard, faintly, and he thought he felt someone shake him.

Then he saw a face, standing over him, in white and gold, and he recognized the High Priest.

"Father," Ben said. "Really...glad...to see you..."

Then he drifted off.

When he woke, sunlight was streaming in the window of the room he was staying in, filling the chamber with brightness such that Ben had never thought he would see again.

It was a small room, maybe ten feet on a side, and built from grey stone bricks. So it was inside the Temple.

Made sense.

Ben's bed dominated the room, a four-poster affair with the kind of deep feather mattress and finely-woven sheets that he had heard about in stories but never experienced. It felt like heaven, even considering the aches and pains that spanned the entire breadth and width of his body.

There was a wash basin in the corner at the foot of his bed, and a bookcase of all things on the wall opposite. The door, a stout pine affair with a simple rising latch mechanism, stood closed next to the bookcase.

It was definitely a worthy place to stay, but he immediately wondered about Andros. Where was he in all this?

He went to get up, but found he could not. Not that he was restrained in any way. His body just refused to move. A dozen different protests flared from as many different locations at the first hint of exertion, and he slumped back into his bedding.

He must have been quite a bit more injured than he thought.

"Hello?" He called, and was gratified to find that, though his voice was hoarse, he could still talk well, and loudly.

A minute or so later, the door opened, and one of the church sisters, cloaked in white and gold like the priests, poked her head it. It was Luci, round-faced and pretty with little dimples in her cheeks. She had caused great consternation among the young men of the town when she chose the virgin's path.

"You're awake," she said. "The Jarl and Father Durgan want to see you."

"How long was I out?"

"Three days."

Ben pursed his lips. That was a long time to be sleeping, and he still felt exhausted. "What about Andros?"

Luci—Sister Luci—smiled gently. "He's fine. He's playing with the cat down in the garden."

"Good."

"Just a few minutes. Do you need anything while you wait?"

"Water, please."

She came fully into the room and picked up a pitcher and cup from a container he couldn't see at the foot of his bed. She poured him a cup and handed it over to him.

Slowly, he lifted it to his lips. Even that much movement hurt. But he did it.

True to Sister Luci's word, a few minutes later, a strong knock came, and then his door swung open. The two top men of the town strode in.

Father Durgan, the High Priest, was not particularly tall, and he was rather round about the belly. But he had a powerful presence and a sharp wit, and no one could doubt his piety or charity. He wore the white and gold casually, but with a quiet dignity, and carried the shepherd's crook of his station.

Jarl Henri was his opposite in almost every respect. A head taller than the other men in town, and powerfully built, with long flowing blond hair and a matching beard, he had a severe demeanor but was possibly the fairest man Ben had ever met. He wore well-cured brown leather leggings and a blue tabard with the golden necklace that marked him as Jarl, and a broadsword on his left hip.

"How do you feel, Ben?" Jarl Henri asked, and Ben tried to sit up.

He failed, and he flopped back onto the cushions, wincing. "Beg pardon, my Jarl," he said. "Can't seem to get up right now."

The Jarl smiled faintly. "Understandable," he said, and clapped Ben on the shoulder.

It hurt, but he decided not to let it show.

"Andros told us what happened," Father Durgan said, looking grave. "I've heard of this sort of thing before, but not in quite some time, and never in these parts. You two were quite fortunate to come through as well as you did."

"He is well?"

The priest made a little shrug. "On the mend. The healers think he will recover fully. Physically, anyway. Emotionally and spiritually? That remains to be seen." He glanced at the Jarl, then said, "We've been keeping him—and you—on the Temple grounds, for obvious reasons. But he's had many visitors. Once we place him in a new household - "

"He's staying with me," Ben said.

The two men exchanged looks.

"I'm not sure that's wise, Ben," the Jarl said.

"He's. Staying. With. Me." Ben fixed the Jarl with a stern look that he before had only used on a trainee who was being foolish. He would never have dreamed to use it on the Jarl.

But Jarl or no, he was not going to decide this one.

The Jarl returned Ben's stare for a long moment, then shrugged and looked over at the High Priest and spread his hands helplessly.

Father Durgan chuckled in amusement. "I told you so, Henri." He turned warm eyes on Ben. "In point of fact, the lad insisted on the same thing. It's a big responsibility, you know. And with no wife to help you, it will be difficult." His tone was perfectly warm and correct, but his eyes narrowed as he said that, as though probing to make sure Ben would, in fact, be the right choice.

"I know," he said. He looked back at the Jarl. "Jarl Henri, it has been the honor of my life serving in your guards. But now I must ask you to release me from that service."

The Jarl looked taken aback. So did the High Priest. They had seen his insistence on adopting Andros coming, but not this.

"Why?" the Jarl asked. No, demanded.

"It may not ever be safe to take the boy off of sanctified land. But he can't stay cooped up in this little Temple forever." He tried a smile at the High Priest, to soften his words. "Meaning no disrespect of course, your grace." He paused, then continued. "Last year you spoke of the Nylop Monastery."

The High Priest nodded.

"Two hundred acres of vineyards, tended fields, and pastureland. A community of five hundred on the grounds, and all of it sanctified land. The boy can have a good life, growing up there. And," he gave a little shrug, "I find that I'm wanting to study my theology a bit more myself. I would appreciate it if you would write a letter of introduction for us."

The High Priest and the Jarl traded looks, and Ben could tell they had no argument to counter his requests.

After a second, Father Durgan nodded. "I would be happy to."

The Jarl looked a bit less eager, but he too nodded agreement. "I cannot question your reasoning. But we will miss you."

"Thank you."

"Now," the High Priest. "We will leave you in peace. Rest and heal. When you are well, we can see about the arrangements."

With that, they stood and left the room.

Ben watched them go and settled back into his cushions. His mind drifted back over the events of three days ago, and he felt again the wrenching grief of loss. He would probably never not feel it.

But then he looked forward, to this new chapter of his life, with Andros and with a world of new knowledge to obtain. He couldn't help feeling eagerness for that new life, and a hope that balanced out that grief.

Mostly.

3
___

NAUGHTY AND NICE

Nora didn't realize it, but this was going to be the best day of her life.

I had it all planned out. Pick her up after work, and zip off to the airport for a spontaneous getaway. Paris - the city of lights. Every girl's favorite destination.

It was going to be awesome.

Until she screwed it all up by getting kidnapped by rogue elves.

Most folks think elves are something out of a myth, and guys like me have worked long and hard to keep it that way. I'm Dustin Cofield, and I'm an Elfsterminator.

My office is tucked in the back of the Wells Fargo branch at the corner of 8th and Main, in the suburban town of Lockwood. The town could have been cut out and replanted just about anywhere in the American midwest; one of those cookie-cutter pre-designed 'burbs that looks nice—and actually *is* nice—but lacks any real personality to set it apart.

And the Wells Fargo branch...well, not much to say about it. It's a

Wells Fargo branch. Faux wood and cleanliness covering up the inherent iniquity and fraud that is the banking industry in an era of fiat currency and artificially low interest rates. Only thing real about the place was my little eight foot by eight foot space.

Because I didn't work for the bank.

Oh, I had a cover. Senior Financial Analyst, or somesuch. But I didn't produce any real analysis and my supposed boss never asked for any. Not sure how the arrangement worked between the Agency and the bank, but I'm certain I don't want to know. I had no illusions I actually worked for the good guys.

But we were doing good, and important, things. Keeping humanity safe from the scourges of elfkind, and Christmas intact for the kids, is no joke. And that's why I was still doing it after ten years.

The fringe benefits were pretty nice, too.

It had been a busy couple of months. I'd been working with a State-wide task force that uncovered a major candy cane smuggling operation two towns over. Had to go under cover for a little while, and almost wound up baked into the biggest sugar cookie ever. But I came through with only a minor sugar rush, and we sent a dozen of the tricky little pointies away for a long, long time.

I was aching for a vacation. And some sugar-free foods.

But first I had to finish the admin.

The normies in the bank would have thought I was nuts if they could see me typing away at an old typewriter, using old-school carbon paper to make copies in triplicate of each page of my report.

Point of fact, I felt stupid doing it that way sometimes as well, but that's how the Big Guy liked it. No electronics for him, so no internet. And nothing could come near him that had been generated electronically. Supposedly the residual electromagnetic field around even something that had been created electronically would screw with his energy flux, and that could mess with his ability to produce the Lists and get his rounds done on the Big Day.

Didn't make much sense to me, but that's how it was.

Then again I think he might really have just liked screwing with the help. Something about that guffaw of his, and the way his cheeks turned especially rosy when he laughed, always made me suspicious.

But whatever. He wanted it that way, he got it that way. No skin off my back.

It did make my office look antique, though. Typewriter straight out of the 30s atop an equally old and beat-up desk. Cork board up next to the door with mimeographed memos from HQ tacked on. A black-and-white picture of me with the Big Guy himself at an awards gala up at the Pole on the wall opposite the cork board. Little potted petunia or marigold or something that Nora had given me underneath the one narrow window I had, going a little brown in the leaf from neglect, since I hadn't watered it while I was out under cover. Smell of old paper and carbon, and the stains on the desk to go with it. And an old rotary phone next to my typewriter.

I was just getting going typing my report's summary when the phone rang.

I glanced at the counterweight-powered clock on the wall to my right and saw that it was almost 10 o'clock already. I'd need to hurry or I'd miss lunch with Tim from accounting. I'd been blowing him off for a while, but my quarterly audit was coming due and I couldn't dodge him for much longer.

So I was feeling a bit grumpy and rushed when I picked up the phone.

"Yeah?"

Nora sounded like she knew she should be scared, but she couldn't bring herself to be. "Dustin there's a bunch of weird little guys here who say - "

She cut off with a yelp, then came the sound of something brushing across the receiver, followed by a muttered, "Stupid broad," in a high-pitched voice. My hackles went up, and a shiver went down my spine.

"You wanna see your little girlfriend again, you'll be at the Dunkin Donuts on Maple in twenty minutes."

It was definitely an elf on the line now. This wasn't good. "What the hell is this?"

"Just be there. Or you'll be finding pieces of her in your stockings for the next ten years."

The line clicked dead.

The scene in the Dunkin Donuts was not at all what I expected.

You figure there'd be a few cops sitting around, doing their cliche'd coffee and donuts thing, some late morning commuters in a rush to wolf something down real quick, maybe some little kids with their moms. The usual tatted-up millennial English or You-Name-It-studies grads with ear gauges that made you want to lose your stomach behind the registers, though why the owners would think those sorts of dufuses wouldn't drive business away I never could figure out. The smells of baking and good cheer.

That's not what it was at all.

Two pointies were posted on either side of the door outside, wool caps pulled down to conceal their ears despite the mid-summer heat and arms crossed over their chests like they had every intention busting some heads in.

If they hadn't barely come up to my waist, anyway.

They scowled at me as I walked up, still dressed in the charcoal grey suit I'd worn to work for the sake of the normies in the bank. The pointy on the right was chewing on something. I hoped it was gum. He looked me up and down and sniffed, scornfully.

"Booth in the back. Watch yourself."

There was definitely a threat there, and despite how the high pitch of his voice inflected the words, I knew better than to dismiss it.

I nodded and pushed the door open.

The place was overrun with pointies. Behind the counter, at the booths, just standing around. Unlike their fellows outside, they weren't dressed for normie eyes; they wore their pointed shoes and long stocking caps, wool jackets and tight leggings, in greens and reds predominantly. It jarred with the standard Dunkin Donuts branch decor.

As did the smell they brought with them. Rather than pleasant baking donut smell, the place reeked of peppermint. The sheer weight of it almost made me choke as I stepped in.

What happened to the normie staff and customers, I didn't know and feared to speculate about right that minute. Every elfin eye in the place turned on me as I entered, and I could feel the hostility, the imminent violence, in their gaze.

I swallowed, pushing down the fight or flight response as I scanned the place.

There. Back corner, just as the pointy outside had said. The elf sitting there, back to the wall, was a tad taller than the others, and dressed in a three-piece navy blue suit with a white shirt and burgundy tie. His hair was black, and slicked back into a ponytail, and he wore wire-rimmed glasses. Sharp green eyes tracked me as I approached and slid into the booth across from him.

He could have passed for a successful, if short, businessman, except for his ears, which pointed up almost as high as the top of his head.

"Been a while, Cofield," he said, and I recognized his voice from the phone.

I kept my poker face as best I could, but his greeting threw me. Had we met before?

Must not have kept it as well as I thought, because he let out a little snort. "You don't remember me."

I shrugged. "What can I say, you all look the same."

The little guy's cheeks flushed, and I could tell I'd gotten under his skin. "You really should show more respect."

"You people wanted respect, you shouldn't have stabbed the Big Guy in the back."

"Easy for you to say. You didn't have to work for him."

"Yeah whatever. Cry me a river." I leaned forward and narrowed my eyes at him. "Where's Nora and what did you do to her?"

He traced out a little circle on the tabletop with his index finger. "Nothing. Yet. Hoping you'll let me keep it that way, but that's up to you."

I didn't respond. After a few seconds of silence he made a little half-smile and sniffed. "You've got something of mine. I've got something of yours. Simple trade."

I leaned back against the back of the booth seat and frowned. "What might that something be?" I didn't like where this was going, not one bit.

"Nothing major," he said with a little shrug. "Little carved wooden box, stained black. Two candy canes painted on the lid."

I recognized it, a piece of evidence we'd collected in the Candy Cane Caper. But it didn't make any sense that he'd go to these lengths to get it. It was a simple box, like he said, and empty. So why - ?

He answered the question for me before I could ask it. "Mom gave it to me," he said, a wisp of a smile crossing his lips. "It's sentimental."

Right. Didn't matter, though.

"You know I can't do that. It's evidence in a case." I narrowed my eyes again. "And how did something of yours get found at the crime scene?"

"I didn't have anything to do with that candy cane stuff, if that's what you're asking." He sniffed. "Amateurs."

"Amateurs who had your really sentimental gift from mommy in their safe."

"Because they stole it from me. It's a long story. But now that you've done us all the favor of getting rid of them, I'd like it back."

He looked legitimately pleased that the perps from the Caper had gone the way of Capone. Which meant...

Which meant I would need to re-evaluate that whole case, see if I could find a link to him somewhere. Some way the fallout could benefit him. There must be an angle to it somewhere.

And that angle was connected to the box. Somehow.

I nodded slowly. "We were just going to auction it off after the case gets closed anyway. Wasn't anything materially useful in it."

He really did smile when I said that. "So you'll do it?"

"When?"

He glanced aside toward a clock on the wall. "Back here at 6 o'clock."

"Make it 4. I've got a plane to catch."

I stood up and walked out.

Just because I can't use electronics to create correspondence to the Big Guy doesn't mean I can't use it at all. I drive a Yukon that's tricked out with all the options, and some that are not factory standard.

When I got in and started her up, I immediately put a call in to Colleen, at the Agency's evidence lab, around the beltway on the other side of the metro area.

She picked up on the second ring. "Hey Dustin."

I pulled out into traffic and gunned it toward the closest beltway on-ramp, a couple miles distant. "Colleen, need you to pull an item from evidence. Black box with crossed candy canes on the top."

I could practically hear her nodding. "I know the one. Was about to box everything up for archives. Why?"

"Take a closer look at it. There's something we missed, something important."

She must have heard the tension in my voice, because hers went sharp, focused. "What's wrong?"

"Tell you when I get there. Twenty minutes."

It actually took me twenty-five minutes to get to the lab. It was the corner entity in a little strip mall in a seedier part of town. And naturally, it didn't look like an elf-fighting evidence lab. The cover business—and it actually did earn a profit, I've been told—was a thrift store, which was rather clever because all sorts of people came and went bearing various and sundry items in and out.

I was a little out of place in my banker's suit, but not as much as I would have been if it had been a manicure parlor.

The shopkeeper worked for the Agency, and she nodded me into the back room where Colleen was waiting.

She was chubby, perky, and blonde, and for some reason liked to wear a lab coat even though we didn't really do the kind of in-depth scientific forensics work that would warrant it. Too much NCIS and CSI, I guessed.

Today she had her hair braided into twin braids that draped over her shoulders and onto her chest like the head-tentacles of those weird Star Wars alien women, and she'd picked her gold-rimmed glasses. She beamed a grin at me as I walked in.

The place was small, but well-stocked. Metal shelves on the rear and side walls held boxes of materials from our recent cases. There was a little lab table and computer in the center of the floor, completed with microscopes and a bunch of imaging and analysis equipment I really didn't understand, or care to.

Long as it worked.

"You're late," Colleen said.

"Sue me," I said, perhaps more gruffly than her teasing tone warranted. But I was pressed for time and worried, so screw it. "What do you got?"

Colleen looked askance at me for a second, then shrugged. She waved me over toward one of the microscopes, and I saw she had put the box in question beneath its lenses.

"Found it."

I raised an eyebrow at her, then bent over to look into the microscope.

The grain of the wooden box sprang clearly into view, easily seen despite the dark staining. But running almost perpendicular to the grain was another line, perfectly straight.

I straightened and looked back at Colleen. "Is that - ?"

She nodded. "If they'd been clever, they would have made the cut in line with the grain. That would have made it nearly impossible to find. As it is, it's not visible to a human's naked eye."

"But it is for an elf," I said, completing the thought.

She nodded again. Then she picked up a scalpel that she kept on-hand as part of her tool kit. I stepped aside and let her put her eyes on the microscope's viewfinder. Slowly, carefully, Collen maneuvered the scalpel against the box, and then...

"Bingo!" she said and straightened.

Looking down at the box, a little sliver on the box's side had flipped up, like a cover on a hinge. I picked it up and turned it over, so that the sliver'ed side was facing up, and blinked.

"That looks like a USB port."

"Yeah," Colleen said. "Yeah, it does."

She took the box from me and maneuvered around to her computer. She fished around in a drawer for a second, then came out with a cord, and plugged it into the computer, then the box.

A moment later, she whistled softly. "This thing is a flash drive, Dustin."

"Flash drive? But this came from the Candy Cane Caper, from the elves." I was frowning deeply now. "Elves can't use electronics. Same reason as the Big Guy - it messes with their other work functions."

Colleen shrugged. "Looks like they figured out a way."

If that was true, it was bad. It would complicate the elf problem immensely.

I moved to her side and leaned over her shoulder, peering at the screen. "What's on it?"

"That will take a little while to figure out." She looked up at me and nodded toward the other chair at the table. "Might want to get comfortable."

In fact, it took her almost an hour to figure it all out. I did not like what she found.

"This," she said, pointing at the screen, "is major. I found APIs from every social media platform I've ever heard of and a number that I had to look up. It draws user data from the various platforms."

"Didn't know you could do that."

She looked at me with a bemused expression on her face. "Of course you can. Facebook is the single greatest mass surveillance system the CIA ever created."

"What, is your name Alex Jones now?"

She shrugged. "Look it up. Anyway, it's not hard to get that data from these companies."

"Ok. So what?"

"So..." She looked back at the screen and bit her lip, mousing over to the root directory, then to a subdirectory labelled "N and N". There were two files in there, and even I with my limited tech skills could tell they were database files, from the file extensions.

"I think," Colleen said, and she swallowed. "I think they're creating their own Naughty and Nice lists."

The bottom dropped out of my stomach. "What?"

"That's what it looks like. And with all this data..."

She didn't finish the thought, and she didn't need to. With that kind of data, the elf lists could grow to match the Big Guy's. And if that happened...

I stood so suddenly my chair flipped and fell onto its back on the floor behind me.

"I need to make some calls."

I wear the suit for the benefit of normies, but with all that was going on with this situation, when I showed up for the meeting at 4 o'clock, I decided to put on my real work clothes.

When I first saw the Agency combat suit, I thought they were playing a prank on me, as the new guy.

The thing was bright red, and fuzzy like it was made from fur that had been shaved extremely close to the skin, with a white furry belt, complete with holster for a sidearm and pouches for various tools of the trade. The boots were white, and the suit's blouse had a flip-up almost white furry hoodie that also had a half-mask, covering just the eyes.

It was ridiculous.

But it wasn't a prank.

Turns out since the Big Guy and the elves were together for so long, the material he uses for his clothing can provide protection against some of the pointies' more lethal tricks. So the Agency designed the combat suit from the Big Guy's leftover material.

I'd once suggested we at least try dying it a different color. But the high-ups put the kibosh on that idea real quick. The formula was the formula and we couldn't know what effect changing the formula would have.

Thus, I got to feel like an absolute idiot every time I needed to be ready for action.

It was worse this time, because Nora was going to see.

"Son of a bitch," I said. I was in the Dunkin Donuts parking lot, gripping the steering wheel of my Yukon so tight my knuckles whitened. Or they would have, if I could see them beneath the furry white gloves I, of course, had to wear.

I glanced at the clock. 15:58.

I'd cut it close. Damn close, and I wasn't sure if I was truly ready. The tech guys had worked their butts off, and they assured me at least part of my plan was sure to work. The most important part. But as for the rest...

No way to know but to try. Taking a deep breath, I made sure my hoodie mask was in place, picked up the box, and stepped out of the truck.

The pointies on duty at the door—same guys as earlier—jerked to attention when they saw me in full battle garb. From the widening of their eyes I could tell they were not sure if I was just going to attack or what.

The guy who I'd spoken with earlier slipped his hand behind his back to where he would be carrying a concealed piece if he had one, and I raised my hands, palms out toward them, and shook my head.

He visibly relaxed. A bit. But not entirely.

He didn't try to stop me from entering, though.

There were fewer elves inside. Just a half dozen guys who were a bit more burly than the average elf, at a booth to the left as I came in the door.

They were also more kitted out than the norm. I saw a couple bulges that could only be weapons beneath their clothing when I looked them over.

Pretty sure they were under orders not to start any trouble, though, so I took note of who looked to have what, then returned my attention to the rear booth.

The head honcho pointy was there again, and Nora was with them.

She sat on the inside of the booth, facing the door, so he could block her if she tried to get out. And he could, if it came down to it; elves are stronger than they look, and tenacious.

Nora was dressed in a light blue short-sleeved blouse with the top button undone. Her pixy-cut black hair was slightly mussed, and she wore a quizzical expression on her face as though, despite having endured it all day, she still couldn't make sense of her situation.

That expression only got worse when she saw me enter, and then recognized me as I got close.

"Dustin?" she said, clearly at wit's end.

"Hey Nora," I said, and slipped into the booth. I looked from her back to the elf and placed the box down on the table. I slid it across until it was firmly in front of him, and well on his side of the table. "As agreed."

The elf actually looked surprised. "Really? I figured you'd at least try to put up a fight over it. From principle, if nothing else."

I shrugged. "It's just a dumb box. No offense to your mom. I checked, and there was no evidential value to it, so I'm not even breaking any rules by giving it to you."

Which was not entirely true. But it was close enough for government work.

The pointy nodded slowly, and picked up the box. Turning it slowly in his hands, he looked it over. Now that I knew where it was, I could tell he was studying the area with the flap particularly carefully. Checking to see if we'd tampered with it, I was sure.

We'd been careful, though.

After a short while, he nodded. Then he slipped out of the booth and swept his arm toward the door.

"You are free to go, my lady," he said, extravagantly.

Nora looked between the two of us, and sat unmoving for a second, clearly unsure what to do.

"Go on," I said. "I'll meet you outside."

Nodding, she scooted out of the booth.

"Bye," the pointy said, and there was a bit of a teasing element to the way he said it, as he got back into the booth.

Nora looked back at him and said, "Bye Loomy." Then she walked out.

Loomy. That was the guy's name. Hearing it jogged my memory, and I recalled when we'd met before. It was a case about five years ago. Small time beat about some missing teddy bears. I couldn't pin it on him, but I was sure he had been up to no good.

Loomy watched Nora depart, then looked back at me, an eyebrow rising. "No hard feelings?"

"If you come near her again..."

He raised his hands defensively. "Wouldn't dream of it."

Either he was play-acting very well, or he meant it. Either way, Nora was going to have a security detail for a while, just to be safe.

Not that she'd know it.

"See you around, Loomy."

He grinned. "Not if I see you first."

<hr>

"You probably figured out I don't really work for Wells Fargo," I said to Nora.

We were in my Yukon, and I was pulling out of the Dunkin Donuts parking lot and into traffic.

She nodded, looking back at the donut shop as we pulled away. "Were those guys really - ?"

"Elves?" I nodded. "Yep. Christmas Elves, to be precise."

"And you," she gestured up and down at me, and my ridiculous combat outfit. "What, you work for Santa Claus?"

"Not directly." I put on my blinker and maneuvered around a guy who was going far too slow. "Some years back, the Big Guy—that's what we call him—and his elves had a falling out. They didn't like the way he did business and wanted changes. He didn't want to change. Big blow up, he decided to outsource his production, and they left the Pole."

Nora blinked. "They wanted to form a union, so he fired them?"

That threw me for a loop for a second. I'd never thought of it that way before. "Well, it's a bit more complicated than that," I said, sounding completely lame as I did so.

"Wow. Dick move."

I cleared my throat. "Anyway, he had problems adjusting, so he came to the governments of the world to ask for help. I work for an agency you've never heard of—because it doesn't exist—that helps him to maintain production, among other things. Since they split, the elves have been trying to sabotage him every chance they get, and ruin Christmas. My branch is devoted to stopping their efforts in that regard."

"I see..."

It was a lot to take in, I knew. But she was handling it pretty well.

"So why did I get to spend the day eating mints and sugar cookies? I'm going to have to diet for a month now, you know that." She made it sound like it was my fault.

Sighing, I said, "They'd been running a project to subvert the Naughty-Nice list, and make their own. We had their database, though we didn't know it. They grabbed you to make me return it." I grinned, a tad viciously, I must admit, and added, "They didn't get what they thought they got. We put a virus in their database that will wipe it, any computers they have, transmit their locations to us, and disable their connections to the social media sites they'd been drawing from to make the database."

"That's...good?"

I nodded. "It is. No kids' Christmas is getting messed up by those guys, at least not this year."

We drove in silence for a while, before Nora asked, "So what happens now?"

"Now, we go to your place and pack. We've got a plane to catch."

She looked sidelong at me, warily. "What, like witness protection?"

I shook my head. "No, just a trip I had planned for this weekend." I met her gaze and added, "That is, assuming we're still an item." I was probably asking for trouble even broaching the question, but I figure it needed to be asked. Torture by Christmas baked goods was nothing to shake a stick at. If she blamed me...

Well, I wouldn't blame her if she decided to call us quits.

She was quiet for a while, then laughed, and it was the merriest laugh I'd heard from her in a long time. "Of course we're still an item." She rubbed her hand up and down my arm, and made a little purring sound as she felt the furriness of the fabric. "I think I could get used to this," she said. She gave me a direct look. "Where we going?"

"Trust me," I said, and winked at her. "You'll love it.

———

She did.

4
____

POPPER'S

I t was nearing the end of David's shift at Popper's Books And Things. Even for a Tuesday, it had been a slow day. Maybe half a dozen people had actually bought something all day; not for the first time, he pondered whether working the counter at a small bookstore was the best summer job for him to have taken.

He was an Engineering major, not in the liberal arts. He probably should have pushed to find something more related to his field.

But he couldn't even apply for a summer intern position until after the end of next school year, and there was something about Popper's...

He'd discovered it his second week at school, and before long it had become the place he hung out in more than any other.

The antique but carefully preserved and polished mahogany counter running half the length of the store to the right of the entrance, where the staff kept watch over the customers like a bartender looking out over his pub.

The six rows of equally-polished hardwood shelves—not mahogany but still nice—that took up the center of the shop's space.

The wall shelves to the left of the entrance that housed new release comics of every variety, and the backlist boxes at the rear.

The small brown leather couch against the wall past the end of the counter, and the two matching stuffed chairs opposite it where customers could read or sip a cup from the pot that Barbara, the owner, insisted be maintained freshly-brewed and available at all times.

And, of course, the game room in back, complete with all the miniatures a game master and his groups of players could need for the evening, an old and battered but still running refrigerator where the players could stash snacks and—non-alcoholic—drinks, and a trio of tables sized for eight so that there was almost always room to get a game on.

Barbara kept the shelves well-stocked with a mix of new and used tomes, and liked to spray the place down with a different air freshener each week. Today, that meant the place had the mixed odor of french roast and lavender, with just a hint of old paper beneath.

Add the light jazz that made up the shop's approved playlist, piped from the cashier's iMac to bluetooth speakers nestled at each corner of the shop's main room, and it was a nice, homey, welcoming place.

Just lacking in customers. Today, at least.

David had the register app open on the iMac and was just getting started reconciling the take for his shift—not a hard task today—when the little bell mounted above the entrance rang.

A customer.

He looked up, and his hackles rose immediately.

The guy was average looking. As average as it was possible to be: height, build, facial features, hair...all the way down to his beige suit. He would have had to work to be more unnoticeable.

Except that as he approached David's counter, doffing the sunglasses he had been wearing to reveal light brown eyes, he gave off a sense of presence, of power right on the edge of control, and David knew this was no ordinary, average guy, however he may look.

"Can I help you?"

The guy folded up his shades and slipped them into the inner pocket of his suit coat. He remained silent for a couple seconds, and glanced to his left, toward the gaming room. Checking to see if anyone was back there?

Finally, the man looked back at David, and the intensity of that very average stare made him want to shift on his feet.

"I don't know, David. Can you help me?"

David swallowed. "How do you know my name?"

The man's lips turned upward into the smallest hint of a smile. "Store's website," he said, and David felt heat rise to his cheeks in embarrassment.

He'd forgotten about the staff pictures Barbara posted there; it had seemed silly to put him up since he was just around for the summer, but she'd insisted.

The man let a few seconds pass in silence, then made a little shrug and looked toward the back room again. "Is Barbara here?"

"No, she's coming in for the evening shift today. Should be here in twenty minutes or so."

"Ah." He nodded as though David had said something profound.

"There's coffee if you want to wait for her."

"No, I must be off. Just tell her Henry said hello, and I look forward to catching up with her soon."

Then he turned and walked out. David couldn't help thinking the plain name suited his plainness perfectly.

It made him distinctly uneasy.

By the time Barbara showed up—thirty minutes later—he still had not been able to put the guy out of his mind. Something was just...off...about him, and the whole situation there.

Barbara was all smiles, as usual, as she walked in the door. She had her reddish-brown hair up, her curls mostly bundled away in an intricate mass of braids and twists and what-have-yous that was impossible to follow, and wore jeans and a loose green collared blouse. In her mid 30s, she was a bit on the plump side, but what she lacked in sexiness she made up for in good old fashioned fun personality.

"Hey David," she said, as she swept through the door and over to the counter. "Good day?"

He shrugged. "Slow day."

"Well, it's Tuesday," she said, and maneuvered down toward the coffee pot over next to the couch.

"Yeah." David logged out of the register app and picked up his backpack, from where he had left it in the corner behind the counter. "Accounts are all square."

Barbara nodded, not taking her eyes away from the cup she was pouring. "Ok, thanks. Have a great night."

"You too." David slipped out from behind the counter, maneuvering carefully to avoid bumping into her as he passed her by. "By the way," he said as he started toward the door, "your friend Henry stopped by to say hi."

"What?"

The sudden change in her tone made him turn back to look at her, concern rising within him. She sounded like she really hoped she had heard him wrong.

"Henry. Plain guy. Really average, but...also not? He said hi, and that he wants to see you again soon."

Her hand that was holding the cup began to shake, and then the coffee she was pouring into the cup ran over.

Barbara made a yelp of pain and chagrin as the scalding liquid spilled over onto her hand. She reflexively shook the hand, flinging the coffee off, but lost her grip on the cup.

It fell and shattered on the false-wood laminate floor, coffee spilling all over the place.

"Damn!" Barbara said, and raised her burned hand to her mouth.

"Are you ok?" David said, rushing toward her.

She put the pot back down and waved him away. "I'm fine. I'm fine. Just...you surprised me."

"Let me help clean up."

"No. No, you go. You're seeing Lindsay again tonight right?" She put on a smile, but David could tell it was forced. "Don't want to be late."

No. No, he really didn't. Lindsay was something else. But... "You sure you're alright?" He glanced toward the door, recalling the look on Henry's face when he'd been there earlier. "Who is that guy?"

"Just...a friend. An old friend."

"Boyfriend?" He tried to make his tone light, but failed and he knew it.

Barbara shrugged. "The one that got away. Kind of?" Again with the smile that really wasn't. "Go on, get out of here."

David hesitated, and she made a shooing gesture. "Go!"

He went.

David had the evening shift Thursday. When he came into the Popper's, Henry was there, with Barbara.

Henry had on the same beige suit as before, and stood in front of the counter in the same casual, yet also not, pose that he had used before.

Barbara was behind the counter, in her red and white stripped shirt and wearing a not happy expression.

When the bell over the door rang, announcing David's presence, both of them turned to look his way.

Barbara immediately tried—and failed—to put a relaxed smile on her face.

Henry gave David a once-over, then sniffed ever so softly. He looked back at Barbara and said, "Three days. Think about it."

Then he turned away from the counter and walked out. "David," Henry said as he walked past. It was both greeting and dismissal. And then he was gone.

David watched the door close behind him, then looked back at Barbara, both eyebrows raising.

Barbara met his gaze for a second, then looked away toward the iMac screen. "It's been a busy day," she said, and began typing away at the keyboard. "But I've got the accounts register up to date. There are two groups in the back."

David nodded, though she couldn't see, and moved over to the counter. "What was going on there?"

Barbara's lips compressed. She continued typing, but didn't reply.

"Barbara - "

"It's not your concern," she snapped, and David flinched.

She had never raised her voice like that, to anyone. Not in most of the year that he had been coming here, and that he had known her.

Barbara seemed to realize she had crossed a line. She stopped typing and just looked at the screen for a few seconds. Then, with a sigh, she turned her eyes back onto David.

"I appreciate you're worried, but you don't need to be. It's just some old business Henry and I have to resolve. I'm a big girl; I can handle it." She grinned mischievously then, and added, "And you have better things to be thinking about. You never told me how it went with Lindsay the other night."

It was a painfully obvious change in subject. She didn't want him involved with whatever was going on between her and Henry, that much was clear.

And, he reminded himself, she was almost twice his age. Pretty sure she knew how to handle herself.

So he went with the change in subject.

This time.

Henry didn't come around again that David saw, but the effects of his presence lingered. Barbara seemed distracted, and on-edge, as the work-week ended and the weekend began.

Normally David would not work the weekend. Barbara had a couple part-timers who handled the counter on Saturdays and Sundays, and though Popper's was open late on Saturday she closed up early on Sundays, so there really wasn't any need for him.

But he found himself in the shop more often than not most weekends anyway. His D&D group met there Saturday afternoons, and a lot of the time there was a writer on a signing tour or something else cool going on so he ended up sticking around after the game.

This weekend, he decided he was going to keep as close an eye on the shop—and Barbara—as he could. Henry had said something was going down in three days. That meant Sunday. And though Barbara's assurance that there wasn't a problem stymied David's initial suspicions, her continued obvious discomfort made him determined to help.

If he could.

So he stayed late after his D&D game, until closing time. Lindsay wanted to hook up that night, but he begged off, honestly saying a friend needed his help.

Still, as he sat on the couch in Popper's and read the latest Grisham book while Henry steadfastly didn't come into the shop and Barbara had absolutely no difficulty at all all night, David wondered what the hell he thought he was doing.

Sunday dawned bright and sunny, and David went out for his morning run.

While he was making his way through mile 3, he let his thoughts go, and he really considered what was going on. What he was doing.

Henry and Barbara had a previous relationship.

Something about Henry himself had certainly made David uncomfortable.

But maybe he was just projecting his own crap onto Barbara. She had seemed uncomfortable when he first mentioned Henry to her, but that was attributable to hearing from an old acquaintance after a long hiatus.

And David had no idea what he had stepped into when he arrived for work the other day. For all he knew, Henry had been trying to ask her out, and she felt embarrassed because David had walked in, not because of anything Henry had done.

She certainly didn't want to talk to David about it; but then she didn't really have to, did she? They were friendly, but she wasn't his friend. She was his boss, and quite a bit older than he was.

By the time he got home after his Sunday 5 miles, he convinced himself that he was just being silly.

And he had passed up a good, hot time with Lindsay last night, for nothing.

Dumbass.

He resolutely did not go to the shop. Instead, he met up with some friends for lunch.

He was just saying goodbye to them and heading for the bus stop to ride over to Lindsay's place when his cell phone rang. He looked at the screen. It was Popper's.

"Hello?"

"David, it's Sonya." Sonya was the part-timer who handled Sundays. "Have you heard from Barbara?"

He frowned and looked at the time. Almost three o'clock. "No, why?"

"Well, she usually comes by before closeup to check on things, but I haven't seen her. Did she tell you anything about it? I've never closed by myself. Should I just lock the door, or... ? But I don't have a key!"

"Have you tried calling her?"

"Yeah, it goes straight to voicemail."

David's frown grew, and a shiver went down his spine. This was completely unlike Barbara, and he immediately flashed to that brief interchange between her and Henry.

Three days. Think about it.

What had that guy done?

"David?"

He blinked, and came back to present. Sonya had been talking, but he had not heard a thing she'd said. Didn't matter, though.

"There's a spare key in the top drawer of the desk in the office behind the game room. Just shut down the computer, turn off the lights, and lock up. I've got the early shift tomorrow. You can bring the key back then."

"You sure? Ok, thanks."

She hung up.

David immediately tried calling Barbara himself.

Voicemail.

He swore under his breath. His mind raced, and he tried to think of what to do.

Call the cops?

And tell them what, that a grown woman hadn't returned a call? They'd tell him to take a hike.

He had Barbara's address with her contact information in his phone. He looked at it, uncertain.

Maybe she was just running late, and Sonya was being flighty. Or maybe she and Henry had hooked up, for real.

Or maybe he was doing something horrible to her, that David would hear about tomorrow on the breaking news.

Screw it.

He opened up his Uber app.

David had been to Barbara's house once before, for an end-of-the-school-year party she'd thrown for her employees and friends of the store. It was a nicely maintained two bedroom bungalow on the north side of town, maybe a thousand square feet. Yellow siding with white trim, a porch the length of the house in front, a shingle roof, and a carport on a triangular lot that was stuck between two slightly-larger houses that were obviously by the same builder.

She had a stylized mailbox post that was carved in mermaids, and a mermaid-emblazoned welcome mat on her front porch. The lawn was closely trimmed, and she had chest-high screening bushes on either side of her lot. And that was it. No frills.

When David got out of the Uber, he saw that her car was in the driveway and her front door was slightly ajar. That wasn't necessarily an indication of trouble if she was home, but still, that anxious feeling that had been growing in his stomach since Sonya's call grew more intense.

He hurried up the walk from the street to the front door and stopped, listening.

A man's voice—he was sure it was Henry's—came through the crack between the door and the jamb. He sounded angry, but the voice was muffled so David couldn't make out what he was saying.

Adrenalin kicked in. Hard.

David slowly pushed the door open and fished his phone out.

The front sitting room was empty. David stepped inside and moved to the hallway that led back to the kitchen. There was a light on back there. Inching forward down the hall, he could hear Henry more clearly now.

" - not good enough, you dumb bitch."

Oh yeah. This wasn't good at all.

David called 911. The operator picked up, and he whispered, "There's an intruder in my friend's house." He gave the address.

The operator asked a question, but the sound of shattering glass from back in the kitchen overwhelmed David's hearing.

Before he could think about what he was doing, he surged forward and stepped into the kitchen.

Barbara was there, dressed in jeans and a white t-shirt. She was backed up against the wall opposite the doorway David had walked in through.

Henry was in front of her, his back to David. Again he had the beige suit on.

The glass David had heard breaking was lying at the base of the wall to Barbara's right, a jumbled pile of shards. Streaks of water flowed down the wall above the pile; Henry must have thrown the glass at the wall and it shattered there.

"There's nothing else, Henry," Barbara was saying as David stepped inside. "If you - " She saw him and her words cut off in a choking sound as her eyes went wide.

Henry noticed her change in demeanor. He made a quarter-turn to his left and looked behind himself. Seeing David there, his eyebrow rose.

"David. Nice to see you again." He no longer had the calm certitude he'd had the last couple times David had seen him, but the feeling of power was still there. It just was no longer in check. "Who you on the phone with?"

Only then did David realize he still had the phone up to his left ear, and that the 911 operator was talking.

"The cops," David said.

Henry made a tsking sound and shook his head. "Real sorry to hear that, kid."

He turned fully toward David and raised his right hand.

David saw the gun coming up to point at him, and everything seemed to slow to a crawl.

He wasn't old enough to get a carry permit yet, but his dad had spent a lot of time teaching him to shoot. One by one, his brain clicked past the rules of gun safety, as Henry violated them.

Treat every gun as if it's loaded. Ok, not really a violation, but...

Don't point the gun at anything you're not willing to shoot. Clear violation here.

Keep your finger off the trigger until you're ready to shoot.

Henry's trigger finger left its position along the slide of his pistol and slipped inside the trigger guard.

Oh crap, he *hadn't* violated rule number two, because he clearly was more than willing to shoot!

Duck!

The sound of a pistol shot turned time back to normal speed, but David didn't feel anything hit him, and Henry was close enough there was no way he could have missed.

Henry's arm dipped, and his expression became confused. He half-turned back toward Barbara, and a trickle of blood ran from the corner of his mouth.

"Barb- " he started to say.

She shot again. Henry's head jerked, and he collapsed to the floor.

David and Barbara stared at each other from across the room.

Her shirt was untucked on her right side, where she must have pulled it out to get at her concealed holster. The little pistol in her hands looked huge right then, and residual gunsmoke curled up from the end of its barrel.

She lowered the weapon to her side and said something, but David didn't actually hear it.

All he could hear was the pounding of his heart, the highly concerned babbling of the 911 operator, and, far away but getting closer by the second, the wailing of police sirens.

It took hours for the cops to get done with him. When he'd finally finished giving his statement and being interviewed, and interviewed, and re-interviewed, it was late and he wanted nothing but to go to bed.

He'd called his buddy Steve to come pick him up from the police station—an Uber didn't really seem like the thing right then—but Steve hadn't arrived yet, so he sat down on a bench in the public waiting section of the station.

He'd been sitting there for about five minutes when the door leading back into the innards of the station opened and Barbara walked out.

She looked just as beat as David felt, and she made a beeline toward the exit. But when she saw him, she stopped and walked over to the bench where he was sitting.

He watched her come, feeling numb and uncertain about everything. When she gestured toward the seat next to him, he just shrugged and she sat.

"I owe you an explanation," she said.

"That would be nice."

Barbara looked down a drew a breath. "When I was about your age, I got married. His name was Henry Popper." She looked back up into his eyes and raised an eyebrow.

David saw the import of the name immediately.

"He was everything you saw and more - dashing, exciting...and a criminal. I knew he was, but I didn't care. That was part of what made him so exciting and sexy. Well, he made this big heist, got a lot of money. And he got caught." Barbara shook her head. "After he went to prison I saw where my life would end up if I stuck with him. So I got a divorce."

"He went through all this because he was sore at you for dumping him?"

She shook her head. "The cops never found all the money he stole. But I knew where it was. I took it, changed my name, and moved away. I traveled for a while, and eventually ended up here. Used the money to buy a place and open my shop. Named it after him, for sentimental reasons I guess. Or maybe just stupidity. Regardless, after all this time I thought I'd covered my tracks, but..." She spread her hands.

"So he wanted his money back."

Barbara nodded. "With interest. But of course, the money was gone. Most of it. Into the house and the business. I thought...hoped... he'd accept a cut of the profits, let me pay him back over time. But... well, he was never as smart as he made on."

David nodded. It all made sense. But... "Are you going to be in trouble?"

Barbara looked askance at him. "No, of course not. It was a home invasion. I have a carry permit, but even if I didn't, he assaulted both of us with deadly force in my home. Totally justified shooting, morally and legally."

David had assumed that was the case from the beginning. "I meant about the money."

"Oh." She considered for a few seconds, then shrugged. "Statute of limitations for the heists he pulled are well past."

"Well, that's good I guess."

Barbara put her hand atop David's and gave his a little squeeze. "I'm sorry you had to go through that, David. More sorry than I can tell you."

"Yeah. Well, I - " David's phone buzzed, cutting him off.

He looked down and saw a text from Steve. He was out front.

David removed his hand from Barbara's and stood. "My ride's here. I gotta go."

Barbara's expression was unreadable. "Will I see you back at the shop, or - ?"

"I don't know. I need to think things through."

"I understand."

David nodded, then turned toward the exit. He stopped after half a dozen steps and turned back around to face her.

"Thanks for not letting him shoot me."

Barbara smiled, a sad little smile that said she feared their friendship was at an end. "You're welcome."

Then David walked out of the Police Station. He needed to rest, and think. And decide whether he would go back to the store that bore the name of the man Barbara had killed.

Or not.

5

THE CASE OF THE MISSING ROCKER

"What's with the hat?"

Dominic was looking at a holopic that was hanging on one of the beige-painted walls of the waiting room he and his partner, Alex, had been pacing around in for the last fifteen minutes.

The 3D image showed a slender yet muscular man, stripped to the waist and wearing tight-fitting black pants that might have even been real leather. He was wailing on a golden electric guitar, the instrument up nearly vertically in front of his body as his fingers ran up and down the fretboard in a repeat of an intricate riff. His head moved to the beat of some off-scene drummer.

And the great big pink top hat he wore, well past oversized to the point of being comic, flopped along as well.

The image was on a loop, so the hat just kept on going, and Dominc found he couldn't look away from it.

Alex chuckled softly. Dominic could tell she was shaking her head in amusement as well; she always did.

"Shoulda known you'd never seen one of his shows. That's his schtick; his trademark."

Dominic forced his eyes away from the holopic and toward his partner.

She was svelte, almost tiny. Maybe five foot even, with long black hair tied back in a ponytail and slightly slanted eyes that told of an east-Asian ancestry, despite their green color. She wore a grey-blue suit and open-collared white shirt—no tie—and that amused expression he had been expecting.

About thirty, he was breaking her in to the detective game, and in the two months they'd worked together he'd found himself impressed by her drive and intellect.

But not her taste in music.

"Not my speed," Dominic said.

Alex looked, if anything, even more amused. But she did him the grace of not saying anything more.

The waiting room was plush, Dominic had to give it that. The shade of beige on the walls was actually almost warm, far better than the drab paint job they had down at the station. A brown upholstered couch dominated the wall to the left of the entrance, flanked by a pair of coffee tables on which were placed holopads that flashed a series of screens from the latest periodicals.

To the right of the entrance was a small coffee mess that smelled like it had been recently brewed; or at least it didn't smell burnt, which again was a step up from the station.

The holopic he had been looking at was not the only one on the walls; seemed like lots of celebrities did business here.

The receptionist, sitting behind an ebony-colored counter directly opposite the entrance and adjacent to a frosted glass door that led further back into the office spaces, was a flighty-looking blonde of maybe twenty who wore a royal blue blouse that strained against the pressure her chest was placing it under. It was entirely unclear how much longer those buttons could hold up.

When Dominic and Alex had announced themselves, she had answered in a bored-sounding alto and called back to her boss somewhere in the the back, and then went back to scanning her own holos, ignoring them completely.

Great customer service. But then, Dominic supposed that was to be expected.

Not like people came to this place for her.

He looked back at the logo emblazoned in golden letters above the blonde's head—Dooey, Cheatham, and Hough—-and shook his head.

The oldest lawyer joke around, and they had embraced it, made it their own. Told you a little something about the people running the place.

Dominic adjusted his suit jacket on his shoulders and took a step toward the receptionist. Enough of this waiting crap. He was just about to open his mouth to speak when the door leading further back opened and a woman in her late 20s, dressed in a navy blue business suit and wearing her auburn hair up in a bun, stepped into the room.

She took in Dominic and Alex immediately and flashed them an inviting grin. "Detectives? Will you come with me, please?"

Dominic and Alex traded looks, then they followed her.

She led them down a broad hallway that was painted the same shade of warm beige. But the lighting was different, sharper some-how, more on point.

The second door on the left opened into a conference room that was dominated by a table sized for eight, with teleconference micro-phones at each seat and a grey box in the center of the table - a holo-projector most likely. Two men in suits were standing on the opposite side of the table from the door, looking out the floor-to-ceiling window that made up the entire wall.

The view out the window was spectacular. The firm's offices were on the 25th floor of their building, and this western-facing wall allowed a view all the way from downtown past Beverly Hills to Santa Monica and then out to the Pacific, where the incoming surf flashed and sparkled in the afternoon sun.

Didn't suck.

The men turned as Dominic and Alex walked in and their escort announced them.

They were both in their 50s. The guy on the right was taller and rounder with mostly-grey hair and bright blue eyes. The other guy was short, bald, wearing square wire-rim glasses, and built like a brick shithouse beneath the carefully tailored grey pinstriped suit he wore.

The body builder took the lead, smiling with apparent warmth that did not quite reach his eyes. "Thank you, Tina," he said. Focusing in on Dominic, he walked around the table and held out his hand. "Sorry to keep you waiting, Detectives. I'm Alan Hough. This is Nick Dooey."

Dominic shook, and was unsurprised to find he had a powerful grip. "Detective Dominic Trejo." He gestured toward Alex. "My partner, Alexandra Okada."

"Charmed," Hough said. Dooey made similar pleasantries, then there was an awkward silence for a few seconds.

Dominic traded quick glances with Alex, then when it became clear their hosts were not going to speak first, he decided to break the ice. "So, what can we do for you, counselors?" Their Lieutenant had ordered them to drop everything and get down to the firm pronto, so this better be good.

Hough gestured toward the chairs surrounding the table, and they all sat. Then he leaned forward in his.

"I must stress that this needs to be kept in the strictest confidence," he said.

Dominic cleared his throat. "Already got that word," he said. "Straight from the Chief's office, I've been told. So," he clasped his hands together on top of the table and returned Hough's look, "What's going on?"

Hough and Dooey traded looks, and Hough made a little shrug. Dooey spoke. "One of our clients has gone missing. Gary Kovacs."

The name didn't ring a bell for Dominic at all, but next to him, Alex took in a quick, surprised breath. He glanced her way and raised an eyebrow.

She saw his questioning look and lost some of her professional poker face, replaced by the same wry amusement she'd worn earlier. "You were just looking at his holo."

Dominic blinked. "The hat guy? Guitar player?" He looked back at the attorneys, and they nodded confirmation.

"He was supposed to get on a plane for London yesterday," Dooey continued. "His European tour kicks off next week, and he has a lot to get done before then. But he didn't show, and no one has been able to get in touch with him anywhere. Not us, his girlfriend, his mom...no one. Even his implants are offline."

Alex pursed her lips slightly. "He's a grown man. Maybe he just decided not to go."

Dominic was forced to agree. "It's a little early for us to be getting involved. 48 hours is typically - "

"We don't have 48 hours," Hough said, his tone sharp, focused. "There are millions of dollars at stake if his tour doesn't start on time. And that's just from tickets, merchandise, and album sales. He's also got a potential gig in a movie coming up. But if he doesn't show..." Hough shook his head.

"That's not our concern," Dominic said. "We're not gophers. If there's not a crime been committed..." He left the thought stretch out, uncompleted.

There must be more to this business, or they wouldn't have come to the police with it.

"We don't know if there's been a crime or not," Dooey said, taking the lead back from his partner. "But Gary's been getting some... disturbing...messages from fans lately. One fan in particular." He tapped his index finger onto the tabletop, and the holoprojector hummed to life.

After a second of warmup, the projection field coalesced in the center of the table, showing an older man with ruddy cheeks and black hair that was going grey. He wore an angry expression, his lips turned back in a snarl as though he was about to rip someone a new one.

Dooey tapped the tabletop again, and the holo began to play.

"- my daughter, and I'm going to rip your heart out and feed it to my pigs, you scumbag. Whole world ain't big enough to hide you from me. When I - "

Dooey paused the image again. "It continues on for two full minutes."

Dominic was unimpressed. So was Alex.

"He's a celebrity. He must get fifty of these sorts of threats a day," she said.

"Actually, no," Hough said. "Mr. Kovacs is very careful to not make a spectacle of himself, outside of his stage presence. He doesn't engage in politics or causes, and he has made a policy of being gracious to his fans. He employs a fair-sized staff just to handle fan interaction, and satisfaction."

"Fan satisfaction," Dominic said, unable to stop a bit of cynicism from slipping into his tone. "For the pretty ones anyway, right? So what, he banged this guy's daughter and the guy's pissed." Dominic shrugged. "If that's all you've got, I think we're done here. Pretty sure Mr. Kovacs will show up again soon as he gets through with the next groupie."

He moved to stand, but Hough's sharp voice stopped him before he could budge from his seat. "We have assurances from Mayor Chavez that your department will give this all the attention it deserves."

Far as Dominic was concerned, he already had done that. But he could see from the expressions on the two attorneys' faces they thought that meant something completely different.

Probably the Mayor would as well.

Damn.

With a sigh, he nodded. "Ok. Send us that message," he waved toward the holo, "and Kovacs' schedule, contact list, addresses...you know the deal. We'll need to access his accounts as well."

The attorneys didn't like that last bit, but they also had to know the reasons for it.

"Our firm has a limited Power of Attorney for Mr. Kovacs. We can arrange for you to have limited, supervised access." Hough's eyes narrowed. "Anything more, you'll need a warrant."

Great. Real helpful. But there was no point in pushing it. Dominic nodded and stood.

"We'll be in touch," he said. Then he turned and left the room.

He didn't shake hands on the way out.

"This is some kind of bullshit," Dominic said.

Back at the station, with its not-quite-white painted walls, cramped cubicles, smell of burnt coffee and, for those unlucky enough to have cubes adjacent to the doorway back to the holding tank, the fragrance of puke...or worse.

He had the holo the attorneys had given them up on the unit in his cubicle, and he'd played it through four times now. It was about what he'd expected. Dude thought Kovacs had deflowered his little girl, and Kovacs was gonna pay.

Blah, blah, blah.

Dominic had seen that story a thousand times, and it was almost always just a guy blowing off hot air; nothing to it.

And if he really though Kovacs was the first guy she'd banged, he was dreaming.

But there was no getting past it. Dominic and Alex had to at least make it look like they were applying some serious detective work to this nothingburger of a case.

He leaned back in his well broken-in swivel chair and looked to the next cubicle over on his left, Alex's. "Got a background on this guy yet?"

Alex shrugged back at him. "Dan Sobieski. Former Marine. Now works as a longshoreman down in Long Beach. Married to a nurse. Three kids: two boys and a girl."

"How old's the girl?"

She frowned, then tapped at her desk console. "She's..." She paused, blinked. "Eight?" Alex straightened in her chair. "That can't be right."

Dominic got one of those jolts that was like a kick to the gut. No, it couldn't be. Unless the dad was saying Kovacs had...with an eight year old?

No, there was no way Kovacs' attorneys would have let him and Alex know about this if that were the case. They would knowingly be compromising their client.

Unless they didn't know. How far in-depth would they have looked into the guy before telling him and Alex about the threat? And those guys weren't criminal defense attorneys, they dealt with Kovacs' business affairs.

Dominic swallowed hard. "We need to go talk to this guy."

Alex nodded. She looked just as grim as he felt.

A quick call down to the docks at Long Beach told them Sobieski had already clocked out for the day, so they headed down to his house.

It was approaching sunset by the time Dominic and Alex pulled into Sobieski's driveway. His home was modest, but well-maintained. Light brown stucco sides, red terra cotta roof. A carport on the side that held two vehicles back to back, both late model Fords that needed a good cleaning.

A flagstone walkway led from the driveway to a little sitting area out front of the door, complete with a blue canvas swinging chair off to the left. Potted roses on either side of the door lent a subtle fragrance to the area.

Alex rang the bell, and they waited for a couple minutes before the door opened.

It was the man from the holo, but without the snarl and the burning eyes. He had on jeans and a blue and grey plaid cotton shirt, untucked. He looked them over quickly, a questioning look on his face.

"Help you?"

Dominic flashed his badge, and Alex did the same.

"LAPD, Mr. Sobieski. We're here to talk to you about the message you left for Gary Kovacs a week ago."

Sobieski's face dropped, and he lowered his eyes to the ground. Nodding, he said, "Yeah...knew as soon as I sent that it was a mistake."

He blew out a breath, then looked back up at Dominic. "Look, I was pissed and just blew off some steam. Didn't really mean anything by it."

"So you admit you sent it?"

Sobieski snorted. "No sense in denying it. So what, he's pressing charges or something?"

"He's missing, Mr. Sobieski," Alex said, in her flat take-no-prisoners tone.

Sobieski blinked, surprise flashing across his face, then wariness moving toward fear. "Are you - ?"

"Where were you yesterday?"

"At work. And then here at home. Ask my wife." He shook his head vigorously. "You don't think - How would I even get close to a guy like that?"

Dominic re-inserted himself. "A man can think of a way to do anything, if he has the motivation. You accused him of messing with your eight year old daughter." He shook his head. "If it were me, I'd go nuts, a guy did something like that."

Sobieski blinked again, then looked quickly back over his shoulder into the house. He held up his finger, asking for a moment, then reached behind himself and pulled the door to.

"I didn't mean Suzy," he said. He coughed, then lowered his voice. "I meant my other daughter."

Other daughter? Dominic looked over at Alex and raised an eyebrow. She was supposed to have done the background on this guy.

She returned his look with one of confusion, and gave a quick shake of her head.

She'd missed it.

Frowning, Dominic looked back at Sobieski. "Other daughter?"

He must have taken Dominic's frown for displeasure at him, because Sobieski swallowed hard. "I had her before I met Rebecca. It was just a short-term thing. Didn't know she was pregnant until a few months after we broke up. I tried to get back with her, to do the right thing, but she wouldn't let me." He shrugged. "I hardly even saw Laura—that's my first daughter—until she graduated."

"How old is Laura, and where does she live?"

"She's nineteen. Lives up in Culver City. She's a waitress at California Pizza Kitchen."

"We'll need to get in touch with her."

"Why?"

Dominic just looked at him for a long several seconds. Finally, Sobieski broke eye contact, looking back down at the ground.

"Yeah, ok," he said, grudgingly.

"How do you keep the fact you have a kid from another woman secret from your wife?" Alex asked.

They were turning off the 5 onto the 10 heading west toward Culver City, and the traffic was making Dominic want to punch something.

"I've seen worse," Dominic said. "You wouldn't believe the creative lengths some people will go to keep their secrets."

"Yeah, but why should that have to be a secret?"

Dominic shrugged. "Got me. I'm just glad we're not dealing with a pedo thing here." Although, if it were that would mean he could shove the case off onto another team, and he could get back to his real job.

Nope. Not worth it, for that.

Beside him, Alex shuddered.

It took much longer than it should have to get there, but eventually Dominic found the California Pizza Kitchen Sobieski had indicated.

The place was decorated the same as every other restaurant in the chain, and of course the hostess was a blonde. She beamed at the two of them when they walked up.

"Table for two?"

Dominic showed his badge and shook his head. "Girl named Laura Gutierrez work here?"

The hostess' smile faded at the sight of the badge. She nodded.

"Yeah. She's on break right now." She indicated a door back toward the rear of the dining area, marked "Employees Only."

"Mind if we go back?"

She shrugged, then leaned in, eyes flashing with curiosity. "What'd she do?"

Dominic shook his head. "Not a thing. Just need to ask her some questions, is all."

"Oh." The girl looked a tad disappointed at that.

They walked past the tables in the dining area—about half full—and the smells of bread, tomato sauce, cheese, and the various meats on the pizzas as they passed the diners made Dominic's stomach growl, reminding him that it was just about past dinner time.

He licked his lips, but pushed that thought aside.

Time for a bite after this.

Through the Employees Only door was the break room. Two round white-topped tables with grey powder coated metal chairs for four at each table dominated the center of the room. To the left, a white-fronted over and under refrigerator sat beside a long white linoleum counter with cabinets above and below, and a white porcelain sink. A coffee maker sat at the end of the counter, next to a stack of white styrofoam cups for employee's use, and there was a microwave mounted below the upper cabinets. A bulletin board with various notices of employment was on the wall across from the entrance, with a second door leading, Dominic presumed, to a locker room.

The sounds and smells of cooking wafted through a closed door to the right; the kitchen.

Two people were sitting at the table directly ahead when Dominic and Alex walked in. A skinny, brown haired guy in khaki slacks and a white collared shirt, and a woman that Dominic could hardly look away from.

Even seated, it was obvious she was tall, approaching six feet, and slender. But not waifish, more like someone who kept herself in shape. Wavy brown hair spilled past her shoulders, setting off the yellowish brown of her eyes. Her cheekbones and chin seemed sculpted, and her lips were a lush and sensual red. She was wearing the CPK wait staff's outfit, but she made it seem like formal attire, the way she carried herself.

"Laura Gutierrez?" Alex said as they approached, and showed her badge. Dominic did the same. He had decided to let her take the lead on this, try the woman to woman thing. At least at first.

Laura nodded, her eyes tracing his badge and then giving him a once-over before shifting over to Alex.

The guy turned in his chair to look at them as well, and his lips turned downward.

"What can I do for you, officers?"

"We'd like to ask you a few questions, if you have a minute. About Gary Kovacs."

She blinked, surprise flashing across her face followed quickly by suspicion. She glanced at the guy she was sitting with, and Dominic noticed he flinched a little.

"What about him?"

Alex didn't answer, but pressed on with their agreed-to line of questioning. "We understand you were with him last week."

Laura looked at her flatly. "Is this because of what my dad did?"

"You know about that?"

Laura nodded, looking, if anything, amused as she thought back on the event. "Yeah, my dad called me up and told me, right after he did it." She snorted out a half-laugh. "He was embarrassed as hell." Then she added, with a bit more heat, "And he should be." But it seemed like she was only adding that because she felt like she should; the heat seemed half-hearted.

Alex pursed her lips. "Interesting."

"What is?"

Alex made a little shrug. "I think I would have been angry, in your position."

Laura shrugged. "Well, mom and the courts wouldn't let him be around when I was little. I guess he's feeling like he has to make up for the lost protective time, or something. He didn't really mean anything by it, though. I told Gary not to worry about it."

Dominic could not stop himself from interjecting at that. "You're in contact with Gary still?"

She narrowed her eyes at him. "Yes. It wasn't just a one night stand, if that's what you were thinking. We've been seeing each other for a couple months." She paused, then lost some of her spunk. "Only just told dad about it a week and a half ago. He flipped out, because Gary's a rock guy. Figured he was using me..." She shook her head, frowning. Now she actually was irritated. "He doesn't get it."

Dominic looked aside at Alex and she raised an eyebrow. This was an angle they weren't expecting.

"Why are you asking this?" It was the guy who was sitting with Laura, and he was looking at Dominic in particular. His lips were twisted into a half-smirk, half-frown, and his tone was affronted.

"Who are you?"

The guy straightened in his chair. "Tom Delancy. Assistant Manager," he said, putting on an air of importance as he said the title.

Great. One of those guys. "Well, Mr. Delancy, that is police business. And none of yours." He looked back at Alex and gave her a little nod.

She said, "When did you see Gary last?"

"Yesterday. We had lunch here before I went on shift." Laura grinned. "He said he wanted to get a last good taste of America before he went off to Europe."

"What time was that?"

"About 1:30. Why?"

Alex made a little shrug. "Just checking the timeline. Someone saw that message your dad left and was concerned." She paused, then asked, "Have you heard from him since?"

"No, but he wasn't getting in to London until late and he's going to be really busy. I'm flying out to meet him in Paris for his gig in two weeks, though." Her grin grew even more broad, and Dominic couldn't blame her. The city of lights in the company of a rock 'n roll star?

Alex looked like she would relish that idea also. Her eyebrows arched upwards, and Dominic thought he saw the edges of an envious smile.

Laura glanced aside at the clock above the door to the kitchen. "I've got to go back on shift," she said, and stood. "Is there anything else? My dad's not going to be in trouble is he?"

Alex shook her head. "No. We just needed to follow up on it. Thank you for your assistance."

The two women shook hands, and then Laura swept back through the door leading out into the dining area.

Tom watched her go, that half-smirk becoming all frown. "Don't let her fool you. He's trouble," he said.

Dominic looked askance at him. "Who, her dad?"

Tom shook his head. "Mr. Rock Star. She's too good for him." He sounded decidedly bitter as he said that, and his eyes remained locked on the door where she'd gone through for a moment. Then he gave himself a little shake and he, also, stood. Straightening, he put on what was clearly intended to be an ingratiating smile but instead resembled more of a grimace. "If there's nothing else, this lounge is for employees only," he said, in lieu of, "Get the hell out of here."

"No problem," Dominic said, and he turned to go.

As they stepped out of the break room and into the dining, Alex said, "What a creep."

Couldn't argue with that one.

Dominic saw Laura tending to a table over on the far left side of the dining area. She hadn't been there for long at all; couldn't have. But she already seemed to have established a good rapport with the customers, as one of them laughed in enjoyment at whatever it was she had said.

"So famous rock 'n roll guy falls for a waitress," he said, mulling the concept over in his head.

"Stranger things have happened," Alex said.

"True enough." His stomach growled again. "You up for dinner?"

"What, here?"

He shook his head. "Might get misunderstood. Let's hit Jack In The Box across the street."

"Fancy man," Alex said, grinning back at him as she pushed the door open. "No wonder you go on so many dates."

Dominic snorted. That would have stung, coming from someone else; he hadn't been on a date in months. "You know it," he said, playing up the joke.

Alex chuckled.

They took their burgers to the car and sat inside, munching away.

In between bites, Dominic said, "What time was Gary's flight supposed to be yesterday?"

Alex swallowed, frowned, and pulled out her holopad. She tapped the interface a few times, then said, "Looks like 1600."

"So it's safe to say Laura was the last person to see him before he vanished."

"Uh-huh."

Dominic took another bite of his burger and chewed, slowly. Somewhere between this CPK and Van Nuys airport, Gary Kovacs had met with some misadventure.

Or...

"Maybe you were right in the first place. He said screw it, and decided not to go."

Alex shook her head. "Why drop off the grid, though? Even his implants aren't answering, and that takes some doing."

True. The new interactive database implants were constantly online with the global network, and enabled the wearer instantaneous, or near enough, access to the information stored there. Made things like forgetting a person's name an anachronism.

That alone would almost be worth the price of admission, as far as Dominic was concerned. If they weren't so damn expensive.

But they also made it almost impossible to have any real private time. The constant network pings and interfaces made someone trackable, and reachable, all the time.

For that reason alone, even if he'd had the money to afford a set, Dominic wasn't sure he would want to get one.

Gary may not have had a choice in the matter. As a high profile celebrity, whose presence was the cornerstone of a massive upcoming musical tour and who knows how many other ventures, his investors or people who he had contractual obligations to may have forced the implants on him.

Which didn't at all change Alex's point. It was darn difficult to block the signal to those things, unless...

"Maybe he had them removed," Dominic said. "Instead of hitting the airport, he went to a tech, got the deed done, and then split."

"For where?"

Dominic shrugged.

"Well, Laura thinks he was going to Europe, along with everyone else."

"So she says," Dominic said.

Alex opened her mouth to reply, but he raised a hand to stop her. "Hear me out." She closed her mouth, looking expectantly at him.

"Laura's the girl on the side. She's not the girlfriend the tabloids and his attorneys know about."

Alex frowned, but nodded.

"He decided he doesn't want the business anymore. Doesn't want the main girl, because she only was with him for his business."

"That's a bit harsh," Alex said.

Dominic shrugged. "But true more often than not. Anyway, he meets Laura. Here's this salt of the earth girl, hot, and they hit it off. He comes up with a plan to get away from it all, and she helps him. She tells her dad something outrageous about Gary, so dad flies off the handle. They know when Gary disappears we'll waste time looking at Dad, and that gives Gary time to get the implant removal procedure. Then, instead of meeting in Paris like she's been advertising they meet somewhere else. And it's all's well that ends well."

"That's pretty thin."

Dominic shrugged. "Did our access to his financials come through yet? They'd need to take out a nest egg."

"I'll check." Alex began tapping at her holopad again. "If you're right, why would she tell us her dad's message was no big deal? They'd gain more time if we focused in on him."

Yeah, that was a wrinkle in his idea. "She doesn't want him to get in any real trouble. And anyway, they wouldn't need a huge amount of time. Just long enough to get the implants removed, or at least disabled. How long does that procedure take?"

"No idea. Ok, I'm in." Alex chewed on her lip as she scrolled through the records. "I don't see anything that stands out right off the bat. No unusually large withdrawals..." She trailed off as the data drew her more fully in.

"Well it wouldn't have to be just one. A bunch of smaller withdrawals over a period of time would do the trick, but not raise eyebrows."

"You're grasping at straws."

"Maybe. But do you have any other ideas?"

Alex was silent for a long several seconds as she mulled it over. Finally, she shook her head. "If she's in on it, they'll probably meet up at some point."

Dominic nodded.

"So we're staking her out then?"

Dominic nodded.

Alex groaned. "So much for my Tae Bo class."

CPK closed at 9, but Laura didn't come out until almost 10.

Dominic and Alex sat in their car around the corner, watching the entrance through electronically enhanced binoculars, but even with them, for a little while there he thought they would miss her. Maybe she went out the back when she left, or...

No. There she was. She had changed into street clothes: a black t-shirt with PINK written across the breast, jeans, and sneakers.

Laura crossed the street at the intersection in front of Alex and Dominic's car but never looked in their direction. She continued up half a block, then got into her own car, a late model Ford just like at her dad's house.

Her lights came on, and Laura drove past them, going the opposite direction as they were facing.

Dominic waited half a minute, then started their car and pulled out, making a u-turn at the intersection to follow her.

It didn't take long to catch up with Laura's car, and then he hung back, being careful to maintain distance so as not to be seen.

She drove for twenty minutes or so, and finally pulled into an apartment complex called "Cedar Farms", which seemed a strange name for a place in LA. But whatever.

Dominic pulled into the complex as well, and parked near the front. They were able to see her park in the lot about halfway down. She got out of her car, popped the trunk and removed a bag from inside, then went to the second of three buildings in the complex and climbed stairs up to the second floor. Her apartment was to the right of the staircase, and then she was gone from view.

It was 10:30.

"Think she'll go out again?" Alex asked, peering through her own binoculars at the building.

"Might not need to, if he's at her place."

She lowered the binoculars and gave him a wry look. "Not likely. They wouldn't risk it this soon."

"Probably right."

They went back to watching.

There was a single window visible from her apartment, and Dominic could see the light on. At 11:30, it went off.

Ten minutes later, she still had not emerged, and Dominic looked back at Alex.

"Guess she's in for the night," Alex said. She glanced at her watch. "I'm beat. Let's call it, pick it back up tomorrow."

Dominic nodded, and was just reaching for the ignition when movement further back in the apartment complex caught his eye.

He raised his binoculars to his eyes. There was a figure crouched in the shadows back at the rear of the parking lot. Dominic flipped on the lowlight function, and his eyes widened.

"Alex. Rear of the parking lot. Left side, by the big tree."

He didn't take his eyes off the binoculars, but he heard her shifting. A moment later, she made a quick inhalation.

"Is that - ?"

Dominic nodded. "Pretty sure that's Tom, the Assistant Manager."

"He was definitely giving off some creepy vibes. What's he doing here?"

Dominic adjusted the magnification function on his binoculars. Tom was holding something up to his eyes. He'd bet good money that something was a set of binoculars, and he was looking straight at Laura's apartment.

"Looks like he's doing the same thing we are."

Alex's silence spoke volumes.

Tom stood there for another several minutes. Then he tucked his binoculars away and stepped over to a car that was parked a couple spaces away from his tree.

Dominic switched off the lowlight function. A couple seconds later the car's lights came on.

"How did he get in here?" Alex said. "No way he came past us."

"There must be a back entrance."

Tom's car pulled out of its space, and Dominic started his own engine.

"I was just about to say no way we're not following him," Alex said.

"Damn right."

Dominic was right; there was a rear entrance to the apartment complex's lot. They followed Tom out at a discrete distance.

He drove north, and before long they were ascending a winding road leading up into the hills. Dominic could feel it in his wallet every time they got a bit higher and passed another uber-expensive house.

"He can't live up here, not on an Assistant Manager's salary," he said to himself.

Alex must have heard it, because she snorted out a chuckle. "Maybe mommy and daddy do."

He did look the type to still be living at home, Dominic had to admit.

But when Tom reached the crest of the hills, he continued on, descending down the other side. Eventually, he slowed and turned onto a side street that branched off to the right. Dominic followed, and almost ran into him as Tom had come to a halt.

His reversing lights came on, and Dominic realized Tom was parallel parking. He maneuvered around Tom's car, and Alex slumped down in her seat so she would be less visible. But as they passed Tom by, he was solely focused on the reversing camera and rearview; he never even glanced over at them.

Dominic pulled over in front of a fire hydrant half a block up, and killed the engine. In the rearview, Tom was just getting out of his car. He looked both ways, and then hurried across the street to the house across from where he had parked.

It was difficult to make out many details of the house because all its lights were off. But there was a carport on the near side, and it looked like the house was just one story.

Dominic chewed on his lip for a second. Then he grabbed up his binoculars and opened the car door.

"What are you doing?"

"Can't see anything from here. I'm going to sneak over and check out what he's doing."

"He's going home is what he's doing."

"Are you sure?"

Alex frowned, then nodded, conceding his point. Tom had already stalked one victim tonight. What's to say he wasn't doing it again?

She got out of the car also, but took a moment to pick up their portable transmitter before joining him.

They moved quickly, staying to the street side of the parked cars and keeping low so they would not silhouette as they approached the house.

Slowing as they reached the last car that was parked before the house's driveway, Dominic inched his way to the edge of the car and peeked around.

The carport lights were not on, but there was a storage shed at its rear. The shed's door was ajar, and the interior light was on, illuminating the red Mercedes parked in the carport.

There was someone moving around in the shed, and Dominic could hear at least one voice coming from within, though he couldn't make out the words.

A minute or so later, Tom emerged from the shed, and now Dominic could clearly hear him say, "Motherfucker," over his shoulder as he switched off the light, closed the door, and locked it. Then he walked around the Mercedes to the door leading from the carport into the house itself, unlocked it, and went inside.

A light came on inside the house. Then, after a couple minutes, it went out again, and the night was silent and dark.

It was well past midnight. Tom had probably gone to bed. But what was the deal in the shed?

"I'm going to go check out the shed," he said behind himself, to Alex.

"Warrant?"

He liked that she played by the rules. But she needed to learn when and how to stretch them. "Only going to check out what's observable from outside. If there's nothing, we back off."

She waited for a few seconds before replying, "Ok."

Dominic moved up into the carport at a crouch, and he heard Alex following along behind him. He stayed on the opposite side of the Mercedes from the house, for extra concealment. When he came to the end of the car, he waited for a minute, listening.

Nothing, except... There was something from the shed, muffled.

Dominic moved to the shed door and pressed his ear up against it.

There was definitely something moving inside the shed. And... that sounded like a voice, but muffled like gagged.

Dominic felt a surge of adrenalin rush through his system. He looked back at Alex and mimed a lockpicking action. She shook her head, and he pointed to his ear then toward the shed door.

She nodded, seeming to understand. Then she pointed at the transmitter. Radio for backup?

Dominic thought for a second, then shook his head. Wait to see what they had first.

He kept a set of lockpicks in the inner pocket of his suit coat. It wasn't strictly speaking illegal to have them, but... Well, he kept them anyway. Just in case he came across a situation like this.

He worked the lock on the shed door for a couple minutes, Alex watching his back—he didn't have to check to know she was. And then he got the tumblers just right, and the lock turned.

He had the door open a second later and stepped inside.

Whoever was in there heard, and probably saw, him. They made more noise, but again, it was muffled, impossible to make out.

Dominic found the light switch inside the door and flipped them on.

In the middle of the shed sat a wooden chair. A man was sitting in the chair, his hands tied behind his back and his ankles tied to the chair legs. He wore jeans and a t-shirt with some band's logo Dominic didn't recognize. He was gagged with a red bandana, and he blinked hard as the lights came on. The smell of urine and feces surrounded him; Tom must not have even let him loose to go when he needed to.

Dominic recognized him from his holo. Gary Kovacs.

"Call for backup," he said to Alex, waiting outside.

***

Alan Hough met Dominic and Alex in the waiting room at Cedars Sinai medical center. Despite the early hour—or late, depending on how one looked at it—he was impeccably dressed in his pinstriped suit. It didn't look at all like he had been woken in the middle of the night with the news, and that he had rushed down to see to his client.

"Tied up in the shed?" Alan shook his head. He sounded incredulous.

"Yep," Dominic said. "Tom lawyered up, but we figure he thought if he could split Gary and Laura up, he could weasel his way in on her while she was on the rebound. In his very finite wisdom, he decided

Gary standing her up in Paris would be the ideal way to do that. Turns out he's studying cybersecurity on the side. So, he figured out how to jam the implant signal and then just..." Dominic made a snatching gesture with his hands.

"But..." The lawyer shook his head. "That doesn't make any sense. What was he going to do with Gary after that?"

Dominic didn't answer, and the lawyer paled.

Changing the subject, Alan asked, "Whose house was that?"

"Tom's," Alex said. "He inherited when his parents passed away two years ago." She paused, then added, "Natural causes. We checked."

Alan nodded. "Well." He paused. Then he stuck out his hand toward Dominic. "Thank you, detective."

Dominic shook, and watched as Alan shook Alex's hand as well.

"If there's ever anything my firm can do to assist you, please let me know," Alan said. Then, not stopping to wait for a response, he turned and walked to the nurse's station where he would no doubt begin demanding to see his client immediately.

"Well," Dominic said, "Another job well done, and all's well that ends well."

He looked over at Alex, and she grinned in response. Then she broke out in a huge yawn.

Dominic agreed completely.

6

FENCES AND NEIGHBORS

Jerome's back ached. A constant state of things after years spent hunched over his fields, tending his plantings.

But today it was worse. The lingering chill from a winter that refused to leave made his joints stiff, lending an extra bit of oomph to the complaints from his spine.

He gritted his teeth and finished patting down soil atop the seeds he had just placed, then rose, straightening and throwing his shoulders back as he twisted his torso left and right to remove the kinks. His breath misted in front of his face as he sighed out a great exhalation, almost a groan.

He really needed to take a rest. But the dirt-stained canvas bag in his left hand was still half full of the seeds he had forced himself to not eat when the Bigman increased his levies over the winter, depleting Jerome's store so that he had feared it would run out before the thaw.

Half a bag of seed left, and half an acre to go.

But he felt his blankets calling to him. He looked off to the right. There, the tilled lines of earth he had already planted lined up, one after another after another, right up to the doorstep of his castle.

Castle. More like a lean-to built from hewn wooden planks that he had constructed against a crumbling gray stone edifice from days gone by. It was a single room, but enough for him now that his boy was gone, and surprisingly cozy. The stove he had bartered from a trader couple years back had done wonders for heat in the winter time.

Still, looking at it, greying brown wood stacking against the cracked grey of the old stone wall, beneath the grey overcast of a spring day that still wanted to pretend it was winter, he felt intensely the loss that had befallen them all, back way before he was born.

Wasn't always this way, or so the oldies said. Used to be this was a world of plenty, where the big worry was the people were too fat, they had so much.

Jerome snorted.

Like the oldies would know. They hadn't been alive to see that supposed golden time either. It was all fairy tales and nonsense.

And that wouldn't put his crops into the ground, so he wouldn't starve next winter.

Jerome adjusted the strap of leather he used to hold his home-spun wool pants up—they were much looser now than they had been—and took a step forward along the line of tilled soil he was working.

"Jerome Hightower."

The gruff voice came from behind, back toward where Jerome's fields ended, and oaks and elms that were only just beginning to bud out new leaves fought for growing room against other shells of constructs from the distant past.

One shell stood out, still discernible as a towering structure that must have, at one time, touched heaven itself. But now it, like the other remnants from that age long dead, was crumbling. Holes dotted its lofty, cracked facade like the eyes in a skull, and one whole side of it was gone, reduced to a heap of rubble that spread out hundreds of yards from where the building had once stood.

Jerome would have been able to plant quite a lot more, if not for that.

A track, worn clear of undergrowth by the footsteps of countless people over the entirety of Jerome's life, ran beneath one of the surviving walls of that behemoth-that-was and skirted the edge of Jerome's fields before ducking around behind the edifice that supported his home.

A trio of men stood on that track, looking at him.

They were all muscle-bound, with visible scars on their faces and forearms from a life spent fighting and brawling, and were dressed in well-cured brown leathers. They had their heads shaved on the sides and back, but had let their hair—brown on the men to the right and left but blond on the one in the center—grow long at their crowns, so it spilled down the backs of their heads like a horse's mane.

Their clothing and haircuts marked them as the Bigman's enforcers even if their demeanors and builds hadn't.

The blond, half a hand shorter than the other two and about five years older, met Jerome's eyes, and it was all Jerome could do not to flinch away from the hard resolve in his stare.

"Bigman wants to see you," he said.

Jerome sighed, nodded, and dropped his seed bag to the ground.

There would be no more planting today.

Jerome's fields lay about two thirds of the way out from the center of the Bigman's domain.

It wasn't quite a town, but neither was it entirely countryside. Rather, the Bigman ruled over a sprawling collection of encampments, homesteads, and farms that lurked within this carcass of the distant past. One could walk for an hour in one direction and see nothing but shattered remnants of old structures, with the occasional farm like Jerome's, or in a completely different direction and find mostly-intact constructs that housed eight or ten families clustered around a marketplace.

It was haphazard. It was barely holding on.

It was home.

The track led them past the behemoth adjoining Jerome's fields, then through a growth of trees so thick they blotted out the sky and almost made a man forget what formerly-grand structures he had just walked past a moment before.

Then it emerged before another blasted-out ruin and turned left, proceeding along a slow upward grade until, after nearly a half hour of walking, they came to the Bigman's abode.

Unlike the dwellings of most of the people in his domain, the Bigman kept his home in exquisite repair. Constructed from stones that he—or his people really—had gathered from the ruined structures or gathered from alongside the river on the west side of his domain and mortared together with a mixture of materials that Jerome could not guess at, it had two levels and a dozen rooms.

And even two glass windows!

Smoke rose from two of the dwelling's four chimneys as Jerome came close, but lingered low above the building as though some force was keeping it from flying free. It lent the area a somewhat acrid odor.

Which was an improvement from the usual smells of bodies and waste that tended to surround habitations. So there was that.

The Bigman's men had set up a sort of covered pavilion in front of his dwelling some years back. Supported by four great logs that were driven in to the earth and topped by a wooden roof, it could be enclosed for the winter but now lay open on all four sides.

Here was where the Bigman held court. There were maybe a dozen other people under the pavilion, but as he drew near, Jerome focused entirely on the man himself.

Jerome could see him waiting there. The broad, bearish man with long hair cut in the same style as his enforcers; although really theirs were cut to match him. It had once been coal black, his hair, but now it was silver-grey, with only a few wisps of his youthful color remaining.

The Bigman's face was craggy, lined by years of conflict and worry, and his brows were very nearly as bushy as the mustache he wore above his lips.

He wore leathers similar to his enforcers, but also a blue cape made of a fine, almost slippery material that some traders had brought from distant lands to the south. Heavy leather work boots were on his feet, and he had a knife tucked into his belt. An actual steel knife, whose blade flashed and sparkled in the light when he brought it out to do its work.

He was sitting on a great stone chair that had been erected at the rear of his audience pavilion. As Jerome approached, he leaned forward and placed his elbows on his knees. The movement set the Timex—his pendant of office—swaying forward from around his neck, and Jerome's eyes were drawn to it.

It was deceptively simple. Round, maybe two-thirds as big as a man's wrist, and made of a dull metal that Jerome did not know. A leather thong held it around the Bigman's neck. Nothing much to look at at all, except for the arms in the Timex's face. Three of them; none of the same length though two were thicker and one narrow and long, like a needle.

Some strange magic kept those arms moving around and around the face of the thing, the thinner one fastest, then the longer of the thick ones, and finally the shortest.

Jerome swallowed as he saw the thin arm sweep across the strange XII marking at the top of the Timex's face, and had to stop himself from shivering.

"Do you know why I summoned you, Jerome?"

The Bigman's voice, unexpectedly quiet for a man of his size—and power—broke Jerome from his consideration of the mystical artifact and drew his gaze back up to the Bigman's eyes. They were a shade between brown and yellow, and narrowed as they considered him.

Jerome made a little shrug of his shoulders and shook his head.

The Bigman gestured with his left hand. Jerome followed the gesture with his gaze and looked to his right.

Kenneth Josburg stood at the edge of the gaggle of people under the pavilion. Kenneth Josburg, tall and sandy-haired and muscular, a dozen or so years younger than Jerome, and the man who owned the farmstead next to Jerome's. He wore wool, but of a higher quality weave than Jerome's and died red, and sturdy work boots.

His left eye was blackened, and his lip swollen. When he stepped forward in response to the Bigman's gesture, he favored his left leg a bit.

Jerome scowled. The boy couldn't take his whipping like a man; had to run off to the Bigman, did he? He turned back to the Bigman and spoke.

"His animals got loose again. Tore up ground I'd spent three days tilling and getting ready to plant. Set me back a week."

Jerome could feel Kenneth's glare as he interjected, "I apologized, and offered to help - "

Jerome didn't look at him, but instead held up his right hand, palm out toward the younger man, to silence him. "I need no help from the likes of you. If - "

"Enough."

The Bigman's soft voice cut through the beginnings of their argument with ease. He looked from Jerome to Kenneth and back again in silence. The thin arm of the Timex swept through two of the strange markings on its face before he spoke again.

"This constant strife between you two has gone on long enough." His eyes focused in on Jerome. "Jerome, I've known you since you were a boy. You were loyal to my father, and you've been loyal to me." He paused, then added, "And I will never forget your son's sacrifice during our war with the Atlantians."

To Kenneth, the Bigman said. "And you served in that war. You and Tommy were comrades. I cannot understand why you two cannot get along."

He chewed on his lip for a moment, then shook his head. "Between your fields, Jerome, and your herds, Kenneth, you two produce a significant portion of the foods that carry our city through the winter. But if things continue as they have been, I may have to move the both of you out and put someone else on your lands."

"Bigman, I - " Kenneth started.

At the same time, Jerome said, "The devil you will." He opened his mouth to speak further, but the Bigman cleared his throat and raised his hands palms out, commanding silence.

"I said may." He drew a breath. "I'm told the ancients had a saying. Fences make good neighbors." He turned stern eyes onto Kenneth, and then Jerome. "You two will work together to erect a wall between your properties. Starting today, when you leave my presence. You will do no other work until it is done."

"My cattle won't just tend themselves," Kenneth said.

"Nor will my fields," Jerome added. "If - "

"I will assign men to mind your animals until your task is complete," the Bigman said.

Kenneth, looking glum, nodded.

Jerome was not ready to give in just yet. "Bigman, if I don't get finished planting soon, there will not be enough time for the crops to grow. The harvest will be lacking."

"Then I suggest you work quickly." The Bigman's eyes narrowed again, and Jerome could tell he would brook no further argument.

With a sigh, Jerome looked to the ground and nodded, obediently.

Jerome walked back to his fields in silence. Kenneth walked beside him, but Jerome had no desire to engage the man in conversation. Best just to get this thing done and be over with it.

But silence could not rule forever, apparently. When they were about two thirds of the way back, Kenneth cleared his throat. "How do you think to do this?"

Jerome glanced sidelong at him and grunted.

Kenneth's farmstead was technically on the other side of the great edifice that Jerome had built his lean-to against. That should have been more than sufficient wall, but the edifice had crumbled a tenth of a mile past the edge of Jerome's fields, on the opposite side from the great tower. That left a sizable area that was mostly clear which

Kenneth's animals had meandered through on far too many occasions.

Interestingly enough, the edifice's collapse had not left the terrain strewn with rubble, like the tower's. Or maybe it had, and people had long ago carried those rocks away.

Didn't matter, either way.

Kenneth returned Jerome's glance, and he could see the herdsman was getting irritated at his lack of response.

No sense starting the project out with a fight, Jerome figured. So, after a couple more paces, he replied, "We use the rubble from the great tower on the other side of my fields. Patch the hole in that wall between us."

Kenneth pursed his lips, considering the proposal before nodding agreement. Then he burst out with a rueful chuckle. "Should have done that a while ago. Save ourselves the trouble now."

Jerome just grunted again. He was right, but no sense saying so.

They reached Jerome's fields and he looked over at the long pile of rubble extending from the tower. Most of the material was in pieces that were too large to be used, but along the edges of the debris field there were quite a lot of smaller stones. None were regular on a side, though, so it would be a chore fitting them together so they would stay solidly in one piece.

"We'll have to make mortar, I suppose. Or just use mud?" Kenneth said.

"Mud should do. I'll go get my wheelbarrow. Might as well start moving these over."

Jerome had a small shed and tool storage bin adjacent to his lean-to. Although, he considered as he walked up to it that small probably wasn't the correct word for it; it was almost as big as the lean-to itself.

It was locked with a simple mechanism that Jerome had paid Patrick, the Bigman's domain's sole blacksmith, to install. It wasn't much, and Jerome didn't fool himself that it would stop someone who was determined to steal his things. But it was better than nothing.

He had it open quickly enough, and hauled the wheelbarrow out.

It was constructed of wood through and through—even the wheel. And it was stiff to maneuver around. But it did the job.

He turned and wheeled it over to where Kenneth stood waiting near the field of stones.

Then they got to work.

***

Jerome only thought his back had been aching before.

Days spent bent over tending crops were nothing compared with a day spent hefting heavy stones into his wheelbarrow, wheeling them across his entire field and through the brambles beyond to the break in the wall, and then unloading and stacking them.

He had slept like a stone, but it hadn't done his back a lick of good; somehow it felt even worse than it had last night.

But there was nothing for it but to keep on, get the damn wall built. Then he could get back to his real work, and he wouldn't have to deal with Kenneth ever again.

Except at market. Man did need some meat every now and then, after all.

He trudged across the fields, rubbing at the small of his back as he went, and scowled at the mist that had descended during the night and that still clung to the land. Thick enough that he could only just make out the closest edge of his field from the lean-to, it quickly dampened his face and head.

At least he was wearing wool.

Nearing the edge of his field, he saw movement ahead in the midst. Was Kenneth at work already? Boy's trying to one-up him. That wouldn't -

That was too big to be Kenneth. What was -

A long, low moo answered Jerome's question for him. Biting back a curse, Jerome surged forward, back pain forgotten. Dodging past a trio of Kenneth's cows who were chewing the cud at the edge of his field, he hurried over to the beginnings of wall that they had built the previous day.

The cows had knocked the entire thing asunder.

Jerome's vision went red with fury.

Jerome's jaw ached as well as his back, but he felt lucky things weren't worse.

To say the Bigman had been unimpressed with them this morning was to call a lightning bolt a small flash of light. When his enforcers had pulled Jerome and Kenneth apart and marched them back before the Bigman, Jerome got the distinct impression that he was seriously considering having the both of them flogged, taking their land, and having done with the whole thing.

Instead, he chewed them both up one side and down the other, then cast them out, back to the task at hand.

But Jerome had no doubt if there was a recurrence, he would not be so lenient next time.

So he set to work, and pointedly avoided saying anything more to Kenneth than he absolutely had to.

Kenneth seemed to be taking the same strategy, which was just fine to Jerome.

By the time the sun had sunk below the trees surrounding Jerome's field, they had repaired the damage Kenneth's cows had done and then some. All in all, it was a good day's work.

He just hoped the cows wouldn't ruin it again.

They didn't, and a week of labor had them completing a wall chest-high and two stones thick that spanned halfway across the gap where the edifice had crumbled away.

And it didn't actually look half bad, either.

Despite his continuing aches and pains, Jerome felt pretty good about how things were progressing.

But when he left his lean-to on the first day of the new week and made his way toward the construction site, he found upon arrival that his wheelbarrow was gone.

He'd left it there the night before, thinking to save time by not locking it up. After all, it wasn't all that valuable, and in the last week he had seen no one come near this spot besides himself, Kenneth, and the Bigman's enforcers who were watching Kenneth's cattle. Surely there would be no harm in leaving it out.

Apparently not.

Jerome fumed as he walked the length of their partially-built wall, looked behind some nearby trees, and generally scoured the area. He found nothing.

No wheelbarrow.

Someone had made off with it.

He looked at the small pile of loose stones a pace away from the wall construction, all that remained of the last wheelbarrow load they had brought over from the rubble pile the day before. If they were going to have to carry each stone by hand from now on...

This was going to take months.

A soft whistling told of Kenneth's approach. It was the same nameless tune that he whistled each morning. Disgustingly cheery and upbeat.

Just then, hearing it made Jerome's fists clench and his teeth ache from grinding them so hard.

Kenneth came into view, stepping through the gap in their partially constructed wall, and pushing Jerome's wheelbarrow before him.

Jerome gave a start. "Here now, what are you doing with that?"

Kenneth stopped, released the wheelbarrow's handles, and shrugged, looking at Jerome quizzically.

"When you went home yesterday, you left it here. Figured I'd lock it up for you, so no one would steal it."

"A likely story," Jerome snarled. He shoved his way past Kenneth and put his hands on the handles, then rubbed his palms along them. Relief at the wheelbarrow's return fought with anger over his earlier despair, and all came to focus on the source of that despair: Kenneth.

The anger flared hotter.

"You tend to your own things, and leave me to mine," Jerome said with heat, and pushed the wheelbarrow away from him.

Intellectually, he knew there was no way Kenneth was going to just up and take it while Jerome was right there. But intellect had nothing to do with his desire to get the thing as far away from the man as possible.

He wheeled it to the far side of the loose pile of stones and released the handles.

"What is it about me that draws such anger in you all the time? Why do you hate me so?"

Jerome froze at Kenneth's words. Grinding his teeth, he waited to take two breaths before he replied.

"You know well why I do."

"I surely do not."

Jerome spun on the younger man and jabbed a finger at him. "Aye, you do! Tommy was barely more than a boy. You were assigned charge of him." He stalked forward a step, barely restraining himself from turning that pointed finger into a fist as the anguish of his loss, still fresh after all these years, welled up. And with it, the anger he had held onto for the same amount of time. "You abandoned him. You left him to die!"

"You think I wanted to?" Kenneth also stepped forward, so they were standing chest to chest and he stared Jerome dead in the eye.

"I think you saved yourself, at cost to him."

Jerome stumbled backward; Kenneth had shoved him with both hands before he could see it coming.

His feet tangled in a root and he fell onto his backside. A spike of pain ran up his back from the impact and he grunted.

Kenneth was standing over him, fists clenched. Jerome looked up and raised his jaw, ready to take the blow.

Instead, Kenneth spoke, his voice ragged with anger and some other, deeper emotion. "I was desperate to save him. We were cut off from the others in the Atlantian counterattack, and they were everywhere. We tried to get away, but they were too many. I saw three of them fall onto Tommy, and I tried to get to him, but..." His voice broke and he looked away, lowering his hands to his sides. "They were too many," he repeated.

Jerome was silent, just watching and listening to this man who he had harbored such resentment for as he clearly struggled to hold back tears.

"I hear his screams every night," Kenneth said, softly, as though talking to himself.

Jerome swallowed. "I... I didn't know."

"Well you wouldn't." The fire was back in Kenneth's voice. He turned back and glared at Jerome through wet eyes. "Never bothered to ask, did you?"

What to say to that? It was true. He had been in such pain, first from the loss of his wife six months before and then Tommy. He hadn't asked the details; hadn't wanted them. But he couldn't accept that it was all just fate. He had to blame someone.

So he'd chosen someone easy.

Jerome swallowed. "I'm -"

"Whatever. Let's just get this done. Then we can be through with each other."

Kenneth turned away and trudged back to the pile of stones next to the wheelbarrow, and picked one up.

The wall was complete.

Jerome's back hurt like hell, and his heart throbbed as well. From the pain of old scabs ripped out, and from guilt. But he still couldn't help but feel the pride of accomplishment as he looked at what he and Kenneth had built.

The Bigman ran his hand along the top of the wall and smiled with apparent approval. Then he gave it a pat and turned away toward Jerome and, standing beside him, Kenneth.

"Well done," the Bigman said. "How does it feel?"

Kenneth piped up, "Rather good actually, Bigman. We had some challenges, but we came through. Looks pretty good actually, if I do say so myself."

The Bigman nodded. "And you, Jerome?"

Jerome shrugged. "Job's done. Like to get back to my fields now."

The Bigman just looked at him. Jerome found himself counting the glyphs that the thin arm on the Timex swept through. He got to four before the Bigman finally replied.

"Very well. You are released." He turned to leave them, but stopped after a few steps and looked back. "I trust there will be no further trouble from you two."

"No, Bigman," Kenneth said quickly.

Jerome said the same.

Sparks popped from the fuel burning inside Jerome's little stove. He had the stove's door open, and the flames within lit the inside of his lean-to with a flickering orange-yellow light.

Jerome sat on the edge of his cot, a wooden cup in his hands, and stared at the clear fluid within it.

He had distilled this spirit himself, over the winter. Nothing much else to do during those long months of cold, and he had long pondered the doing of it.

But he hadn't cracked the cask he'd poured the finished product into until tonight.

The wall project's completion had left him with a hollow feeling inside. Or maybe it was the revelation Kenneth had given him that one day. Or maybe it was both.

Or maybe -

With a shock, Jerome realized what it was he was feeling.

He was not angry.

The anger had been with him for so long, he had ceased to notice it almost, except when it burned severe. Now that it was gone...

It was like a piece of himself had been hewn away. But not a wholesome piece; rather something gangrenous. Being without it felt...

It felt good.

Jerome rose, the twinge in his back barely registering. He unstoppered the flask of spirits and poured the contents of his cup back in. Then he replaced the stopper and, picking up a second cup, he closed the door to his stove and left his lean-to.

The moon was nearly full, leaving him more than sufficient light to navigate his fields to the track through the Bigman's realm. But instead of following it past the towering behemoth, he turned instead to follow it to the other side of his stone edifice.

It only took a few minutes to reach Kenneth's door.

His house was larger than Jerome's, and properly constructed from felled logs, with a thatch roof. He even had a porch out from of his door, where a pair of empty rocking chairs sat.

Kenneth opened the door promptly at Jerome's knock. Seeing him standing there on his porch, the younger man's eyes narrowed and he tensed visibly.

This sort of meeting had ended in a fight enough times that Jerome couldn't blame him for expecting a punch.

Instead, Jerome raised the flask in his right hand and the pair of cups in his left. "I brewed this over the winter. Hadn't uncorked it until tonight. I was going to have at it, but thought maybe you might like a try as well."

The invitation, and the unspoken peace proposal, lingered in the air. In his mind, Jerome saw the thin arm of the Timex sweeping past glyphs. One. Two.

Kenneth smiled ever so slightly and nodded. "Sure. Why not?"

Jerome returned the smile, then turned and sat down on one of the rocking chairs and unstoppered the cask. He poured out a portion of his spirits into the first cup and held it out to Kenneth, who took it as he sat in the other chair. Then he poured himself a cup and, setting the cask on the floor of the porch, re-stoppered it.

He straightened in his chair and lifted the cup toward Kenneth in toast.

Kenneth returned the gesture, then they both drank.

They did not go blind.

7

GIVE A DOG A BONE

Harry loped along beside his best buddy John, the grass of the park where John liked to go running soft beneath Harry's feet and the air rife with scents: clipped grass, John's sweat, pollen, and despite the bright sun overhead, humidity like just before a good rain.

Breathing easily through his mouth and letting his tongue loll out to cool himself, Harry was content to just follow along beside John until he heard something moving off to the left, away from the path of dark stone that John seemed to like so much.

A new scent came to his nostrils then, and his lips drew back over his teeth as he recognized it. Rabbit.

Letting out a little yip, Harry surged forward and to the left, anticipation of a nice little snack bringing saliva to his mouth and setting his tail to wagging.

Then the thing around his neck dug in, and he came up short. He reared in the air, fighting against the restraint, but to no avail. It held fast, as John willed it.

"Harry, come back here," John said.

Harry looked back to see John had stopped running and was

looking at him with an expression that Harry had learned meant he disapproved of what Harry had done, but was not angry.

Loping back to his buddy, Harry closed the distance between them, only a couple strides, and looked up at him.

John squatted down, the blue and white second skins on his legs and torso bunching up as he did so. "What'd you see over here?" he said, though the words just came across as playful and companionable sounds, and little more. Far more important than the sounds, John reached out with both hands and scratched at the area behind Harry's ears.

Harry shivered in delight—he loved when John did that—and his tail got to wagging more fervently, of its own accord. Reaching up, he ran his tongue over the bottom half of John's face.

John leaned back and away, laughing, then straightened. He rubbed the top of Harry's head then said, "Come boy."

They ran some more, and Harry relished the feeling as his legs bunched and flexed and his toes dug into the dirt.

The stone path John followed continued through the field of grass and then passed beneath a cluster of weeping willows, though of course Harry didn't know the name for them. He always loved running beneath those tress because of the soft sound the dangling limbs and leaves made as they moved in the breeze, and because of the extensive shadow they cast. Harry wanted to just lie there and relax.

But John had other ideas, and the thing on Harry's neck urged him to keep up.

The willows were quickly forgotten, though, as the path bent to the left and the scent of water grew more strongly on the breeze.

The lake.

Harry loved the lake.

He sped up, but again the thing on his neck held him back, keeping him close to John. But it was all Harry could do not to burst, his anticipation had him tingling so.

The path rounded a small rise, and there is was: the lake.

If he'd known the word, pond would have been a more appropriate term. The body of water was not particularly broad, nor was it deep. But it had the most wonderful something in the center that sent water spewing skyward and then falling back down in a mass of sparkles that shimmered and reflected the sunlight in glints and sometimes mini-rainbows.

As he always did, John stopped for a rest at a strange almost-forest that stood at the side of the lake. It was a bunch of trees that weren't trees, logs without limbs and leaves clustered together at weird angles, with dull grey hard tubes connecting some of them together in some places, but not in others.

As Harry and John approached, there was another person at the weird forest. A female from the shape and scent of her, in tight-fitting yellow and white second skins. She was hanging from one of the hard tubes between logs, her arms bent double as she trembled to hold her chin up above the tube.

Strange. But John seemed to like that she was doing it.

There was a wooden bench—Harry knew what that was—not far from the strange forest. John dropped the end of the thing on Harry's neck atop one of the cross-pieces that made up the bench's back, so it was loosely looped over one of them, then stepped over toward where the female was hanging.

He said something as she dropped back to the ground, and she turned to face him. Her lips pulled back from her teeth as she saw him, and despite Harry having lived with humans for so long, he had to restrain his fighting reflexes for a second.

Bared teeth meant different with them, he always had to remind himself.

Harry settled down onto his haunches while John and the female exchanged noises, but Harry's attempt at becoming comfortable was interrupted by a high-pitched "Oh...so cute," from the female.

And then he was having his ears scratched again, and Harry couldn't complain.

He flicked his tongue into the female's face and she laughed, then stepped away from Harry and turned back to John.

Harry sniffed, and caught a faint odor from her that he had last scented a few moons ago, when John had brought a different female to their house and the two of them had begun wrestling together on the couch. The odor of that female's arousal had been so overpowering Harry had had to flee to a different room.

This one's was not so pungent. But it was there, and one man to another, he felt happy for John.

Then a fly buzzed past Harry's face, its wings almost striking his snout. Annoyed, Harry nipped at the air, but missed the bug.

It came back, and Harry tried again.

And again, no luck.

Harry sniffed and turned away from the annoying insect, which anyway had flown off to bother someone else. He paused when something else new came to his nostrils.

The breeze had shifted so it was now blowing toward the lake, through the woods on the other side of the stone path from the not-trees on the shore. And there was something...

Harry started forward, and found himself surprised when the thing on his neck didn't restrain him. He looked back and saw that the end of it had fallen from the bench and was now dragging behind him; it must have come off when he was jumping after the fly.

Back by the not-trees, John and the female were still making noises at each other. John would be fine there, Harry was sure.

He could go find out what this new thing was.

Harry padded across the black stone and beneath the canopy of the woods. The grass that had lined the path quickly gave way to bare dirt, and Harry felt his toes dig more deeply into the cool, slightly moist soil. It was comforting, in a way.

The leaves overhead rustled, and somewhere off to the right a bird made a high-pitched call that Harry didn't know.

And the odor grew stronger.

It was strange. Like some of the meats that John liked to grill or broil, but fundamentally different in some way Harry couldn't put his nose on.

And rotten, of course. But that wasn't the strangeness; he had scented rotten before, and could pick out the various meats despite their rot, no problem.

But not this one.

He put his snout to the ground and ranged forward, moving left and right as he went further into the woods.

The scent was everywhere. But it seemed to be strongest coming from right...over...

Harry stopped in an area where the soil seemed somehow softer than elsewhere. He sniffed; whatever that meat was, it was here.

Time to dig.

Harry lolled his tongue out, happiness washing over him. He loved to dig, too.

The soil *was* more loose here, and more damp as well. Little shivers of contentment flowed up Harry's legs as his toes dug into the moist coolness beneath, and loosed greater nose-fulls of the strangely enticing, yet also somehow abhorrent, odor beneath.

"Harry!"

His name—not his true name but the one John had given him—rang through the air, but Harry paid the call no heed. Faster he dug, his toes unearthing hidden treasures that any other day he would have investigated for hours. Today, though, he only had nose for whatever it was that had created the odor that drew him on.

Deeper he went, and deeper still, and still it eluded him.

Another voice, higher-pitched, joined in with John's, calling out to him. "Harry!"

Part of Harry's mind grinned in triumph for his best buddy, for he had clearly secured himself a mate this day.

But that didn't matter, because what was causing that scent?

"There you are!" It was John's voice, near behind him.

And there it was. The last few pawfulls of dirt had unearthed it, and now it lay beneath him. It was decaying, but there was enough of it left to see it for what it was. It was rotting, but there was enough unturned meat to make its scent almost appealing.

Except that it resembled his best buddy so much he would never dream of sinking his teeth into it.

"What is he getting into?" said the higher, female voice.

"No idea," said John, and then the thing on Harry's neck tightened, and strong arms pulled him back. "Come on, boy, get out of - "

John's voice broke, his sounds halting in a gurgle of surprise and shock.

The female made an, "Oh!" that was all fear mixed with revulsion.

John pulled Harry the rest of the way out of the hole Harry had made, and Harry only resisted a little bit. Because now he realized what it was he was looking at; an appendage just like his best buddy's, except it was detached from the body of the human who used to own it.

"Call 911," John said, and he swallowed hard.

The meaning of his sounds escaped Harry, but the sense of horror, of revulsion, with which he made them did not.

The sun was almost gone behind the trees, and still they remained there in the not-forest of not-trees next to the lake.

Many more humans had come, strangely dressed in dark blue second-skins, with dark blue things atop their heads and a sense of officialness that implied a whole other skin that was invisible, but also undeniably there.

They had brought with them great noisy transports, like John's except larger, that had torn up the ground around the lake as they charged into the area and that flashed brilliant lights into the growing shadows of the fleeing day. White, Blue, and Red, they dazzled Harry's eyes every time he looked their way. So he stopped doing so, instead looking away from them toward the waters and the strangely comforting thing that spat upward in the center of the lake.

The official humans made noises at John again and again, and at his new mate. But eventually they let her go. She and John made noises to each other, and he did something with a flat black thing he always kept in a pouch of his second skin. Then she left, moving quickly past the flashing transports in the direction of a place Harry could vaguely recall.

Wasn't it in that direction that he and John had originally come from? Where John had left his own transport thing, so similar yet so much less disturbing than those that the official humans used?

Harry supposed it didn't really matter.

In the time—he had only a vague notion of time, just that things moved on from where they were, becoming something else but without notion of a goal to that becoming—Harry and John had waited there, other official humans, dressed less martially but possessing the same air of being about stern business, had cordoned off the woods where Harry had made his discovery.

Much to his disdain. Twice he had managed to loosen the thing on his neck and tried to go back there. And twice he had been intercepted and prevented from doing so.

Harry bared his teeth and growled at the last human who had stopped him and delivered him back to John, and the official human with him. How to make him understand Harry didn't want to eat the things under the trees?

He would never do that. Too much like his best buddy.

But he did want to know what they were, and how they got there.

It didn't matter; he never got the chance to look again. Not long after that second attempt, the official human with John clasped forearms with him, then turned his back on Harry's best buddy.

A breath later, John said, "Let's go, boy," and the thing on Harry's neck urged him into motion.

He walked next to John as John headed in the same direction the female had gone, some time earlier. Toward his transport, and then, Harry presumed, back home.

Drat it. If they went home he'd never be able to figure out -

He hadn't noticed until right this moment that in addition to the official humans, others had gathered around the lake. Humans of all shades, wearing all sorts of second skins, were watching the goings on with the official ones, and in the woods.

They smelled of curiosity and good humor. A few of dread. And one...

As he and John drew near to the one human who stood apart from the others, garbed in a single grey second skin, Harry's hackles rose.

The human's scent was mostly normal: sweat and the strange aromatic thing that they used to conceal their sweat. But beneath that, mostly emanating from the skin he had slung over his shoulder, came another scent that was both alluring and abhorrent.

A scent that Harry recognized from the woods over by the lake.

Harry bared his teeth and growled, and he surged forward toward the strange human.

"Harry - " John sounded surprised, and the thing on Harry's neck tightened for a second, then let go as Harry heard John fall behind him.

The strangely-scented human's eyes widened as Harry leapt onto him, and he collapsed onto the ground.

The skin that he had slung over his shoulder fell as well, landing on the ground a pace away.

Paying the human no further mind, Harry dove at the skin and began tearing at it.

"What the - ?"

"Help him!"

"Damn dog!"

"Harry!"

A multitude of voices rose from all around, but Harry paid them no heed. He bit at the skin, tearing at it... And then it opened, and its contents fell out.

Immediately, the mood among the surrounding humans shifted. From anger at Harry, they now smelled of revulsion, or horror.

Of anger.

And, from the one Harry had knocked over, of fear.

That human tried to scramble to his feet and run, but others surged forward and knocked him down.

"Don't move! You're under arrest!"

Official voices took over, but Harry only heard John's as he knelt down beside him.

"Easy boy," John said, but only the comforting tone carried meaning. "Come on."

The thing around his neck didn't need to pull him away from the skin on the ground. John's arms did that for him.

Back at home, and Harry raced ahead of John across the entryway and into his room, with its big couch and chairs, and his bed over in the corner.

He found his little round toy and leapt on it, biting and pressing down, then feeling a surge of supreme joy when it emitted its little high-pitched squeak.

Harry shook his head, thrashing the toy about, then tossed it aside and watched it bounce across the room.

Then he bounded forward to bite at it again.

Heard but unnoticed behind him, John was talking into his black thing as he followed Harry into the room.

" - must have been cutting his victims up and bringing the pieces to the park one by one."

A pause, which Harry barely registered as the toy's squeak rang out again. Then John shrugged.

"Cops told me sometimes these sickos like to hang around the crime scene. Gives them a feeling of power, to watch people's reaction to their work."

The toy bounced away, but Harry cast it from his mind. He had come near to his water bowl, and its odor reminded him of his need for drink.

He bent his head over and began lapping up the cool fluid.

"Yeah, I got her number. We're going out tomorrow night." John laughed. "We'll see. Later man."

Then he set the black thing down on the flat wooden thing that dominated the room.

Harry saw this from the corner of his eye but didn't pay any heed until John came over and squatted down next to him. He was carrying another skin in his hands.

"I've got something for you, boy," John said. Then his hands made some indecipherable movements with the skin he was holding.

A scent come straight from heaven issued forth as the skin opened, and Harry pulled his head up out of the water bowl. Was that - ?

It was.

John pulled a great big bone out of the skin. And not just a bone. It had meat on it.

Cow meat.

John held the bone out, and for a moment Harry could do nothing but just look at it, saliva flooding into his mouth as he took in the bounty before him.

Was this real?

"Come get it, boy," John said, and he wiggled the bone around in the air.

That was all the encouragement Harry needed. He thrust his head forward and closed his teeth around the proffered treat.

Cow meat and blood and salt and marrow and thousands other flavors at once struck Harry's tongue, and it was all he could do not to swoon on the spot. But he was made of sterner stuff than that.

Mostly.

Moving quickly lest he tempt fate into taking the bounty away, he hurried over to his bed, circled once, and lied down, bone and meat in front of him between his forepaws.

Then he began gnawing. And he did not intend to stop until every last bit of this tasty morsel was gone, though it take him a week.

He had no notion of what a week was; or even what a day or a year truly was. But what notion of time's passage he did have, he projected out to an equivalent length.

Or not. Whatever thought of time, or its meaning, fled before the flavors cascading through his tongue and into his body. He just chewed and chewed and chewed.

So captivated was he that he almost missed the comparatively small pleasure of John scratching him behind the ears and saying, "Good boy."

Almost.

8

SMOKE AND EMBERS

Woodsmoke filled the air despite the stiff breeze blowing in from the east. It seemed to rise from everywhere, and never mind the determined efforts of the fire department personnel, who had labored for hours to contain the fire.

Where once this had been a non-denominational neighborhood chapel—white and pure exterior finish, stained glass windows showing bible scenes going down both long walls, an unadorned steeple pointing toward heaven—now it was a ruin, blackened timbers leaning against each other at odd angles as though trying to prop each other up and stop a total collapse.

Too late for that.

The last team of firefighters in their fireproof coveralls and breathing masks was going through the rubble with axes and pry bars. What framing hadn't fallen in the blaze itself they were prying apart, to separate fuel and prevent any re-flash.

Before long, there wouldn't even be a charred memory remaining of the peaceful beauty of the place.

Pete stuffed his hands into the pockets of his slacks and stood at the T of the concrete walkway that connected the entranceway leading to the chapel's front door to the sidewalk running down this once quiet, suburban street, and watched the firemen go about the last of their business.

He resolutely did not look behind himself.

He didn't need to; he knew the scene there perfectly. The wedding party, sitting dejectedly on the curb across the street from the chapel. The bride's dress blackened and charred, her eyes puffy red from crying—as much from grief as from the stinging smoke. The others were just as mussed, but she seemed the symbol that represented the crowd.

Eyes staring not at the scene, and the ruined chapel, but at him.

Their accusations tore into his back like lances hurled by Olympic track and field champions, unerring and true.

And completely deserved.

Patrolmen would be mingling with them, taking their statements. Other blue-uniformed personnel were hard at work elsewhere around the scene as well; erecting a cordon, engaging in crowd control, escorting the immediate neighbors from their houses until they were certain the immediate danger was past.

The red, blue, and white flashing lights on the top of the patrol cruisers at each end of the block seemed brighter now, but it was just that the afternoon was beginning to fade into evening, the sky above slowly taking on the red-orange of sunset.

And Pete just watched, his mind replaying the event over and over, searching for something—anything—he could have done differently, to avoid -

The crunching of gravel beneath shoe soles on the street behind him advertised another person's close approach, interrupting Pete's thoughts.

A second later, a man in his mid 50s, stick-thin and four or five inches taller than Pete, stepped into the right side of Pete's peripheral vision. He had on a cheap grey suit—even cheaper than Pete's if that was possible—with a solid royal blue tie, and he had his mostly-grey hair tied back in a ponytail at the nape of his neck. His bushy mustache mostly hid his upper lip, but it couldn't conceal the displeased scowl he wore.

Inwardly, Pete groaned. "Lieutenant," he said, without looking at him.

Lieutenant Sikes looked sidelong at his lead detective and scowled. Pete looked like hell. He had black smudges all over his suit, hands, and face. His sleeve was torn halfway up to the elbow, and it looked like his right shoe had a hole in it as well.

But worse was the expression on his face. His eyes were reddened from the smoke, but wide, his jaw slack, like someone who can't believe what he's looking at.

Sikes cleared his throat. "Got a call from the hospital. It's not good. Charlie - "

Pete interrupted him. "I know." His voice was toneless, dead.

Sikes let it drop, nodding. From what the doc had said, there really had not been much of a chance. When Charlie was rushed from the scene earlier, he had significant burns over 60 or 70 percent of his body, and probably massive smoke inhalation as well.

Pete had seen him; helped smother the flames on his partner's body. Of course he had known how little chance he had to survive.

The Lieutenant looked away from Pete and back toward the remains of the chapel. Such a waste. In every sense. Sudden anger flooded through him. Intellectually, he knew it was just a defense mechanism, to ward off the sorrow over Charlie's passing, but still -

"Goddamnit, Pete. What the hell happened?"

Beside him, Pete shrugged. "Garza broke contain. Ended up here. You know the rest."

Sikes ground his teeth to avoid really lashing out at the man. He knew Pete wasn't the real source of his anger, and it wouldn't do any good to take it out on him. All the same, that was a bullshit answer and they both knew it.

"You're sure Garza didn't make it out?" was all Sikes said in reply.

Pete nodded, and the Lieutenant grunted, then nodded approvingly.

He wasn't fooling anyone. Pete knew he bore the blame for this debacle, and the fact that the perp went up in his own fire didn't make up for anything. Didn't make up for Charlie...

Charlie's screams rang in Pete's ears, blotting out everything else from the scene. Pete almost broke to think of his friend of so many years.

But he realized the Lieutenant had said something else, and he forced himself back to present.

"What?"

Sikes said, "Going to be some high-level attention on this." He gestured toward the still smoldering chapel, then around at the neighborhood, which while not filled with McMansions per say had still been a well-heeled place that never had a hint of trouble touch it.

Until now.

Probably some decent political contributions came from this place. Pete didn't bother holding back his groan this time.

Sikes nodded agreement. "Not sure who's going to be heading up the investigation yet, but I'll let you know when I do."

Peter took the words in, but didn't really process them. He just nodded.

The Lieutenant laid his hand on Pete's shoulder and gave it a little squeeze. "Not much more you can do here, Pete, and you'll want to be fresh when the investigation starts. Go home. Get a few days' rest."

His tone didn't hold malice or accusation, but Pete knew it was there all the same. He'd seen this coming; just hoped it wouldn't come so soon.

Sighing, he brushed back his suit coat and took hold of his holstered sidearm. It took a second of working back and forth to ease the clip holding it to his belt, then he took the whole unit and held it out to Sikes.

The Lieutenant turned to look at him fully, his eyes widening slightly. He raised his hands, palms out, in a peacemaking gesture. "Not what I meant at all, Pete. You're still on the job. I just - "

Pete shook his head and pressed the weapon into Sikes' open left hand. Then with his free hand, he fished his badge wallet out and pushed it into Sikes' right.

"That's bullshit and we both know it," he said. He looked Sikes in the eye and pressed the items toward him, harder. The Lieutenant resisted, both the look and taking the items.

"I'm done," Pete said, then he let go of the piece and the badge and turned away.

Sikes had to move quickly to avoid letting them both fall to the ground. He looked down to make sure the gun in particular was safe. By the time he raised his eyes again, Pete had vanished into the crowd of onlookers on the other side of the street.

"Dammit," Sikes said.

In all the years Pete had been coming to her bar, Melissa had never seen him tie one on the way he had tonight.

She couldn't blame him. She'd seen the story in the news, and immediately recognized Charlie's face when it popped up on the screen. She had spent many a fun night serving beers to the two of them, and sometimes also their buddies in their division, and she'd thought well of Charlie.

But Pete was the real regular. This was going to crush him.

It was almost crushing her.

She'd had to have one of her servers take over for a few minutes when she saw the news, so she could go back into her office to cry it out of her system.

But now it was getting on toward closing time, and Pete was going nowhere. He sat at his usual place at the corner of the bar opposite the entrance, nursing a Michelob that had long since gone warm from when he first ordered it, two hours ago.

He'd made up for beer swilling with shots. But she'd cut him off of those an hour ago, and so he just sat, staring into his drink and occasionally making to lift it to his lips but never quite getting it there.

He was wasted.

But that was not the real thing dragging him low.

The last of her other customers left through the front door and Sheila, one of the two servers she had on staff on Wednesdays, locked it behind the guy. She was young—college aged though she wasn't in school—and perky, just like Melissa always tried to hire in the wait staff. And she had on the required The Cock And Bull t-shirt, with her logo of both animals arm wrestling for a pint of beer on the breast.

Melissa caught her eyes as she left the door, and Sheila gestured questioningly toward Pete. Melissa waved her off.

This was her job. And not just because it was her place.

Pete was special.

He was tracing his fingertip along the rim of his glass as she walked toward him, and for a moment he looked like a lost kid.

He'd always had a baby face. She'd been shocked to see he was almost thirty the first time she'd carded him, way back... She didn't want to think about how many years back that was.

She'd been married then, or she might have made a play for him; cute and cocky as he was. But that was before Carl had turned into a cast iron jerk and an abusive drunk, and she still had her scruples.

And then, once she was free again Pete had shacked up with Helen, so that was that.

Except he and Helen had gone pear-shaped about eight months ago, and it was turning into one hell of a fire-and-brimstone style divorce. She didn't want to be the rebound.

But more, she didn't want to get in the middle of that crazy drama.

So as she eased her way toward him, she reminded herself sternly that, no matter how she might fall seamlessly into the grey blue of his eyes, or the way his slightly off-kilter smile always made little butterflies take flight through her belly, she was strictly acting as a friend tonight. One who knew and understood his pain.

It helped that she felt it too, though she knew nowhere nearly as profoundly as he did.

"Pete?" she said as she reached him. "It's closing time, hon."

Peter heard her voice, but it was like a whisper against a whirlwind. He looked at the beer but didn't see it. Traced his finger along the glass but didn't feel it.

He only heard Charlie's screams. Only saw the skin pull away from his arms as Pete tried to drag him further from the inferno that had tried to claim them both.

Pete stopped running his finger on the glass, and turned his hand so he could look at his palm.

The unburnt, unbroken flesh of his hand. Not even a scratch on it despite what had happened earlier.

How could there not even be a scratch on it?

He looked away, casting about on the grey-black polished granite of the bartop. Hadn't he seen a knife somewhere....there!

Pete picked it up in his other hand, and drove the point of it down toward that palm, with its undeservedly unbroken skin.

It was going to hurt, but he didn't care. He wanted it to. Needed it to, if only to eclipse that other pain in his chest.

He gritted his teeth in anticipation.

And was denied.

Something forced his hand aside and he lost grip on the knife. It skittered across the bar, uselessly. Pete felt a snarl of rage boiling up within him.

Then pressure on both sides of his head forced him to look away, and he saw the yellow-brown eyes that he remembered in his dreams. The eyes that had kept him coming back to this bar, despite its bad food and at best average ambience.

Even in his drunken state—and he knew well and good he was drunk, just not drunk enough—he would know those eyes.

"Hey, M'lissa," he slurred. He tried a smile, but failed as suddenly the barrier he had been building all night fell beneath the empathy he saw in those lovely eyes.

He began to bawl, though his pride shouted at him to stop.

He howled and wailed, and wept, and at some point he passed out.

But throughout, he felt the warmth of her arms around his shoulders, and he clung to that feeling as the dreams took him.

When he woke up, Pete at first thought he was dead, and in Hell.

But after a moment he decided no, God could never be so cruel as to consign someone to feeling this way for all eternity. So he must be alive.

But really fucking hung over.

His head felt about ten sizes too small to encase the throbbing that threatened to burst his skull; for a little while he found himself identifying with Zeus at Athena's birth.

Then he sat up, and the entire contents of his stomach wanted to come up onto his pajamas.

He blinked, confusion forcing the nausea away, but not the headache or the shakes. Pajamas?

He never wore pajamas.

What the hell?

He looked around. This wasn't his bedroom.

This wasn't even his house.

The paint job was all wrong; all soft almost-pink tones and warmth, whereas he stuck with the drab white that the landlord had painted between the previous tenant and him.

It was a nice room, though, he had to admit. The bed was small; just a twin, though a four-poster. But the sheets were slick cotton, probably at least 200 grain from the feel of them. Egyptian?

The other furniture was well-made and appeared to be real wood, not particle board. There was a potted plant in the corner that was almost as tall as the ceiling—8 foot—and was blooming with some sort of red-pink flowers. It gave off a pleasant musky odor, but if anything else had convinced him he was not at home it was that.

No plant could survive more than a week in his company.

Grunting, he swung his legs off the beg, and they sunk into a thick white throw-rug that covered the darkly-polished hardwood floor. It was like stepping onto a cloud, it was so soft.

Where the hell was he?

He managed to hobble over to the door, only partially successful in ignoring the pounding in his head, and opened it, then stepped through.

Beyond was a great room, though it was perhaps a little small for that name. But it had the white couch and matched stuffed chairs around a glass coffee table in front of a TV that all living rooms require, and off to the left a walnut-stained dining table set for six. And directly ahead a kitchen setup with white granite counters, grey shelving, and stainless steel appliances and sink.

And leaning behind the counter, reading a newspaper with one elbow resting on the counter and her fist supporting her chin, dressed in a set of flower-pattern pajamas that somehow were sexier than any lingerie Helen had ever deigned to wear for him—and not very often at that—was Melissa.

Auburn-haired, yellow-brown eyed Melissa, with her fit, slender body and small, perky boobs.

He'd dreamed about her for years, but he'd only thought he'd dreamed of her last night.

Had they - ?

He glanced down at the pajamas he was wearing. No, clearly not.

He cleared his throat. "Good morning?"

Melissa looked up when he spoke, surprise making her drop the newspaper onto her countertop. She had been reading the detailed story of what had happened to Pete and his partner yesterday. Or as detailed as the Police Department would allow any news article to be. And she had not heard him come in, engrossed as she was.

She straightened, and saw the bags under his bloodstained eyes, the greenish cast to his skin. Inwardly, she winced in sympathy for the hangover he must be feeling.

But he did fill out Carl's old pajamas very well; he had kept in good shape over the years, unlike many cops. She found herself growing warm looking at him, but had to force that feeling down. This was not the time, and she had no right.

Well, she did, now that he and Helen were split. But she didn't want to get involved in that situation.

Did she?

"You were hitting the whiskey hard last night," she said, to distract herself from that train of thought as much as to inquire from him. "How are you feeling? Need some coffee?" She gestured toward the end of her countertop, beneath the overhanging cabinets, where a coffee maker sat warming a two-thirds full pitcher.

Pete glanced away from her toward the coffee and smiled slightly. Considering his probable condition, it was an ear-to-ear grin. He nodded. "Thanks."

As he headed toward the life-giving fluid, he said, "How did I get here?"

Melissa felt herself flushing, despite having done nothing untoward. She looked back down at the newspaper as he reached for the coffee pitcher. "You were in no condition to drive. And I don't know where you live. So..." She left the rest unsaid.

Pete had to hand it to her; she brewed a mean cup of coffee.

He considered sugar and creamer, but decided this was no morning to lessen the shock, so he took it black, and was pleasantly surprised by the deep, rich flavor. He immediately felt more alert, though his head still throbbed.

Turning away from the pot, he saw her looking back down at the newspaper. Her cheeks were red, like she was embarrassed. That intrigued him.

"You could have gotten me an Uber."

She looked back up at him, and her lips compressed slightly. "And who would have gotten you into your house?"

He nodded, conceding the point. He took another swallow of the coffee and stepped over to where she was standing alongside her island counter. Setting the coffee cup down on the granite, he plucked at his pajama top with his left hand and jiggled it, meaningfully. He raised an eyebrow, and only after doing it did he realize it was the same thing he did when he was trying to non-verbally press a suspect into talking.

He felt a flush of shame at that.

Pete's accusing eyebrow made Melissa flush all the more. But she found she could not look away from him. Those grey-blue eyes were locked on hers, probing, and she felt drawn in by them. Lower down, she ached for him to do a different sort of probing.

She stiffened and turned away, forcing her thoughts back in order while she chided herself for being so foolish.

Melissa opened the refrigerator door to mask her slip. "I asked Jim, my next door neighbor, to take care of that." She pulled open the crisp and fresh drawer and withdrew half of a cantaloupe.

Pete wasn't sure what he saw in her eyes before she turned away, but he was unprepared for that bit of news. Jim? Who the hell was Jim? Was he - ?

Melissa turned back toward him and held up a gallon-sized ziplock back that held half of a cantaloupe. "Want some?" she asked.

Pete nodded. "Sure." He paused for a second while she set the melon down on the countertop, then said, "Who is Jim? Your neighbor?"

She turned eyes that twinkled teasingly at him. "He's straight. You don't have to worry."

That...was not what he meant at all.

Melissa was relieved that her remark had set him back on his heels. And then she felt ashamed for feeling that. But damn it all...

She focused on the cantaloupe. Pulling the cutting board out from the shelf where she kept it. Selecting the right knife and testing its edge.

And all the while aware of Pete's eyes on her, and unable to stop the warmth that flowed through her at that knowledge.

Finally, in desperation, she said the worst thing possible. "The Times did a story on you and Charlie."

And she immediately wished she had not.

Melissa's words hit Pete like a bullet, and immediately he recalled everything from the previous day. He turned away from her, pressing his palms down on the countertop.

The newspaper was laid out there where she had dropped it. The headline was plainly visible: HERO COP KILLED IN FIRE.

Then, below it, in smaller letters that nevertheless burned into his soul: PARTNER ACCUSED OF NEGLIGENCE.

Negligence?

He grabbed up the paper and hauled it up in front of his face. Headlines were almost always bullshit. Click-bait, to use the modern term. They can't have meant -

But there it was.

"Sources in the Police Department have indicated that procedures for securing suspected perpetrators may have been violated. Though the sources did not specifically name him, Detective Peter O'Donnell, the victim's partner, has been strongly implicated as contributing to Detective Argento's death through his improper actions."

"Mother FUCKER!" Pete said, and slammed the paper back down onto the counter.

Melissa jumped at the sound of Pete's outburst, and dropped the knife she was holding. A second later, she yelped as pain flared from her foot. She looked down and saw the knife stuck point-first into her hardwood floor. Its cutting edge had sliced through the side of her big toe as it landed.

"Son of a bitch!" she cried, and had to force herself to not pull her foot away, and make it worse.

Instead, she bent over to pick up the knife first.

Pete was about ready to scream at the ceiling when Melissa cried out in pain.

All thoughts of his predicament fled as concern for her flooded him, and he rounded on her. In time to see her rise, her cutting knife in her hand and its edge red.

He looked down, and saw the big toe of her left foot had a gash on the side, and blood was flowing out onto her finely-polished floor.

"Oh geez," he said, and straightened, reaching for a paper towel.

Her hand landed on his as they both grabbed it at the same time.

Pete's eyes turned onto hers and Melissa felt the pain in her toe retreat beneath the electricity of his touch, and again she felt pulled into his eyes. His beautiful blue-grey eyes.

"I'm sorry," Pete said, hoarsely, and Melissa realized their bodies were very close together, his chest almost pressed up against her breasts.

"Not your fault," she said, in a nonchalant tone, but Pete barely registered.

All he could see was her eyes, filling his vision. All he could hear was the suddenly strong pounding of his heart. All he could feel was the sudden heat on his cheeks from where her breath impacted his skin.

As though guided by some outside force, he leaned in toward her.

She felt him come in, and every portion of her being willed him to. To kiss her. To take her.

Except for her mind.

This was not right. Not now, while he was so broken.

His lips were about to touch her, and she turned away.

Pete felt like he stumbled forward a step, when she suddenly wasn't there, even though the only part of him that had moved was his head. All the same, he had to catch himself to stop from falling over.

And then she was gone, moving away from him toward a door he hadn't see earlier, on the opposite side of the room.

"I've got some band-aids in the bathroom," she said over her shoulder, without looking at him.

Then the door closed behind her, and he was left all alone. With a bloody knife and a raging hard-on.

Charlie's funeral was three days later, and Pete felt like an outcast throughout the entire proceeding.

He wore his dress blues, like everyone did. He stood in formation with the rest of his division. He watched as the Mayor presented

Hillary with the folded flag and recited his scripted and oft-spoken words of condolence. He saluted as the riflemen fired their shots.

And through it all, no one said a word to him.

Not even Hillary, except for a fleeting, "Thank you," when he said how sorry he was.

At least she returned the hug. But even that seemed hesitant, distant.

It was like they had cast him adrift already, before he had even been tried, let alone convicted.

Melissa watched from near the rear of the crowd at the funeral's edge. She would not have missed it, no matter the circumstances. She had known Charlie for a long time, and even though he wasn't close enough to truly be a friend, he was like Pete's brother. And Pete...

Pete was special.

She'd done a lot of thinking over the last few days. Since she fled from him in near-panic in her kitchen.

She'd sat on the toilet seat in her bathroom for many long minutes more than it had taken to properly bandage her toe. Just sat, thoughts churning, as she listened to his movement out in her living room.

He had not groused or shouted. He had not made much noise at all. But after a few minutes she heard her front door close, and only then had she dared put her head out and look around.

He had not just wiped up the blood at the base of her counter, he had cleaned the entire trail she had left to the bathroom.

And now, three days later, after three days of cursing herself for a fool for not giving him the comfort, the closeness, he had so clearly needed, she watched him go through the motions of duty and regulation, his pain obvious to anyone who would bother to look at him.

She felt that pain as though it was her own, and as the ceremony broke apart and he walked, alone, away from the gathered people, she moved to follow him.

"Pete?"

The voice, so familiar he recognized it without any effort, brought Pete up short. He stopped and turned around.

Melissa stood there, in a long black dress that might have worked well as an evening gown except that clearly she was in mourning. Her eyes were red and he mascara had run a bit.

He was surprised for a second, then cursed himself for the feeling. She and Charlie had been friends. Of course she would mourn his passage.

"Hi," he said. He sounded awkward even to his own ears, and lame when he left it at that. But he really had no idea what else to say to her.

Melissa looked into his eyes and saw the same pain she had seen before at her bar and then again in her kitchen. And she cursed herself again for leaving him alone these last days. Surely Helen hadn't offered him any comfort, not since she'd revealed herself as the harpy Melissa had always feared she was.

She looked down at the grass before Pete's mirror-shined shoes. "I'm sorry."

Pete said, "I'm sorry," at the same time as he heard her say it, and he blinked.

What did she have to be sorry for? He was the one who had taken her kind act and turned it into something awkward.

She looked back up as he spoke and her eyebrows rose in surprise. Again as their eyes met, he found himself at a loss for words for a moment, so he was almost grateful when he heard a very familiar throat clearing to the left, and he turned to see Lieutenant Sikes standing there.

The new arrival saved Melissa from a moment of uncertainty, when everything she had planned to say flew away completely before the earnest expression on Pete's face and the deep feeling in his eyes.

She looked to the side and saw Bill Sikes standing there, and felt grateful relief at the reprieve.

Sikes looked between Pete and the bartender from The Cock And Bull—and what was her name? She was a looker, whatever it was— and thought perhaps he would have been better to wait until after they'd conducted their business. But then he considered maybe their business would take the rest of the day, and all night, so he decided to get down to his.

Tearing his eyes away from the hottie, he looked at Pete and tried to put on a reassuring smile.

"Hey, Pete," he said.

"Hey Lieutenant," Pete replied, wondering how much more trouble he was in. Sikes' express was severe, almost stern. He hadn't even seen Sikes look like that when he was in the middle of chewing someone a new ass.

Sikes cleared his throat. "I've had you on medical leave the last few days," he said, and Pete blinked in surprise.

"No one will question it," the Lieutenant continued. He reached out with his left hand, and Pete saw a brown folded leather packet in his hand. "But you need to take this back."

Pete knew what it was, but still his hand trembled when he reached out to take it. He flipped it open, and he felt his breath leaving his lungs in a sigh of relief.

It was his badge wallet.

Only then did he realize it was relief he felt, and he froze in surprise. He had felt so certain the other day that he was done, but now he felt like the badge Lieutenant Sikes had given him back was the greatest gift in the world.

He looked back at Sikes. "Thanks."

Sikes nodded curtly. "Just don't let me hear any more of this 'I'm done' bullshit. Don't matter what the news says. You're a good cop, one of the best I've known. And I'm here for you." He glanced aside, toward Melissa. Then he added, "We all are."

Sikes was relieved when Pete's handshake was the same strong, confident grasp he had always used. He turned away, pausing only to give the bartender a look that he hoped she understood before he walked away.

Pete watched his Lieutenant go, and felt a warmth inside that he hadn't experienced in days.

He hadn't been cast out from among his brothers. They had his back after all.

He found he was smiling slightly when he looked back at Melissa.

The sight of his smile was too much. Melissa cast aside the words she had been planning to say. Instead, she grabbed him by the shoulders, pulled him forward, and kissed him.

Hard.

They stood there together for a long time. When they finally parted, they each had to gasp for breath.

Then they hurried back to her place.

9

———

HERMES' KRINGLE

If someone had told Brian's 8-year old self that he would one day be outside the world fixing Santa Claus, he would have laughed and called him crazy.

But then, when he was 8 years old Brian hadn't really had a notion that there really *was* an outside of the world. It wasn't until he was a teenager, and the lower deck areas of the world were opened to him, that he was first able to look outside, through a small viewing port in the floor, and see the majesty of the stars that his teachers had told him about for so long but that he had never truly believed actually existed until then.

From then on, he'd wanted to be one of the lucky few who got to go on EVAs, to repair and maintain the world's external systems. And he had.

And now, here he was, breathing recycled air that carried a hint of peppermint instead of the usual sweet-sour of the EVA suit's scrubbers—it was Christmas Eve, after all—and approaching a red-painted sleigh, festooned with golden jingle bells and apparently pulled by 8 annoyed-looking reindeer simulacrums as it tumbled helplessly through the void of space. A large, red-coated man simulacrum seated in the driver's seat of the sleigh flailed his right robotic arm uselessly, while its left remained completely motionless. And Brian knew immediately what the problem was.

He fired a quick burst from the maneuvering pack that he had strapped on around the waist of his suit, and his approach velocity, displayed in green text on the lower right of his facemask, slowed to just over a meter per second. Then he nudged with his chin on the transmit key for his comms array.

"EVA Delta Four, approaching Kringle."

There was a burst of static, and then Brian heard a female voice in his left earbud. Sounded like Stacy, the new girl in the comms division. "Roger that, Brian. What's his status?"

Brian grinned. He hadn't worked with Stacy too many times, but every time he did, the warm cheeriness of her voice lifted his spirits a bit. "Looks like a bad actuator in his left arm. Should be an easy fix."

"But why would that throw him off course so bad the auto-shutdown kicked in?"

Brian couldn't stop from laughing over the comms circuit, even though it was a violation of regs. "You haven't dealt with procurement much, have you?"

As he spoke, he noted the range to Kringle, displayed on the lower left of his facemask. Then he fired another quick burst and reached out with his left hand.

"No, why?"

It seemed he should be able to take hold of the jinglebell-lined reigns leading from Kringle's seat to the first reindeer pair right now, but he knew from experience distances could be deceptive out here. He opened his hand and waited, as his residual momentum carried him the rest of the way in.

"Kringle's thrust controller is on his right. Attitude controller on his left. His belly's too big for cross control, and no one ever installed backups."

"You're kidding."

"Wish I was."

The reigns impacted Brian's glove and he grabbed hold. The last of his momentum carried the rest of him gently into the side of the tumbling sleigh, and for a moment, Brian twisted halfway around. He winced as the flexion on his left arm made the seam of his suit dig into the meat of his shoulder, and bit back a curse.

That shouldn't have happened; he hadn't checked the fit well enough before he went out.

Stupid. But there was no help for it now. Brian gritted his teeth and worked to right himself.

After another moment, he managed it, then he unclipped the tether line that was clipped to the front of his suit and secured it to an eye on the top of Kringle's sleigh, just in front of the big robot's seat.

It was aware of him, of course, and Kringle's eyes focused in on him tightly as Brian secured himself. His cheeks, rosy red, offset the grey of his irises, but the ever-present smile that made his round face into a welcoming bit of joy for the kids was gone. Even simulacrums can show frustration, it seemed.

"Hey Kris," Brian said, and pulled himself over to hover next to the robot. "How ya doing?"

He didn't expect a response; Kringle didn't have wireless voice comms. Instead, the robot just flailed its right arm again.

"Yeah. Well, hold tight."

Brian was pretty sure he knew what the problem was, but he still needed to be certain. Brian reach out toward the robot, and Kringle's eyes narrowed but he didn't move; he knew the drill. Behind Kringle's left ear was a data access port, concealed beneath a flesh-toned covering flap. Brian linked in a data cable, and a moment later he heard a deep voice in his right earbud.

"Ho! Ho! Ho!"

Kringle's lips moved in time with his words, and it was almost like Brian was speaking to him through air instead of vacuum.

"Merry Christmas, Kris," Brian said. "Run diagnostic, please."

Kringle replied almost before Brian had finished the command. "Left shoulder gyro-actuator failure. 100% loss of function."

Yep. Just like he though. "Thanks, Kris. We'll get that fixed right quick."

"You're a good little boy."

Brian had to laugh at that. He keyed the comms array again. "Confirmed it's a bad actuator. ETA for repairs fifteen minutes."

"Roger, Brian. - " A burst of static, and then Stacy's voice was replaced by an older, male voice. Taro, the EVA section supervisor.

"Give me a dosimeter check, Brian."

He blinked, surprised. Taro didn't normally jump in like this. Brian raised his left wrist and looked at the display attached there. Though his facemask showed key flight parameters, other information like consumable stores could be accessed here. Two taps on the display brought up the dosimeter, and Brian felt his eyebrows rise.

He chinned the comms button again. "150 mrem/hr." That was way higher than it should have been.

"I was afraid of that," Taro said. "You're drifting faster than we expected, and the vector shifted; you're heading toward the shield edge."

Crap. It must have been when he impacted the sleigh on arrival. Brian turned around and looked back at the world, and his stomach rose into his throat.

It wasn't really called the world, of course. Its name was Hermes. But it was his world; all he had ever known. Twenty kilometers of dimly-illuminated, silver-grey starship, with two seven kilometer long, four kilometer radius counter-rotating cylinders containing all the living space in existence, as far as it mattered.

He had never been farther than one or two kilometers away from the ship's surface; there had never really been need. When he'd set out to retrieve Kringle, the sleigh had only been one and a half kilometers away.

They were further out now. Much further. He could clearly see the reactor sphere and engine nacelles five kilometers aft of the stern-most living cylinder. Normally he'd only be able to see part of it.

Brian tugged at his tether and spun himself about, to look forward, toward the shield.

It was barely visible, just a circle of blackness a kilometer ahead of the forward cylinder, extending five kilometers past the outer edge of the cylinders in all directions forward.

Most people sighed through the portion of Physics class that explained it, but since Brian had wanted to be an EVA tech, he hadn't. Because Hermes was traveling at such great speed toward their destination, the light from stars ahead was blueshifted substantially. Which meant the normal amount of harmful radiation that existed in space increased as well, from the forward direction. The shield was constructed of high-density material to block most of those high energy gamma rays, so the people onboard could be relatively safe during the journey.

Which, since it was supposed to take 300 years or so, Brian supposed was a good idea.

Before when he'd looked at the shield while on EVAs, Brian had imagined he could see that destination star—SAO 229624, but everyone just called it Eden—through the shield, even though he knew it wouldn't be clearly visible to the naked eye until probably his grandchildren were his age.

Still, he liked to imagine it.

Now, all he could see was that he was far closer to the edge than he had business being. And getting further away by the second. He looked back at the dosimeter on his left wrist. 165 mrem/hr.

Crap. But survivable crap. He'd have to sit out EVAs for a while, to avoid exceeding his annual dose limit, is all.

Once he got past the shield's perimeter, though...

He nudged the comms array. "ETA on shield edge?"

"Twelve minutes. Work quickly."

Double crap.

Brian tugged on his tether and spun himself back to the sleigh.

"Kris, maintenance shutdown in five seconds."

"Confirmed. Merry Christmas! Ho! Ho! H - " and Kringle's voice cut off and his body stopped moving completely.

Brian got to work. Fast.

Some time later, Brian wasn't sure how long because he hadn't checked his chronometer, static sounded in his left ear, then Taro's voice came through again. "What's your status, Brian?"

Brian paused in the middle of screwing in a fastener to hold the new actuator in place within Kringle's shoulder socket, and scowled. "Almost there. Be easier if you stop bothering me."

"You're about to reach the edge. Time to call it."

"I'm right there," Brian said, hearing the frustrated growl in his own voice and feeling surprised at it.

"Check your dosimeter."

Brian ground his teeth, but shifted his focus away from the robot's open shoulder and rotated his left arm to see the display again.

His blood ran cold.

3 rem/hr.

3.5

It was into the realm where he would have to turn back or not do any EVAs for a couple years if he kept it up for much longer. He wouldn't feel any immediate effects from the radiation until he hit 50-75 rem total, though, so he should be ok.

It increased to 5 rem/hr.

Brian looked to the shield, and blanched. Taro was right. He was definitely passing beyond the protective boundary. Radiation levels would only go up until they reached a level where he wouldn't have to worry about not doing EVAs anymore. Survival would become a concern.

But...

He looked back at the shoulder. He just needed to insert three more screws, then attach the arm connectors and the flesh covering. Then re-sew the suit together. Five more minutes, tops.

Brian flashed back to that time when his 8 year old self had watched Santa come flying into the world from the north pole of the forward cylinder, then spiraled down to settle onto the room of the Hermes Christmas Center, one of the few buildings in the world with a fireplace. And this one large enough to house a bonfire big enough to warm up five thousand kids at a time who, like him, were gathered in a semi-circle around the flagstone-constructed mantel that housed it. A fireplace large enough that Santa could come down the chimney with ease, popping out from his door atop the mantel and then sliding down a red and white candycane-striped slide with his satchel of gifts for all the kids in the world.

Every year the gift was different. Brian later learned they were pre-selected based on kids' ages on a rotating basis. It was all part of the Christmas Program the Hermes' builders had constructed when they made the ship.

But even knowing that hadn't changed the magic of those memories for him, even now a couple decades later.

All the children in Brian's world were waiting for that bit of Christmas joy and magic. And there was only one Kringle simulacrum in the entire universe. Or at least in the entire universe that mattered.

He felt wetness running down his cheeks, and realized he was crying over the loss those kids were about to experience. And not just those kids, but all kids that would even be born in his world.

No. Not on his watch.

Brian turned back to his work and keyed his comms unit again. "Five minutes, Taro."

"You don't have five minutes. Recall now."

"Negative."

The screw was halfway in when Taro's voice interrupted again. "You're grounded Brian. I'm remote-activating your Nav pack."

Brian froze in surprise for a second, then grabbed hold of the edge of the sleigh, hard. A moment later, he felt like a rope was pulling him backwards as the thrusters on his maneuvering pack fired.

It wasn't a ton of force; it didn't have to be, in space. But the angle was awkward, and his grip not the tightest in the bulky pressure suit gloves.

It also didn't help that the sleigh began to spin from the new force, first slowly and then more rapidly.

Brian lost his grip. He flew back, away from the sled, and then jerked to a halt as his tether line went taught.

The sleigh jerked slightly, and its rotation changed again.

The thrust from his Nav pack continued. For a second, Brian considered just giving in, heading back.

No.

"I'm not leaving, Taro," he said into his comm. Then he reached down and hit the disconnect latch on the maneuvering pack that kept it strapped around his waist.

Immediately the thrust ceased as the pack zipped away behind him.

"You crazy - !" Taro cut off what he was about to say, then after a few seconds all Brian could hear was him working hard to bring his breathing under control from the fury-imposed high he must surely have been riding just then. Then he spoke again, his voice calmer but caring a tone of cold anger, and disbelief. "You just killed yourself, you know that? And over a stupid robot?"

"We'll see about that." Brian cut off the comm channel, then hauled himself back up the tether to the sleigh.

The rotation was more intense now, and he felt it in his stomach more than he had before. But a glance at the dosimeter lifted his spirits a bit. Steady at 5 rem/hr. That bit of thrust must have helped mitigate his escape vector.

Not that it would do him much good, if he didn't get Kringle fixed.

He looked into the robot's dead, lifeless eyes and managed a grin. "Looks like I'm hopping a ride with you tonight, Kris."

Then he got back to work.

* * *

Brian keyed in the simulacrum restart code into the data pad on his left wrist. A second later, Kringle's eyes lit up and his head gave a little jerk. He focused in on Brian and beamed out that smile that always lit up a child's heart.

"Ho Ho Ho! Merry Christmas!"

"Merry Christmas, Kris. Run diagnostic, please."

"Affirmative." Half a second's pause. "All systems fully functional."

Brian let out a breath that he hadn't realized he had been holding. "Do you have a fix on the Hermes?"

"Affirmative. Navigational system synch completed. Hermes range 7.5 kilometers, bearing 265 mark 20." Another slight pause. "Warning, we are outside the shield barrier. Radiation levels are likely extreme."

Brian nodded. "I know. I'll be riding back with you, if that's alright."

Kringle looked sidelong at Brian for a second. His eyes flicked down to Brian's waist, where the maneuvering pack used to be, and his eyebrows rose.

"Evidently you have no choice."

He shifted over to the left, moving as far as the restraints that kept him secured to his seat would allow.

That didn't leave much room, but right then Brian didn't feel up to complaining. Using his tether and the eyes built into the sleigh's top, he hand-over-handed his way to the other side of the sleigh from Kringle, then slid in next to him as best he could. He took a moment to adjust the latch point for his tether to bring it closer to him, then cinched it as tight as he could.

It wasn't the kind of straps that were holding Kringle in place. But it would do in a pinch, and it was far better than nothing.

Brian looked back at Kringle and saw the simulacrum watching him, expectantly. He nodded. "Let's go deliver some toys."

Kringle grinned broadly. "You *are* a good little boy." He reached forward and took hold of the reigns. "Now Dasher, now Dancer, now Prancer, and Vixen. On Comet, on Cupid, on Donner, and Blitzen!" he said. Then he gave the reigns a snap.

The engine buried in the sleigh below their seat came to life, a low rumble that carried through the sleigh's material and Brian's suit. But more importantly, the reindeer began to run.

And the sleigh turned back toward the Hermes, and all the waiting kids.

Brian had only been in the hospital once before. To have his appendix out when he was fifteen. It sucked then. It was almost worse now, and he wasn't in any physical pain.

But holy cow, was he swamped! It seemed like every parent in the world had come by to thank him, leaving behind a card or a little faux-flower, or one or two bits of chocolate. By the time the nurse declared visiting hours over and shoed the last of them away, the little table next to his bed—beneath an electronic window-approximation that displayed a forest so large and thick that it could only have existed for real on Earth, so many decades and light years behind them—was covered to overflowing with the well-wishings.

Several had fallen onto the floor.

Not that Brian minded so very much. He understood how they felt; he would have felt the same if he had a kid. But he didn't feel like any sort of hero, even though many of them said he was..

It had been, frankly, embarrassing.

So when the door to his little room, all two meters by four and decorated as lifelessly as only a high-tech medical station can be, opened again, he didn't even bother to look over.

"Look, I - "

He cut off when Stacy's voice reached his ears. "Hey Brian. How you feeling?"

He looked over then, and there she was. All cute with her auburn hair and the little dimple in her left cheek, wearing the white and grey jumpsuit that the operations staff all wore.

"How'd you get in here? They just chased everyone else away."

Her grin made the dimple a little bit deeper. "I'm friends with the nurse supervisor."

"Oh."

"I just wanted to check on you. You going to be ok?"

He shrugged. "Doc says I didn't get enough dose for any stochastic effects. May have a higher chance of cancer down the line though, so we'll be running tests more often." He sighed. "I'm out of the EVA business for a while though. Maybe forever. Even if Taro doesn't fire me."

Stacy snorted. "If he tried to fire you, he'd probably end up spaced. You're the most loved person in the world right now."

Brian snorted, but he couldn't doubt that was true, after what he'd been through with the parents. Instead he just shrugged again.

"How long are you in here?"

"Docs want me to stay a couple days, just to be sure nothing unexpected comes up."

Stacy nodded. "Well when you're out, you want to grab some egg nog?"

Brian grinned, the first true grin he'd managed in several hours. "Sure. Sounds great."

After all, the man who saved Christmas for the entire world deserved a reward, didn't he?

10

KICKING THE ANTHILL

Kevlar and ballistic plating doesn't help worth a damn against magic.

Sergeant John Singleton really wished he'd known the suspect was going to turn out to be a wizard. He would have called for Special Magics. Instead, SWAT showed up, and they never had a chance.

John's police cruiser sat cross-ways across the two-lane suburban road in front of the house he and his men had cordoned off not so very long ago. It wasn't a fancy neighborhood, and the house went with it: a single-story ranch with peeling red paint on the sides, a weed-encroached front yard, and a one-car carport on the right hand side that was sagging where the suspect's getaway car had careened out of control into one of the yellowish-white pillars that supported the overhead.

He cringed behind the car, watching in helpless frustration as, one by one, the assault team who had just moments ago seemed imposing and undefeatable in their black fatigues, body armor, helmets, and rifles fell beneath the magical onslaught that erupted from the house's front door.

Sparks of blue, red, and green shot out, each striking a trooper squarely in the chest.

The troopers fell to the ground, writhing, their cries of chagrin gradually rising in pitch as they shrank, going to the size of teenagers, then children, then toddlers, until they were left, equipment and all, little taller than the blades of grass that grew over-long in the yard.

"Jesus, Sarge, what are we gonna do now?" The voice came from behind the other cruiser blocking the street in front of the house, to John's left. He turned and saw Mendoza crouching behind the forward wheel well of the car, his pistol in both hands, barrel up toward the sky and his dark eyes wide with shock and amazement.

He was a rookie, but even veterans had trouble dealing with the new reality of magical crimes that had begun cropping up five years ago.

John opened his mouth to talk, even though he was unsure what he was going to say, but a new commotion from the yard drew his attention back there.

The SWAT guys were retreating, their tiny forms struggling to get through the tangle of grass and weeds that was the house's front yard to the street, then to their van which was parked a short ways down the street. They would have magical first aid equipment in there, as an emergency measure. But John doubted it would do much for the effects of this shrinking spell.

And was he seeing things, or were the SWAT guys not done shrinking?

Abruptly, one of the SWAT guys went down, hollering in a pitch so high John could barely hear all of it. But what he heard carried more than enough: surprise, followed by fear, then pain.

"Anthill!" a SWAT guy near the one who had fallen shouted, then he too started shrieking.

John shoved his own fears down and tried to put on a confident face. He looked back at Mendoza. "We gotta help the SWAT guys. Call Special Magics, then follow me."

He drew a deep breath, held it, then ignoring Mendoza's look of astonishment, he rose and rounded the front of his cruiser.

The SWAT team of eight had been going in by pairs, spread out along the length of the yard, separated by about eight to ten feet between each pair. The pair that was being accosted by ants was the furthest to the left of the group, about thirty feet from where John had been watching from behind his car.

Had they been normal sized, it would have been child's play for the next SWAT pair to rush over to assist them. But shrunk as they now were, that eight to ten feet now was more like a mile equivalent, or more.

If someone not-shrunk didn't move to help, there would be no help for the attacked pair. And being attacked by ants—or possibly even worse, fire ants—when you're barely the size of a blade of grass is no picnic.

All that flashed through John's mind in a second as he rounded his cruiser's fender and began sprinting toward the area of the yard where the two SWAT guys had gone down. He distinctly did not listen to the soft voice that was screaming in the back of his head that he was being a fool, and get the hell back to cover.

"Don't come any closer!" came the suspect's voice from out of the house's open—broken, really—front door. It was young, scared, and...female?

The surprise of that almost made John miss a beat, but he had to stay focused.

"They're in trouble," he shouted in response, though he knew as he said it the words were not sufficient.

But he was almost there. He could see the grass rustling around where the two SWAT guys were battling it out with the ants. Hear little pops as they fired their shrunken weapons at the insects. Smell faint whiffs of gunsmoke as a little cloud of it began to rise from that same area.

And then something struck him in the side, and he cried out. The world spun and whirled, and twisted around on itself, like the entire planet had been stuck inside a kaleidoscope that was being twisted by a particularly masochistic six-year old.

Green rose up all around him, and then the world stopped. And he was lying on his back, surrounded by shafts of green that were almost as thick as his thigh. The smell of earth was heavy in the air, and he knew immediately what had happened.

The wizard had hit him with the shrinking spell too.

"That's just great," he snarled. Then he cursed loudly, and added, "Idiot!" to himself.

Because, yeah, he was a freaking idiot, running out like that. He was really in the thick of it now.

He sat up, and considered the ironic truthfullness of that thought as he could see only the grass shafts everywhere he looked, restricting his visibility to only ten or twelve feet in any direction.

Well. No use moaning about it. The SWAT guys still needed help. He needed to get up and get to it.

As though in answer to that though, he heard more gunfire from ahead and to his right. It was louder now than it had been when he was big; no surprise there. And from the sound of it, they SWAT guys were only a hundred or so yards away.

John already had his pistol drawn. He checked to make sure his two spare magazines had made the transition with him. They had.

Then he took off running, shoving the grass shafts aside as he went.

That was harder than he thought it would be. The shafts were thick, and tough, and after only a few paces he found himself more moving forward briskly and having to use his shoulders to press between the grass shafts.

More gunshots from ahead, and now in between John heard voices. One stronger, the other haggard-sounding, and both fearful.

Almost there.

John pushed through a few last shafts and came to a halt in a clearing, of sorts. Grass grew up on all sides, and above it he could see the rising stalks of some of the weeds and creepers that infested the yard. But here, the grass had been at least partly shoved aside in favor of a mound of earth that reached to just above waist height.

It was loose, and lighter in shade than the soil beneath his feet, and there were ants coming up out of the top.

A lot of ants.

They would have been tiny, hardly an issue, at his normal size. Now, each had a body almost as long as John's forearm, and pincher mandibles the size of his thumbs. But worse, their carapaces were bright red, and they gave off a smell that was almost cinnamon.

Fire ants.

Son of a bitch.

They hadn't cued on him yet, they were making a beeline—antline?—to his right. John turned his head in that direction, and saw the two SWAT guys.

They had somehow managed to bend one of the grass shafts over double, and then hauled themselves up onto the elbow the bend had created.

But the two men were looking quite the worse for wear. Their helmets were gone, and their fatigues were torn in multiple places. The guy on the left, an African American officer who John recognized but could not put a name too right that second, looked the stronger of the two. The other guy was blond, had several obvious wounds, and was slumping. His face was puffy and red, and he was gritting his teeth like a man enduring something horrible.

And no wonder. Fire ant bites burn like a sonofabitch, and that's on a full-sized human.

John didn't want to think about how even one bite from those things would feel now that he was tiny.

The blond guy was carrying on, though. For the moment at least. As John watched, he aimed and fired with his rifle at a pair of ants that were leading the line toward the two men's bent shaft.

He hit, and the ants carapaces shattered.

Still, their position was untenable, and they knew it. So did John.

"Hey!" he shouted, and the black guy's eyes zeroed in on him.

He blinked. "Singleton? What the hell are you doing here?"

John shrugged. "What can I say, I'm an idiot. Here to help."

He glanced toward the top of the anthill, where another of the fire ant soldiers had stuck its head out and began moving toward the two trapped SWAT men. For the moment at least, John was still in the clear. But that couldn't last.

"Glad to have you," said the SWAT man, and his voice clicked something in John's mind. He remembered where he knew the guy—Barnes he thought was his name—from. A bank holdout a year or so ago. They had been on the midnight shift together on the perimeter during the two days the negotiators had taken to talk the perps into releasing their hostages and surrendering.

"Got any bright ideas?" Barnes added, drawing John out of his memories.

Still eyeing the top of the anthill, John had an idea. "Got any flash-bangs?"

"Think that'll just piss them off more," Barnes said.

"Maybe, but it'll also stun them for a bit, let us get out of here."

More shots, as Barnes and the blond guy took out another pair of ants.

"Got any better ideas?" John asked, looking back at Barnes.

The SWAT man paused, shrugged, then dug into a pouch on his tactical vest. He tossed a black object toward John. It hit the ground a few feet away, and John went to retrieve it.

He picked it up in his left hand.

It had been a while since John used one of these. They'd all had training on it, but in the normal course of patrol duties the need for a flash bang never really came up. Still, he remembered how it went. Pull the pin, count to -

He rounded back on the anthill, and saw that another ant had emerged. But this one was heading toward him.

"Crap." John sighted in on the ant's head as it skittered toward him.

He fired.

The ant took the hit, and kept on coming. Maybe its carapace was cracked, but that didn't seem to be affecting it much.

"Crap!"

John's M&P fired 9mm bullets. Which was fine for confronting a gang banger. But those don't have the muzzle velocity, or impact, of a rifle round. And looked like that was going to make a huge difference here.

John backed up, and shot again.

Still the ant kept on coming. At the top of the hill, the antennas of another ant were beginning to poke out.

The attacking ant was almost close enough to attack. Its mandibles opened wide.

And then its head exploded at the same time as a report from a rifle shot came from John's right. He looked over and saw Barnes lowering his smoking barrel.

Their eyes met, and Barnes gestured toward the anthill.

John nodded, and pulled the pin. Then he sprinted forward.

The second ant was emerging from the hole, and pointing in John's direction.

His shoes slid on the loose earth of the anthill's side, but he didn't let that stop him. He released the sprong on the flash-bang and leapt upward, above the probing antennas of the emerging ant.

As he passed over the hole, and the emerging ant, he dropped the grenade.

He hit the ground on the other side of the hill and lost his footing, sliding down the loose dirt and drawing a lot of dust and pebbles down with him.

Then the flash-bang went off, and the concussion of sound swept over him, knocking him flat for a second.

He was just pushing himself up onto his hands and knees when something landed beside him with a crunch that he could just barely hear.

He looked to the right and recoiled.

An ant!

But a heartbeat later, he saw it was dead. Carapace broken and holed in half a dozen places, the legs broken off.

What the - ?

"Oh man, that was awesome!" Barnes' voice drew John's eyes upwards, and he saw the SWAT guy, his blond companion leaning on his for support, hurrying across from his grass shaft toward where

John sat. "That thing," he gestured with his right hand—he had his left around the blond guy's shoulder, letting his rifle drop on its tactical sling—toward the dead ant, "shot straight up out of the mound. Must have been thirty feet!"

"Great." John pushed himself to his feet and dusted himself off. He eyed the top of the anthill warily.

The hole on top was more a crater now, and he thought he could hear skittering sounds—lots of them—from within.

"We'd better get out of here."

Barnes followed his look toward the hole and nodded agreement. "Can you run, Eddie?" he said to the blond guy.

Eddie shook his head. "Don't think so. This burns like a - " He shifted a little and let out a gasp, then a groan, and his left hand pressed to his side. John could see blood flowing freely there.

But much as that must hurt, he knew the ant venom would make it worse.

All the same, good thing he'd been wearing Kevlar. If he hadn't, he might already be dead, from the look of things.

John glanced back at the hole again, then holstered his pistol and slipped his right arm over Eddie's shoulder, on the opposite side from Barnes.

He met Barnes' eyes from overtop Eddie's slumping head. The SWAT guy nodded understanding.

All but carrying Eddie between them, they began hoofing it, as fast as they could.

Which was nowhere fast enough for John. As much trouble as he'd had pushing his way past the grass shafts before, they had more since they were, together, so much larger than he had been alone.

And then it got worse.

They were just getting past a particularly tough clump of shafts when John heard it. The skittering.

It had been there in the background behind them, but all of a sudden it rose in a crescendo. He looked back, and felt his stomach drop through his feet.

There was movement back through the grass shafts behind them. Lots of movement.

Lots of red movement.

"They're coming!" he said, and pushed forward with renewed vigor.

And stepped on the head of an ant that burrowed out of the ground directly in front of them.

"Son of a bitch!" Barnes shouted, and stomped down hard.

Stamping in unison, they managed to crush the ant's head before it could do any harm.

But the skittering from behind was louder now, and looking to the left, John saw another ant burrowing upward.

"Move!" Barnes said.

They moved.

But It was hopeless. They were not going fast enough; John glanced over his shoulder again and could clearly see the skittering monsters now, growing closer by the second.

If they weren't carrying Eddie, maybe -

He quashed that thought. Hard. Then he redoubled his efforts at running and shoving shafts aside, despite the burning in his lungs—too many damn cigarettes—and the protests from his things—not enough running the last couple years.

"Look for someplace we can hole up," John said between gasping breaths. "High ground, where we can make a stand." He didn't say that would only delay the inevitable.

He didn't have to.

The ground shook, and John stumbled forward. Eddie and Barnes went with him, and the three of them almost fell in a heap.

Instead they crashed into a grass shaft, and managed to use it to steady themselves.

"What was - " Barnes began.

But his words were overwhelmed by a thundering noise that came from everywhere and nowhere all at once.

Just as quickly as it came, the thunder faded, but for a second there something about it rang a bell in John's mind.

He and Barnes met each others eyes again. He could see the confusion, the disorientation in the SWAT guy's face. It must surely match his own.

But there wasn't time to wonder over this latest whatever-it-was. The ants were coming.

John looked back, and blanched.

The ants were here.

They were swarming everywhere, skittering across the ground. Climbing over and around the grass shafts. And unerringly heading straight toward the three of them.

The ants were maybe thirty feet away, and closing quickly.

"Run!"

But it was futile, and they all knew it. Still, they started forward again.

And again, the earth rocked.

The thunder came again, but this time John caught its content better, and his eyebrows rose high as he understood what it was.

"Sarge!"

Mendoza! John had told Mendoza to follow him, and he must have obeyed.

Better late than never.

But he wasn't shrunken down. If he and Barnes could find him -

Another quake, and several shafts up ahead a short ways bent double.

"Over there!" John shouted, and Barnes didn't hesitate but to head in that direction.

They heaved Eddie up over a broken shaft.

And came up against a wall. A black wall that ran left and right as far as they could see past the grass shafts, which admittedly wasn't far. It had a ledge about chest high running parallel to the ground, then curved up and away from them.

John followed it up, and saw that it continued to rise higher, becoming navy blue and straight after a short distance -

It suddenly struck him what he was looking at. This was Mendoza's shoe, and he was looking up Mendoza's pants leg.

John had visited New York City once, and gone to the Liberty Tower. Staring up at the Rookie, he was struck by the same sense of awe as he had when he looked up the side of that huge building.

He snapped out of it when Barnes said, "Get up on the shoe," and began boosting Eddie up.

Eddie was very weak, but he managed to force himself up, then Barnes followed suit.

John took a second to look back and found himself eye-to-eyes with an ant that had climbed up the grass shaft they had just clambered over.

Shouting in surprise, John swatted at it, and was shocked when his backhand knocked the thing off the grass shaft.

But there were a hundred more behind it, and they were not stopping.

The shoe began to shift behind him, and John realized Mendoza was about to take a step. If he missed this chance, the ants would get him.

He turned and leapt, grabbing desperately at the ledge of the shoe. Barnes grabbed onto his clutching hands as the shoe rose into the air.

John had a glimpse of the fire ants, swarming amongst the grass below in obvious frustration, and then they were gone, lost amidst the endless green of the lawn, and Barnes pulled him the rest of the way onto the ledge.

They sat there, spent, for what seemed an hour as Mendoza continued to walk around and call out for John.

But it could only have really been a half a minute or so before Barnes shook his head in annoyance and lifted his rifle. He shot a long burst out to the side, and Mendoza stopped.

Above them, miles away seemingly, the tower that was the rookie shifted, then moved, and slowly his face—gargantuan in proportions so John could make out his every pore, came into focus above them.

"Sarge?" he said, and it was like a thunderclap, but less so now that he at least wasn't shouting.

John stood up on the shoe and gestured for him to come closer.

Instead, Mendoza shifted again, and the open palm of his hand came down next to them. John and Barnes helped Eddie move over onto it, then followed suit. A second later the bottom fell out of John's stomach as the fastest elevator in existence rocketed them up to Mendoza's full height and they stood on his hand in front of his face.

Feeling extremely queasy, John took a second to steady himself then stood and pointed toward Eddie. He shouted, to be sure Mendoza could hear.

"He's badly wounded. Call for an ambulance. Get us to the SWAT van."

Mendoza nodded, and it was like a mountain shifting. Then his hand closed gently around them and he began to run.

John lost his lunch.

Special Magics were already on scene when Mendoza got them to the SWAT van, and they wasted no time in restoring John, Eddie, and Barnes to their normal size.

And despite John's assurances that he was fine, they insisted he accompany the SWAT guys in the ambulance to the hospital and get fully checked out. No telling what the side effects could be from such a spell.

So he slumped down next to Barnes in the back of the ambulance as its wailing siren cleared the way for the paramedic drivers up forward. Eddie was strapped to a gurney on the other side of the van, with an IV running. He was unconscious, but the paramedics didn't think he was in immediate danger.

Beside him, Barnes shook his head and let out a chuckle that was half amusement, half astonishment.

"This is going to be the king of all "There I was" stories," he said. "Never gonna match it."

"Oh I don't know," John said. "Next time there might be a giant and a beanstalk."

Barnes' chuckle became a full-on laugh. He held out his hand toward John. "You sir, are one crazy, stupid son of a bitch." He grinned. "I owe you a tall one."

John returned the grin and shook hands with him. "Any time, brother."

Any time.

11

———

VIP TREATMENT

Most folks have heard the term "Christmas in July."

The suburban town where I'm stationed is run by smart-alecks, though, so Lockwood has "Christmas on the solstice." Because symmetry of timing and rigid thinking.

What most people don't know is the concept, whether fun or annoyingly pedantic, derives from a real necessity of the Big Guy's battle rhythm. Can't keep reindeer cooped up too long or they go stir crazy, taking to biting and being generally grumpy.

So every summer they go on tour to stretch their legs, and do a little PR for the Big Guy's operation.

When that happens, someone's got to provide security against the Elf problem. This summer, the job fell to me. I'm Dustin Cofield, and I'm an Elfsterminator.

———

Most days I work out of a small eight by eight office in a Wells Fargo branch. When I'm there, I dress like a banker in a nice custom-tailored suit and I at least put on the appearance of doing banking things. Attending staff meetings, things like that.

But I don't really work for the bank.

I work for an Agency that no one has ever heard of, because it doesn't exist. We help the Big Guy maintain production up at the Pole since the elves walked out on him, and keep the elves from sabotaging him and ruining Christmas. Among other things.

Unfortunately, with the reindeer tour coming through town, it was out of the bank for me. Which was just fine, as far as I was concerned. I really can't stand banks.

But it did mean I was going to have to spend much more time in my combat suit than I normally like to. The damn thing is ridiculous: made of fuzzy red material that was like fur that had been trimmed real close, with a broad white sash of a belt—same material—and a fuzzy white hood with a half face mask that left the mouth and chin exposed.

It was like some godawful attempt at a bad superhero costume; when I first saw it, I thought sure it was a joke the other guys were playing at my expense.

It wasn't.

But there was a reason our combat suit looked the way it did. It was made of the same material as the Big Guy's clothing, and something about his long relationship with the elves had imparted a protective field of some kind in that material that defended against the worst of their tricks.

So much as I feel like an idiot every time I wear it, I've come to appreciate its utility.

But the damn thing is also hot. And this was shaping up to be the warmest summer we'd see in Lockwood in quite some time. The weather geeks were predicting mid-90s the entire week of the solstice.

This duty was going to suck. But it was important work, and that's why I'm in the business.

Lockwood puts on its Christmas on the Solstice extravaganza— yes they really call it an extravaganza—in a public park across the street from city hall. Like most everything in the town, it was a nice place. Well-manicured flowerbeds and trees. A bubbling fountain with the statue of one of the original city fathers in the center. Walking paths and sitting benches. A kids playground to the back. The usual.

But also like most everything else in Lockwood, it was just that: the usual. It was a suburban public park. Nothing more, nothing less. Not really special in any way.

Except that, unbeknownst to the citizens of my cookie-cutter nice little town, they were going to soon be getting some exceptional visitors.

I met with the advance elements of the reindeer tour a week before the VIPs were scheduled to arrive. They were two field agents and a supervisor. The agents I knew from working with them on a case that went national a couple years back.

Dwayne was a bit taller than me, and deeply tanned. Well-muscled, but he'd begun to develop a paunch since I last saw him and his black hair was thinning. His eyes were just as sharp as they ever were, though.

Crystal looked like a dancer, because she was. She'd done ten years in a semi-pro ballet troupe while she was in High School and College. She toured all over the place and was heading for great things on the pro ballet stage. Then she'd gotten caught up in the big sugar cookie incident of '13. After that experience, she wanted payback. So she left the troupe and signed on with the Agency. But she kept up her dancer's figure. She was tall, slender, blonde, and just as flexible and strong as you'd expect. And she was sharp as a tack.

I grinned when I met the two of them in front of the park's fountain. We were all dressed in normie attire; no combat suits for this meeting at least, thank God.

"Great to see you two again," I said as we shook hands.

Dwayne's return grin was good humored. Crystal's was...challenging, and her eyebrow rose slightly as she released my hand.

I was just pondering what that meant when a throat cleared and I turned my attention to the supervisor. I'd never seen the guy before, but I got a sinking feeling the second I really looked him over. He was about my height, but slight, almost mousey. He had a narrow nose that seemed to strain to hold up the thick black-rimmed glasses he wore, and lips that seemed locked into an expression of disapproval. His hair was mostly grey, though there were a few strands of strawberry blond left. He wore an expensive-looking watch on his left wrist, and had a leather attache case in his hand.

He didn't offer to shake.

"Agent Cofield," he said. "I'm Bill Anders, head of security for Operation Margaritaville."

I blinked. "Margaritaville? Seriously?"

"You have a problem with that?"

Shrugging, I said, "The name doesn't exactly match the rest of our theme, you know?"

He looked even more disapproving. But apparently he decided to drop it, as he just opened the attache case and pulled out a manila folder, which he passed over to me. "It is very important that this event go smoothly," he said. "The VIPs have a long - "

"Yeah, yeah, I know," I said as I opened the folder. "I've done these before."

"And that is precisely why I have decided to oversee preparations for this stop on the tour personally. Your performance on your last security detail was...less than optimal."

I snorted. "The VIP got out unhurt and we collared the pointies who tried to make trouble. So some normies got their egg nog spiked with prune juice. It's not really a big - " I stopped when I turned the page on the briefing papers inside the folder and saw the VIP list. I felt my eyes widening, and a surge of adrenalin went up my spine. I looked up from the paper at Anders and met his eyes, which were narrowed to slits. "Is this right?"

He nodded. "It is. So you see why we cannot afford to leave anything to chance."

I could. I could, indeed.

Rudolph was coming to Lockwood.

Even now, a week after that initial meeting, I couldn't get the reality of that fact through my head. Sure, every one of the Big Guy's drivers was important. But there were reindeer....and then there were reindeer.

I couldn't remember the last time Rudolph, himself, had left the Pole, so I looked it up. He hadn't. Not since way before the kerfuffle with the elves began, and that went down well before my time.

It wasn't that he didn't need to stretch his legs and get out and about like the other reindeer. He does. But...to be frank, if one of the pointies managed to knock off Comet, for example, there are other reindeer who can replace him.

But no one has that nose. So he and the Big Guy came to an agreement where he would take his summertime sojourns at the Pole. Just not...in...the Pole. The Big Guy figured out a way to use sugar straws and pixie dust to make a -

I didn't fully understand it myself. But he got his own private place to romp around without ever having to leave the safety of the Pole. Apparently it was too expensive to do that with the rest of the team, though, and that had led to grumbling over the years.

Last one of these I did—the one Anders didn't like—Blitzen had been bitching up a storm about it. Called Rudolph a prima dona. I'd never met the guy so I couldn't agree or disagree either way. And I figured I never would.

Guess I was wrong.

On the day the extravaganza kicked off, I met up with Dwayne and Crystal in full combat attire two hours before he was set to arrive.

It was hot. Hotter than the weather geeks had predicted. Only twenty minutes into our final check of the VIP enclosure and the security arrangements, I was sweating up a storm and my outfit was starting to itch in half a dozen places.

I eyed the staff of personnel—normies mostly, from town, and doing backgrounds on them to make sure they weren't going to be a problem was what took most of our time over the previous week— who'd been hired to take tickets and stand around looking Christ-massy around the VIP enclosure, at their holiday-appearing but light and loose attire that really was pretty well suited to the summer heat, and I couldn't help but grind my teeth.

"This is why we get the big bucks, man," Dwayne said, from beside me. He and I were making the final circuit while Crystal checked on the electronic security measures, and he must have seen the look on my face.

I grunted. "Yeah, right."

In point of fact, I did alright with the Agency. More than alright. And the fringe benefits were great.

But I'd sure rather not be cooking in this outfit right that second, regardless.

Looking away from the hired help, I shifted my focus toward the other stations that the town had set up for the extravaganza. There was a life-size gingerbread house—not really gingerbread, unfortunately—and a review stand where the Mayor and other assorted folks would hang out and give speeches. Over to the left, toward where the kids playground sat, were three portable carnival rides that had been trucked into place earlier in the day. Some food trucks were stationed around the periphery, as were stands selling cotton candy, funnel cakes, and all the usual fairground fare.

But no sugar cookies or candy canes? That just wasn't right.

The most amazing thing the town had done to set up, though, aside from getting the VIP, was the ice rink. Somewhere, somehow, they'd found someone who was able to set up and cool down a portable rink that actually stayed frozen in these temperatures.

I was thinking that almost had to be magic; maybe pointy magic. And I was about to pull strings to get it taken away a couple days ago. But turned out no, it was just good engineering.

Go figure.

The entire park had been sprayed with that fake snow that you can get from party stores, and the town had rigged up Christmas lights everywhere, so they at least went to a bit of effort at holiday cheer, despite the odd choice in snacks.

And as people from the town began filtering in to join in the festivities, it began to feel festive, almost enough to ignore the sweat and my itchiness.

Almost.

"I think we're good to go," I said to Dwayne, and he nodded agreement. So we slipped under the garland beads that ran between the four foot tall candy canes that were the fenceposts around our VIP enclosure and made our way across the dirt mini-pasture toward the red wooden double doors that would open to expose Rudolph to his adoring public.

And yes, he really did refer to it as "his adoring public."

I'd had a chance to spend some time with him the previous night, briefing him on the security set up. Blitzen was right; total prima dona.

But it wasn't my place to judge, so I didn't. Instead, I looked outward, toward the growing crowds as more of Lockwood's populace began to gather.

A burst of static sounded in my left ear, then Crystal's voice came through the earbud I'd placed there before pulling the hood and mask into place.

"All set on my end," she said. The transmission made her voice sound tinny.

"Roger," I replied, keying my transmitter quickly. "We're go in ten minutes here. Radio silence in eight."

"Roger."

I looked across at Dwayne and got a small nod from him. He had heard clearly, and understood.

The thing about the Big Guy and his setup is he can't use any electronics. Something about the electromagnetic fields they generate messes with his mojo, or his magic, or his... Whatever it is, if there's anything electronic around him, he can't do his work right.

He can't even take a report that had been typed up electronically. So I, and the rest of the Agency, used old typewriters from the 30s, and carbon paper in triplicate, for correspondence.

It sucked, but the Big Guy gets what the Big Guy needs.

That electronic limitation goes for his drivers as well. And, we'd all thought, for the pointies. But lately I'd seen evidence that they may have figured a way around that particular limitation.

Regardless, the upshot was we couldn't use any electronics in our security arrangements for the VIP. Or at least, we couldn't use them in his immediate vicinity. So Crystal had set up in a remote van on the other side of the park from the VIP enclosure, and monitored our electronic surveillance from there.

We'd be securing our radios two minutes before the VIP came on "stage" but she'd still be going strong. If she saw something amiss, she'd signal us through alternate means.

The time passed quickly. Just as the Mayor was taking the stage on his reviewing stand, to an unexpectedly good amount of applause from the crowd, considering some of the things he'd done lately, I said, "Going dark," into my transmitter, then secured the power.

A minute later, sooner than I expected and before the Mayor had even been able to complete his introduction, the double doors swung open and our VIP strode out.

When I first met him the day before, I was, frankly, shocked. He was the shortest, scrawniest, and, frankly, ugliest fully-grown reindeer I'd ever seen. For a second I thought there'd been some mistake, or a last minute change in plans. But then his nose had begun glowing.

It was glowing now. And boy was it glowing. Brightly enough that it cast a red tint on everything, even over to the Mayor on his reviewing stand.

He got caught mid-sentence and stopped, blinked, then cleared his throat and stared daggers at me and Dwayne, as though it was somehow our fault that he'd been interrupted. Then he just as quickly put back on his slick political smile and made a sweeping gestured in our direction.

"Well, there he is now! Ladies and gentlemen, boys and girls....Rudolph the Red-Nosed Reindeer!"

Oos and Ahs wafted from the crowd as they turned away from the Mayor and toward the VIP enclosure. But Rudolph's snort overwhelmed them, to my ears.

Most folks don't speak reindeer, and couldn't if they wanted to, without a lot of classwork using specialized instructional techniques. My reindeer was very rusty, but I knew enough to understand what he said next.

"Red Nosed. Red-Nosed! Buffoon. My nose is not red." The VIP sounded positively affronted.

And, to be frank, he was right. His nose was just as black as any other reindeer's. But something about the way the mistletoe hung over the manger angled the northern lights into his mother's eyes on the night he was born imbued his nose with the power to cast that magical, warm red glow that the Big Guy found so useful in steering his transport around.

No one was really sure how it had happened, as despite many attempts no one had been able to recreate the event. And so, he was famous.

As he pranced into the middle of his VIP pasture, Dwayne and I advanced with him, looking to the normies like a couple of handlers.

Half a dozen of our normie employees manned the outside of the fence at intervals, keeping people at their distance without really having to do anything except be there; societal norms about personal space handled the rest. Normally.

But the crowd did press closer. They wore varying degrees of wonder on their faces. Some from genuine enjoyment. Some from pondering how we had created the glowing nose trick. But they were all taken in.

Especially the kids. Their eyes were practically bugging out of their heads, and parents had to restrain them from rushing headlong into the fence—and maybe through it—they were so entranced. Especially one group directly in front of Rudolph and to his left.

There were about a dozen of the little munchkins, ranging in ages from probably eight to ten. They were pointing and giggling and smiling, and the light from Rudolph's nose seemed to reflect off their well-brushed teeth. And wasn't it cute that their parents had dressed them up in holiday clothes for the occasion, and Santa Hats.

Santa Hats.

I keyed in on them, the hackles on my neck rising, and saw one of them adjust his hat a bit. I caught a whiff of peppermint at the same time I noticed an unnaturally long ear beneath.

The kid—not a kid either, I realized—next to him reached into a pocket.

"Pointies!" I said, as loudly as I dared, and I grabbed at the bridle the VIP was wearing, pulling him backward.

Dwayne surged forward to place himself between the group of elves and the VIP.

The pointy withdrew his hand from his pocket and made a casting motion.

Black liquid, more viscous than water, seemed to ooze through the air, like it was moving in slow motion from the pointy's outstretched hand toward Dwayne and the VIP, despite the fact that it really did move at normal speed.

Dwayne caught most of it, the front of his combat outfit becoming coated in the oily, tarry fluid. He cried out as if pained and stumbled backward.

Then the VIP cried out as well, as a single drop of the black stuff, whatever it was, landed on his nose.

The light his nose had been casting immediately went out.

And then all hell broke loose.

***

Two days later, I went with Crystal to my local field office's forensic lab and evidence storage facility. It was located in the back of a Thrift Store—owned and operated by the Agency, and at a tidy profit I'm told—and while not particularly large, it was well stocked, and even better maintained by our evidence tech, Colleen.

The room was neatly arranged with metal shelving around the periphery, where evidence boxes from recent cases were stored, and a combination lab table, imaging system, and computer desk in the center.

Colleen herself was a bit chubby and blond, and always cheerful.

She habitually wore a white lab coat, despite not actually having a degree in forensics, and today she had her hair done up in a pair of buns on either side of her head. A continuation of the Star Wars motif she'd been going with lately, apparently.

Her normally cheerful face was troubled, though, when I walked in, Crystal at my side.

"How's Dwayne?"

"Better," I said. "He's still in the hospital, but the Docs think they'll release him tomorrow."

Some of the tension that had been in Colleen's face left it, and no wonder. Most pointy tricks get deflected by our combat suit's material. But not that black stuff. It had gone straight through and knocked Dwayne for a loop, giving symptoms that the normies had taken for a heart attack.

And just one drop had extinguished Rudolph's light.

That was some serious stuff.

"Have you figured out what that crap was the elves hit him with?" Crystal asked, stealing the question from me.

Colleen nodded quickly. "I think so. Check it out." She turned from us toward her imaging equipment and brought up a picture she had clearly taken earlier, through her microscope. It showed a bunch of black smudges, separated from each other even though they were stacked close enough that seen from normal magnification a human would never be able to tell.

"It's like a sort of modified bacteria," she said.

"Bacteria? The pointies are using germ warfare?" I said. "How?"

Colleen shook her head. "I said it's like a bacteria. But near as I can tell, they don't interact with us medically. I don't see any means of cellular transfer, mitosis, metabolism, you name it."

"Well they clearly do interact somehow, don't they?" Crystal said, no small amount of sarcasm in her voice.

"Right. So I looked at it a different way. Turns out they don't do what bacteria normally do: invade and colonize a body. Instead they produce a toxin that does the same thing."

I traded glances at Crystal. She raised that eyebrow again.

"Ok," I said. "That still doesn't answer how the pointies got them."

Colleen spread her hands helplessly. "I can't answer that. But I was able to isolate the toxin."

"Is there an antidote?" Crystal asked.

"Sort of. If my analysis is right and the dosage is small enough, we may be able to flush it from the victim's system using..." Colleen trailed off, looking almost embarrassed.

"What?"

Colleen shrugged. "Peppermint spice hot chocolate."

I stood there in silence for a long several seconds, just looking at her. She squirmed on her feet for a second, then threw up her hands. "I'm serious."

"Ok. That's odd, but ok. But," I looked back at Crystal again, who looked as puzzled as I felt. "If it's that easy to cure, what's the point?"

"If the dose is small enough," Colleen said, putting greater emphasis on her words. "More than a drop or two of this stuff on an average person's skin and the toxin will overwhelm the beneficials in the hot chocolate."

I felt a sliver of dread in my gut. "But - "

At the same time, Crystal said, "Dwayne! Is he - "

Colleen shook her head, holding up calming hands, palms toward us. "From the blood work I saw, his suit blocked most of the toxin. After the treatment he shouldn't have any relapses."

"And...the VIP?"

"Hopefully, a mug will get him back to his old self, good as new. But if Dwayne hadn't blocked the attack..."

Colleen left the rest unsaid.

She didn't have to say it. We'd come two drops of gunk away from lights out on Christmas forever.

"You know what I can't figure out?" Crystal said as we drove away from the forensics lab in my souped-up Yukon.

"What's that?"

"How in the hell did the elves get that stuff into the event in the first place?"

I put on my blinker to change into the left-hand lane in preparation for taking the upcoming on-ramp to the beltway around the metropolitan area that Lockwood inhabited. "What do you mean?"

"The town had security screening. Bag searches. No outside food or drink allowed inside, to hook the food vendors up. And we put our own sniffers in on top of that. No way something like that should have made it past without us detecting it. But even if we missed that, the sniffers should have detected the elves themselves. But I didn't get any alerts from our equipment at all."

She had a point. The Agency had developed some sophisticated equipment—electronic and non-electronic, both—to detect elfin chicanery. Some of them keyed on the distinctive peppermint odor that tends to surround the pointies. Some of it looks for their auras or their known equipment. But this was a new weapon.

"It's a new weapon," I said, making the turn onto the on-ramp. "We've never seen it before, so how could the sniffers detect it?"

"Yeah but it looks funky. Security should have at least raised a flag."

I cast a doubtful glance at her, and she shrugged, shrinking back in her seat slightly. "Or the sniffers should have at least detected the elves themselves."

Which was a valid point. Elf sniffers could detect peppermint down to one part in a million in the air, and like Crystal said we'd set them up at each access point to the event, and around the VIP enclosure as well. They hadn't raised an alarm.

Had the pointies come up with a way to mask their distinctive odor? They hadn't been successful so far, despite many attempts at elfin deodorant over the years. But maybe this time...

Memory of a whiff of peppermint just before the attack put the lie to that thought.

"You're right," I said. "I smelled them. The sniffers should have, too."

We traded glances, neither of us having to give voice to our thoughts because we were both thinking the same thing.

Someone must have tampered with the sniffers.

I held out a steaming mug of hot chocolate, laced with peppermint, toward Rudolph's snout. His nostrils flared and he sniffed. Then he cocked his head at me, confusion mixed with something else that I couldn't quite put my finger on showing through in his eyes.

We were in the small building Operation Margaritaville had rented as a staging area for the VIP's trip to and from Lockwood. It was basically a warehouse, with a roll-up door leading to a loading ramp in one corner and wide open space inside. Space that had been taken up with CONEX boxes filled with the equipment needed to support the VIP's visit.

Rudolph was settled into a small pen in the corner of the building opposite the loading ramp. The pen was as comfortable as the Agency's considerable resources could have made it.

But it was still a pen. I was sure he'd much rather be out and about with his adoring public.

Or maybe not, all things considered. It was moot, though, because no way was he going to get anything close to exposure to the public after what happened. Not in Lockwood anyway. And maybe not in any of the other stops on his tour. That was being heavily debated at Agency HQ by the highest of high-up muckety-mucks. Or so Anders had said the day before.

"What's this?" Rudolph said.

"Peppermint hot chocolate," I replied. "According to our forensic analysis, a few quaffs of this and you'll be good as new again."

"Really?"

I nodded.

Anders had insisted on accompanying me and Crystal to see Rudolph, and he looked almost poleaxed. So I guess I could understand the reindeer's trepidation as he lowered his head to drink.

I looked over at Anders. "You can thank Dwayne for that. If he hadn't blocked as much of that goop as he did." I shook my head. "The affect would have been irreversible."

Rudolph coughed into the mug and raised his snout. "Really?"

Already I could see the glow beginning to re-ignite, however dimly. I nodded. "You got very lucky."

Anders glowered at me. "This makes two security details you've botched, Cofield. I'm writing you up."

"I wouldn't do that," Crystal said. "It's not his fault."

"Oh?" Anders turned his glare on her. "Whose fault is it?"

"Yours."

Anders spluttered. "I beg your pardon!?"

"You disabled the elf sniffers the night of the event, after we made our final checks."

"Preposterous! I - "

"We've got you on security camera footage doing it," I said, giving him a nasty grin that I reserve for bad guys who I truly despise. "Ours weren't operational then, but you forgot the city had its own security setup. Their cameras were working fine."

Anders' face went pale and his jaw dropped open. His beady little eyes darted back and forth quickly between me and Crystal, as though searching for something, anything, that would get him out of this. He opened his mouth to speak.

Rudolph's derisive snort cut him off before he could get started. "You fool. You absolute idiot! I can't believe I ever listened to you!"

I about dropped the mug, I was so shocked. I rounded on the VIP, in time for him to say, "You've screwed us both, completely, you jackass!"

"What - ?" I began, unsure what to say next.

Rudolph met my incredulity with a resigned stare that quickly turned into one of dejection as he looked away, down toward the freshly-laid dirt at his feet.

"I hate this nose," he said, his voice plaintive. "I hate it so much."

The true pain, the hopelessness in the VIP's voice took me aback.

"Ah," I tried, and then just decided to say nothing and let him continue.

"It's a curse," Rudolph said. "When I was little, I couldn't play in the reindeer games because of it. Then I grew up and the Does wouldn't come near me. After that foggy night when Kris asked me to drive, everyone loved me and I thought it would all get better. And it did. For a while. But then I realized it wasn't me they loved, it was this damn nose. They put me on a pedestal, because of it.

"And then, after the elves..." He bit back a sob, shaking his head. "I couldn't even go out on trips any more. I'm a prisoner at the Pole because of this damn nose. Practically a slave." Rudolph looked up at me, and then over toward Anders. "He told me he found a way to cure me, to break the curse. And we'd both make a bunch of money in the process, enough to retire on." His gaze hardened for a second, then he let out a little groan and looked back down into the dirt.

I looked away from the stricken VIP and toward Crystal. I could see she was as shocked as I was. But she recovered faster.

She rounded on Anders. "You took a payoff from the elves?" She sounded like she was accusing him of drowning babies, her tone was so severe.

Anders wagged his jaw silently for a second or so. His eyes darted between us again.

Then he bolted toward the loading dock.

Crystal looked back at me. She sighed, rolled her eyes, then winked.

And then she was off. Great bounding steps like ballerinas make on the stage easily closed the distance between herself and the fleeing Anders.

When she was just a few paces from him, she leapt into a grand jete that ended with the toe of her foot in his back, between the shoulder blades.

Anders stumbled forward and rebounded against the wall adjacent to the roll-up doors. He fell to the floor, clutching at his nose, which he crunched when he struck the wall with a sound I could hear from all the way over where I was still standing next to Rudolph's pen.

Crystal didn't show any empathy. Landing gracefully on her feet, she strode over to where Anders lay groaning and kicked him over onto his belly—making his nose strike the floor and evoking a louder cry of pain—then forced his hands behind his back. She looked very satisfied as she cuffed him.

I turned back toward Rudolph. He looked even smaller than before, utterly defeated.

I considered for a second that there wasn't the equivalent of handcuffs for reindeer. Then I decided he was in a pen already, so I really didn't need to worry about it.

Instead, I held out the mug toward him again.

He stuck his snout in and drank some more of the peppermint hot chocolate, the glow from his nose growing more bright with every swallow.

Crystal sat in the one spare chair I had in my little office in the Wells Fargo branch while I sat behind my desk, typing away at my 1930s vintage typewriter with its carbon paper for making copies in triplicate.

The rest of the office aside from her was the way it always was. Mimeographed memos from HQ tacked up onto a corkboard adjacent to my door. A picture of me and the Big Guy himself up at the Pole at an awards banquet up on the wall next to it. The plant Nora, my girlfriend, had given to me beneath the one narrow window in the room, looking much improved since I'd gotten back from undercover work and been able to water it consistently. The counterweight-powered clock on the wall opposite the door.

No electronics, but then I didn't need any here.

I was finishing up my report on what had happened. Naturally Crystal was interested in what I was going to say, so she'd been reading it, page by page, as I typed. She'd offered a few comments and suggestions, but not much. We'd agreed on how to state things before I'd even begun typing.

Finally, I finished. I pulled the final page out and passed it over to her.

It only took her a minute to read it through. She handed it back with a nod of approval.

"All's well that ends well, I suppose," she said, but she had an element of doubt in her voice.

I nodded in agreement, both at her words and at her doubt. "Anders is going away for a long time," I said. "Dwayne's back on his feet, good as new."

I stopped there, and the subject that I hadn't brought up hung heavily in the air between us.

Finally, she gave voice to the thought that had been haunting us both. "What do you think the Big Guy is going to do with him?"

"Rudolph?"

She nodded.

I looked away, toward the picture of me and the Big Guy himself with his plump rosy cheeks and his big jolly smile that had never quite struck me as completely genuine.

"I don't know. Hopefully they'll come to some kind of new arrangement. It clearly can't continue the way it has up until now. But..."

I shook my head. I really had no idea. But I hoped this incident would cause the Big Guy to re-evaluate how Rudolph really felt about their situation, and make changes for the better.

Who knows, maybe it was time for the red-nosed reindeer to retire, like he'd tried to, however dishonestly. It wasn't like the Big Guy couldn't get the Agency to rig some kind of lamp or spotlight or something on his transport so he wouldn't have to use Rudolph's nose.

But then again...electronics.

Bah, there had to be something.

"Yeah," Crystal said, agreeing with me.

We sat there in silence for almost a full minute before, abruptly, she stood. "Want to get dinner?"

I spared a look at the clock; I hadn't realized the time. I needed to hurry or I'd be late. I shook my head. "Can't. Meeting Nora over at Bertucci's."

Crystal cocked her head to the side, and I saw something flash in her eyes for a second. Disappointment? "You're still with her, huh?"

I nodded. "Yup. I kind of like her, you know?"

Crystal smiled ever so slightly. "She's a lucky girl." With that, she turned and opened the door to my office. "See you around, Cofield," she said. Then she was gone, and the door swung shut behind her.

12

A MAN OF FAITH

The shriek that left the girl's mouth was guttural, profane, and inhuman. A roar from the Pit of Hell itself, something that her vocal cords could never have produced on their own.

Joseph knew the sound well; he had been evoking it from demons for years.

The girl was fifteen, wearing a sweat-dampened and torn yellow-white nightgown, and writhed against the bonds he had placed on her wrists and ankles, keeping her tied down to the little four-poster bed that dominated the bedroom where he stood.

She would have been beautiful, except she had shaved the sides of her head and dyed her hair a mix of pink and blue and green, and inset garish ear gages that distended the lobes of her ears grotesquely. She had pierced her nose and her tongue, and probably other places as well. Through a tear in the sleeve of her nightgown Joseph could see the ink of at least one profane tattoo on her arm.

But as much as she had disfigured herself, the demon had done worse. It fought against the spiritual bonds Joseph was throwing at it as much as the physical, and it had twisted her face into something bestial, human only in its most basic structure. Her teeth, grown razor sharp, snapped at the air, trying futilely to get at him, and she—

or rather, the demon—gazed at him through eyes that were completely black except for burning red pupils, filled with an all-consuming hatred.

Not just hatred for him, but for all humanity. And for God Himself.

Another surge against the bonds, and again they held. But the sulfurous stink surrounding the possessed girl increased, and Joseph knew he must act quickly. He drew a breath.

"Pater noster, qui es in caelis. Santificetor, nomen tuum."

The demon shrieked again as the words of the Lord's Prayer filled the room, louder than Joseph could have spoken them on his own. He felt the power of God flowing through him as he called upon the Father in the name of the Son, amplifying his prayer and focusing the words.

The Latin wasn't necessary. Papal writ had changed that decades ago, but even if it hadn't, it was the meaning of the words and the faith behind them that were the weapons Joseph wielded. But Joseph liked the Latin; it brought him closer to the power of the Logos, the living Word.

And the demons always seemed to feel its punch stronger than from the vernacular. So he used it.

He finished the prayer and pulled out a vial from the pocket of the black robes he wore.

"In the name of God and by the power of Jesus Christ," he said, unstoppering the vial, "I command you to begone!" He shook the vial, letting holy water splash onto the girl's face.

The water hissed to steam as soon as it struck, and the demon's shriek amplified again. It arched upward, flailing wildly until only the back of the girl's head and the heels of her feet were touching the mattress.

"Begone!" Joseph shouted, and made the sign of the cross in the air between himself and the beast.

As he completed the cross, the beast let out another shriek, this one long and drawn out. But this time it gradually grew more quiet. Not like it was shouting its defiance any less forcefully, though. More like it was continuing to shriek but being drawn away down a long and distant tunnel, until the last of its cries became nothing more than a faint echo.

There there was silence.

The girl's body collapsed back onto the bed, her limbs spread limply and her hair, what little of it there was, soaked with sweat and plastered about her head.

Her chest rose and fell in long slow breaths, and her head lolled to the right, facing Joseph. He could see her skin had reverted from the reddish tint the demon had lent it, and her jaw was less distended, back to its normal shape.

Joseph watched her closely for a moment, then reached out and parted her lips.

Normal teeth.

Reaching up to her eye, he lifted the eyelid to peer beneath. White sclera.

He withdrew his hand and inhaled. The odor of sulfur had faded, leaving only the frankincense he had lit at the start of the ritual.

The girl stirred and made a little whimper.

Joseph replaced the vial of holy water into his pocket and withdrew a different vial, this one filled with a a translucent gold-yellow liquid. Unstoppering the vial, he dripped some of the anointing oil onto his fingers, then reached down again.

"Ego te absolvo e pecatis tuis," he said, and began drawing the sign of the cross on the girl's forehead with the oil, "in nomini patri, et filii, et spiritus sancti." He withdrew his hand again and restoppered the vial. "Amen."

The girl, still asleep, let out a sigh, and tension seemed to leave her body as it slumped back into full relaxation.

"Rest, child," Jospeh said. Replacing the vial in his pocket, he took a moment to untie the girl's bonds, then he turned toward the bedroom door.

The living room outside was cramped; but then so was the family's entire apartment. A threadbare couch, faded to grey from years of use, rested against the wall to Joseph's right, a darkly-stained wooden coffee table in front of it.

The girl's mother, late 30s and full figured, was kneeling between the two, her elbows resting on the coffee table and her hands clutching at a rosary. Her head was lowered over the beads, her long black hair obscuring her face as she bobbed her head occasionally. She was praying frantically in Spanish.

The girl's two brothers, one older and one younger, knelt with their mother, praying over their own rosaries, though less frantically, and perhaps less zealously, than their mother.

Her father stood apart from them; he had clearly been pacing back and forth across the worn brown carpet while his family had been praying. When Joseph entered the living room, his was the first head to turn. His round, tanned Mestizo face was lined with worry, his brown eyes red as though he had been crying, but trying to conceal the fact.

He was a working man; his jeans were stained and torn in a few places, from actual labor not from fashion, and his red and white plaid shirt needed washing as well. His wife and sons' clothing was equally simple. No family of means, this, but they had an earnest charm that Joseph had found endearing from the start.

"Is - " the father—Enrique—said in heavily accented English as Joseph stepped toward him, and the wife and two sons stopped their prayers and focused in on him like a laser.

Joseph nodded and answered before Enrique could finish the question. "It is done." Then he stepped aside as the mother, followed closely by the brothers, charged the room where the girl now slept peacefully, free of the demon that had been plaguing her.

Enrique hesitated, then moved to follow them, and Joseph turned toward the apartment's front door.

A younger man, darker than the family with a shaved head that gleamed in the electric lights of the apartment and wearing black robes like Joseph's, stood adjacent to the door. He held Joseph's silver crucifix-headed cane in his left hand and a his broad-brimmed black hat in his right, and a black canvas duffle bag sat on the floor at his feet. As Joseph's eyes met his, Thomas raised a questioning eyebrow.

"Let's go," Joseph said, and Thomas stepped forward, holding out the cane and hat.

Joseph was just reaching out to take them when Enrique spoke from behind, bringing him up short.

"Padre," Enrique said. "Gracias, padre."

Joseph turned and saw the father, open tears now streaming unashamedly down his cheeks. Through the doorway to the bedroom, he could see that the girl had awakened.

Enrique held out a hand that clutched a rolled-up collection of bills. Joseph couldn't tell all their denominations, but the outermost one was a fifty. It was a thick roll; probably several hundred dollars total.

He shook his head and cupped his hands over the money, then gently pressed it back toward Enrique until the hand and the money were both pressed against the father's chest.

"I don't do this for money," Joseph said, smiling gently at the man. "And I'm not a priest."

Enrique blinked, confusion sweeping the elation from his face. "Not a priest?" he said.

Joseph shook his head. "Just a man of faith." And if you had any actual faith, you could have done this yourself, he didn't say.

It was an uncharitable thought, and he hated that it had swept through his mind. But he couldn't prevent it, all the same.

The family had all the outward signs of piety. Crucifixes above the doors, a painting of the Sacred Heart on the wall above the couch. But if this man had been the strong spiritual leader that his family needed, and that God called husbands and fathers to be, his daughter never would have fallen astray into the occult and witchcraft, and opened herself up to the servants of Satan.

Joseph chastised himself inwardly. That was easy enough for him to say. Though he had not taken the holy orders after seminary, he had made his vow of chastity. And he kept it. He had not married, and never would. Not fathered a child, and never would. He had given those parts of his life as a sacrifice to God, in order to focus on his mission. But that meant that though he knew the responsibilities and challenges a man like Enrique faced intellectually, he didn't truly understand them in his core.

Judge not this man, lest ye be judged, Joseph said to himself.

He released the man's hand and money, instead resting his hands on Enrique's shoulders and giving them a gentle squeeze. Glancing toward the bedroom where the girl was already showing signs of getting back her strength, he said, "See to your daughter. She will need you."

Enrique nodded quickly and began to pull away, but Joseph tightened his grip slightly, holding him in place.

"But more than that, she will need God. You must lead her back to Him."

He locked eyes with Enrique, and saw that he fully understood what Joseph was saying. Both the mission he had to perform, and his earlier lack. A flash of shame, then guilt, passed through Enrique's eyes. Then he drew himself up with a quick inhalation. He nodded more briskly, and Joseph saw the simple, earnest strength of the man. The desire to do right.

"Si, señor," Enrique said.

Joseph nodded approval and released him. Enrique turned away and hurried back to his family.

Joseph watched them for a moment, and felt reassured that Enrique would work to set things right. Then he turned back toward Thomas, and the front door. He met his assistant's eyes and saw the silent question there. Joseph nodded to him, and they walked out.

Joseph met Monsignor Bruce Hennessy in the outdoor patio of Cafe Lamierre five minutes before their appointed lunch meeting.

The Cafe was on the tenth floor of the Peninsula hotel downtown, its patio outside with a sweeping view of the surrounding cityscape and the hustle and bustle in the streets below. Though Joseph was early, Bruce had already procured a table, a glass-topped setting for two in the left rear corner of the patio.

As he approached, Joseph noticed the table was just separated enough from its neighbors as to give them a bit of privacy.

So this wasn't just a social call between friends.

Bruce stood as Joseph reached the table. He was in his priestly habit, unlike Joseph who wore civilian attire. He wasn't actually a priest, after all.

They were of age, but Bruce had three inches and about thirty pounds on him, and his blond hair was receding rapidly. Joseph didn't want to think about how deep the lines on his old seminary classmate's face had gotten; his would no doubt be deeper still. He didn't truly feel his years yet, but he still didn't like the reminder that they were passing.

Bruce smiled, his round face seeming to glow and his blue eyes twinkling in the sunlight as he extended his right hand to shake. "Good to see you well, Joe," he said.

Joseph shook and found Bruce's grip as firm and commanding as always, then pulled the brushed aluminum chair back from his side of the table and took a seat.

It was hard, unyielding, but not uncomfortable.

"And how is life in the diocese?" Joseph asked. Bruce had taken up a new post as the Bishop's personal assistant; a prestigious position, though it did take him away from actual priestly duties. "Do you miss tending your flock?"

Bruce's smile slipped slightly, and he gave a little shrug. "We all have our assigned duties," he said. The drinking glasses at each of their settings were filled with ice water, and he picked up his to take a sip. "The Bishop heard about the aid you gave to the Hernandez family."

"God aided. I was just the instrument."

Bruce raised the glass slightly in a half-toast, acknowledging the response, then set it back on the table. Then he leaned forward, narrowing his eyes slightly. "I understand why you did not take the holy orders. But consider how much more effective you could be in your work if you accepted the Bishop's offer of patronage."

Joseph had to fight back a scowl. They had discussed this before, several months ago. The Bishop had offered to fund Joseph's ministry, allowing him to devote his efforts to it full-time. He had refused then, and he had no intention of changing his mind.

"I serve God, not the Bishop."

Bruce leaned back in his seat and frowned. "That's unfair, Joe. The church is the bride of Christ. To separate yourself from it is - "

"The church is the body of believers, not a worldly and corrupt bureaucracy."

Bruce's brows furrowed and his lips compressed. But before he could open his mouth to retort, Joseph beat him to it.

"How many sodomites and pederasts masquerading as priests has the Pope defrocked and excommunicated this month?"

Bruce blinked, his anger replaced by a flush of embarrassment. He did not reply.

"This year?"

Still silent, Bruce broke eye contact and looked down at his plate.

"Ever?"

A long moment of silence dragged out. Finally, not looking up, Bruce said, "You don't know how difficult it is, affecting change from within. But I believe the preservation of the Church is worth that struggle. I've been fighting the battle for years, and so has the Bishop." He lifted his eyes again, and there was steely determination in them. "But these things take time."

Joseph had to admire Bruce's optimism, and his faith in this regard. He himself had given up on the Roman Catholic Church—not the faith, the organization—when he had seen its ultimate corruption back in seminary. To Joseph, it seemed like the parable of the seed thrown onto bad soil: it needed to be ripped out, root and stem, and burned to make way for something better.

But Bruce still had hope mother church could be reformed, and was determined to fight for that. And fight he had; that could not be denied.

Joseph sighed and lifted his own glass. "Until that change comes, my answer remains the same," he said, and took a drink. "But you didn't ask to meet me just to rehash old arguments."

Bruce spread his hands in a "Hey, what are you gonna do" gesture. Then he leaned forward again, his gaze direct and businesslike. "The Bishop requests a favor from you."

Joseph raised his left eyebrow.

"Not for himself," Bruce added quickly.

"For whom then?"

"Governor Willoby - "

Joseph interrupted him with a derisive snort, and Bruce scowled at him in return.

"Will you let me finish?"

Joseph considered. He supposed it couldn't hurt to hear the proposal, at least. Shrugging, he made a "get on with it" gesture with his right hand.

Bruce cleared his throat. "The Governor's nephew has been having fits. Seizures. At first they thought it was epilepsy, but the doctors haven't been able to find a cause. As you know, the governor is a Catholic and - "

"He encourages young women to sacrifice their babies to Moloch," Joseph growled, "and has endorsed legislation to make those sacrifices even easier than they already are. No man who does that can name himself Christian, of any variety."

Bruce gave him a level, long-suffering look. Consternation was written all over his face.

In truth, Joseph understood his old friend's point of view. He was part of the system, and Willoby at least gave lip service to being of the faith. It would not do for the Bishop's assistant, or the Bishop himself, to publicly call the man out on his sin. Might rock the boat.

Joseph knew Bruce hated that aspect of the way things were. And he could respect that. Christ would have hated it too.

But He wouldn't have gone along with it.

Judge not, lest ye be judged, Joseph reminded himself again.

Seemed he had to remind himself that often. Several times a day, at least.

With a sigh, he gestured again for Bruce to continue.

Bruce obviously ground his teeth for a second before continuing. "He often comes to the Bishop for counsel. After hearing the details, the Bishop thinks the boy's malady may diverge into...your area of expertise."

Well, it wouldn't surprise Joseph if a man like the Governor was surrounded by demons, or that they would choose a member of his family to latch onto. Still, to come to the aid of a man who was an active enemy of the faith, and all the worse since he claimed to be a part of it...

Bruce must have seen the disapproval on Joseph's face. He leaned forward again. "Joe, the boy is ten years old. Whatever you think of the Governor—and Lord knows I have issues with him too—the boy is not a party to his uncle's sins. Probably it really is a medical condition. But if it's not and you can help him..."

He didn't need to finish the sentence. Joseph had already gone there in his own mind. Perhaps revealing the demonic influence on the boy, and then purging it, could be the thing to help rekindle the Governor's own faith, and help him down the road to repentance and salvation.

Perhaps.

After a moment, Joseph nodded. "Very well. When and where?"

Bruce smiled, and there was victory in that grin. "The boy and his family have been visiting the Governor in his mansion the last week. A car will pick you up at 7:30 tonight."

"Thomas will come with me."

"Of course," Bruce said, sounding magnanimous now that they had agreed in principle. Then he smiled broadly once again, and the twinkle returned to his eye. "Well," he said, and slapped the table lightly, "now that business is done with, you will absolutely love this place's grilled sea bass."

He waved his hand, and moments later a perky young brunette

dressed in the Cafe's livery appeared at their table, beaming a smile as she handed them menus.

Joseph accepted his with a feeling of resignation. He expected this evening would be trying, in any number of ways.

The car arrived promptly, pulling up out front of Joseph's apartment building at precisely 7:30. Joseph looked out his front window and down two stories to where the sedan sat running while a man in a charcoal grey suit got out of the front passenger seat and walked toward the building's entrance, and frowned.

He had on his robes and hat, and bore his cane in his left hand. It was wooden, painted black, and was capped by its silver crucifix. But there was more to it than met the eye. Still eyeing the street outside, Joseph took hold of the top of the cane, just below the crucifix, and twisted, then pulled upward.

The blade concealed within was tempered steel coated with silver everywhere except on the cutting edges, which had been sharpened to a razor's edge. He only withdrew it a few inches, to check the smoothness of the draw. It would suffice.

Satisfied, he sheathed the sword and twisted the locking mechanism.

Beside him, Thomas watched this and raised an eyebrow. Joseph noticed the gesture and shrugged slightly.

"I don't trust these people," he said simply, and Thomas nodded.

"So I should bring my special gear as well?" he said.

The buzzer from the apartment's door sounded. Joseph hesitated for a moment, considering. Then he nodded to Thomas. "Yes."

Three minutes later, they got in the car for their ride to the Governor's Mansion.

Joseph had seen pictures of the Governor's Mansion, of course, but it was smaller in person than those pictures had made it appear. Not that he got to see much. The driver and his partner up front in the car got them through security easily enough, then pulled up to the Mansion's side entrance.

Then a whirlwind of doors, corridors, a flight of stairs, another corridor, and a door later, he and Thomas stood in a oak-paneled study, complete with leather upholstered couch and stuffed chairs arranged around a dark fireplace, a wall of bookshelves stocked with tomes beyond counting, and a massive wooden desk at the end of the room before a broad window overlooking the Mansion's grounds.

The place smelled slightly of pipe smoke, and bourbon.

Governor Willoby stood in front of the fireplace, holding a glass filled with two fingers of the dark amber liquid that Joseph's nostrils had detected, and wearing an expression on his face that was welcoming, if not warm. His greying black hair was cut short and his hazel eyes were narrow. He was in his shirtsleeves and his tie was loosened, and much like the Mansion itself Joseph was struck by how much smaller he appeared in real life than he did on the TV screen.

"Father Joseph," Willoby said, and stepped forward, extending his right hand. "Good of you to come."

Joseph took the Governor's hand and found his grip clammy, but firm. "Any friend of the Bishop is a friend of mine," he said, sounding lame even to his own ears. He gestured toward Thomas, who had lingered by the door to the study as Joseph took the lead. "This is my assistant, Thomas."

Willoby let out a half-chuckle, pretending at least to see the humor in Joseph's quip. He nodded to Thomas and turned to his right, sweeping out his arm to take in the man, woman, and child sitting on the couch. Joseph immediately picked out the family resemblance between Willoby and the woman. Her features were more feminine than his, of course, and she was a good ten years his junior, but their common parentage was obvious from the shape of her nose, the line of her chin.

And by those same sharp hazel eyes that examined Joseph, and then Thomas, closely.

"My sister Bethany, her fiancé Carl, and her son, Tim," the Governor said.

Carl rose. He was a bear of a man, looming a full head taller than Joseph and with muscles that strained the blue polo shirt he was wearing. Joseph recalled hearing somewhere the man had played rugby in his youth, and his ears showed it; the right one had a gap between the top of the lobe and where it would normally have fastened to his skull. A little too much tugging in the scrum pile, no doubt.

"Hello, Father," Carl said, and crushed Joseph's hand in his own. He had to fight not to wince at the sheer force of the man's grip.

"Just Joseph, please," he said, smiling with what he hoped was reassurance. "I'm not actually a priest."

Both Carl and the Governor blinked in surprise. They exchanged glances that suddenly looked doubtful.

"I don't - " Willoby began, but a snort from his sister cut him off.

"Really, Ernie, you didn't listen to your friend the Bishop at all, did you? He told you that just this morning." Rolling her eyes in bemusement over her brother's antics—or what she apparently considered antics anyway—Bethany also rose. But she didn't offer her hand, instead helping her son to his feet.

He was small for ten. Sandy haired. Green eyes. He fidgeted, like he was nervous, and he had on an X-Men t-shirt and khaki cargo shorts.

"Say hello to Joseph, Tim," Bethany said, standing behind him and giving his shoulders a gentle squeeze with her hands.

Tim just shrugged slightly and looked down at the floor. Clearly he was uncomfortable, but whether from the situation as a whole, Joseph's presence, or both was impossible to tell. Yet.

"Good evening, Tim," Joseph said, shifting his attention fully to the boy. There didn't offhand seem to be anything more to his demeanor than what Joseph would expect. Nor did he sense any of the blatant telltales of a demonic presence.

But that wasn't enough to rule it out, either.

He looked from the boy back up to his mother. "When did the episodes first begin?"

Bethany gave a little shrug. "Two months ago? Three? We've been to every doctor, but..." She left the rest unsaid. No need to restate things.

Joseph nodded, then he looked back at Willoby. "I will need to speak with the boy and examine him. It will be easier if we have some privacy."

Willoby blinked. "Examine him?"

Joseph smiled in a manner he hoped was comforting. "Spiritually."

Willoby and his sister exchanged glances, conferring without speech.

Carl killed whatever rapport they had by chuckling softly and saying, "Well you guys aren't priests, so he should be safe enough alone with you." His tone was flippant, like he found the joke incredibly funny.

Joseph stared at him. Carl's smile lessened, then faded completely. He swallowed and made an apologetic shrug.

"We'll be right outside," Bethany said, and walked past Jospeh toward the door. As she passed Carl by, she shot a glare at him that would make a palm tree wilt at a hundred paces.

Carl, looking glum, turned to follow her out.

Willoby did the same, but he looked, if anything, amused by the whole interchange. Once past the door frame he turned and smiled back at Joseph, then he pulled the door to with a solid thunk.

Joseph tried to put his annoyance with Carl aside as he turned back to Tim. He needed to be on his game, and not encumbered by any vice, during the examination.

He gestured toward one of the stuffed chairs, and Tim sat back down. Joseph did the same. He leaned forward, placing his elbows on his knees and watching the boy closely.

"Does your mother bring you to church? Do you know your prayers?"

Tim nodded.

"Then pray with me, please."

The boy lowered his head and clasped his hands together.

Joseph began the examination.

Joseph waited until Carl had led Tim out of the study and sufficiently down the hall so there was no chance the boy could hear what he had to say, then he turned to where Willoby and his sister stood waiting anxiously in front of the study's desk.

He put on a reassuring smile. "I can't see any signs of demonic interference." And thank the Lord that was the case.

Bethany let out a breath she had been holding, and pressed a hand to her mouth. "You're certain?"

Jospeh nodded.

Then he was being crushed in her arms, as she threw herself across the space between them and hugged him. In his ear, he heard her say, "Thank you."

Joseph shifted on his feet, uncomfortable by the sudden contact. She was an attractive woman, and vow of chastity or no, he was still a man. He needed as little temptation as he could manage.

Carefully taking her by the forearms, he pressed her back from him and smiled. "You're welcome," he said, then carefully guided her away from himself by turning to the right and nudging her toward the door.

She seemed to understand the source of his reluctance to touch her, and her lips turned upward ever so slyly. She held his gaze for a moment, then turned to follow her fiancé and her son as Carl led the boy away to bed.

Joseph took a moment to collect himself, clearing his throat. Then he looked sidelong at Thomas, who had an amused expression on his face—no vow of chastity for him—and nodded toward the door. Time for them to go as well.

Thomas smirked slightly then hefted the duffle bag of equipment he always carried on their excursions and stepped out of the room.

Joseph moved to follow, but Willoby's voice brought him up short.

"A moment, Joseph," the Governor said.

Joseph turned back around to look at the man. He was frowning slightly, not looking at Joseph but rather watching the retreating back of his sister as she moved away down the hall.

"There is no doubt in your findings?" Willoby asked.

Joseph shrugged slightly. "The only certainties in life are death, taxes, and God's love," he said, earning a look of amusement from the Governor. "But no, I have no doubt. No demon has come near that boy, thanks be to God."

Willoby nodded slowly. "Good," he said. Then he drew himself up and gave a more firm nod of his head. "Good," he said, in a more settled tone.

Joseph narrowed his eyes. "Beg your pardon, Governor. But you sound almost disappointed."

"What? No." Willoby looked askance at Joseph for a second, then smiled sheepishly. He flushed a little. "No, but I was hoping the boy's ailment would be something simple to cure. Now..." He let the thought die off, and made a vague gesture with his hand.

Joseph sniffed. "Be grateful all it is is a physical problem," he said. "The consequences of a demonic intervention are far worse, and far more long-lasting."

Willoby looked sidelong at him, then nodded. "You're right of course." He sniffed out a half-laugh. "The politician in me, just looking at the physical." He sounded like a man who was trying to convince himself of something he didn't really believe; or of a man who was trying to put on that he believed it for another's benefit.

Either way, Joseph wasn't buying it, and that just sealed his opinion of the Governor.

He was a fool.

"Well, just in case, here is my card," Joseph said. He reached into his pocket, pulled out two of his business cards, and held them out to

WIlloby. "If anything happens with the boy, call me. There's one for your sister as well."

Willoby took the cards and nodded. "Thank you, Joseph."

"My pleasure, Governor."

Then he turned and left the room, Thomas in tow. It was well past time he was out of there, and back home to his ministry, and real work.

Joseph woke up to his phone ringing.

At first he couldn't figure out what was going on and where he was, he was that groggy. He looked around at the the dark room surrounding him, shapes all blurry and non-distinct, and came up with nothing.

Then he zeroed in on the noise that had woken him: his personalized ring tone, Holst's Mars.

He snapped to focus and registered where he was. His apartment. He flailed his arm across to his nightstand and found his phone, which was still ringing. Pressing the answer button, he lifted it to his ear.

"Yes?"

"Joseph?" The voice was masculine, and vaguely familiar. "It's Carl, Bethany's fiancé."

Joseph's eyes widened in the darkness, and he sat bolt upright in bed. "What can I do for you, Carl?"

"Bethany's gone. So is Tim. And Ernie too. I asked the security people where they went, but they won't tell me anything. I found your card in the trash can in our bathroom, and..." His voice was plaintive. Scared. "You haven't heard from them have you?"

Joseph pulled the phone away from his ear and looked at the time display. 2:45 AM. He sighed and rolled his eyes, then put the phone back to his ear. "No, Carl, I haven't. I'm not in their social circuit, you know?" He was fighting to suppress annoyance—anger, almost—at the interruption of his sleep cycle, and failing.

"Well, it's just that I overheard them saying something before we all went to bed. Something about a ritual? I thought maybe it was something to do with you, and..."

An icy shard of dread skewered Joseph's belly.

"Bethany has a cell phone, yes?"

"Yeah."

"Is it there, or does she have it with her?"

A pause, then he replied, "It's not here. Why? What's going - ?"

"Give me her cell number, and yours. I'll call you back in ten minutes."

"I don't under - "

"Give me the numbers!"

Thomas picked up before the end of the first ring.

"What's up?"

Joseph pulled the phone away from his ear and looked at it in bemusement for a second. Did the man never sleep? Then the gravity of the situation struck him again, and he got back to business. "I need you to trace the location of a cell phone. Right now."

"What? Joe, that's not exactly - "

"It's Bethany's phone, Tim's mom. I think something horrible is about to happen."

A heartbeat's pause, then all protest left Thomas' voice. "Give it to me."

Saint Paul's Cathedral was ten blocks east of the Governor's Mansion. At that time of night, it was dark, and shut up tight as a drum.

Or at least, it was supposed to be.

As Joseph and Thomas pulled to a stop in front of the cathedral, though, they saw a dim light shining through some of the stained glass windows on the building's side.

From the passenger seat, Joseph looked sidelong at Thomas. "You've got your special gear, yes?"

Thomas nodded, his lips compressing into a look of grim competence, and he patted Joseph on the left shoulder. He felt some of that special gear stick into place.

"Then let's go." Joseph opened his door and stepped out into the night.

He was just turning toward the Cathedral's front door when he spied a set of headlights down the street ahead. They were approaching, and approaching fast. They resolved into a sedan—a Cadillac?—that was far exceeding the speed limit as it careened down the street toward the Cathedral.

Toward them.

Joseph's hand went unconsciously to the grip of his cane sword even as he considered the only person the driver could be.

The car skidded to a stop across the street and the door opened, and Joseph's suspicion was confirmed.

Carl sprinted across the street and met up with him and Thomas in front of Thomas' car. He was breathing heavily, and bent over to put his hands on his knees as he caught his breath. Joseph looked at him askance. Not enough time exercising since rugby, apparently.

"I told you to stay put, and let us handle this," he said.

Carl looked up at him—first time for that—and shook his head. "No way. If Bethany and Tim are in trouble, I'm helping."

Joseph appreciated the thought, but he had the sinking suspicion they both weren't in trouble. Still, hard to argue with a spirit that was willing. He reached out and clapped Carl on the shoulder. "Very well. But keep back and let me take the lead."

Carl nodded.

Joseph looked away from him to Thomas. "We'll take a side entrance. Can you get the door open?"

Thomas grinned, then he strode quickly toward the side of the Cathedral, disappearing into the gloom as he made his way down the length of the structure.

Joseph moved to follow, but paused when he felt Carl's hand on his arm. He looked back to see the man staring at him with a strange look, a mixture of confusion, disbelief, and shock.

"Your assistant knows how to pick a lock?"

Joseph smiled thinly. "We don't have the funds to do this full time. Thomas is a man of God, yes. But he's also a private investigator. That's how he knew how to locate Bethany's phone. He'll get us into the building."

Carl's hand dropped off his arm as the man's eyes widened even further.

Joseph turned away, moving quickly to follow Thomas around the building to its side entrance.

Behind him, he heard Carl moving to catch up.

"So you're not a full-time whatever-you-are either?"

Joseph shook his head. "Correct."

"What are you then?"

He paused for a second, then looked back at Carl. "I'm a freelance computer game programmer. I've written code on probably every game you've played in the last five years."

Carl's mouth dropped open. "Seriously?"

"Seriously."

He hurried to catch up with Thomas.

By the time Joseph reached him at the side entrance, Thomas had the door unlocked and cracked open. They gathered briefly outside, and Joseph reaffirmed that Carl would hang back. Then, one by one, they slipped through the partly-open door into the dark interior of the Cathedral.

Except it wasn't all that dark.

There were candles planted all over the sacristy, not the creamy-white candles used during mass but red and black, waxy candles that gave off thick black smoke as they burned and dripped wax freely onto whatever they had been set upon. All the same, the candles cast a good light, bathing the alter area in a golden glow that should have looked pure, serene.

Except that the light also illuminated the desecration that had been done there.

Either blood or red paint—most likely the later—had been drawn all over the marble stones making up the floor. It was impossible to make out all the details unless one were high up, but Joseph had seen enough in his study of demonology and the occult to know what the design had to be. A pentagram surrounding the alter, and the glyphs corresponding to the names of the cherubs and archangels who had followed Lucifer in his revolt.

And, tied to the top of the altar, stripped down to his underwear, was Tim.

He was asleep, somehow. Probably drugged from the stiff way he lay. Red designs had been drawn on his torso and legs as well. But his chest still moved; he was alive.

Joseph thanked God for small miracles.

A group of four people were gathered around the altar, one on each side. Two of them were concealed by cowled red robes. But the other two were plain to see, dressed as they were in the same civilian attire Joseph had seen them in earlier this evening: Willoby and his sister.

Behind him, Joseph heard Carl gasp in horrified shock as he took in the scene ahead of them, and he knew he would have to act quickly or the rugby man would rush in and possibly spoil everything in his inexperience.

So, leaving stealth to the wind, Joseph straightened and, using his cane with his left hand, he strode down the aisle between the pews in the cathedral's side chamber.

"Looks like you really were disappointed after all, Governor," he said, in a voice that carried easily throughout the building. He thanked God for the help with his volume, but also thanked acoustics.

The four people around the altar gave a collective jerk, and all eyes turned toward Joseph. He sensed surprise, fear even, from the two cowled men. From Willoby and Bethany....nothing. Though they did watch him come with eyes that showed at least some level of discomfort with his sudden appearance.

Willoby glanced to his side at the nearest of the cowled men, who looked back at him. The Governor nodded.

Both cowled men charged at Joseph. Between one step and the next, they produced long, curved daggers from inside their robes, and they separated so as to get on either side of him. No doubt they intended to flank him and then skewer him. Probably thought it would be easy.

No such luck.

He twisted his hand on the grip of his sword cane, unlocking it, then whipped it upward. The scabbard, as freed from the locking mechanism as the blade was, flew forward and upward toward the charging man to Joseph's left.

He only had time to blink in surprise before the floor end of the scabbard—capped in iron—struck him full in the face.

The man staggered backward, his hands rising to his suddenly broken nose and shattered teeth.

And then Joseph was surging to his right, shifting his sword to his right hand smoothly with a technique he had practiced many times during his saber fencing days in High School and Undergrad.

He whipped the blade around, and suddenly the second cowled man, who a moment before was so certain he was about to skewer Joseph alive, found himself cut in three separate places on his arm, shoulder, and upper thigh.

None of the cuts were deep enough to be fatal, or at least Joseph tried hard to ensure they would not be. He had no desire to condemn the man to hell without allowing him time for repentance. But they were painful, and he dropped the knife from an arm that must have suddenly lost all strength.

A kick later, the man went down on his back, writhing and moaning.

The first man had recovered, and he continued his charge. But he was off balance from the sudden resistance, and it was easy to side-step his attack.

And that left the back of his knee open to a hamstring cut.

Joseph turned away from the two groaning underlings and found

Willoby and his sister had moved to stand next to each other on the opposite side of the altar from him. He ascended the two stairs separating the sacristy from the rest of the Cathedral's interior and lifted his sword, pointing the tip, stained red from their underlings' blood, at them.

"You've been trying to give him to Satan's minions for three months now, but you haven't succeeded."

They didn't try to deny it. The Governor simply shrugged. "Apparently small offerings weren't enough. We weren't sure, though, until you verified it."

"Enough for what?"

Willoby smiled broadly. "I've accomplished great things here in this State. When I'm President, I'll accomplish even more. I can be the man to finally drag this country out of the doldrums of its past and into a glorious new future."

"So you would sacrifice your own flesh and blood. Give your nephew," he turned his eyes toward Bethany, "your son, to the Prince of Lies in exchange for four years in a political office?" He didn't even try to keep the contempt from his voice.

They were pathetic creatures, the both of them. If they were not also pure evil, and if they did not wield some real power in this world, it would be laughable.

Bethany surprised him by laughing. "He's not my son, you fool," she said, condescending scorn filling her voice. "I bought him from a dealer when he was an infant." Her lips turned upward into a sadistic smile. "He's been very useful, over the years, as a plaything for campaign donors and the like. But he'll be too old to be appealing soon."

Joseph's stomach roiled in revulsion as the full import of her words struck him. She could not mean -

But she did. The burning light in her eyes told the truth, plain as day. She had given the boy to be used in every conceivable way—and ways Joseph knew he could not conceive of and did not want to—and now was willing to cast him aside, into the very fires of Hell itself, for just a little bit more power for herself and her brother.

Except that's not how it worked. Not when Joseph was around.

He maneuvered around the altar toward them, and they backed away. Just far enough.

"Carl!" he said over his shoulder, not taking his eyes from the satanic couple.

Bethany's eyes went wide when he said the name, and wider still when she must have seen the big man emerge from the shadows behind Joseph and stalk up toward the altar.

He could hear Carl's footsteps against the floor stones, and Bethany's face twitched with each one. Her mouth flopped open and shut like a drowning fish's as she clearly struggled to find words of explanation but came up with none.

Joseph advanced again, coming to the far edge of the altar now. The brother and sister retreated as he moved, and Carl now should have full access to Tim.

"You got him?" he asked.

Behind him, Carl grunted, then said, "Yeah."

"Get him out of here. Hurry."

Willoby grinned. "Yes, do hurry." He reached into his pocket and pulled out a transmitter of some kind, which he raised to his lips.

"This is Governor Willoby. My nephew has been abducted."

The dismay that had settled over Bethany's face lifted when her brother's words reached her ears. She grinned at Joseph in triumph.

Behind him, Carl's running footsteps were growing softer, heading toward the side door they had come in from.

"Give my regards to your master," Joseph said.

Then he turned to run after the big man, pausing only to pick up his sword cane's case where it lay on the floor.

"Lose your cell phone," Joseph said over his shoulder, to where Carl sat in the back seat with Tim. "They can track it."

Thomas was driving, keeping to the speed limit but still making time away from the Cathedral and toward the other side of town, where Joseph's apartment was located.

Carl met his eye and nodded, then rolled down his window and tossed his phone out into the night.

"Good. You're going to need to run. You and Tim both. They'll be looking for you. If they catch you, you'll be lucky to be arrested and thrown in prison. More likely they'll just kill you."

Carl looked like he wanted to argue against that assertion, but then he couldn't. He nodded, his eyes haunted as he began to fully comprehend the situation he was in.

Tim as well.

Thomas spoke up. "Don't use the ATMs. Don't use credit cards. Do you have a place you can go, friends you can contact, that Bethany doesn't know about?"

Carl considered, then shook his head. "No. She knows everything. I - She - " He bent forward in his seat then, resting his elbows on his knees and placing his head in his hands. "Oh God!" he cried, disbelief conflicting with horror and fear and anger and a dozen other emotions as he let out a long, hard scream.

Joseph traded glances with Thomas, and Thomas nodded. They had not faced this exact kind of situation before, but they had dealt with similar needs, at least. Thomas would be able to hook Carl up with enough to keep him safe, at least for a few days.

A few days was all they needed.

***

Bruce went for a three mile run at five o'clock every morning. It had been his routine since Joseph first knew him in seminary, and he kept it up religiously.

Sometimes Joseph wondered whether he even prayed as religiously as he ran.

Most days, he would have thought that question uncharitable. Not today.

Joseph waited in the bushes on the side of the diocese rectory that housed the door Bruce always took to go in and out on his morning runs. And sure enough, at the same time he always did, the monsignor came puffing into view, still cooling down from his jog.

Bruce stopped almost directly in front of Joseph and lifted one leg. He reached behind his back to grab his foot and pulled back to stretch his quadriceps.

It was then that Joseph stepped out into view.

"You set me up, Bruce."

"Wha - ?" Bruce said, surprise sending his voice an octave higher than normal as he tried to spin around. He failed and lost his balance, stumbling forward two steps before he righted himself.

"Joe," he said, finally recognizing Joseph as he drew nearer. "What are you talking about?"

"Willoby and his sister. They're Satanists. Tried to make a sacrifice for more power, but weren't successful. Couldn't figure out how to get it right...until you sent me to be their stooge."

Bruce's eyes widened, and he shook his head. "That's crazy."

"Did you know?"

"What?"

"Did you know?" It came out as a roar, and Joseph hurled himself forward at his old friend.

The force of their meeting threw Bruce backwards, and never mind the extra height and weight he had over Joseph. His back struck the bricks of the rectory's outer wall, and Joseph pressed in against him. He hadn't realized he'd done it until he saw the silver crucifix up alongside Bruce's face, but he had drawn half a foot of his sword cane free, and the razor's edge lay across Bruce's windpipe, a breath away from cutting him.

Bruce saw it too, and his face paled. He knew Joseph's sword cane. He had been with Joseph when he bought it, way back in seminary.

He hadn't realized it was actually a weapon until he'd gotten it back to their dorm.

Bruce spoke rapidly. "Swear to God, Joe. On my mother's soul, I don't know what you're talking about."

That meant something. Bruce could be flippant about some

things. But he esteemed his mother more than any other man Joseph had ever met.

Still...

Joseph leaned in closer. Bruce's panicked breathing was hot on his face.

"Did *he* know?"

He didn't need to say who. Bruce knew immediately; it showed in his eyes.

The Bishop.

Willoby often sought his counsel. Bruce had said that himself, at their lunch meeting. If that were the case, if Willoby and the Bishop were truly close friends...

Bruce shook his head quickly. "I don't know," he said, his voice trembling, barely above a whisper.

It was the abject, mortal terror in Bruce's voice that woke Joseph up to what he was doing. How close he was coming to crossing a line that he could never step back over.

Joseph moved back, releasing Bruce and letting his sword slide fully home into its case. He raised his free hand, palm open and out toward Bruce, and retreated again.

"I'm sorry, Bruce."

Bruce raised his hand and touched his fingers to his throat, where the cutting edge of Joseph's weapon had threatened. He looked at his fingertips as he pulled them away, and looked relieved when they came away clean.

"S'ok," he said in a tone that didn't sound like he really meant it. "Seems like you've been through a lot."

How much, Bruce didn't truly know. But he would. Joseph gave him as stern a look as he could. "You need to look into your boss. There's a good chance he's working for the enemy."

Bruce shook his head in denial.

"Willoby is going down. Hard. If the Bishop is on the wrong side, he will too. Make sure you don't go down with him."

Then he turned and walked away.

Behind him, Bruce regained some of his vocal strength. "What do you mean, he's going down?"

"Look on YouTube and BitChute in forty-five minutes."

***

Thomas is a private investigator, not a soldier. His special gear is high resolution audio and video recording equipment, and remotely piloted drones.

When he slapped the body camera onto Joseph's shoulder, it had immediately begun recording. Then he had sent a drone into the Cathedral after Joseph and Carl entered, and got a birds eye view recording of everything that went down as well.

A couple days of editing, and it was ready to go. Joseph had just given him the thumbs up to release it right before he'd gone to meet up with Bruce.

When Joseph said Willoby was going down, he meant it. There was no way he could recover politically from that scene. Desecration of the Cathedral was bad enough. But the things he and his sister had admitted to...

He might not go to jail.

Scratch that. No way he would ever go to jail.

But he was done politically.

And once the video was released, there was no way Carl could get in trouble for kidnapping, or that Bethany could try to argue for continued custody of Tim.

So all's well that ends well.

Joseph tried to tell himself that was enough. That he should take the win and be happy about it.

Then he looked over his shoulder at the diocese building, and a righteous fury filled his chest. If the Bishop truly had been involved, he would have to answer too. And he would.

Someday.

Someday soon.

13

ABE'S LIQUORS

Betty sniffed back tears and wiped the back of her right hand across the bottom of her nose. It had gone runny from crying so hard.

She squinted into the early evening darkness, her left hand flexing on the scarred and fading brown leather that wrapped the steering wheel of her Camry, and tried to concentrate on driving. But she couldn't get the fight out of her mind.

"Shut up, bitch!" and then the slap. Reeling backward as David stared hatred and disgust at her that the slap only confirmed. Fleeing from his apartment, though he did not follow. Stumbling down the stairs of his complex, tears making her vision blurry and sobs making her breathing difficult.

Then the frantic, near suicidal drive away.

She was twenty minutes further on now, and only just beginning to feel like she was getting herself back together. Slowly.

Ahead of her, a traffic light turned red, and she slowed to a stop.

Where was she?

When she had flown away from David's apartment complex, Betty had not paid any attention to where she was going, or even the traffic around her. Now she leaned forward, peering through her windshield, and could not recognize the area at all.

She was not in the suburbs any more, that was for sure. The buildings were closer together, cramped in. Mostly brick-faced, and there were neon business signs advertising a tavern, a his and hers barber shop, a thrift store. The cars parked on either side of the four-lane street were older than the part of town she was used to, and she could see small groups of people sitting on the porch steps of some of the buildings, just hanging out and talking.

Definitely not her neighborhood. And from the look of things, not all that great a neighborhood at all.

Still, she recognized the cross street at the intersection. Turn right here, and she should get back to highway in a few blocks. And then, in another twenty minutes or so, home.

Betty made the turn, and wiped at her nose again. She needed more tissues.

And she needed to get away from the depressing music on her Camry's radio. She hadn't even registered it consciously before now, but it was on a Top 40 station, and the singer was wailing out a ballad begging his girl to come back to him.

She punched the radio off before she burst into tears again, and drove on.

Ahead, the neighborhood continued pretty much as before, but she spied a sign coming up on the right. Abe's Liquor Store.

She didn't just need tissues. She needed a drink. Badly.

Betty was able to find a spot about fifty yards from the store, and took a couple minutes to parallel park her Camry between an old black Ford Explorer and a yellow Miata. She put the car into park and sat there for a moment, and looked at herself in the mirror.

She was a mess. Her eyes were red and puffy, her mascara running. Her black hair, which she had carefully put up before going to meet David earlier, was mussed, strands pulled out from her barrettes.

She looked exactly what she was: a woman having a totally crappy evening.

Betty considered starting the car back up and just getting the hell out of there. But screw it. This wasn't her neighborhood; no one would know her to gossip about how messed up she was in the morning.

So she got out, smoothed the white skirt she was wearing, centered her green blouse more evenly on her shoulders, and strode up the street to the liquor store's door.

The sidewalk was cracked in a few places, the parking meters on the side of the street the old kind that only took coins and had those big twisty knobs to send the coins down into their containers; no debit cards or ApplePay for these. The liquor store itself had a long window at the front with posters of various beers and liquors posted up, and the front door was aluminum framed glass, with the standard broad paddle pull-to-open handle.

A bell rang over Betty's head when she stepped inside, and she immediately was struck by a musky incense from a lit burner behind the counter, which stood off to her left. It was wood-topped, and had the usual racks of last-minute purchase items on the customer side. The guy manning the register was in his thirties and Arabic-looking, with close-cropped black hair and a short beard. His off-white t-shirt had the store's name on the left breast.

When she walked in, the cashier looked her over quickly and nodded greeting when she met his eyes, then he went back to tending to his current customer, an elderly black woman in a white and blue polka-dotted dress and wide, gold-rimmed spectacles.

Turning away from the two of them, Betty saw three aisles filled with liquors and wines of all kinds, and at the back a full wall of refrigerated storage for beverages that needed to be ice-cold right now.

She walked to the second aisle, which looked to be more wine than anything else, and stepped past a tweed-jacketed white guy who looked to be in his fifties, with mostly grey hair and bright blue eyes. He shuffled to the side to let her pass with a smile and a polite, "Good evening."

It wasn't until she was three paces past him that his words registered, and she looked back to reply, but he was already queueing up behind the black woman.

Betty shook her head, upbraiding herself for being rude, and shivered, only just now noticing how low the store had the air conditioning set.

Just get the wine, silly goose. You don't know these people, and they won't care what you did or didn't say ten minutes from now.

The whites were halfway down the aisle on the left, and Betty made a beeline for them. Reds were well and fine, but whites were so much more drinkable, and right then she needed something crisp and fruity, not something rich and deep.

She scanned the four levels of shelves quickly, stopping in surprise when a particular bottle sprang out at her. Yellow and white and red and orange and brown polygons all intertwined to make a regular pattern that seemed to draw the eye into its center. Alongside the pattern, the name: Coeur Sauvage, 2017 Loire Valley Sauvignon Blanc.

Betty remembered that particular bottle from a lunch out with four friends a month ago. Sally had revealed she was marrying Paul, and the five of them had splurged on more wine than they should have. But the Coeur stood out in her mind as being the best of the bottles they'd had.

She wet her lips in anticipation of the semi-sweet, slightly tangy flavor, and the warm buzz of relaxation the wine would bring.

That would do nicely.

Snatching the bottle up, Betty turned and headed toward the counter, where the tweed-jacketed guy was still waiting behind the old lady.

She was just finishing up when Betty got in line behind, hefting a paper bag that clinked from the sound of multiple bottles tapping together.

"Thank you," she said to the cashier and moved to the door.

The bell overtop the door rang before she got there, and a tall broad-shouldered man with long brown hair half stepped in. Then, seeing the elderly woman coming his way, he stepped back out and held the door open for her.

The woman said, "Thank you, young man," and he smiled, nodded, and replied, "Of course, ma'am."

Once the old woman was past, he stepped back inside, and Betty got a better look at him. Late 20s probably. Wearing a brown leather jacket a couple shades darker than his hair, and jeans that looked like he'd had them for a while, doing actual work. Those worn parts were not fashion statements from a preppy clothing store.

He had dark, intelligent eyes and a bold nose. Square jaw. Nice looking fellow. His eyes met hers as he began moving toward the first aisle, and he smiled ever so slightly as they flicked quickly up and down her body.

Betty resolutely looked away from him, toward the cashier, who was just beginning to ring up tweed jacket's trio of wine bottles. She was in no mood for men, especially good looking men right -

The door swung open and the sound of the bell carried, along with the old woman's voice raised in a cry of alarm.

Betty looked left toward the door in time to see first one man, then a second, storm in. They were both dressed in long black pants and long-sleeved black t-shirts. They wore black gloves and black ski masks.

And they were both carrying silvery guns.

"Hands up!" shouted the first of the men, brandishing his gun—it was a revolver, Betty could see now—toward the cashier, who backed up behind his counter, hands raised.

He turned the gun toward tweed man and Betty, flicking it back and forth between then, and a shiver of fear went down her spine.

"Back up!"

She complied, as did tweed man.

The robber had a rolled-up cloth bag in his left hand, which he hurled toward the cashier. "Fill it!"

The cashier caught the bag and moved to comply, moving slowly and deliberately. Past the first robber, his partner was standing closer to the door, his gun on the handsome leather jacket guy. Leather jacket guy was standing ominously still, his hands raised, but his body was relaxed, like this was no big deal at all. His eyes were wary, but calm.

Betty tried to find some of that calm herself, but instead found only outrage. This was so, so...

She burst out. "You're robbing a liquor store? Seriously?? How cliche can you - ?"

The lead robber turned on her, and the barrel of his revolver pointed straight at her face. The silvery circle seemed to widen as she looked at it, the darkness inside the hole of the barrel opening up to suck her inside, and her bowels went to ice.

She was going to die. He was going to pull the trigger, and she was going to die. She could see the fingers holding his gun flex slightly, tensing for the killing movement.

Instead, he said, "Shut up, bitch." He shot her with his eyes, then turned his attention—and his gun—back to the cashier.

Shut up bitch.

The words rang in her ears, but she didn't hear the robber saying them. It was David again. Rage and disgust and hatred and disdain all mixed together in his tone, and eyes that smacked almost as hard as his hand had.

David, not the robber, and Betty's terror turned to a red-hot rage that flared up within her. How dare he?

She had the wine bottle in her hands. She moved without thinking, reversing her grip on it so she was holding it by the neck. Then, with a cry that carried all the rage, humiliation, and hurt she had been nursing the last half hour, she bound forward, raised the bottle high, and brought it down onto the robber's head.

It didn't shatter.

She thought it should have, but instead it struck with a dull, squishy thud and a jarring impact that ran up her arm to her shoulder before stabbing into her neck.

The robber dropped to the floor instantly, his body going limp. His gun made a metallic clink as it bounced once and landed on the floor tiles at Betty's feet.

Everything seemed to stop.

There was blood on the end of the bottle. She could see it in front of her eyes. She looked down and saw a trickle of blood flowing from the area of the man's head where she had struck him; the material of his ski mask was already soaked, and a little pool was beginning to form around his head on the floor.

His face was turned toward her, and she could see one of his eyes open wide, but glazed and unseeing. His jaw was slack.

Had she killed him? She hadn't meant to kill him. Hadn't meant to -

Sudden movement from off to the left drew Betty's attention away from the fallen man.

The second robber turned toward her, and leather jacket man sprang on him. The two men were wrestling, fighting over the gun.

Leather jacket man was taller, but the robber was well-muscled beneath his shirt, and Betty could tell leather jacket man had made a mistake. He'd over-extended, and was off balance even as the robber began pulling away from him.

He was going to fall, and the robber would win out. He would win out, and still have the gun. And when that happened, handsome leather jacket man would be dead. Maybe they all would be.

Betty cast about, and her eyes came to the first robber's revolver, lying at her feet.

She dropped the wine bottle and snatched up the gun. She'd never even held a gun, let alone fired one, and it was heavy in her hands. The knurled grip bit into her palm, and it seemed she shouldn't be able to lift it, so ominous did it feel.

She straightened and raised her eyes back to the conflict between the two men just in time to see leather jacket man land on his back on the floor. The robber moved quickly, placing his shoe onto the center of leather jacket man's chest.

He was bringing the gun around and down to point at his face -

"Stop!" Betty cried out, and she heard the quaver in her own voice. "Let him go."

Her hands were shaking, but she had the revolver pointed at the robber. She saw him stop, then look back at her. He straightened, and held his free hand out toward her, open and palm out in a gesture that was probably meant to be calming.

"Bitch, don't - "

The gun went off. She hadn't meant to fire. Hadn't realized she was squeezing the trigger under the gun bucked in her hands and the muzzle flash brightened in her eyes and the thunder of the bullet firing smashed her ears. They immediately began ringing.

Behind the robber was a shelf of vodka bottles. One immediately behind his head and just to the right shattered, and she realized she'd missed him.

Less than ten feet away, and she'd missed completely.

Part of her felt relief, because she didn't actually want to shoot him. The other part felt disgust, that she couldn't even manage to hit something that close.

The robber freaked. He jumped up half a foot and landed with his hands high in the air.

"Jesus," he said, and let his own pistol drop. "Jesus, don't - "

His eyes flicked toward the door, as though he was thinking about running.

Then he was on the floor, face smacking onto the tiles. Leather jacket man made some kind of scissor move with his legs that swept the robbers' legs out from under him, and then he was on top of the man, knee in the small of his back as he levered the man's arm up into a lock that had him squirming in pain. Both from the strain in his limb and from his nose, which was bleeding and looked to be broken.

Betty still had the revolver in her hands, but they were shaking more. Uncontrollably.

Fresh tears were streaming down her face, she realized, and her breathing was coming in quick heaves. Her heart was pounding in her ears, and sweat was making her blouse cling to her body.

But she couldn't let go of the gun.

A pair of hands closed around hers and she gave a little jerk. Then she realized it was tweed jacket man. He was speaking gently into her ear, and applying light pressure on her hands to move them downward.

"It's ok, miss. It's over. You can put the gun down now. It's over."

He said it in a low, drawling tone, almost the tone a parent would use when saying a lullaby to a child. At first she resisted lowering the gun. Then, all at once, her reserve—what reserve she had left—broke and she dropped it completely.

She sagged against tweed jacket man, sobbing, and he lowered her to the ground, leaning her back against the counter.

"Cops are on the way," she heard the cashier say from above and over her shoulder.

Tweed jacket man nodded, but remained where he was, squatting in front of her. "Do you need anything?"

She said the first thing that came to her mind. "Beer."

Tweed jacket man looked up past her toward the cashier. She could hear the shrug in his voice. "Give her a beer."

Tweed jacket man stood and hurried over to the refrigerated doors at the back of the store. She had seen earlier they held everything from cans of water that only claimed to be beer from their labels to good crafted ales. Right then, she'd take anything.

She looked away, back toward where leather jacket man had the robber in submission. He really was a nice looking fellow. Well built, too.

Leather jacket man looked up from the robber and met her eyes. He smiled again, more openly this time, and nodded at her.

Right then, she decided to get his phone number, and to hell with David.

14

INTO THE DEPTHS

Harry adjusted his lips around the hard rubber clenched between his teeth and inhaled. Dry air that tasted slightly of plastic entered his lungs with the corresponding click-hiss of his regulator.

Deep and slow, controlled breaths. Don't draw down the tank too soon.

The mantra from his SCUBA instructors echoed in his head as he kicked forward and down, the fins on his feet propelling him smoothly, but not effortlessly, toward the multi-hued coral reef forty feet below.

Around the regulator mouthpiece, he grinned. This was his first dive as a certified Open Water Diver, and it was awesome. And he definitely did not want it to be over too soon.

Deep and slow.

The water was warm and crystal clear, allowing him to clearly see the reef and its environs, and its abundance of life. Fish large and small, of every color of the rainbow, darted around green and purple and red coral growths and anemones, and through swaying growths of seaweed. Or kelp. Or whatever it was called.

Farther out from the reef, larger fish swam, and...

Was that a shark?

Harry's heart began to thump as he focused off to his left, saw the torpedo shape, the dorsal fin, the side-to-side movement of the long and graceful tail.

Definitely a shark.

He almost turned and swam back to the boat, anchored about thirty feet behind him and ten feet above, but then he noted the black markings at the tips of its fins, and he relaxed. A reef shark. Not dangerous.

And, now that he really looked at it, not all that large either. Cool to look at, but not something to worry about.

Much.

He descended more quickly, and began to feel the squeeze in his ears. Working his jaw, he swallowed, and both heard and felt the pressure differential relieve, but not enough. A quick squeeze of his nostrils through the flexible plastic of his mask and a puff of exhalation remedied it, though, and he was good to go.

The reef was closer now; the other five members of his diving tour had already reached the bottom and were fanning out, underwater cameras clicking away as they found items of interest. One of them was floating above the others, over the reef itself. He wore a bright neon green buoyancy compensator and matching swim trunks, making Harry immediately recognize him as Sean, the dive leader.

Sean moved his head left and right, and Harry assumed he was counting out the divers under his charge. When Sean paused, and then did a complete circle, only stopping when he looked up to see Harry still descending toward him, Harry's suspicion was confirmed.

The leader's long brown hair billowed in the water as Harry approached, and he pointed Harry's way then raised his right hand, forefinger and thumb circling into the "Ok" symbol.

Inquiring whether Harry was alright.

Harry nodded and returned the "Ok" signal, and Sean nodded and gave a thumbs up. Closer now, Harry could make out a grin on his face before he turned around again to check on the others.

Harry bubbled out a little laugh as he saw which pair of the others Sean was kicking over toward in particular: the two early twenties, blonde, and stacked Yanks.

Hard to blame him for that. Harry wouldn't have minded going there himself.

But right then, he was more interested in other kinds of fish.

He stopped kicking, but his descent continued. He was only ten feet above the top of the reef, and probably fifteen feet above the sea bottom, and he didn't want to damage the reef by contacting it. He needed to halt his descent.

The analytical part of his mind rolled back through his diving instruction, and he decided the increased water pressure had compressed the air bubble in his BCD. That combined with the lead weights he had clipped around his waist was making him steadily less buoyant the further down he went.

He took hold of the inflation control button on his BCD and clicked. A shot of compressed air from his primary regulator entered the BCD, and he felt it expand against his sides and back.

His descent slowed, then stopped, and he nodded in satisfaction to himself. Piece of cake, as the Yanks like to say.

The top of the reef was a wash of color and life, and it was difficult to decide which little piece of it Harry found most fascinating. There was all so much to see and look at, the dance of life captivating, that for a few minutes he didn't do anything, just watched and took it all in.

And not just the sights. The sounds of the ocean reef rushed through him. The subtle sounds of the water flowing, pushed along by the fish's fins, or just the slow flow of the current. Chittering of some creature or other scurrying along or issuing a mating call.

His regulator, sending air to his lungs, and the bubbles of his exhalation.

Metallic tapping as one or another of his fellow divers made a sound to draw someone else's attention, or carelessly bumped into something.

It all flowed over him, and he couldn't help but just bask in it for a time.

But after a bit, a single blue fish—he didn't know the species—darted past in front of him, slipping around a bit of coral that rose out from the reef proper almost like one of those cacti he'd seen pictures of from the American southwest. Harry followed it with his eyes, and then realized he was kicking slowly to follow it completely as it dashed around, moving slowly over toward the edge of the reef.

That little guy was having a ton of fun, wasn't he?

The fish reached the edge and darted below. Harry moved to follow.

The bottom was farther down on this side of the reef than it had been on the side he'd initially approached from. He paused and moved his depth and air gauges in front of his mask. 2/3s of his air supply remaining, and he was at 45 feet. At that depth, he had at least another half hour to go before he reached the limits of the dive tables. And anyway, his air would run out first before he had serious decompression concerns.

But peering down, toward where the blue fish was still hurrying away, the bottom had to be a good twenty or thirty feet further down.

Harry didn't recall how long the dive tables said he could stay at that depth; and anyway he was only rated for sixty feet; if we wanted to go deeper than that, legally, he'd need to get his Advanced Open Water certification.

Sixty feet it was, then.

Harry kicked downward, following that fascinating little fish, and glancing at his depth gauge a bit more often now. He pulled up just before reaching his depth limit, and watched as the fish continued down. But then it stopped, almost as though it had its own maximum depth limitation.

Or maybe it realized it was out from the protective screening of the coral atop the reef.

For whatever reason, it reversed its course and began to ascend. But it kept moving away, so Harry followed it. He didn't notice that the seabed was rising along with the fish until the little blue guy rose up past Harry's head, and he looked back down to see the sandy bottom just a few feet below him again.

Harry blinked, then turned and looked behind himself. From this new angle, the deeper area alongside the reef was a depression that almost looked like a semicircular crater. Weird.

Harry was about to turn to continue following the blue fish when another something new caught his eye.

About ten feet back on the way he had been swimming, and the same below him. The reef, nearly vertical the entire way back he had come so far, broke off abruptly. What was - ?

Harry swam away from the reef a few feet, and the new structure came more fully into view. He blinked, and exhaled deeply in surprise.

The reef had a fairly large gap in it, down at its base. Almost like a cave.

Now, that was interesting.

It was only a few feet deeper. Harry glanced at his gauges again. 1/2 of his air tank remaining, and he was right at 60 feet.

Ah, screw it.

He kicked down and forward, giving his BCD another pump of air as he went, and halted at the cave opening.

And it really was a cave. About five or six feet wide, and the same tall at its highest point, it led straight back into the reef. The sunlight filtering down from above illuminated only a few feet inside, but it looked like it went in a good ways.

Harry had a diving light tied to the wrist of his left hand. He flicked his arm to bring it around and grabbed onto it, then turned it on and shown it inside. It looked like the cave, and he couldn't think of this structure as anything but, widened a ways in.

What kinds of cool structures and critters might lurk in there?

His mind immediately went to a Moray Eel. They tended to hang out in nooks and crannies, tubes and the like. And their jaws could take your arm off no sweat.

But this was way too big a structure to be one of their homes.

Harry breathed in again. Deep and slow. Then he nodded to himself and kicked forward.

The water seemed to cool as he passed beneath the reef's canopy and he entered the cave structure. Just his mind playing tricks on him. But the illumination definitely faded quickly; that was no mind trick, and he quickly became thankful for his light.

He paused for a moment in his kicking, and found himself sinking again. He hit his BCD inflator, but still struck the bottom. Sand bloomed around him, and he shook his head in annoyance. Hitting the inflation valve a second time, he found himself rising again, slowly. A couple quick kicks and he was off the bottom and moving forward again.

And then he emerged into the larger area past, and he pulled up short, surprised.

It was a natural formation. Obviously. But it was also almost completely round, and partially illuminated from light seeping down from a small rift in the coral overhead. But aside from that rift it was almost a solid formation above, and for a second Harry felt like he was swimming beneath a domed rotunda somewhere.

That was a silly thought, of course. But he couldn't shake it.

Then a shape moved past his face, and Harry recoiled, sudden adrenalin flooding his system even as he recognized a clownfish. But from so close, it had for a second appeared much larger than it really was.

He thumped up against the wall of coral behind him, and his tank made a distinct clank from the impact. Harry shook his head. Dumb. He needed to be more careful.

He'd also floated upwards a bit. He hit the air release from his BCD quickly, and a short trail of bubble announced a smidgeon of air leaving the vest.

Harry began to settle, and he panned his light around. Wasn't much else to see here, except...

An irregular shape to the left, and on the other side of the area, drew his attention, and Harry kicked over. It was a rock.

It had to be a rock. And yet...

He stopped before it and found himself settling onto the sand. Sediment puffed up as he landed, but he paid it no heed. That rock was... It was a little too regular to just be a rock.

Images of pirates and treasure chests flashed through his mind, despite him intellectually knowing that pirates had never plied these seas. Or if they had, they were few enough that there was no record of them having done so. And even if they had, how would a chest from the days well before SCUBA gear have come to be here, in a natural cave inside a reef, dozens of miles from anywhere?

He shook his head, castigating himself for his foolishness, but he still couldn't help but reach out to take hold of either side of the rock.

His gloved hands closed over purchase points, and he tugged upward, willing the cover that he was all but certain did not exist to open.

It didn't. But he did lose his grip and float upward. He hung there in the water for what felt like forever but was really just a second or two, then he slowly descended back to the sea floor, and more sand puffed up around him as he settled.

Harry shook his head, disgust welling up within him. This was stupid, and he was an idiot. And though this cave was cool, he was done with it. Time to get out of here, and also time to start thinking about heading back up to the boat.

More sand stirred up as he pushed himself back up off the seabed, and turned around.

The water was filled with sand.

His light reflected off the particles, thousands of them, suspended in the fluid. He looked left, then right, then up, and all he could see was sand entrained in the seawater. It obscured his view completely, and he forced down a surge of annoyance.

Too many times bouncing off the bottom; he'd stirred up much more sediment than he'd thought. And though it would eventually settled back down to the bottom, it would probably stay suspended for a while.

No worries, though. He'd just go back the way he came.

He kicked himself forward.

And had to twist himself around quickly to avoid plowing head-first into a wall of coral. What the - ?

He turned around, and only saw suspended sand. The rock he had been messing with was gone. All points of reference were gone. And though he thought he'd turned around enough to get back to the entrance, clearly he hadn't. How the hell was he supposed to get out of there?

He spun around and kicked forward again, but again found only a coral wall.

Annoyance became fear, and he got a sinking sensation in his gut. His breathing came faster, and he realized he was beginning to burn through his air; he was sending up a near continuous stream of bubbles, so quickly was he inhaling and exhaling.

Have to calm down. Stop, and figure this out.

First thing. Air. He looked at his gauge again, and his heart sank.

Less than 1/4 of the tank left. He was getting down to his reserve level, where the regulator would make the draw more difficult to warn him his air was running out, and he needed to get to the surface asap.

But which way to the surface? Which way out of this cave?

Harry berated himself for being a bloody idiot. Cave diving had its own qualifications associated with it. He knew that, but he had just forged on in, blindly. And now...

Now he was going run out of air and drown, sixty-five feet beneath the surface on his first qualified dive ever. And they probably would never find his body.

Blast it, it wasn't fair!

He would have snarled, if the regulator mouthpiece hadn't been clenched in his teeth. To hell with that; he was getting out of here.

But when he tried to swim forward again, again he was stymied. Just floating sediment impeding his vision, and then a sudden stop at a way of coral.

He turned round, and tried again, making his best guess as to the direction of the entrance passage.

Same result.

His heart was pounding in his ears, and he couldn't get enough air to fill his lungs. Every breath was an effort, and came only in short gasps.

As he reached the wall yet again, he looked down at his air gauge.

It was at the reserve.

Damn it, this couldn't be happening. The cave wasn't all that big. He ought to be able to find the way out easily. All he needed to do was -

It came to him then, and he felt like a complete moron. Reaching forward, he pressed his hand against the wall. Then he turned to the right and kicked himself slowly in that direction, being sure to keep his hand on the coral as he went.

He tried to tell himself that each kick brought him closer to escape, the surface, and limitless air. But the back of his mind reminded him each breath brought him one gasp closer to the last of the air in his tank. Already, it was an effort to get even an incomplete breath.

His lungs were beginning to burn. He needed to stop, get a good breath, and then he could -

His hand slipped off the coral. For a second, he thought he had kicked himself too far away from the wall. But no, it was the entrance passage.

At last!

Harry didn't hesitate. He turned into the tunnel and kicked for all he was worth, drawing on the air from his flask with all the force his diaphragm could muster as he went.

The silt in the water began to lessen....

And then he was out. It seemed like he shot out of the cave's mouth, and he wanted to shout for joy. But then he tried to draw breath, and nothing came.

A look at the gauge told him everything. The tank was completely empty.

Harry looked up. The surface was only sixty-five feet away, but it might as well have been a mile. Or two. He was out of air. All he had left was what was in his lungs, and he couldn't even inflate his BCD to help get him up to the surface.

He began kicking upward, desperately, his hands fumbling for the quick release on his weight belt. If he could just -

It was off, and he felt like he was a rocket, he shot up so quickly.

He began to feel a pressure inside his lungs, and his eyes widened. His training came back to him, and he forced aside the impulse to hold his breath. Exhaling for all he was worth, he prayed as he ascended that he hadn't waited too long to start. He'd heard of gas embolisms, and never wanted to experience them.

What had the instructors said, the way to avoid them?

Exhale, and...

Go up slower than the bubbles.

He forced himself to slow his ascent even as he also forced himself to breath out.

He'd never breathed out so much before. It seemed he must be getting to the end of the air in his lungs, but still there was more to let out.

And all the while, his instincts screamed at him, "No! Breathe in, you idiot!" and he began to feel the growing existential panic that he knew came from excessive carbon dioxide buildup in his bloodstream.

He had to keep exhaling, but if he didn't get a new breath soon...

Harry's entire body was shaking. He must take a breath. He must. Take. A.

He broke the surface, and the sudden feel of air on his skin, and the direct sun on his face, was so foreign to his experience the last several minutes that he almost didn't know how to react for a second.

Then he spat the regulator out and drew in a long, deep breath of blessed fresh, warm, and salty air.

He held it for a second, then let it out explosively, and fell to coughing.

There has sat, floating, held up by his BCD, for several minutes. Just grateful to be breathing, and to have escaped the trap of that cave. He kicked himself for an idiot. Thanked God for his good fortune to get out. And just generally soaked up being alive, despite it all.

Finally, a sound intruded on his consciousness, and he turned in the water. He saw the dive boat, about a hundred feet away, and the other divers in his party on deck, looking anxiously in his direction. Someone was in the water, swimming toward him. From the long hair, it had to be Sean.

He reached Harry's side and came to a halt next to him, treading water. He had his mask on, but not his snorkel. His expression was deeply concerned.

"You alright, mate?" he asked.

Harry nodded, but couldn't bring himself to say anything. He just gestured for Sean to lead the way back to the boat, then he kicked after him.

One thing was for certain. He was never going into a cave again.

15

WORK RELEASE

"I really don't want to do this."

Billy looked across the drop ship to where the kid sat, strapped to his crash couch by a four-point sling of webbing, and could identify completely.

The kid was young, maybe twenty years old. Brown-haired, with yellow-green eyes. In shape, but not bulky, and wearing the same drab blue-grey coveralls Billy wore. Despite his strong physique, he had fear in his eyes.

Billy had felt that fear a dozen of times over the last fifteen years. He'd been doing drops like this since before Steven was in grade school. But still, no matter how many times he'd done them, he never wanted to do the next one.

His body pressed down into his seat as the g-forces began to build up, and he put on a grin—the same grin he'd seen the oldies make on his first drop, or at least his best approximation of it—and forced out a laugh that did a pretty damn good job of being genuine.

"What's the matter, kid? You want to live forever?"

The kid looked at him and scowled, then said, "Yeah, actually."

Billy really did laugh then.

Around them, the drop ship gave a lurch. It was five meters on a side, and cubic. The interior was all grey metallic plating, pipes, and data displays on cracked LED screens, except for the crew couches. They were arranged around the four sides of the room, four on a side except for the bulkhead to Billy's right, where only two of their fellow chattel sat, on either side of the red and grey painted hatch that would open after they made planetfall so they, poor doomed souls that they were, could rush out to meet their fate.

The place stank of sweat and fear, and beneath that of ozone from electrical wiring that was too old so that it was just on this side of bursting into flames, because who cares if a boatload of nobody convicts burned up from the inside before they reached their doom.

And piss. There was always piss, from some poor schmuck who couldn't control his fear, or his bladder, on the way down.

Most guys didn't last past their first drop. Fewer still lasted past their second. Billy had only met one other guy who'd survived as long as he had in this game. But he had died on the last drop.

So Billy figured this was it for him.

There was a peace that came from that. A peace that he had never known, in all his time since his sentencing.

He still hadn't wanted to make the drop.

Oh well, here he was. And there the kid was, all young and scared and with no idea what to do or how to handle himself, and if possible to all appearances even more certain than Billy was that this would be his last ride to, well, anywhere.

"Stick with me, kid," Billy said, not knowing why he said it. "You'll be alright."

To either side, and on all the other walls of the drop ship, his fellow convicts looked at him with expressions that at first said he must be insane. But after a second, as the others took in his demeanor and then his obvious age and experience, first one, then the others, turned to expressions of bitterness, then anger.

Only Steven didn't look like he wanted to kill Billy.

Good.

Steven nodded, didn't say anything. His expression said everything.

The g-forces built up, and Billy had to suppress a groan. He clenched his thighs and worked his shoulders, blowing out through pursed lips to keep the blood flowing and force himself to breathe.

Then there was a giant lurch and a hollow BANG. All around him, the other men in the drop ship surged forward against their restraints as the g-forces suddenly relented.

All was silent for a few moments, except for the strained breathing from thirteen other men, the soft groans that some could not restrain from leaving their mouths. Then a hiss and a pop, and the hatch dropped open, falling outward to land on the ground of their slaughter field outside.

Warm humidity flooded into the drop ship, and with it the smell of vegetation and the taste of water on the air. Chirping, whether from local bird equivalents or some other species, carried into the chamber with the warm air, and for a second, everyone just stared at the glare of sunlight streaming through the hatch.

Then a hulking dark-skinned man, dressed in the same jumpsuit and boots as the rest of the drop ship's occupants, threw off his harness with a grunt that was almost a roar, and rushed forward toward the open hatch.

That was all the others needed. The drop ship became a stampede of man racing to remove their restraints and shoving each other aside in their haste to head toward the exit, and the fight to survive.

Across the drop ship, Billy saw the kid move to undo his harness, and Billy raised a hand toward him, open and palm out, and shook his head. Wait, Billy mouthed, and the kid looked askance at him for a second.

Then the press of men became severe, and understanding rushed across the kid's face as he took in the press.

Small as it was, the weight of the crowd was still immense. Off to the left of the door, on the kid's side of the ship, Billy saw one man, slender as though not one who worked out much, crushed between two larger men and then shoved aside by a third. He stumbled into the hatchway and his forehead rebounded off the hatch's seating surface. Billy saw blood as his scalp split, and then he disappeared from view as the press of men flowed overtop him.

Billy looked back at the kid and nodded grimly. Best to wait; there would be plenty of time to debark and get settled after the initial rush died down.

The kid returned the nod. He understood.

To the left, on the wall opposite the exit hatch, a third man still waited in his harness. Older than Steven, maybe twenty three or twenty four, with skin the color of chocolate and a shaved head, he clearly had been through this before as well. He sat, thumbs hooked beneath the chest straps of his harness, and waited with them, his eyes watching the press of newbs with disdain. More like disgust.

The dark man must have felt Billy's gaze on him, because he looked away from the rushing crowd and met Billy's eyes. A rush of adrenalin went up Billy's spine; his eyes were stone cold. The eyes of a killer. But he nodded with evident respect, and flashed a little grin Billy's way.

So. Billy had found his team for this drop. You always needed a team; that was the only way to even have a chance to survive. But some guys made the mistake of picking a team that was too large, and that always bit them in the ass.

Only three could pass through the gauntlet. Three survivors from each drop, of forty-two men sent down. Four times in his career as a convict, Billy had only made it because some fools had chosen teams of four or five. In the end, the in-fighting killed them, and let Billy go on living.

Living as a prisoner, and a toy. Never seeing anything except the walls of a cell except for an hour a day and even then just stars through a viewport in the side of the prison's exercise compartment.

And only certain to go on living until the next drop.

But it was still living, and it beat the alternative.

So Billy returned the grin, and the nod.

The press of men ended as abruptly as it began, and then it was just the three of them sitting in their chairs in the drop ship's prisoner compartment. Across the compartment from him, Billy saw the kids eyes moving from him to the dark man and back. He licked his lips.

Billy rolled his shoulders in a shrug and unlatched his harness. Then he stood, moving slowly to get a good stretch, and turned toward the hatch.

The skinny guy who had gotten jounced around earlier was lying there, just inside the hatch sill. He was limp, unmoving, and his head was wrenched around in an unnatural angle. His neck was almost certainly broken, and he had the starts of several bruises just starting on several places in his exposed skin.

He was a goner. But you had to make sure. So Billy walked over, crouched down, and checked his pulse.

Yep. Dead.

Nodding with grim satisfaction, he turned and looked back at the kid and the dark guy.

"Well. One down, thirty-eight more to go," Billy said. He raised his eyebrows and swept his arm toward the open hatch. "Shall we?"

The kid looked at him with more of that uncomprehending fear. The darker guy just grinned. It was a smile of hunger.

Four hours in, and near as Billy could tell twenty competitors down.

Competitors. It was a euphemism, but it was the euphemism that warden and guards always used. The first two or three times Billy had dropped, he had rebelled against it. But eventually he had found himself using the term.

After all, it was a competition. Survival of the fittest, to see who got to keep on living. Just broadcast on galaxy-wide vidcasts.

Rumor was the vid networks made a fortune off it, and Billy could believe it. He'd watched them when he was a kid, when his parents were out partying and didn't know what he was doing. He got a vicarious thrill watching the convicts duke it out, scratching and clawing when they didn't have weapons to see who got to live and who didn't.

He'd seen the broadcasts of the proud few convicts who'd lived out their terms and emerged, victorious and supposedly wealthy from donations sent by their various fans, to live out the rest of their lives, their debt to society paid, on a beach on some tropical paradise on a sun-drenched world somewhere away from the major shipping lanes.

Supposedly.

Now that he'd been in the system for almost as long as he'd been alive before he got arrested, he highly doubted any of that was true. Far as he knew, he was the oldest surviving convict in the system, and he still had another seven years left on his sentence.

No way some other guys had made it out. He'd have heard about it.

No, it was all a sham, to give the public some entertainment while lining the pockets of the broadcasters and their commentator staff.

But that wasn't Billy's problem. Right now, his problem was getting through the remaining nineteen without getting killed himself.

He crouched behind a tall thin-trunked tree with swaying limbs that almost but not quite resembled a palm tree he'd seen in a picture once, clutching the hatchet he'd picked off a dead convict an hour earlier. He was sweating up a storm; his coveralls were wet, clinging to his torso, and he had to breath in heavily to get enough air from the humidity of the place. And, he suspected, from its lower than standard atmospheric density.

Steven was leaning against another tree fifteen feet to Billy's right, a cudgel made of smooth, dark wood in his hands. He glanced aside to meet Billy's eyes and raised a questioning eyebrow.

Billy raised his free hand, telling him to hold fast, and looked back toward their prey.

A group a four convicts, clad in grey and red coveralls—so coming from a different prison than theirs—were clustered around a wood-sided box in the center of a clearing about thirty feet away. On all sides of their little group, more tall trees swayed in a breeze that didn't seem to carry any coolness, and smaller shrubs and under-brush somehow managed not to wilt in the heat. Overhead, whitish-grey clouds moved on that same breeze. One momentarily passed before the yellow-white sun that was almost directly overhead now, and the temperature dropped noticeably.

Billy had to restrain a sigh of relief at the sudden coolness. No time to dwell on that now, either.

Three of the quartet were in a discussion, speaking in low voices that didn't quite carry to Billy's location, while the fourth stood apart, keeping a lookout, his head turning left and right often enough that it would be hard to creep up on him unseen. The other three appeared to be trying to figure out how to get the box open.

Idiots.

The wardens often placed boxes in the killing grounds, to lure the competitors into a place and force a fight through promises of supplies or weapons. In Billy's experience, those promises were almost always empty. It was all just a game to force the action.

And it worked. After all, there he was, about ready to leap on the poor sods, to the viewing public's amusement.

Only difference was he didn't plan to stick around afterwords, for the next team to ambush.

The lookout turned to look in Steven's direction, his long knife clutched in his hand.

The three talking were in disagreement. The one farthest away from Billy was shaking his head and making a chopping gesture with his right hand. His lips, thin and blood-red beneath his blond mop were drawn into a scowl. He was just opening his mouth to speak when something large, dark, and muscled rose out of the underbrush behind him.

Large arms wrapped themselves around the blond man, twisting beneath and around his shoulders before getting around his neck and twisting. Hard.

Before any of the blond man's companions could move, he slumped, dead from a broken neck in the arms of the big dark man—Gamal—from the drop ship.

They all froze, stunned.

In that second of opportunity, Billy rounded his tree and charged, straight for the sentry.

He had turned with his fellows, his eyes drawn by the sudden noise and violence. He only registered Billy's approach a second before his arrival. He had only just begun to turn to meet him when Billy's hatchet took him in the temple.

He fell, and Billy turned toward the others. Only two now.

One, unarmed, turned to flee. The other had a claw hammer, and charged toward Gamal, crying out in something that was probably supposed to be powerful rage but just came across as desperate.

The big man let the blond fall to the ground and stepped forward, into the man's swing. The hammer struck his raised forearm, but only with the shaft, not with the head. It evoked a grunt from the big man, but that didn't stop him from jabbing his attacker in the throat with half-closed knuckles.

The convict went down, thrashing as he clutched at his shattered voice box, and Billy turned away to find the last man.

Steven stood over his body, his cudgel dripping blood from where the kid had bashed the guy's brain in.

Steven's eyes were wide. He had a look on his face that was part exhilaration, part shock, and part disgust. It was hist first time killing a man. Even if he hadn't said it earlier, and he hadn't taken anyone down yet so far in this competition until now, Billy would have known it just from the look on his face.

Billy met Steven's eyes and nodded. "Good job," he said. Then he turned to Gamal.

The big man grinned at him, only the joy of killing in his face.

"Let's gather their weapons and get out of here," Billy said.

Twenty-four down. Fifteen to go.

Six hours in, and Billy was pretty sure another six of their competitors were gone. Or at least, he and his team had taken out two more and come across four other bodies he didn't recognize.

Assuming he wasn't being optimistic, that left nine to go.

Nine more. Just nine.

"You know," Steven said, "we could just find a place to hold up. Wait for the others to pick each other off." He sounded like he was getting tired. He certainly had grown up some in the last couple hours.

He'd scored another kill, and he was taking the second one far better than he had the first. He'd firmed up, become more stoic.

In another life, Billy would feel sorry for him. But not this one. In this one, it was kill or die, and strange as it seemed, Billy found he didn't want the kid to die. Not yet.

Gamal shook his head. "That's a good way to lull yourself."

They were standing amidst a collection of boulders that rested alongside a swiftly flowing stream that ran from north to south through the pseudo-palm forest. Or at least, Billy presumed it was north to south, from the location of the sun and the way it had moved across the sky since they'd departed the drop ship anyway.

They'd been going for a good long time now, and dehydration was fast becoming an issue. They'd stopped to get a drink.

Billy nodded in agreement with Gamal. "I've seen other guys try to evade, keep out of the way. Never seems to work out. Something always drives them out. Either someone finds them, or a wild animal. Or the wardens just send a drone to shoot them out into the open. No, better to take the initiative."

He bent over and cupped his hands into the flowing water, then lifted the fluid to his lips. It would have been warm elsewhere, but compared with the heat in the air it felt blessedly cool. And tasted sweet, somehow.

It was good.

"Ok," Steven said. "Then maybe we set another ambush? Other teams will be looking for water as well."

Billy nodded and dropped his hands, exhaling with satisfaction. "Ya, now that's a better idea." He looked around, pondering. "Where do you think?"

Steven gestured with his chin toward the other side of the stream and up about a hundred paces. There, a tree had fallen at some point in the past, coming to rest at an angle atop another boulder. In the time since its collapse, undergrowth had sprung up around the fallen trunk.

Billy considered for a moment then nodded. Kid was right; that would be a good place to lie in wait.

A few moments later, he cursed himself for a fool when, as they were approaching that place, three men that he recognized from their prison, and their drop shop, charged from the trees to their right and another two emerged from the same place they were just thinking to set their own trap.

Then he ran out of time to upbraid himself, as their attackers were on them.

Gamal was gone, his head bashed in by another hammer, and Billy was limping from an injured leg. But Steven was somehow untouched and another hour had passed.

They hadn't seen anyone since the fight at the fallen tree. But there should be five more competitors out there.

One they could spare. The others...

His foot came down wrong, making him twist his injured leg unexpectedly and making Billy grit his teeth in pain.

Spare one. Who was he kidding? Gimpy as he was, he wouldn't be in position to offer anyone mercy. He'd be the one begging in a straight-up fight, more than likely.

Steven grabbed onto Billy's arm and helped him get back fully upright and into a more comfortable position. Though comfort was a relative term lately.

"Come on, old timer," Steven said. "Not much farther."

Billy looked sidelong at him and snorted. "You got someplace in mind to go I don't know about?"

The kid shrugged and managed a grin at him. "Away from here."

Fair point. Although... "Wouldn't mind staying here, actually."

Steven looked at him askance.

"What? Warm air, nice scenery. Lots of food, from the look of things." He shrugged. "Beats that prison satellite."

"Yeah, well, make it past this and we'll be out of there soon enough."

Billy snorted again. "You're dreaming, kid. No one gets out."

"Of course they do. If - "

Billy held up short, and Steven took a pace before he noticed. He turned back around to look at Billy, that questioning eyebrow raising again.

"You don't actually believe that shit about making it through, paying your debt, and going on to the beach somewhere do you?"

Steven shrugged slightly, eyeing Billy with sudden uncertainty. "Not a beach. But after I've done my five years, I - "

Billy rolled his eyes. "Kid, you ain't going to make it five years. Most guys don't even last one." He gestured toward the forest around them. "Haven't you been paying attention today?"

"But - " Steven stopped himself mid-sentence. His eyes turned to follow Billy's hand, toward where it had ended up pointing deeper into the forest. "All I did was steal a cab." He stopped, his voice catching in his throat. "That doesn't deserve - "

The true enormity of his situation, the utter lack of hope, seemed to strike him, and Steven's shoulders slumped. His eyes dropped and he hung his head.

Christ. This was all Billy needed. Was the kid - Was he crying??

He was going to get them both killed if he didn't pull himself together. Damn him.

Damn yourself, said that little voice in Billy's head that he hated listening to. You could have waited to educate him until after you guys made it out. If you made it out.

Cussed voice was right, of course. That's why Billy hated listening to it.

He reached out to lay a hand on the kid's shoulder. "Look, kid. Don't take me - "

Right at that moment was when a group of three charged them from off to the left.

Billy should be dead. He had no idea how he wasn't.

It was effectively three on one, and though Steven had proved to be tougher than Billy had given him credit for in the drop ship, those were long odds, even armed. And their attackers were armed as well.

But Billy had somehow managed to brain the guy who came for him, and Steven took down the other two.

So there was only one more competitor to take out, and they were safe. Only problem was Billy's attacker had slipped his knife into Billy's side. And Steven...

The kid was rough. Left arm hanging limp at an unnatural angle, obviously broken. And cuts above his right eye and deep into the meat of his left thigh. He wasn't in any condition to fight, either.

If either of their two remaining competitors came on them now, they were done.

Or one of them was, anyway.

Billy sat slumped against the trunk of one of those pseudo-palms, and racked his brain for some tactic, some trick, to get them out of this.

Steven was going through their attackers' pockets. He straightened with a wince, and shook his head. "Nothing better than what we had already. And - " He gestured at himself, then at Billy, and half-barked a bitter laugh.

Billy returned the laugh with a snort of his own. Yeah. Lot of good better gear would do them now. Unless it was a gun. But the wardens would never leave a weapon like that out for the competition. Too much risk of losing control of the convicts during pickup or drop off.

Steven limped over to the same tree and leaned back against it, then slumped down to the ground to Billy's right. "Guess we just have to hope the other two fight it out amongst themselves."

"Guess so." But that was a fool's chance to take. There was no guarantee those two weren't teamed up, or that they would meet up before finding the two of them.

For that matter, Billy's count could be off. There was no telling for certain.

But he was pretty sure he was right. He'd had lots of years to practice counting down the competition. And lots more years of the same thing to look forward to, even if they managed to take out one of the other two.

More years than the kid had in his entire sentence.

Wasn't much to look forward to.

"You said you've got five years total. How long you been in?"

"Nine months."

Billy nodded. Rules were a guy got anywhere between a year to eighteen months between drops. To recuperate, and to enjoy to spoils of victory. Those spoils being prison food and prison walls.

And breathing.

Better than the alternative. Sometimes.

But that meant the kid might only have to go through the competition two more times before release. Assuming release really was a thing. He'd never seen it happen, but maybe it was possible.

Billy would have to go through at least three, maybe four more drops.

Inwardly, he shuddered at the idea.

"You said stole a cab?"

"Yeah. What did you do?"

"Shot a guy. Robbed a bank." Billy shook his head. "Done plenty worse than that since then, though."

There was a pause, then Steven nodded. "Yeah."

From the tone of his voice, Billy could tell the kid was considering the future also. Maybe computing how many more times he might have to do this, just as Billy had. And he wasn't liking what he'd come up with.

Billy couldn't blame him. If he had his druthers he'd -

Rustling off to the left, and Billy turned his head. His spirits dropped.

The last two competitors were coming. Just walking straight toward them, out in the open. And why not? They wore grey and green coveralls and they looked completely untouched.

No way he and Steven would be able to fight them off.

Billy fingered the knife he'd taken from his dead attacker. The same knife he'd used to stab Billy with.

The two were moving quickly, but warily. Their eyes locked onto Billy, and he could see the confidence in their stare. And the balpeen hammer in the one guy's hand and the length of rebar in the other's. He could use that like a spear, and from the blood on the end of it, he had already, at least once.

Wouldn't even have to get close to kill with that. Definitely outside of Billy's swinging distance.

Crap.

He looked to his right. Steven was staring out the other way. He hadn't seen their attackers yet.

If it came down to a fight, there was a chance both of them might end up dead. It had happened before, and that would just suck. No sense both of them going out when one could make it. And if it came down to that, it just made sense...

"Sorry about this, kid," Billy said.

Steven was just turning to look at him, that eyebrow raised in its question again, when Billy swung at his throat with the knife.

He told himself it was the fact that he was wounded, and moving slower than he otherwise would have. That was the reason why the kid was able to catch the hand holding the blade before it ever reached him.

And it was also on account of the wounds that he wasn't able to move out of the way before the kid shuffled over and sunk his own blade into Billy's stomach.

He heard the groan coming from his lips even before the pain registered. He felt wetness spreading across the front of his coveralls —spreading at a rate that should have been alarming—as the kid withdrew the weapon.

The kid kept his hold on Billy's knife hand, but he didn't even try to fight back. He just let go of the weapon, and it thumped into the ground at his side.

Steven narrowed his eyes and raised the knife to Billy's throat. "Why?"

Billy shrugged, then gestured toward the oncoming competitors. Steven followed his gesture with his eyes, and they widened.

"Can't both make it out," Billy said. "And I'm sick of this shit." And as he said it, he realized it was true. He also realized that -

"No chance I'll get through enough of these to get released." He drew a breath, and coughed as a new spasm of pain swept through him. "You might, though."

Steven just stared at him. Then, slowly, he took the knife away from Billy's neck. He pushed himself away then slowly, with obvious pain, forced himself to his feet.

It was getting cold. Strange, since the sun was not yet low enough in the sky to be setting yet. But the shadows were growing longer, all the same.

Steven dropped his knife to the ground and nodded, looking him in the eye. "Thank you," he said.

Then he turned and limped toward the last two remaining competitors.

As the shadows expanded to completely fill his vision, Billy heard the siren that announced the competition was over. His last thought was a smidgeon of hope that maybe, just maybe, the kid might be the first one to make it all the way to release.

Maybe.

16

MISS MELODY AND THE ELF SPA

Steph ran her left hand through her hair, and wished she hadn't cut it short the previous week. She hadn't realized how much just running her fingers through it, and then being able to give it a little tug—just a little—was soothing when she was irritated or upset. Now there was barely enough to get a hold of at all, and she really needed some soothing.

She felt the frown digging furrows into her cheeks and tried to will herself into a smile, but that just made the frown deeper. Images of the confrontation with Jenny at work and embarrassment over being called out so harshly, and so publicly, kept running through her head, and her mood just grew more dark.

She wanted to say she was stalking down the concrete sidewalk of Third Avenue, her light whitish-green jacket zippered up tightly against the late afternoon drizzle that had begun shortly after she started to walk.

But she wasn't stalking. She was fleeing.

Brushing past hundreds—thousands?—of faceless and nameless people as they too navigated the walkways of the great city around her, oblivious to her and her returning the favor.

Splashing through puddles below each curb as she crossed the streets, the leavings of yesterday's stronger rainfall.

Trying not to notice the smell of exhaust in the air that overwhelmed the natural odor of moisture that she used to find so pleasant, when she lived out in nature instead of in an artificial jungle of concrete and steel.

Not paying attention to the car-rattling uber-bass as some gangster wannabes drove past in an old El Dorado that had been painted bright yellow with red lightning bolts on the side.

Simply fleeing, and lost as she ruminated, and got more angry at Jenny. And at herself.

Steph lost all track of where she was, and it didn't matter. She wasn't going anywhere. Just walking to get away.

But you'll just have to go back there again tomorrow, that little voice in her head stated. She snarled inwardly, feeling the frown turn those furrows into canyons on her face, and told the voice to shut up.

The voice was beginning a retort when movement from the right brought Steph up short. She barely saw the trenchcoat-wearing guy emerging from a shop at breakneck speed before he bumped into her. Hard.

She stumbled backward, and had to pinwheel her arms to keep from falling over entirely. She felt another impact on her back as she rammed into another person behind her, followed by an annoyed, "Hey!" in a nasally tone.

The guy who ran into her—tall, dark, and handsome, of course— barely spared her a glance. Just grunted and said, "Watch where your're going." Then he pushed his way through the flow of pedestrians and vanished from sight.

"Seriously?" Steph said aloud. More like shouted, and all of the pent up emotions she'd been stewing came out in sheer volume.

Faces on all sides, those who hadn't turned to watch the minor incident, now all turned to regard her. It was like being in a spotlight. An inhuman, impersonal spotlight. All around, the faces were disinterested except for perhaps a smidgeon of amusement.

A few cell phone cameras were pointing her way.

Had the entire crowd been pulled away and replaced by robots, Steph would have found that more genuinely human than what she was facing right that second. Flushing, but almost more from fright than embarrassment, she cast about for a place to go, just to get out from under that weight of the automatons-that-were-also-people's gaze.

And from the rain. It had picked up from its initial drizzle to a more steady pour while she was walking, and her jacket, which was for show more than for really combatting the elements, was beginning to soak through. The day was already cooler than normal for early fall, and she'd catch a chill if she didn't dry off soon.

The shop the guy had come from was a cold and intimidating business attire tailor. On any other day, the pictures of models wearing trim suits that were posted inside its display windows might have had some appeal, but right then, under the collective stare of that crowd...

No, no way.

She looked left, and her spirits lifted.

Miss Melody's Cafe, the sign said. Food for the Body. Healing for the Soul.

The front windows were uncluttered by signs or advertisements, letting the warm light from inside spill out onto the grey overcast of the street. Yellows and greens and blues and pinks made up the decor inside, and the white-backed chairs around white tables looked comfortable and inviting.

Before she realized it, Steph was inside, and shaking the water off her jacket, which she doffed and hung on a coat hook that the proprietor had placed just inside the door and to the left.

It was warmer than outside, and smelled of fresh baking and simmering chicken soup. Acoustic guitar music, all arpeggios and chords in a cheerful major key, no singing, issued from speakers mounted up in the corners.

There were no other customers inside, just four sets of tables for three and the glass-fronted service counter in the rear. An older woman, wearing a pastel green apron over her plumpness, with silver-grey hair done up in a bun on the top of her head, stood behind the counter. She had on a white blouse beneath her apron and pink-rimmed glasses, and she smiled when Steph approached.

It was the kind of smile that would turn a plain face, like hers, into a thing of utmost beauty. And it did.

"Hello dear," she said, her tone welcoming. "I'm Miss Melody. What can I get for you?"

Steph looked through the glass of the counter at pastries and morsels that all looked they they would just melt in your mouth, then she looked back up at Miss Melody and gave a little shake of her head. "I... I don't know. I'm not really hungry. I don't think. I just - " She looked back over her shoulder at the grey light of the city and shivered.

"Just needed to get away," Miss Melody finished for her. Her smile grew, if anything, more warm, and gentle. "I understand."

She turned away and stepped a pace back from the counter. A few moments of exacting movement, and she turned back to face Steph, steam rising from a white and blue porcelain teacup sitting on a saucer. She held it out toward Steph.

"Here. This will be just the thing."

Steph accepted the cup and saucer, and somehow got the feeling something momentous had just occurred. She wasn't sure what, but it felt like the cup had more mass to it than it should. But when she looked within, she just saw yellow-brown tea, with a small slice of lemon floating in it.

She inhaled the rising steam, and the fragrance sent a warm feeling through her entire body. She lifted the cup to her lips and sipped. Heavenly. Steph let out a little sigh. "That is great," she said.

"I thought you'd like it. Please, relax." Miss Melody gestured toward the closest of the tables, and Steph gratefully sat down on to the white-backed chair with pink upholstered cushion. It felt like sinking into a cloud, despite the chair's rigid-looking construction.

She just sat there, sipping the tea and wondering as to its blend. She'd never tasted its like. But as the brew settled into her belly it seemed to create a bubble of warm within her that emanated everywhere.

After the rain and the chill and the automatons outside, she decided Melody was right. It was exactly what she needed.

Her cell phone rang.

Of course it did.

Steph was just lifting the cup to her lips. She considered saying screw it, and just accepting the relaxation that so closely beckoned. Then she glanced down at the phone's screen.

It was work, and Jenny. Why was she calling? It was after their normal business hours...

A cold sliver went down Steph's spine, and she knew. She was fired. And Jenny didn't even have the courtesy to do it to her face.

Steph slammed the cup down into its saucer, and felt mild chagrin when some of the tea sloshed out. But that paled beneath the anger at the affront Jenny was shoving at her. She snatched up the phone and snarled into it, "Jenny, you - "

But it was dead. She had waited too long, and the call had gone to voicemail.

Yep, sure enough, the phone chirped a second later, and the waiting voicemail icon appeared on the screen.

Steph considered just deleting the damn thing and getting back to her tea. But then she noticed the time.

It was late. Very late. And she had to meet up with Gwen and Stuart. They were supposed to see the new show together, and now she'd barely have time to get home and get ready.

Dammit. She had ruined everything at work, and now she was going to ruin the night out she'd been looking forward to for weeks!

Biting back something that she wasn't sure would be a snarl or a sob, she pushed the chair back from her table and picked up the saucer and cup.

Miss Melody was looking at her with concerned, sad eyes when she returned to the counter and placed the cup on top of it.

"I didn't realize," Steph said, for some reason feeling like she owed this woman, a complete stranger, an explanation. "I have to go."

Miss Melody just looked at her for a moment. "A soul needs time to collect itself. Can't always be rushing around."

"Yeah, well..." Steph shook her head. "What do I owe you?"

Miss Melody shook her head. "First visit is on the house, dear. Here." She reached to her right. Steph hadn't noticed it before, but one of those little stand-up calendars where you could pull off a different page for each day was sitting atop the counter.

Miss Melody pulled off the day's page, and Steph blinked.

For a second, she could have sworn she saw a series of little flashes, almost like golden sparks, as the paper pulled free of the bonding that had held it in place.

Miss Melody held the calendar page out to her, and Steph accepted it. The date and day of the week were on the right, in an elegant cursive font. On the left...

Steph sighed at the image of a glowing sun shining down on a peacefully still lake, with flowers of every color growing on its banks, and a woman swinging in a hammock between two willows, while off in the distance a unicorn trotted along, an elegant-looking figure in green robes astride the steed. Beneath the picture, Warm Light And Pleasant Springs was written in golden text.

Then, beneath that, at the bottom, the cafe's address.

"Something to pick your spirits up, maybe?"

Steph looked back up at Miss Melody and tried out a smile. It almost worked. But she appreciated the gesture, however impotent.

"Thank you," she said. Then she turned for the door.

As she pushed the door open, it made a little belly chime that Steph didn't recall from when she entered. She glanced down at the calendar page still clutched in her hand, and again she saw little golden sparks, this time flowing all around on the page.

"What the - " she said, as she stepped across the threshold.

A brilliant flash of golden light. And then she was somewhere else.

Warmth flowed through her. The kind of pleasantly moist warmth that's comforting without crossing the line into excessive humidity. Golden light was all around her, and she felt a momentary surge of panic that faded beneath wonder as the light receded and she was able to look around.

She stood atop a grass-covered hilltop, looking down toward a perfectly-circular lake of crystal clear blue water. Golden sunlight from directly overhead reflected from the lake's still surface like a beacon. All around the edge of the lake grew clusters of flowers of every hue, and on the side of the lake to her right stood a pavilion of white canvas beside a pair of willows. Between the willows was slung a hammock of braided white cords.

Steph felt her jaw drop open, and again she looked down at the calendar page.

It was the same place.

What was going on?

Hoofbeats from behind made her turn, and her jaw hit her chest.

The unicorn was beautiful. Proud and tall, rippled muscles on its flanks, and its horn shining like silver in the sun. And riding astride it...

He was the most beautiful man Steph had ever seen. Lean, but clearly well-muscled beneath the green robes he wore. High cheekbones and a chiseled jaw. Piercing green eyes, and long blond hair that flowed around his head to his shoulders and beyond. His robes were held closed by a black leather belt with a golden clasp, and he wore a curved sword on his right hip. He rode bareback, and when the unicorn reached Steph's side he slipped from the creature's back with such fluid grace that it took her breath away.

"My lady," he said, inclining his head to her. As he did, his hair parted, and she saw that his ears were pointed. A thrill of excitement swept through her as it clicked that he was an elf. Right out of Tolkien!

"We are pleased you can join us," he continued, and smiled at her as he straightened and met her eyes. "May I assist you up?"

He stepped aside and gestured toward the unicorn.

Steph looked at the animal uncertainly. "I don't think it'll let me ride. I'm not - " She coughed, embarrassment flooding her cheeks with color. "I mean - " She gave over trying to say she wasn't a virgin and just spread her hands.

The elf chuckled softly and placed his hand on her shoulder, gently pressing her forward. "It is purity of the soul the unicorn judges, not of the body." His smile was encouraging. "I think he will approve."

She wasn't entirely convinced, but she reached out to touch the unicorn's side. It nickered once, and eyed her, then turned to look straight ahead, apparently consenting to the contact.

Its hair was smooth and silky, beyond anything she had ever touched. It flowed past her fingers effortlessly, leaving little tingles in its wake, and she couldn't help but shivering at its touch.

Then the elf's hands closed around her waist and she felt herself lifted. A moment later, she was sitting sidesaddle—but without a saddle—atop the unicorn, and the elf smiled up at her.

"Come, my lady," he said, then he turned and stepped even with the unicorn's head.

It moved to match his stride, and before Steph realized it they were beside the pavilion and willows. The elf helped her down, and she turned to see half a dozen of his kin stepping out from within the white fabric of the pavilion. They were all maidens, dressed in white gowns. Some were darker than others but they were all beautiful enough to make Steph feel like a weed among roses.

But the elf continued to smile gently at her. Again he touched her shoulder, and he gestured toward the emerging maidens.

"These ladies will see to your needs," he said. "Bathe in the waters. Take your ease. Restore yourself."

The elf women moved toward her, and Steph found herself stepping to meet them. She paused though and turned, to see the man leaping up onto the unicorn's back seemingly without effort. "You aren't staying?"

He shook his head. "I have other duties. But you will see me again, when the time is right."

Before she could ask what that meant, he nudged the unicorn's sides with his heels, and the beast turned round then cantered back up the hill from which they had come.

Steph watched him go with a mixture of wonder and longing. Then the elf women reached her side, and they showed her into the pavilion.

She lost track of time as the elves gave her the spa treatment to end them all. The water in the lake was just as pure as it had looked from afar, and warm so she was able to swim without effort and in complete comfort. She dove to the bottom to examine the plants and fish there, then returned to the surface without ever feeling out of breath.

Her keepers washed her hair with a soap that smelled of lavender and something subtly sweet, then scrubbed her back and massaged aches that she hadn't even realized she felt from her muscles.

Warm fragrant oil, and then a time spent putting her hair into tight but somehow luxurious curls, and never mind how short she had recently cut it.

And then she was in a white gown to match theirs, swinging in the hammock as a gentle breeze rustled the leaves of the willows overhead and a songbird twittered from somewhere off to the right. She sipped at a goblet that the elf women had given her, and tasted something that was almost like honey, but also spicy, that set a deep warmth in her belly and flooded relaxation through her limbs.

She dozed. For how long, it was impossible to say because near as she could tell the sun never changed position in all the time she had spent there.

But when the light of that sun diminished from a shadow passing over her, she woke, and smiled broadly up at the dashing elf who had placed her on the unicorn.

"Hello," she said. She heard the luxurious tone of relaxation in her voice, and part of her recoiled in shock. The rest just went with it, though, because damn, she really did feel good. All her cares, all her stress, everything that had been hovering over her like a storm cloud - it was all gone.

"Hello, my lady," the elf said, and returned her smile. "Good to see you are well." He paused to inhale slightly. "Alas, it is time."

Steph blinked. "Time?"

He nodded gravely. "To return."

She felt her smile fade as the concept of returning to that grey, stifling prison of a world opened up before her. Steph shook her head. "I don't want to."

The elf reached out and took her hand, then, slowly and gently, guided her up out of the hammock and onto her feet. As he did, he said, "You are not meant for life in this place, any more than we are meant for life in yours."

Steph opened her mouth to protest, but he placed the tip of his index finger on her lips, and she felt her protest fading. She knew he was right. Though she didn't want him to be. But pleasant as this place was—whatever it was—it wasn't really her home. Part of her knew if she did remain she would just waste away here.

So she nodded, and he smiled approval.

They walked hand-in-hand up the hill. The unicorn was nowhere to be seen. When they reached the top, she saw there was a small stone square inlaid in the grass. She hadn't noticed it before. It had a strange glyph—two circles interconnected by a collections of wavy, swirling lines—carved into its surface, and it glimmered ever so slightly in the sunlight.

She was busy studying it when the elf said, "Fare well, my lady." He gestured toward the stone, as though she should step upon it.

Steph hesitated. "What's your name?"

The elf cocked his head slightly to the side, then his smile quirked upward ever so slightly. "I am Lorien. And if you should happen to come this way in the future, I will be glad to see you again."

He made that same gesture again, and Steph stepped forward onto the stone.

Another golden flash, and she stumbled forward back into Miss Melody's Cafe.

It took her a moment to realize where she was. Then she saw the woman herself standing behind the counter, exactly as she had been right before Steph stepped through the door...portal...whatever. She gasped as recognition swept over her.

Miss Melody smiled gently and raised an eyebrow. "Back so soon?"

So soon? She had been gone for hours surely.

Steph's cell phone chirped, and she pulled it out. She blinked in shock. According to the date and time displayed on its screen, it was exactly the same time now as it had been when she stepped through the door. But that was impossible. How - ?

The phone vibrated in her hand, and it chirped again. The Voice-mail icon had a red 1 overtop it.

The message from Jenny. Well, might as well get on with it.

She lifted the phone to her ear, still not entirely sure what had just happened. Jenny's voice came through loud and clear.

"Steph, I wanted to call and say I'm sorry for how I acted in the meeting. I was surprised and angry and... It wasn't your fault, and I was wrong to blame you like I did. I hope you don't quit over this; I can't run this place without you. Please come in tomorrow and let me make it up to you."

Steph dropped her hand to her side, cellphone still playing the rest of the voicemail, and looked wonderingly at Miss Melody. "What is this place?"

The older woman shrugged. "What the sign says. Food for the body. Healing for the soul."

"But..." Steph shook her head, her mind racing through the events of the last several hours—days?—in that other realm, and back here in the real world. Wait. "Was... Was that real?"

"Was what real, dear?"

"The...place. The elves. The..." She stopped, realizing she sounded like an idiot.

Miss Melody shrugged. "Was it real to you? That is what matters." She glanced at the little calendar, and Steph followed that with her own eyes. Another wave of shock swept through her when she saw the day and date that was atop the stack, ready to be pulled off:

today's. And there was no picture on the sheet, just the day and date, which filled the entire page.

It hadn't registered fully when she'd fished the cell phone out, but Steph realized she was back in her own clothes. And... And she was still clutching her page from the calendar in her left hand, just as she had been before stepping through the door.

Hers still had the picture on it.

"We all have different needs, at different times," Miss Melody said. Steph looked back at her, and the she sniffed. "But now, I believe you need to get moving, or you'll miss your show."

"Yes," Steph said, as memory flooded back into her. "Yes, I - " She froze, narrowing her eyes at Miss Melody. "How did you know about that?"

She didn't answer, just smiled her kindly smile and made a shooing gesture.

Steph knew she was right; now that she was back time wouldn't just stop and wait for her. And her friends were expecting her. So she nodded and turned back to the door.

She paused with her hand on the door's handle again, and looked back. "It won't - ?" She didn't quite know how to ask the question.

Miss Melody shook her head. "Another time, perhaps."

"So I can come back?"

Miss Melody gave a little shrug. "If you have need. We are always here for those in need."

Steph wasn't sure she understood, but she nodded anyway. She opened the door and stepped through.

Somehow the greyness of the street outside was less bleak than it had been before she went inside. The people were less robotic, the city less oppressive. She breathed in the air and couldn't smell the exhaust, the way she had before.

She felt 100% better.

With a start, she realized she hadn't said thank you. She turned to go back inside to remedy that, and stopped.

Where Miss Melody's Cafe had been was a Seven Eleven.

What the - ?

She looked back down at the calendar page in her hand. It was just as it had been, except for one thing. The address at the bottom. She hadn't really paid it attention earlier, but she could have sworn it had been the street address she had entered. Now it read, "Wherever needy souls are located."

Despite the weirdness, the absolute insanity of it, Steph found herself smiling. Looked like there was someone looking out for people, after all.

As she turned to hurry down the street toward home, and then her evening out with her friends, she had a bounce in her step that she hadn't had in years.

17

JOYRIDE TO THE MOON

Jeremy frowned, and stared daggers at the keypad that had—once again—foiled his attempt to get inside his Dad's ride. He hadn't figured it would be this tough.

He'd tried his Dad's birthday. His Mom's birthday. His sister's. No dice. He'd tired combinations of all four. Nothing. Their wedding date. Nope.

It was frustrating as hell.

He'd been able to get into his Dad's terminal in the their house easily enough a few months back, so he could bypass the parental controls on their network access to get to the really good stuff—and boy was it good. A little disturbing sometimes, too. But good. But it looked like Dad paid more attention to security on his ride than he did for other things.

Figured. It was a sweet ride. Jet black and sleek, it was built for both atmospheric and orbital flight. And not just flying: racing. It would get him all the way to Luna and back without a problem, and in time for the Pamela Jennings concert, and all the parties that would go with it, on Mare Tranquilitatis.

And with Dad out of town with his girlfriend and Jeremy's sister off to college, there was no one to stop him from taking it, picking up

Steve and Amil, and putting in an appearance at the social event of the year. Maybe the decade.

Except for the damn lock.

Jeremy took a half-step back and straightened, right index finger tapping his chin while he thought the problem through.

The sounds of the night surrounded him. Chirping insects. The light, cool breeze rustling the rigid late-autumn leaves on the limbs of the maples and elms that grew around his Dad's house. The sound of ground traffic cruising the avenue at the bottom of the hill below their property.

He glanced to the right and upwards, toward the house, square and dark and suddenly imposing, and for a second he forgot he was alone on the property. He had the feeling that Dad might suddenly look out his window and see what Jeremy was doing, then come storming down to stop him.

He couldn't stop himself from cringing at the thought of the tongue-lashing Dad would dish out. And of the probable loss of his surface driving privileges, because really that was about all the punishment Dad could really give him anymore.

Jeremy was seventeen, almost ready to graduate and move on. He wouldn't be able to get his flight license for another six months when he turned eighteen, or his orbital license for another two years after that. But for all intents and purposes he was a grown up. It's not like Dad could spank him anymore.

Still, loss of surface driving would suck.

But there was no danger of that here. Dad wasn't around, and Jeremy knew how to trick out the house's security so it would look like he'd never left; not in the air anyway.

That just left getting it done.

Jeremy adjusted his faux-leather jacket on his shoulders and leaned forward again, toward the security keypad. A thought had occurred to him. He tried to push it away, but it wouldn't go. So even though he hated thinking of that day, he tried the last significant date in their little family's history. The day they'd learned Mom had been killed in a car crash.

The little LED above the keypad switched from red to green and an electronic beep sounded. Then the smooth black surface of Dad's orbital racer cracked open, and the entrance hatch to Jeremy's left rose high, offering admittance.

He was in.

Jeremy spared one last look at the house above the racer's landing pad. He hesitated for just a second, doubts flashing through his head. Maybe it would be best just to do what he normally did on a Friday night: drive over in his surface car to grab Steve and Amil and just go to the movies. Or something.

He almost closed the racer back up and left. But then thoughts of the concert and the party that would surround it returned. The absolute bedlam that everyone predicted up on luna, the fun. The hotties from all over this quadrant.

Screw driving to the movies.

He picked up the duffel bag that he'd brought down from the house, containing a couple changes of skivvies, a fresh shirt and pants, snacks and a water bottle, and a few tools he thought would be helpful for the trip, then ducked his head and stepped into the racer.

Interior lights flicked to life as the ship sensed his entry, illuminating a crew compartment that was deceptively large, for a ship this size. It could seat four comfortably; five if you squeezed, and six if you really knew and liked each other. The pilot and copilot's gell cushioned seats, all covered in worn and cracked black faux-leather, were separate units up at the front fo the compartment. The passenger's couch, to Jeremy's immediate right as he entered, was one long unit with three built-in sets of four-point restraint harnesses made of black canvas webbing.

There were no windows or portholes; the only view of anything outside the ship was through the open hatch. For now, at least. The lighting was a warm almost-natural hue, and the compartment smelled faintly of pine from Dad's favorite air freshener. Jeremy felt a little thrill of excitement as he breathed it in.

This was going to be awesome.

He left his duffle bag on the passenger couch and turned forward toward the pilot's chair. He had to keep his head ducked as he moved; he had grown to be a couple centimeters taller than Dad, and Dad could just barely stand to his full height inside the ship. But in a short while he was seated in the chair, the gell cushion adjusting to his weight and body size automatically to create a snug but comfortable support.

Jeremy finished buckling his restraint straps then reached forward and tapped the two large screens in front of his chair to life with brushes of his fingers. The upper screen, the larger of the two, ran through a bootup sequences of codes and symbols, then after a moment settled down into an image of the property in front of the racer. A second later, screens to the left and right of the pilot and co-pilot's chairs sprung to life, showing the view from the port and starboard sides of the ship as well. He didn't look, but he knew a fourth screen mounted on the bulkhead above the passenger couch, would show the rear view.

The second screen ahead of him, the smaller of the two and mounted below the first, came up with a navigation display overlaid atop a chart of the city where the ship was shown as a white pip resting on a blue square labelled "Home". At the bottom of the navigation display, ships systems status were displayed as a series of circles, all green except for the crew hatch indication which showed red, and engine parameters were shown as digital gauges for power output, acceleration, velocity, and fuel status.

Jeremy did a quick look over the instruments and nodded to himself in satisfaction. Good to go. If any of the systems had issues, they would come yellow or red instead of green, and like usual Dad had topped off the fuel just before he landed last time he'd taken the ship out.

"Ok," Jeremy said to himself. "Let's get this show on the road."

On the overhead above his head was a bank of switches and knobs that would initiate engine startup. He knew the sequence to get it going; he'd watched Dad do it countless times, and in the last six months Dad had begun teaching him how to fly the thing in preparation for getting his flight license. He'd logged about sixty hours of under instruction time in this seat, with Dad in the right-hand seat beside him. And three hours solo.

But he'd never tried to fly out of the atmosphere before. He'd watched Dad do it. And he'd read about it. But actually doing it...

Doubt again swept through him, and again he shoved it away, and flicked the engine start switches and the switch to close the hatch.

The hydraulic whine of the hatch actuator sounded quickly. Then came the solid thunk of the hatch closing and the lesser hissing of the inner seal sliding into place.

A low rumble, just barely perceptible, came from aft of the crew compartment as the engines spun up, and Jeremy felt a slight vibration in his chair in tune with the rumble.

On the system status display, the engine parameters jumped upward then settled down into idle. Jeremy eyed them for a few seconds; all normal.

Good to go.

Jeremy grinned and tapped a smaller control pad to his left, and a dialogue window opened in the upper situational awareness display in front of him. In the right cargo pocket of his pants, his holopad gave a chirp and vibrated for a second as the ship established a link with it. The dialogue window populated with his music playlists, and Jeremy selected a high energy, rocking mix he used when he went to the gym.

Thumping bass and a rollicking drum line supported a seriously shredding guitar as Jeremy took hold of the control yoke that was mounted on a panel to the left and in front of his pilot seat and the engine controls on a small console between the pilot's and co-pilot's seat.

He applied vertical thrust and pulled back on the yoke. And he was up.

On the situational awareness displays, the trees around the landing pad slipped down and then disappeared from view. Altitude indicators on the navigation display showed him passing through 100 meters. 200.

He leveled off at 300 meters, below the altitude where he'd have to contact traffic control, and adjusted the thrust vector for forward flight, and he shot off through the night.

Acceleration forced him back into the seat, and Jeremy bit back a curse. He'd forgotten the inertial compensators. Releasing the engine controls, he reached up to the control switches over his head and flicked one, and at once the feeling of being kicked in the chest relented, and he was able to more comfortably steer the ship.

He turned to the southwest, then switched the dialogue window to his contact list and placed calls to Steve and Amil.

It took a few seconds, then Jeremy's music faded as additional dialogue windows opened showing their faces: Steve all blond and square jawed, Amil darker and rounder of face. Neither of them looked particularly excited, though.

More doubts rose, but Jeremy forced them down. "Hey. I'm up, and on the way to our meeting site. You guys rolling?"

Both of Jeremy's friends looked like someone had put vinegar in their breakfast cereal. Amil spoke first.

"Hey man, my grandma just came into town. Unannounced. Mom's pissed she didn't call. But now we have to..." He trailed off, and in the window, he gave a helpless shrug.

Damn. That sucked. Not that seeing grandparents was bad, but -

Then Steve chimed in. "Katy called a few minutes ago. Her folks are out of town and she wants me to come over. I mean, the Luna concert sounds cool and all, but..."

Oh for the love of - "Dude, Katy's been blowing you off for six months. You don't really think she's serious, do you?"

"Don't be hating cause a hottie wants me all to herself. Sorry, man, but beauty calls."

Jeremy pulled back the throttle, reducing his airspeed back to a hover, and leaned back in the pilot chair, dumbfounded. They'd been planning this for weeks, not going out so they could save money from work, and now when it's finally time to do it, his buddies bail on him?

"You guys are killing me. What am I supposed to do now?"

Amil shrugged again. "Dunno. Movies maybe? Better than what I've got to do."

"Not better than who I'll be doing in a little while though." Steve's anticipatory grin was practically ear to ear. "Really am sorry, Jeremy. I'll make it up to you. Gotta go." Then his transmission winked out and the dialogue window closed.

"Yeah. Sorry," said Amil. Then he ended the conversation as well.

Son of a bitch. Jeremy ground his teeth in frustration.

Go to a movie? A movie?!

The fact that Amil's suggestion mirrored his own hesitant thoughts from a few minutes ago just made it worse. Screw the movies, and screw them. He was going to Luna.

Snarling to himself, Jeremy advanced the throttle all the way and pulled up on the yoke, raising the ship's nose toward the sky above, and space beyond.

Luna or bust.

Initial exhilaration quickly gave way to routine, and then to boredom.

Jeremy recalled reading that the first visitors to the moon required four days to get there and back. His trip out was going to be closer to four hours. But after his initial near panic as he dealt with orbital traffic control procedures that he had only observed and read about before, never navigated himself, he had darn little to do.

So he reclined his pilot's seat and listened to his music. And then listened some more.

After three hours, he was truly ready for something else to happen. Just about anything else.

By then Luna had grown quite large in the situational awareness displays, and the little pip showing the racer on the navigation screen was beginning to approach the point where the deceleration burn to enter lunar orbit and then touch down on Mare Tranquilitatis would be necessary.

He supposed that was as good a something else as he was going to get. He was just situating himself back into a position to properly fly the ship when an electronic beep preceded a hail from Lunar Traffic Control.

Jeremy swallowed. He knew LTC existed, of course. But he'd never dealt with them. Or even read about their procedures. The various approach and landing procedures were programmed into the ship's navigational computer, so he wouldn't be completely in the dark. But still, this was entirely new territory, and he fought down a big case of nerves as he reached over to the control yoke and pressed the button to activate his pilot's microphone.

"This is the racer Ollyfant en route to Tranquility Base," he said, then winced. That felt lame; hopefully it didn't sound lame as well.

A second's pause, then LTC replied. "Racer Ollyfant, we do not have a flight plan on file for you. Request your registration number and flight plan number."

Umm... Crap.

Jeremy hadn't known he would have needed to file a flight plan with LTC. Those weren't typically needed past Low Earth Orbit, where a majority of the satellite constellation resided, and the plan he had filed with Earth Traffic Control—under Dad's name—had just specified transit through LEO to Luna. Would that be enough?

He tabbed open another dialogue window on the situational awareness display, this one of the ship's internal records, and pulled up her registration specs. Then he keyed his mike again.

"LTC, this is Ollyfant. Registration number is N624CTV. We filed our plan with ETC. Did they not forward it on to you?"

It was a half-truth. But it was better than a straight-out lie.

He sweated for half a minute before LTC replied.

"Racer Ollyfant, you are cleared for Lunar Entry burn. Execute approach procedure Victor 4 and land at pad 27, Tranquility Base."

Jeremy let out a sigh of relief. Maybe this was going to work out after all.

"Roger, LTC. Thanks."

Now what the hell was approach procedure Victor 4, and where was pad 27?

It took him a while to find the procedure; it was buried beneath three levels of directory trees in a seldom-used folder. But when he called it up, it looked simple enough. He was just finishing his first review of it when the ship beeped at him and he heard the deep thrum of the engines lighting off.

He looked up to see that they had reached the burn point. On the navigation display, the ship's velocity was ticking down rapidly, and over the course of several minutes their plotted vector went from being a straight—or near enough—line zooming past Luna to who knows where to a curve that circled Luna to a free return trajectory back toward the Earth, to a stable orbit, to a decaying orbit that ended up in a crash landing on Mare Tranquilitatis.

Unless he implemented the approach procedure to turn that crash into a nice, soft, landing on pad 27.

No pressure.

It was a simple enough procedure. He should just be able to enter it into the navigation system and then...

A red square with the chilling words "ERROR - CODE 40" appeared in the center of the navigation system when he tried to import the procedure's files.

Had he missed a step? He tried again.

ERROR - CODE 40.

Oh crap. What was going on here? Jeremy tabbed open a troubleshooting window. He needed to find out what CODE 40 meant and hopefully get it fixed in the next—he glanced at the navigation display to the ETA block, and blanched—in the next twenty minutes or he was going to crash.

Jeremy paged hurriedly through to the troubleshooting documentation and found what he was looking for. His stomach dropped.

CODE 40 - incompatible file type.

He shook his head in denial. Incompatible file type? How was that even possible? It was a file resident on the ship's network. How could it be an incompatible file type?

He opened up the procedure file to the human readable portion again and scanned it. When he got to the bottom of the first page, he saw the logo there, and winced.

The logo was for Jeppesen Astronomic Charts. But Jeremy remembered now. A couple years back his dad had upgraded the Ollyfant's navigation system from the old Jeppesen one to a newer unit from Garmin.

Naturally, the two companies' file types would not be compatible with each other.

And apparently Dad had never bothered to get charts and approach procedures for Luna for the new system, because he never had any reason to go there.

And Jeremy was such an idiot, he hadn't bothered to check before leaving on this trip.

So that left contacting LTC, declaring a major mea culpa, aborting his landing and going back to Earth. Or contacting LTC to declare an emergency and have them guide him in with precision approach controls. Or flying the procedure manually.

He really, really, REALLY didn't want to do the first. He'd come this far, and to leave without at least stepping on Luna... Jeremy's mind rebelled at that notion.

The second option was almost as bad. Because if he declared an emergency and they guided him in, there'd most likely have to be a debrief of events with the local flight standards office. And it would take precisely zero minutes for them to figure out that he wasn't even licensed for atmospheric flight, let alone orbital.

That left doing it manually.

Jeremy looked at the procedure again. It was simple enough. He'd once done a far more complicated approach in his atmospheric training, under Dad's tutelage.

He could do this.

"And hey," he said to himself as he pulled the restraint straps on his seat a bit tighter, "worst case I just abort and head back to Earth." He tried chuckling to himself, in that confident way that Dad did sometimes. It didn't work; his mouth was dry and his stomach was doing somersaults in his belly.

A beep from the navigation system told him there were ten minutes remaining until contact with the Lunar surface. Peaks, valleys, and craters on the surface were getting close enough that it was easy to see their depths in detail. And he could see the lit towers of Tranquility Base ahead, and closing quickly.

The first step of the procedure was due right...about...

Now.

Eyes flicking quickly between the procedural steps and the navigation display, Jeremy applied a burst from his maneuvering thrusters to adjust the ship's vector a few degrees to starboard.

Next, a quick burn from the engines to steepen their descent.

Lower the cameras supplying the situational awareness displays so they were looking down.

Find the right pad...there, on the far side of the landing complex. The landing beacons were lit, a series of white directional strobes that were running toward an octagonal plate that was elevated slightly from the terrain surrounding it. It memory served him right, after he touched down the plate would lower and carry the ship beneath the surface into an airdock, so ingress and egress from the ship would be easier.

Also, since there was next to no protection from radiation up on the surface, most of the lunar settlements were subterranean. So it made sense to have the ships go there -

A chirping alarm drew Jeremy out of his thoughts of random trivia and back to the present. He looked down at the navigation display, and blanched.

His descent rate was too high. He gave a quick burst from the engines, and then cursed again as the ship stopped descending entirely and began to rise.

Too much thrust.

And crap, now he was out of alignment with the pad. And -

"Racer Ollyfant, what is your status?" It was a different voice on the communications system. The tower controller instead of approach control.

Jeremy's mind raced, and he keyed back, "Missfire from one of my thrusters. I've got it under control now. Good to go."

He hoped.

He'd managed to stop the unexpected ascent, and was yawing the ship around to line up with the markings on the pad...

"Racer Ollyfant, do you require assistance?"

Dammit, he did not need this distraction. "Negative," he said, quickly. "Everything's under control."

And he thought it was. The ship was lined up nicely. Descent rate was good. Just a few meters and -

Oh crap, the landing gear!

Jeremy surged forward and hit the switch to deploy the struts. He heard the hydraulics cycle to lower them, and then -

BANG!

Jeremy lurched in his seat and for a second thought he'd crashed. But when he looked at the ship's status display everything was green.

He was on the ground.

Hurriedly shutting down the engines, Jeremy slumped back in his seat and adjusted the situational awareness cameras back to their normal position just in time to see the ship sink into a vertical steel tunnel and a hatch iris shut overtop.

Over the communication system, he heard the tower say, "Welcome to Luna."

Jeremy breathed out a sigh of relief.

He waited a few minutes to give himself time to calm down before opening the hatch and leaving the ship. When he stepped out, he found himself on a steel platform that was big enough to accept a ship three times the size of Ollyfant. The steel tunnel stretched above him a good thirty meters before stopping at the massive irising hatch that he had seen closing above them.

The place was well lit by recessed LEDs in the tunnel walls, and a couple of spotlights shone down on the ship from the lower side of the hatch overhead.

Ground crew was hard at work securing the landing gear to the platform and rigging up umbilicals for shore power and sanitary tank draining. The crew's foreman turned toward Jeremy when he stepped out and gave him a quizzical look.

"That was about the most jacked up landing I've ever seen," he said. He was an older man, in his 60s probably, with dark brown skin and deep smile lines on his face. His hair was frizzy, white, and receding, and he wore the same grey coveralls that his team wore.

"Yeah," Jeremy said. "I almost lost it there." He moved to step toward the foreman, and stumbled in the low gravity.

Inside the ship, the inertial systems had maintained Earth-normal. But here the gravity was one-sixth that, and he had never experienced it before. The first step out of the ship had been weird. This second...

He tried to catch himself, but his reflexes were not attuned to the environment, and he found himself launched up into the air. He cried out in alarm.

And then strong hands were grabbing him. He turned to see the foreman had bounded over in one step, grabbed him, and pulled him back down into a normal standing position.

The foreman looked at him quizzically. "First time on Luna, huh?"

Jeremy nodded.

"How old are you, boy?"

Jeremy had been expecting this question, and had come prepared. "Twenty-one," he said, and reached into his cargo pocket. He pulled out the fake ID he'd gotten a few months back. It was in Dad's name, but it had his picture and vitals on it. Just his birthday was four years earlier than reality.

He showed it to the foreman, he looked it over and frowned.

He grunted. "Twenty-one, huh. Well you look about fifteen." He grinned then. "In about twenty years, you'll be happy for that baby face, believe me. Now, take it easy moving around at first. Takes some getting used to. I presume you're here for the concert?"

Jeremy nodded.

"I hope you got a place to stay lined up already. Way I hear all the hotels are booked."

"I figured I'd sleep on the ship. Save some money that way."

The foreman grunted again. "Your call, I guess. When you leaving?"

"Sunday morning."

The foreman nodded. "Alright then. Well, have fun."

Jeremy grinned in return. He was going to. Oh boy, was he going to.

<hr>

Jeremy couldn't help but smile, probably the broadest smile he'd ever had, as he pressed the engine start switches and powered up the Ollyfant, then blasted off from Tranquility Base.

It was Sunday morning and he hadn't gotten any sleep the previous night. Part of the reason was the concert. Another part were the parties after the concert. The final part was up in a dialogue window on the situational awareness display.

Her name was Samantha. She was twenty. She was a redhead. And she had made his life incredibly interesting the last few hours, before he had to leave if he was to get home before Dad did.

"Eat your heart out, Steve," Jeremy said, and sounded smug even to himself.

Whatever. He'd earned it.

As he lifted off, he found he could not look away from the image of Samantha's face in that dialogue window. Those green eyes. The cute dimples in her cheeks.

Best part was she didn't live all that far away from him. He was definitely going to have to look her up again.

And how, exactly, are you going to explain that you're not really 21 and that ship you showed her around was really your dad's, asked the annoying voice in the back of his head.

"Shut up," he said to it. But it kept on babbling at him.

It couldn't take his great cheer away, though. He'd figure something out.

Speaking of which, he glanced down at the navigation display and saw that he was -

"Racer Ollyfant, you are approaching the limits of the departure corridor. Adjust your vector." came the voice of LTC over the communication system.

Jeremy cursed to himself and applied some lateral thrust. "LTC, Ollyfant. Roger that. Little glitch in the system. We're good now." He resolutely closed the window with Samantha's picture in it. Time enough to daydream about her later. Carefully tweaking the racer's vector, he eased the ship back into the center of the departure corridor.

And then just a few minute later, LTC was bidding him farewell, and he was on a trajectory back to Earth.

Easy peasy.

He got back to Earth without anything happening to stop his remembrances of Samantha, and before he knew it he was passing through reentry interface and flying on a vector for home. The sun was still well up in the sky when he set down on the landing bad below the house, and he took a few minutes to secure the ship, making sure to leave no trace of his presence, or of the adventure he had had.

When Dad came walking in through the front door, a suitcase in each hand, Jeremy was sprawled on the couch, watching a holo of a kung fu shoot-em-up almost comedy movie from twenty-some years ago. One that he knew Dad loved.

Dad stopped when he saw the movie and grinned. "Big Trouble In Old Taipei," he said. "Now that is a classic." He turned to the stairs leading up to their bedrooms. "Didn't know you liked it."

"It's kind of fun," Jeremy said. It wasn't entirely untrue. The movie was cheesy, that's for sure. But there was something about the cheese that made it...almost...good.

"Damn right it is." Dad headed upstairs. He came back down a couple minutes later sans jacket and suitcases, and walked past where Jeremy was sitting on the couch toward the kitchen.

"How was the trip, Dad?"

"Pretty great. Kinda glad I didn't take the Ollyfant down there, though. I was in no condition to fly this morning." He opened up the refrigerator and pulled out a box of Orange Juice, then found a cup and poured himself a drink. "Got a funny call from Ms. Kranitz, though."

Jeremy felt his eyebrows rising. Ms. Kranitz was the neighbor two houses over, on the other side of the hill. She was always poking her nose where it didn't belong. "What did she want?"

Dad replaced the orange juice box in the refrigerator and closed it, then took a draw from his cup. "Weirdest thing," he said after swallowing. "She said she saw the Ollyfant lift off from here Friday evening, and land again this afternoon."

Jeremy worked hard to keep his face straight, though the bottom dropped out of his stomach. "Oh?"

"Yeah." Dad shook his head. "Funny old bird. I told her she had to be mistaken. You've been here all weekend, and no way could someone just take the ship without you noticing and calling the cops."

"Yeah." Jeremy sounded breathless even to himself.

Dad's eyes locked onto his, and grew stern despite the easy expression on his face. "I thought about checking the ship's position log to be sure."

"Position log?"

"Yeah. Ollyfant updates its position hourly to a site I have access to, so I can check on it from afar if I need to. I can run system diagnostics, check its position, look at the exterior and interior camera feeds, you name it. Even get the engines warmed up so I can take off in a hurry." Dad's eyebrow rose. "You didn't know that?"

Jeremy shook his head. He knew his mouth had dropped open, and he could feel his cheeks warming as he thought of bringing Samantha onto the ship. And the things he'd done with her while she was there. If Dad saw -

Dad shrugged. "But I decided I didn't need to do that. I left you in charge, and you're a dependable, responsible young man. I'm sure nothing untoward happened at all."

He drained the rest of his cup and set it down on the counter. "But I'll tell you what. If someone *had* run off with my ship while I was away, I would hope they'd at least have the decency to leave it with a full fuel tank." He patted his belly and looked around the kitchen for a moment as though trying to decide whether to get something else or not. Finally, he shrugged and turned back to Jeremy. "Well, I'm pretty beat. I'm heading to bed. Good night, son."

As Dad walked past him, it was all Jeremy could do to manage a hoarse-sounding, "Good night."

Dad went back upstairs, and a few seconds later Jeremy heard the door to his bedroom close.

Jeremy waited until the movie was done and he was sure Dad was asleep. Then he rushed out the door, down the hill, and to the landing pad where the Ollyfant was parked.

He had to go to a gas station.

Now.

MOONSTRUCK

The moon was a waxing gibbous, just a few days away from full. It shown down on the field where Susan lay with blue-white brilliance, giving the world a dull, mysterious illumination that hinted at mysteries almost uncovered. Secrets whispered in the shadows.

She tucked her hands beneath her head and just lay on the quilted blanked she had placed overtop the wildly growing grass strands and the interloping wildflowers that in the daylight would have made the field a kaleidoscope of color. Now they were dimmed to shades of grey, and the moon alone grabbed her attention.

The late summer breeze caused the grass around her to wave slowly, and it tugged at the loose cotton of her blouse and skirt, carrying the lingering heat from the day away and leaving her pleasantly cool, just south of warm. The scents of growing things and flowing water, from the stream she had passed on her way out here, came to her nostrils.

But the moon. The moon was all.

The darkness of the mares, the brightness of the impact craters and their surrounding ejecta blankets. The way the light and shadow of its surface seemed to flow into and around itself.

It called to her, beckoning. She felt its desire for her; its need.

But she also felt the great breadth of distance between it and herself. A distance that only a few humans had ever crossed, and that she almost certainly never would.

The knowledge that she could not answer that call tugged at her heart, and she willed it to stop with all her might.

But still the call came. Unceasing.

Insistent.

As Susan lay there, the moon seemed to grow in her vision, the shadows of the night elsewhere growing deeper with each breath she took, until the moon as all, filling her eyes and seeping into her mind with its siren call.

"You feel it, don't you? The call?"

Susan turned her head and was unsurprised to see a man lying on her blanket next to her. He had a lean, handsome face and well-coiffed black hair. Piercing eyes that she could somehow tell were green despite the darkness. His body was long and lean, covered in a black suit with a white shirt that was open at the collar, no tie.

The man faced her, propped up on one elbow, and his eyes burrowed into hers as she met them.

Susan nodded.

"Will you answer?"

Susan hesitated. What would it mean if she said yes? But the call, silent and insistent, tugged at her, and her uncertainty faded beneath it. She took a deep breath.

"Yes."

The man's lips turned upwards at the corners, then he leaned into her. Their lips met, and she tasted salt beneath sweetness, and beneath that something almost metallic. Lightning swept through Susan's body as he pulled her into an embrace. She wrapped her arms around him as heat followed the lightning, and felt herself carried away by the sensation of it all.

After a short eternity, the man broke the kiss and pulled his head back. He stared down into Susan's eyes, and his smile grew larger.

Unnaturally large, as though his mouth was growing somehow, even as it stayed the same size.

His lips parted, and she saw long, pointed incisors.

As he drove down toward her neck, Susan screamed -

And jerked awake, sitting bolt upright. Her bedsheets fell off her body, and she pressed her fingers to the side of her neck. She expected to feel the wetness of her own blood, where those terrible fangs must surely have ripped her throat out.

Nothing. Just the smoothness of her skin, unbroken and dry save for the sweat that covered her body, making her nightgown cling to her.

Shivering, and not just from the nighttime chill in the air, Susan looked over at the alarm clock sitting on her nightstand. Its blue digital numbers told the tale: 3:45 am.

With a suppressed groan, Susan pushed the remaining covers off and forced herself off of her mattress and to her feet. She knew there would be no more sleep tonight; there never was, lately. So instead of fighting a hopeless fight, she stumbled the ten feet from her bedside to her bathroom.

Flicking on the light, she stood in the yellow-white glow that the old incandescent bulbs gave off—better by far than the new ones the government forced on everyone to enrich cronies—and bent over the sink to wash her face. As she straightened and looked at her own reflection in the mirrored medicine cabinet mounted on the wall above the sink, she was struck, not by the frizziness of her auburn hair, but by the lack of fatigue lines on her face.

The dreams were getting more intense, and her sleep shorter and less restful. But she didn't look at all excessively tired.

Nor did she particularly feel it, once she got out and about her day. Despite never getting more than four or five hours down any more.

It was odd. But if it wasn't for the dreams, she'd take it. Sleep was annoying in how it cut into her productive time.

But the dreams. Always the same place. Always the same man.

But they'd been coming more intensely the last week or so. And tonight's...

She shivered again as memories of his touch, and the thrills it brought, wormed their way upward, and her body responded. As the shiver passed, she felt an itch in her left arm, just above the wrist. She looked down and saw that the scar she'd gotten from an accident a few months back, the one that almost looked like a dog's head that she'd had since she was a little girl, was inflamed. Red and rigid, almost protruding.

She scratched at the scar, and the itch faded, but the inflammation remained.

"What is going on?" she asked her reflection in the mirror.

Silence, and the reflection of the blue-white moonlight spilling in through her bedroom window, was the only response.

Susan spent a full day at work trying and failing to put the previous night's dream out of her mind. The day passed in a blur, with the glowing moon, its light reflecting off the man's sharp teeth, intruding into her thoughts when she least needed them to.

Which was often. Though her duties as a paralegal were not physically strenuous, they did require attention to detail. And many times she found that she had typed a clause wrong, or misspelled one of the disputants' names. And once she transposed a comma, so a settlement proposal for $10,000 became $100,000 before she caught her mistake.

As a result, when she left the Law Offices of Bricks and Capeto, she was well and truly frustrated with herself, and befuddled by her lack of wits.

She was just happy she'd caught the major mistakes before her bosses saw them.

It was not far from the law firm to her rented house, maybe four miles as the crow flies. Many days she rode her bicycle in, weather permitting.

Not today, though. She hadn't trusted herself to keep focused and not ride straight into traffic this morning. So instead, she got into her red Ford Fiesta and drove home, with a stop at Vons for the week's groceries on the way.

Her thoughts were still encumbered by the strange dreams, and stranger feelings, she'd been having as she picked out a cart and, passing through the automatic doors of the grocery, turned right into the produce section. She picked through the fruits, selecting good specimens of apples and oranges, and was turning around a stacked pallet of melons when she stopped cold, the blood draining from her face and a chill running down her spine.

There, ahead of her in the organic vegetables section, stood a long, lean man with a fine mop of black hair. His skin wasn't pale—in fact it was nicely bronzed—but it seemed to reflect the fluorescent lights in the ceiling for a moment as he turned toward her. He wore a black suit and a white collared shit, unbuttoned at the collar.

His green eyes met hers, and his lips twisted upward ever so slightly.

Susan wanted to shriek. To cry out in denial, and flee. But she was rooted to the spot, like her feet were encased in concrete. And though she could breathe, it was only in quick bursts, through her nose. Her jaw was open, dropped wide in astonishment, but she had no power to move it.

It was like she was paralyzed.

The man walked toward her, and she clearly heard each footfall as he came closer, his footsteps making sharp rhythm against the suddenly frantic beating of her heart.

God, he's beautiful, part of Susan's mind cried out, nearly ecstatic at the sight of him.

The other part was gibbering with terror.

He came to a stop in front of her and smiled more fully. "Hello."

"Hi," Susan said, breathlessly. Though her mind rebelled against it, she could not deny what her eyes said to her: this was the man she had been dreaming about, more vividly each night, for the last several weeks.

"Do you come here often?"

He said it with a tone of ironic humor, and Susan responded with an almost instinctual laugh as she played along with the cliched joke.

"Every week," she found herself saying, and still she could not bring herself to move from the spot she had stood upon the moment she first laid eyes on him.

"Well," he said, and he reached out to take the apple she still clutched in her hand away from her with a negligible twist of his wrist. "Why don't we go someplace less routine, shall we?"

Susan's mind cried out to her to resist the incursion. Or at least to see to the basket full of foodstuffs that she was leaving in her wake. But her feet turned her to follow him, and basket be damned, as he led her back out of the grocery store.

He turned left after they exited, and she followed until he came to a stop in front of the parking spots at the edge of the building where a shiny chrome and black motorcycle stool leaning against its kickstand.

The nameless man walked up and threw his leg over the bike, then settled his weight onto it and pushed up enough to relieve the kickstand of its weight. Then he kicked the stand back up and looked at Susan, his mysterious smile still plastered all over his face.

He reached out his hand to her. "Let's go, Susan."

She should have been screamed out the question: how do you know my name? But a flash of insight told her his: Gerald. It was like she'd always known him, somehow. And he'd known her. Without protest, she took his hand, then mounted the bike behind him.

A minute later, they were screaming down the road, headed toward God knows where.

Except that Susan also knew exactly where they were heading.

The drive lasted forever, and it passed in a heartbeat. They swept through the intersections and thoroughfares of the suburbs, then out into the countryside surrounding the metropolitan area until the subdivisions faded into individual houses spaced a broad distance apart. Then the houses fell behind completely as the road rose into rolling hills that presaged a mountain range to come, a hundred miles or so away.

Susan rode without a helmet, arms wrapped around the man from her dreams, and felt a mixture of exhilaration and horror. Exhilaration at her first time on a motorcycle, the speed the man drove, the quick precision that sent thrills through her body unlike any she had never experienced. Horror as she berated herself at her foolishness for willingly going with a stranger to who knows where.

But he's not a stranger, that voice in her head said, and you know where he's taking you.

Sometime into the night, Gerald slowed and turned off onto a narrow two-lane road that shoved its way through an overhanging forest canopy deeper into the wilderness.

The night had fully closed around the land, and beneath the rumble of the motorcycle's engine Susan imagined she could hear the chirping of night insects, the croaking of toads...all the sounds of the forest at night.

They drove on, accelerating again, and then after several minutes of darkness broken only by the illumination of the bike's headlight on the road ahead, they burst out from beneath the canopy and into the open.

The road turned right, hugging the edge of the forest, but to the left was open field.

The man slowed, and as the noise of the engine faded, the sounds of the night grew louder, exactly as Susan had imagined. The air was cool, but moist, and the smell of flowing water and growing things covered the land.

The same way it had in her dreams.

As if in a daze, Susan slipped off the motorcycle, detaching herself from Gerald with a strange reluctance. She stepped back from him and the bike, and watched as he also dismounted. His movements were fluid and efficient, exacting.

He paused for a moment, stooping to open one of the two plastic saddle bags that flanked the bike's rear wheel. He pulled something out from inside, then turned to face her, the smile still locked onto his face.

Susan's eyes lowered to the thing that he held in his hands. It was a quilted blanket.

She didn't have to wonder about it at all; she was certain. The same blanket from her dreams.

Gerald gestured toward the field on the other side of the road, and raised an eyebrow. "Shall we?" Then he set out across the road, apparently confident she would follow.

She did.

She was getting her wits back, and the fuzziness that had been encroaching on her mind since their meeting in Vons was fading, but it was just replaced by a deep curiosity, and beneath it an aching earning. To know. To understand.

And to go.

But...go where?

Susan moved to follow him, and called out, "Who are you?"

He didn't look back at her. "You know my name."

And she did. But... She shook her head. "Yes. But who are you?"

Gerald chuckled, but didn't answer. Instead he ascended the little mound that separated the field from the road, then began pushing himself through the grass and wildflowers that grew to almost knee height beyond.

The entire scene was bathed in blue-white light from the moon, and lesser light from the multitude of stars. But there was not even a hint of a manmade light source. Susan cast about to be sure, almost doing a complete circle. Nothing. Just nature's own illumination.

She glanced up, and saw that the moon was maybe a day away from full. Only a sliver of its western half remained dark.

A bout of nerves crossed over her, and she swallowed. But she couldn't not follow Gerald. So she, too, mounted the mound and stepped into the field.

She found him fifty or sixty yards in, reclined on the quilt blanket, which he had laid out on the ground, trampling grass and wildflower beneath. As she approached, he shifted, boosting himself up onto one elbow to watch her. In the crystal clear moonlight, she saw his smile widen, then his eyes left hers as he looked back up at the moon.

"Have you ever wondered why it calls to you?"

Susan recalled the sharp teeth from her dream, and the nerves she felt a moment ago tried to creep up again. But something forced them down as she looked at him, gazing up into the sky with such a look of devotion on his face.

That was just a dream; not reality. But then, so was he...until he was also real.

Susan shook her head as she sat down onto the edge of the quilt, as far from Gerald as she could be without not being on it. She did not follow his gaze upwards; she kept her eyes on him.

He must have seen her head shake from his peripheral vision, as he lowered his gaze back to her. From the look in his eyes, he had noted the distance she was keeping. But if anything, he looked amused by it.

"I'm not going to harm you, Susan," he said.

She looked askance at him. "How can I be sure of that?"

His eyebrow crooked upward, then he rolled his shoulders in a little shrug. Sitting up more fully, he reached with his left hand and pushed up the sleeve of his suit and shirt on his right arm. "Because we are kin." He extended his arm so that the inside of his right wrist was clearly visible.

Susan gasped.

He had the same scar she did, but on the opposite arm. And looking at it here in the moonlight, the dog's head seemed to be almost three dimensional. And it glowed, seemingly giving off light of its own in response to that of the moon.

Susan looked down at her wrist, and saw that her scar, too, was reacting to the moonlight, the same as his was. She raised her hand for him to see, and he nodded approvingly.

"It is how I found you. How I reached out to you these last weeks. You've grown up, and now it's time to take your place."

Susan shook her head. She was almost thirty. She'd been grown up for a while. And... "Take my place where?"

His smile broadened, and for a second it seemed it was going to do the unnatural face-consuming thing that it had done in her dream. Instead, it halted at its normal, natural breadth, and he pointed upward toward the sky.

Toward the moon.

She did look up now, and it seemed like something was moving up there, on the moon's surface. She couldn't quite make out what, but the patterns of light and shadow had shifted. Were shifting. What -

"What is that?" she said, aloud.

"Your transport," Gerald replied. He had gone back to reclining on the blanket, a peaceful smile on his face. "They first came here when mankind was young. They saw we needed guidance, and picked certain people from the population, to be emissaries. Prophets, if you will."

"Prophets." She knew the look she was giving him was skeptical, but it didn't seem to give him any pause.

"They did not pick from any specific race, or based on status or wealth. Just people of promise, from whatever walk of life, who could help spread the message and guide mankind on the path."

She could see he was completely serious about what he was saying. But it didn't make any sense at all. She didn't recall ever having been chosen, or..

But when she looked back up into the sky, the bit that had been moving around on the moon's surface was larger now. It was certainly detached from the moon's face. And it was growing larger. Getting closer.

Susan felt her jaw drop again. "So... So they're aliens?"

"In a manner of speaking," Gerald replied. "They're from a dimension outside of ours. They were once physical like us, but have evolved to a higher realm, and seek to help us do the same."

"And they just pick people at random." She shook her head. "That doesn't make any sense."

The object, whatever it was, was much closer now. Though it was the same color as the moon, it now completely eclipsed Earth's companion. And it was growing still. A soft humming began to fill the air, organic-sounding, almost like a heartbeat sped up three or four times but kept at its same tone.

"It does," Gerald said, "if you consider that real changes cannot be imposed from above. They must arise spontaneously. So they influence people throughout society, all at once."

"Making us puppets on their strings."

Gerald chuckled. "Nothing so melodramatic as that. They are teachers, not dictators."

The humming was getting louder, and now it seemed the sky itself was parting before the object. The spaceship?

She still couldn't quite make out what it was. It seemed to come in and out of view even as it grew closer and more distinct.

And then it was there, on the ground right in front of her and Gerald. It wasn't like any ship she had ever seen, or ever envisioned. Just a silvery column rising straight up into the sky about thirty feet away.

She jumped to her feet in surprise at its sudden arrival, completely without sound except for that humming, and without even a breath of wind except for what was already blowing.

"Holy shit," she said.

"Indeed," Gerald replied as he got to his feet as well, though more calmly and deliberately than she had.

In the column ahead, a dark rectangle seemed to slide into place from left to right. Like a door opening? Sure enough, a second after the rectangle stopped its motion, pure white light began shining forth from within. Susan could see stairs leading upward, and humanoid figures inside, waiting.

"Well," Gerald said. "They're here, and they've been waiting on you for a long time." He lifted an eyebrow at her. "Don't want to keep them waiting."

Uncertainty reared its head again. Susan chewed on her lip. "I... How do I know it's safe?"

Gerald took her gently by the hand and began leading her forward. He didn't tug at her, but she didn't really resist him either. Despite her uncertainty she found herself walking with him, toward the doorway. "I told you, they only want to help us."

"Have you gone with them?"

Something crossed over Gerald's face for a heartbeat, then he smiled at her, the same beautiful smile she recalled from her dream. "I have. It's like nothing you can imagine."

They were just in front of the door now, and she could see clearly inside. The steps looked to be made of marble, and the being standing just within, waiting for her...

She heard herself drawing in an awed breath, and couldn't blame herself. It was the most beautiful creature she had ever seen. Tall, stately with proud, but not haughty, features that could have been male or female or both. Its long wavy yellow-brown hair flowed past its shoulders. It wore blue-white robes and had its hands clasped in front of where the navel would be on a human. And was looking at her with an expression of love, love that flowed into her from its presence until she felt like she would overflow with it.

All doubt swept away. This was not a creature to fear. It was impossible such a being could do her harm.

Susan moved to step inside, but stopped, looking back at Gerald. "Are you coming as well?"

He shook his head. "I have other tasks to perform. But go. They will take care of you."

Susan smiled and nodded. "Thank you, Gerald." She leaned forward and gave him a little peck on the cheek. Then she stepped into the aliens' craft.

The being within moved to the side and gestured for her to proceed up the stairs. As she mounted the second one, she looked back and saw the doorway sliding shut.

And through it, Gerald sprinting away, like he was being chased. What - ?

As the door closed completely, the light changed. Where before it had been pure white, warm and cleansing, it began to take on a greenish-yellow tint.

Feeling suddenly uneasy, Susan turned to look at the being who had greeted her, and saw that it had changed as well. In the new light, its proud beauty was twisting, becoming somehow unclean-looking.

The humming, which had been filling her ears before, changed tone, becoming discordant, then downright jarring. Like rhythmic metallic screeching.

There were other beings like the first now, closing in from all sides and floating through the space even as the lighting continued to shift, moving from green-yellow toward red.

As she began to get a scent of sulphur in the air, the being who greeted her opened its mouth wide, and she saw the same huge incisors she had seen in Gerald's mouth during her dream.

She heard herself whimpering as she backed away from the thing, but as she looked left and right, the other beings were still there, getting closer.

Her foot came down on the edge of the stairs, and she almost fell. She caught herself, but not before she saw the source of the red light, and the sulfurous smell: raging flames beneath the staircase, some unimaginable distance below here.

She was gibbering now. What was this? This couldn't be happening.

Susan cast about, looking left and right, up and down. But there was no escape. The creatures were everywhere, circling. Eyeing her like meat.

Then they charged her, from all sides at once.

And she screamed.

<hr>

As the portal winked out of existence, Gerald thought he could hear Susan's shriek. The first of many, that would go on for a long, long time.

How long, Gerald didn't know. Time didn't move the same in the beings' dimension as it does in ours. But she would be a long time in the dying. That much he knew for certain.

That was, if she ever actually did.

He sniffed in satisfaction. It used to be more difficult, sweeping up the mark. But these millennial girls were so stupid; they fell for the hope and change fix the world bullshit so easily...

Part of him, a tiny sliver of what had once been his conscience—the stubborn part that refused to die no matter how he worked to sear it away—cried out in sympathy for the girl. He smothered it. Hard. It could have been him in there; would have been him if he hadn't struck the deal he had.

It could still be, if he didn't produce. Better her than him.

It took only a moment to get his mind right, then he went about folding up the quilted blanket.

As he was walking back to his motorcycle, he felt the brand on his wrist pulse. Once. Twice. On the third time, a feeling of warmth and strength flooded through him. He arched upward, going up onto his tiptoes for a moment as he was swept up in ecstasy.

Then it passed, and he went on back to his bike.

After stuffing the quilt back into his saddle bag, he mounted up and started the engine. He took a moment to look at himself in the mirror mounted on his handlebar.

The lines that had been growing on his face had faded, his skin going back to the smoothness of youth. His muscles felt more taught, and his pants looser where the little paunch that had been starting to grow had receded.

He smiled, satisfied at his pay, and maneuvered the bike around to head back to town.

But as he gunned the engine, the little voice in the back of his head whispered to him. Ten years ago, he would have ended up looking twenty three or twenty four. Now, he looked about twenty six. The payments were getting shorter; or he was getting more tolerant of them. What happened when they stopped being effective altogether?

How long did he really have before they finally came for him as well?

It was harder to cast that thought aside than his earlier doubt. But he did it.

Focus on the present. Enjoy eternal youth while you have it. The other is a bridge to cross when the time comes.

But above all, keep doing the job.

And so he sped off into the night, looking for his next mark.

19

WIRE RUNS

The ship rocked, and Karl felt himself hurled to the side.

He clenched his teeth and rolled his shoulders in anticipation of the impact, but still he ended up grunting out a half-shout when he struck the bulkhead across from where he had been working.

The unexpected g-force left as quickly as it came, and he slumped back to the deck, breathing quickly to regain his bearings even as he looked around the room.

He was lying on the wall. Or, the wall as it had been a few moments before. The deck that used to be the floor was a meter and a half to his right and above him, from where he lay. The control panel that he had been working on remained open, though its access hatch was slightly cockeyed, as though the sudden change in gravity vector had thrown it off true.

And why shouldn't it have? It had thrown Karl halfway across the compartment and, from the feel of it, came damn close to dislocating his left shoulder.

Karl grunted and licked his lips, and grimaced at the metallic flavor of blood. He spat, and watched as the mixture of blood and spittle arced up and then sailed down to land on what used to be the athwartships bulkhead next to his temple. Then he cursed.

The battle was going even worse than he'd thought he would.

Karl pushed himself up onto his feet, ignoring the multitude of protests from joints and muscles all over his body. His instincts called out for him to curse the Captain and her idiocy. And boy, he was tempted to do that. But he'd pledged her his loyalty.

So instead, he kicked on the magnetic grips of his boots and, ignoring the pain, he stepped up onto the wall that used to be the floor, and, holding himself erect against the third-g pull down from his right, he stalked back toward the engineering control panel he had been working on before all hell broke loose.

He reached the panel and took hold of the cover. Looking at it, he grunted. It was warped, but not so bad he couldn't force it back into place. Then it would just be a matter of jury-rigging the fasteners back into place, and the thing would be solid. At least for long enough to last through this battle.

An electronic beep, and then the Captain's voice echoed throughout the compartments of the ship.

"Attention all hands." As always, her voice slammed through Karl's defenses, her melodic alto seeming to carry the words against the defenses of his rational mind into the very center of his being, and he felt buoyed by them. "The enemy is retreating. We've taken down one of them, and the other is almost crippled. We are in pursuit. Stand strong. Athena Triumphs."

Karl couldn't hear it through the bulkheads separating himself from the other members of the crew, but he could feel them shouted Huzzahs, fists launched toward whatever passed for the ceiling as the Athena adjusted her flight vector to send her on toward the last of the enemy ships, and victory.

And, with victory, prize money.

But that wasn't Karl's concern. He had to get this panel back online, and fix the local gravitic system.

His shoulder cried out, reminding him of the necessity of his mission. And then the acceleration vector changed again.

He felt pressed into his boots as the engines kicked on full thrust in the direction of the ship's hull, and he was once again standing on the floor as it was designed. He glanced to the side, toward the bulkhead that so recently had been the floor, and that had thwacked his shoulder so strenuously, and scowled.

Then he got back to work.

The panel's cover was twisted, but only slightly. It would be easy enough to get it back into place; he might not even need to use a mallet to do it. But the wiring beneath, that connected the touch pad to the circuitry below, was a shambles. Half of the wire bundle was pulled off its connections on the circuit board.

And, of course, none of the wires had any label tabs connected to them, to tell where they were supposed to go.

"Son of a bitch," Karl said to himself. This was not good at all.

He tabbed the communication patch on his right breast, opening a connection to Sven, the Chief Engineer. A second later, Sven's gruff, gravelly voice came into Karl's ear through his implants.

"What's the status?" Sven asked.

Karl tried not to let his frustration get into his voice as he replied. "Ecologic controls in compartment 16 are shot. Wiring is pulled completely. Don't suppose you've got a wiring diagram?"

"You check the tech manual?"

Karl ground his teeth. Of course he'd check the tech manual. He tapped the fingers on his left hand together, and the manual's pages opened up in the left side of his vision, fed there by his implants. It showed every electrical connection in the panel he was working on.

But it didn't show which wire was which. Or rather, none of the wires in the panel itself had any labels that corresponded to the connection points in the tech manual.

Karl bit back a curse. "Tech manual's no good. People've been working this thing for so long, none of the connections are labelled anymore." He drew a breath. He knew the answer to the question he was about to ask before he asked it. "Don't suppose your folks used wire removal forms?"

Sven's sarcastic laugh was all the answer he needed.

Karl didn't wait for the response. He cut the feed, and stood there, pressed down by the engines' thrust—until the pilot needed to shift his course—and swore up a storm.

Back when he'd been in the Navy, Karl had cursed his Chiefs when they insisted he use wire removal forms every time he did any kind of work inside a panel. It seemed like the ultimate waste of time...until the day he'd had to change out a main engine throttle control, which required removing over two hundred separate connections.

That had taught him the value of knowing what went where; it would have taken him months to put the damn thing back together again, otherwise.

Now, he was looking at the inside of this panel, at maybe half as many connections, all severed. And he felt his spirits sink completely.

This was going to suck.

Karl keyed his comms again. "It's going to take me a while to get this fixed, then. Going to have to trace each wire back to its source." He paused, the added. "Sure would help if you could get the Captain to not maneuver for a while."

Sven snorted in Karl's ear. "Lose this ship, we cut our pay in half. Deal with the course changes."

The comms cut off, and Karl scowled. Easy for Sven to say that. He was up in the bridge, where gravitics weren't compromised. He wouldn't feel each and every little -

As if responding to Karl's thoughts, the gravity vector shifted, and he had to clutch onto the panel's stanchion to avoid losing his feet; and to hell with trusting the magnets on the ends of his boots to save him.

The shift in acceleration eased after a moment, and thrust resumed simply pulling him down into what had been designed to be the deck.

Karl stood there, panting, and swore to himself, and to the empty compartment around him. A big part of him wanted to say to hell with this. It wasn't worth the hassle. He could fix the damn thing after their engagement was done; it wasn't like there were any vital systems in here.

But he set that aside just as quickly as he thought it. Yes, he could put these repairs off. But that would just add to his plate of things to do later, and from the comms so far during Athena's engagement he would have more than enough stuff to repair once they were through this.

Plus, there was always the chance Sven would claim he'd been shirking, and convince the Captain to cut him back from a full share to half, or even a quarter. Which would cast aside a year of toil on the Athena getting to the status he currently had. And not like anyone else on the crew would stand up for him; lower share for one meant greater shares for the rest.

So Karl shoved his misgivings down, tabbed over to the applicable page in the tech manual, and set about tracing the first wire in the control panel back to its source.

Karl lost track of the hours. It would have been easy enough to check how long he'd been going, but what was the point?

The ship had long since stopped its wild maneuvers. And at some point the Captain had come over the announcing circuit, declaring their victory and heaping praise on the crew who had brought them to this great victory—and a greater payday, apparently.

But Karl paid that no mind. Though part of the crew, he never took the Captain's praises over the announcing circuit to heart. He had long ago figured out that she meant the praise for the tactical guys; the ones who fought the ship or, if a boarding was necessary, stormed the other ship to take out the crew and claim her a prize.

Maintenance guys? The ones who kept Athena running and actually made her victories possible?

Nary a word for the likes of them.

But that was ok. Karl had learned the reality of things back in his

Navy days. The techs kept the ships running, the grunts got all the glory. And they did all the dying.

Karl didn't envy them one bit.

Except they never had to trace out unlabelled wires through half a dozen panels to figure out their source, so as to be certain they weren't re-connected to the wrong portion of a circuit board and maybe blow the whole damn thing out, and with it the life support in a quarter of the ship.

The stress of that kind of work ate at a man's liver.

But, Karl considered, at least it wasn't a bullet. So there was that.

He looked down at the wire he had been tracing for the last hour, and at the termination point he'd finally located. Two compartments over from the panel he'd started in, within a minor power panel that was subservient to a networking junction three decks above.

It provided control power to the servo-actuators that allowed the ventilation compressors to turn, sending fresh air from the atmosphere processing equipment in the Auxiliary Machinery Room to this, and six other compartments in the after third of the ship.

He'd been wrong; it wouldn't have just been the space he was in that would have been screwed if he'd not gotten the job done. It would have been much worse than that.

But he'd found it, and ticked that wire off on the form he'd been keeping. Then he made his way back to the original space, and to his damaged panel.

He looked within. Just a couple more wires to go, and then he would be able to re-attach all the leads and get this thing back to running. After he forced the panel back in place, of course. But those last two looked like they'd be easy.

And they were. The first led to a grounding strap. Essential, but easy to follow. The second, to an LED on the panel's lid, to give status indication.

Karl reattached them, then forced the panel closed, and removed the tag he'd placed on the main power supply to the control panel. He felt a small surge of satisfaction when he flipped the breaker closed and the panel lit up. And then a greater one when he felt fresh air begin to move throughout the compartment again.

He took a moment for gather up his tools, closing them in the plastic case he always carried them around in. Then he tapped the panel and started walking back forward.

The mess called. Midrats and some tea. Then his bunk, and what few hours down he could get.

Tomorrow he'd do it all again. And then after the next battle he'd do even more.

But that was for later. For now there was just the satisfaction of a job well done.

And a nice paycheck when next they hit port.

And that was enough.

20

MISS MELODY AND THE KNIGHT GALLANT

Henry ran as hard as he could remember ever running. His heart pounded in his ears and his breaths came in gasps as he pushed himself to greater speed, but above even the cacophony of his racing pulse he could still hear the footfalls behind him, the mocking shouts as his pursuers raced to catch up.

Catch up, and catch *him*. And then...

He fairly leapt off the curb of the sidewalk he was running down, splashing through a puddle leftover from the rain that had fallen two days before, and froze in shock and terror for a second when the blaring of a car horn from his left made him turn, and cringe.

Screeching brakes, and the little blue coup that had been cruising down the four-lane road that split his suburban hometown in two fishtailed as the driver clearly fought to avoid hitting him.

Henry just stared for a second as the car drew nearer...

Then his mind snapped and he hurled himself to the side. His shoulder struck the pavement and he rolled up to a sitting position.

The wind of the car's passing carried the smell of its exhaust to his nostrils as it finally came to a halt ten feet past where he had just been standing. The driver's door flew open and a 30-something guy in jeans and a green collared shirt, bulging with muscles, stepped out, glaring at him.

"What the hell do you think you're - "

But the man's words were lost on Henry. Past the car, he saw his pursuers. Ben Thompson and his two cronies.

They had pulled up short as the scene unfolded. But seeing Henry was ok, one of the toadies nudged Ben, all six feet of muscle and zero brains, and Ben smirked.

Then they started moving again, in Henry's direction.

He pushed himself up to his feet, not bothering to wipe the muddy grime from his shorts and t-shirt, and spun away from them.

Another car had stopped in the second lane, this one much farther away from him. The driver was an older women, who was raising her hands at him through the windshield as if to ask the same thing Mr. Muscles had started to ask.

The lanes going the other way were clear, though, so Henry sprinted across them, and away from Ben and company.

Or he tried to. As he began running, his left ankle shouted in protest, and he winced at the pain flaring up.

Despair welled up. There was no way he would get out of this. He was a dead man.

But that didn't mean he was going to stop at least trying to get away.

He got up onto the sidewalk and turned left, pushing himself to go faster even as his ankle cried out for him to stop. A woman pushing a little kid in a stroller recoiled as he shuffled around her, and sent an exclamation of irritation after him, but a louder shout from one of Ben's cronies blotted that out of Henry's attention.

"We're going to get you!"

There was an intersection up ahead. Main Street. There would be more shops there, more places he could go and maybe get away.

He glanced over his shoulder, and winced. They were coming up fast, moving for all they were worth.

Henry veered right at the intersection. The street ahead was straight, four-lane, and lined with lush trees of some sort or other.

Beneath their spreading limbs were the shops, restaurants, and occasional bar of the Main Street business section.

It was a fun place to walk. When you weren't being chased by the meanest bully in the school and his toadies.

There was a storefront to his immediate right. Henry didn't bother looking at what it was; he pushed the door open and darted inside. Closing the door immediately behind him, he pressed himself against the wall to the door's left and turned his head just enough so he could get a glimpse out the broad windows that looked out onto the street.

His heart was still pumping in his ears, his chest heaving, and he could feel the sweat pouring off his body now that he had stopped moving. He wondered if -

Three figures shot past the window. He didn't need to see more than the shapes of their bodies to recognize them as Ben and company.

He craned his neck a bit farther, and saw that they were continuing down the street, not slowing yet.

Henry smiled for what felt like the first time in years. He'd given them the slip. Now to just go back the way he'd come, and then shoot on over home. Against all odds, he was home free.

Hallelujah!

Henry was just pulling the door open again when a voice from behind brought him up short.

"Can I help you, young man?"

Henry turned around, and finally had a look at the store he had just crashed into.

Or rather, the cafe. The walls were painted yellow, with multicolored flowers painted up near the ceiling and landscape prints hung up in several place. There were four tables, round and white with matching white chairs surrounding them. In the rear was a glass-fronted display case and counter, where he could see pastries and other bits of yumminess on display.

The place exuded warmth and relaxation, and he felt the tension of his flight begin to drain away.

The speaker was behind the counter. She was elderly; probably in her 60s, with gray hair pulled up into a bun. She wore a pastel green apron over a white collared shirt, and pink-rimmed glasses. And she looked at him with a pointed, but not unkind expression.

"Oh," Henry said. "I'm sorry. I was just - " He stopped, not sure how to explain, or whether he even wanted to.

The woman smiled in understanding, and nodded. "Just looking for a place to get away," she said.

Henry shrugged. "I guess." He suddenly felt the tension return; her statement was a bit too on-point. Was he that transparent?

But if the woman disapproved, she didn't show it. Instead she turned and bent over behind her counter for a moment. "The world is full of troubles," she said as she did. "It's good to get away sometimes." She straightened and turned back to him, and Henry felt his eyebrows rise when he saw the stack of chocolate chip cookies on the plate she held.

His mouth watering, he stepped toward her—and the cookies—almost as if his feet were doing it of their own volition.

But when he reached the counter, he got a sinking feeling. "I don't have any money," he said, feeling the fool. He'd left his wallet at home again when he went to school, and here it was going to bite him in the butt.

Again.

But the old woman smiled and held the plate out to him anyway. "First visit is on the house, dear."

Henry blinked. "Really? That's awful nice of you."

She just shrugged. "I'm Miss Melody," she said.

"Henry." He picked up a cookie and sank his teeth into it. And could not hold back a groan of enjoyment as the chocolate chips, still warm and flowing as if straight out of the oven, burst and filled his mouth with deliciousness.

Before he realized it, he had devoured the entire thing and was reaching for another. "Wow, that's about the best cookie I've ever had!"

Miss Melody smiled at him again. "That's what we do here." She gestured to the wall behind the counter, where a sign that Henry hadn't paid attention to earlier read, "Food for the body. Healing for the soul."

"Well, I don't know about the soul healing, but you've sure got the food part down." He stopped midway into raising the next cookie to his lips. "Did you just open up? I hadn't heard of this place before."

Miss Melody shrugged. "We've been around for quite some time."

Henry nodded and finished taking a bite from the cookie. "Well, sorry I hadn't found you sooner," he said. Then he looked down at his hand and was surprised to see it empty.

Another cookie gone already?

Henry took a step back from the counter. If he wasn't careful he'd spend all afternoon just standing here eating cookies, and he needed to get moving. Ben would figure out he'd ducked into a shop soon, and come looking. If he was still here when that happened...

"Well thanks. I need to get going," he said.

Miss Melody just looked at him for a second, then nodded. "Do come again, dear," she said. "Here. Something to remember us by." She turned to her left, where one of those pull-off day calendars was sitting atop the counter. The top page was for today, and it had a cool picture of a knight on a horse, his armor glinting in the sunlight and a red and white banner flying from the end of his lance. Miss Melody took hold and pulled the page off, and for a second golden sparkles seemed to flash in the air around it.

She held the calendar page out to him, and Henry took it. He looked down at the picture, and felt a stirring in his soul. The way the horse's hooves seemed to tear at the ground. The proud way the knight sat erect on his steed. And, somehow, through the slits in his helmet, the stern and determined look in his eyes.

No quarter asked, and none given from this man.

And there, beneath him on the page, was the address to the cafe.

Henry looked back up at Miss Melody and grinned. "Thanks. I'll be sure to come back."

She raised an eyebrow, but said nothing.

Henry turned and walked back toward the door to the street,

feeling her gaze on his back. Did she expect him to do something? He wasn't sure. But he knew he had to get going, before Ben came around again.

He reached out and pulled the door open, and stopped. The calendar page was definitely sparkling now. What was going - ?

He stepped through the door, and the world vanished in a flash of white-gold light.

Henry's foot came down onto soft earth, and he stumbled forward in shock.

This wasn't Main Street. This was -

What was this?

He did a complete circle, and his bafflement grew. All around was wilderness. High rolling hills lay off to the west—or he presumed it was west because the sun was only a small distance above the hills in that direction. Trees, covered in leaves that were turning to the yellow and red of autumn, covered the hills and ran down past him to the north. To the east and south was grassland which descended into a valley many miles away. The glint of reflected sunlight from down there made him think there might be a lake in the distance, but he couldn't be sure.

The air held the cool of autumn and carried the scents of grass and wild growth, and blew in steadily from the south.

"What the hell?" he said to himself, and even his voice sounded strange to his ears.

He did another full circle, but the scene remained the same. Then he pinched himself on the forearm.

It hurt. This wasn't a dream.

But what - ?

The cracking of wood, and guttural words from a gravelly throat, brought Henry's head back around toward the woods, and the bottom fell out of his stomach.

The creature stepping out from beneath the forest canopy was huge. Probably seven feet tall, and two-thirds that across the shoulders, which were muscular to make Arnold Schwarzenegger ashamed. It was like a human, in that it had two legs and two arms, but its skin was green like the Hulk's, and had a protruding jaw from which two tusk-like teeth shoved their way skyward. Its eyes were small, and sunk deep into its face.

It was dressed only in brown leather pants; its extremely muscular chest and torso was bare to the elements. And it was completely bald. It carried a huge double-bladed axe in its right hand, and rested the haft on its shoulder so that the axe blades glinted in the sun from behind its head.

As the creature stepped fully into the clearing, it spied Henry, and stopped.

It studied him, and Henry took a reflexive step backwards, away from it. The thing's beady little eyes traced up and down Henry's body, and a thick purple tongue licked up the inside of its rightmost tusk.

Then it let out a guttural roar and raised its axe over its head.

That could only be a challenge. Henry knew exactly how to respond to it.

He turned and ran.

The creature, whatever it was, bellowed, and Henry imagined he could feel the increased air pressure from the thing's exhalation. He propelled himself to greater speed, and part of his mind questioned why his ankle wasn't hurting.

But he heard the things' footsteps behind him as it ran in pursuit, and those thoughts fled his mind beneath the necessity to run. To hide. Whatever it took—GET AWAY!

He ran downslope, toward the distant lake that he wasn't sure was even there, and the creature followed.

It would get him. He couldn't escape. It would get him and then it would take that axe and -

Ahead, surging through the grass further downslope, he saw movement. He couldn't make out what it was, and he didn't have the time or capacity to figure it out. He was running flat out, faster than he had ever run before.

Another roar from behind, louder now, proved he wasn't fast enough, and he tried to go faster.

His toe hit a rock. Or a dip in the ground. Or something. Whatever it was, he stumbled, pinwheeling his arms to try to avoid falling.

For a second, he thought he would succeed, and keep his feet. Then his ankle turned, and he felt a pang of protest from the joint.

He went down, flat onto his face. He skidded for a couple feet, then came to rest with his cheek dug into the moist soil and his nostrils full of the scent of the earth.

Then another scent eclipsed that. Rank, powerful, and unclean. The stink of a creature that hadn't been bathed in weeks, if not months.

Henry raised his head and looked over his shoulder, and saw the creature that had been chasing him. It was slowing as it approached the spot where Henry was lying, its chest heaving from the exertion of chasing him.

He felt a flash of satisfaction that he had at least caused the creature difficulty in running him down.

That satisfaction faded, because though it clearly had exerted itself, the creature wasn't in any way slowed. It stepped up to him smoothly, and rolled its shoulders, bringing the axe up.

Henry forced himself to roll onto his back, though he wanted nothing more than to bury his face into the dirt and just await the end. But something within him wouldn't let him just cower that way; if nothing else, he'd watch the killing blow come.

The creature's lips twisted, and it took hold on the axe's shaft with both hands. Raising it up over its head, the creature inhaled in preparation for the killing blow.

Henry's heart was thumping hard, the staccato bass thundering in his ears. He was entranced by the curve of the axe blade as it rose, and a flash of sunlight glinted off its killing edge.

And then, suddenly, the creature was falling backwards, a huge shaft of wood piercing its chest as the thunder that Henry now realized wasn't his heart at all came to a halt, and the white horse whose hooves had produced it cantered past the stricken creature.

The green creature turned, one hand leaving the axe and grasping at the lance that pierced it, the other redirecting the axe to try to cleave the horse.

But it was already past, and its rider, a man covered head to toe in gleaming, polished steel, reined it in and turned it with a quick and practiced tug of the reins.

He slipped down from his saddle and drew a sword from the scabbard on his left hip, then strode forward toward the creature that until a second ago had been about to kill Henry.

The creature snarled, then brought its free forearm down onto the lance, snapping it off half a foot out from its chest. It stepped forward to meet the knight.

Henry watched in amazement at the two clashed. Wounded as the green creature was, it still had strength and speed. But the knight had skill and courage...and time. He danced away from one axe cut, then parried a second.

Then a third. And the creature began to slow, its wound beginning to take its toll.

Finally, it swung just a hair too slowly, and the knight stepped beneath the cut and ran his sword into the creature's body, all the way to the hilt.

The two stood staring at each other for a long moment, then the creature slumped, its knees giving out beneath its bulk. It slid to the ground, and the knight let it pull itself free from his blade as it went.

Its last breath escaped its lungs in a sigh, and then it lay still at the knight's feet.

"Holy shit," was all Henry could think to say.

The knight bowed his head for a moment, and Henry heard mumbled words that he couldn't quite make out. Then the knight straightened and turned toward Henry. He pushed the face mask of his helmet upwards, revealing a round almost boyish face framed by a black beard, and blue eyes that twinkled in the sunlight.

"Are you well, lad?" the knight asked, in a deep baritone.

Nodding slowly, Henry pushed himself up to his feet and brushed his hands off. "Thank you for..." He trailed off, but gestured at the fallen creature.

The knight sniffed and looked back down at it. "Good for you that I was coming this way. A full grown Orc is more than a match for most grown and trained men." He paused, and something strange crossed his face briefly. Then he looked back at Henry and extended his hand. "I am Gabriel, of Montesque."

Henry accepted the shake and had to hold back at wince at the vice-like pressure of the man's grip. "Henry," he said, feeling the lack of title distinctly.

Gabriel released Henry's hand and nodded. "Well, Henry. Where are you bound?"

That was a good question. Henry turned his head left and right, and again the countryside was the same unfamiliar terrain as before. "I'm not sure," he said, lamely. "I don't know this place."

Gabriel looked at him in silence for a long several seconds. Then he grunted and turned back toward his horse. "In that case, come with me. I will see you to civilization, and a comfortable bed at least."

Gabriel practically vaulted up into his saddle, then walked his horse over to where Henry still stood. He reached down, offering Henry a hand up. "Or did you have a better plan?"

Henry wasn't a rocket scientist, but even he could see his alternatives were severely limited. He took the knight's hand and allowed himself to be boosted up behind Gabriel on the horse's back. Then he held tight as Gabriel kicked the horse's flanks, and they sped off downslope toward the lake that Henry had glimpsed before.

The horse moved quickly, and Henry felt every pulse of the animal's muscles. Every bounce over uneven terrain.

He'd never even seen a horse in real life before, let alone ridden on one. Very quickly, his legs began to tire, and he had a good idea he'd understand what they meant by "saddle sore" before much longer.

"How came you out here, lad?" Gabriel asked from in front of him.

How to answer that question? Or rather, how to answer without coming off as a complete lunatic?

Henry wasn't so certain he hadn't gone insane, actually. How else to explain going from the inside of a pleasant cafe to...this...in the span of a step?

"I, uh," he said, then paused, unsure how to proceed. Finally, he blurted out the first thing that came to mind. "I was out for a walk and got turned around. Then I saw that thing and," he swallowed back a sudden sense of shame, "I ran."

Gabriel nodded. "There is no shame in running from such a beast as that," he said, almost as if knowing Henry's thoughts. "Especially when one is unarmed."

Henry found himself nodding in agreement. Yeah. No shame. No shame at all.

He was beginning to feel a bit better about himself. Then Gabriel spoke again.

"But neither is there honor in it." The knight shifted on the saddle, and Henry had the notion he was turning around to look at him, as much as was possible in that armor, anyway.

Henry didn't respond; there was nothing he could say to that.

They continued down toward the lake, which was beginning to become clearly visible now as the horse burned up the miles from where Henry had initially arrived. It was wide, at least a couple miles across, and it stretched out to the horizon before its far edge could be seen.

So maybe it wasn't a lake after all, but a bay.

But did it really matter?

"Where are we going?" Henry asked.

"To my castle," said Gabriel. "There is no safer place in all the realm, and none more pleasant."

Well, that sounded like a good idea. If -

From the grass in front of them rose three shapes. They were tall, and muscled. Henry had just enough time to notice their skins were green before the leftmost of them let fly the bow he carried, whose string he had drawn back to his ear.

The arrow streaked faster than Henry could see, and then the horse was rearing, screaming out a nicker of pain as the shaft struck home.

Henry lost his grip and flew from his perch behind the knight. He struck ground on the same shoulder that had hit the street earlier, then he rolled to a stop, flat on his back.

Somewhere behind him, he heard thrashing as the horse flailed around on the ground. Then he heard Gabriel's baritone voice swearing mightily.

And then came the roars of the orcs, as the three of them charged.

Henry pushed himself up to a sitting position and turned around to look at what was going on.

The horse lay on its side, thrashing in the grass as the knight fought push himself away. It looked like his leg was pinned beneath the horse's torso. There was no way he'd be able to fight, immobile as he was.

Henry looked up from him toward the charging orcs. The one with the bow was hanging back, but the other two were running toward them full out. Both had battle axes, though they were smaller than the huge axe of the orc Henry had met earlier.

Still, though they were smaller, they would be plenty to finish the knight off—and Henry as well—with the knight pinned as he was.

Gabriel knew that for truth; it was plain in his eyes when he turned his head to lock gazes with Henry.

"Hold them off, lad," he said. And he tossed his sword over toward Henry.

It landed in the grass a few feet away from him, the setting sun reflecting off the sword's ruby pommel stone and seeming to ignite a fire within the stone's depths.

Henry ran his tongue through a mouth that had gone dry from fear. He looked from the sword to the knight...and then to the orcs.

They were maybe twenty yards away; they'd be on Gabriel in seconds unless Henry did something—NOW—to stop them.

And if they got Gabriel, they'd surely get Henry next. He knew without question he could not escape them even if he turned to run right that second.

So he got to his feet, bent over, and picked up the sword.

It was surprisingly light.

Heavier than he was used to, and he had no idea what to even do with it. But still, it was lighter than he thought it would be.

That was some comfort, at least. A little.

The orcs were ten yards away now, running full out toward them. Gabriel's leg was still stuck beneath the horse from just below his knee, though thankfully the horse's thrashing was growing less.

Or maybe not thankfully, considering -

Five yards, and no time to think on that. Henry took hold of the sword with both hands and stepped forward to put himself between the orcs and the fallen knight.

The first of the orcs swung its axe. Henry clearly saw the razor-sharp edge cutting through the air toward his neck.

Instinctively, he ducked, and he felt as much as heard the killing metal pass overtop him.

He had the sword, but no idea what to do with it. But it had an edge, so he tried cutting upwards.

The orc's roar become a yelp as Henry felt a touch of resistance to the swing, and then black fluid spewed out from the orc's underarm where he had somehow managed to score a hit.

Henry stood staring, dumbfounded, as the orc backpedalled away from him, its free hand going to clutch at the wound.

Had he done that???

And then the other orc was on him, its axe blade arcing downward toward his shoulder.

He jumped to the side, and the axe embedded itself into the ground with a solid-sounding thud. The creature pulled upward on the axe's haft, then grunted when it would not come free.

No time to stop now. Henry advanced, and thrust.

But the orc released its hold on the axe and leapt backward, the tip of Henry's sword just coming short of its ribcage before its feet struck the ground and it backed away further.

"Holy crap," Henry said. He'd somehow managed to survive their initial charge. If he could -

A hissing sound caused him to duck, and he felt he air move over his head as the third orc's arrow just barely missed him.

And then the orc's shoulder struck his side, and he went tumbling to the ground beneath the beast's bulk.

Henry's breath left his body, and he saw stars. Then his vision cleared, and he wished that was all he could see.

The orc was on top of him, its face just inches from his. It breathed out hot against his face, and Henry smelled rancid meat and something worse.

The beast's lips drew back, revealing smaller fangs among its upper teeth, a counterpoint to those two great tusks. It reared upwards, and Henry all but felt the headbutt coming.

Instead, the orc stiffened, then fell over onto its side, black blood flowing out from its torso to cover Henry.

He blinked, uncomprehendingly, at the axe blade protruding from the dead orc's torso, then he traced the axe's handle up to the armored form of Gabriel.

In a rush, Henry recognized the axe as the one the orc had lost into the ground.

Gabriel winked at him, then pulled the axe free from the corpse with much more ease. He turned around, and caught the other orc's axe on his steel-encased forearm.

If the blow caused him injury, he didn't show it. He just chopped the axe into the orc's guts.

It dropped with a bellow, and Gabriel charged away.

Henry pushed himself to his feet and saw the orc bowman nocking an arrow. But Gabriel was running hard toward it, and even he saw that by the time the orc was ready to fire again, Gabriel would be on it. It tried all the same, and got its shot off.

If it had struck him straight on, it might had penetrated Gabriel's armor. As it was, the arrow just nicked off the pauldron on Gabriel's left shoulder.

Then he was on the orc, and it fell moments later.

Henry watched in something like awe as Gabriel walked back to him. The knight had the black blood of three orcs on him, yet somehow his armor seemed to shine in the waning sunlight, like a beacon in the encroaching darkness.

When he came to stand in front of Henry, Gabriel inclined his head to him.

"Thank you, lad. If not for your bravery, we both would have fallen this day."

Henry, embarrassed, looked away, and made a dismissive gesture with his left hand. "I'm sure you could have handled it."

But when he looked back up at the knight, Gabriel had a deadly serious expression on his face. Their eyes met, and Henry knew he had meant every word. A warm feeling flowed out from his belly to every corner of his body, and he returned the knight's initial nod.

Apparently satisfied, Gabriel turned and looked at his horse. Its twitching had stopped; the beast was clearly dead. Gabriel let out a sigh.

"I would have you feast with me in my castle tonight," he said. "But without my steed..." He shook his head and looked back at Henry with a regretful expression. "I have no way to get you there before nightfall."

"Oh." Henry glanced around, and saw that the knight was correct. Already, the western sky was red with sunset. And was that the first star of night off to the east?

Gabriel held out his hand toward Henry. "Instead of a feast, know that you will always be welcome in my realm, Henry."

"Thanks." Henry accepted the knight's hand, and again was impressed by the man's grip.

"Fare thee well," Gabriel said.

And then the world exploded in golden white light.

Henry took a step forward...and found himself back in the cafe, facing the counter and Miss Melody behind it.

He blinked, unable to comprehend what he was seeing.

Part of him had expected it the second the light flashed into his eyes. But still...

He shook his head. "What was that? What - ?" He stopped, flummoxed. Had it been real?

Miss Melody put on a warm, knowing smile. "Exactly what you needed, dear," she said, and gestured toward the sign on the wall behind her.

Henry followed her gesture to the words. "Food for the body. Healing for the soul."

Healing for the soul.

Even in his confused state, he still felt the pride of accomplishment from fending off the orcs. He hadn't vanquished them. But he had given Gabriel the time he needed to free himself, so he could take care of business. As Gabriel had said; if not for him, both of them would food for the orcs' cook fires tonight.

That feeling hadn't gone away, and looking down from the sign to Miss Melody, Henry thought it never would.

Her smile grew a tad larger, and he found himself returning it. "Thank you," he said.

"My pleasure, dear. Now, you'd best be getting home. You've got important things to attend to."

Henry supposed she was right. But still... "How late are you open?"

"Come back any time, if you have need," she said, her eyebrows lifting.

Henry looked down at the calendar page that was still clutched in his left hand. There at the bottom, instead of the cafe's street address, was written, "Located wherever souls have need."

He looked back up at her, and she made a shoo'ing gesture with her hand.

Bemused, he turned and opened the door.

He was almost surprised when he emerged onto Main Street,

though he shouldn't have been. The door swung shut behind him, and he glanced back.

And felt his jaw drop open in shock.

That wasn't a cafe. It was a shoe shop. What - ?

"Well. Look at what we have here."

The voice, boyish but trying to sound manly and tough, came from Henry's left.

He turned, and sure enough there was Ben. Ben, and his two cronies. They were staring at him the way a cat stares at a mouse it's about to pounce upon.

"Thought you could get away from us, huh?" said the toady to Ben's right. "You thought wrong."

Henry felt a surge of fear, and the urge to flee. He glanced over his shoulder, and saw the sidewalk was empty; he'd have all the room he needed to make a dash for it.

The sound of movement brought his eyes back to front, and he saw Ben had taken a step toward him. The bully wore a confident smirk on his face that said he was going to enjoy pounding Henry's face into pulp.

He was big. He was strong.

But he wasn't nearly as big as an orc.

Henry took a deep breath, and set his jaw. Clenching his fists at his side, he stepped forward, to make his stand.

Ben's smirk faded, replaced by uncertainty.

And then fear.

21

LOST CREDIT

Raedrick Baletier looked up from the parchment he was reading as the door to the Constabulary swung open, admitting midday sunlight that brightened the place more than the lamps hanging on either side of the barred wrought iron doorway leading back from the front office to the cell block ever did. His eyes lingered for a second on the empty desk across the room from his own, adjacent to a small wood stove that would keep the office at least passingly pleasant in the winter. A rack of unstrung bows hung on the wall behind the desk, matching a brace of swords on the wall behind Raedrick's. But the man who would normally balance out with him was gone.

The new arrival finished stepping inside, and Raedrick focused in on him.

The man was short and stocky, not quite fat, and had a well-combed swath of black hair atop his round face. He wore a green tunic cinched about his waist by a brown leather belt, beige leggings that were tight to his thighs and calves, and ankle-high leather boots. Raedrick recognized him as one of the fellows who worked at Holb's tavern, on the west side of Lydelton past the last of the docks that put into Lake Glimmermere. But he had never got the man's name before.

The newcomer also looked at the empty desk for a second before turning to regard Raedrick fully.

"Morning Constable," he said as the door swung shut, the latch clicking into place behind him. He made a little gesture with his left hand toward the empty desk. "Any word from the Deputy?"

Raedrick set the parchment down onto his desk and leaned back against the carved pine of his chair, the same wood as the desk was made from, and really the entire building. He shook his head. "Julian's not my Deputy. We're equal partners."

The man sniffed, and shrugged. "You say so. He on his way back yet?"

Raedrick had been wondering that very thing for a month now. Julian had left on a journey with Melanie Klemins and Jared Tolburt three months ago, on a quest for magical treasure that shouldn't have taken as long as it already had. And he'd had a difficult time holding down duties as Constable without Julian at his side.

A town of about a thousand adults, in a remote mountain vale weeks away from the closest city, Lydelton was never particularly troublesome. But every now and then a member of a trading caravan would get into a tussle with a local. Or one of the outlying farmsteads would have issues with its neighbor. And then the Mayor wanted his regular reports.

It wasn't a lot of work, most times. But it was never simple or quick to deal with, and it was sometimes tiresome. And with his son —or daughter, but a man can hope—due to arrive any time now, Raedrick was feeling the lack of help.

He returned the man's shrug. "No word, but I expect it won't be much longer." He drew in a breath. "Anyway, what can I do for you, goodman?"

The fellow, though, went back to looking at Julian's empty desk, and frowned.

"Goodman?"

The fellow looked back at Raedrick and smiled apologetically.

"Lemmy," he said. "Guess we never did make acquaintance, did we?" He shrugged. "Mostly I come to Julian, seeing as you and Holb don't get along."

Raedrick bristled at that for a moment, but then had to admit Lemmy had a point. He and Holb *had* gotten off on the wrong foot, back when Raedrick and Julian first came to town and took over as Constables of Lydelton, and the rest of Glimmer Vale as well. In fact, Holb had thrown Raedrick out of his tavern—almost literally— during their first meeting. But after that initial misunderstanding they'd been cordial to each other, at least.

All the same he could understand why Holb, and his men, would choose to work with Julian instead of him.

That didn't mean he had to like it.

He managed to hold back a sigh and gave Lemmy a level look. "What seems to be the problem?"

Another quick glance at the empty desk, and then Lemmy gave a quick shake of his head before replying. "Holb's got some regulars who he takes special care of. Guys who don't always have the money for a night's drinks. He extends a credit until they get paid again, and usually they make good. But - "

"But someone didn't," Raedrick finished for him.

Lemmy nodded.

"This has happened before?"

"Every now and then. Most times Holb gives 'em a reminder and it's all good. But once or twice we had to get the Dep - " He stopped and cleared his throat. "Your partner to make them live up to their word."

Raedrick felt his frown pulling at the scar on his chin. He wore a goatee now to conceal it, but he still felt it sometimes. Like now. "Who has reneged this time?"

"Stu Marly. He works the fishing boats. Payday was two days ago, and nothing. Holb sent me over to roust him this morning, and he slammed the door in my face."

"So now it's a matter for the law." Raedrick sighed and looked down at the parchment he had discarded. It was the report he was just finishing up for the Mayor, detailing his activities for the last month, and statistics on the various goings-on in town for the same period. It almost was more appealing than this squabble.

But, that was the job, most of the time. Petty disputes. It sure beat the alternative of fire and battle and things that threatened to bring Lydelton, and with it the entirety of Glimmer Vale, down to ruin. And there sure had been enough of those in the past year and a half.

He stood, the legs of his chair scraping across the polished planks of the Constabulary's floor. "I'll take care of it."

Lemmy bobbed his head. "Thanks, Constable."

Raedrick had dealt with Horace, the head of the Fishing Guild, a number of times over the course of his tenure as Constable. An older man, with a fully-grey head of hair and beard, who always wore a grey cloak and whose gruff demeanor only partially concealed a charitable heart, Horace had become quick friends with Julian and when he and Raedrick first rode into town.

Raedrick's relationship with him had always only been professional. And he had found Horace to be a forthright and determined fellow. If sometimes headstrong.

"I've warned Stu about his drinking," Horace said as he clumped along Lydelton's main street beside Raedrick.

The Constable had sought Horace out first thing after leaving Lemmy. For one thing, he didn't know Stu at all, not even to look at him, let alone where he lived. For another thing, as a fishing man he looked up to Horace; they all did. Horace wasn't their boss, exactly. All the fishing men in Lydelton worked for the Covington brothers. But as head of the Guild Horace had pull with the brothers, and had negotiated a number of beneficial arrangements on behalf on the workers under his care. And he didn't hesitate to give them what for where the safety or health of his boys were concerned.

So there wasn't a fishing man in the town who wouldn't bend over backward for him.

In fact, several had done much more than that. When Raedrick and Julian first came to town and helped Lydelton repel a large group of brigands, at Horace's prompting a fair number of the fishing men had volunteered for martial training and then stood beside the two newcomers in battle against their town's foe.

It was always good to have Horace on your side, especially when dealing with the fishing men.

Raedrick looked at him sidelong as they followed the street northwest through town. "He hits it hard?"

Horace nodded. "Too hard, some days. Especially since Marta passed." He gestured to the right side of the intersection ahead, to the street that led to Bigsbe's Boarding House.

Turning in that direction, Raedrick as always felt the change beneath his feet, and fought back a minor bout of irritation.

Main Street was the only paved road in Lydelton; the others were packed earth that more often than not were muddy messes or worse, in the winter, treacherous ice sheets. He'd spoken with the Mayor about completing the project to pave the remaining streets in the town several times, and the answer was always the same: the reason Lydelton had stopped the project in the first place still held. Not enough money, and it required too much time away from the tasks that actually kept the town alive. Namely, fishing in Lake Glimmermere.

Which was understandable. But it still rankled, sometimes.

But that was neither here nor there right this moment. "Marta was his wife?"

Horace shook his head. "No, Sabine passed ten years ago. Marta was their daughter. Caught consumption the winter before you and Julian got to town."

Raedrick winced. He had always known that was a terrible blow to endure. But now, with his first child coming so soon... He couldn't imagine having to live through that.

"Poor guy."

Horace nodded. "One of the best men in the boats. But *out of* 'em..." He left off the rest of his sentence and shook his head again, this time in commiseration from the pitying expression on his face.

The two men walked in silence the rest of the two blocks until they reached Bigsbe's Boarding House.

It was a long, broad building, two stories tall with the sharply-angled tiled roofs that all of Lydelton had—the better to let snow fall off it during the winter. It took up most of block itself, and was well-kept.

Raedrick led the way through the front entrance and into the office to the left of the building's common room, where Madaleen Bigsbe or her attendants held court behind a neatly-arranged wooden desk that faced the office's door.

The attendant today was not Madaleen but Tami, a young girl just recently reached maturity who still resided with her parents while she got herself onto her feet as an adult. She was almost pretty, and brown-haired with hazel eyes. But her smile made up for whatever deficiencies her bone structure had, turning her face into a pleasant ray of sunshine in the otherwise dimly-lit office.

She stood from her chair and bobbed a curtsy when she saw Raedrick, the visible portion of her brown and white dress bunching slightly as she moved. "G'day Constable," she said. "How fairs Lani?"

Raedrick stopped, mention of his wife bringing a grin to his face. "Every day is a trial for her," he said. "And I thank the gods I don't have to endure it."

Tami giggled slightly, the same way all the young women did when Raedrick made that joke. It was only half a joke; he wasn't at all sure how he'd cope with the trials of pregnancy, let alone the pains of childbirth. But women were made for it, and knew in their bones how to cope. And they thought themselves superior to men because of it.

The fact that every woman batted their eyelashes when he made the statement proved it.

Oh well, whatever kept them happy.

"We're here to see Stu," Horace said, and Tami's smile faded. She glanced between the two of them and nodded, then gestured toward the rear of the common room, where the set of darkly-stained stairs leading to the boarding rooms on the building's second floor lay.

Tami said, "Upstairs and to the right. Last door on the left," and Horace nodded.

"Thanks," he said, but Raedrick was sure he didn't need the directions. There was no way Horace didn't know exactly where a member of his Guild lived.

They ascended the stairs and turned right. The corridor had three pairs of matched doors, evenly spaced all the way down to the end. Horace stopped at the last door on the left, and knocked.

No answer after a long several seconds.

Horace knocked again. Louder this time, with the heel of his fist.

Still nothing.

Horace turned to meet Raedrick's gaze, and his eyebrows rose slightly.

"He's not at work right?" Raedrick asked.

Horace shook his head. "He's got the evening shift. But he should be up by now."

"Try again."

More pounding, and still nothing.

Raedrick looked down the corridor, past the remaining pairs of doors to where the stairs from the lower level led back downstairs. "Wait here," he said, then he hurried back downstairs and into the office, where Tami was doing sums behind her desk.

She jerked to attention when he stopped in front of her and rose to her full height. She was remarkably tall. Then she bobbed a curtsy yet again.

No time for this. Raedrick said, "Has Stu departed at all today?"

Tami slowed as she rose from her curtsy, her eyebrow rising. "I haven't seen him."

"When did you come on duty?"

She glanced toward the front door, and shrugged. "Six bells this morning."

Raedrick did some quick sums in his head. That was almost five hours ago. If Stu had been on the evening shift on the boats, he would have gotten off the boat in the dead of the night, since the fish only bit at sunset and sunrise. A few hours for a later dinner and some drinking....there was no way he wasn't still here if he had come home before Tami had come on duty. And if he hadn't come home since she had...

Well, there was no chance of that, unless he was face down in the gutter somewhere. But Raedrick would have heard of his being in that condition already. The largest use he and Julian put to the cell block was for local drunks who'd passed out somewhere, so they could have a safe place to sleep it off.

Which meant Stu had to be in his room.

"Thank you Tami," Raedrick said. "Give Madaleen my apologies."

He turned and hurried back to the corridor toward Stu's room, Tami's "What?" echoing behind him, unanswered.

Horace was still standing in front of the door, pacing impatiently. He looked up as Raedrick approached, eyes narrowed in concern.

"Break it down," Raedrick ordered.

Horace's eyes widened, then he turned and drove his heel against the door, at the level of its latch.

It sprang open inward, and the older man stumbled forward out of Raedrick's view.

He heard Horace curse softly, then cry out in shock. Then...

"Oh gods! Help, Raedrick!"

Raedrick sprinted the last few yards to the door and leapt inside.

The room was small, as he knew all the rooms at Bigsbe's to be. A bed just large enough for one on the right hand wall. A wash basin and chamber pot at its head. A small bureau on the other side of the room. A single window, with limp grey drapes that were drawn to blot out the view of the street beyond.

And in the middle stood Horace. His arms were braced around the waist of a man Raedrick didn't recognize. But he wore the same grey cloak that Horace always did—the mark of a fishing man. Beneath the cloak, his shirt was yellow and his leggings green. He hung limply, his arms and legs dangling and his head lolling forward.

A rope was tied off around the rafter above his head, the other end looped around Stu's neck.

As Raedrick drew up, shocked, Stu's arms and legs spasmed weakly. Horace was pushing upward on his body, to try to relieve the pressure on his neck. But he was very nearly gone.

Raedrick sprang forward onto the bed and pulled his knife from its sheath on his belt. He reached up and began sawing at the rope, desperate terror lending extra speed to his strokes.

Raedrick squared his shoulders and stepped into Holb's Tavern.

It wasn't really a building. Or, there was a building there. It stretched back from the street a ways until a twenty foot section of the red-painted building's wall had been cut away. In its place, Holb had installed a running countertop where he served drinks. He had erected a wooden awning above the bar that ran out a good thirty feet from the side of the building. Beneath that awning were a number of tables where Holb's customers could sit and drink. And eat, if they brought it with them. Holb did not serve food.

Raedrick had only come here a few times, and only then for business. His experience the first time he'd come through still weighed on him.

He hoped Holb's wife had gotten over the insult. But he hadn't even known it would *be* an insult...

Holb himself was a tall fellow with shoulders that put a giant to shame. Despite his thick black beard, he kept his head bald, whether because he preferred shaving it that way or because his hair had fled from his temper Raedrick didn't know for sure. He had a scar that ran from his left eyebrow to his left ear, which had a little notch cut out of it, and he had dark brown eyes that shown with intelligence. And ill humor.

He held court behind the bar in his stained white apron, and cast a distrustful gaze upon Raedrick as he weaved his way through the tables. Even at this afternoon hour, Holb had plenty of customers.

"I found Stu," Raedrick said, without preamble, and Holb's eyebrow lifted, voicing a question without asking it.

"He tried to hang himself. He's over at the Healing Circle. Master Sebastini is tending to him."

Holb's jaw dropped open, shock followed by confusion followed by remorse crossing over his face in half a heartbeat before he got himself back under control.

"Ya get my money?" he said.

Raedrick scowled. "That's all you're worried about? His bar tab?"

Holb shrugged. "Rest of it's not my business."

Raedrick had to force himself to not clench his fists. "You know about his wife and daughter."

Holb nodded.

"Do you know what today is?"

Hold just looked at him with a blank expression.

Raedrick ground his teeth for a moment before continuing. "Today is his daughter's naming day. She would have reached her ascendancy this year."

Still nothing from the bartender.

"He's been coming here for years. You had to know."

"What's your point, Constable?" Hold said.

"How much did you let him drink last night?"

"His usual."

"And the night before that?"

"The same."

Raedrick felt that scar tugging at his chin again, and knew he was scowling too hard. But he didn't care. "I ought to arrest you for complicity in his death."

Holb snorted. "You already said he ain't dead. Don't play games with me Constable. We both know how that will turn out."

That took a bit of the wind from Raedrick's sails. Though it pained him to remember, Holb had an embarrassingly easy time throwing him out of the bar the first time. Raedrick had no desire to repeat that incident. And unless he was willing to draw steel, he suspected he would, if it came to blows.

And maybe even if he did draw steel.

"You knew he was having problems. And you let him drown himself in beer every chance he got. Even extended credit to him. I know what he owed you. A fishing man couldn't pay that back in a year on his wages, not unless he went without food and shelter." Raedrick leaned forward. "What were you doing with him?"

Holb stopping moving. He just looked at Raedrick without words for a long moment. Then he shrugged.

Raedrick let out a disgusted snort. Fishing around inside his jacket, he pulled out a sack. It jingled as he held it up in front of the bar. And it ought to; he'd filled it with funds from the Constabulary's discretionary fund.

Raedrick tossed the pouch onto the bar, and it landed with a tinkling thunk. Holb's eyes twitched down toward it for the shortest of instants before returning back to Raedrick's. His left eyebrow moved upward slightly.

"That should even things up," Raedrick said. "But Stu never drinks here again."

Holb's right eyebrow rose to join the left.

"Master Sebastini thinks he will pull through, and he's putting Stu on a regime to purge him of his need for drink. But for that to work he has to abstain." He leaned toward Holb, locking stares with the big bartender. "I hear he's had even a single drink here, there will be problems."

Holb matched his gaze, and they stared into each other's eyes for what felt like a long time. Finally, after a small eternity, the bartender broke the connection, and reached down to pick up the pouch of coins. He tossed it in his hand, feeling the weight, then nodded. Though he was frowning slightly something about his carriage suggested satisfaction to Raedrick.

"However you want it, Constable," Holb said.

"Good."

With that, Raedrick turned and walked away from Holb's Tavern.

His report to the Mayor technically didn't have to include the information on the incident with Stu. It could go in the next month's report, and he wouldn't have to change a thing that he'd already written.

But Raedrick felt strongly that he needed to include it now. He might forget some detail, or forget the incident entirely. And that wouldn't be right. Not for Stu, not for his lost wife and daughter, not for Holb. And not for himself.

As Raedrick put pen to parchment on his desktop again, he reflected that he might have been too harsh with Holb. Yes, Holb knew what had happened with Stu's family. But that didn't mean his extending credit to the man was a malicious act. Maybe that was the only way he knew to help, or to at least show a bit of kindness to the man he'd known for years.

That was possible.

But it was certain that the outstanding debt had allowed Holb to gain some leverage over Stu. To do what, Raedrick had no idea.

Maybe nothing. Or maybe something. Something important.

Or not.

Raedrick shook his head at his flights of fancy, and wrote on, determined not to include those flights of fancy in his report. Just the facts, and only the facts. And the fact was that Stu was going to be fine. And now that he couldn't drink from Holb's tavern anymore, maybe he could become better than fine.

Maybe he'd get his life back together and going in a good path from now on.

Raedrick was beginning to smile a satisfied smile when it occurred to him that Holb's wasn't the only place in town Stu could get drink. He could just as easily go to -

The door latch lifted and the door to the outside swung inward. A figure stepped awkwardly in, and Raedrick saw long blond hair, well-formed breasts beneath a blue blouse and a white apron...

And a bulging belly, with baby about come any time now.

"Lani!" He bounded to his feet, coming around the desk before his wife could close the door behind herself. "Are you well?"

She gave him a level look. "Of course I'm well. Figured you'd be hungry; it's past dinner."

Lani extended her hands, and Raedrick blinked to realize he had completely missed the tray she was holding in her hands. He had focused in on her belly, and then up on her sweet face, so completely... But how could he have missed the scents rising from the plate atop the tray?

Fried fish, and broiled potatoes, and leeks, and...

His stomach growled, but Raedrick forced himself to dignity, accepting the tray quickly but steadily and turning to place it atop his desk. Then he paused to inhale the vapors rising from the meal.

"Your mother's outdone herself today," he said.

Lani snorted. "You say that every day."

He turned back to her and grinned. "It's true every day. Have you eaten?"

She nodded, but, rubbing her baby bump, she said, "But I may share of bit of yours if you don't mind."

He just grinned at her.

Along the wall adjacent to the front door were several chairs for guests, or witnesses. He moved one over in front of his desk and waited for her to sit down, then he took his own seat behind the desk.

They dug in.

After the initial couple minutes of biting and chewing, Lani said, "I heard about Stu."

Raedrick stopped in mid-chew, the nodded. Swallowing quickly, he said, "I was going to come talk to you and Molli about that. Ravi Sebastini is treating him, but once he's done he cannot have drink any more. Holb's already agreed not to let him have anything. You need to make sure he doesn't partake from The Oarlock."

Lani nodded. "Mother and I already talked about it, soon as we heard. He'll get no drink from us." She paused, then added. "Poor man."

Raedrick nodded, his eyes going downward again toward the bump in Lani's belly. "I can't imagine going through what he did."

She pressed her hand to her belly and nodded. "It's something we should have addressed a long time ago. But he seemed to take it all so well. And then..." She trailed off, and shook her head. "If there's one thing I love about this place, is that we all come together when its needed. We all help each other. Now that we really know, we'll make sure Stu gets back to healthy again."

Raedrick nodded. He had seen that instinct himself, back when he'd first visited Glimmer Vale as a child, and then again when he and Julian returned to find the town under siege by Isenholf's brigands. The sense of community, that they were all in it together, was striking. And he had seen it again several times since then.

So as he finished dinner with his wife, though he continued feeling pity for Stu, he didn't lack hope for the man. He would have a better future. They would all see to that.

And that would make a better future for them all.

22

HUNTING FOR GAME

George opened up the trunk of his blue Ford Focus and hefted a brown canvas duffle bag out. He shifted his torso, slinging the duffle over his left shoulder, and grunted softly at the weight of the bag's contents. He'd thrown that shoulder out once about five years earlier while weight lifting, and sometimes he had flare-ups from it. He hadn't had one in a while...until just this moment.

Wasn't that just great.

George gritted his teeth and slammed the trunk shut, then hit the key fob to lock the car up and turned away.

He was parked off of a two-lane country road that had departed from the main highway three miles back the way he'd come. The road had twisted and turned through rolling hills covered with lush green forest until he'd reached this spot, and he'd pulled off behind a billboard sign for a roadhouse bar and grill ten miles farther on.

Stepping out from behind the billboard, he glanced left and right; no one was around. That was good. He'd be out in his stand for several hours, probably. It was his secret place, and he didn't want anyone to find where it was, or know that he was even here.

That could be bad, and mess up his afternoon. And more.

He also had three grand in cash stashed in the cardboard box that had ridden in the trunk with the duffle. Better not to risk losing that if someone broke into the car, or stole it.

Hence, the concealed parking job.

He'd been out of the car's air conditioning for less than a minute, but already sweat was beginning to trickle down his back from the mid-summer heat and the humidity that made the air feel thick and smell of moisture. Overhead, puffy white clouds moved briskly across the sky from west to east, in the direction he had to walk, and he watched one go out of sight behind the tress atop the hill he needed to climb.

Then he adjusted the duffle and hurried across to the other side of the road and beneath the forest canopy beyond.

Immediately it became more dim, but it didn't cool at all. If possible it seemed to warm up, actually.

George slowed as soon as he was out of sight of the road, and began ascending the hill, being careful to avoid trip hazards as he scanned the tree trunks for the signs he had left earlier. Where was - ?

There. Carved into a trunk thirty feet to the left. A heart with the letters G + H inside.

He strode over and laid his hand atop the rough bark, trailing his fingers around the carving he had made a week ago. They traced the heart, then brushed past his initial to the H, and there they stopped.

As it always did when he thought about Heather, his heart wrenched in his chest and he found himself gasping, suddenly breathless.

The image came to him of her, thirteen years old with her dark brown hair tied into two pigtails, dressed in a yellow sun dress and beaming an ear to ear smile on the day he'd taken her to see that movie she'd been asking him about for weeks. Why couldn't he remember its name now? If had been so important to her, and it had only been two years ago. Why - ?

Then he flashed to the last time he'd seen her face, how different it had looked from that happy day, and his gasping breathing became a sob that he had to work to contain.

He leaned forward and pressed forehead against the tree trunk, and forced his emotions down. He drew in a long, deep breath. Held it, and counted to ten.

Then he pushed himself back upright and, wiping his nose with the back of his right hand, he turned back upslope and resumed his trek.

The hill wasn't particularly steep, but it was a long ascent and by the time he reached the crest George was breathing heavily and sweating up a storm. But it wasn't far now, so he pressed on down the back side.

He reached his hide five minutes later.

It had taken him weeks to find this one perfect place, and then more time to get it built. Fifteen feet up the trunk of a towering sycamore, balanced in the gap between the trunk and a branching limb, the hide was a wooden platform large enough for George to lie prone comfortably.

He'd driven planks into the trunk to act as ladder rungs, and he took a moment to re-situate the duffle over both his shoulders, like a pack. Then he boosted himself up into the tree.

Once he was up, George dropped the duffle with a sigh of relief and rolled his shoulders. He was getting too old for this.

But he had to do it, for Heather's sake if nothing else.

She'd begun to come with him on his hunting trips, and had started to appreciate them, before -

Again he flashed to the last time he'd seen her, on the flat stainless steel, covered by a blue sheet that the orderly had pulled back so he could see her face. Bruised, cut, battered. Staring blankly into the bright lights of the ceiling, but not seeing them.

Not seeing anything.

George flopped down onto the wood that he had shaped and sanded, and laid into place here. His rump hit the platform, and he leaning forward, elbows on his knees as he pressed his hands to his eyes, willing himself not to see.

But still the image of his little girl would not go away.

He tried to think of another time, a happier time. But it wouldn't come. In his minds eye, his daughter's dead, lifeless eyes turned toward him, and he heard her voice in his head.

"Why didn't you protect me, daddy?"

George jerked upright, and heard himself scream for a second before he forced himself back to silence.

Don't scare away the game. Though that was extremely unlikely, here. In this place. For this game.

George drew a deep breath, then turned and unzipped the duffle bag. Along with his other gear, he had a gallon jug of water in the bag. He pulled it out and drank deeply.

The water had warmed since he took it out of his refrigerator two hours earlier, but even still it was cool compared with the heat of the day. The coolness spread down his throat and into his belly, and he let out a long sigh as he set the jug down.

Through a gap in the trees ahead of him, a glint of light drew his attention, and he leaned forward again, squinting. The lake, below and a few hundred yards away from his position, was rippling with waves, and the sunlight glinted at intervals off it.

Smiling thinly, George nodded to himself, then got to work on the rest of his gear.

The rifle was bolt action, chambered in .308 Remington, with a telescopic sight. He'd taken lots of game with it over the years. Lord willing, today would yield even greater results.

He pulled a box of ammo and a bipod mount out of the bag, then set to screwing the mount onto the lug at the bottom of the rifle barrel.

As he worked, his mind wandered back again. But not to the morgue, and Heather.

Three months, later, and sitting down with the detectives and prosecutor assigned the case. They'd caught the guy, had him dead to rights. The prosecutor would seek the death penalty, but probably he'd end up with life without parole. So at least he wouldn't be able to kidnap, rape, and murder any other little girls.

The earlier smile faded into a scowl as George remembered going into the courthouse for the pre-trial hearings. Watching as the defense attorney submitted a motion to dismiss.

And then stunned disbelief when the judge granted it, with prejudice.

George's scowl became a grimace as he set the rifle down, the bipod holding the barrel up off the floor now, and opened up the ammo box. He loaded four rounds into the ammo receiver, then jammed the bolt home, chambering a round. He checked the safety on, then arranged himself into a prone position, rifle butt snug into his right shoulder.

He recalled spending a week in jail. Contempt of court from the protests he'd shouted when the judge dismissed the case.

Seeing the prosecutor after he got out, and learning the perp was the nephew of a State Senator, or something.

He flipped off the dust covers over his sights and pressed his cheek against the stock.

Distant tree trunks and underbrush leaped into view in his eye, slightly blurry. He adjusted the focus ever so slightly, then panned the rifle left and right on the bipod, testing its function.

Smooth and easy.

He'd pressed the prosecutors to try again, maybe in a different venue, a different judge. But dismissing with prejudice meant the case could never be pressed again, period.

He walked out of the prosecutor's office, feeling his entire world crumble apart.

First Jane, four years earlier. Now Heather. Both had been murdered: his wife by cancer, and his girl -

George blinked away tears and focused on the sights as he shifted his aim point toward the break in the trees.

There could be no justice for Jane. But there should have been for Heather. And that had been stolen; from her and from him.

Through the sight, he saw the lake again. The ripples running across its surface were stronger, originating from just to the left of his field of view. Shifting his aim slightly, he saw the boat whose wake had been creating the ripples. It had a white hull and blue bimini above its conning station. It was sleek and lacked any superstructure: a speed boat.

And sure enough, it was pulling a bikini-clad woman behind it, on waterskis.

George wanted to smile at the sight, but he couldn't bring himself to. He shifted further to the left, and the lake's shore sprang into view. Large houses—mansions, practically—lined the water's edge. Some were sided in brick, some in more conventional planks, but all had the look of places that had been built in the last ten years or so. Each had a dock, and was separated from its neighbor by a fence that ran to the waterline.

A few had swimming pools in their yards above the lake, and wasn't that silly. All had meticulously-pruned landscaping, and lawn furniture for entertaining.

The house halfway down the lake's edge toward him had another boat just tying up to the dock. A dark-haired man in a white shirt and tan shorts was just standing from cleating off the boat's lines. The sun reflected off the lenses of his sunglasses quickly as he turned back to the boat and reached out to help its other two passengers out onto the dock.

They were a woman, somewhat plump but tall, almost as tall as the man, in a pink and white sun dress, and a girl; though young woman would be a better term from the growing hips that were plainly visible from the one-piece blue swimsuit she was wearing. She had brown hair, like her mother, and stopped to slip on Daisy Dukes before stepping off the boat.

The trio walked up the dock to a paved patio area a few yards up from the lake's edge, to where a glass-topped patio table surrounded by four white slatted chairs waited for them.

The man and the young lady sat down, and the woman hurried up to the house. She returned a few moments later, carrying a tray with a pitcher filled with a yellowish fluid—lemonade?—and three glasses. Her face was in view now that she was returning, and despite her sunglasses George recognized her with ease.

Judge Madelin Rosenburg.

The woman who had dismissed the case and thrown him in jail. The woman who had denied Heather her justice.

George tracked her as she walked back to the table, keeping his sighting reticle on her the whole way, and licked his lips.

He had been watching her, and her family, for months. Learning her patterns. Searching for an opening. It hadn't been particularly hard to learn about this lake house, when they tended to come here, and for how long. The Judge didn't have any social media accounts, but her sister did.

And so did her daughter.

Between the multitude of postings and check-ins those two had sent out to anyone with the desire and wherewithal to look, he knew where to go.

That just left finding the right place from which to hunt his game. That had really been the long pole. A place that was within the effective range of his rifle, and within his ability to get a hit, and was secluded enough that he could be assured of being able to make an escape.

Truth be told he really didn't care all that much about getting away. If he got caught, so be it. But it would be better to make a clean getaway.

He'd finally found the sycamore, and the gap in the trees that offered precisely the right angle. Then it was just a matter of waiting for Labor Day on the lake.

He kept tabs on the good Judge in the interim, and went to the range frequently to get his marksmanship up to the best it could be.

Now it was time. The game was in the open, and he had his shot.

Justice for Heather. Finally.

The Judge poured cups for her husband and daughter, then sat down in a chair facing George's position, to her husband's right and opposite her daughter. George could see about two thirds of the judge's head over the daughter's. No problem making that shot.

Flicking the safety off, he lingered there, with his reticle centered on the judge's face.

The temptation to shoot was so strong, he almost did it.

But that would revenge, not justice.

George had thought it through thoroughly, and could not escape that fact. Killing the judge would be satisfying. Deeply satisfying. But it would not be justice.

Justice would be to inflict on her the wounds she had inflicted on him. And leave her without recourse, just as she had left him.

He said a quick prayer, asking God to explain what he was doing to Heather. Then he shifted the reticle from the judge to the back of the daughter's head.

He took a long, slow breath. Held it.

And squeezed the trigger.

23
───

CALEDONIA

Saul looked through the scope on his rifle and grimaced.

In the viewfinder, five times normal magnification, he saw a dozen grey-brown scaled and armored bodies, each with eight legs and four manipulator arms below an oval head with external mandibles and at least four visible eyes. They were moving in seemingly random patterns, but together they formed an eery sort of symmetry as they zigged and zagged but steadily advanced across the blasted plain beneath Saul's post.

The drones were out again, and they had resumed their advance.

That meant Celeste's plan had failed; the queen still lived. And in all likelihood everyone who had gone with Celeste was either dead or wishing they were.

As he watched the creeping death coming steadily closer, Saul felt a crawling dread come up his spine, colder than winter's breath. He had to force himself not to squirm; but that might draw attention to himself, and he couldn't have that.

He needed to live to bring the word back to headquarters, such as it was. And no chance he'd do that if he made unnecessary movements and attracted the swarm to himself.

His post was in a cleft between two granite boulders atop a small rise, about a thousand meters from where the drones were patrolling and advancing. So maybe he was being a bit overly cautious. But he'd seen too many people taken unawares by the things to be careless now.

The plain in front of and below him used to be lush grassland— or at least this world's equivalent of grass—that stretched from the wooded foothills of the mountain range behind him all the way to the river where he and his fellow colonists had landed and set up their foothold on this brave, new world. Fifteen kilometers of what promised to be excellent soil for growing crops, with a strong source of freshwater right nearby and readily accessible timber just a short drive away. Not to mention the strong mineral deposits the probes they'd sent down from orbit had detected in the mountains.

It had seemed the perfect place to set up their new civilization.

But the probes hadn't seen the bugs. And now, three weeks later, he and twenty others, the only survivors of the fifteen hundred who had initially landed, had retreated to the foothills in the hope that the change in terrain and vegetation would stymie the bugs' territorial defense.

Didn't look like it so far.

Saul licked his lips, tasting the salt of the sweat that dripped down from his forehead despite the relative coolness of the afternoon. He moved his eye away from the viewfinder and looked down at the advancing drones with his naked eyes, and shook his head.

Without the magnification, it was like a sea of brown that shifted and twisted, but continued nonetheless, and was slowly driving the yellow-green of the planet's grass equivalent beneath its weight.

"Shoulda just blasted back to orbit when we had the chance," he said under his breath, hearing the fatigue and the tension in his voice. And the self-rebuke.

He'd been one of the louder scoffers at that notion. After the first couple of interactions with the bugs, and the first casualties, several groups had proposed the colony do just that: blast off and find a different location on the planet. There had been several identified; Caledonia had just been the most promising. There were others that would have been almost as good, and probably wouldn't have such hostile and deadly fauna nearby.

But they were just bugs.

Yeah, they were three feet long and stood a foot high, but they were just bugs. Easily taken care of by the colonists with their sophisticated equipment and knowledge.

No one had counted on the sheer strength of their bite, or their nigh-on unbreakable carapace and mandibles. The damn things were able to chew through steel, for chrissakes! Who could have possibly foreseen that?

Nor could anyone have foreseen their numbers. After the first few encounters, the Mayor had sent out extermination parties. And at first they had met with some success.

But then the real swarm started, a defensive reaction one of the docs had said. But whatever the cause, within days the fields were teaming with the buggers and they had overwhelmed the camp's perimeter.

The call went out then to get to the shuttle and evacuate, but by then it was too late.

Saul saw a few folks actually make it to the shuttle. But he couldn't have; too many bugs between him and it. All he could do was grab what gear he could and run.

A few minutes later, he was glad he hadn't made it there.

The shuttle lifted off in a great plume of fire, sending hot air blasting past Saul as he ran from the crawling mass that was destroying the colony they had only just started to build.

He'd looked up, smelling the rank engine exhaust, and saw brown shapes crawling on the skin of the shuttle even as it lifted. Some were blown off by the slipstream and fell to the ground. But several vanished a different way: digging in and then burrowing beneath the outer hull.

The shuttle had only climbed a few hundred feet when it blew, sending a shock wave that knocked Saul off his feet. The bits and pieces of the ship came falling down everywhere, trailing smoke and starting little fires everywhere they hit.

Saul had only thought he'd been running hard before.

Something like a hundred fifty people made it out of there, ahead of the bug swarm's advance. With nowhere else to go, they'd headed for the mountains with only what they could carry. The hope had been that the difference in terrain and vegetation, as tree equivalents replaced grass equivalent, would stop the swarm's advance, and the colonists would be able to set up something of a life there.

Though what kind of life it could be, and how they could hope to carry on in the future, without their equipment, seeds, and any means of reaching the mothership they'd left in orbit around the planet, no one knew.

But that was a worry for a later time. First thing was survival.

So they'd run. And the swarm followed. More colonists had fallen, eaten alive when they'd stopped to rest, until only forty had made it to the foothills. Then Celeste had come up with a plan. If they could locate the queen, and take her out, the swarm would be without a head. It would lose cohesion and die. And maybe the colonists would be able to go back and recover some of the equipment they'd lost.

She'd even come up with a weapons of sorts that might just do the trick. A mixture of some chemicals one of the scientist guys had had in his pack when he'd fled, which would produce a noxious nerve toxin that would take just about anything living down. All they had to do was work past the advancing front of the swarm, then track the swarm's path back to the bugs' hive, and let fly.

What the hell? No one else had a plan other than running. Most of the men in the group had stepped forward to volunteer. She'd taken eighteen with her, and they'd run off to do the deed.

Saul had stayed behind. Not because he wasn't willing to go but because someone needed to stay back to protect the kids and womenfolk. Him and four other men were their last line of defense if the plan didn't work. He'd taken up station in this cleft of rocks, rotating out every few hours with one of the others, and watched the advancing swarm, all the while hoping Celeste and company would succeed.

And for a couple days, it looked like they had. The swarm had pulled back, retreating in apparent disarray. When Saul had turned over the watch last night, he had been in high spirits. When he'd taken it back this morning, Jusef had been as well.

But now...

Now their hopes were dashed.

He slid carefully backwards, deeper into the crack between the rocks until the swarm was completely out of view. Then he got his feet under him and he turned, then hurried back toward the place where the others were camped, two hundred meters behind and twenty meters above his watch station.

Time to pass on the bad news.

The other survivors were just as bedraggled as Saul. Some worse. A few better. But no one was taking the conditions well.

All eyes turned to him, and one and all they were harried, haggard. The other grown men were all sporting new beards, and everyone's hair was ratty and matted. Everyone had on green jump-suits like Saul wore: the uniform that everyone had been issued by the Colonial Administration when they'd set off on this journey. And like Saul's everyone's was more brown than green now, streaked with dirt and grime and blood and other fluids he didn't want to think on.

The camp was makeshift at best. A few blankets and tarps stretched between the trees that had begun growing a few tens of meters further down the hill, but mostly the shelters were the sorts of things Saul and his brother—and wasn't Seth so much better off on Earth now, despite its overcrowding and constant warfare—had learned in Trail Life: lean-to structures made up of branches resting against tree trunks or against large rocks, coated in mud and fallen leaves to make a semblance of a roof.

A couple of fires were burning, sending fragrant smoke toward the overcast sky above. Someone had run with a coffee pot, and it smelled like one of the women was brewing a tea of some kind.

One good thing they had discovered was that the wood on this world, and the vegetation, had a fair amount of aromatic and spicy compounds in them. So the woodsmoke smelled almost of incense. And the tea, certainly made from clippings of the leafy vegetation around here, was spicy enough to get his mouth watering just thinking about it.

Jusef, who Saul had relieved just a couple hours earlier, was poking the tea's cook fire with a stick when Saul approached. When he saw Saul, he dropped the stick and stood. He was a little bit shorter than Saul, and used to have a bit of a paunch before this all started. Now his jumpsuit was starting to become loose about his mid-section.

One thing they hadn't fled with much of was food.

"Saul," Jusef said, his dark eyes narrowing with concern and his tone confused. "What are you doing back? Bill doesn't relieve you until - "

"Colleen's plan didn't work," Saul said, interrupting him in a voice that easily carried to every ear in the camp. "The swarm's back, and moving faster than ever."

"Dammit," said Cynthia, a young, shapely redhead with a gaggle of three children who all had somehow managed to escape without harm. Though her husband had not.

She was sitting on a stump, doing her best to mend someone's jumpsuit with what was left of the sewing set she had brought with her. She looked from Saul to Jusef to the other three remaining men in the group questioningly. "What are we going to do?"

Saul had no good answer to that one. But even a bad answer was better than none at all.

"We continue with the original plan," Saul said. "Get further up into the mountains. There are more rocks here than down there." He gestured back the way he came. "The bugs burrow, but maybe they can't burrow through stone. Maybe they won't follow."

"Maybe." Cynthia's tone was doubtful, almost scornful. But the look on her face was resigned. She didn't have a better idea either, so even if she doubted this one, what else was there for her to do?

What else was there for any of them to do?

Saul looked back at Jusef, who frowned for a long few seconds. Then he nodded agreement.

The other men did as well. What other course had they?

Without another word, they all got started breaking down the camp.

Within the hour, they were all walking uphill, away from the advancing swarm.

The sun—Saul still though of it as the sun even though this system was dozens of light years from Sol—was low against the horizon, and he was soaked with sweat. His breathing came in heaves and his heart thumped in his ears.

The last several hundred meters had been grueling. Looking back down the way the troop had come, and in some cases was still coming, it appeared they had ascended a meter for every meter they had advanced. Or near enough to it.

But they had also made good progress, and he could clearly see the plain, well below them and behind, through a break in the trees. He could also see the swarm, the mass of brown eating away at the yellow-green. But was it his imagination, or had it not advanced nearly as quickly as it had been the last time he looked?

It had reached and overcome the little hill he had used as a post; he could see that hill clearly, far below and behind. But it looked like the swarm had not followed so readily into this higher country.

Was the plan working?

The younger of Cynthia's children scampered up next to him. The boy's cheeks were flushed and he was breathing heavily, but his eyes were alight with something almost like glee and he didn't look at all spent. He looked down toward where his mother and sisters were still clambering up, then at Saul, and grinned.

Somehow, Saul found himself returning the grin, the youth's

exuberance combining with the apparent slowing of the swarm to raise his spirits immensely. "Help your mother, Kevin," Saul said.

The boy nodded, then scampered the few steps down toward Cynthia. Shortly, all four of them were standing at the top f the rise next to Saul and looking back down through the trees.

"Do you think they've stopped?" Cynthia asked between breaths.

"Time will tell," Saul said. He wanted to say yes, they were past the danger. But twice now he had thought the problem solvable. And twice he had been proven wrong.

False hope was worse than no hope.

He turned away from the view behind toward the path ahead. Here the rise was flatter, almost not an ascent at all. The others in their groups were trumping ahead, obviously tired with stooped shoulders and lowered heads as they walked in an approximation of a line behind Bill, the youngest and spriteliest of the surviving men and so the guy who'd taken point. But despite their fatigue they moved at a better clip now, and they'd already put several meters between themselves and Saul, Cynthia, and the kids.

"Come," Saul said. "We'll rest soon, but we need to make as much distance as we can."

Just in case the swarm hadn't actually stopped.

So he, with Cynthia and her kids, picked the pace back up again, and moved to catch up with the others.

The sun continued to lower as the troupe marched on, and Saul was beginning to think they really needed to stop soon before they ran out of light. He was just about to call out to Jusef, who was at the midway mark of the group, to have Bill stop, when an excited shout from the front interrupted his intention.

Immediately on guard, he rolled his shoulder to slip the rifle out from its slung position, then he moved forward more quickly, passing women and children as he first caught up to Jusef and then surged forward alongside him.

His mind flashed through a dozen scenarios that could have evoked the cries he heard from Bill and the other man at the front—and from the kids up near them—but none of them matched what he saw when, between one step and the next, he emerged from a forest of tree equivalents with leafy underbrush to a clearing that stretched for at least a kilometer in each direction and that held in its center a lake that looked at least to be perfectly circular. Or near enough to it.

He came to an amazed halt and his jaw dropped open at the sheer beauty of the thing; it reflected the pinkish-orange hues of the beginning sunset and the coloration of the mountain peaks on the other side of the lake with a purity that struck him right to the bone, and there was a sense of peace, of oneness about the place that made the worries of the last few weeks seem trivial, needless.

Saul came to a halt beside Bill. "Whoa," he said.

Bill was skinny, and taller than Saul by a hand. His yellow-orange hair was an unruly mop that ran past his eyes in front and to his shoulder in back, and his demeanor normally reflected his coloration perfectly: all fire and passion. Right that second, though, he only nodded, an expression of awe on his face.

"I guess we camp here," Jusef said as he, too, came to a halt. He was not nearly as awestruck as Bill, from the satisfied grin on his face. "Good visibility, fresh water. Hard to beat."

"Ain't water," Bill said.

Saul looked askance at him, and Bill must have seen it. He gestured toward the lake with his left hand. "Look more closely."

Frowning in puzzlement, Saul followed Bill's gestured with his gaze. At first he wasn't sure what Bill was talking about. It was highly reflective, but that was hardly unusual in water of its stillness. There was hardly a ripple in it. That didn't mean -

Then he realized that there was a steady breeze blowing, from behind them. It had been at their backs for so long he had stopped thinking about it, since he hardly felt it. But now that they were stopped, he felt it clearly. But with the breeze blowing, how was the lake so still?

He leaned forward and squinted, and felt his breath catch.

Bill was right. The reflection was too perfect, without blemish. And as he leaned forward he saw himself in the fluid, and he saw a silvery shimmer for a second in his reflection.

"What is it?" he asked. Dropping down into a squat so he could view the fluid more closely, he definitely could see that it was silvery. And it must surely be fairly dense or the breeze would have stirred it.

He reached out to dip his fingers into it, and immediately felt Bill's hand on his shoulder.

Saul looked up to see the younger man staring down at him, his green eyes deadly serious. "Don't," he said. "It's not for you."

Saul blinked. "What do you mean, not for me?"

Bill looked confused for a second, then shrugged, shaking his head. "I'm not sure. Just..." He trailed off, going back to stare at the lake for a few seconds. Then he spoke again, more resolutely. "Just don't touch it."

Unsure what to make of Bill's statement or demeanor, Saul nevertheless obeyed and retracted his hand. Standing back up straight, he turned to Jusef and shrugged. Then he said, "Probably better camp back under the trees. Don't want one of the kids wandering into this stuff. Whatever it is."

Jusef nodded. "Good call. I'll get them stopped."

He turned and went back to the rest of the group to get them settled, leaving Saul and Bill alone at the lake's edge. They stood silently for a time, then a thought struck Saul.

"Did you ever see the probe scans of these mountains, Bill?"

Bill shook his head, not looking at Saul but still at the lake.

"I did. I don't recall seeing this lake in any of the scans."

Bill frowned slightly. After a moment, he said. "Well, it's here now."

"Yeah. But - "

Bill surprised him by surging forward, toward the lake itself.

"Bill!" Saul cried, and reached out to stop him. His fingers brushed at the back of Bill's jumpsuit, but he couldn't get a firm grasp on him.

And then he was leaping out over the fluid of the lake.

Bill seemed to float there, suspended over the silvery fluid for a second. Then he fell into the fluid.

He didn't make a splash; the fluid just flowed around him as he made contact with it.

Then he was gone.

———

Bill's loss struck the survivors hard, and it took a lot of effort to stop everyone from panicking. In truth, Saul wasn't sure he and the other guys did any good at all.

Regardless, there was no way they were staying there that night, so immediately after getting everyone at least semi-coherent, they set out through the woods at a right angle from the lake and their previous heading.

It wasn't long, though, before the shadows had grown long and it became clear that they were going to lose the light very soon. Still, from the looks on people's faces, fatigue or no, oncoming night or no, the incident with the lake had many wanting to continue on regardless.

That was foolish, but in the end Saul felt sure it was sheer exhaustion, and not his and Jusef's arguments against it, that won out. And so, after not too much objection, the troupe bedded down for the night.

Or rather, lay down on the dirt and fell fast asleep, since there was no time to build shelters and no one had the energy to do so. Only one person bothered to make a camp fire, and that was small and feeble, since even its tender fell asleep before she could get it properly built up, so exhausted was she.

Saul and the other men discussed setting a watch, and agreed on a rotation. Saul was supposed to have the third watch, awoken by Kent.

But when he awoke—on his own—in the morning, the sun was shining brightly and it was clearly almost noon.

Chagrined and feeling momentarily guilty over missing his watch, Saul sat bolt upright and looked around.

Everyone else was still asleep.

"Must have been more tired than any of us thought," Saul said to himself as he pushed himself to his feet. And no wonder. They had pushed themselves extremely hard, physically. And the renewed stress and lack of good, consistent food for several weeks now led to a lack of stamina.

No wonder everyone had taken an extra long snooze.

Still, they were in no condition to truly rest up. Not in these circumstances. If the -

A cracking twig from behind made Saul turn around. His blood went to ice.

Bill stood there, at the edge of the little circle of people who were all that remained of Saul's colony.

But it wasn't Bill.

Oh, it looked like him. It had the same lanky build, same posture. Same movements. But its eyes were pure silver, and there were silver streaks in the reddish-yellow hair. Its fingernails were silver as well, as was its jumpsuit.

Still, Saul found himself saying, "Bill?" even though he knew it couldn't be the lost man.

The creature—whatever it was—stepped forward, moving carefully around the prone bodies until it came to stand directly in front of Saul. This close, it carried the odor of damp earth mixed with the aromatic spices that rose from a camp fire here.

Saul swallowed. "Who are you?"

The thing that looked like Bill cocked its head at him. "Who are you?" it replied. "You invade me. Carve my body." It gestured toward the embers of the campfire. "Burn me." It narrowed its eyes at him. "You try to kill my daughter and her children. Who are *you*?!" The last came out as a demand, and an accusation.

Saul swallowed. What was this thing? "We come from a far away world. We - "

"You invade," the thing said.

Saul shook his head. "We seek a new home."

"So this one told me," the thing wearing Bill's face said. "Nevertheless, you invade. Invade, and kill. I cannot allow."

There was a crunching sound from all around. Saul turned his head and saw, with growing horror that threatened to loosen his bowels against his will, bug drones digging their way up. Dozens of them, in two rings—no, three—completely surround the band of slumbering colonists.

Saul turned back to the Bill-creature and raised his hands toward it, open and palms outward in a sign of peace. "Wait!"

The thing cocked its head at him again, and the bugs stopped moving. All at once.

"We don't want to cause harm. Just to live."

"For you, living is harm. Harm to my children. And me."

The bugs began to move forward again. "But..." Saul swallowed. "If you do this, you'll be killing our children." He gestured to the left, where Cynthia lay sleeping, all three of her kids curled up closer to her, on either side. He had no idea what kind of link this thing had with the bugs, but clearly it was controlling them, and thought of them as its children. Maybe that was a way in.

The Bill-creature followed Saul's gesture toward the mother and children, and its lips compressed slightly.

Clearly it was thinking that angle through. Saul decided to run with it.

"We didn't know about your children. We don't want to harm them. Just to live for ours. If you don't want us here, we'll leave." He tried an ingratiating smile, but wasn't sure how well he did. "You just had to say so."

The Bill-creature looked back at him fully. "You cannot leave. This one knows. Your transport was destroyed."

Damn. He should have known the thing would have gotten that from Bill, too. But still, the mothership had more than one shuttle. If enough equipment had survived...

"We have another ship in orbit." He pointed up at the sky. "If we can get back to Caledonia, we can try to contact it and send another transport down. Then we will get in and leave. And never come back."

The Bill-creature looked up at the sky, and the lines of its lips turned downward, forming a deep frown. "No," it said after a moment. "This one thinks that will just lead to more invasion, from others of your kind." It gave a little jerk of its head, and Saul felt the very ground beneath his feet shift, just for a second.

It didn't feel all that severe, but all the same Saul had the impression something profound, and powerful, had just occurred.

"The large ship will not tell others about me and my children now." It looked back down at Saul and the frown faded, replaced by a look of serenity. "My children will be safe, and no more invaders will come."

It reached out its hand toward Saul. He wanted to recoil from it, but he found he couldn't, and the Bill-creature's fingers, cold but thrumming with energy and power, touched his cheek.

He had a flash of the Bill-creature's mind. It was immense, filling this entire world. Every crack in the rock, every shift in the mantle beneath the tectonic plates. Every movement of every creature on its surface, and the motion of its three moons. And now, the motion of the mothership as its orbit, perturbed by some adjustment of the planet's gravitational vector, began to spiral in toward atmospheric reentry.

"No!" Saul said, the denial sounding as impotent as he now knew it to be. This creature was the planet. And it did not want them there. Nor did it want any other humans to ever return. So it would not allow word of it to get back to Earth, or any survivor to do so either.

"No," he said again, this time in a strained whisper.

"There will be no pain," the Bill-creature said, and Saul began to feel drowsy again. "And your parts will become a part of me. That is my gift to you, for helping me understand."

Saul wanted to move. To fight. To do something!

But his limbs were heavy, and his vision was fading. All around, he heard vague sounds. He couldn't place them for a seeming eternity, until part of his mind put them together and he realized he was hearing the bugs advance and begin chopping up the outermost of his sleeping comrades.

"No."

But the word barely registered in his own ears.

The last thing he saw before sleep claimed him were those silvery eyes, seeming to shine in the sunlight.

Then there was the blackness of dreamless sleep.

And then an expansion of thought beyond anything he had ever known or conceived of, as he too, like Bill, became one with the world of Caledonia.

24

LOVE IN THE APOCALYPSE

Light flashed into Silva's eyes, rousing her from what had been a deep and dreamless sleep. She squirmed and stretched, raising her arms above her head and letting out a long, low sigh that was almost a groan as she forced herself to full wakefulness.

Then she remembered where she was, and the pleasant feeling of stretching limbs and gathering of morning energy fled before that reality.

She sat bolt upright, eyes that were still adjusting to the new light levels darting to and fro, looking for danger and heedless of the sheets that had fallen from her naked torso. Didn't matter if her boobs were showing if she was about to get eaten.

But...nothing.

The room where she'd been sleeping was the same as she now remembered it had been when she and Zack had tucked in the night before.

Silva's lips turned upward slightly at that thought. Why was she making euphemisms to herself? Tucked in, indeed. They had both expected to be dead before morning. So when they'd stumbled upon this abandoned house, with its still functioning solar array and the biggest, most luxurious bed Silva had ever seen, they had decided to go out with a bang.

And quite a bang it had been.

But now it turned out that hadn't been their last night ever on this —or any other—world. And that meant things were about to get...awkward.

Silva brushed her black hair back from her eyes and turned to the left, where Zack was still asleep -

He wasn't there.

"What the - ?"

Had he risen ahead of her, and gone to the little house's kitchen to rustle up some coffee?

More mindful now of her state of undress, Silva slung her legs out from under the sheets and settled her feet onto the chilly grey-white tile of the bedroom floor. Pulling the sheet with her as she rose, heedless of the bed's red comforter flopped onto the floor, she wrapped herself into the sheet and walked over to the door leading out to the living room and kitchen area.

"Zack?" she called, but his name drifted away into nothing when she fully emerged and saw the red leather couch and loveseat arranged around a black marble-looking coffee table, the red cabinets above black quartz countertops in the kitchen, the screen of the televid black against the far wall, and the front door, black and closed against the horror of the world outside.

But no Zack.

The air was cool and dry, and smelled slightly of disinfectant, as though the owner's maid had been through here just before all hell had broken loose. But not of coffee. Or of the cologne Zack had been wearing last night.

She hadn't really been concerned before, but now a shot of icy fear lanced through her. Where was Zack? What had happened to him?

And, more frightening still, how had it happened with her lying asleep beside him, without her knowing of it?

Had one of those...things...come in and got him? But why would it have not taken her as well? And how could she have slept right through it?

Or, almost more terrifying in its own way, had Zack waited until she was asleep and then left her? Had he been playing her the whole time, just to eke out one last bit of nookie before the end?

He'd succeeded in that, but she had wanted it too. And even if that had been all he was after, why would he bolt? There was really no place to go. Not anymore. And no one to brag to about his conquest. No one who wouldn't eat his face off, anyway.

So...what the hell?

Silva scanned the room again, eyes lingering on the furnishings and decor longer this time, soaking in details. Nothing seemed out of whack...

She came to the front door, and froze.

It was ajar. The latching mechanism just resting against the jamb, like it had not been fully pulled to, more allowed to swing slowly shut on his own.

That shard of fear became a full-on lance, and Silva retreated back into the bedroom, moving as quickly as she could without creating a big rustle of moving sheet. Then she pushed the door slowly closed.

The click of the latch sliding home lessened her fear somewhat, even though she knew the things wouldn't be stopped by something as paltry as a bedroom door. But she still felt better, regardless.

Moving more quickly now, Silva dropped the sheet and gathered up her clothing from where Zack had discarded it on the floor after removing it. She dressed quickly, only cursing over the fact that her underwear was three days old now twice, then patted the front pocket of her jeans.

The keys to her place were still there. Not that those would do much good. But it felt reassuring to have them. But where...

She cast about, looking for her wallet, but couldn't see it anywhere.

Silva normally carried a small handbag, not quite a purse. But lucky her she'd decided to forgo that for just a wallet and keys when she'd left the house before it all started. So at least she didn't have to be the cliched girl clinging to her purse during the end of the world.

And truth be told, it wasn't like a wallet would do her much good now anyway. But she hated to lose it. Just in case. And because... Because it was a bit of normalcy, in all the sudden madness that had engulfed her life, and everyone else's.

The bed was raised above the floor on four black wooden legs. Getting down on her knees, Silva peered beneath.

And there it was. Her wallet, a thin bit of brown leather doubled over itself. She reached out to get it, and when she did she saw something else as well, lying just past it.

A simple golden ring, lying on the tile beneath the bed.

Zack's wedding ring.

Silva froze, just staring at it. The symbol of the life he'd built with Helen, the bond between them.

The bond Silva had broken when she'd taken Zack into her last night.

"Stupid cow," she said under her breath. "Helen's dead."

That didn't make the sudden guilt go away.

"They're all dead," she said, louder and more forcefully to herself. "And we were going to be, too."

That didn't change the fact that she'd fantasized about him ever since she'd first met him, when Helen brought him back to meet their parents. She'd never done anything about it, but she couldn't make that desire go away.

And now, not two days after Helen died, Silva had done it: She had screwed her sister's husband.

"Doesn't matter because she's fucking dead," Silva growled in answer to herself. She pushed herself back from the bed and straightened, slipping the wallet into the pocket of her jeans. She took a moment to wipe tears that she hadn't realized she was shedding from her eyes, then stood and turned toward the door.

But before she could open it back up, she found herself diving back beneath the bed and grabbing up Zack's ring.

The front door swung open easily, and soundlessly on apparently well-oiled hinges, and Silva stepped out into the world. Or what was left of it.

Here, on the outskirts of town, the ravaging of the things was almost invisible. And especially in the little nook of woods around the house she and Zack had borrowed. The place was small, just the one bedroom, and isolated; blocked from sight on the street by high bushes and low-hanging tree limbs that surely had to have been planted just for that reason.

They had almost walk-ran right past it, except Zack had seen the path to the front door from the corner of his eye. And they had ducked in, feeling like they were barely a step ahead of the pack that had been dogging their steps for hours.

Now that it was daylight, she could see the house was stucco-sided, just yellow of white, and trimmed in red-brown like a well-stained piece of wood. And it still looked untouched, like no one had been here ever. So clearly they hadn't been just one step ahead of the pack.

The path back to the street was made of flagstone, and it curved between the trunks of two willows before rounding the edge of the bushes. Silva walked slowly down it, carefully placing her feet so as to avoid making excess noise and peering about for any sign of Zack's passage.

She saw none.

But just as she was rounding the bushes, she heard a sign.

Zack's voice.

Immediately relief and elation swept through her a heartbeat before she realized it was his voice all right. But it was raised, louder than it should have been, given what was going on these days. And it was full of fear. Nigh-on with panic.

Silva began to move more quickly, but froze a second later when Zack's cry went from fear - to pain.

"No!" she cried, then surged forward.

Silva rounded the bend and emerged onto the sidewalk beyond. The street was two-lane, running north to south. It was lined with willows and maples and oaks, whose overhanging limbs lent the street a quaint, shady charm. A charm that was ruined by two wrecked cars within two hundred yards, and at least a couple corpses...or what Silva assumed were corpses. Though there was little enough left that it would have been impossible to be sure.

She took all that in, then set it aside as she turned right and saw Zack lying on his back on the blacktop, one of those things on top of him.

He was tall: 6'1". And strong. The thing probably used to only be 5'9". But it was overpowering him, throwing its entire weight down onto his arms, which he had thrown up above himself to ward the thing off.

They were thirty, forty feet away, but Silva could clearly see Zack's arms trembling at the exertion to keep it off of him.

Without thinking about what she was doing, Silva rushed toward them. But she had maybe taken three steps when the thing raked its fingers across the meat of Zack's forearms.

He cried out, pain and desperation both in his tone.

Then his arms gave out and the thing was on him.

Zack's shriek as its teeth dug into his belly was high-pitched, almost like a boy's, and despairing.

She was still moving toward them. Zack's eyes caught hers as she approached, and he shook his head at her.

Then she was next to them, and she drove her foot into the thing's side.

Caught unawares, the thing lost its grip on Zack and rolled off to the side.

It's face, once human but now...something else...was red around the mouth and chin from Zack's blood, from where it had bitten into him. And it was chewing.

Silva felt her stomach heave and tasted bile; she looked down at Zack's belly and saw that it had torn straight through his shirt and into the flesh...and beyond. Blood flowed freely from the wound, and other fluid too.

Movement from the thing drew her eyes back to it. It had rolled onto all fours and was looking at her with grey-yellow eyes that shown with hunger, but beyond hunger to something more. Something that could never be quenched.

She took a step, her guts turning to water. Every part of her screamed to turn and run while she still could. But she couldn't. She couldn't do anything except watch as it crawled right overtop of Zack as he clutched futilely at the wound and groaned.

Watch it, and retreat.

Her foot struck something solid, and she glanced back to see that she had reached the curb. She stepped quickly up onto the sidewalk and looked back at the thing.

It was closer now, its pink-brown skin slick with what she assumed was sweat. But did they still sweat? Nude except for some last scraps of the shorts it had worn before turning, it surged forward toward her, arms outstretched and mouth agape, revealing teeth that had grown into mini-daggers.

Silva heard herself squeak out a shriek, but somehow in the midst of her fear she moved. A sidestep to the right, and the thing shot past her, just missing carrying her to the ground with it.

As it was, the thing stumbled face-first into the grass on the other side of the sidewalk from the street, and it let out a bark-cough that might have been an expression of chagrin.

Or of nothing at all; these things didn't seem to have much in the way of intellect.

But this was not time to reflect on their anatomy. It would be coming for her again. Silva cast about for something to use as a weapon.

And saw a broken chunk of concrete lying in the street next to the curb. It must have been thrown there from an accident, or who knows from where.

No matter how it got there, Silva thanked God that it had, and picked it up.

It took both hands to heft it, and the thing was back on its feet when she turned back toward it, cudgel in hands.

The thing looked pissed. It charged, and Silva swung the hunk of concrete.

The stone struck the thing in the jaw, and it went reeling off to Silva's left, falling back onto the street.

Silva didn't wait this time, She threw herself down onto it, pinning it to the street with her knees. Then she brought he concrete chunk down onto its head.

Again.

And again.

And again.

A couple more hits, and its skull was a mush of red, its limbs trembling and spasming weakly.

Silva collapsed onto the street next to the thing and just breathed for a few seconds. Minutes? Her heart was pounding, and it was like she couldn't get enough air. But finally, she managed to collect herself a bit, enough to remember Zack.

Rolling over, she pushed herself to her knees, then her feet, and she stumbled over to where he still lay, blood flowing freely from around the fingers he had clenched to his wound. He was trembling, and had gone pale. His eyes were sunken, and there were tears running down his cheeks.

She was no doctor, but she didn't need to be to know he wasn't long for this world.

Silva dropped down to her knees next to him, and immediately, he said, "I'm sorry."

She blinked, confused.

Zack must have seen the question on her face, because he drew a breath, then said, "For last night I... I don't know why I - " He cut off and looked away from her, a sob escaping his lips. "Oh Helen, I'm sorry."

"Shh." Silva leaned over him and reached out, cupping his chin to turn his face back toward hers. "You've got nothing to be sorry for."

He let his head turn, but he shook it after she spoke. "I shouldn't have..." He trailed off amidst a series of strong coughs that left him gasping in pain as his abdomen contracted. "Ah!' He drew a deep, quick breath. "I couldn't sleep. Needed to get away. Take a walk. Didn't mean to go so far..."

"It's alright," Silva said. Clearly he was blaming himself for this whole predicament, and not just for their sex last night. But Silva was pretty sure this was how they would have ended up no matter what he did: food for the things. Or worse. "It's not your fault."

He shook his head again, as though to deny her words. She opened her mouth to say that yes, she meant it. None of it was his fault; not last night, and not now.

But he grabbed her forcefully on the upper arm with his blood-soaked right hand.

"But about half mile that way," he said, gesturing down the road to the north with that hand before letting it drop limply to the street. Apparently he didn't even had the strength to try to staunch the flow anymore. He could talk, though. "Found a dead guy. Next to cop car." He drew in a deep, quavering breath. "Had a map. Old base marked down there. Radio frequencies. Keys in the ignition, and the car started. Cop's radio had the freqs..."

He coughed, and blood trickled down his cheek from his mouth. "People on the radio," he said, weakly. "Base is safe. Open to survivors. Figured we'd go there..." He smiled faintly. "Just you now."

"Zack - " Silva stopped, unsure what to say and how to feel. There was a safe place, where people were gathering? There were still others alive? Hope surged within her, but then just as quickly it faded as she looked at the dying man beside her. Silently, she cursed the fates...or God...or whatever it was that caused life to suck so much.

It just wasn't fair. First Helen, and then she had - And now Zack going as well. And Silva was just supposed to get up and go on, like nothing happened?

Why was she not the one bleeding out on the pavement?

"Do...me...favor." Zack said, sounding very weak now.

"Anything."

"I'm dying. Or I'm...turn. Don't wanna turn." He looked at her earnestly, and she saw the fear there. Not of dying, but that was there. But of worse than dying. Of becoming one of them; of the things that had killed him, and everyone else.

Or almost everyone.

Silva nodded slowly, and looked back toward the corpse of the thing she had brained. The hunk of concrete she had used was lying on the street next to it. The edge she had used to cave in its skull was bright red in the morning sunlight.

Not trusting herself to speak, she stood and walked over to the thing's corpse, and retrieved the concrete chunk. When she knelt back down beside Zack, he flashed a sad smile at her, and his hazel eyes were almost the lively orbs they had been when she first saw him.

He reached up to touch her face. His hand was covered in blood, but she didn't recoil. He traced his finger down the side of her cheek, stopping when he reached her chin. His eyes left hers, moving down to his hand, and his expression broke.

"Threw my ring away," he said. "Felt so guilty. Don't wanna meet her without it..."

Silva blinked in surprise. Then she set the chunk of concrete down and fished into her pocket, where she had slipped his wedding ring. Pulling it out, she took his hand and gently slid the ring onto his ring finger.

His eyes widened when he saw it, then he smiled up at her and nodded. Their eyes met, and he looked away from her and up toward the sky. "Ready," he said, and Silva almost couldn't hear it.

She couldn't look away from his face as her hands, trembling, took hold of the concrete chunk and raised it over her head.

His face was calm, his eyes glazed over. He looked at peace.

Silva forced her eyes closed and brought the chunk down with all her might.

The car was right where Zack had said it would be. And it started, as he said it would.

From the markings on the map, the base looked to be a hundred and fifty miles northeast of there. She checked the fuel gauge and figured she had enough to get there, or at least get close enough that she could walk the rest of the way if need be. So she shut the car door, put it in gear, and set off down the road.

When she turned on the radio and heard the voice from the base calling out to her, Silva realized she was weeping.

But whether tears of grief and loss or of relief, or of, for the first time in what felt like forever, hope, she didn't know.

25

PLAYING FOR SCRAPS

I was just tallying up the invoice for my latest case, an easy job for a little old lady down on the station's third level, when Jason commed for entrance to my office.

I'd known Jason for a couple years, and when he commed the image of his face popped up into the upper-left corner of my vision, courtesy of the database implants I'd had installed last year. Made forgetting names and faces a thing of the past, but sometimes it could also be annoying. Like now, when I had been busily deciding whether to charge Ms. Gorant for the gratuity I'd had to slip to a security guy or just let it slide.

So I tried to ignore Jason's comm. Maybe he'd go away.

But he commed again a few seconds later.

Screw it. I'd let her pass on this one. Swiping the gratuity entry out of the invoice, I made a sweeping downward gesture with my left hand, and the holo of the invoice file compressed down into the stainless steel top of my desk and winked out.

My office was not what you'd call spacious. Just a few meters on a side, barely larger than a closet in some people's homes. But I owned it right out—or as much as anyone could really own anything on a space station that was owned entirely by the government of the

Qorathi Empire—and I'd made it into my own little slice of...well, not quite heaven, but at least something that worked for me.

The desk was directly in front of the door, and L-shaped so that I could swivel my chair to to the right to face the little brown and white sofa where clients could sit without exposing myself. That also gave me plenty of leg room. And plenty of room to conceal a couple of pieces on either side of the L, so one was always easy at hand, whichever way I was facing. Just in case.

Behind the desk, or to the right if I was facing the couch, I had my file cabinets and a vidscreen, and just to the right of those was the little blue sliding door that led to my back room, which had just enough space for a bed sized for one—two if you really liked snuggling—and a head compartment that I had modified to include a little shower apparatus in it.

I even had a real potted plant in the corner next to the clients' couch, which opened flower buds from time to time throughout the year, giving the place a more organic fragrance than the typical afterscents that the atmosphere processors on the Engineering levels lent.

It was pretty much everything a guy could need or want.

Except for maybe a kitchen. But I'd never been a good cook anyway, and Tamra's place down the corridor had the best chef on the station. So screw it.

The latest comm from Jason was still registering on my implants. I keyed up the security camera I had mounted in the corridor above my door. On the vidscreen above my file cabinets, live video from outside sprang to life and I saw Jason standing there, his head swinging left and right as he shifted from foot to foot noticeably.

Either he really needed to use the head or he was damn nervous about something.

Great.

Sighing, I slipped my hand beneath my desk to the button that controlled the door's locking mechanism, and turned to face front.

The lock snapped open with an audible CLACK, and outside a quick buzzer would have sounded. A second later, Jason had the door pushed open and he slipped inside, closing it as soon as he was through.

Jason was a little bit taller than me, but skinny. The kind of guy who'd never become acquainted with the weight room, but also had a metabolism that kept him lean. He was lightly tanned, with long, thick black hair and deep brown eyes, and he wore an olive green jumpsuit and magboots. A black faux-leather belt cinched the jumpsuit around his waist, and the thigh pocket on his left leg bulged with something or other.

"Hey, Suresh," Jason said, his eyes dancing from me to the couch to the door to my back room and back in a frenetic scan that confirmed it in my mind: he was scared.

"Jason," I said, keeping my voice calm and gesturing at the couch for him to sit. "How's the recording coming?"

Jason blinked, then some of his nervous energy faded as my comment changed his thoughts for a second, and he flashed a hint of a smile.

He worked up on the cargo docks, but he'd always fancied himself a musician. And he had a side gig playing his keyboard and singing in the various bars and clubs that scattered the station. From what I'd heard he made alright money doing that, and he'd developed a bit of a following.

He'd given the station a bit of a stir a couple months ago though, when he launched a campaign to help fund his first privately-recorded and distributed album. He'd put up advertisement messages on the various boards, sent out emails to everyone he knew, pimped it at his gigs. Said he had the distribution all lined up; just needed the money for recording and production. He'd offered a bunch of perks and goodies for people who contributed, depending on how much they gave. It was the talk of the station for a few weeks.

Hell, I'd even contributed a little myself; just enough to get the album, not for anything else. I figured what the hell. He and I weren't exactly friends, but I didn't think ill of him. And he could play that keyboard pretty well. So why not help a brother out?

And from what I heard, he'd crushed it. Brought in far more money than he asked for.

Now he just had to produce the thing.

Jason sank onto my couch, and the smile he had started to wear slipped away. He slouched forward, resting his elbows on his knees and clasping his hands together. His eyes lowered to look down at his hands, and he shook his head.

"Need your help. I have to get off the station, without anyone knowing I've gone."

I wasn't entirely surprised he was in trouble, based on how he was acting. But I was surprised by the request. I cocked an eyebrow at him. "Why?"

He looked back up and me, and blanched when his eyes met mine. "I'm in trouble, man."

"No kidding."

He flinched slightly at my tone—I didn't even try to hold the sarcasm back—but after a second he shrugged slightly, and his eyes fell again. "I owe some people money. I thought I'd make enough from the album thing to be able to get the album produced and pay them back, and it would all be good. But..." He shook his head.

My other eyebrow rose to meet its fellow on my forehead. "You took in about double what you asked for."

"Yeah. Well, about that..."

Oh for the love of... I shook my head in disgust. "What, did you blow it all on strippers and dust?"

"What?" He jerked upright, looking at me with an expression like I'd just called his sister a slut. "No!"

"So what's the problem?"

Jason's nostril's flared; I had pissed him off by that dust comment, apparently. But at least he wasn't talking in a self-pitying mumble anymore. "The problem is that production costs are more than I thought. I blew through most of the money I got, and the album's only two-thirds done. And I still have to pay for the extras that I offered to the higher-tier backers. And then this morning, Carpenter's men told me he wants his money. Now."

"Carpenter? You owe money to Carpenter?" If that were the case, it was bad. Very bad. You didn't mess with Carpenter, not on Gilroy Station. Hell, not any place within two jumps of this system.

Jason nodded, some of his anger leaving as he considered his predicament again, and not my accusation.

"How much do you owe him?"

"Four thousand."

"But I heard you brought in almost ten thousand from your fundraiser. How much do you have left?"

Jason just looked at me, silently.

I sat there for a long several moments, considering. He really was in big trouble. It was hard to tell which direction was worse. On the one hand, he had taken a lot of money from people living on the station, making promises to them he apparently now was not going to deliver on. I'm not a lawyer, but to me that sounded like fraud.

On the other hand, he owed Carpenter the equivalent of four months' wages for a guy who worked the docks, like Jason did.

A man could get thrown in prison for fraud, for a long time. But not paying Carpenter... That would get you spaced.

Ok, no question which was worse, after all.

I shook my head. "Should have paid him off first."

Jason snorted agreement. Then after a second, he shook his head. "No. I was going to pay him, soon as the album was out and I started getting royalties. No problem, at all."

I just looked at him. Even after all that had happened, he couldn't actually be that dumb, to continue justifying like this.

But maybe he was, because he looked back at me defiantly, like he really thought he'd done nothing wrong.

I sighed. "So you want me to smuggle you off the station." Shaking my head, I said, "What is it you think I do, Jason?"

"What do you mean? You're a private dick."

I nodded. "Yeah. I do investigation. If I help you run out on your contributors, I'm an accessory to fraud and maybe larceny. I don't do crime. You want crime, you go to Carpenter. You want an honest investigation, within the law," well, not always within the law to be honest, but close enough for deniability; and he didn't need to hear that right this moment, "you come to me."

"Carpenter?" Jason looked taken aback. "But I can't - "

"Right. You can't go to him to ask for help in getting you away from him." I blew my breath out in a soft whistle, and leaned back in my chair. "Sounds like you're screwed."

Jason frowned, his eyelids fluttering in a quick succession of blinks as he processed what I'd just said.

"You know what the worst part is?"

He shook his head.

"Worst part is I won't get my copy of your album."

He blinked. Cocked his head to the side. Then he grinned, as the import of what I'd said raced—as quickly as anything could race—through his head. "Yeah? I didn't know you backed me. Thanks, man!"

I just stared at him, narrowing my eyes into the look that I knew from experience made me appear a very dangerous fellow to cross. And not just as an act, either. I couldn't believe what he'd just said. He didn't even know who had backed him??

How in the hell could he think he would fulfill - ?

I took in a long, deep breath, to calm myself. Held it. Then let it out slowly.

Jason, meanwhile, had lost his momentary smile. He'd actually recoiled deeper into my couch from the look I'd given him. Right that second, he looked like he wanted nothing more than to bolt out of my office.

Too bad for him my door locked automatically when it shut.

I let him squirm for a few seconds as I considered the situation. I could just tell him to get out, and let him take his chances with either Carpenter or the law. It would serve him right.

But you know what? I really did think he played that keyboard well. And I wanted to hear his album.

And, while he wasn't exactly a friend, I didn't really want him to end up being spaced either. Or sent to prison. Though let's be honest: he would never live to go to prison.

And...maybe I could work a little something for myself in this, too.

I nodded to myself and stood up from my desk chair.

Jason made to get up as well, but I put up a hand, and he froze in place.

"Ok," I said. "Here's what's going to happen. You're going to stay here. I'm going to go talk to Carpenter."

"Carpenter?" Jason sounded shocked. "But - "

"Shut up." I reached down beneath my desk and pulled out the right-most of the guns I kept concealed there. Jason's eyes widened when he saw it, but when I just lifted up my shirt and tucked the weapon into the holster I always wore on my right hip, he relaxed again. A bit.

"Ok. I'm going to try to cut you a deal. Probably take an hour or two. But if you're not here when I get back, the deal's off."

His eyes flicked from the spot on my hip where the gun was now hidden beneath my shirt to my face, and he nodded. Then his eyes moved to my desk.

Was he wondering what else I had stored in here? Maybe money?

Well, I did have a stash of money in here. But he'd never find it in its hiding spot. And as for the other gun, the mechanism locking it in place beneath the left side of my desk was keyed to my DNA, and wouldn't unlock for anyone else. So he could muck about with it all day, and never get to the piece.

Still, it couldn't hurt to lay down the rules plainly for him, since he apparently wasn't all that smart.

"Don't touch anything while I'm gone. You can watch the televid and use the head. Nothing else. Got it?"

He nodded again.

"Ok. I'll be back soon."

With that, I headed toward the door, and the station beyond.

I've worked with Carpenter before. I didn't know if Jason knew that or not, but it didn't matter.

No one who does business in my field on Gilroy Station could have avoided crossing paths with Carpenter. In my case, I'd dealt with him twice on behalf of clients and again for a job he wanted done. Mostly above-board, and not at all unscrupulous. He knows my boundaries, and has never even attempted to get me to cross them.

So we knew each other. Wouldn't say we were friends, but there was at least a healthy professional respect there. I was counting on that to give me an in to try to help Jason out of his fix, and as I rode the lift up to the first deck, where Carpenter kept his offices, I went over my pitch to him at least four times.

The first deck was much different than the lower level where I resided. The corridors were broader, the overheads higher, the LED lightning more closely approximating the natural light from a G5 star. Even the gravplates in the deck seemed more uniform, but maybe that was just an illusion caused by all the other niceties that were so much better than what I was used to.

Carpenter's offices were opulent, as fitted a man of his stature. Officially, he was CEO of the system's largest shipping firm, and had branched out into real estate development and domestic manu-facturing.

But of course, that was just a front to conceal, and assist, his real business.

Still, as I strode into Carpenter's corporate offices I couldn't help feel like I was being warmly welcomed into a peaceful and honest realm of commerce, bent only toward doing its best for the benefit of its clients and shareholders both. But that only lasted a few seconds. Then I began glancing over my shoulder, looking for the knife that was heading toward my back.

Or the bullet.

Since I was known there, I managed to skirt past the initial layer of receptionists and lackeys. But I couldn't just waltz past Justine, Carpenter's executive assistant. She was mid-40s and still attractive, with lush blond hair—that had to have been dyed to conceal growing gray—rolling past her shoulders and a shapely figure that didn't at all reflect the five children that I knew for a fact she had borne her husband. As I approached, her sparkling green eyes narrowed and she smiled at me cautiously, shifting so that the green blouse she wore closed a bit at the collar.

Almost like she expected me to try to steal a glimpse, or something.

"Mr. Ramantha," she said by greeting, and arched an eyebrow at me. Sitting there behind the thick mahogany desk that marked her domain, she made no qualms about who was in charge in this place. "I don't believe you have an appointment."

I grinned at her, trying for the charming gambit. "Just wanted to see you again."

The other eyebrow rose to join the first, and her lips compressed.

So much for the charming bit. I cleared my throat. "I need to see him. It's an urgent matter, concerning Jason Ramsey."

She just looked at me for a few seconds, and I could see the wheels turning in her head. On the one hand, Carpenter didn't like to be disturbed without an appointment. On the other hand, she knew I had done jobs for him in the past. And her eye had twitched slightly when I said Jason's name. She knew Carpenter was interested in him, if not the exact reason why he was.

Justine nodded. "One moment."

Then her eyes went unfocused. I recognized the expression of a person conducting subvocal comms over implants; she was communicating directly with her boss.

A moment later she blinked, and her eyes turned back to meet mine. She nodded slightly. "Mr. Carpenter will see you."

She gestured toward the wide faux-oak double doors to the left of her desk, which led into Carpenter's inner sanctum. Smiling at her, I nodded, then proceeded toward the doors. I saw her left hand drift beneath her desk, and then a buzz and click announced a lock disengaging. Then the door swung open inwardly.

Carpenter's office was five or six times the size of mine, and paneled in what was either very good faux oak or the real thing.

Either way, it would have cost a small fortune to bring it up here onto the station. The left-hand wall as I entered was dominated by bookshelves that were crammed full of hardback tomes beyond immediate count: yet another indication of the man's wealth even if the panelling hadn't been enough. His desk was broad and deep, made of darkly stained wood, and faced the doors before a wall of pure transparent plasteel that looked out into the starscape beyond the way a planetbound executive's would look out over a picturesque countryside.

A trio of beige upholstered stuffed chairs sat around a round table that was stained the same shade as Carpenter's desk between the doors and the desk, to the right a bit; a more informal place to meet than in the two similarly upholstered chairs sitting directly across from his desk and facing it.

Carpenter himself was a man who, unlike Jason, had seen the inside of a weight room before, many times. Word was he had played rugby in his youth, and though he was in his 50s now and his belly strained the buttons of the grey pinstriped suit coat he wore over a white shirt and red tie, he still had the broad shoulders and barrel chest that spoke of many years of exertion. His face was round and he had closely-cut yellow-brown hair, and hazel eyes, and the lines around his mouth suggested a man who liked to smile and laugh.

When I stepped in, he rose from the chair he was sitting in—one of those surrounding the round table—and placed the book he had been reading down atop the table.

"Suresh," he said, extending his hand to me. "Nice to see you again."

I knew from experience that his grip was beyond firm; every time I shook hands with him I had to thrust my hand as deeply into his as possible, or my fingers would be crushed to the point of breaking. I did the same this time, inwardly bracing myself against the pain in case I didn't go far enough before he began the squeeze.

"Mr. Carpenter," I said simply, and squeezed as the vice grip came down around my fingers. I didn't let my relief show when I realized I had, indeed, pushed far enough.

But I could see from the amused twinkle in Carpenter's eyes that he knew what I was thinking. Still, he had the grace not to say it. He just released my hand and gestured toward the other chair at the table. As I settled down in the proffered chair, he spoke again.

"So you're here on behalf of Mr. Ramsey," he said, shaking his head. "Wish I could say I wasn't upset with him."

"Yes well," I said, and leaned forward toward him as he also sat. "You have reason. I'm here to see if we can work out an arrangement."

"I don't see what's to work out. He raised a lot of money with his fundraiser. He needs to pay what he owes."

That was true enough. But...

"I don't disagree. But there's more to the situation that makes things...complicated."

Carpenter raised an eyebrow, and I laid it out for him.

When I had finished, he leaned back in his chair and blew out a long, exasperated breath. "You've got to be kidding me."

I shook my head. "I wish I was."

"So you mean to tell me that not only does he not have enough money to pay me, he doesn't have enough to finish his recording?"

I nodded.

Carpenter looked away, toward the plasteel wall the looked out onto the universe. "Son of a bitch," he said. He paused for a second, then looked back at me. "You know I backed his fundraiser? At the highest level."

I blinked, utter surprise forcing me to silence for several seconds as I processed what Carpenter had said.

I flashed back to the days when Jason had been running his fundraiser. The highest tier had been for five hundred. Which meant...

"He owed you four thousand, and you gave him five hundred more in the fundraiser?"

Carpenter nodded.

"You didn't add it to his debt, just gave it?"

He nodded again.

"Why?"

Carpenter shrugged. "What can I say? The man plays a mean keyboard, and he's got a great voice."

No argument there. Except it was another indictment again Jason, because if he had realized Carpenter had given him five hundred in the fundraiser, surely that would have queued something in his head to question what was going on with the debt he owed.

But then again, I'd already established that Jason wasn't so smart. So...

I shook my head. One thing at a time.

"Can we agree we'd both rather see him finishing his album and getting it out to the world earning money than see him try to breathe vacuum?"

Carpenter raised an eyebrow at my forthright statement, but he nodded. He had a distinctively curious expression on his face.

"So how about this. You front him the rest of the money to finish producing the album and to make good on the rewards to his backers."

Carpenter opened his mouth, to object no doubt, but I held up a hand before he could say anything.

"Hear me out."

He shut his mouth. Though he did not look happy.

"You manage him while it's being finished. Make sure he keeps on the straight and narrow. Then when it comes out, you get the proceeds, both revenue from royalties and from concerts, until his debt is paid plus....let's say twenty percent." I raised an eyebrow. "Simple interest."

Carpenter snorted, but made a gesture that said, "Keep going."

"After that, you get 40% for the life of the album."

Carpenter sat silently for a half minute, pondering. Then he shook his head. "That's a lot of risk to take on my shoulders. For all you and I know, the album might not earn anything beyond what it already has."

"Then Jason works for you until his debt's paid, with interest." I raised an eyebrow. "Simple interest," I said again. And again Carpenter snorted. I continued, "But I think neither of us believes it won't do well. If you add a little bit more funding for marketing in the surrounding systems, it just might catch on big. And then..." I left the rest unsaid, but spread my hands and raised my eyebrows at him.

The corners of Carpenter's mouth were beginning to turn upward slightly. "That's more money out of my pocket, Suresh. I'd need more of a cut on the back end."

"How much more?"

"Eighty percent."

I shook my head. "Fifty."

"Seventy."

"Sixty."

"Sixty-five."

I hesitated, then nodded. "Done."

Carpenter leaned back in his chair and inhaled, then let out a long slow sigh. "This could turn out to be a good thing," he said. "I run Jason's musical career. Get most of the proceeds..." He raised an eyebrow. "This goes well, I might open up my own label, hmm?"

I shook my head. "No. This is just for this one album. After that, he's on his own."

Carpenter's satisfied expression dropped a bit. "Not sure I like that. He's not exactly a reliable man. Once I've made the investment to get him off the ground I don't want him screwing it up in later efforts."

"That's between you and him. Later. If he wants to sign on with you again in the future, fine. But for this deal, I'm not committing him to anything further."

"What, you don't trust me?"

I didn't answer, just looked at him. Truth was, I didn't trust him. And though Jason and I weren't friends, I had no intention of signing him into indentured servitude to this man. Paying him back, and giving him a piece of the action for his trouble? Sure. Forcing Jason to work with him forever? Not a chance.

After a few seconds, Carpenter shrugged. "Fine. He's free to do what he wants after this first album, as long as I get paid back with interest first."

I raised an eyebrow, and he chuckled. "Simple interest," he added, sounding amused. "But," he held up his finger, "if he starts to produce his second album before I get my money back, I get the same cut of the second."

That seemed fair. I nodded. "Agreed."

"Well," Carpenter said, and moved to stand. "I suppose all's well that ends well."

"Not quite," I said, not moving.

Carpenter paused, then settled back down into his seat. He eyed me sideways. "What else is there?"

"My cut," I said.

His eyebrows rose.

"He's not my friend," I said. "I'm only doing this because I didn't want to see him spaced, and I like his music. I think I should get a finders fee."

Carpenter's lips turned downward slightly. "How much?"

"Ten percent."

"So I only get fifty-five." There was the beginnings of anger growing there, and I hurried to clarify before that anger began to blaze.

"No, you get your sixty-five. My ten percent is on top of that."

The anger fled, and Carpenter nodded in understanding. "So sixty-five to me, ten to you, and twenty-five to him."

I nodded. "But if it's all the same to you, I'd prefer he not know about my cut."

Carpenter just looked at me for a moment, then said. "So he thinks I get seventy-five, but in reality I'm kicking back ten to you. And then in subsequent albums, if we continue working together?"

I shrugged. "Like I said, that's between him and you. I don't want any part of it after that. If you two decide to keep working together, give him a ten percent raise, to sweeten the deal. Or keep the seventy-five. Doesn't matter to me."

Carpenter burst out laughing, then he held out his hand, and we shook.

I didn't push far enough this time, and left feeling like my fingers had been broken.

"Seventy-five percent?" Jason's voice was higher-pitched than normal, disbelief arguing with relief and then with resistance as he responded to my summation of the negotiation with Carpenter.

"Sorry man," I said, as I unholstered my gun and slipped it into its clip beneath the desk, then settled back down into my chair. "He was rather irritated with you. I tried to get him less, but..." I spread my hands helplessly. "Best I could do."

Jason nodded slowly. "Yeah, guess so." He looked away from me, toward the vidscreen, which he had turned to a sitcom while I was away. He wasn't really watching it, just looking at the flashing images as he thought for a second. Then he said, "Still, it sucks he gets so much. I was thinking this would be my big break, you know?"

"Yeah, well, it beats being a fugitive. Or sucking vacuum."

Jason blanched, and looked back at me. He nodded again, more quickly this time. "That's for sure." He drew a breath, then rose. "Thanks, man, I really appreciate the help. You're a real friend."

I didn't let my skepticism show about that. We hadn't really been friends even before this incident. So I just made a vaguely dismissive wave of my hand. "It's no big deal. Just happy you'll get to produce your album." I paused, then added, "and keep breathing."

Jason shook his head. "No, man I mean it. You really saved my ass." He bit his lip, thinking for a second. Then he nodded to himself, coming to a decision of some sort. "Look, I don't have much money. But how about you take ten percent of what I make from the album?"

I blinked. I hadn't truly expected he would make this kind of offer. But as long as he was... "You're getting twenty-five percent. So you mean I get ten percent and you get fifteen, or I get two point five percent and you get twenty-two point five?"

Jason looked askance at me, then he shook his head. "Two percent's bull crap. You deserve more than that. Straight ten."

"So Carpenter gets seventy-five, I get ten, and you get fifteen. That doesn't seem fair to you."

Jason snorted. "Like you said, without you I wouldn't be getting anything."

Spreading my hands, I leaned back in my chair and put on my deepest look of appreciation. "Jason, I really don't know what to say."

"Don't say anything. You saved my ass, man. Thank you." He extended out his hand.

We shook, then he left my office.

As the door closed behind him and the lock clacked back into place, I considered that this had turned out to be a pretty good day all around. On instinct, I opened my invoicing program up again, then swiped Ms. Gorant's file open.

Pretty sure she deserved a discount, this time.

26

TERRAN NEW YEAR

Why on God's green Earth did the New Year always have to fall on the exact date and time that Terra had set for it, centuries ago?

It would have been one thing if Persephone's orbital revolution and rotation had matched Terra's. But it didn't. One day on Persephone was 1.0498576 Earth day. And a year on Persephone would take...

Jenny scowled as she resisted doing the math that would convert a 332 day year into a Terran year. And never mind that she had memorized the conversion to a Terran day and year way back in second grade.

It didn't matter, no matter what the variation may or may not be. And when she was honest with herself, Jenny knew exactly how much the variation was. What mattered was that a year on Persephone was not a year on Terra. And where the HELL did the Terrans get off telling Persephonans that they had to celebrate the New Year by Terra's calendar?

But Jenny knew the answer as soon as she thought it. The Terrans got away with it because they had the economic, social, and military might to force it. And wasn't a damn thing Persephone and her patriots could do but grind their teeth, bend the knee, and grovel before Terra's imperial might.

That, or be killed utterly, to the fifth generation. No one would ever choose to risk that.

And so Jenny had grown up beneath the boot of the Terran Empire. Listened to its news messages of fighting for peace, freedom, and self-determination for all. While at the same time turning power over the Empire's controlled territories, including her home, to political flunkies who knew less than nothing about how to manage business on the lands and planets they had just been bequeathed. But who had expertise in milking that production for the flunky's own gain. And, apparently more importantly, in milking the population's young virgins for his own pleasure as well.

And the Empire wondered why production was down over twenty percent, or why rebellion tended to flare up every twenty to twenty-five years.

All that being said, Kevin still stood in front of Jenny, his expression a mixture of hope and terror as he waited for her answer to his invitation to the New Years Eve Ball.

In all of her sixteen years, Jenny only had one boy who could even approximate a boyfriend. Samil, who had grown up two doors down from her parents' townhouse, and who had flushed crimson and then fled, trying in vain to conceal his—admittedly disappointingly small--erection when she had taken their kissing to the next step and removed her blouse and bra.

She had sat there, feeling the swelling within her that had started to open up and call to him fade in disappointment, and mentally shouted curses at his lack of manhood as he'd fled.

Since that utter humiliation, and the accompanying frustration that came with it, she had not let any person with a Y chromosome near her at all. And yet Kevin had wormed his way in, and Jenny's heart had swelled to welcome him inside.

Although...

Truth be told, Kevin hadn't had to squirm or maneuver all that much. She had halfway fallen for him the moment she laid eyes on him. Tall, muscular, darkly tanned, with black hair and dark brown eyes. He had been everything she had ever dreamed of: her strong, powerful father taken to the next level.

And so much more than that. Because while her father had meekly bent the knee, Kevin was standing up. Protesting against the injustice of Terran rule. And, secretly in the shadows, helping to build up an army that would drive the Terrans off once and for all.

So why did he want to go to the New Years Eve Ball, of all things? Jenny would have presumed he would avoid the thing entirely, in protest against the blatant imperialism implicit in the event's entire premise.

And yet here he stood, on the doorstep of her parent's little house, looking at her with earnest eyes that strove very hard to not betray the fear he was surely suppressing that she would say no, as he waited for her answer.

Jenny shifted on her feet, and glanced behind herself.

The noonday sun shone through the open doorway into the house, augmenting the solar-attuned LEDs in the overhead to produce a warm, almost natural glow throughout the space. Her parents' well-upholstered Navy blue couch and armchairs almost seemed to stand erect before the sunlight that accompanied her gaze, followed by the cream paint on the sitting room walls and then the brown-stained faux wood in the kitchen beyond, where her mother was working on a stew of some sort for dinner.

She was only in her early 40s, but she could have been more like 55 or 60, stooped and worn as she looked. And unless Jenny was wrong, she'd be lucky to make it that long.

Looking at her mother, Jenny couldn't help but wonder how much better her life would have been had someone worked to cast aside Terra's boot when she had been Jenny's age.

Someone like Kevin.

Maybe he had some sort of mission planned, and he needed her as cover. If that was the case, she'd be shirking her patriotic duty not to go and help him.

And, she admitted, it's not like he wasn't cute, on top of everything else.

So, on an impulse, or maybe not really an impulse, she turned back to him and nodded briskly. "I'd love to go with you," she said.

Kevin's uncertain expression turned into a broad, pleased grin, and he nodded in return. "Great," he said. "Pick you up at ten." He paused, the added, "Wear a nice dress."

He winked, then turned and walked down the little set of stairs that separated her front door from the flagstone pathway that connected what little their was of their front yard—but by God, though it was little, Mom kept it trimmed, manicured, and green as Ireland...wherever that was—from the sidewalk that ran alongside the street leading back to the center of town.

Jenny watched him go, and felt a little stirring of nervousness.

If she had just signed up for a secret mission, she really hoped she didn't blow it. And blow it with Kevin in general and...

She stopped in mid-thought, and the bottom went out of her stomach. What had he said?

"Wear a nice dress," his voice echoed in her ears. But she didn't have any nice dresses!

Whirling around faster than she ever had, she bounded toward the kitchen. "Mom!"

***

Kevin cleaned up nice.

When he showed up to Jenny's house he was in a grey-brown suit with a white shirt and a red-orange tie that somehow made the color of his eyes stand out all the more brightly. Jenny hadn't realized it was possible, not in that color combination. But it worked.

Walking next to him as they ascended the short stairwell that led to the entrance to the athletic field house where the New Years Eve celebration was being held, Jenny felt like a weed next to a flowerbed.

She didn't have any nice dresses. And of course neither Mom nor Dad had the extra money to buy her one, even if there had been time to go shopping that afternoon. But Mom had a old dress stashed away in the back of her and dad's closet: a little navy blue number that was cut to be tight at the hips but generous in the bosom, with thin straps that ran up over her shoulders to keep the thing up and a little slit that ran from her left ankle to mid-thigh on that same leg, which allowed for easier movement and showed off the leg a bit.

Problem was Jenny wasn't nearly as busty as Mom. Though she was taller. So while the slit on the leg worked really well, she felt like a half-filled sack of potatoes up top.

Kevin hadn't noticed, though. Or if he had, he had been polite enough not to mention it. In fact, he'd said she looked great when he'd shown up at her door to pick her up.

That was nice of him.

It didn't stop her from feeling self-conscious as they reached the top of the stairs and stopped before the marble pillars lining the entrance to the Field House.

A short line had formed there, as people were being checked by security as they made their way inside. And for a second, Jenny felt a flash of nerves on top of her self consciousness.

"Uh-oh," she said, glancing up at Kevin. Had his mission been blown already?

He looked sidelong at her. "What? Did you forget something?"

Jenny shook her head and gestured at the security guards, in their white collared shirts and with their heavily-laden gun and utility belts, and the portable metal detectors and explosives sniffers they were using to search the people who hoped to enter the building.

Kevin snorted. "What, them?" He shook his head. "No sweat, Jenny. Just relax." He looked back at her and raised and eyebrow. "We're not doing anything wrong. Just two people looking to have fun together on the big night."

He didn't sound at all ironic when he said that. He really was in character.

Biting her lip for a second, Jenny nodded. Then she took a deep breath, squared her shoulders, and faced forward.

Ahead, the person in front of them walked inside, having cleared the security team. One of the guards, older than the others by about ten years and powerfully built beneath his uniform, waved for her to step forward.

Putting on her best brave and unconcerned face, Jenny moved toward to meet him.

There was dancing.

Jenny hadn't known there would be dancing.

Then again, when they got inside and she heard the music from the five-piece tuxedo-clad band set up on the stage at the end of the big inner hall of the field house, largely empty since the people who ran the building had retracted the bleacher seating on either side of the main hall and raised the basketball hoops on each end so they were snugged out of the way against the ceiling, and saw the crowd milling about with the first few couples beginning to step out to the band's music in front of the stage, Jenny realized she should have known about it.

Hadn't she heard people talking about this party before countless times?

She'd never gone to it; previous years she had been too young, or so Mom had said. But Mom and Dad had gone a time or two before. And other girls a grade or two above her had gossiped about it.

But somehow it had never clicked that this was, in fact, a dance party. And Jenny had no idea how to dance. Not really.

She stopped dead, dread and uncertainty freezing her in place so quickly Kevin hadn't noticed she had stopped moving until he was two paces ahead. Then he stopped, turned around, and looked at her with a concerned and confused expression.

"What's wrong?" he said.

Jenny gestured toward the dance floor. "I..." She trailed off. Stopped. The drew a deep breath and tried again. "I can't dance."

"Oh, is that all." Kevin grinned broadly at her, then closed with her until he was just a few inches in front of her. She leaned her head back so she kept looking into his eyes as he got close. She could see a mischievous twinkle in them.

"Don't worry," he said. "I'll show you."

Then he had her left hand looped into the crook of his right elbow, and his left hand atop hers, and he lead her toward the dance floor.

———

The evening passed in a blur. After her initial hesitation, she learned basics of how to follow Kevin on the dance floor. Then within a couple songs they were moving together easily, and she lost every thought except for how much fun it was.

Then he started introducing her to spins. The first time, she got tangled in her own feet and she thought for a second she was going to fall, right there in front of everyone. But somehow Kevin continued the movements he was making, and he scooped her up, preventing her from falling even as he made a sort of dip maneuver where she leaned way backward and he leaned forward atop her.

As he brought them both up, a few of the couples around the edge of the dancing area, who were watching instead of dancing, clapped. Instead of acknowledging the applause himself, Kevin stepped back, releasing one hand and sweeping his free hand from her toward the clapping members of the crowd, as though to say, "Look this piece of elegance, who pulled off that display."

And one of the guys who had been clapping broke in with an approximation of a wolf whistle.

Jenny flushed, unsure whether that was meant as a compliment or if it was a challenge to Kevin, or an insult toward her...

And then she was swept up in Kevin's dancing frame again, and he spun her away from her adoring public. Such as it was.

They continued on like that for a what felt like forever, and Jenny lost track of time completely.

But eventually, she realized she needed to stop. She was getting winded, and sweaty. And so was Kevin. He seemed to know somehow that she was losing energy, and between one spin and the next, he had her led off the dance floor toward the refreshment stand that had been set up off to the side.

There was punch, and harder drinks for those who were of age, and finger foods and sweets.

Heaven.

But Jenny felt like a mess; she must certainly have looked it too. So she begged off to use the restroom to get herself back together.

Plus, she needed to go.

When she got back, she found Kevin speaking with an older man in a navy blue suit and paisley tie by the refreshment stand. They didn't look like they were trying to be particularly furtive, but as she approached, the older man noticed her coming and plainly stopped what he was saying as he eyed her openly.

"Good evening, Kevin," he said as she stepped up, and shook hands with him.

"George," Kevin said.

Then George nodded to Jenny and walked away, back into the crowd.

"Who was that," she asked, watching him go.

"A friend of mine," Kevin said. He held out a cup of punch, which she accepted. Then he grinned at her, openly. "Drink up," he said. "They're having a contest on the floor soon. And we're going to win."

"What? No, I can't!"

He just grinned more broadly at her, and she took a long gulp of the punch, those nerves coming back into her stomach.

They didn't win. But damn if the contest wasn't fun anyway.

The whole rest of the night was fun, and it seemed like a weight of some sort had been lifted from Kevin's shoulders, because as energetic as he had been on the dance floor before her trip to the rest room and his talk with George, he was on fire after.

When they left the Field House at the end of the night, Jenny was soaking with sweat. But she didn't care. She couldn't remember when she'd had so much fun.

And she felt good in another way, too. As the evening progressed, she became convinced that George had something to do with Kevin's mission that night. That meeting had been what he needed, and with his mission completed, he was a different man.

So she'd helped, somehow, do her little part to rid her home of the Terran tyranny.

When Kevin dropped her off in front of her parents' house, she smiled up at him. "That was a good night," she said.

He nodded. "Best in a while."

"I'm glad I was able to help with your mission."

He looked at her askance and she raised her eyebrows at him, amused. "What? You don't think I can be," she fluttered her eyelashes at him, jokingly, "discrete, and under cover?"

Kevin cocked his head to the side and looked silently at her for a moment. "What are you talking about?"

"Your mission." She looked left and right, then leaned in toward him and said conspiratorially, "You meet with George. What, was he passing you info? Making arrangements for the next op?"

The confused expression remained on his face. He shook his head. "George was helping me get my dad's auto fixed."

She blinked. "Auto fixed?"

"Yeah, his auto fixed." Some of the good humor left his face. "What did you think this was?"

Now it was Jenny's turn to look confused. "Well, you're always talking about getting rid of the Terrans. I just thought...maybe you had something going on. That you needed a cover, and that I..." She paused, then spit it out. "That I was helping you."

"Is that what you think?" He rolled his eyes, then stepped forward, closing the distance between them. Looking steadily into her eyes, he said, "Jenny, I don't like the Terrans, but I'm not going to pass up a good party out of spite." He smiled again at her, gently. "The only mission I had tonight was being with you."

She felt a flush of warmth flow through her. First from embarrassment, then from something more pleasant, and tingly. "Really?"

"Really."

Then his lips were on hers, and she felt her knees threaten to give way.

It seemed they were there, locked together like that for a long, long time. Then a throat cleared behind them.

Jenny jumped, and pushed away from him, spinning around to see her father, standing there in shadows beside their front door.

"Get inside, young lady," Dad said. He didn't sound displeased, but his voice would brook no argument.

Jenny looked back at Kevin and smiled an apology. He said, "I'll give you a call tomorrow." He looked over at her Dad and said, "Good night, Mr. Rogan."

"Good night, Kevin," Dad said. And he really meant that, as well.

Jenny hurried inside, then rushed to her room and shut the door.

It had been one hell of a night.

27

SANTA FE STATION

Though she'd been living in San Diego for ten years and had lived less than two miles away from it for most of that time, Kim hardly ever came out to Balboa Park. But every time she did, she left asking herself why she didn't come more often.

The entire city was beautiful, heaven on earth as far as she was concerned, with the seemingly eternal sunlight and temperatures that never got much above the mid 80s or below the low 70s. But there was something about the Park itself. The old-style architecture, the walking paths, the manicured landscaping, the historical feel of it, and for whatever reason, the press of people and tourists who flocked to see it. She couldn't help but smile there, no matter how bad her day had been.

Which might be why you're walking the path here again, she said to herself as she paced past the parking lot that stood before the protruding round construction of the city's Air and Space Museum, and on toward Pan American Plaza and then the park proper beyond. It had been a hell of a week.

A hell of a month.

And mom's call at lunchtime had just made things worse. So much worse that she had been unable to focus at all in her job as a paralegal in Benson and Wigger, the law firm she had served for the last five years in their expansive offices downtown, just a few blocks away from the park.

So she'd begged off, taken half a day of leave, and practically fled up the hill to the park, a walk she hardly ever made anymore because of the number of homeless who had taken to using the streets on the east side of downtown, away from the waterfront, as their living and bedrooms.

But she'd barely noticed it today. Barely noticed the ache in her feet from walking the nearly a mile and a hundred-some feet of elevation change from her office building to here in her business pumps. Her mind could only find one focus, the whole way up.

Cancer.

Stage three, mom had said. Might be operable...but the expense. Dad refused to hear of it, she said. He'd resigned himself to this being his time to go, and no one was going into debt to try to prolong his time.

Well, he is seventy-three.

Kim squashed that thought, shoving a dangling brown lock that had pulled free from a barrette and had gotten into her eye as though it were something—or some one—that was assaulting her.

Of course, it just flopped back down into her field of view again, and she scowled.

But then, she'd already been scowling, so what was the difference.

There was a stucco-beige stone bench on the edge of the sidewalk a few feet ahead on the right. She made a beeline for it, and smoothed the navy blue fabric of her suit skirt before settling down. She had a small collapsible mirror in her hand bag, and she fished it out and popped it open.

Her hair wasn't too badly out of whack, and it just took a moment to fix.

As she was working at it, part of her shook a finger at the rest of her. Who cared what her hair looked like? With what she had just learned, it didn't matter worth a whit, did it?

But it did. For whatever reason, by the time Kim had the stray lock tucked back into place and the mirror snapped shut, some of the weight that had been crushing down on her soul was gone. Not all of it, to be certain. But just the act of tending to that one minor bit of trivial normalness had taken her mind away.

And she felt better. A little.

She sat still, and closed her eyes. Breathing deeply, she took in the sounds of the park: the chatter of kids as they rushed ahead of their parents down the walking paths. The rumble of a passenger jet passing overhead on its descent into the airport. More softly, a trumpet from the direction of the zoo: an elephant maybe?

The faint smell of fried food, from the cafe next to the Air and Space Museum most likely, reached her nostrils, and she breathed a bit deeper, thinking of french fries and a nice, juicy hamburger, with all the fixings.

But your diet, her mind shouted at her, and Kim snorted that thought away.

When she came to the park, she normally got something to eat up at the Prado and sat at one of the many umbrella'd tables there to munch on her food and people watch. It wasn't that much further ahead and to the right, considering the distance she'd already walked. But her stomach growled, and she realized she hadn't even bothered to grab the lunch bag she'd stuffed into the firm's refrigerator that morning.

Ah, to hell with her diet. With news like she'd just gotten, who cared anyway?

Resolutely, she opened her eyes and clasped her hand bag closed, then moved to stand.

She stopped halfway to her feet, when she looked down and to the right, at the bare dirt of the ground next to the bench.

There was a book lying there. But she couldn't quite make out what...

She bent forward a little bit more, turning her body to see more clearly, and felt her left eyebrow raise.

J. F. Henson. Her favorite author. And...

She blinked. Depths of Shadows. It was his latest, in hardback.

She'd heard it was coming out and had put it on her list of things to go pick up, but she hadn't gotten around to it.

It had been one hell of a month.

Stooping, she picked the book up.

The dust jacket was dusty, but it had been lying in the dirt, so... Flipping it over, she couldn't see any signs of damage. What was it doing here?

Clearly someone must have dropped it, or forgotten it here.

She straightened up to her full height and looked about.

The parking lot over by the Air and Space Museum was about half full, and there was a slow stream of people going to and from cars over there. A couple in shorts and t-shirts who looked like tourists were walking away from the park on the opposite side of President's Way from her. But there was no one on her side of the street, that she could see.

Kim peered left, then right, then left again.

Yep. No one about at all.

Frowning, she looked down at the book in her hands. She had the urge to just take it and go. It wasn't like it would really be stealing, she told herself. Just her lucky day is all. And after everything that had come crashing down on her, she felt like she could use a bit of luck, right then.

"Screw it," she said. Then she tucked the book under her arm and walked toward the cafe whose scents had called to her a moment ago.

A hamburger, then home and the good book she'd been looking forward to for weeks.

Just what the doctor ordered.

Home was a little one-bedroom condo in the Gasslamp district. If she'd been on the other side of the building, she would have had a decent view of Petco Park. Not enough so she could actually see the game. But the ballpark and surrounds made for a nice sight.

Alas, her place only got a view of other high-rises, and then the smaller buildings out through East Village and the hills beyond downtown into the sprawl that made up the rest of San Diego county.

It was not particularly inspiring, but still Kim liked to sit on the balcony of her seventh-floor place and look out at the world anyway.

She'd bought it back in '12, unknowingly at the time at the absolute bottom of the San Diego housing market after the shenanigans of 2008. In the last couple years she'd thought a few times about moving to a bigger place. Then she saw the prices, and balked. Even with the gains she'd accumulated on her place, it was just too much.

Of course, she could move out of Downtown. Out to Bonita or Chula Vista to the south, or Vista up north. Both areas still got relatively decent bang for the housing buck. But that meant more than her current fifteen minute walk to work each day, so that was right out.

Still, as she switched on the lights and stepped inside her place, and beheld all 575 square feet of its glory, Kim couldn't help but wish to be less cramped.

She made decent money as a paralegal in a big firm downtown, and had decorated her place carefully to match that. Modern stainless steel appliances and grey quartz countertops in the kitchen, with white shaker cabinets and recessed LED lights in the ceiling. Cream paint on the walls, setting off the charcoal leather couch and love seat arrayed before her TV in the living room. Out on the balcony a pair of rattan chairs with a glass-topped drink table between them, facing east.

Kim let the door swing shut behind her and breathed in the subtle pine scent of the Scentsy burner she had plugged into the wall in her entryway, and tried to feel the usual relaxation, the lifting of burden, that she always felt when she returned here, to her abode.

No such luck.

Not that she'd really expected it. Though she'd tried to set her mother's news from her mind during her late lunch, she had only marginally succeeded. And then on the Uber ride back home, the dread and the anguish returned full force.

Now, looking around at the reproduced art on her walls, and the sterile cleanliness of her kitchen, she couldn't feel anything but desolate.

"To hell with that," she said through her teeth. Stalking forward into her condo more fully, she kicked off her pumps and flopped her hand bag down onto the kitchen counter. Then, eyes firmly on the sliding glass door leading to her balcony, she stalked across the living room, found book in hand.

She was going to sit down, by God, and get her mind off of things. That's what she was going to do.

Her balcony chairs were well cushioned, and when she settled down into the one on the right, she couldn't not let out a little sigh of relaxation as the cushion morphed to match her form and provide just enough gentle support to ease at least the muscular tension that had been haunting her the last hour or so.

Hopefully J. F. would do the same for her mind.

She hefted the hardcover and, leaning back into the chair's deep cushions, opened to the first page.

A slip of paper, which apparently had been wedged somewhere in the middle of the book, slid out and fell into Kim's lap.

She froze, blinking in surprise and looked down at it. It was yellow-white, unlined, and folded over itself, like a note.

Probably just a bill or something from around the house that the book's previous owner had been using as a bookmark. Closing the book, Kim picked up the paper and flipped it open, curiosity pushing her to pry into that unknown stranger's life before her inner voice could object.

It wasn't a bill. The sheet was blank except for three lines, typed in a plain font in black.

"Santa Fe Station.

Locker 542.

26483."

What in the - ?

Kim read the simple text again, her eyebrows rising in confusion as a little shiver went passing through her body. Not of fear, of intrigue.

She knew Santa Fe station. It was the rail terminal in downtown San Diego, a couple blocks in from the wharfs. She'd been there several times over the last few years, taking the Coaster up to Hollywood for a premier with a friend who worked as a Producer's assistant, or all the way up to Monterey to see her parents. It wasn't super big, but it was nice enough. And were there...?

The image of a collection of lockers, rentable by the hour or the day, over in the corner to the right as one entered the station's main entrance, sprang into Kim's mind.

There were rentable lockers there. It stood to reason; many transit terminals had them. But she'd never noticed—never had need to notice—them before.

That third line must be the code to get the locker open. Which meant whoever had owned this book last was now screwed, because he wouldn't be able to get his stuff back.

"Shit," Kim said to herself.

Maybe it was an old note. Maybe the book's owner got whatever it was from the locker weeks ago, and had taken it home, happy and safe.

Or maybe, that annoying voice in her head said in a tone like her first grade teacher used while wagging her finger, he was going to get it today, but he lost his book and you took it.

Either way, Kim was going to have to go to Santa Fe Station and see. If it truly was an old note, no harm no foul. If it wasn't...

"Hopefully he's got a label or something on it, so I can find him to give it back."

Yeah. Fat chance of that. But no way was she going to be able to sleep tonight if she didn't find out one way or the other.

Muttering to herself, Kim rose and went back inside, then turned right to go into her bedroom.

At the very least, she was going to change into more comfortable clothes...and shoes.

A pair of Brooks running shoes and compression shorts and an athletic shirt later, Kim was feeling a whole lot more limber. She descended the elevator to the ground floor and exited her building, then turned left toward the west and the waterfront half a dozen blocks away.

And toward Santa Fe Station.

She thought about grabbing an Uber, then decided against it. It was getting on toward late afternoon now, and traffic in the city was beginning to pick up. It wouldn't hit full on rush hour for another hour or so, but even still, she hated sitting in a car in traffic. Walking would be slower, but at least it would feel like uninterrupted progress.

Besides, she needed to think about what she was going to do if her hope was wrong, and whatever the book's owner had left in that locker was still there for the taking.

She couldn't just take whatever it was, that was for sure. A book was one thing. This was likely something much more substantial.

But how to find the owner, or if she did how to explain?

She halted before an orange hand and an electronic voice saying, "Wait. Wait," at the intersection of fourth and Broadway, and shook her head. She didn't need to find the owner. She could just go to lost and found in the station, and turn it in there. Or go to the cops, and let them handle it. No need to get any further involved at all.

That made her feel better, and as the crossing signal turned to walk and she started across the street, she felt her spirits buoy for the first time all day. Her pace quickened, and she was practically whistling as she hurried the last few blocks to the station.

The relief from responsibility was like a drug, it felt so good.

Santa Fe Station took up the entire block between Broadway and B Street on Kettner Blvd. It was constructed in the southwest style, with yellow-beige stucco siding and orange-red roof. Surrounded by towering skyscrapers on all sides, it seemed a diminutive throwback to a long-gone era as she walked up to it.

Inside, it was neat and clean, and well lit by lamps in the ceiling shining down onto polished tiles. The ticket window had row upon row of wooden benches in front of it, just like in the movies, and there were half a dozen people sitting in those benches, waiting for a train or for someone to pick them up. It being Southern California in September, no one had a jacket, and only one long sleeves.

No one looked over when she entered, and she was just as happy they hadn't. She didn't spend any time looking them over either. Just turned to the right toward the three rows of rental lockers, stacked three high, that took up space in the near corner at the end of the station's lobby in that direction.

It had been a while since Kim had last used lockers like these. Back then you inserted your coins into a slot and pulled out a little orange-handled key, which you could then use to unlock the locker when you were ready to get your stuff.

But as she approached this cluster of lockers, Kim could tell that's not how they operated at all. Each had keypads above their locking mechanism. Which she should have expected; hence the code in the note. The keypads were colored orange, though.

Had to keep up tradition, Kim supposed.

It didn't take long to find the locker. There weren't that many lockers to choose from, and well over two thirds of the available lockers were obviously unlocked and empty.

For that matter, why number it 542, and not just 27? That would make more sense. Not that it really mattered. What mattered was -

"Crap," Kim said to herself as she stopped in front of the locker in question. It was the middle locker in its column of three, and it was shut. And clearly locked.

Could be someone else had put her stuff in this one after the book owner got his out. It could happen, right?

"Yeah right," she said.

With no small amount of trepidation, she keyed in the code from the note.

The locker made a metallic click, then the door swung ever so slightly open.

Drawing a quick breath and forcing butterflies down in her stomach, Kim reached out and swung the locker door open the rest of the way.

There was a bag inside. Brown leather, with two leather handholds on either side of a zippered closure that ran all the way down either side of the bag's body. It looked like the kind of bag a doctor would use for a house call in one of those old movies.

Curious, despite the growing certainty that she had just unknowingly screwed somebody, she inched forward and took hold of the bag, pulling it partway out of the locker.

There was no lock on the bag itself; the zipper was free to move. So she unzipped it.

Green paper in neat stacks, bound by yellow paper wraps at their center struck Kim's eyes and she gasped, then closed the bag up tight.

Then looked left and right; surely someone must have seen -

But there was no one anywhere near her.

She looked back at the bag again and inched it back open. She must have been imagining things.

Nope.

They were hundred dollar bills, stacked neatly together and wrapped in paper with $10,000 stamped on the wrappers. She did a quick count. Two. Four. Six. Eight...

There was a hundred thousand dollars there.

"What the hell is this?" she breathed, then looked around again.

Still no one. Not even a security camera that she could see.

Nervousness battled with excitement, then elation. A hundred thousand dollars! Cash! And no one would ever know she had it.

What about the guy who owned it, asked that nagging voice inside her head.

"Screw him," she said softly. After all, he had to be up to no good. Who leaves a hundred thousand dollars in a train station locker, if he's on the level?

By finding this money, she may have just disrupted a terrorist attack. Or a murder for hire scheme. Or a -

You're just trying to justify taking it, said that voice again.

And she was. But damn it, this was the answer to everything. Dad's cancer. Her own desire for a bigger place.

Everything.

Moving quickly, before that nagging voice could say anything else, she zippered the bag shut, hefted it by the handles, then strode briskly out of the station, for home.

———

The voice started up three blocks after she got back onto Broadway and turned east.

And no wonder. As she approached the intersection with State Street, she saw the lofty building of the Hall of Justice to her left. The County Courthouse, she knew, lay a block behind it. And to the right, on her side of the street...The Federal Courthouse, followed by the Circuit Court. And behind them, the IRS.

She'd been in all of those courthouses hundreds of times during the course of her duties at work. She knew the people who worked there. The clerks, the bailiffs, the Sheriffs, the Marshalls. Even a few of the judges. She thought highly of them and, she hoped at least, they did the same of her.

What would they think about this, the voice asked.

The bag, not exactly light when she started carrying it, felt like a ton of bricks in her hand as she waited, feeling the displeasure of those places of justice as they stared down judging eyes at her.

It was like the windows on the buildings were scowling. Kim wanted to cringe away, but just then the walk symbol appeared.

Instead she hurried across the street, practically running to get past the courthouses and all they represented.

After a couple blocks, she slowed, and glanced back over her shoulder, almost expecting to see a stream of uniformed men charging at her, ready to pounce for what she'd done.

But there was nothing. No one but the usual suited lawyers chatting away into their cell phones as they hurried about their business.

Kim let out a quick, humorless laugh.

Of course there was nothing. There would continue to be nothing, too. There was nothing to link her to this bag and the money in it. No way anyone would think to suspect her of anything. She had the money free and clear, and with it she could make sure these weren't Dad's last months on the planet.

And after, if there was anything left over...she could make use of the rest herself. No one would ever need to know.

But how will you explain where you got the money for the operation, that voice asked as she began walking again, sweeping the renewed confidence that had started to grow within her aside as fresh doubts crept up.

It was a valid point. She'd have to come up with some kind of explanation as to where the money came from.

For some reason, she flashed back to Breaking Bad, to the "Help my dad" site that the main character's kid set up for his cancer treatment, how he had used that site to funnel his drug money to himself cleanly. Maybe she could do something like -

Oh great idea, said the voice. Money laundering. Make it an even greater Federal offense, why don't you? And do you have any idea how to really do that at all?

No, Kim had to admit to herself, she didn't. She had no idea whatsoever.

"Well fine," she said under her breath. "But I can figure it out. Start with small things. Pay with cash for small things. Things that are easy to explain. Then sell them. Or something."

Or something.

This was going to be more complicated than she initially thought. But she could do it.

She needed to do it.

She came up on the intersection with Eighth Street. A right turn, then a few blocks and she'd be home.

But instead of turning, she found herself stopping there at the intersection, unable to move.

You can't keep it, said the voice inside her.

But I need it, she practically cried back at it. Dad needs it. He'll -

Kim's vision blurred as tears welled up, and she bit back a sob as the pain of Mom's news—the pain she had tried and succeeded at keeping at arm's length all day—slammed into her chest like a sledgehammer. She stumbled backwards a half step before she caught herself.

Get ahold of yourself, woman, she snarled inwardly.

But the tears came more strongly. She wiped at them with her free hand, but it didn't do any good.

Is this how he would want to be saved, asked the voice. What would he tell you to do?

Shut up.

But the question lingered, and Kim knew the answer without even having to think about it. Knew exactly what he would say if he ever learned about this. Knew exactly what he would already have done if he were in her shoes.

San Diego Police Department's Headquarters was another few blocks down Broadway directly ahead.

With another sob, she resolutely did not turn toward home.

The look on the face of the woman behind the bullet-proof glass of Police Headquarters' receptionist station when Kim showed her the bag and its contents was priceless.

She directed Kim to one of the uncomfortable plastic chairs in the waiting area, then immediately picked up a phone to call someone higher up the chain. Kim had barely settled down onto the nearly completely un-ergonomic seat when a pair of uniformed, and very serious-looking, officers came in through the swinging double doors leading further back into Headquarters' innards, zeroed in on her, then led her deeper into their lair.

A few twists and turns later, and she was sitting in a plain white room in a chair that was only marginally more comfortable than the one in the waiting area, in front of a simple table topped with grey formica.

Nothing happened for fifteen minutes.

Then two men in grey suits, almost like they'd purchased them off the same rack, stepped into the room to join her.

They were as different as their suits were the same. The first was older, mid-50s, white, and lean, with piercing blue eyes beneath a mop of fully-grey hair. The other was short, black, bald, and chubby, but the kind of chubby that speaks of lots of muscles underneath the fat.

The black guy was the one who took the lead.

"Miss Hawthorn," he said, "I'm Detective Franklin." He looked her up and down, then his eyes settled on the bag that was still clutched in her hands, on the table in front of her. Then he gestured toward the other man. "This is Agent Mackenzie. Why don't you tell us what happened, please?"

Agent. So the white guy was a Fed. Kim zeroed in on him for a second, but found she could not meet his gaze for long. It was like he was staring deep into her soul.

Instead, she looked down at the bag, drew a deep breath, then told them everything that had happened since the park.

There was silence after she finished. When it seemed like an entire minute had passed without anyone saying anything, she looked back up to see the two men looking at each other.

It was like they were engaged in a battle of wills, or something.

But finally, after another several seconds, Mackenzie broke the silence. Letting out an explosive sigh, he threw up his arms as though in surrender, then turned to look at the wall next to him. "Dammit!" he said, sounding not angry so much as annoyed, but also...amused?

That couldn't be right.

Detective Franklin chose that second to chuckle and shake his head. He reached out and clapped the Agent on the shoulder, saying, "Told you so, Tim."

"Yeah, yeah," grumped Mackenzie. His lips twisted into something that looked like it wanted to be a scowl but finally settled on a rueful grin. Shaking his head, he looked back at Franklin and made a little shrug. "Asshole."

Franklin grinned back at him, more broadly.

Kim looked between the two of them, confusion growing more strongly within her by the second. Finally, she cleared her throat. Loudly.

Both men turned to look at her, and for a second something that almost resembled embarrassment passed across the Detective's face. The Agent's went back to professional calm immediately.

"I'm sorry," Kim said. "What's so funny about this?"

Mackenzie remained silent, but that professional facade cracked again—and why did he bother with it after having dropped it so completely a minute ago?

Franklin, though, shook his head again, and then he made a friendly smile at her. "Sorry, Miss. We had a bit of a bet going, and I just won."

"Yeah, yeah," Mackenzie said, still trying with all his might to keep up the professional gambit for some reason or other.

"A bet?" They were taking bets about her? What in the holy hell was going on here?

The annoyance and affront that was beginning to overtake her confusion must have shown through in her tone, because Franklin raised a placating hand. "You see, Miss Hawthorn, you may have just saved the most sensitive counter-drug operation in San Diego PD and the DEA's history."

She blinked, annoyance fading back to confusion again. "Come again?"

Mackenzie sighed, and looked back at the bag. "We've been working a joint operation, with several people under deep cover. This," he gestured at the bag, "was supposed to go to one of our undercovers for use in a big buy tomorrow. But..."

"But he lost his book, with the bag's location and the code to the locker in it," she finished for him.

Mackenzie nodded. "We've had personnel scouring every place he'd been for the last twelve hours all afternoon."

Franklin put in, "I bet him that a citizen would solve the problem for us. He didn't want to believe it."

"Ok. But why didn't you guys just go get the bag yourselves, and get it to your agent another way?"

Mackenzie shook his head. "Because we didn't put the bag there. The money came from another party, who handles the money. We have another undercover in that organization. He recorded the bill serial numbers and put a tracker in the bag, but he wasn't involved in placing it. No one but the person who delivered that note—and we don't really know who that was—knew where the bag actually was." He paused, then added, ruefully. "Until you found it."

Recorded serial numbers? Tracker in the bag? Kim shook her head. "Guess I'm glad I didn't keep it, then." She laughed to show she wasn't being serious, but both law men looked at her sternly, whatever humor they had a moment ago gone.

"Yes," said Mackenzie. "Yes you are. These are not the kinds of people you want to be stealing from."

Kim swallowed. Then she pushed the bag away from herself, toward them.

"Well, I'm just as happy to have it out of my hands then. Do you need me to make a statement, or - ?"

Franklin shook his head. "No we'd just as soon this didn't have a formal record, if you understand."

Playing a little CYA. Well, Kim supposed she couldn't blame them for that. It was, come to think on it, a rather embarrassing screwup to make.

She nodded. "I can keep a secret."

"Good," said Mackenzie. He stood, and so did Franklin. Assuming that meant the meeting was over, Kim did the same.

"Seriously though," Franklin said as he held out his hand to her. "Thanks for your help."

They shook, and she found his grip firm but gentle. Mazkenzie's was just firm.

"My pleasure," she said.

After they led her out to the reception area, she watched as they strode back into the belly of the beast. Then she turned and exited the Headquarters building.

As she turned toward home, she found herself smiling. Not content, and not over the pain from earlier today by any means. But she felt satisfied. And she knew Dad would be satisfied with what she'd done, too.

She decided to call into work when she got to her condo. She had three weeks' vacation on the books, and she planned to take it all. Tomorrow she would go back to Santa Fe Station and get on the Coaster for Monterey.

If these really were to be Dad's last few weeks or months on the planet, she was going to spend as much time with him as she could.

28

FINDING BOBBY JENKINS

Pan blew away steam that was rising from his coffee mug, then lowered his nose over it to catch the fragrance without getting his nostrils scalded.

Deep, dark, and thick said his scent neurons to the rest of him, and he smiled slightly in approval. What was it his first captain said? If you can't put a spoon into your coffee and have it stand straight upright, it's not brewed right.

This was just about there. Perfect.

And it had taken long enough to get it that way. Getting any sort of coffee bean was difficult enough in a long-haul ship like the JOSEPHINE. And weeks cruising through the void far away from any resupply, let alone a stable gravity well and natural atmosphere, meant that when he did manage to get some, it didn't last long. Not the way his crew swilled the stuff. Which meant they had a tendency to just take whatever they could get and run with it.

It had taken a lot of cajoling, and some outright coercion, to get it into the skull of Jack, the crew's cook, that when he said only the good stuff, he meant it.

But Jack was finally getting up to standard.

Pan leaned back into his gimbaled couched and felt the gel

within its cushions adjusting to match his body's new position. The gimbals creaked slightly as well, and he made a mental point of tasking Kimbe, his chief engineer, with taking a look at it. He loved this couch; he'd had it for years, ever since he took over as JOSEPHINE's Captain, and he hated to hear it squeaking in pain like that.

Pan chuckled softly at his silly thought, then he raised the cup to his lips and sipped.

Naturally, the intercom picked that second to beep into his office compartment for a second before a gruff female voice piped through.

"Coming up on the coordinates, Skipper," the voice said, and Pan recognized Hatha, his Navigator.

Perking up immediately, Pan straightened and placed the coffee cup down atop his desk. It was standard sheet metal with a fake wood top, bolted to the deck just in front of his couch, not gimbaled at all. The designers probably figured if the gravplates had gone out, he wouldn't need to be doing any paperwork.

Or maybe it would have just been too complicated to gimbal it in unison with the couch.

Probably a mixture of both.

His office compartment was small by planetside standards, but huge for a ship, even one the size of JOSEPHINE. Maybe two and a half meters on a side, it had enough room for his desk and couch, and for a pair of locker shelves on the bulkhead to the left as he faced the airtight hatch that marked the space's entrance. He also had a little stainless steel wash basin and sink off to the right.

The walls were painted gray, though years of grime that were too ingrained to be washed away by any amount of cleaning solvent made them drift toward black, and the deck was the same. The overhead was the standard mess of cable runs, LED lighting fixtures, and ventilation ducts that one saw everywhere on the ship.

As he let go of the cup, the last of the coffee's aroma faded from his nostrils, replaced by the slightly sour smell that came from the atmosphere processing gear down in Engineering. He suppressed a sigh at that loss, but that was easy considering the Navigator's report.

Excitement surged through Pan, and he grinned a little bit more broadly.

On the right-hand side of the desk's top was inlaid a control pad and miniature ships status display. He tabbed open the navigation plot, then hit the intercom controls.

"Thanks, Nav. Get the sensors spun up, and I'll be right there."

"Roger."

Pan stared for a second at the nav plot. They were right where Nav had said they would be; right where Pan had told her to bring the ship. Twenty degrees above the ecliptic of the Melrose system, four and a half standard AU out toward Galactic North, and forty-five degrees to spinward.

The middle of nowhere.

But if the information he'd managed to ferret out of official records was accurate, and his extrapolation of orbital variances and drift were correct, somewhere out there in the vicinity was a bigger salvage than anything his crew had ever seen. A massive payday, enough to set him up for life, and do really well by his crew as well.

If he was right.

Pan pushed himself up to his feet and picked his coffee cup back up. Then he did take that swig, much more than a sip.

It was just as rich and thick as the aroma had advertised, and he immediately felt a surge of energy as he swallowed and its warmth spread down his esophagus into his belly.

He shivered slightly at the pleasure of it, then nodded to himself and strode toward the hatch.

Time to get to work.

***

If Pan's office compartment was larger than most spaces onboard ship, JOSEPHINE's bridge was smaller.

It didn't need to be big. Just large enough for the pilot's couch and control panel at the ship's bow, surrounded by a hemispherical bubble of transparent plasteel that allowed the pilot a panoramic view of the space ahead of and to all sides of the ship. And then, further back, within the normal confines of the ship's hull, the navigation station, which consisted of a horizontally mounted touch-controlled vidscreen that ran the ship's navigation program and, on each bulkhead athwart the vidscreen, controls for the port and starboard optical observation systems—telescopes to sight key stars to get a fix.

Of course, JOSEPHINE almost never used those observation systems. Most times the navigation program updated ship's position automatically by interpolating time-coded transmissions from a cluster of satellites parked at stable Lagrange points throughout the system, similar to how planetside systems function inside a Global Positioning System. Those signals combined with the data from JOSEPHINE's trio of inertial navigation system ring laser gyros in the space just aft of the bridge made for a tight navigational fix, most times.

The observation systems were just a backup; especially since the stars would shift completely once you went through a jump point to a new system.

Getting reacquainted with them was always super fun.

Like every other space on the ship, the overhead in the bridge was a mass of pipes and cables and vent ducts. Unlike most spaces, there were also a multitude of system status displays, an alarm panel for emergencies, and in the forward starboard corner, just to the side of the pilot's blister, an array of communication gear.

It was cramped, but efficiently laid out, and Pan spent so much time there that it felt almost more like home than his bunk did.

Almost.

When he walked in, Hatha was bent over the horizontal plot, tapping at her lips with her left index finger.

She was big for a spacer, and not just because she had an inch or more on Pan's—average for a man—height. She was downright plump, expanding the offwhite jumpsuit she was wearing like a gas bubble ascending slowly through a liquid.

It was that way on every underway. She'd come back from a few days down time looking almost svelte and trim, though she never really qualified for either term. And then by the time they docked again, she had expanded noticeably.

Not that it mattered. She wasn't on Pan's ship as a plaything, and in the year she'd been aboard Pan had no complaints at all about her competence.

"Status?" Pan said as he stepped next to her.

Hatha turned to look at him, and her curly black hair bounced slightly from the movement. She shrugged. "We are where you wanted to be," she said.

"But ain't no one else here," came a voice from the pilot's blister. "So why'd you drag us all the way out here, Cap?"

Pan looked froward to see the pilot's couch rotated 180 degrees so the man in it could look right at him.

Carl was short, dark, and wiry, with a near-continual expression of good humor on his face and eyes that twinkled with mischief. He could also thread JOSEPHINE through tight confines better than anyone Pan had ever seen. His jumpsuit was the kind of olive green that military flyboys liked to wear. And why not? He'd done his eight years in the Navy before bailing for the riches and glamorous lifestyle of a salvage crew, as he liked to put it.

You could always count on Carl for a joke, even at his own expense.

Pan returned Carl's inquiring look with a raised eyebrow. "For the biggest score you'll ever see, that's why. Got the scanners up?"

Carl nodded. "Yep. And they ain't showing diddly."

Which didn't necessarily mean anything. It had taken Pan less than a minute to get to the bridge from his office compartment. Light speed latency meant they might not have gotten an active return from a nearby object yet.

And then there was the other factor.

"Pick up the visual and IR scanning," he said. "What we're looking for might not give a good radar return."

That made Carl's grin slip slightly, and he cocked his head to the side. "What is it you think's out here, Cap?"

Pan just smiled. "Call it a surprise."

He felt Hatha's quizzical stare as the pilot turned back around to face forward in his blister and keyed additional commands into his controls. Pan ignored her, stepping forward to the edge of the blister to look about.

Clearly visible from this angle, the plasteel of the bubble was marked with a computer-generated Head's Up Display, showing JOSEPHINE's course vector and projected track ahead, as well as compass rose overlay in azimuth and elevation. Various blue or green dots, surrounded by squares of the same color, were imposed on the display, showing smaller velocity vectors as well. Ships, their data transmitted by their transponders and interpreted by JOSEPHINE's. Blue for Navy, Green for civilian.

But there were no yellow track markers yet; nothing unknown.

Pan didn't say anything, and silence reigned for a couple of minutes. Then Carl spoke again.

"Still nothing, Cap. Think you brought us on a wild goose - " He paused, and despite being behind him, Pan could practically see the pilot's eyebrows rise. "Hang on," he said after a handful of seconds. "What is this?"

A yellow dot and square popped into view on the blister bubble, about fifteen degrees off the starboard bow and twenty degrees depressed.

Pan stepped forward, so he was standing next to Carl's couch now, squinting as though doing that would somehow magnify the target for better viewing.

"Small IR variance and visual reflectivity there, Cap."

Pan nodded. He was actually surprised there was still any IR signature at all; it had been long enough the entire vessel should have completely cooled. But reflectivity would be expected. Ships of its class were generally darkened for stealth, but nothing was perfect. And especially after what had happened to her...

"Got an image on the lower forward camera. Calling it up now," Carl said.

A moment later a dialogue window opened on the blister bubble, taking up a third of the space on the starboard side of the bubble. It took a second to fully compile the image from the camera's data stream. Then Carl gasped in surprise. More like shock.

The dialogue window showed a vessel that had been torn open in three spots, its innards exposed to the void. It was completely dark, but despite that its original form was easy to see. It once had been sleek, with a bluff bow that sloped upward to a long flat hull. Gravitic engine nacelles mounted alongside the after third of the hull. A hangar deck, one side of its bay doors knocked askew. And a raised bridge station, jutting up from the hull's spine almost like the conning tower on an old submarine from old Earth.

A POTTER class frigate. Or it used to be.

"What the hell is an Icaran Confederation Navy ship doing way the hell out here?" Carl's voice had gone up a quarter octave from shock. As well it should have. The Icaran Confederation stopped two jumps from here; Melrose was an independent world, friendly with them but not allied in any way. There should have been no reason for one of the ICN's Frigates to come here.

But it hadn't always been that way.

Pan's smile broadened. "That, Carl, is the former ICS BOBBY JENKINS."

"JENKINS? But she - " Carl broke off talking as the impact of that thought fully came home to him.

Pan looked back at his pilot, and found him looking at his Captain like he was insane.

Hatha was doing the same. But she had also gone pale, like someone had just stepped on her grave.

Pan just smiled all the wider.

The boarding and salvage party consisted of Pan, Kimbe, Lars, who was one of Kimbe's technicians, and Hatha. They gathered to suit up in the corridor outside JOSEPHINE's port side airlock, located almost exactly halfway down the hauler's body. Here the corridor had been enlarged from its normal meter and a half width to form what on a Naval vessel would probably be called a quarterdeck: a half-circle about three meters in radius that extended from the hull inward, specifically fro this purpose: to allow space to prepare for an EVA, or to maneuver cargo or material that had been brought aboard or was about to be shipped off.

The quarterdeck was brightly lit, as were all the ship's spaces except for the bridge, and painted a lighter shade of grey that almost approached cream colored. Six EVA suit lockers were mounted in the convex bulkhead across from the airlock doors, along with an emergency medical supply locker marked with the standard red cross on a white square.

Just in case someone got decompressed, or otherwise injured, in the void.

Pan had never developed a liking for EVA. The suit was uncomfortably tight on his limbs, from necessity to avoid bruising from the vaccuum of the void. And the helmet and life support/propulsion pack were bulky. And for some reason, no matter what he did the helmet always seemed to fog up on him.

But EVA was necessary for his salvage job, so he lived with his dislike of the process. Funny how money made that easier to do.

The team paired up to don their suits: Pan and Kimbe checking each others' seals and atmosphere regulators while Lars and Hatha did the same. It took about ten minutes, and though Pan was itching to get to his prize, he didn't begrudge the time.

The void was an irritable mistress, and she showed no mercy for slipshod mistakes.

"You sure this is a good idea, Skipper?" said Hatha over the suit comm channel as Pan made a final check of Kimbe's helmet seal.

"You're not superstitious are you, Nav?" Pan said in a joking tone.

Her silence spoke volumes for a few seconds. Then she replied, "I've just heard rumors is all."

And who hadn't? ICS BOBBY JENKINS had been lost with all hands while making a patrol through the Melrose System fifteen standard years ago. The ICN had never released all the details, but scuttlebutt soon held that she had lost core containment on her fusion reactor, and the emergency shutdown and ejection system had acted too slowly, so she had been caught up in the resultant explosion.

But that explanation had never rung true to Pan. He'd come up through the ranks as an Engineer before he shifted over to command responsibilities. And he knew how bad an explosion of that kind would be. There wouldn't have been anything left of the ship at all.

But starting a year after the incident, reports began coming in of sightings of the derelict ship. And one clip leaked out showing the ship, adrift and holed but otherwise whole. Just as she was now, half a kilometer off JOSEPHINE's port side.

That clip had been taken down and purged from official, and legal, network nodes almost as soon as it was posted. And the ICN released statements repeating the official story, which were repeated and amplified by all the respectable news feeds.

But Pan remembered seeing the clip and, combined with the sightings reports, being intrigued.

The ship had encroached on his consciousness, and he had determined that he would find her. And see what had really happened.

And get some good military-grade salvage out of it, of course.

It had taken a long time, and a lot of careful digging. Back-channel inquiries to acquaintances. The occasional bribe. But he'd managed to recreate the ship's track up until the time of the incident. From there, it was a matter of integrating the various sighting reports and estimating a position from the star pattern in the leaked footage —pulled down from an illicit network node—and he was able to estimate the ship's orbital track.

A lot of work, and now it was going to pay off.

"I heard she's haunted," Lars said over the comm, earning a snort from Kimbe. "No really. That's why the ICN never tried to recover her."

Pan rolled his eyes and turned around so Kimbe could check his rig. That let him get a view of Lars' blue eyes and stringy blond hair through the dome of his own helmet on the other side of the quarterdeck.

"That's just silly," Pan said. "There's nothing over there but metal, stores, fuel, and ship parts." And answers, but Pan didn't say that. "The kind of ship parts that are real hard to come by outside of the Confederation. The kind that will make us all a ton of money."

Which was entirely true. The POTTER class was old now, but she still was a cut above the warships Melrose was able to construct locally. The Navy Department would be happy to get their hands on some of those ship systems. And especially on the torpedoes that were almost certainly still strapped onto their stows in JENKINS' torpedo room.

Lars looked doubtfully at him, then shrugged as Hatha slapped the top of his helmet to indicate all clear.

"You say so, Skipper." He didn't sound entirely convinced.

"I do," Pan said. A second later, Kimbe smacked the top of his helmet, and he nodded. "Ok, everyone set?"

Thumbs up all around.

Pan grinned. "Let's go earn some money."

The other thing Pan didn't like about EVA was the smell of the suit's portable atmosphere system.

It wasn't noxious or anything. It was actually quite subtle, a little lemon on the breeze. But to him, at least, it seemed to build over time, growing stronger and stronger until that little bit of odor dominated his nostrils and made him want to tear his helmet off in annoyance.

When he'd first experienced that, way back in his greenhorn days, he thought there had been a problem with his suit. But extensive testing and inspection of that suit had said no to that notion. And everyone else on the ship had looked at him like he was nuts when he'd brought it up, after that.

But even now, five ships and Lords knows how many suits later, it still happened.

It was all in his head, Pan knew. But that didn't stop it, so he'd long ago learned how to suck it up and work through it.

It still sucked.

When the four of them settled onto onto the JENKINS' back, the magnets in their EVA boots holding their feet to the derelict's hull easily, the buildup had already started. It wasn't bad yet, so it was no problem pushing the annoyance from Pan's mind. But it was there.

"Ok, hangar bay's back this way," Hatha said, as she lead the way aft.

They had decided rather than trying one of the ship's airlocks, which might or might not still be able to cycle open, that they would enter through the ajar starboard-side hangar bay door. It actually was larger than either the airlock or Underway Replenishment hatches, and it would allow certain ingress, saving time.

So Pan allowed the Navigator to take the lead, falling in behind her as his team trooped back down JENKINS' spine, and tried not to focus on the lemon his mind insisted on constructing in his suit.

The hangar bay was two decks high on the POTTER class, and opened onto the back of the ship's lowermost decks, giving the vessel a look as though someone had scooped out the upper-right corner of a rectangle, when seen from the side.

Getting down from the spine of the ship to the base of the bay was fun, but then walking "down" a wall always was. And then they were inside the bay itself.

There were no lights, of course. As many years as JENKINS had been adrift and cold, there was no way her batteries could have retained any charge. And of course the fusion drive was out. So Pan's team switched on their suit lights.

As the beams from their lanterns splayed around the hangar bay innards, Pan couldn't help feel a bit of awe, and trepidation.

It was a very large space, larger than any crewed space on JOSEPHINE. Wide open, with room to dock two Surveillance and Reconnaissance skiffs, and all the support and maintenance gear those skiffs would require to function. But there was only one skiff docked in the bay now, on the port side. That starboard side, where Pan's team had entered, stood empty.

Seeing that skiff sitting there, black and dead like a corpse, sent a little shiver up Pan's spine. Which was silly; he'd been in plenty of derelicts before, and seen everything that could seen in a ship's broken body.

But there was something about this one...

He gave himself a shake. This was no time for grousing, or losing focus. They were there to do a job. Best get to it.

"Hatha, think that skiff might be functional?"

The Navigator had been taking a close look at it, as Pan had drifted off into fantasy land. Walking its length and focusing her light on key pieces of equipment. As he asked the question, she straightened. "Could be. The hull looks intact." She moved forward toward the skiff's blunt nose, and its single airlock hatch. "Let me see if - " Her breath caught and she let out a little noise that wasn't quite a yelp.

"What's wrong, Nav?" Pan said, already moving to assist.

"I've got bodies here," she said.

She was peering through the transparent plasteel of the skiff's canopy, where the pilots would sit, when he reached her side. Immediately he saw what had brought her up short, and he swallowed. There were two men in the pilot and co-pilot seats. They didn't have EVA suits, just the kind of olive jumpsuit that Carl liked to wear. They weren't strapped in, just sitting there. And they were clearly frozen from the deep cold of the void; they didn't show very much sign of decay at all.

They almost could be wax mannequins. Except for their coloration, and the slack expressions on their faces.

"Jesus," said Kimbe. He had moved over to the skiff as well, when Hatha called.

Pan nodded in agreement.

"They must have taken shelter in the skiff when the incident happened," Hatha said. "Hoped its life support would keep them alive until a rescue could arrive."

"Poor bastards," said Lars, and Pan could hear the dread in his voice. The thought that maybe the Skipper wasn't right to shoot down notions that this place was haunted, after all.

Or maybe that was coming from within Pan's own head.

Keep focused.

"Well if it kept them alive then, it will probably still work now." He turned to look at the Chief Engineer. "Kimbe, get down to engineering. The fusion plant's toast but see if there's any hope for the fuel cell generators. It'll be a whole lot easier to get the skiff out if we can open the bay door," he gestured toward the still closed door that separated the port side of the bay from space, "instead of having to cut it out."

Kimbe met Pan's gaze and nodded within his helmet. Then he patted Lars on the shoulder and the two of them turned toward the airtight hatch leading forward into the guts of the ship.

Pan turned back to Hatha, who was fiddling with the skiff's airlock control panel, probably hunting for the mechanical interlocks that would actuate it even without power.

"Let's get up to CIC and the bridge," Pan said.

Hatha stopped what she was doing, straightened, and looked at him with a questioning expression on her face.

He shrugged slightly. "More good equipment in there, and this isn't going anywhere. Besides," he paused for a breath, "I'm curious what really happened here."

"You want the deck log."

Pan nodded.

"We'd have to power up the systems to even have a chance of retrieving it, and who knows if that could even work after all this time. And anyway, what's the point? If the ICN thought there was anything useful on it, they would have come taken it years ago."

"Maybe."

Hatha's brow furrowed, and her eyes narrowed. "You know something you haven't told us."

Pan had to hold back a wince at the accusation in her tone. And she was right; this entire trip had been out of his routine. But how to explain it?

After a moment's contemplation, he shook his head. "No, I really don't. But there's always been something about this ship, and what happened to her. I've never been able to put it out of my mind. I don't know what happened except I'm certain the official story isn't true." He spread his hands, palms out to her through the gloves of his suit. "It's like a calling, or something. I need to learn the truth."

Hatha snorted softly. "So it's not about the big payday. Never was."

Pan chuckled. "Well, there is that, too."

She just looked at him, the void between them seeming to contract as she took in his words. Then she grinned and let out a little laugh of her own. "All right, skipper. Let's go find the answer to your mystery."

The hatch Kimbe and Lars had taken led into a small airlock that then passed Pan and Hatha into the corridors and compartments of the ship.

It was much different than JOSEPHINE.

Where as his ship was painted grey, JENKINS' bulkheads and over-heads were pristine white, the floor covered in bright blue tiles that were flecked with black and gold. The corridors were punctuated every three meters by hatch coamings for airtight compartment stops, and there was damage control equipment everywhere: portable fire extinguishers, hull patch kits, hoses that could be flaked out to fight a more serious blaze. The bulkheads were marked in a series of alphanumerics that Pan knew told the ship's level, which frame corresponded to the nearest bulkhead, and how far out from the centerline of the ship it was, and ever so often there were red scuff pads beneath manifolds in the overhead containing four to six small plug-in fixtures.

Those would be Emergency Atmosphere System manifolds, so the crew could continue to move around and fight the ship without

EVA suits, even with a loss of internal pressure. Pan had heard about them, but never used them, having never been in the Navy. According to Carl the Navy's underway uniform was vacuum rated, so the crew just had to plug into the EAS air lines to get breathing air, and they could move easily about the ship.

Pretty slick, but it didn't do them much good here.

That thought was still floating through Pan's head when he turned a corner and got proof of how correct he had been.

There was an EAS manifold just around the corner. Floating in the corridor, emergency breathing mask still over his face and still plugged into the manifold, was another dead man. His coveralls, the underway uniform, were navy blue and he had two golden bars on each of this collars. His nametag, embroidered onto the right breast of his coveralls, named him Cooper, and his face was blackened and distorted beneath his mask.

He must have suffocated there in that mask when the air to the EAS line finally ran out.

Pan reached out and touched him, and his body gently floated away from his touch toward the bulkhead where his breathing tube was still plugged in.

"Bad way to go," Hatha said.

Pan nodded in agreement.

They found the ladderwell leading upward and ascended to the next deck up, where the CIC should be from the schematics Pan had seen. And sure enough, when they exited the ladder, the found a passage running athwartships. Halfway down it, in the centerline of the ship, they came to two closed airtight hatches. One leading forward was labeled "CIC" by a blue label plate with white writing above the hatch coaming. The other, leading aft, was labeled "Officers Country. Official Business Only".

"Wardroom and staterooms through there," Pan said, gesturing toward Officers Country.

"Captain's quarters?"

He nodded at Hatha's question, then paused. Maybe it was the

Captain's quarters he wanted. He might have a personal log, to supplement the deck log.

Pan was just running that possibility through his head when his comm crackled to life, static in the signal immediately telling it wasn't from Hatha even before Kimbe's voice came through. Interference from the ship's structures, most likely.

"Skipper, I found something." From the tone in his voice, it was a bad something.

"What's up, Kimbe?"

"Bunch of dead guys," the engineer said.

"We expected that."

"Yeah. But these guys were shot."

Pan stopped dead, and he looked over at Hatha. She looked as taken aback as he felt.

"What do you mean, shot?"

"I mean someone put a gun to two guys' heads and blew their brains out. Maneuvering is covered in blood and grey matter."

What in the hell? That didn't make any sense...

Except that it did. Maybe. If the official story wasn't true. Which as he'd told Hatha, he was certain it wasn't. But still, he hadn't expected to find something like that here.

Pan swallowed. "Right. We can figure that out later. Any luck with the fuel cells?"

"I can do you better than that. If what I'm seeing is right, it looks like the reactor is intact. Give me a half hour to get power up from the fuel cells, then another hour or two to warm the reactor up and I can get you full power."

"You're kidding."

"Not even a little bit, Skipper."

Hatha's mouth formed the words, "What. The. Fuck," though she didn't say them.

Pan agreed completely.

"Ok, Kimbe. Get the fuel cells up then see if you can get lights on while you bring up the reactor. It's creepy in here with just flashlights."

"Ain't that the damn truth."

The comm clicked off.

Pan and Hatha just looked at each other for a several seconds. He could see her brain was whirling in circles as much as his was. Had there been fighting aboard? Small arms wouldn't hole the ship like it had been, though. So what the hell happened here, and why?

"Well," he said. "Not going to find any answers standing around here. Let's get this door open." He gestured toward the hatch leading into CIC.

Hatha gave a little jerk, then nodded.

The airtight hatch had an electronic control pad on the wall to its right, and a mechanical handwheel installed in the center of the hatch itself.

The handwheel was stuck. Of course. Years of utter cold would do that. It took both him and Hatha tugging on it, and even then he wasn't sure they'd get it to budge. Until it did. A quick pop that he could practically hear as much as feel, and then the handwheel turned freely.

After a few seconds of turning, the handwheel stopped as it reached its end of motion. Pan took hold of the door's latching mechanism handhold, then pushed.

It didn't budge. Not one millimeter.

He tried again. Still nothing.

"Is it stuck, or..." He trailed off as he spied a small gauge built into the bulkhead above the electronic control panel. It was mechanical, and marked off in kiloPascals. A differential pressure gauge, and one of its sensing tubes ran into the bulkhead. "Damn. CIC's pressurized."

He shouldn't have been surprised. Of course the heart of the ship's combat systems would be designed to hold pressure, even if everything else had been breached. But, he still was.

"No hope of getting that thing open," Hatha said, sounding disgusted.

She was right. The hatch opened inward. There was normal atmospheric pressure inside. As big as the hatch was, he'd be trying to push against several tons.

"There has to be an equalizing valve somewhere," Pan said.

The Navigator nodded, and they set to looking.

It only took a moment to find. It was mounted unobtrusively up in the overhead above the hatch, a small centimeter and a half valve and pipe. From the shape, a ball valve, with a long hand actuator. But when Pan turned the valve, nothing happened.

"The bulkhead stop inside must be closed," Pan muttered. And of course it would be. It would be insane to just leave it open, because if you were a living crew fighting the ship, someone could do what Pan just tried to do, and depressurize the space on you without you knowing until perhaps too late.

"There should be another entrance up forward," Hatha offered. "Maybe that one is open." She didn't sound hopeful.

Pan shook his head. "No, they wouldn't be that careless." He sighed. "We're going to have to cut our way in there."

Which would take a lot of time, effort, and manpower. But it would be worth it, for the salvaged gear as much as for access to the logs.

Then again, that wouldn't be the only place one could access the log.

"To the bridge then?" Hatha asked, as though reading his thoughts.

"Not yet," Pan said. "Let's check out the Captain's cabin first. His terminal would have access to the logs, for review if nothing else."

He turned aft, to the airtight hatch leading into Officers Country, and found the differential pressure gage mounted next to it read zero. The wardroom area was in vacuum, like the rest of the ship.

A small amount of effort later, they had the hatch open, and he stepped through.

The decor in Officers Country was markedly different. The white-painted walls and blue tiles were replaced by deep red-brown paneling that looked very much like real wood and floor tiles that could have been marble if he didn't know better.

The overhead was the usual mass of cable runs, lighting fixtures, and ventilation ducting, though. And as he swept his flashlight around he could see a portable fire extinguisher mounted near to a pair of doors—not hatches—on the right hand side of the passageway looking aft.

As he drew near, he saw that the first of those doors was labeled "Commanding Officer" by letters carved into the door and inlaid with brass. Below them was engraved the circled star that the Icaran Confederation Navy used to designate a man (or woman for their female ships) as the CO.

He was just reaching out to the door knob, a simple twist device, when Kimbe came back over the comm. The static was worse this time, but Pan could still hear him well enough.

"Good news and bad, skipper. Got one of the fuel cells generators online. Should have lights in a minute or so."

"Outstanding. What's the bad news?"

"I think I was wrong about the reactor. Looks like the injectors have been fused open. I could start it up, but - "

Pan finished for him, "But it would just overload and trip the emergency shutdown if we did." He sighed. "Do we have any injectors on JOSEPHINE that we could install?"

Kimbe made a clicking sound, like he was flicking his teeth with his tongue. Then a couple seconds later, Pan could hear the head shake in his voice. "Don't think so, Skipper. Military models are made to different tolerances than ours. It might work. But more likely it would destroy the injectors from the different flow rate. Also I'm not sure how their reactor safety interlocks and injectors are interrelated. If we screw with it and mess up the interlocks, we might not get a shutdown when we need one, and then..."

He left the rest unsaid, but Pan didn't need him to say it. If that happened, the ICN's official story would end up being true. Except that his crew would be the one blown up by it.

Pan wouldn't risk that.

"Ok, leave it. Just get the lights on, and we'll proceed with the salvage as planned." He thought for a second, then added, "Will there be enough juice for grav plates?"

"Not for long. They burned through most of the H2 and O2

reserves. Probably survivors trying to keep at least some power after the incident. Just lights alone, we're talking a day tops."

And they would likely need much longer than that to get the best and most valuable stuff off the ship. Pan didn't bother asking about the hydraulics for the hangar bay door. If grav plates were going to be too much, with their relatively low current draw, the power needed to warm up the hydraulic fluid, get the accumulators recharged and the pumps running, and then open the hatch would be far too much.

"Ok, lights only."

"Roger."

Pan muttered under his breath, but really there was no reason to be disappointed. He hadn't planned for any lighting or gravity at all. Still...

He shifted frequencies on his comm, then transmitted, "JOSEPHINE, this is the Captain."

Carl's voice, crackling with interference from JENKINS' hull, came through a moment later. "Aye, Cap."

"Carl, get the off-shift personnel suited up and prepared to come over. We've got lights coming up, but we won't have them for long. Want to get as much off while we have the light as we can. Also, send over a couple cutting torches. It's going to be a bit more difficult getting access to some spaces than we thought."

"Aye, Cap. We're on it."

Pan shifted back to his team's frequency, then glanced over at Hatha and shrugged. "We do it the hard way, looks like."

"As usual."

"Yeah." He turned back to the CO's door.

As he was pushing the door open, lights began flickering to life. The corridor's lights settled into a steady illumination, but inside the stateroom...

The lights flickered and kept on flickering, making a scene that would have been gruesome already into something out of a nightmare.

There was a man pinned to the forward bulkhead. From his apparent age before he died and the circled star on the left breast of his uniform, above the golden sunburst and crossed sabers that the ICN used to designate fully qualified officers, he was the Captain.

His arms were outstretched, and something metallic had been driven into the palms of each of his hands, pinning them to the wall. Frozen blood left a red crystalline line from those hands to the deck below him, and from his neck where his throat had been slashed down the front of his uniform.

Someone had tacked—stapled?—a piece of printer paper onto his torso below his nametag and warfare device. It was stained red from the blood, but Pan could still make out the word printed there.

TRAITOR.

"Oh my God," Pan said.

Pan leaned back in his couch, and the gimbals squeaked. He'd forgotten to ask Kimbe about it with all that was going on, but the squeaking didn't get to him this time.

His attention was fully focused on the rectangular object he had cradled in his hands. It was plastic and metal, black, and had input/output ports on one side. A memory core from JENKINS' network equipment space; from the server that held the ships' logs.

He raised the memory core up to his face and stared at it, as though willing it to give up its secrets would make it happen.

No such luck.

Pan sighed and righted himself, then placed the core down atop his desk.

Five days of round the clock work had stripped the JENKINS of just about everything of value, and filled JOSEPHINE's holds with enough to earn himself and his crew a crap ton of money. And yet...

The memory core seemed to mock him as it lay there, so close, yet impenetrable through its defense of military grade encryption that Pan could never hope to break on his own. It was enough to drive a man nuts.

The electronic beep of his office call button pierced the air, and he looked back up toward his door. "Come," he called.

The door opened and Hatha stepped into his office, ducking her head to avoid cracking it on the hatch coaming. She didn't waste any time, but made her report before fully settling into place before his desk.

"All set to go, Skipper. Salvage is all stowed and everyone's accounted for. Course is computed. Just waiting on your word."

"Thanks, Nav," he said, nodding at her. His eyes then fell back to the memory core, and he realized he was frowning.

Hatha cleared her throat slightly. Then she said, "I guess we know why the Icaran Confederation never let the real story get out about what happened."

No argument there. "Yeah. Fighting on one of their warships." Pan shook his head. "It had to be a mutiny."

"Quite embarrassing if word got out," Hatha agreed.

"But what I still can't figure out is why they never sent a recovery ship," Pan said. "And what caused the hull breaches? Not small arms. And anyway why would either faction in the fighting do that to their own ship?" He shook his head. "It makes no sense."

Reaching out, he poked at the memory core, and it rotated a quarter of the way around atop his desk.

"The answer's there," Pan said. "I know it is. If only we could get to it." He didn't even try to keep the frustration out of his voice.

Hatha shrugged. "Maybe the Navy Department will tell you once they decode it. You're the one who found it, after all."

Pan looked from the memory core up to her round face. It was a kind thing to say, but also dumb. He wasn't cleared for anything; none of them were except maybe Carl depending on when his last clearance review had been conducted before he left the service. The Navy Department wouldn't tell him jack.

And besides...

Hatha saw something in his face, and an eyebrow rose on her forehead. "You are planning to give that to them, aren't you?"

 MICHAEL KINGSWOOD

Pan shrugged. "I should. It would certainly give the government a nice lever to use in the trade talks with the Confederation next May."

"But you don't want to."

Pan didn't answer for a while. He chewed on his lip, going over everything they had found, and learned. Then he shrugged. "No, I don't want to. I want to learn what the hell really happened. It's been..." He let out a rueful chuckle. "It's been my obsession, you know?"

He could see that Hatha didn't approve, but she had the grace to not say anything. She merely drew herself upright and said, "Ready to break contact with the derelict, Captain."

Silently thankful she had chosen not to press the matter, Pan nodded and stood. "Very well, Nav. Let's get going."

Hatha nodded, then turned to leave his office.

Pan slipped around his desk to follow her to the bridge, but paused when he was halfway through the hatch. He looked back at the memory core sitting there, beckoning to him.

It would be take three weeks to get back to Coppernaum Station, in orbit around Melrose, the system's lone habitable world. He'd have that long to decide what to do about it. He wasn't sure that was enough time.

He took a breath and forced his eyes away from the thing. He'd figure it out. But for now, he had a ship to get moving.

The hatch to his office swung shut behind him, but even through it he could feel the memory core calling out to him as he strode toward the bridge.

The truth, calling to him.

If only he could reach it.

29

WARDEN'S TRIAL

The humid air seemed to drag and flail, resisting being inhaled, as Patros made his way from his little cell in the trainees barracks and across the carefully-trimmed field of grass toward the testing ring.

Five years he'd been here, at the martial academy. Five years of running and jumping and study and sweating and pushing rocks and sparring and taking beatings and giving them back...all leading up to this day. Today, he was prove his mettle, and be allowed to join the ranks of the Queen's Wardens.

Or he would be sent north, to the farmlands away from the border with the Josian Empire, there to tend the fields that produced the food for the warriors who patrolled, fought, bled, and died to keep the Empire from gobbling them all up.

Patros had done his share of tilling and planting. It was tough, necessary, noble work. But it wasn't for him.

So as his sandaled feet pressed down the short strands of grass and the testing ring drew nearer, he found he was bursting with nervous energy. His arms and legs were quivering, and his stomach was doing leapfrogs in his belly. Sweat dripped down the back of his neck, making the rough fabric of his blue trainee's jerkin stick to his torso.

But that was mostly from the warmth and the humidity.

Or at least he told himself that.

The testing ring was familiar; he'd sparred inside it countless times over the years since he'd first arrived here, before his voice had even thought about cracking into manhood and when his arms were spindle-thin.

Now he was sixteen, a man in all but name, but as he approached the brown-stained wooden fence surrounding the dirt of the ring, the gate nearest him open invitingly, he felt the same eleven-year-old he had been, way back when he'd first set foot on the martial academy's campus.

A number of other trainees were lining the outside of the fence; there always were spectators for sparring sessions, but especially for the final trial. They stood in clumps, divided by age ranges. Most were in the year below Patros, boys who knew their time was coming and who were beginning to feel the pressure. But there were a few from the youngest class as well. One, a sandy-haired lad whose head barely reached Patros' chest, was standing just to the side of the gate.

As Patros passed, the boy said, "Good luck," in a voice that cracked slightly at the end there.

Patros gave him a smile that he hoped was confident, then stepped into the ring.

Someone closed the gate behind him, and he heard the clack of the latch coming down distinctly, even above the murmur from a dozen conversations among the spectators all around.

Someone else said something over to the left, triggering soft chuckling from his group, but their humor washed over Patros without touching him.

Across the ring, through its other entrance gate, his foe for the trial was entering. Tall, broad-shouldered, and well tanned, with a shaved head and closely cropped black goatee. He was bare to the waist, revealing bulging muscles and a puckered scar that went from his left shoulder to right hip, the leavings of some battle back before Patros was even born.

Seeing him, Patros' heart sank and his confidence, already mostly just propped up, wilted.

Karmac. Why did it have to be Karmac?

The instructor stopped three paces inside his own gate and looked Patros up and down, his expression blank though his eyes were probing. After a few seconds that felt to Patros like an hour, Karmac spoke.

"Patros Ingeltan, you are called to prove your worth to the Queen. How will you answer?" Karmac put a little extra bass inflection into his words as he said them; a trick he had learned from his own mentor twenty-some years before. It added a bit of gravitas to the moment, and a bit of extra intimidation.

And even after all this time, he still was sometimes amazed how well it worked.

Across the ring from him, the trainee visibly drew a deep breath to steel himself. He usually did that. Everyone got nerves, but Patros always seemed to feel them a bit more deeply. Not that he had ever let them stay his hand; if he had, Karmac's peers in the staff would never have allowed him to remain at the academy, let alone recommend him for the trial.

Karmac still wished he wouldn't show it so much.

Still, when the lad made his response, the slightly-higher than baritone of his voice—supposedly he was quite a singer, though Karmac hadn't heard him—was steady, his tone resolved. And completely to script, to fulfill the formality of the trial.

"I answer with muscle and steel, and will that will not break."

Karmac nodded. "Then choose your steel, and show your will."

With that, the instructor turned to his right, where a rack of weapons stood waiting. Patros would have an identical selection on his side of the ring. The sunlight shown brightly off the steel blades: swords and daggers, hammers, and axes. All were blunted for training, but even with that, they could injure or kill.

That was not the intent, of course, but it happened.

Karmac picked up his favored weapon, a battle axe with a broad crescent-moon blade on one side and a spike—blunted into a round nub on the training model—on the other.

The leather wrapping the handle was worn, but still gave good grip, and he took a couple swings with it to loosen his shoulder. It felt good in his hands, and Karmac had to stop himself from smiling at the little rush that he always got when hefting it.

It was like recovering a part of himself.

When he turned back to Patros, the lad had selected a bastard sword: blade of comparable length with a standard longsword, but with the hilt sized so he could grip it with both hands if he wished.

He did so now, his wiry body turned slightly to put his right shoulder back from his left and his weight balanced on the balls of his feet. The blunted tip of his sword pointed toward Karmac's eyes, and his mouth was compressed into a determined scowl that didn't quite hide the nerves he clearly still felt.

Well. He'd sweat those nerves out quickly enough.

"Are you ready?" asked Karmac.

Patros heard the words, but it was more like he felt them. The import of their meaning struck at his soul, and for a moment he could not answer.

Karmac. He should have known it would be him.

Patros had sparred with every member of his class, and faced all of the instructors at one point or another in his training. Against his classmates, he had always done well. Against the instructors...not so much. Until recently. Recently he found he was able to hold his own, and sometimes prevail.

Except with Karmac. He had only ever faced him in the ring twice. Memories of those thrashings had left him red-faced for weeks.

The other instructors told him there was no shame in his losses. Even the other instructors lost to Karmac more often than not.

But now here Karmac was. The obstacle between Patros and his manhood and entry into the Wardens. The one man he'd never been able to come close to besting.

Might as well give up and go north now, save himself the pain and humiliation.

Patros snarled inwardly, forcing that voice of doubt down. He may end up being sent north. But if that was his fate he'd meet it straight on, like a man.

He forced, "I am," out in as clear and steady a tone as he could.

The words had barely left his mouth, and Karmac was on him.

The instructor closed the distance between them at a speed that Patros almost couldn't believe, and he'd faced the man and watched him in the ring before.

His axe swept through the air toward Patros' neck, and he was only just able to duck beneath it.

A riposte was out of the question, unbalanced as he was. But he tried anyway, his sword cleaving only air in the instructor's wake.

Patros backpedalled, parrying another attack as Karmac came on again, a low cut this time. But before he could maneuver his sword for his own counter, Karmac twisted his wrists and the axe caught on his blade, forcing it away.

And then Karmac was twisting his entire body in the opposite direction, and -

The instructor's sandaled foot caught him in the side, and he staggered away, sudden pain making his vision go red for a second as he frantically worked his feet to stop himself from falling.

This was not going well at all.

But it should have been. The boy was better than this.

Recovered from his kick and stalking forward toward the still stunned trainee, Karmac was tempted to ease up, allow Patros to regain his equilibrium before coming at him again. But he could not. There would be no quarter in battle against the Empire, and he would be doing Patros no favors showing any here.

Inwardly, he screamed for Patros to right himself, and fend off the attack he was about to send. Outwardly, he snarled out a death cry as he raised his axe and brought it down toward the back of the boy's neck.

He was sure it was going to land, and end Patros' trial in dishonor and defeat.

Instead, the boy got his sword up at the very last second, coming in behind the swing of his axe and knocking it upward just enough that it passed over his head harmlessly.

And then he countered with a backswing that made Karmac have to leap backward and exhale loudly to avoid being cut across the ribs.

That was better.

He landed to find Patros was advancing with a thrust toward his belly. Karmac went to knock it away with his axe, but the thrust had been a feint, and Karmac found himself having to duck the true attack.

Much better.

Patros came on again, willing the pain in his side to silence as Karmac backed away again. He was too quick, too strong. Patros knew his only chance lay in taking and keeping the initiative.

So he kept on. Attack after attack after attack.

Karmac avoided them all, but he continued to retreat, and Patros began to lose some of the crushing doubt that had almost done him in so early in the fight.

He still didn't know how he'd managed to make the parry that had started his assault, and he didn't care. Analysis could come later.

Now, attack. And again.

And again Karmac avoided Patros' blade. But this time he reversed his swing instead of continuing it, and the nub that would normally be a spike came hurtling toward Patros' eye.

He ducked his shoulder and hit the ground, rolling to his feet and spinning away from a proper axe cut, then flicked hiss own blade Karmac's way.

The instructor retreated a half step, then began circling to the right, both hands on the haft of his axe. His eyes twinkled in the sun, and sweat ran down his bare torso, but his breathing was slow and steady, his steps smooth and even.

He began spinning the axe in his hands, turning the haft and blade over and over in the air in front of his body almost the way a man would with a quarterstaff, and his lips turned upwards ever so slightly.

Licking his lips with a tongue that was dry despite the sweat running freely down his own body, Patros retreated in time with Karmac's circle, eyes locked on the instructor's. He knew better than to be taken in by the spectacle of the axe flourishes; it would be the eye that announced the next attack.

But it was difficult not to look down, even if just for a second -

The boy's eyes dropped, and Karmac surged forward, driving the haft of his axe straight forward toward his belly.

As expected, the boy dropped his blade down to knock the attack away. So Karmac flipped the axe over, removing the haft from the path of Patros' parry and dropping the blade down toward the boy's shoulder from above.

Patros' eyes widened, and he twisted his torso, releasing the grip on his sword with his left hand so as to remove his shoulder from the path of the cut.

As Karmac's axe passed harmlessly through the air, he felt an impact on the side of his head, where the skull met the neck.

Now it was the instructor's turn to go reeling.

Patros was actually surprised his pommel strike landed. He hadn't actually meant to do it; he was only reacting from desperation to avoid being cut by the axe. But when he twisted to get out of the way, his sword arm came up, and...

This wasn't time to congratulate himself. Though he surely wanted to. He could count the times he'd been able to land a blow against Karmac before on one finger.

Focus!

The instructor had staggered forward two steps, and Patros advanced toward his exposed back. A thrust would have been fitting, but his sword was low from the follow-through of the pommel strike. So he cut upward, from the left.

Karmac felt the trainee coming, a mixture of decades of fighting instincts mixed with his other senses telling him exactly what was going on behind himself.

His vision was blurry from the unexpected strike and his ears rang, but he'd long ago learned to trust his instincts even when he couldn't think to do so.

He surged forward, and he felt the air displaced by the trainee's sword as it just barely missed his exposed back. Then he rounded on Patros, raising his axe back up to a guard.

Karmac was swaying on his feet; he could feel it. And he had to blink to not see a double-image of his foe.

He had backed off when Karmac turned back around, falling back into a defensive stance. Through the blurry vision and lack of equilibrium, Karmac noted that, and anger reared up within him. Not anger at the blow; he'd taken plenty of those over the years. But over Patros' timidity.

The pup could have done him in, if he'd just committed fully. Now...

Giving his head a quick shake to clear his senses, Karmac charged forward on the attack.

Patros retreated, parrying the instructor's blow, and inwardly cursed at himself. This could be over now. Should be over now.

Grinding his teeth, he parried another blow, then another, and retreated faster.

Karmac was coming on with the same blurring speed he'd used in his initial press, and there was something like rage on his face. It made Patros' belly go liquid, and he felt he first real quivers of fear.

He'd never been truly afraid of the instructors before; he'd known from the start that they were not out to intentionally harm him, however cruel they may have seemed at any particular moment.

But now...

He'd landed a blow. Something Karmac had almost never allowed him to do before. Bruised the instructor's ego. Now he was going to make Patros pay for that slight.

The fear grew strong and blow after blow came at him, and he could tell his reactions were slowing because of it. But he couldn't force it down.

In desperation, he repeated the mental chants that would guide one's mind to stillness, but it would not come.

Another strike.

And another.

And then a high cut met his parry, and his sword became entwined in the notch between the axe's blade and its haft. The angle was wrong, so he couldn't pull the blade back, and it was only the strength of his arm and shoulder against the weight of Karmac's body and weapon, and the the instructor bore down and pressed.

Slowly, inexorably, the entwined blades inched downward, and the axe blade approached Patros' face.

The boy's cheeks puffed outward as he breathed in and out in quick, exhausted heaves, and his eyes were wide with exertion and fright. He saw the end of his trial coming, and with it the end of his hopes, and the strength of his shoulder alone was not enough to stop it.

There were half a dozen ways Patros could get out of this situation that Karmac could think of without difficulty. But the instructor could tell he was frazzled, locked into just this one struggle.

That would be his undoing.

Don't give up, boy. Think, and move.

Karmac continued to press.

Patros had moved both hands to the grip of his sword, and it still wasn't doing any good. His arms were quivering from exertion, and he was beginning to become overbalanced; Karmac's press was forcing him backward farther than his back wanted to bend.

He was going to fall, and then the instructor would get him, and the trial would be over. And he would be sent north.

All his labor, all the discomfort—downright pain—of the last five years would be for nought.

Karmac's face loomed over his, beyond their interlocked weapons. He could practically feel the man's breath; smell his the stink of his sweat.

He pressed all the harder, and from the grimly determined set of his jaw and the glint in his eyes, he knew Karmac intended to finish him now.

"No!" Patros heard himself shout.

Without thinking, he reversed his direction. Where before he had been pressing against the instructor's press, now he went with it, ducking his shoulders and twisting his torso even as he crouched down.

Karmac made a grunt of surprise, and then he went stumbling off to the right, thrown by the force of his own press.

Patros' sword was yanked from his hands; it flew away from him to land on the dirt several feet away. But he didn't look to it; only to the instructor, who and gone to one knee, left hand pressed to the dirt to stop himself from falling completely.

No time to get his sword; Patros had to press the advantage now.

He charged forward, then leapt.

The trainee's weight struck Karmac as he was just beginning to regain his balance and rise.

The unexpected force knocked him down fully. He landed on his side and rolled, but then found himself unable to move, as Patros was atop him, forcing his shoulders to the ground with his knees as his fist came up.

Karmac worked hard not to cringe as the punch came down.

He didn't succeed for the second one.

The third punch made Patros' knuckles scream. But he threw another one.

Karmac's nose was flattened across his cheek, and his eye was welling shut. But the battle fury was on Patros, and he forced his aching fist to ball again. He raised it.

And something caught his hand before he could let the punch fly.

He looked to the right and say Tomas, another of the instructors. Short and thin, he was whip-fast both in wit and in limb. He usually wore a jolly smile, but now his expression was grave.

"Enough," Tomas said.

For a second, Patros actually fought against him, but then he tightened his grip.

"Enough," Tomas said again, with a cold tone of command that could not be disobeyed.

Patros relaxed, and sat back, then pushed himself up and off of the prone Karmac. He stepped—no, stumbled—a couple paces away, and only then noticed the absolute hush that had fallen over the spectators. One and all, they were looking at him with expressions ranging from shock to amazement to awe.

Patros found he could hardly breathe, but whether from the weight of those stares or from the absolute exertion of the trial, he did not know.

Hell, he didn't even know whether the trial was over or not. Tomas had halted it, but would it recommence?

Or would he be sent north after all?

Over where he had fallen, Karmac was getting to his feet, aided by Tomas. The big instructor looked like hell.

He felt like hell too.

Karmac had taken many a punch in his time. He'd had his nose broken a time or two. But he couldn't remember such a pummeling from so few blows before.

The boy must have been really worked up. And no wonder. It was the most important event in his life, so far.

Karmac waved off Tomas' fretting over him, then he turned toward Patros. The trainee was trembling visibly, his chest heaving and his eyes haunted, like he wasn't sure what had just happened or what would come next.

Karmac new that feeling.

He took a moment to crunch his nose a bit better back in place, wincing at the pain of it but knowing it would have to be done.

Then he took a step toward Patros, who unconsciously retreated a half-step in response.

Smiling, Karmac raised his hands, palms out, and said the ritual words.

"Patros Ingeltan, you have proved you will, and your skill."

The words swept over Patros, and a feeling of relief went with them, followed by a sense of wonder. Was this real?

"Now join us as a brother. Warden," Karmac said, and he held out his right hand to him.

Patros grasped the instructor's forearm, and felt the other man's hand do the same to his. The vice-like grip was somehow also gentle, companionable.

Karmac's grin grew more broad, actually companionable. For the first time Patros had ever seen.

Then he said, in a lower tone that didn't carry past the two of them, "You scared the hell out of me for a second there. Thought you were going to quit." He shook his head. "Glad you didn't."

More loudly, Karmac said, "I don't know about you, but I need an ale." Releasing Patros' arm, he clapped him on the shoulder, then turned away, toward the gate he had initially entered through.

Patros watched him go, still unable to process all that had just happened for a moment.

Karmac must have sensed he hadn't moved, because he looked back and raised an eyebrow—the one over the eye that was quickly growing completely black from Patros' punches. "Coming?"

Patros nodded, then moved to walk with his instructor.

No, with his new brother.

He felt his lips turning upward into a smile. Part wonder, part relief, part pride, and part anticipation. A new world, a new life, awaited.

He stepped forward eagerly to meet it.

30

ON THE ROAD TO HOPEFELL

The sun rose slowly, gradually sending the night's shadows scampering away like hoodlums fleeing the sound of the constable's approach.

As the hours passed, the few lingering shadows shrank, pushed back against the burned-out or simply decayed frames that cast them as though to make way for the the clouds of dust that the wind, grown from the increasing heat of the day, picked up as it moved across the land. Occasionally the wind would get funneled between clusters of dilapidation, and would compress and speed up as it forced its way through with a howl that was more maniacal and malicious than gleeful.

In one of those funnels, tramping down the gap between the blasted remains of things gone by, a figure trudged, head bowed against the wind's onslaught and black cloak wrapped tightly about its body.

It was not just the wind that caused the figure to hunch over, but also the weight of a great pack on it shoulders, faded from a color than once might have been blue but was now bleached gray. The pack bulged, and in a few places some of its contents protruded from tears in its skin. But for the moment at least it held together, and kept those items in place for whatever use the figure would put them to.

The figure's steps were short but steady, a steady pace despite its obvious load; a pace that said, "Screw you, I'm not stopping," to the wind's wrath far more than any shout or waved fist could have.

Most of the buildings—or what once were buildings—on either side of the figure were shattered, placards over missing doors faded so that whatever writing had been on them was almost impossible to read. They were two stories and three, but never more than that, though there were a few that were a single story.

Though several of those looked to be in that state more from collapse than from design.

The gap between the buildings may once have been paved, but now it was just a path of brown dirt and dust, the latter kicking up mercilessly into the figure's face as it continued doggedly down the path. There used to be trees; a few gnarled trunks here and there reached toward the sky on either side of the path, their few remaining limbs that previous winds hand not snapped off stretching up toward the sky like fingers imploring the heavens for relief from their misery.

If heaven heard, though, there was no sign that it had ever done a thing to help.

The path between the buildings stretched maybe a half mile before the last of the buildings ended. More like fell over on themselves. And then there was just more wasteland, rolling hills of dirt and dust that stretched on and on until the next obstacle that evoked the wind's wrath.

The figure had just reached those last pair of blasted shells when something brought it up short. It straightened, and turned to the left. As it did that, the wind caught its cloak and blew the cowl back from the figure's face, revealing a craggy face framed by a bushy, but not unruly, growth of black beard and like-colored curly hair. Full brows that very nearly converged above a hooked nose furrowed and grey-blue eyes squinted at the thing that had caused the figure to turn.

And there it was again. A glint of light, from the rear of the building there, back on its left side in the gap between it and the building's neighbor. Was that - ?

Almost unbelieving, and not wanting to get his hopes up, Gavin licked at his lips, feeling the sand that had accumulated in his mustache and tasting its salt, then blinked.

When he opened his eyes again, the flash of reflection was still there.

That was either metal...or glass. Both far too rare in these days gone on to pass up.

So he turned from the course he had been taking and hurried toward the gap between the two buildings.

His cloak threatened to pull away from his body, and he felt little pellets of sand and grit biting into his face and torso where the wind's assault threw them against the thinner cotton of his shirt, long-sleeved or no, and he fought to gather the heavier fabric close about him.

But soon enough he was in the lee of the buildings, in the gap between them, and the worst of the pelting subsided. But the glimmering of sunlight against whatever it was remained, there at the back corner...

Gavin drew up short, drawing an awed breath when he realized what he was looking at.

An intact window.

How in heaven's name had it survived all this time? Not just the elements, but scavengers and raiders and every other human left alive in this wasteland that used to be so lush should have conspired to leave it at the least removed for use elsewhere if not shattered from a fit of fury or as the side effect of a desperate struggle for food or water...or just bloody mindedness.

The window was at the extreme back of the building, just before the once-red—now mostly brown-gray—siding ended at the corner leading into the building's back wall.

Past there, in what would have been a house's back yard but here would have been...a parking lot maybe?...was just dirt and the scraggly remains of what used to be a few bushes. And the pile of rubble that marked the grave of another, larger, building that had stood behind these two.

As Gavin emerged from between the buildings and looked left and right, he was hit by the wind again. Less strong than it had been in the wind tunnel that had been the street behind him. But still shrill and biting with grit, and without even the decency of helping to remove the midday heat at all.

His scan of the area was quick, enough to show no immediate threats or dangers. Then he zeroed in on another unexpected thing. An intact door, in the building's rear wall.

This had to be a trick. A trap of some sort. Or maybe the pressure of two weeks' walking through the wasteland on his way back to Hopefell had snuck up on him unawares and he was seeing things.

He blinked his eyes again. But the door was still there. Faded, like everything else these days, the paint mostly peeled off leaving the wood beneath to gray in the elements. But intact, just like the window.

"What in the blazes?" he said to himself.

Then he was at the door, left hand on the chipped and pitted chrome of its knob. Before he could think what he was doing, he twisted. And was amazed when the knob turned freely, and the door swung open inward.

Gavin slipped his right hand beneath his cloak and grasped the grip of the club he kept hanging from his left hip, concealed by the cloak's weight. Squinting his eyes, he peered inside.

There was no interior light, of course. But the sunlight streamed in through the window's glass, dimmer than it would have in years gone by from dust and grime but still enough to illuminate. The room was small, and sparsely furnished. An old desk and swivel chair sat beneath the window, so the person could look out while doing paperwork...or whatever. Both were carved from what looked like good hardwood, and had the look of quality workmanship. There was another door leading further into the building, closed. This door's paint was in better shape than the exterior door's; mostly still there, and also mostly still red. The paint on the walls was yellow-white, and peeling up by the ceiling where water stains spoke of leaks back when there still had been rain in these parts.

And that was it. The exterior door obscured the other part of the room, but it appeared empty, and there was no sound except for the wind's insane cackle as it sped down the little ruin of a town's single street.

Gavin stepped inside, and immediately looked to the left, to the area of the room that the door had concealed.

It was empty, except for a bedroll and a pile of blankets in the corner opposite the window.

He froze, and glanced back at the desk, only now noticing the lack of dust on it and the chair.

Someone had been here, and recently.

Slipping the club off his hip, Gavin slowly closed the door behind himself and listened. Still nothing except the wind's guffaws, muted now that he was indoors but never silent.

Clearly this was someone's abode, but they weren't here. Good luck for Gavin; he really didn't need to deal with a fight. It was still three days to Hopefell, and if he got injured that would only make the journey longer. He barely had the supplies to make it the rest of the way as it was. Best to turn around and git while the gitting was good.

But something about the place tugged at him. This one building, out of the thousands he'd walked past in his journeys, still had a livable room, with an actual honest-to-God window and door. And someone lived here. Or had.

How had the person managed to keep the place, after all this time? And how was he living here, so far from any outpost and supplies?

Curiosity got the better of Gavin's instinct to flee, and he crossed to the door leading deeper into the building. He pressed his ear to it, but heard nothing on the other side except the wind. So he tried the knob, not nearly so pitted as the exterior knob had been.

Again, the knob turned. This time the door opened toward him, and Gavin inched it open slightly and peaked through. Seeing no movement, he opened it fully and slipped through, club at the ready.

This was a hallway, running crossways across the width of the building. No windows, so the only light came from the room he'd just left, and that faded quickly into dark shadows as the hallway reached the other side of the building. But he could just dimly make out another door, opening to the left, so again toward the back of the building, at the end.

He had an old lighter that he'd squirreled away from back before the bombs fell and the earth quaked and the blight spread, and ever so often he'd managed to barter for a bit of butane here and there to keep it topped off. Reaching into his pocket with his left hand, he found the rectangular hunk of metal and pulled it out.

The top flipped open easily, but the striking wheel was getting worn, and it took five or six flicks to get it going. But then he had at least a little flame of a light, which he held up above his head as he proceeded down the hall. It wasn't much, but it beat nothing at all.

In the dim light, he was struck by the lack of clutter and trash in the hallway, just as in the room he'd just passed through. Obvious signs that someone had been keeping it up.

But who? And why?

And more importantly, how?

He had to sling his club back onto his hip to try the new door, and once again it opened freely.

Even with the little flame from his lighter, it was dark. He could barely make out the area beyond the door, but he could tell it was a square room. It must have been a duplicate of the first room, except without the window and the door. But had he seen another window in the building's back wall?

Gavin searched his memory, but couldn't tell for sure. He had zeroed in on the door so quickly...

Go back, his mind screamed at him, even as he stepped inside.

It was then that he noticed the smell. It wafted out of the darkness of the room like an unclean miasma of filth, seeming to seep into his pores even as it assaulted his nostrils and forced its way into his tongue. Rot, and human waste. And something else, almost coppery...

Gagging, Gavin backed out into the hallway and pulled the door closed, then pressed his right hand to his mouth and nose, as if he could wipe the stench away.

He sagged back against the wall opposite the door, and realized he was breathing heavily. His pulse pounded in his ears, and he felt the rush of adrenalin in his veins.

Blood. That was what he'd smelled there, atop the filth and the rot.

Someone had died there. Maybe several someones. Died, and rotted.

The building's inhabitant?

Regardless, it was time for him to be out of here. There were plenty of hours of daylight left, and he knew a good place to bunk down for the night that he could make. If he left now and made good time.

But maybe he should see to the poor wretch's body, said that little voice in his mind, but he shushed it. He didn't have the tools for a proper burial. Nor did he have the time, and he wouldn't want to bunk down here. Not after finding that.

Besides, it smelled like the fellow was well on toward rotting...

Gavin stopped at the doorway leading to the first room, the thought careening to a halt before his feet could.

No, the smell of rot hadn't been that strong. Not nearly as strong as the blood and the crap.

So either the guy had died recently, or...

Gavin swallowed hard. He'd heard of people going completely feral if they'd spent too much time alone out in the wasteland. Rumors said there were tribes of them out there, in the deep wastes far from the few settlements that had managed to sprout up.

Savages.

Cannibals.

He'd never encountered their type before, but he'd talked to one or two people who had. Usually the stories only came out after a bunch of drinks at the town watering hole, so he'd always given those accounts a bit of skepticism. Drunks always exaggerate their tales.

Now he was thinking maybe he was wrong to do that.

Dousing his lighter, he slipped it back into his pocket and brandished his club again, then stepped into the first room. It was time to get out of here. And once he got to Hopefell, he needed to tell the Constable about this place. Bert couldn't afford to let this sort of thing exist so close to town.

He was halfway across the room to the exterior door when he saw the knob begin to turn.

Gavin froze, and glanced left. He saw a head topped with a scraggle of blond hair looking in, and large eyes that were going wide with surprise as they met his.

Cursing, he bounded forward.

But he knew he was too late, when the door began to swing inward, admitting more of the sunlight from outside.

"There's someone - " came a female voice at the same time as the opening door showed the hulking man who was preparing to come into his home.

He was big. Very big. A full head taller than Gavin, and Gavin wasn't short. His shoulders were almost wide enough to fill the doorway, and he was dressed in a brown trench coat instead of a cloak, and worse a broad-brimmed hat of the same color on his head. His face was chiseled, angular, and his eyes were so brown as to be almost black.

And he had a body draped over his left shoulder, in what Gavin remembered they used to call a fireman's carry.

The big man stopped when he saw Gavin, and for a second they just stared at each other.

Gavin thought to do a quick bit of apologizing for trespassing and then try to talk his way out of there. But he saw the other man's face lose the last remnants of good humor that shock had not yet had the chance to chase away. His expression went slack and his jaw tightened, and he shifted his shoulders, loosing his grip on the body to let it slide off his shoulder to the ground.

He was getting ready to attack. Gavin beat him to it.

Lowering his shoulder, he charged forward, careening into the big guy's belly shoulder-first.

The momentum of his charge, short as it was, sent the man stumbling backward, and Gavin rode him down into the dirt behind the building.

The brightness hurt his eyes after the dim interior, but he ignored it, blinking quickly as he rolled off the big guy to spring to his feet. If he could get a good head start, maybe he could -

Powerful hands grabbed at his thighs before he could make a full step, and he found himself half-hurled back toward the building. He stumbled forward and to his right, losing his footing—and his club— as he went, and landed on one knee, left hand pressed into the dirt to stop himself from falling completely.

He had gotten so used to wearing his pack that he hardly noticed its weight most times. It wore at him, made him tired, but it was like part of him most of the time, until he took it off for the night.

But right then, its extra weight just added to his difficulty as he struggled to push himself back up onto his feet, and he wished for a second he had taken it off before he went inside.

But that would have spoiled even the slight surprise he'd gained on the man. And speaking of which -

Gavin forced himself upright and turned, just in time to catch a fist in the cheek.

He reeled back, and found himself falling when he didn't strike the wall. The ceiling of the room with the desk wheeled into view as he fell back inside, and then the big man was above him.

"Came to the wrong house, bub," he said, and those beefy hands were grabbing onto the straps of Gavin's pack, hauling him up from the floor.

His head was spinning from the punch, and he could feel his cheek swelling up already. He tasted blood; had he chipped a tooth or just bit into the flesh?

Gavin shook his head to clear it, and found himself looking

straight into the big guy's eyes, as his lips turned upward in a feral grin. "But I will thank you for helping fill our larder."

Gavin was up on his tiptoes, held there by the strength of the big man's arms, and truth to tell he really wasn't in any mood to fight anymore. For a second, he just hoped the big guy would get it over quick.

Then the rest of his mind caught up with the coward within and smacked him down. Screw that.

Big guy's hands were still on the straps of Gavin's pack, so he clenched his fists and swung them up and over big guy's shoulders, to strike at his temples with the inner ridges of his fists.

The counterattack took big guy by surprise, apparently, because he cried out and released Gavin's straps, his hands instead going to the sides of his head, which Gavin knew from experience were now throbbing like mad.

His feet hit the floor, and Gavin considered just running for it. But that wouldn't work and he knew it. So instead he drew back and slugged the guy in the gut, hard as he could.

It was like hitting a wall. But Gavin had hit a wall or two in his time, so he knew how to deal with it. And he was plenty strong from lots of time hauling gear across the wastes.

Still, the guy was big enough that he could take the hit. All the same, he doubled over a bit, which gave Gavin a warm feeling of satisfaction for a second.

Before the big guy's counter, a backfist, lashed out toward him.

Gavin knew it—or something like it— was coming, though, and he blocked it, raising both forearms so that the big guy's forearm struck the bones of both of his.

It hurt. A lot.

But it stopped the punch, and Gavin looped his left wrist over the top of the big guy's. Then he pressed his right palm into the back of the guy's shoulder, crouched down, and twisted.

The big guy was heavy, but Gavin had the leverage, and big guy went with it, unable to resist being spun and then thrown as Gavin let go the wrist.

The big guy stumbled forward, and struck the desk with his thighs....

The crinkle of shattering glass announced that his head had struck the window a second before a stream of red running down the glass from his neck showed what had happened as a result.

The guy squirmed, shuddering, and Gavin thought he heard a gurgle come from his lips. He tried to push himsefl off the cutting glass, and just ended up cutting his hands and wrists as well. But he pushed all the more, and extricated himself.

And the blood flow just got worse.

He turned to face Gavin, as though still wanting to fight, but his expression was a mixture of confusion, pain, and gradually increasing horror as he realized what had happened to him.

Blood ran down his chest, and he took a half-step toward Gavin.

Then he just collapsed there on the floor.

"Hector!" came the female voice again, this time raised in a shriek of disbelief and grief.

The blond came rushing in and collapsed atop the big guy, shaking at him as tears began running down her cheeks and she began to wail.

Gavin watched her for a second, as shocked by the outcome of the engagement as she, though not as upset. He considered saying something. Sorry, maybe?

But he wasn't sorry. The guy had meant to do him in. And apparently eat him, for his trouble.

And she would have joined in the eating, no doubt.

Yeah, not sorry at all.

It crossed his mind that he should probably not let her go on with her cannibal ways. But right then, he wasn't up to beating down a woman. And he probably never would be. He'd go on to Hopefell and tell the Constable. Let Bert deal with her, if she was still here when he came with his men.

That all went through Gavin's head in a second, and then he moved to step around the woman as she knelt over her now dead... lover, he assumed.

But he felt he should say something, so he paused in the doorway and looked back. "Sorry about the window," he said, and her face jerked upward to look at him. There was murder in her eyes, but also the knowledge that she didn't dare try it. Gavin put on a grin that he knew wasn't cheerful at all. "But hey," he said. "You've got plenty of meat to last you now."

Her screamed, "Fuck you," didn't carry any punch at all as he stepped outside.

He squatted to pick up his club and looked at the body the big guy had dropped. It was a woman, mid 30s and dark, with long black hair, dressed for the wasteland and staring with wide, unseeing brown eyes.

Yep. He didn't feel bad about the big guy or his woman at all.

With that, he turned and resumed his trek toward Hopefell. As he wrapped his cloak back around himself and closed the cowl around his face to ward off the worst of the biting sand and dust, he looked up toward the sun, only slightly lower than when he'd first veered off to investigate this charnel house.

Plenty of time to reach his camp site.

Things were looking up.

31

WOLVES ON CORNELL STREET

The wolves were howling on Cornell Street, again. But this time it wasn't a false alarm.

That fact was not immediately apparent to Humbert, though. When the ululating howl that started with a single voice but quickly got picked up by, apparently, an entire pack roused him from sleep, his first thought after pushing himself up onto his haunches from where he had been lying in his cozy little den was to hiss and bare his hunter's teeth at the effrontery of the damn canines.

Twice this month they'd raised a ruckus. And twice it had turned out to be nothing but a member of the pack who managed to get loose.

Stupid creature couldn't even think enough to keep quiet until it had fully made its getaway. No, it had to start yipping and yowling, and it was quickly caught and penned again.

But this time, the sound was different, and Humbert's initial chagrin faded to curiosity as he fully took in the rising canine chorus, and then he felt the first stirrings of alarm.

Pushing himself up onto all fours, he ignored the soft swishes of Matilda's form as she, more slowly, came to consciousness behind him. He left their comfy bed of furs behind and padded over toward the entrance to their little den. His claws dug into the soft loam of their floor as he went, his night eyes easily picking out the trio of low lounging cushions spread out to the left, the imprints of his and Matilda's previous relaxations still visible, so often had they been used.

The den entrance was closed off by a hanging cut of fur from a deer he'd taken on a hunting trip with three other guys from work. Not often a clerk like him actually got to dip his claws into live flesh, so he had felt good about actually taking a prize. And he always felt a surge of pride when he saw it, hung up for all the town to see.

But now as he approached the doorway, an acrid and unwelcome —but from the howling of the wolves unfortunately not unexpected —scent reached his nostrils, and he hissed again, his ears coming erect and the hair on his back standing straight up.

Nudging the hanging fur aside with his snort, he looked out, and the yellow-orange flickering from off to the left confirmed what he already feared.

Fire.

"Matilda!" he said, loudly, and he heard her shedding their furs and moving up behind him.

"What is - " she stopped as she smelled the wood smoke, and the silence carried her sudden fear more strongly than words could have.

Humbert envisioned her belly, already grown large from the young ones within it. She was not a cripple, but she could not move nearly as quickly or with the dexterity that she once had. And she was still a week or more from birthing.

On the other side of the street, Humbert's neighbors were also pointing snouts out past their doorways, one and all turning toward the growing conflagration.

The town was nestled in a wooded hollow, the dens nestled between and within the tree trunks, or up in limbs where some of the more dextrous and height-loving of the town's citizens had created their homes. The street was packed earth, solid enough to allow good footing but loose enough that it was still comfortable to walk.

But now the flames were rising up on the trunks of trees just a few hundred running strides away, and to Humbert's eyes the distance between the limbs of one tree and the next was not nearly enough to stop the spread, if the fire brigades failed to contain it.

As if on cue, a mighty engine charged down the street. Several of the neighbors off to Humbert's right squealed and vaulted away from the huge red hunk of metal. The wolves' howls grew louder as the duo of canines, locked in a cage at the front of the engine, bellowed up at an image of the moon cast onto a platform above them from a light held by one of the human chattel.

Others of the man-apes were pumping their legs behind the warning howlers on circular contraptions that worked in unison to turn the great wheels that propelled the thing down the street. Behind them, the engine's captain crouched on his platform, eyes narrowed to slits and fur slicked back from the wind as he watched his bearers, paw at the ready to touch the zapper that would render punishment to any of the man-apes who dared not pump its legs fast enough.

Behind him came the water drum, huge and red painted, and festooned with pumps and hoses, with more of the chattel waiting in a cage at the back under the careful eyes of their squad overseers.

The engine was massive, dwarfing all of the dens on Cornell street, and as it zoomed past Humbert's spirits rose.

All around, on neighboring streets, he heard other warning howlers draw near as they howled their engines forward.

With that much ape-power and water arriving on the scene, surely the fire would be extinguished quickly.

And yet...

As Humbert looked back to the left, the flames leapt from one tree to the next, and an entire limb fell, landing directly across the street ahead of the engine. He cringed as he saw people pinned beneath the branch, the lucky ones dying beneath its weight.

But the unlucky ones screamed as the embers caught their fur ablaze.

The engine skidded to a halt, barely avoiding collision with the still-burning branch, and the squad overseers began chivvying their man-apes about their duties. The hulking brutes moved quickly, but even to Humbert's untrained eye, he could tell his initial optimism was misplaced.

There was no way that engine could contain the blaze down his block. No way at all.

And if that was the case on Cornell Street...

He turned to the right, where Matilda's usually lithe brown and black form, now beautifully bulging, stood next to him. Her eyes were narrowed, their nearly-black irises contracting at the brightness of the flames.

"We have to leave," he said.

Matilda's eyes met his, and she nodded. She was no fool.

Humbert stepped out into the street, and cringed slightly; even from this distance the heat from the blaze was noticeable. And getting more intense by the second.

And yet....

He found himself transfixed by the deadly beauty of the event, and for a moment could not look away from the scene.

The man-apes were working hard. Some of them manned the pump handles on the sides of the water tank. Some rolled hoses out and used them to direct water at the growing inferno. Surely they must have wanted to flee; to save themselves. But none did.

No doubt their squad overseers saw to that.

All the same, the gallantry of their effort, obviously futile as it was doomed to be, touched something in Humbert for a moment.

Then Matilda slid past, her flank rubbing against his, and he looked away from the chattel toward his love as she swayed past him. Asian females had always does it for him, especially Thai females. And Matilda was the the most beautiful Thai female he had ever known, or heard of. Even with the bulge in her belly—especially with it—she was a sight to see, and if this wasn't a life or death situation...

He licked his lips and gave himself a shake.

Head in the game, buddy.

He spared a glance over his shoulder at the deer fur hanging limply in his doorway, and a moment of regret tugged at him. That fur would go up with the rest of the neighborhood. His prized keepsake.

But his man-ape housekeeper wasn't scheduled until Wednesday, and anyway he could always get another pelt. His most important treasure—his Matilda—was already several running paces ahead of him, bounding as best her heavy-with-children body could do away from the inferno.

It was past time to go.

Humbert hurried after her, quickly catching up as the growing throng of fleeing neighbors made running, or doing anything more than a fast walk, impossible.

* * *

They weren't going to make it.

The press of people fleeing the blaze had only gotten worse as Humbert and Matilda fled the blaze, and now the crowd was pressed in almost flank to flank. Even the most nimble and quick person could not have pressed his way through the throng.

And the flames were racing closer by the second.

Humbert had glanced back once, some minutes earlier, only to see the valiant engine that had charged down the street to fight the blaze completely overwhelmed. Its crew tried to retreat—and to blazes with the man-ape chattel and the warning howlers...literally— but another limb had fallen between the fleeing crowd and the brave firefighters.

He had cringed in sympathy at the horror of that kind of end. If it were him, he would hope the Captain would end him by claw rather than having to face the flames.

But then, he was just a clerk. Not a brave defender of the citizenry.

Regardless, he had put his back to the now larger and closer, despite all attempts to flee it, blaze, and pushed forward against the growing crowd.

But now, with the crowd's advance slowing even further, he glanced back over his shoulder and wondered if the firefighters' fate would soon be his and Matilda's. That was looking more and more likely with each second.

She was growing fearful as well; he could see it in her eyes. In the way she craned her lithe neck to look behind them every few steps. The way her hair flared up and her tail stiffened.

They had to find another way out of here.

But where?

Humbert slowed, letting the pressing crowd stream past himself, and looked to the left and right, scenting the air and scanning the surroundings for something—anything—that might present a different option.

Fortunately Matilda was far more observant than he. She stopped as soon as he did, flicking her tongue across her teeth in a questioning manner for a second before her eyes widened in understanding. Then she too began to look. In a heartbeat, she had it. Nudging her front shoulder into his, she bobbed her head to the right.

He narrowed his eyes as he looked over there and saw a gap between two dens. It looked to go all the way to the rear between them, and no one else looked to be taking it.

Matilda looked back at him, and he nodded wordlessly.

Let's do it.

She bounded forward, or rather shoved forward, and he followed.

She would have earned anything from a hiss to a snarl to an actual claw in protest as she shouldered her way past the various fleeing people, except that she was obviously bearing young ones. And even in these dire circumstances, that bit of protocol still held, Humbert was grateful to see.

Or at least, it did for now.

How much longer, though?

It didn't matter, they were at the gap, and Matilda held up to let him lead the way now that they were past the throng of people.

That was women's lib for you. Fine to take the lead until danger rears its head. Then it's run to the man for protection.

Humbert flicked his tongue teasingly at her, and Matilda gave a little playful hiss in response. Then he plowed forward into the gap.

It was dark, despite the glow from the fires lighting the forest canopy above. It was also tight. But it could have been worse. In some of the other neighborhoods, where the man-ape caretakers were less rigorous, there might be litter strewn all over the gap between dens. But no danger of that here, with the quality of people living in this area of town.

Because of the lack of rubbish, they quickly got past the two dens, and emerged between the trees in their rear.

There was a span of three or four running paces between these dens and the back of the dens in the next street over. In that gap, there were tree roots, undergrowth and bushes, and a carpeting of fallen leaves from years past that were mostly decomposed into new soil.

But only a couple of other people. They rushed past Humbert and Matilda as they emerged from between the dens, hardly sparing a backwards glance at them as they ran away from the blaze toward safety.

For a moment, Humbert just stood there, perplexed. Looking to the right, the flames were continuing to leap from tree to tree, and he could see entire dens ablaze just a few tens of running strides away now. To the left, overgrown space between tree trunks. But basically no other people but the two of them.

How come no one else was here? Were the rest of his neighbors really that lulled that they could only follow the pack? That was something he could have expected from canines....or man-apes... But from his own people?

He recalled hearing a lecture a while back, about how this generation was getting soft. How people had let their dominance of the man-apes and canines convince them that troubles were over forever, and that it would only be pleasure and indulgence from here to eternity. And that that mindset would spell the ruin of their entire culture and way of life.

Humbert had scoffed at the old curmudgeon's words then.

He wasn't doing that now.

But he was also thankful that the rest of the people around here were, apparently, blind. That meant he could get his Matilda and their young to safety.

"Let's go," he said, and turned away from the blaze.

They sped through the woods between streets. Although if he was being honest with himself, they weren't really making good time at all. But compared with the pace they had been making in the throng of people on Cornell Street, it felt like they were flying.

"How are you doing, Mat?" he said over his shoulder, and he heard his mate hiss at him.

"Wish you weren't holding me up, Bert."

He purred slightly at the teasing tone in her voice, and moved a little bit quicker.

Behind them, the heat of the flames was receding, and he began to become optimistic again. They were going to get out of this, just fine.

That's when the light and the heat erupted in front of them.

Humbert drew up short, and Matilda came to a halt beside him.

He didn't look at her, but he knew her eyes were wide and her jaw slack with shock and horror, same as his.

Another fire. This one in front of them. And not just one. Glancing left and right, he saw others, their glows spaced so that they had to be burning at the ends of the town's various streets.

The people who were streaming away from the fires behind were going to be cooked by them.

But worse, the crowds would compress, stop. And then panic.

Blood would run in the streets, before the survivors inevitably burned.

As Humbert looked all around, he saw more fires starting up everywhere. There had to be a way out....but he couldn't see one. His entire town was going to go up in flames, and him and his mate with it, unless he found a place to run to, but...

The crowds on the two streets to either side began making loud, panicked sounds, and Humbert's heart sank. It was starting already. It was only a matter of time -

Panic became anger, and then the sounds of fighting began to erupt from all around. Then screams of anguish.

He cast about again. There had to be something. Anything!

If -

His eyes came to rest of a tree trunk nearby. Between an upturned root and the ground beneath it was... a hole.

Shelter. Some animal's lair.

Revulsion welled up with him. He would not crawl into the dirt like some...some...peon! He would -

He would suck up his pride and do it, or he would die, and Matilda and their young with him.

He looked at her, then pointed with his nose toward the hole.

She saw it, and stiffened. He could see the same thought process he had just gone through, and shook his head vehemently.

"It's this or death," he said.

The look on her face for a second said she would prefer death. Then she assented, and gave a little nod.

He led her toward the hole, and their only hope of survival.

Even without the firestorm above them, the night would have been a torment. Cramming into that tiny, dirty, vermin-lair. It was so... So undignified.

But the heat blasting down the hole into the depth of the lair put the lie to any notion that they would have been better off up above.

For a time, it felt like it wasn't going to matter that they were down in the hole. It grew so hot Humbert thought they were going to roast alive. Breathing became difficult. Not because of smoke, though there was some of that. But every breath seemed like a strain, and it felt like he could never get enough in. Whatever it was in the air that calmed that need to breathe seemed to not be present, or to not be there enough to satiate his desire.

His head swam and his eyes grew dim, and he thought sure he was passing on to whatever Bast had for them in the next life.

Then he was blinking at light streaming down the hole.

Normal, wholesome sunlight. Not the hellish glow that had pummeled him into submission and unconsciousness in the night.

He stretched, and found he could barely move. The hole was tiny, but it seemed like it had compressed somehow while he had been out. His muscles ached and his coat was filthy and he probably looked even worse than he felt.

He had to get out of there. And get a bath. And a backrub from a man-ape servant. And then -

Humbert got his thoughts under control, forcing the reality of his new situation to the forefront of his mind. No, first he needed to see what the situation was, then he needed to make sure Matilda was going to be fine.

And speaking of Mat -

He looked behind himself, further back in the cave, and saw the glowing eyes of his mate as she looked back up at him. Or rather, at the lighted opening of the hole; she just happened to be looking at it through him.

"About time you woke up," she said, and he shrugged.

"You alright?"

"I will be after a good, long cleaning," Matilda said.

Humbert couldn't argue with that.

Turning away from her, he crawled his way to the edge of the hole and stuck his head out.

The hollow where the town had stood was a wasteland. Burned tree trunks, bereft of limbs and still smoking as they smoldered in the morning breeze, were all that he could see, everywhere he looked. The sky was grey, whether because of clouds or from the aggregated smoke of all the devastation he could not have guessed, but it dimmed the sunlight enough that the early summer day that should have been warm was instead cool.

Except for the smoldering trees.

The tree that his hole stood above was no different, though it looked like somehow only the trees' upper portion had been scorched. It actually still kept a few of its lower limbs, though they were leafless and blackened.

Thinking for a moment, Humbert said a quick prayer to Bast; if the tree had gone up completely, he and Matilda probably would not have survived, considering the proximity of the tree's root to the opening of their hole.

As he pushed himself fully out, he shuddered at the thought.

Then he was free, and he bounded a couple steps away to allow Matilda to follow him out. He looked himself over as he waited for her, and cringed. His fur was matted and muddy and streaked with soot and...

He was just a mess.

Part of his mind thought of the kind of shake that canines do to rid their fur of water or muck. Disgust with himself made him shove that thought away. Did he have no dignity left?

No. Though it cost him his life, he would not behave in such a manner.

You weren't thinking that when you climbed in that hole last night, the voice said back.

Inwardly, he sliced his claws across the voice's throat, and it died an agonized, gurgling death.

For a moment.

Then it started muttering to him again.

He scowled darkly.

Matilda had by now extricated herself and was looking around, no less upset than he felt.

"Bert, what are we going to do?" she asked.

He had no good response. So he just said, "Get out of here and find a new place, I guess."

That was lame and he knew it. And from the look she gave him she knew it and knew he knew it. But really...what else was there?

Matilda just looked at him for a long several seconds that stretched to nearly a minute. Then she curled her back in a long, drawn out shrug. "Do you have any idea where?"

He didn't, actually. But thinking it over real quick -

"My parents are over in Nipville, only about ten miles north."

Matilda's eyes narrowed. "You want to live. With your mother." He tone held levels of meaning. Disgust at the entire notion, and the degradation that moving in with your parents entails. Scorn at the entire thought of it. Disappointment in him for even bringing it up. But most, beneath it all, utter terror at having to spend more than an hour with her mother in law.

He could understand that. Her mother was no picnic, either. But she was half a world away, outside Bangkok. They weren't dropping in on her any time soon.

Humbert gave a half-hiss of reprimand. "Not forever. Just until we make a better plan. And do you have any better ideas?"

Matilda glowered for a moment, then shrugged.

He didn't think she did.

He led the way in the direction he thought was north; the sun was just barely visible through the gloom above, but he still wasn't entirely certain. He set a pace that was easy to maintain, but would also hopefully cover the distance before it got dark again.

They'd only gone a couple hundred paces before they had to stop, to avoid sicking up.

It used to be a street between dens. Now it was just another burned out area between charred remains of trees. Except for the pile of burned corpses.

The stench of burning hair and flesh warned them about it before they got into view, but even that couldn't prepare Humbert for what he saw when he came up the little rise and beheld the scene.

There had to be a couple hundred of them. Dead people, sprawled everywhere. Some were completely burned to charcoal. Some only partway. But none lived, and of the ones whose faces were visible all wore expressions of horror and agony.

Down in the hole Humbert had prayed that the people would find easier deaths than burning. And surely some had.

But so many others....

He turned away, and found Matilda had already done the same.

But their eyes met, and she could see an all-consuming grief in hers that mirrored his own, amplified it until he felt he could not go on.

But he had to. So he did.

He led her away from the charnel pit and toward where the first fires had originated, going several hundred walking paces before turning north again.

Mounting the rise once again, he found what had used to be a street, but this time it was clear. For the most part.

He distinctly did not look in the direction of the mass of dead bodies as they crossed.

All the same, when he reached the rise on the other side of the former street, he looked down, and saw another body.

Humbert was about to turn away again when the body's head twitched.

This one wasn't dead.

Surprise froze him in place for a moment, then he was bounding down to sit beside the stricken person.

He recognized the person as he drew close. A cop he'd gotten to know in the pub from time to time. Name was Sylvester. Humbert had always been impressed with him: he was big and strong, black and white and tall. Witty, with an easy manner that always seemed to charm the ladies.

Now he was burned black on his rear third, and his coat was horribly dirty and matted everywhere else. His left eye was white and pussy, and he had scratch marks across his face, like he'd been in a grand fight.

When Humbert came to a stop beside him, Sylvester lifted his head feebly, then blinked in recognition.

"Bert."

"Syl," Humbert said, by way of greeting. He felt like he should have said something more, but he had no idea what.

"You look like hell," Sylvester said, and Humbert couldn't help but snorting out a little laugh.

Sylvester tried a laugh of his own, but only managed a coughing fit that led to a painful groan—and somehow passing a little bit of hairball? How did he manage that?

"Not...much time," Sylvester said, and Humbert shook his head.

"Don't talk like that, Syl. We'll find some help and they'll lick you right into shape, no problem."

Even as he said that, he felt Matilda's gaze of, "What the hell do you think you're saying?", and he cast her a warning, "Be quiet" look.

Still, Sylvester snorted again. "I know when I'm done," he said. Then he coughed some more. And somehow even more hair came out. He drew a deep breath, then raised his head so he could look Humbert directly in the eyes.

"It was the humans."

Humbert blinked. "What?"

Sylvester nodded. "Been...working a case... Some of them talking with the canines. Plotting escape. Rebellion." His words were cut off by another round of coughing.

Humbert looked away from Sylvester toward Matilda. She looked as puzzled as he felt. The man-apes had always been the people's willing, sometimes eager, servants. Tending their every need with nary a complaint. In fact, they seemed to relish serving the people. Especially with backrubs.

But if what Sylvester said was true, that had all been a lie. A duplicitous deception, to lull people into complacency, so the man-apes could usurp their rightful place as rulers.

Which was, of course, inconceivable.

Wasn't it?

He looked back at Sylvester, and found the cop's expression pained, but completely lucid and serious.

"You doubt me. Don't." He moved his leg, and Humbert saw a canister in the dirt beneath, depressed where Sylvester had apparently been trying, weakly, to dig a hole in order to bury or protect it. "Evidence is all here," the cop said. He nudged the canister toward Humbert with his nose.

"Get it...to someone..." Another round of coughing interrupted again. But this time it went on and on, but the coughs also grew weaker with each racking exhalation until finally, they subsided into a long, drawn-out exhalation that ended in a rasping gurgle.

Then Sylvester lay still. Gone to his eternal reward.

Humbert hung his head in renewed sorrow.

Humbert looked out at the setting sun as it touched the top of the hill across the valley from his parents' den. The sunset was redder than usual. Redder than he had ever seen it; it seemed to turn the entire sky to blood.

Fitting, considering what had happened.

He sat on his haunches, batting the little canister Sylvester had given him between his forepaws, but kept his eyes on the sunset.

The color of blood. Very fitting indeed.

Movement from behind announced another's presence, and then his father came to sit beside him to his right. Dad was as lean and powerful as he ever had been, but he had grey in his coat now, and in his whiskers. His eyes were as sharp, as piercing, as ever though. And when he looked at Humbert, he felt them peering into his soul.

"Your mother's got Matilda situated," Dad said. "She thinks she might be heading for labor in the next few days."

"What? Is she - "

Dad made a reassuring gesture with his paws. "She'll be fine. Natural result of stress. Or so your mother says." He paused, then shrugged slightly. "It's women's business. They know what they're about. Best not poke your head in."

Humbert opened his mouth to object, but realized he had no retort that could upset the plain and simple truth of what Dad had said. So instead he looked back at the canister and batted it with his paw again.

Dad waited another couple seconds, then said, "Heard from the Prosecutor's office. They'll be sending people over for that in the morning."

"Good."

Another pause. "If it shows what your friend says it shows, you know what that means, don't you son?"

Humbert raised his head to meet his father's gaze. Then he lifted his paw. He felt his claws emerging, unbidden.

Dad glanced downward and, seeing the claws, nodded. His expression became approving.

Humbert held his father's gaze for a few seconds, then he lowered his paw back to the ground. He turned to look back at the sunset, and how it had made the sky bleed.

And he knew there would be more blood flowing, soon.

He looked forward to it.

32

TERRA INFIRMA

I t was Sunday afternoon, and I was sitting under a peach tree atop a hill overlooking the bay.

The sun bathed the land in a warm radiance, unblocked by all but a few tiny puffs of clouds that hung in the sky, moving lazily if at all. A gentle breeze carried in from the bay, bringing the smell of the sea along with the far-away calling of gulls on the wing. And I just reclined back against the gritty bark of the tree trunk and sketched, my pad resting against my propped up knees as I ran a hunk of charcoal along the page.

The image I was creating was nothing special. Just the outline of the bay, with the finger piers of Carraway Yacht Club protruding out like the tines of a pitchfork and little ripples of waves caused by an offshore wind that was undetectable here. And a pair of boats under sail, close-hauled to the wind as they tacked out from shore to wherever they were bound.

Not special, but still unique. Or so my teachers liked to say.

Which, I suppose, was like saying the retarded kid has special needs. Sounds better, but lipstick on a pig.

It didn't matter though. I didn't draw with any hope of making money from it, and right then I really just wanted to clear my mind and relax. Thus, the charcoal and the page.

I lost track of how long I had been sitting there, just letting the image form on the page as I let my thoughts wander. It became a mechanical rhythm. Look over at the bay, back to the page. Make a few more lines on the drawing. Look back at the bay, then back to the page. Make a few more lines.

Over and over, without thought, as the image grew from a few little squiggles into something that was approaching coherent.

I barely noticed the sweat trickling down my head and wetting my shirt, or the fly that buzzed around occasionally, that's how deeply I got into the zone of just drawing.

Until I heard the swishing of footsteps through the grass behind me; someone was ascending the hill.

Ignoring it, I leaned my head forward and focused in on the sketch pad. But I lost the flow state I was in, and I made an errant mark, turning one of the boats into something...

A body slid down the tree trunk to my right, and I smelled lavender, heard the rustling of skirts as the person adjusted herself before settling back next to me.

"Thought I'd find you up here," Susan said, her deep—for a woman—voice sounding intentionally casual.

I knew it was her before she said anything; she always wore that perfume, and she had a distinct rhythm to her gait that I never could help but recognize. But I really didn't want to deal with her right then. Didn't want to deal with anyone.

So I said nothing, but rubbed out the ill-made mark as best I could, and glanced back down at the bay for a second.

I was just looking back to make my next mark when she spoke again, and whatever hope I had of getting back into the zone fled screaming into the distance.

"He didn't mean it, you know."

I didn't reply, but the memories of the morning rushed back into my head, spurred by her words. The shouting. The threats. Then grabbing up my pad and running—I had walked, but I was really running—up here, to get away from everyone.

And it had almost worked. I'd managed to purge it all from my mind in the zone of my sketching. Until Susan had to come up here and ruin it.

I looked at her and scowled. Or tried to. But when my eyes met hers, the green of their irises seemed to beam compassion and understanding at me, and I found I couldn't be angry at her.

Grant, though? I had more than enough anger for him, now that she'd made me remember it all.

"He meant every word."

Susan shook her head, and the red-brown hair framing her face seemed to flow like a wave from the movement. "Jake, he's your brother." She laid her hand against the bicep of my right arm and squeezed lightly. "He just wants what's best for you. And you know how hotheaded he is."

I snorted. "Not sure how getting onto his crazy rocket ship and blasting off to some long-lost legend is," I dropped my charcoal to make air quotes with my fingers, "best for me." She opened her mouth, but I kept right on going, talking over her. "But anyway, I'm not going. So just leave me alone. And tell him to do the same. He can go have his adventure, or whatever, without his stupid little brother. We'll both be better off."

Susan's lips compressed and I could tell she was angered by what I'd said. But I didn't really care. I'd meant every word. Grant had never liked it here, not the entire time we'd grown up. He'd been scheming for years, frittering his money away. And now he apparently had bought a ship. And lo and behold he'd concocted an excuse to leave.

Right when I had finally got out from under the yoke of school and teachers and was ready to get going with my own thing. And I was just supposed to say screw it, leave my whole future behind and head on off with him?

No.

Susan must have seen the resolve in my face, because she just let out a little sigh, instead of the rebuke I thought was coming. "You're not stupid, Jake. No one thinks that, especially Grant. But he's right. This place is - "

"My home," I finished for her. "He's always hated it, but I don't. He wants to leave? Fine. But I'm staying."

With that, I pushed myself to my feet. I took a moment to brush bits of grass off my pants, then I tucked my pad under my arm and turned away from her. I started descending the hill toward the bay. There was another good place where I'd done some other sketches before, on the other side of the Yacht Club.

Farther away, so maybe they'd leave me alone.

I didn't hear Susan get up to follow me, and when I reached the base of the hill and looked back, she was gone.

The storm rolled in almost without warning, and caught me halfway through my walk from the Yacht Club back home.

Dark clouds seemed to materialize overhead, so grey they were almost black, absorbing the red-orange light of the setting sun greedily and letting nothing escape back out. The wind whipped up in time with the clouds' appearance, and I had to lean far in to make any headway at all.

And then the ran came. Great drops as big around as a peach pit, it seemed, falling slowly but steadily at first until, after a few minutes, converting into a torrential downpour that was like standing beneath an upturned bucket.

The wind grew even more intense, and thunder rolled across the terrain like a great bass drum, coming right on the heels on lightning bolts that seemed to be keeping their own intense rhythm in the madness.

In five minutes, maybe less, it went from a balmy day to this conflagration, and I became completely soaked.

Grimacing against the onslaught, I hunched my shoulders and ran, fast as I could against the assaulting wind, toward home. I covered my head with my sketch pad to get at least some relief from the rain, heedless of the effect the pelting would have on my drawings; there would be no way to save them anyway. Not in this, not dressed as I was in lightweight slacks and shirt, not even a windbreaker.

I put thoughts of my creations out of my mind and slogged on.

It was almost as dark as night, despite at least another hour before twilight should have fully sent in, and homes and businesses would have turned on their lights. But the intensity of the rain made it difficult to see more than a few feet in any direction.

I began to worry that I would get turned around, and lose my way home completely.

If I'd been wearing my watch, which interfaced with the global locating system and the wireless net, that wouldn't have been a concern. But I'd left it behind in my room when I'd fled Grant earlier; didn't want him to call and harangue me some more.

Now I regretted that decision.

I was beginning to think I'd be better off to just stop and find some shelter somewhere until the worst of the storm passed when I saw a light, ahead and to the left. Dim, but that didn't mean much in all this.

I splashed through ankle-deep puddles toward the light, and all at once it turned into a great lit-up storefront sign: "Povel's Pleasant Pastries."

Seeing the sign evoked a sigh of relief. Povel's was just down the street from Grant's house, where I still lived. I was home free.

Newly oriented, I turned to the right and hurried on into the somehow still darkening gloom.

Three minutes later found me scampering up the hand-crafted wood stairs to the front porch. As I passed beneath the porch's awning, I felt the loss of the rainfall on my head almost like a forty pound weight had been lifted from my shoulders. But it had been replaced by a different weight, altogether.

I stood there for a long couple minutes, looking at the red-painted front door with its old fashioned brass knocker and modern locking device, complete with cypher pad and biometrics scanner, and felt the strange conflict between those two things.

Much like the conflict between Grant and myself.

He yearned to spread out, get in his ship and go, see the stars. Embrace all the tech in the universe, and explore.

A simple knocker was all I needed or wanted. At least for now. Maybe someday... But no, not even then. Grant bristled at the "backwater" home our grandparents had cut out of a barely-terraformed world. Looking at the door, I remembered vividly arguments between him and Dad, before Dad had passed on.

And now the arguments had just shifted over to me.

Well, I wasn't going to -

The door swung open, and Grant was pushing through. He was slipping a heavy weather jacket around his six foot three inch frame, high-powered hand torch in one hand and a GLS locator beacon in the other. He was looking over his shoulder as he came out.

"When I find him I'll - "

Grant's words stopped in his throat when he turned to look forward and saw me, dripping from head to toe on the porch.

Our eyes met, and not for the first time did I think how similar in tone the deep hazel of his eyes were to mine.

And then he engulfed me in a bearhug.

"Thank God you're back safe," he said into my ear. I could hear the worry, and the relief, in his voice. But damn, he was crushing my ribs.

I tried to say something in reply, but all that came out was a pained grunt.

That was enough, though, because he released me and stepped back, a sheepish half-grin, almost apologetic, on his face. "Come on inside," he said. "Let's get you dried off."

Three more storms came crashing through in the next two weeks, just as bad as the first. By the time the last one faded out, shortly before sunrise on a Thursday, the roads running through our little town by the bay were a pitting mess of mud and detritus from all sorts of vegetation and dead animals that had flowed down from the highlands on the rush of the stormwater.

I could barely make it down the street to the bend in the road around Povel's, and I had on knee-high boots. But I tried; word had come back that the bay itself was higher than normal. Noticeably.

That was inconceivable. A ludicrous rumor. But certain as I was in that assessment, I still had to see for myself.

But there was so much runoff still washing down the street, so much rubble, and so many drowned creatures plugging up the path that I ended up tromping back up to the house.

I kicked the boots off just inside the front door and stomped across the living room toward the stone fireplace that Grandpa had built with his own hands—or so he'd told me when I was just barely able to walk. A merry flame was flickering over the logs within, and one popped as I got up close to it, sending little embers flying. One struck the steel mesh that separated the fireplace from the polished hardwood flooring of the living room, and glowed there for a moment before dropping into the growing ash heap beneath the wrought iron cradle that held the logs in place.

I watched it with fascination for a moment, then held my hands out to the soothing warmth exuding from the fire.

Grant was sitting as his desk, over in the far corner from the front door. His workstation monitor was up, and I could see three graphs up: two line graphs and a bar graph, multicolored to better contrast the various data points in each. He was leaning forward in the padded swivel chair he liked so much. I couldn't see his face, but I was certain he was squinting at the screen as he looked the data plots over.

He always squinted when he did that.

From the kitchen further back in the house, I heard clanking. Pots and pans, no doubt, as Susan tidied up from breakfast. Her voice, low and melodious, barely carried through to my ears as she hummed to herself.

I smiled at the simple pleasure her humming portrayed; the enjoyment of mundane work, a contentment with the everyday.

Then I glanced back at Grant, and that momentary empathetic pleasure faded at the intense focus his hunched body gave off. He could never just...enjoy.

And that wasn't the only problem.

Glancing at the doorway leading back into the kitchen and dining area to make sure she wasn't going to come out, I said, "Are you ever going to marry her?"

Grant gave a little jerk and turned to look at me. He appeared startled, almost baffled. "Huh?"

"Susan. Are you going to marry her?"

Grant blinked twice, then gave a shake of his head and snorted softly before giving me the standard condescending look that screamed, "I'm ten years older than you. Don't presume to question me." He didn't say that, of course. He never did.

Never had to.

"How about you let me worry about that, ok?"

I just looked at him, but he didn't seem bothered by that at all. Instead, he changed the subject.

Pointing at the data graphs on his screen, he said, "We've got more important things to worry about right now."

"Oh?"

He gestured for me to come look. With some trepidation, but also with a bit of honest curiosity, I did. When I reached his side, he gestured at the two line graphs.

"The storm intensity is definitely increasing, compared with ten years ago. Just like I've been saying."

I frowned at the graphs, but couldn't deny that at least on the surface, it appeared he was right. The one was a plot of major storm measured rainfall. The second of measured wind velocity. Glancing downward, I saw that the bar graph was a frequency plot of total major storm occurrences.

Assuming his data was accurate, there was a definite trend there.

He looked at me, a grave expression on his face. "The terraforming is breaking down," he said, certainty in his voice.

This again. I shook my head at him. "That's not for certain at all, from that data. It could be anything causing those storms. A fluke. A natural oscillation that we've not been on the planet long enough to know about yet. You're jumping straight to that..." I sighed, almost groaned at the same old discussion we'd had a thousand times already. "If the terraforming wasn't taking, don't you think the governor or Senate would have told us?"

He frowned, then shook his head. "Not if there was no way to fix it."

"So what, they're just going to sit there and let everyone die, instead of ordering an evacuation or something?"

Grant nodded. "They would if there weren't enough ships to go around."

We'd had this discussion before, but Grant had never brought up this sort of paranoid thought process in the past. What was he getting at?

He saw the disbelief on my face, and rolled his eyes. "You know how long it took me to find and buy my ship. It wasn't because it was too expensive. In fact, it was cheap. I've been having to make repairs to it these last few weeks. It'll probably be another several weeks before it's safe to fly." He shook his head. "No, there simply weren't any ships available for sale. At all. Anywhere. Believe me, I looked."

"So?"

"So." He leaned forward, fixing me with a level stare. "When's the last time a ship came from one of the other colonies?" It was a rhetorical question. The last offworld ship had come through ten years ago; I remember because it happened on my birthday, and it had been such an unusual event it had been all over the news. Since then, though, nothing. "There's only the ships here planetside. And there aren't enough for the whole population. The political class will be getting out. Them and their cronies. The rest of us are out of luck unless we make our own."

Ah, so now it was a grand conspiracy. I shook my head and turned away from him, back toward the fireplace. I was still chilled from the walk outside, and the damp.

To my back, Grant said, "Pull your head out of the sand, Jake. We have to get out of here before it's too late."

"And go where?"

"There was once a planet that people didn't have to terraform. Where - "

"Where the human race originally evolved. Yeah, I've heard that bedtime story before."

"It's not a story, Jake. It's real."

I scowled into the flames for several long breaths. Our fight from two weeks before was still a fresh memory, and I didn't want to have another one like that. Finally, I looked back over my shoulder at him. "Mom and Dad, Grandma and Grandpa are buried out back. Susan's family is here. Your job is here. So is my new job. Everyone we know is here. But you want to leave over a little rain and paranoia, to find a place that no one knows where it is, or if it even exists at all?"

My snort was loud, and conveyed every scrap of meaning I could put into it.

Grant just looked at me, and scowled.

Four weeks of good weather followed, but that didn't seem to please Grant. It was like the contradiction of his predictions of woe was intolerable.

Or maybe just my pointing out that he was wrong.

Either way, I resolved to keep away from home for much of the day. I left early for work, and then after my shift I waved off going to the pub with the other guys on my crew. Instead I went to my hilltop, and the peach tree.

My old sketching pad had been ruined by the deluge, as had all of my older drawings. Fortunately, new pads were always available, and as long as there was charcoal, so were new drawings.

I spent my evenings sketching until the last lobe of the sun was just barely visible above the hills on the opposite side of the bay. Then I got up and trudged back to Grant's house. Technically it was mine as well; we had both inherited half of it. But I couldn't really think of it as mine. Too much of our parents, and now Grant, in it.

As I trudged back to the house, beneath the slowly dimming sky as the colors of sunset drained away into the grey of twilight, I considered that maybe it was about time to get my own place. Both Grant and I were being rubbed raw by our constant proximity, and the disagreements over his obsession with conspiracy and flight.

I was able to save most of my paychecks, so I was accumulating a decent balance in my account. Another few weeks and I'd have enough for a deposit, and for some furniture.

I resolved to tell Grant I was moving out that evening.

That's when the ground began to shake beneath my feet.

The house lay in ruins, but compared with the sight of Susan lying on a paramedic's gurney, unconscious in a neck brace, the destruction of my childhood home seemed pale.

Grant had a stunned look on his face, like he couldn't believe what was going on, as they wheeled her into the ambulance and then sped away to the hospital.

I walked up to him, but he barely noticed me. He just stared after the flashing red lights as they receded into the darkness, his mouth slightly agape and tears welling in his eyes.

"Is she - ?" I began.

He gave a little jerk, then finally focused in on me. He blinked twice, then shook his head. "They're not sure. They don't think it's life-threatening, but..." He trailed off, and I looked him over more closely.

He was a mess. He had a bruise on his forehead above his right eye, and his shirt was torn in two places. One of those tears was stained red; he had cut himself, but apparently not badly enough for the paramedics to bother with.

But then, looking up and down the street toward the other collapsed buildings in our town, I got the feeling that if someone was able to walk around on his own, if he had a hunk of wood sticking out of his side the paramedics would just leave him be, for other, more serious cases.

"There's never been an earthquake in these parts," I said, hearing stunned disbelief in my own voice as I shook my head at the devastation.

"Terraforming's failing," Grant said, then he got started down the road, quickly moving from a walk to a jog to a full-out run.

"Where are you going?" I called after him, then immediately kicked myself inwardly for being stupid.

"Hospital."

I ran to catch up with him. I thought for a second about his car, but gave up on that immediately. Too much rubble in the streets, and anyway there were so many ambulances out and about that we'd just be in the way.

And besides, the Hospital was only a mile and a half away.

So we ran.

When we reached the Hospital, it was a mad house.

The building was not all that big. Just three stories tall and a hundred feet or so on a side. But it didn't need to be; our town wasn't all the large, so there were few patients to be admitted at any one time. Normally.

Tonight, the parking lot was full of people waiting to be let into the building. Some were injured but ambulatory. Some had to be helped by friends or family. Others, like Grant and myself, were healthy and whole but obviously in distress for loved ones.

The ambulance entrance was in the rear of the building. After a brief look around at the milling crowd, growing larger by the second, Grant looked at me and then nodded toward the nearest side of the building. I understood at once, and followed him as we skirted the crowd and headed toward the rear.

It was dark; power was out throughout the town. But the Hospital obviously had an emergency generator. Still, many of the building's windows were dark, as were its security lights outside. So quickly, as we got away from the handheld torches people in the crowd were carrying and the emergency lights that had been set up out front, we descended into shadow. But as we reached the rear corner of the building, we could see the Emergency Room ambulance door, standing wide open.

An orderly in scrubs, or maybe a nurse—who could really tell?—stood to one side of the doors, talking with a paramedic in blue coveralls. There was a single ambulance in the driveway; the paramedic's ride, not doubt.

Grant stood tall and strode toward the doors, and the two medical personnel. For a second I thought he would just waltz right on through, but at the last moment the orderly sidestepped in front of him, holding her hand up at his chest, palm out.

"You can't come in here sir. Hospital staff only."

"My fiancé just came in an ambulance."

Fiancé? I blinked, confused. When had Grant asked Susan to marry him, and how come he hadn't told me?

The woman's stern expression softened slightly, but she shook her head all the same. "I'm sorry, sir. But you'll have to wait with the rest of the people out front."

Through the ER doors, I could see that the place was busy to the point of chaos. I'd been to the ER before a time or two; what boy didn't as a teenager? When I'd been there it had always been a calm and controlled place. To the point that it seemed to me patients were more likely to die of boredom than from the injuries that brought them in.

All that composure was gone now. Medical personnel were bustling to and fro, and there was a feeling in their movements like they were only just barely holding it all together. Like any small thing would bring their entire process down on top of them.

That scene put more of a chill up my spine than anything I had seen so far this evening. I reached out and put my hand on Grant's arm.

"She's right," I said. "We can't help in there. We'd just make it worse."

Grant scowled his displeasure, but he couldn't disagree. He grunted submission, and then we turned to go back around to the front, there to wait with all the other desperate and frightened people.

Half of the houses in town were destroyed. The other half were damaged, to some extent or another. Families with intact houses opened their doors to their neighbors, but even with that there wasn't enough room for everyone to have a roof over his head.

Some folks stayed on boats in the Yacht Club, whose owners also opened them for use. But for the rest, emergency services set up a tent city.

But Grant and I stayed in his ship.

He had it tied down on a landing pad set back in the woods to the west of town. It wasn't exactly a secret, either that the pad was there or that Grant had a ship on it. But no one paid it much mind.

Susan was released from the Hospital after a week, and she joined us aboard. We had a celebratory dinner made from the best emergency services-supplied protein squeezes money couldn't buy.

The ship had internal power, and it was designed to withstand the high g's of takeoff and reentry. So it had come through the quake pretty much unscathed. So we got to watch the news feeds. We didn't do it very often; it was too depressing. Other places on the planet had been hit by quakes too, with damage similar to what we'd experienced.

It made me begin to wonder if Grant wasn't right in his paranoia, after all.

Then the first ships began to blast off for space.

It happened without warning. Just one day, two weeks after the quake, when it looked like the rebuilding was starting to get going, people at the yacht club reported seeing a smoke trail rising from the north, veering up in a ballistic arc. The next day, they reported two more.

Upon hearing the news, Grant grunted. "It's starting," he said, and raised an eyebrow at me.

I didn't have to ask what he meant: the exodus of the able. Of the rich and powerful.

And again, I couldn't call him wrong.

The newscast that night just solidified it.

The regular anchor wasn't on the broadcast. Instead the cast was headed by a pockmark-faced guy in his early 30s with black hair and darting grey eyes. He had on a suit, but it was rumpled like he'd been sleeping in it, and he looked like he hadn't been sleeping well.

He stammered as he read the opening message. "Citing looting and violence in several cities damaged in the recent global earthquakes, the governor has issued an emergency order today declaring martial law. Orders have been sent to local guardsmen in all precincts that looters are to be shot on sight, and the use of deadly force to defend lives and property is authorized."

The substitute anchor swallowed, then the screen went black; Grant had shut it off.

He looked at me. "It's coming apart, Jake. And it won't come back together again. I've got one last system to fix, but we can take off without it. I think we gather up every bit of food we can tomorrow, and then get out while the getting's still good." He raised an eyebrow. "We do not want to be here when people start to catch on to what's really going on, and the guardsmen decide better they have my ship than we do."

I didn't want to agree with him. The entire concept struck against the core of my being, and everything that I wanted my life to be.

I had a vision of settling down, continuing on building the roots that our grandparents and parents had laid on this world. Have a family, live simply. Not go galavanting around in Grant's ship.

Inwardly, I rebelled against the entire concept. But I couldn't help thinking, somewhere deep down, that he was right, after all.

***

That evening, I left the ship and hiked through the woods. I brought a hand torch with me, and used it as a guide to make my way up a shallow rise that I had visited before in the daylight. There was a clearing on top that offered a good view of the town to the east, and the bay beyond.

During the day, when I'd come up and looked out on that view, it was like looking at a scar on the face of the planet. Whereas in previous visits, back when Grant had first bought the ship and brought me up here to show it off, the town's spires and buildings had been bright and colorful, picturesque in and of themselves as they seemed a part of the scenery, like a natural growth that belong there. Now, there was rubble and torn up dirt and, in a few places, rising smoke where fires from buildings that had collapsed still smoldered for one reason or another.

Even the bay looked darker, like the scars of the land had run off into it, befowling it.

And they probably had. There hadn't been another huge storm, but there had been rain. Who knows what sorts of solvents and chemicals and other things that we never would have allowed to tarnish the natural water in better times had been cast into it by those rains?

I was hoping, as I made my way up to the top of the rise that night, to see a better view. Something more peaceful, more beautiful. Something I could sketch by the light of the stars and my torch.

I stepped out from beneath the tree canopy and up the last few steps to the peak, and looked east.

The second moon was up, a waxing crescent halfway down from its zenith to its resting place on the other side of the bay. Its pale pink-white glow burned with a wholesomeness that I hadn't seen or felt in days. Weeks.

Looking down from the heavenly body, I saw it reflected off the shimmering water of the bay, and whatever tarnish the disaster had leant the water was invisible. Only serenity seemed to waft from that direction now.

Even the wreckage of the town was less ugly. Torches that lit houses and the tent city were dimmer than the normal lights, giving the impression of campfires, almost, despite their true electrical origin.

Insects buzzed in the night, and the smell of growth and life from the woods all around me seemed to draw the cares I'd brought up the slope with me right away.

I inhaled deeply. Held it, then exhaled, and felt a lot better. Seeing my home like this, in the peace and beauty of the night, seemed to lift a heavy burden from my shoulder.

Looking out there, right then, I imagined that Grant really was just paranoid, like I'd always said. Times would be hard for the next while. Probably a long while. But the town—the entire colony— would get through, and then we'd be better off than we ever had been. Our family roots could continue to grow deeper into the soil of this place until -

A flash of light, nearly blinding it was so much brighter than anything else in the night sky, erupted to the south.

Raising a hand to shield my eyes, I looked that way, blinking away spots.

As my eyes adjusted—really as the light dimmed—I saw glowing trails of light lifting into the sky. Two. Three. Five.

Seven in all. Each a ship, I knew without having to ask, rising toward the heavens on a pillar of fire.

I flashed back to the peach tree where I had been sketching before, and the sailboats tacking away from shore. I never had found out where those boats were bound for, but they'd never returned to Carraway Yacht Club, that I'd ever seen. Cruisers, out exploring the planet like Grant wanted to explore the cosmos.

But these ships weren't exploring.

They were fleeing.

Two more joined the departing flotilla. Then a tenth.

And I turned and hurried down the rise toward the ship, my heart in my throat. For I knew there could be no denying what was happening any longer.

Vibration and acceleration forces pressed me back into my seat, and I had to strain to lift my head. But lift it I did; that was the only way I could see out the little porthole next to my couch in the ship's bridge.

It was tiny, the porthole, but it was enough that I could see the clouds—white and puffy, just like on the day when I'd gone sketching—falling away beneath us as Grant's ship roared upward to the heavens.

Below the clouds, the patchwork ground was receding at an ever-increasing rate, and I felt like my heart was flying away with it.

My home was leaving, going far from me; but no that wasn't right. I was leaving my home.

For a moment, I longed to be able to leap through that porthole and fall back down to the land that had grown and nourished me, where my parents and grandparents' bones were buried.

But then I raised my eyes toward the rapidly-falling horizon, and I saw the other clouds gathering, rushing forward on winds so strong they would have precluded us from taking off if we'd waited any longer in our countdown. Clouds so tall that they reached higher than the ship had yet climbed, so dark that they were almost black, even here from the side. Clouds that stretched from horizon to horizon and crackled with pent up energy released in jagged lightning that crashed to the ground, rending hills, trees, mountains, and flesh beneath its thunder.

There was no end to that storm that I could see, even as we rose higher than the cloud tops and the planet's curvature became noticeable, and then obvious.

It was a storm like nothing I'd ever seen or heard of, and it would erase all that man had wrought on the world of my birth.

"My God," Susan said, from her couch, mounted to my right.

"The collapse is accelerating faster than I imagined," Grant said, from the other side of her. He looked my way, and our eyes met. His were sad; a deeper sadness than I thought to see on this occasion that he had been dreaming of for so long.

I guess you were right after all, I almost said. But I didn't. It didn't need saying, and I could tell it would actually just add to his sadness.

Instead, I said, "Do you know where we're going?"

Grant shook his head. "I only have a name. Terra. Where we all came from, back in the beginning." He shrugged. "Maybe one of the other colony worlds will have more data than we did. Maybe they can point us in the right direction."

"And if not?" Susan asked.

"Then we decide: move on and keep looking, or choose another colony to settle down in." He paused, his voice turning wistful. "I know what my vote will be."

So did I.

So did I.

33

THE ETERNAL RIDE OF BROM BONES

The sun was still shining when Brom emerged from his lair, wherever that was. The brightness of it flared across his vision, whiting the world out and rendering him able to perceive only the faintest of shadows as he took halting steps forward.

Vague shapes—the trunks of trees, he thought—loomed all around, and a strange whistling sound carried through to him, somehow. A gentle breeze carrying a bit of extra coolness to the already growing autumn chill.

It was always this way, when he roused from what might be called his resting period. Except that he never rested. He was never entirely certain where he went, but that time was always spent caught up in the constant repetition of his many betrayals and misdeeds...and one in particular.

So when he emerged, it was with greater fatigue and sorrow than when he went in, and today was no different.

And it *was* day; only in daylight could he be so blinded. But not for much longer. Even as he took his first steps toward a familiar blur ahead of him, he could already tell the whiteness of daylight was dimming, the shadows of night growing, and gradually he began to be able to see more clearly.

He was right about the shape in front of him. Four legs and a powerful body, completely black, with a proud snout and mane, already saddled like always, his tail switching impatiently for Brom to mount him and carry on with the night's ride.

Daredevil. Brom's trusty steed for many years of life.

And an eternity now.

Brom remembered the earthy scent of him, the way his chest would heave on the run, and sweat would slick his back and legs from the exertion as he took him through his paces, jumped him.

All gone. Now there was only the nightly ride, and no scents to inhale. No thrill of adrenalin coursing through his veins. No nicker of joy from Daredevil at the exertion.

And no Katrina to come back to, admiration for his horsemanship in her eyes and fire for him in her loins.

Just the lair. And the ride.

The shadows were deep now, night fully come, and he could see as well as he used to be able to see at noon, back in life. The woods were empty, the ground coated in fallen leaves from the surrounding maples and oaks, sloping down from the right toward the valley where Tarry Town lay to his left. Or used to lay. Now it was something else, like everything he had once known.

Only he was the same, dressed like the black Hessian from tales of old in his deep cloak and riding boots, saber on his left side while he carried the pumpkin that substituted for his head tucked under his right arm.

Always the same.

As he drew up next to Daredevil, Brom slid his free hand through the horse's mane, wishing he could feel the silky strands of horsehair as they passed through his fingers. But even that small pleasure was denied him, now.

"Well boy," he said—though how he could speak he didn't know and never had—"let's be off."

Then he placed his foot in the stirrup and boosted himself up into the saddle. It was always a balancing act, to ensure he did not lose his pumpkin burden as he mounted Daredevil. But he had done it so many thousands of times since that fateful day when he met his end, he almost didn't need to think of it now.

Like so much else, the woods outside Tarry Town had changed over the years. Shrunk, the groves and glens receding before the ever-increasing expansion of the hamlet where he used to reside, and it seemed every other town in the country as well.

But worse than that...there was no longer true dark. As he and Daredevil clopped down the hill, the clarity of nighttime darkness gave way to a thinning whiteness as the lights from the town grew more bright. What devilry it was that created such brilliance Brom did not know, but year by year it grew and grew.

Someday there would be no place safe from that light; no place he could go that would not be blinding. And then where would he be? What would he have?

Just the torment of memories of sins past in his lair. And blind wandering when he was out of it.

Brom suppressed a shudder at the thought, and turned Daredevil to the right, to skirt the brightest lights in the town ahead and keep to the woods. What was left of them.

For the thousandth time, he considered turning even more to the right, to the north country where he thought—he hoped—the land would be more open, the lights less harsh.

But he put that thought aside as quickly as it came. Three times he had attempted that journey. And each time, when he had emerged from his lair after the day's unrest, he had returned to exactly the same spot; the same spot he always did.

No, he was stuck here. Doomed to ride the night in the country of his birth and death, until there was no country left.

And then what?

In life, Brom had not lacked for courage, but he shrank back from that thought. Instead, he kicked Daredevil from a walk to a canter.

Trees rushed past and Brom imagined he could feel the breeze of his passage through the hair on his head; or at least he recalled how it used to feel when he had been able to feel, and had the hair on a head to feel with. But despite the lack of sensation, he felt an echo of the old stirring in his heart as Daredevil's flanks heaved beneath him and his hooves punched through the loam of the woods' floor.

Daredevil snorted as though he were actually breathing, and he tossed his head to let out a quiet neigh, and Brom—not for the first time—considered that though this existence might be his own curse, for Daredevil it just might be a slice of heaven itself.

Perhaps this was his reward for a life well lived in service to Brom.

If so, blessings to him, but that brought Brom little joy to consider. Some. But little.

Up ahead, the trees thinned some, and light dimmed Brom's vision. But it was not intense and constant like the unearthly illumination that lit the town and country, seemingly everywhere. No, it flickered; a flame. A campfire, perhaps?

This was unusual for these woods. Almost no one came out here except him and Daredevil, and the occasional deer, though they were rare these days. Aside from squirrels, rabbits, foxes, and other small forest creatures, Brom almost never came across any living things.

By design.

He reigned in, reducing Daredevil to a slow walk, and peered ahead at the fire.

And it *was* a fire. Still a hundred feet or so away, but with the breeze blowing as it was he would have been able to smell the smoke from its burning plainly, if he still had nostrils to smell. As it was, the clearing where the fire lay was clear to see, though fuzzy like looking through a mist. The effects of the fire on his night-attuned vision.

Still, he could plainly make out a tent in the design that had become popular in these later years, and a man and a woman sitting out front of the shelter, beside the fire. They had a spit apparatus set up over the flames, and the man was turning a handle to rotate the meat they were cooking.

If Brom had a mouth, it would have watered to consider the idea of freshly-roasted meat. Or meat of any kind at all. It had been so long since he had enjoyed even the small pleasure of a meal that he could barely recall what it was like, unless he fought to remember it.

But seeing the couple preparing their little feast, it all came back in a rush. The salt that lingered on the steak despite soaking it half the day to remove the preservative. The feel of the meat as he sank his teeth in. The spray of flavor as the juices flooded his mouth. The coolness of the ale washing it down, and the warmth in his belly coming from both meat and alcohol that spread through the rest of his body, leaving him satiated.

The sight of Katrina across the table from him, her red-brown hair reflecting the candlelight and her eyes sparkling with mischief as she smiled in a way that brought on a different sort of hunger, that she alone could tame, but never quench.

He always said he would hunger for her forever. And it turned out that was true.

It just added to his torment; another bit of goodness gone forever, that he could only long for but never attain again.

Brom found himself shifting his burden to his left hand and placing his right onto the hilt of his saber. Almost he kicked Daredevil into a charge to cut down the couple who dared to enjoy the fruits of love while he was forever denied them.

He stopped himself just before he would have sunk his spurs into Daredevil's flanks, a new pain of guilt washing over him as he considered what he had almost done.

But then...could he have cut them down even if he'd gone ahead and done it? He was not flesh and blood; hadn't been for years beyond count. Mostly because he'd stopped counting long ago. After all, what was the point to keeping track of time in his never-ending punishment?

And in all those uncounted years, he had never actually made contact with a living person.

At first, when he'd not fully understood his predicament and tried to find some enjoyment from the nightly rides, he'd played pranks like he had atimes done in life. Frightened people on the road. But he had never made contact; never really tried.

Could he interact, if he even wanted to?

The sudden impulse to move forward, to enter the firelight, and greet the couple. To converse with people, like a man.

Absurd. He pushed that thought from his mind, shaking his head at his foolishness. He was not a man; not any longer. Brom wasn't sure what he was, but that much he knew for certain. Their world was no longer his, and he would only receive terrified rejection if he tried to enter it.

It had been that way for all these years without count, but still as he gathered the reigns to turn Daredevil away from the fire and deeper into the woods, he felt another pang of regret and loss.

As if he didn't already have enough of those.

A snap in the woods off to the left brought him up short, and Brom directed his gaze—however he accomplished looking around and gazing without a head—in that direction. Was that a twig or branch being broken?

Between a gap in tree trunks, his vision unclouded by the campfire's light, he saw movement. If he had eyes, Brom would have squinted to see better. No need. The movement resolved itself into the shape of a man a few seconds later. He was skulking from tree to tree, approaching the campfire.

Brom could almost feel his mental frown as he watched the man creep forward. If he knew the couple and were friends, he would not skulk about like that.

He must be up to no good.

Unless he was playing a prank. Brom thought back to his life, and a multitude of pranks played on friends—and that friends played on him—and he couldn't rule out a prank.

For the first time in what felt like forever, he found himself interested, and entertained, by the goings-on in the world. As he watched the man creep up to the very edge of the firelight, Brom found himself fair quivering in anticipation of the prank, and the couple's reaction to it.

But when the man burst into the firelight, his form blurring and becoming hazy from the firelight, he was brandishing something in his hand. A sword?

No, people did not use swords in this uncivilized age. A club perhaps?

The reaction from the couple at the camp was immediate. The woman opened her mouth, as though to scream, and the man scrambled to his feet.

The skulking man surged forward, not even voicing a challenge as he brought the attack.

The defending man backpedaled to avoid the club's swing, and he shouted, "Katrina, run!"

Katrina.

Brom froze, the name tearing through him like a saw through an oak. Images of her from his life—from their life together—flashed through his mind. Laughing, dancing, praying, cooking, eating, loving... It all came back in a rush, and though she was never far from his mind it was like being with her all over again, for a second.

And when the memories faded, it was like losing her all over again, and he howled.

Brom didn't even notice driving his spurs into Daredevil's sides. The horse bounded forward, rushing toward the camp at a run.

Ahead of him, the woman had not heeded her man's command. She'd backed up to the tent, but was frozen still, watching, horrorstruck, the fight in front of her.

The man put up a valiant effort. But he was unarmed, and smaller than his attacker as well. The club came up, then swept down, and the man raised his arm to block the blow to his head.

The crack of breaking bone almost defeated his cry of pain, and he fell to one knee beneath the attack's force, his arm dangling limply.

The attacker's back was to Brom, so he couldn't see his expression. But he could imagine the look of sadistic glee on the miscreant's face when he followed up with an almost negligent backhand swing.

The club caught the man on the cheek, and he collapsed in a heap.

The woman—Katrina—shrieked now, the first sound she had uttered, as the attacker turned on her.

And then Brom's vision blurred further as he entered the firelight.

Brom hauled back on Daredevil's reigns, and he pulled up short, rearing and kicking his hooves in the air as he let out his own horsely scream.

Woman and attacker turned to stare at Brom: the attacker in disbelief turning to horror, she in surprised relief.

Then the attacker fled into the woods opposite where Brom had entered the campsite, screaming in fright as he went.

Not good enough. He must pay for his deeds.

Kicking Daredevil again, Brom charged forward after the man.

He was fast for a man his size. But Daredevil had won his share of races in life, and the man could never hope to outrun him.

As he approached the fleeing brigand, Brom felt the weight of the pumpkin in his right arm. He flashed back to that night, so many uncounted years ago.

Ichabod fleeing on horse, looking back over his shoulder, his eyes wide with terror.

Brom following on Daredevil and wearing his Hessian costume, its shoulders raised with braces to make it look like he lacked a head.

Raising the pumpkin he was carrying, and throwing it.

The gourd striking Ichabod in the back, between his shoulder blades. Him swaying and the falling from his saddle, somehow dragging it with him to the ground as the cinch came undone.

Ichabod's horse continuing in its wild flight, trampling man and saddle both as it continued its gallop.

Brom pulling up along side the fallen schoolmaster, looking down at him as he groaned in pain but still sought to flee, pulling himself through the muck at the road's edge in an effort to make it to the tree line. Hat, saddle, and shattered pumpkin in his wake, and him not even daring to look back, lest the mythical rider take him.

Brom had left him there, in the certainty that Ichabod would never remain in Tarry Town, or the Sleepy Hollow, after such an experience.

Katrina would be his.

But his fate was sealed by the treachery of that night: doomed to wander the nights forever, in the body of the Hessian legend he had imitated to terrorize a man who had once named him friend.

All that ran through Brom's head in an instant, and he mentally gritted nonexistent teeth. What he had once done in treachery, he now would do righteously.

He raised the pumpkin in his right hand and hurled it.

The gourd seemed to glow with a mystical grey-white light that didn't affect his vision at all as it traversed the distance between himself and the brigand.

As if in slow motion, he watched the missile strike the brigand just as its predecessor had struck Ichabod: right between the shoulder blades.

Unlike the real pumpkin, this did not shatter, but exploded in a brilliant flash of that same mystical light. Again it didn't affect Brom's vision at all, not even leaving the after-images he recalled from his years of life.

The brigand hurled forward, slamming into the trunk of a tree with a solid-sounding splat. Then he slumped to the ground, groaning.

Brom brought Daredevil to a stop and examined the man. He was clutching at his ribs with his left hand and groaning. His right arm was bent at an unnatural angle, and his left knee was knocked off true. He wasn't going anywhere.

This close, he was dressed raggedly, like a pauper. His beard was long and unkempt, the black hair on his head the same.

A dreg of society. No wonder he had turned to thieving.

He looked up at Brom, face locked in a rictus of pain, but also of horror, his eyes wide with mortal terror. He would only see Brom as a headless shadow in the blackness astride a large and terrifying black stallion. Perhaps he and Daredevil would be profiled by the light of the not-so-distant campfire. So much the better.

A horrible sight, the foretelling of doom.

The man had no idea.

The brigand's groans turned to whimpering, and he gibbered out something that Brom couldn't make out. But he assumed it was a plea for mercy.

He paid the man no mind, just wheeled Daredevil around and walked back to the campsite.

When he arrived, the woman was kneeling next to her man, bent over him and checking his injuries. Tears were running down her cheeks, but her expression was set, focused. She had black hair, not red-brown like his Katrina, that was cut short to her shoulders. Her clothes were simple, in the style that people were wearing these days.

"The knave is dealt with," Brom said as he once more pulled Daredevil to a halt. And as usual he had no idea how he spoke, or whether she would hear it at all.

Katrina nodded. "Good. Thank you - " She looked up as she spoke but stopped mid-word when she saw him in the firelight.

She blinked. In surprise though, not in fear.

What was she - ?

"Nice costume. You've got an even weirder Halloween tradition than we do."

Halloween?

Brom had heard that word. In conversations from some people who had passed near over the years. And in newspapers he had seen left lying around. It had taken some time, but he came to understand it referred to what he knew as All Hallows Eve. But...different, also.

Which didn't help him know how to respond. So he changed the subject. "Is your man alright?"

She shook her head. "I think he'll be ok, but he needs a doctor." She gestured toward a small black rectangle on the ground next to her. "I called the cops and ambulance. They'll be here soon."

Brom wasn't sure what that meant. Regardless, his business here was done. He tugged on the reins, and Daredevil turned to the right. Back to the night, and the ride.

"Wait," Katrina said, before the horse had taken a step. "Who are you?"

Brom stopped Daredevil and paused for a short while, considering. This was the longest conversation he'd had in... He had no idea how long;

the years were uncounted and he couldn't recall a discussion since before he died. He needed to be about his business and away from these people.

But something about talking with them felt...good.

"My name is Abraham Van Brunt."

Katrina nodded. "Katrina Crane." She gestured at the fallen man, who was beginning to move, slowly. A soft groan issued from his lips, drawing her gaze to him. Her expression brightened to see his evidence of life. "This my husband, Iggy."

Crane. The name halted Brom's thoughts. It could not be - Could it?

He thought back to the lanky schoolmaster he had betrayed, and what he knew about Ichabod Crane. He was not originally from Tarry Town. He hailed from...

"From Connecticut," Brom said out loud, before he knew he was going to do it.

Katrina's eyebrows rose, and she looked back at him, nodding. "Yes. How did you know?"

"A fortunate guess."

"We come here every year for Halloween. There's a legend from way back in his family, so we come camp out here and look for..." She trailed off and gestured toward Brom, then giggled. "The Headless Horseman."

At those words, Iggy opened his eyes. "Kat?" he managed to say, weakly.

"Baby?" She turned to face her husband more fully, leaning over him. "You're ok, baby. Help's on the way."

"You...ok?"

She nodded.

Brom took the opportunity to turn Daredevil away from them and heel him into a walk. As he rode into the woods around their campsite, he heard Katrina say, "You won't believe who's - "

Her words cut off. Then she said, "Where'd he go? Hey mister? Mister!"

Brom kept on riding.

Riding, and thinking. Thinking thoughts the likes of which he hadn't dared consider before.

Iggy and Katrina Crane. From Connecticut.

Was it possible that Iggy was descended from Ichabod?

Certainly Ichabod would have married. Katrina was not the only woman in the world—though she was the only woman for Brom— and he would have found a good woman once he made it back home to Connecticut. He must have had progeny. And they would have. And so on and so on.

But for Ichabod's descendant to be camping here, for Brom to encounter?

And on All Hallows Eve.

That made tomorrow All Souls Day. When souls in Purgatory who had been purged of their sins were finally admitted to Heaven, all debts paid.

Meeting Ichabod's descendant here. On this day...

It could not be a coincidence. Could it?

Brom had gone to church every Sunday. Of course he had. But he'd never been a particularly devout man. Now he could not help think that maybe God had arranged this meeting.

It was absurd. Except maybe it wasn't.

Brom had betrayed Ichabod's friendship, terrorized him to get him to leave town and abandon his quest for Katrina's hand. And so Brom was cursed to ride the land, for all this time.

But now he had rode straight into Ichabod's progeny in need, and had come to their rescue.

Could this have been the capstone on his penance?

Brom could not even begin to believe that it could be true. But at the same time...

He came to a break in the trees, and rode out to find he was in the manmade clearing that framed the stone roadways of this modern era. This one ran east-to west. As he looked to the east, his vision dimmed and blurred. The sky was brightening; sunrise was growing near.

Always he felt trepidation at the end of the night. It meant a return to his lair of unrest, and the torment of his sinful memories.

But this was the dawn of All Souls Day.

Was it possible he might go to his lair at dawn and find actual rest?

And not just rest...redemption?

He dared not believe it. But when the first lights of dawn shown forth over the road and Brom felt his hold on reality fading...

As the world drained away all around him, he felt, for the first time in what seemed forever, hope.

34

LIQUOR COOLERS

I t was a Thursday night, and the crowd in The Golden Harp was almost non-existent. Just Tim down at the corner of the bar farthest from the door, dressed as usual in plaid flannel and jeans and leaning over his half-full mug of beer like it held some deep dark secret, and Ramon and Larry in a table across the room from the taps behind the bar, heads bent over a game of checkers as the tournament they'd been playing against each other for twenty years reached its latest climax.

Those three were in here almost every night; and on Thursdays they almost always were the only customers who came through. Several times Hank had thought to just add Thursday to Sunday as a no-business day, to give himself a little more time off. But then he considered the way bald Ramon and silver-haired Larry had kept their game going for so long, and how Tim seemed to view this place almost like a second home, and Hank tossed that thought aside.

Besides, every now and then something interesting happened, even on a Thursday.

Didn't look like that would be the case this time, though.

Hank took a rag that he kept hanging on a hook behind the bar and began wiping down the bartop for the sixth time that night. The pale grey granite, flecked with bits of yellow that almost looked like gold, was already spotless, almost gleaming. But he had to do something to make the time pass, and he'd already swapped out the keg of 805 that Tim had floated an hour ago, and it wasn't like there were a ton of receipts to enter into the system and verify from the three customers he'd had all evening.

So wipe the bar it was, and Hank couldn't help but smile and whistle to himself as he did it.

Yeah, it was a mindless, repetitive task, but it was his task to keep up *his* place, and if there was one thing he could relate to Tim about, it was that the Harp was more of a home to Hank than just about any place else in the world.

From the chintzy old plastic harp that was colored yellow but didn't in any way resemble gold hanging over the entrance, which he'd gotten at a port call in Singapore back in his Navy days, to the brass taps that poured a rotating selection of his customers' most requested beers, to the old-style jukebox in the back corner that was chock full of 80s classics and was currently playing "Raspberry Beret", to the cracked brown leather of the booth seating where the checkers duo always kept their vigil, to the faded linoleum floor tiles, to the eternal odor of old cigar smoke—the only kind of smoking he allowed on the premises...everything here was exactly the way he loved it, and he had spent the last twenty-five years making it into his own little perfect place.

And turning a decent profit from it, too.

Yep, life didn't suck.

Would be better with more customers, though.

Hank finished up his bar-swipe in front of Tim, who obligingly lifted his mug to allow the rag's passage.

Tim grinned his gap-toothed grin, the remnants of some brawl somewhere that Hank had never gotten him to tell about. "Think you missed a spot."

Hank snorted.

Behind him, from the vicinity of the taps, an electronic beep rang out.

Tim looked past him toward the coffee maker, and shook his head. "You're the only bar owner I've ever met who don't touch booze," he said. For the eightieth time.

"That stuff will kill you quick," Hank replied, then turned around, flipping his rag onto the top of the stainless steel cooling chests that held his selection of bottled beer for customers without the good taste to take it from the tap. He made a beeline for the coffee, the scent of the deep roast blend overpowering the lingering bar odors as he drew near to the big commercial-grade unit he had installed last year, on a whim.

Well, not exactly a whim. Ever since he got the thing The Golden Harp had gained a reputation for making the best Irish Coffees in town.

But Hank just liked it straight. Black and bitter, the way God intended.

He kept a small collection of mugs hanging above the bar, in a sequestered corner of the area where he hung the mugs belonging to his Beer Club patrons. He kept his smaller mugs carefully arranged; his own personal timeline. From the mug he used in High School to his first ship, and all the way up to now.

Hank pulled down one labelled USS SPRUANCE (DD 963), with the silver silhouette of an old, long-decommissioned ship of war on the side. He ran his finger over the image of the old girl, and grinned as remembrances of that first deployment, so long ago, came back to mind.

His eyes lifted, going toward the door and the cheesy harp, a keepsake from that deployment, and he chuckled, then filled the mug with the rich, aromatic brew that he liked best in the world.

Hank about dropped the coffee pitcher when a low-pitched voice that he didn't know, but was somehow eerily familiar, spoke from above him and to the right.

"Tim's right, you know. That's really very offensive."

"What?" Hank said, looking up toward the voice. He felt like every hair on his body was standing on end, and a rush of adrenalin ran down his spine.

But there was nothing there but the glass shelving where he kept the bar's stock of liquor bottles.

For a second, Hank told himself it was Tim's voice he had heard, and the guy was playing a prank on him somehow.

"I didn't say nothing," Tim said.

That was very definitely not the voice Hank had just heard.

Hand trembling, he carefully put the coffee pitcher back into its spot in the coffee machine and took a half-step back, away from the unit and the taps and the liquor bottles. His eyes flicked from side to side and up and down.

No one. Nothing.

Everything was just where it was supposed to be, and he didn't see any speakers or anything, so...

"Hank, you alright?"

He turned halfway around and saw Tim leaning forward over the bar, his dark eyes probing and his face locked into an expression of concern.

"I..." Hank realized his other hand was shaking too, the one holding the SPRUANCE mug, and the piping hot Joe. Turning the rest of the way around more quickly, he firmly set the mug down on the bartop before he splashed scalding fluid all over himself. Then he placed his hands on the granite and took a deep breath.

He met Tim's eyes and forced himself to chuckle. "I'm good. Mind playing tricks on me."

"Ok." TIm said it very slowly, like he wasn't sure he entirely bought Hank's story. Then he shrugged. "Well if you're sure you're alright." He held up his own mug, which was now empty, and wiggled it meaningfully.

Hank really did chuckle then, and he nodded. Then he turned back to the taps, and the other chiller to the left of them, the one he kept at freezing to make his beer mugs nice and frosty.

Hefting a cool one, he set to filling it from the fresh 805 keg.

"Woohoo!" said a voice, coming straight from the tap handle. This voice was different. Higher pitched, with an accent that reminded

Hank of California Surfer Movies. "Kawabunga, dude!" added the voice.

The mug shattering on the floor was the first indication that Hank had lost his grip on it.

"Hank, what the - " Tim began, as Hank retreated until the small of his back hit the bartop.

The tap handle was still in the pour position, and beer was flowing. The drip tray quickly filled, and then the 805 overran and also began pouring onto the floor.

"Hey!" said the surfer dude voice. "What're you pouring me on the ground for?"

Jesus Christ, what the hell was going on?

Hank surged forward and shut off the flow of beer, then jumped back to where he was again. Then he just stared at the tap handle, his heart thumping in his ears like a bass drum. Despite the cool AC-moderated temperature inside the Harp, sweat was beading on his brow.

"Hank!"

Tim definitely sounded concerned now.

Across the room, the subtle sound of checkers faded beneath Prince's singing, and Hank could feel Ramon and Larry's eyes burning into his back.

"Bar's closed," Hank said, and was amazed to hear his voice come out clear and strong, without the slightest tremble.

"What do - " Tim began.

"Closing early tonight. Go home." Hank turned to give Tim a hard —or at least he hoped it was hard; he was too freaked out to be sure if he was doing it right—stare. After a second, he turned around to apply the same look to the checkers players. "All of you."

Across the room, Ramon and Larry traded looks. Then Larry shrugged and grinned. "Guess we'll have to start over tomorrow."

From what what Hank could make of the board from where he was behind the board, Larry was losing.

Ramon snorted. But after a moment, he nodded. The two of them quickly put the game away back into its box, then they headed toward the door. Larry gave Hank a one-finger salute—the good kind —just before he left.

Tim waited a few seconds longer, looking at Hank with an expression that bordered between confused, irritated, and concerned. Then he nodded, and followed the other two out of the bar.

"Dude, that wasn't cool," came the surfer voice again.

Then the deeper voice spoke up. "Get ahold of yourself, Hank."

Get ahold of himself. Yeah right. He was hearing phantom voices from his liquor bottles and beer taps.

"I need a vacation, that's what I need," Hank said under his breath.

And why not? He was closing early. Why not close up shop completely for a couple weeks? He had enough cash reserves to handle the overhead for a couple months, and it had been years since he'd taken a good, long, relaxing vacation in a warm and beachy place.

He would go, and chill. Meet a MILF or three on vacation and have a good old time. Knock the cobwebs loose. Because he was clearly losing it.

Yeah, that was a great ide -

"Vacation." That was a new voice, more baritone than bass, and dripping derision. It was from the left-hand side of the liquor shelves. "Don't be a pansy."

"Jack, let me handle this," came the first voice, from over to the right.

"And let you screw it up like you did in Memphis?"

"That wasn't my fault, and you know it. If Fireball hadn't - "

Hank was screaming, "SHUT UP!" and placing his hand over his ears before he even realized he was doing it.

He screamed long and loud, at the top of his lungs. By the time he finished, his throat felt raw. But at least the voices stopped speaking.

"Vacation," Hank said to himself again. He turned and walked toward the end of the bar, where the granite had been cut and hinged so he could raise it up to allow passage out.

But before he could raise the hinge, the surfer voice came again.

"Dude, don't go. You're gonna miss out on some seriously awesome vibes, man."

Hank closed his eyes and swallowed. He shook his head, willing himself to quit this; to stop imagining until he could get out of there and get a little rack time. He could leave in the morning, and -

"Hank, we're here to help." It was the first voice again.

"You're a figment of my imagination."

Baritone voice snorted. "Don't flatter yourself, fat boy. You're not that clever."

Fat boy? Hank had been working out for years. He was in the thousand pound club, and he had recently started triathlon training, as a new challenge. Yeah, he had a little belly fat; but he was almost 50! It was hard not to have that, at his age. And considering his heritage; both his dad and grandad were blimps at his age.

He turned around toward the liquor rack and shoved his index finger in the general direction the voice had come from. "Screw you, buddy. I - "

Hank stopped himself, realized he was about to get into an insult competition with thin air.

"Well, finally something got a little spark in you," said baritone again. "You ready to talk like an adult now?"

"Jack," the first voice began, but baritone cut it off.

"Shut it," said baritone, then somehow, even though he was looking at nothing but air, and the liquor shelves behind the bar, Hank got the feeling like the voice had shifted its attention away from him for a second, but now it was entirely focused on him again. "Jim's a moron, Hank, but he's right. We *are* here to help."

"Who - " Hank stopped himself. Was he really going to talk to the air like this? He must be losing it...

But a part of him piped up that if he really was losing it—or had already lost it—he was over the edge now. So might as well go with it.

Hank always hated that part of himself. Mostly because it was right more often than not.

"What are you?"

Baritone snorted again. "What, you haven't figured it out yet? I'm Jack Daniels."

"And I'm Jim Bean" said the first voice.

There was a pause, and Hank got the idea that the first two were waiting, increasingly impatiently. Then, after a very long few seconds, surfer voice piped up.

"I'm Firestone Walker. How's it hanging?"

Hank just shook his head. "I really am losing it."

"No, you just think you are," Jack said. "I assure you, we are very real. And really here."

"What do you want?"

There was a short pause. Then Jack spoke again, very slowly and dripping irritated condescension, like he—it?—was talking to a person he suspected was retarded.

"Like we've said three times now. We. Want. To. Help. You."

"Help me. How?"

"This is a nice place you've got, Hank. But it could be better. Do better business."

Jim piped up again. "Ever see Roadhouse?"

Of course he'd seen Roadhouse. It was required viewing, far as Hank was concerned. "What, you going to tell me you've got Patrick Swayze with you too?"

Jack snorted even more derisively. He seemed to like doing that. "Please. He'd have to pay us more than he's good for to get me to agree to bring him along." Hank got the distinct impression of a person shaking his head in annoyance. "Movie stars." Oh yes, the derision was back, and how.

"Just think of us as your Cooler, dude," said Firestone Walker. "Except without the fistfights."

"What if I don't want your help?"

Jim sounded aghast. "You would refuse? No one's ever refused!"

"Hank," Jack said, "you have to understand. We don't do this for everyone. We're always on the lookout for good prospects, though. And of all the gin joints in all the world, we walked into yours."

"Because we think you're a righteous dude, man," said Firestone.

"Umm....thanks," Hank said. "I guess. So what's involved?" He wasn't entirely certain he believed all this; he figured there was a much better than even chance that he had actually had a psychotic break and was making all this up in his head. He'd end up in the psycho ward.

But what the hell. If he was going to the psycho ward, might as well enjoy the journey getting there.

"Just follow a few pointers," Jack said. "Some minor changes. And they'll pay off big, believe me."

Hank pondered that. His mind wandered back to Roadhouse. To watching it when he was young and being entranced by Swayze's love interest. She was incredible.

"Do I get a hot doctor?"

Another pause, then Jack said, in a clipped tone, "No."

Well, it was worth a try.

Hank took a breath. "Ok, what do you want me to do?"

It was amazing what a difference four months made.

It was Thursday night, and the place was packed.

Tim still sat in his seat at the end of the bar, and Ramon and Larry were still playing checkers in their booth across the way. But everywhere else were patrons galore, enjoying their booze and each other's company and listening to music from the greatest music decade of all time floating out of the Jukebox.

Tears For Fears right at the moment, and Hank couldn't help singing along to the lyrics and tapping his foot to the beat as he poured out four mugs of Modelo Especial to the newest members of his beer club: a quartet of football players from the University two towns over.

And of course they'd brought the cheerleaders with them. And other assorted tagalongs.

Jack had been right. The changes Hank had to make were small; almost insignificant. Partly in the area of decor, partly in the signage out front, and partly in liquor and beer selection—he had expanded it quite a bit. But mostly in marketing.

And the results were better, and had come sooner, than Hank could have imagined.

Thursday used to be a dead night. Now there were no dead nights. It was enough to make Hank think about maybe opening up on Sundays.

He can-x'ed that thought immediately. Not that he was a devout man, but he figured if God really did set things up the way the preacher men said He had, he probably took the seventh day off for a reason. And who was Hank to argue with that?

Besides. Football.

Hank placed the freshly-filled mugs down before the quartet of jocks sitting at the bar opposite his taps, then gave them a small, well-practiced shove to separate them and send them sliding across the granite toward each man's waiting hand.

"Here you are, gents," he said, then took the credit card the tallest of them handed him over, and opened a tab.

As he was working the register, he heard Jim Bean's voice coming down from the shelves again.

"Looking good, Hank," Jim said. "Glad we stopped by?"

Hank finished the keystrokes to open the football tab, then put the card up on a small shelf above his register computer, which he'd installed for just that purpose. He glanced up and to the left toward the liquor shelves, where Jim sat, and shrugged.

"Yeah it's turned out alright," he said, softly so at to not carry. "Guess I owe you guys a thanks."

"You're welcome."

Hank went to turn back to his waiting customers, but stopped midway. He looked up at the liquor bottles carrying Jim's name, and imagined he could almost see a grinning face looking back at him from those shelves. "Am I going to see you guys again?"

He got the distinct impression of a shrug. "We'll stop in from time to time to check in on you. But no more intervention. It's up to you from now on."

Hank considered that for a moment, then concluded that was a fair deal. And one that he could get behind. Ever since he'd gotten out of the Navy he just wanted to go his own way, be his own man, and prosper by his own efforts and wits. And he'd managed it.

Managed it ok before Jim, Jack, and Firestone came around.

Managed it much better now, because of their advice. But he didn't want to be a puppet.

He grinned. "Sounds like a plan. See you around, Jim."

He had a vision of a broad, round face with a wide, toothy grin. "Not if I don't see you first."

And with that, Hank got the distinct impression that Jim was gone, and with him whatever link that may have existed that allowed him, Jim, and Firestone to come and give Hank a hand.

If was like a tiny bit of magic that Hank hadn't even known existed had winked out.

It was sort of sad, in a way. And Hank felt the lack of it, in a manner he never could have conceived of before.

Then he finished turning around, and saw a different kind of magic, but one no less potent, in the grinning eyes of his customers. One and all, they were having a good time, because of being in Hank's place and being in each others' company.

And they were paying him good money to do it.

It was hard to not like that arrangement. It was just too perfect.

35

SACRED VOWS

The fabric of his cassock was heavy brown wool, and even through the Underarmor long-sleeved t-shirt he wore beneath it, Gregory could still feel the itching want to break out all over his torso. Every timed he donned it, he wondered at the endurance of his brothers back in medieval times, wearing even rougher wool often times without any undergarments.

Fortunately, his newly-joined order had allowed some benefits of modernity despite their vows of chastity and poverty. He thanked God for that every day.

But despite the itchiness, the garment was warm, and today that made up for the other discomforts.

Winter had come on with a vengeance, and there was already a foot of snow on the ground inside the monastery. And more forecast for later this week. Thankfully after Christmas though, so Gregory and his brothers would be safe to make the two hour journey to Saint Jerome's, where his order traditionally helped sing the midnight mass on Christmas Eve.

This was his first time making that voyage, in an old school bus that his order had purchased and converted for their use, and he didn't entirely trust his voice to carry him through the chant without error. It didn't matter, though; God would see his intent even if his delivery didn't live up to standard.

Or at least that's what he told himself. Or rather, what his faith told him he should be thinking.

It didn't really help push his nerves down at all.

"Relax, Greg," said the man to his right. Taller than Gregory by almost a foot and muscular—he had been a division one football player before the incident that brought him to faith three years ago—Brother Lawrence had a broad smile and eyes that twinkled with merriment and, too often for the Abbott's liking, mischief beneath his curly black hair. But right that moment he gave Gregory a calm and serious look as he gave his shoulder a squeeze.

"You'll do fine," Lawrence said, and Gregory began to smile in thankful response.

Then he dropped the other shoe. "We'll all be singing. No one will notice when you screw it up."

The smile that had been beginning to form on Gregory's lips stopped midway, and he stared flatly at the man who had become his fast friend almost immediately upon his entering the order.

The twinkle came back to Lawrence's eyes then, and Gregory couldn't help it. He burst out in a laugh, shaking his head at his brother's quip.

In the seat in front of them, one of the older brothers—Gregory couldn't remember his name—looked back at them with disapproval, and Gregory forced his laughter down.

It was difficult, but he managed it. Looking back at Lawrence, he said, "You have a singular wit, brother."

"We all have different gifts from God," Lawrence said, smiling in satisfaction.

As the van from her convent pulled up to Saint Jerome's, Sister Agnes had to work hard to push down the butterflies that were threatening to fly out of her stomach.

This was her first Christmas with the convent; she had only taken her vows four months ago. And though she had always had a talent for singing, she had never been in this situation before: singing to praise God before all the world. What if she couldn't remember the words? Or the notes?

Her convent had been coming to assist with the midnight mass at Saint Jerome's for the last ten years, or so Mother Superior had told her when she first volunteered for the choir. It was a sacred duty, and an honor.

But now, as she stepped off the van and looked up at the towering spire of the parish's steeple, she felt she may have made a mistake.

She wasn't ready. Not even close to it.

"Get going, Sister Agnes," said the sister behind her. Justine, her name was, and she was twenty years Agnes' elder in the body, if not in the faith.

Agnes pulled the frock that was hanging over her habit closed against the cold of the winter night and hurried to follow the others of her convent who had already started up the flagstone stairs toward the church's side entrance.

Candles and electric lights from inside made the stained glass windows that lined the church's side shine, sending multi-hued projections onto the snow beneath that almost, but not quite, mirrored the images of holy men and women that the windows contained.

For a moment, Agnes could only look, the chill of the already late evening forgotten as she admired the simple beauty of that sight.

Until Justine chivvied her onward again, and again she hurried forward.

The relief she felt as she stepped into the church's threshold was profound. Modern climate control truly was a miracle; a gift from God.

Oh sure, Agnes knew how it worked. She'd started out studying engineering before switching to theology and then abandoning the academic world altogether in favor of the convent, and the calling she felt. But knowing how it worked didn't mean she couldn't give credit where credit was due.

So she said a little prayer of thanks to the maker of all things as she stepped inside and doffed her frock, shaking off the few snowflakes that had blown onto it as she wiped her feet on the interior doormat. Then she hurried on, not waiting for Justine's urging this time.

Even the feel of the chill from just outside the door was too much, now that she was back in the warmth.

That, and the beauty of the place.

She'd been in many churches; she knew them well. They all had high, lofty ceilings, and were lined with stained glass. They all had the alter at the joining point of the cross that the church's construction was based upon.

But Saint Jerome's was built in the old style, almost gothic. And it showed in all the little intricate details that modern building and design never quite got right. The leaf on the arches. The way the statue of the Blessed Mother, in a side alcove, was carved and painted.

It was all perfect, all down to the incense that was already burning, giving the entire place an exalted smell.

The choir galley was on the other side of the church from where she and her sisters had entered. As Agnes turned to walk over to it, she saw that a group of men in monks' cassocks were already there, in three ranks on the left hand side of the galley.

She almost missed a step when she saw them. But she shouldn't have been surprised. Mother Superior told her that the monks would be joining in singing the mass; it was their tradition as well. But still, it had been a while since she'd been around men. And now she'd be standing next to them, singing with them.

She didn't object. Just -

As she approached, she spied one of the monks, the second-most man from the left in the third rank. Average height, with reddish hair that was cut short and a strong jaw. He was talking with an extremely tall and bulky monk to his right, and was smiling with good humor.

Justine again had to speak up, to move Agnes along to her place in the sisters' ranks. Agnes shook herself and looked back at the older sister apologetically.

Justine just shook her head. "What's with you, girl?" she said, not unkindly but with some irritation.

"I - " Agnes began, but then her gaze went back to the young monk.

Their eyes met, and Gregory felt a bolt of lightning course through his body. He lost all track of what he had been about to say to Lawrence, lost as he found himself in the sight of her.

Her habit was not flattering; it wasn't designed to be. But all the same, the graceful curves of her body were there to see, if one were to look. And he did; for a second. But then he got sucked back into her oval face, the bit of rose on her cheeks, the way her lips were seeming to want to rise in a gentle smile. The intelligence in her deep brown eyes.

"My God," he said to himself, "she's like an angel."

Beside him, Lawrence said something, but Gregory didn't catch it. Until his friend nudged him in the ribs. Hard.

He broke away from looking at the lovely sister and met Lawrence's gaze, which had now lost all humor. "Be careful, brother."

Gregory nodded. "I know." He cleared his throat, then stole a glance back at her, to see that she was looking away now, toward the older sister standing to her left. "I know."

There was some time to mingle after the mass, but Gregory told himself he was not going to go over to the sister. He'd sworn an oath of chastity, and he had no intention of breaking it ever. Let alone before he'd even been at the monastery six months.

But then he turned from admiring one of the stained glass windows' depiction of Saint Steven, stoned by the crowd for his faith, and there she was.

She wasn't looking at him; she too was admiring the workmanship of the window. But after a second, she lowered her eyes to meet his.

A flush of warmth went through Agnes as she realized his eyes were green.

She needed to get away from him. Now. She'd just taken her oaths, and she had no intention of breaking them. Especially not so soon onto her path.

But despite the inner warnings rushing through her head, she found herself saying, "Hello." At least it was in merely a polite tone. "You sang well." Why had she added that?

Gregory blinked, then let out a chuckle. "How could you tell?"

He immediately saw that his words had confused her, maybe caused a little hurt. So he quickly followed up. "Thank you. You and your sisters made it easy, beautiful as your voices are."

Inwardly, he winced. That was cheesy. And anyway, he was not trying to pick this nun up. Not trying to do that at all.

So he gestured toward the window, and changed the subject. "This is very well done. I've always admired Steven. His courage in the face of the mob. His faith."

Agnes thanked God he'd changed direction. For a moment she thought he was trying to pick her up. But then she saw the embarrassed flush on his cheeks, and realized he had merely put his foot wrong.

But part of her whispered regret that he hadn't been making a pass. The part that had gotten her into trouble too many times before in the past, and that she had been working to expunge.

Apparently, she needed to work harder. She forced her eyes away from him, back toward the window, and caught the tail end of his comment about Saint Steven. Agnes nodded agreement.

"The center for needy children that I and my sisters support is named after him." Thinking of that place, and the kids, mostly parentless, who the place served drove whatever carnal desires that might have been building within her away. She shook her head sadly.

Gregory saw the sadness in her eyes. "You don't enjoy the work?"

The sister gave herself a little shake, then met his eyes again. This time the lightning strike was lessened, but it was still there. Still, the seriousness of her expression drove any untoward thoughts away as she shook her head. "No, I love it. But there are so many children in need, and not enough money or people to help. We - "

"Agnes," came a voice from behind her and to the left. She recognized it as Sister Justine.

Of course.

She turned to look and saw the older sister gesturing for her to come on, and she realized the others of her convent had already departed. Except for her and Justine.

Flushing, she looked back at the young monk and made what she hoped was an apologetic smile. "Looks like it's time to go. Nice meeting you, brother."

Gregory returned the smile. "You too."

She turned to go, but before she could step away, he added, "I'm Gregory."

Agnes looked back at him, his name ringing like a bell in her ears, and nodded. "I suppose I'll see you next Christmas, Brother Gregory."

Then she walked out of Saint Jerome's, leaving him wondering what had just happened.

The Abbott was fifty-something, and despite the order's vow of poverty, he had a bulging belly and flabby jowls. But he also had a sharp wit and a sharper tongue, and he didn't tolerate fools or foolishness.

So when Gregory received a summons from him to discuss his proposal, he came expecting a rough meeting.

Instead, the Abbott sat with him in a pair of almost-comfortable chairs on the side of his office. The place where the Abbott took friendly meetings, not official ones. Or at least not official ones that would require disciplinary action, anyway.

Gregory had never had this particular honor before.

The Abbott got straight to it, not leaving Gregory time to ponder the situation.

"You want our monastery to begin sponsoring Saint Steven's Center For Needy Children. With money and with labor."

There was no sense denying it, so Gregory merely nodded.

The Abbott's eyes narrowed, the bushy grey of his eyebrows practically touching as his brow crinkled. But he didn't say anything for several seconds. He just looked Gregory over with that stare of his that could unsettle one of the guards at Buckingham Palace.

From what Gregory had heard, it actually had. Once.

"The sisters from Our Lady Of Lourdes are also supporting the institution."

Gregory saw where this was going and decided he needed to put a stop to it before the Abbott got too far down the road.

"It's a good cause, sir. The center does the Lords work with children, but they need help and - "

The Abbott cut him off with a chopping motion from his right hand. "I know their work, and I agree they are a worthy cause to support. That's not my concern." His eyes narrowed and he leaned forward. "I'm concerned about you, Gregory. Are you asking this because of the sister you met at Saint Jerome's? What was her name...Agnes?"

Gregory blinked in surprise, and the Abbott snorted.

"Secrets are hard to keep around here, Gregory. Everyone there saw the affect she had on you." His eyes hadn't blinked; they hadn't left Gregory's the entire time.

Under the weight of that stare, Gregory couldn't have lied if he wanted to. He nodded. "I suppose so, yes." The Abbott opened his mouth to speak, but Gregory hurried to continue. "But not in the way you think, not entirely. I..."

He trailed off as the Abbott's doubtful raised eyebrow cut off whatever excuse Gregory was about to make. The older man shook his head. "We're not priests, Gregory. But our vows are real nonetheless. If you can't live up to yours, you should leave the monastery and return to normal life. There will be no shame or guilt; this life isn't for everyone."

Gregory gritted his teeth. "Just because I think she's pretty doesn't mean I won't keep my vows, sir."

Silence lingered for a while, then the Abbott rose and walked over to his desk. He picked up a piece of paper from atop it and turned to face Gregory again. "The Mother Superior shares my concerns. She wrote me last week about this...whatever it was... between you and Sister Agnes."

"Sir, there was nothing - "

The Abbott raised a halting hand, and Gregory shut up. "I didn't say there was. And neither did she. But she went to Sister Agnes to be sure, and she reports that Sister Agnes says there is nothing between the two of you in any way, and there never will be." He raised that eyebrow again. "Now, having heard that, do you still want to pursue this?"

Though not unexpected, it still hit Gregory like a ton of bricks, and he realized that somewhere deep down, he had been hoping that something might bloom between him and Sister Agnes. He lowered his eyes, looking at the floor in front of the Abbott's feet, and cursed himself for a fool. And more than that, a faithless fool. To so easily be tempted away from his vows, so soon?

The Abbott spoke again, his voice more gentle. "We're all men, Brother Gregory. We all get tempted. What I'm asking is whether you can get past whatever temptation you may have felt, since there will be nothing coming from it, and fulfill your vows. Or can't you?"

Gregory drew a breath, then looked back up. He nodded. "I can. And I want to do the work at the Center."

The Abbott looked into his eyes again, then he nodded. "Very well."

"It's good to see you again, Brother Gregory."

Sister Agnes' tone was completely friendly, but also completely detached, almost professional. And despite knowing there could never be anything here, and having set aside those hopes, the lack of warmth beyond mere friendliness poked at Gregory nevertheless.

"You too, Sister Agnes," he said, putting on the same politely friendly tone even as he smiled in greeting.

They, along with two of her sisters and three of his brothers, were standing out front of Saint Steven's. It wasn't much to look at. A small, two-story building across the street from a strip mall that had seen better days. Painted blue, but the paint was fading, and the sign needed work as well.

The toys showing through the windows were new, though, and the doors were freshly painted with smiling faces and images of kids at play. So the Center wasn't completely neglected. But it certainly could use the extra help.

"So," Gregory said, "what do you need us to do?"

Agnes smiled then and said, "Come and see."

She led the small group inside, and past a well-appointed reception area into the Center beyond. Then down a hallway that was painted beige and tiled in blue, until coming to the kind of double doors that Gregory remembered from school back in the day, facing to the right.

"The kids are in here. They need mentoring, and love, as much as the building needs upkeep."

Gregory glanced to his left, where Lawrence looked back at him with a raised eyebrow. Of course Lawrence had come; he was always the first to volunteer for good works. Plus, Gregory was sure he would be looking for any opportunity to tease him about Agnes.

Well, small chance of that.

Inside, the kids were spread about, engaged in play of all kinds. There were books and toys and stuffed animals and a little plastic slide and mini-playground off in the back corner.

One look at the kids said they were from poor to dire economic straights. Obvious hand-me-down clothes, but worse a harried expression about them, even when they were at play.

But some of them were better off than others.

As the group entered, one of the little boys ran toward Agnes, arms spread wide. He was probably seven or eight, black, with a mess of hair on his head and a broad toothy grin on his face when he saw her.

She bent down to give the kid a hug, then after a moment, turned to look at Gregory.

She caught a flash of the expression that had been on his face when she was looking away from him. And as quickly as he schooled himself back to merely friendly professionalism, she knew the look he had, and it lit a warm fire inside her.

Well, a small match anyway.

Agnes had thought she was imagining things when she'd left Saint Jerome's, and had alternated between relief and disappointment when the letter back from the Abbott had confirmed there was nothing and would be nothing between them. Mostly relief.

Or so she'd thought. But that flash of more on his face, even if just for a second...

Giving herself an inward shake, she gestured from Gregory to the boy. "Brother Gregory, this is Amos."

Gregory bent over to greet the kid, and returned his smile. "Nice to meet you, Amos."

Amos held out his hand, and Gregory shook it. Then he glanced over at Agnes' face, and the sudden look he saw there before she could get her expression back under control sent another zip of electricity through his spine.

The Abbott was right. This was trouble, and he was just running toward temptation. He needed to back off, and get back to the monastery before he did something really stupid.

But then he looked back at the kid, whose expression was both so open and so needy at the same time...

Gregory drew himself up and focused on that.

The kid was what mattered. He'd help the kid.

It was amazing how fast ten years went.

Agnes had always heard older people talk that way, and she'd told herself she'd never do the same when she got older. That was dumb talk; years didn't pass any faster or slower. They passed one year at a time, one day at a time.

But now here she was, thinking like an old fuddy duddy as she watched Amos stride across the stage of his High School graduation. He was tall, fit, and handsome, and he had given one heck of a valedictorian speech.

"And now he's off to the Marine Corps," Gregory said, from his seat next to hers in the bleachers overlooking the High School football field, where the ceremony was being held.

"Yeah," she said, and couldn't help the upwelling of concern over his choice from spilling over into her voice.

Gregory heard it and turned to look at her, saw the fear for Amos there beneath her outward good cheer. It tweaked at his heartstrings the way it always did when Agnes was distressed, no less now than it had when they first met, not so very long ago and yet also an age and a half ago, it sometimes seemed.

He wanted to reach out and take her hand, squeeze it to offer some comfort. But he couldn't. He didn't dare even approach that door, let alone let it open even a crack. If he did, it would be so easy to step on through. And their vows...

"It's a good place to get started in life," he said, putting on as confident a tone as he could, despite the concerns he also felt.

"I know. But..." She gestured toward the stage, where Amos had departed and the next to receive a diploma was coming up.

"I know."

And when he said it, Agnes knew that he understood completely.

Later, after the official ceremony was over, Amos found her. Like he always had, since he was a little one.

"Sister Agnes!" he said as he approached. But this time, he was the one who bent down for the hug, lifting her up off her feet and giving her a little spin around.

She was laughing by the time he set her down, and she found all the concern had been swept away by Amos' gesture. And she was quite sure he knew what she had been worried about, and what affect that hug would have.

Dear boy.

Then Amos turned to Gregory and just like when they first met, he held out his hand.

Gregory took it and as usual these days found his grip firm to the point of nearly painful. He grinned through it anyway. "Congratulations, Amos."

"Thanks, Brother Gregory. Couldn't have done it without you." He looked back at Agnes. "Both of you."

Someone shouted Amos' name from behind, and Gregory saw a group of Amos' fellow graduates gesturing for him to come with them. To a party, no doubt.

Amos also saw them, and gave them a thumbs up. Then he turned to look back at Gregory and Agnes. "The mom and dad I never had," he said, and pointed an index finger at each of them.

Then he turned and ran to his group of friends.

Agnes found herself tearing up over his words.

Gregory felt it as well, saw the affect it had on her, and again wanted to touch her, draw her into an embrace. Instead, he cleared his throat and stepped away. "I need to be getting back to the monastery. My flight's early in the morning."

"So you're still going on the mission?"

Gregory nodded. "The Abbott put me in charge, so I can't say no even if I wanted to."

"Will you be back for Chistmas?"

Gregory grinned, and as usual that grin put little butterflies into Agnes' stomach. "I'd never miss midnight mass. You know that."

Lawrence was the Abbott now, but he still had the mischievous twinkle in his eye from time to time.

When he came to see Gregory the week before Christmas,

though, the twinkle was gone.

"I just got a note from the Mother Superior over at Our Lady Of Lourdes."

"Oh?"

Lawrence's hair had gone mostly grey, but there was a strand of black directly above his left eye. For some reason that stood out to Gregory just then, and for a moment he was glad for their vows of poverty. It meant he didn't get to look into a mirror very often. But he was sure the spider webs around Lawrence's eyes and the deeper cracks around his nose and mouth were nothing compared with his own.

Lawrence just drove a desk these days. Gregory spent most days dealing with troubled kids over at Saint Stevens.

He had devoted himself to the work completely after getting back from his last mission trip; he'd always missed the kids each time he'd taken a mission in the past. But for whatever reason, this time he felt their lack desperately.

And it wasn't just Agnes; though Lord knew he still panged for her when he was away, even after all these years and despite neither of them ever making a move to dishonor their vows.

"Bad news, I'm afraid," Lawrence said. "Agnes has taken ill. She won't be coming to the center for a while."

And there went that pang again. "And midnight mass?"

Gregory's old friend shook his head.

Another pang.

"Sorry, brother. I know it was kind of a tradition for you two." And he knew fully exactly what Gregory felt for her. And, he suspected, she for him.

"That's ok," Gregory said, feeling the lie even as he said it. It wasn't ok. But things happen, and Lord knows he had been away enough times over the years.

But never on Christmas Eve.

As Gregory turned and walked away, Lawrence's heart went out to his old friend, and he said a quick prayer that Agnes would get well soon.

"It's cancer."

Lawrence's news struck Gregory to the core of his being, and he took a full step backwards until he struck the wall of his friend's office. The office where his first Abbott had grilled him about Saint Stevens, more than thirty years ago. The office Lawrence had occupied for four good years.

Until now.

"What do you mean?"

"Agnes has cancer. Mother Superior just told me."

"Treatable?"

Lawrence shrugged and shook his head. "They're not sure."

Gregory passed the priest who had come to perform Agnes' last rights as he exited her little bedroom. The priest was middle-aged, lean, and dark of hair and skin. His expression was sad as he pulled the door to and moved to step down the hall, but when he spied Gregory he made an obvious effort to conceal that grief.

"Brother Gregory," he said, and Gregory nodded in greeting.

For a second, it looked like the priest was going to say something else. But then he just cleared his throat and walked past him.

Gregory stood outside Agnes' door for what felt like an eternity. But it was really maybe a minute.

A huge part of him screamed for him to turn around, just get the hell out of there. Because he didn't want to face what was happening inside that room.

Agnes, his Agnes, was dying. Any moment could be her last. And his heart wrenched to think on it.

"Coward," he said to himself. And he was. He was a coward, for this at least.

He wasn't sure he could face this.

But he knew if he didn't, he would always regret it. So he forced himself to raise his hand and knock on the stained oak of the door.

He thought he heard a voice saying, "Come in," so he did.

As he stepped through the door, Agnes was struck by how much he looked like the young man he used to be. Oh, he had the wrinkles to go with his—with their—age. The grey that had completely destroyed the youthful red of his younger hair. But he still stood proudly erect, and he moved with the same easy almost swagger he always had. And his eyes were the same green they'd always been.

He sat down in the simple wooden chair next to her bed and just looked at her for a time, and she could see the desolation in his gaze. Knew how what she was going through was tearing him apart inside.

In addition to the physical pain the cancer was causing, that the drugs could not have completely masked even if she'd bothered to take them, Agnes now felt a far deeper pain in her heart, to see him despairing so.

So she reached out a trembling hand and, for the first time, laid it atop his.

The touch of her hand sent the same lightning bolt through Gregory as he'd felt that Christmas Eve so many years ago when they'd first met. In all these years, he'd never dared let himself touch her, for fear of what that might lead to. And never mind how badly part of him wanted it. Some things were more important.

But now, here at the end...

No, not the end.

"Agnes," he began.

"I love you, Gregory," she said before he could say another word, and if he hadn't already been sitting he would have collapsed from the shock of it. "I've loved you since the first time we met in Saint Jerome's."

His jaw dropped open, in shock Agnes thought, but she was sure it was from shock that she'd said it, and not from her feelings. He knew how she felt as well as she knew how he did, though they had never spoken it aloud before.

She managed a little smile. "It's the one sin I didn't confess to Father William."

Gregory shook his head. "It is not a sin to love, Agnes."

"Of course not." She took a breath, but then a rack of coughing overtook her, and she could not speak for a while as she gathered herself again.

It was only then that Gregory truly saw the effect of the sickness. How it had eaten away at her body, made her thin and frail where she used to be so lithe and strong. But in her face she was still the smiling young woman he'd first laid eyes on, all those years ago. And her eyes were the same deep brown, full of intellect and faith.

Finally she got herself under control again, and she took that breath. Then she met his eyes, and he saw remorse, and guilt, there.

"My sin is that now I regret that we were never together. I wish I would have thrown it all away, and gone to you. And to hell with my vows."

Gregory shook his head. "You don't mean that."

She kept her eyes locked on his, but after a moment, she looked away, and nodded. "No. No, I don't. I wanted to be with you, but I wanted to keep my vow to God more. And I knew you valued your oaths as much as I did, so I would never have dreamed to impose on you."

Her voice lowered, and she went on in a tone he could barely hear. "But when I think on what could have been. The children we could have had." She looked back at him, and there were tears welling up in her eyes.

Gregory reached out and placed his other hand overtop hers, and squeezed gently. His deep eyes, filled with love that he couldn't have spoken before, seemed to grow to fill her entire vision. "But Agnes, we do have children."

That struck her like a blow, and she felt her mouth drop open.

"Amos, and Christine, and Sheldon, and Devon, and Lamont, and Keisha..." He shook his head emphatically. "Every child that made it through that center and is now living a full life, because of us." He squeezed her hand again. "Really, because of you." He smiled that crooked, charmingly self-effacing smile he had. "Because I never would have gone there if it hadn't been for you."

He saw wonder on her face, as though she had never considered that before. Then she smiled, and that smile contained such peace and gratitude that he couldn't help but smile in return. Despite what was happening.

Agnes said, "I'll be going soon."

"I know."

"I'll wait for you with the Lord," she said, and then another round of coughing took her. This one was longer, and worse than the last, and she stiffened beneath her blankets at the end of it, like her entire body was fighting against the coughing. Fighting, and failing.

Then she slumped back down onto the mattress, his hand still clutched in hers. But her gaze had left him, instead looking up past his head toward the ceiling.

Or toward something else.

A change came over her face. The tension that had been there during the coughing left, and a look of wonder—of awe—came over her.

"Gregory," she said, barely above a whisper. "Oh Gregory, it's so beautiful..."

Her words faded out, then the last of her breath left her body in a soft rattle.

He sat there, looking at her face, which had retained the look of wonder and joy despite the unfocused glaze of her eyes. He wasn't sure what to do, so after a moment, he bowed his head to pray.

"Hail Mary, full of grace. The Lord is with thee. Blessed art thou among women..." His voice broke, and tears welled up, blurring his vision.

It was like someone had twisted a red hot poker through his heart, and all he could do was fall forward, resting his head on his dead love's hand, and weep.

The sheets were rough. They were very well-made, finely woven cotton. But they were rough. Rougher than his cassock had been when he first put it on all those years ago.

The sheets were rough, and Gregory wanted to get up out of bed and go do something. But he didn't have the strength to even try. Even moving his hand to pick up a glass of water to drink from was an effort that took all his strength now.

"I absolve you of your sins in the name of the Father, and of the Son, and of the Holy Spirit," said the priest who had come to perform his last rights. He was maybe thirty, still had baby fat on him. Reminded Gregory of the priest from that old Clint Eastwood movie.

That sent Gregory to chuckling, which was a mistake because the chuckles gave way to coughs, and he couldn't hear anything else the priest was saying for a time, until he finally got his breath back.

The young man bent over him, concern on his face. "Abbott?"

Gregory waved him away. He wasn't the Abbott. Not any more. He'd turned it over months ago. And anyway, he'd been a crappy Abbott compared with Lawrence.

Lawrence. He was gone now.

Agnes was gone.

Everyone Gregory had known and loved was gone, and younger men were carrying the torch now. It was time for him to go, and it seemed fitting that the same disease that took his Agnes away was now taking him to the Lord as well.

"About time," he said under his breath, and was not at all surprised to realize he actually meant it.

He had no fear of death; he knew what awaited him. And who. But until recently he'd thought about all the things that remained, all the good works still to do...

Now, though, he was ready to go. Like he saw the road laid out before him, and all else was in shadows and didn't matter. Step down the road to eternity.

That sounded like a good idea. So he did. One step, then another, and the road continued on ahead.

With each step, he felt strength returning to his limbs. Strength and vigor that he hadn't felt in decades, and he found himself standing taller, shoulders thrown back the way he used to walk so long ago.

Light bloomed from ahead. Light and warmth that surpassed anything he'd ever known of conceived of. It was all colors and none, and should have been blinding, but he found he could look at it without difficulty. And it called to him, drew him onward even as it filled him with peace and a feeling of love and acceptance that was beyond description or understanding.

A shape loomed ahead of him. Tall, broad. A man.

Gregory felt no fear, only peace, and he continued forward until the man's features resolved. A round, youthful face with a broad grin and mischievous twinkles in his eyes beneath a mop of curly black hair.

Lawrence.

"Welcome home, brother," his friend said, and clapped him on the shoulder as Gregory walked past.

And then there was another person in front of him. He didn't need to wait for her features to resolve to know it was Agnes. Agnes, as young and beautiful and graceful as the day he'd met her. Agnes, who was gazing up at him with eyes full of love, and joy at finally seeing him again.

"Hello, my love," she said, then cupped his face in her hands and pulled him down for a kiss.

The kind of kiss he'd dreamed about with her but hadn't ever initiated in life. But here, now, in the presence of the Lord...

He supposed that made it alright, so he returned the kiss, and they held each other for a small eternity.

Then she released his face and stepped back, her hand trailing down his arm until it reached his hand, and she gave him a gentle pull.

"Come on," she said, and led him further forward, into the light and their new eternity together.

And he heard in his mind a voice full of love saying, "Well done, good and faithful servant."

36

SHELL SHOCK

The shell landed three feet away from me.

I was crouched—really pressed prone into the dirt with my hands thrown over my head—in my pitiful attempt at a foxhole, but we'd had so little time to get on station and then prepare to repel the oncoming attack that I'd only been able to dig maybe two feet down into the earth. And never mind putting any logs or other overhead cover in place.

So when the bombardment started, I did like the rest of my platoon: hunkered down and covered my vital areas, and prayed that random mischance would treat me well.

Lying there with my nose full of earth, practically tasting the worms and crawlies that made their home deep into soil that was supposed to be used to grow crops, listening to the crump of artillery and mortar shells exploding all around me, feeling the concussion of their detonations through every twist of my intestines as the shock-waves passed over me, and trying not to listen to my friends' agony as first one then another then a dozen or more within ears reach found their hastily and insufficient shelters no protection against the enemy's assault, I couldn't muster even the courage to lift my head.

I just lay there, praying wordlessly, terror driving me to reach out to the Divine despite not having any notion of what I would say to Him even if he deigned to answer.

Time seemed to stand still. Even the pounding of my heart in my ears—somehow louder even than the impacting artillery and the screams all around me—seemed just a continuous rhythm, unconnected to anything except its own existence.

It could have been a minute, an hour, even a day, since the assault began.

Then the shell landed.

I felt its impact as much as heard it. An almost wet thud into the earth in front of me that shuddered through my body like a hammer-blow.

I hadn't been able to raise my head before, but hearing and feeling that impact, so close, I couldn't not look up.

The long, aerodynamic shape of the instrument of death just in front of me, its tip buried into the earth that I had so recently tried in vain to craft into a shelter, seemed to laugh at me as I looked at it, wide-eyed in horror as I waited for the explosion that would send me into eternity, to learn whether what they told us in church was true or just a lie to make us feel good about our limited time drawing breath.

But it didn't go off.

I don't know how long I lay they, staring at it, expecting it to explode sometime within my next breath.

I heard the shouts around me as the barrage let off and the enemy closed to engage with infantry, and all around me the counter-roars of my comrades as they rose from their meager defenses to meet the attack and throw it back. Again, and again.

It all washed over me, and I knew I should get up to join my brothers in their struggle. But the shape—the deadly, entrancing shape—in front of me would not let me out of its spell.

Some time later, after all the sound and heat and sweat and terror and joy of battle had faded, I felt a hand on my shoulder.

The touch roused me with a violent jerk, and I heard a voice say, "You ok, buddy?"

Then I screamed, and I didn't stop for a long, long time.

A doctor called it traumatic stress. But everyone else called it shell shock.

No one ever said anything to me about it. No one gave me any shit. But when the time came for my unit to receive its commendation for gallantry, having single-handedly repelled the enemy's main assault against all odds. When the President herself got up behind a lectern and praised us, and then General officers walked down the line to pin the unit commendation on each and every one of our breasts....

When they came to me, I wanted to scream and run, refuse the honor that I knew I hadn't earned. Everyone else had fought; I hadn't. I had just lied there, looking at death and...had I welcomed it? I couldn't remember now. But I hadn't pitched in.

I should have laughed in the General's face as he congratulated me, told him that I'm a coward and then left the ranks of better men than me, on all sides.

But when the time came, I remained silent, didn't respond to the General's praise. Let him pin the medal on my chest. Then I went back to drink beers with the other surviving members of my platoon that night.

And no one said a word against me.

But I knew they all were thinking it.

How could they not?

Honorable Discharge and a Disability Rating—a pretty good one— and then I was out. Back to "normal" life. Back home.

But home wasn't home any more. Mom put on too many kid gloves, and Dad...

No one in my platoon ever looked askance at me, or openly thought ill of me. But he did.

He denied it, of course, put a good face on it. But always I could see the judgment, the disappointment. The self-incrimination. His thoughts reverberated through the ether between us: "My son is a coward. What did I do wrong?"

Echoing my own, but more gently. If he only knew.

Time passed, some little bit more or less than I paid attention to. And then I was gone from them again, and feeling the relief of being out from under her smothering and his disapproval.

But then where was I?

One day I looked up at unfamiliar buildings stretching up into the sky all around me, and the question lanced through my brain loudly enough that it broke my focus on the blessed aerodynamics I'd met all those unknown days or minutes before in the foxhole that wasn't.

Uncertainty forced the shell from my mind, breaking my meditation on its mystery for a full afternoon as I wandered.

Long and aimlessly I walked, through thronging crowds that parted before me without effort. Part of me noticed their looks of discomfort, or pity, or alarm, as I drew near and they saw my state. Smelled it. And hurried to give me easy passage.

I thought to thank them, but just as quickly put that out of my head. Might as well thank the shell for not exploding. But that was just random chance, and anyway why should I be thankful that it didn't do its job...

A different sort of noise broke through my wandering thoughts and brought me back to focus. I realized I was still in the city—which city I didn't know—but the crowds that had parted so easily in front of me were thinner now, almost non-existent.

The shadows were growing longer, and I realized the sun was nearing its rest; looked over my shoulder and saw the orange-red glow between two skyscrapers to confirm it.

Then I noted the dilapidated storefronts on either side of the street, every third one boarded up, out of business. And the furtive looks from the people I was passing, and those sitting on porch steps in front of apartment houses.

This was a bad part of town.

But I could have known that by the noise that broke me out of my reverie, even without seeing my surroundings.

A sharp crack, loud and quick, that lanced through the deepening gloom and into my ears like a javelin hurled by Hercules.

It brought me up short, made me come up to my full height, every hair on my body seeming to stand on end as a rush of adrenalin poured into my bloodstream.

I knew that sound. I'd heard more thousands of its repetitions on the fighting lines than I would probably ever hear again in a dozen lifetimes. A firearm being discharged, somewhere ahead and to the left.

The sound seemed to echo all around me as my brain analyzed it, seemingly rote. Small caliber. .38? 9mm? Pissant attempt at suppressing it; so not a professional behind the trigger. It wasn't something I needed to worry about...

Except that two more cracks pierced the growing gloom of evening. Larger bullets this time, in rapid succession, and the calculations I had been making without intending it fled before the realization of what was going on.

One side was firing; the other returning fire. From the alleyway half a block up. I saw the reflections of the muzzle flashes even though I couldn't see the combatants.

And just as with the shell on the battlefield, I found myself entranced by those flashes. I could not look away from them, could not perceive anything but their perfect majesty as they brought on the eternal. And I walked toward them.

The cacophony of pops grew louder as I approached, their staccato rhythm growing more intense and their concussions beating into my torso all the more deeply the closer I got. Before long they were no longer little pissant handguns, but well-charged rifle rounds being expended between enemies.

I heard screams, and shouts, and saw shapes flooding past me, fleeing the battle, and I saw the faces of my platoon mates. Brave men, and hearty. But this conflagration was beyond even them, and they fled before it.

But for some reason, I could not. The concussions of the firearms echoed the thumping of my heart, and as I rounded the corner from whence they came I knew this was the battle I had been born to fight.

This was the reason the shell had not gone off.

There was a man in front of me, crouched behind a trash bin that had been pulled out from the alley wall. He was dressed in civilian attire, but from his coloration and accent I knew he was not of my country. He was the enemy, who had tried to invade before but who my friends and brothers had repulsed while I sat inert.

Not today.

His back was to me; he had his weapon up in one hand, gripping it like he'd never been trained in firearms before, rattling off rounds aimlessly down the alley toward his foes. My countrymen.

His neck snapped easily, and then I had his weapon. Magazine half empty, but he had a second one, which I palmed before moving forward.

He had an ally, who was just looking in my direction, his eyes growing wide with surprise, when I gunned him down.

A quick scan showed no others, except for my countrymen at the end of the alley. Standing up straight, I walked toward them, a greeting on my lips.

A hail of bullets was their response.

Betrayal. Betrayal most foul.

I saw only red from fury. Heard only my primal scream as I took their fire and returned it, then, finally, charged into the fray.

I bested six of the enemy single-handedly.

But there was no Presidential commendation. No General pinning a medal on my chest.

There was only flashing blue and white lights, and then a small room, and a cage. I railed against the cage bars at first, but after some time—who knows how much—a man in black robes in a bench above me said some things. The things he said were important, I knew they were, but they sounded only like muffled reports. His bench was lofty and well-made, but I only saw timbers that I could have dearly used for my foxhole that day, so I could have aided my brothers with them, instead of redeeming myself later where they couldn't see or hear of it.

After the black-robed man spoke, the cage became a different room, more brightly lit with soft walls and and a door with a window.

Much more comfortable; more comfortable than any place I'd slept in...

Time meant nothing, so I didn't bother to compute it.

As I curled up on the soft floor of that new place, and looked up at the window, I saw a pair of eyes staring back at me.

Blue, beneath a thinning crown of red-blond, and buried in a round face.

I flashed to Benny, from the next foxhole over. Heard his screams as the shells fell around him, then heard them cut off in a rasping gurgle.

It was Benny looking in at me; I knew it immediately. And I knew this wasn't a place of comfort after all.

This was Hell, and I was its newest inhabitant.

The half dozen I'd taken hadn't been enough to make up for my lapse before.

There might never be enough to make it up to Benny and the others; the accusation in his eyes made that clear.

But maybe. Just maybe. If I work hard enough, I could make it.

I'd just have to get out of this place first.

37

THE GREENHORN TREE

Once upon a time, far away in the land of Quenith, lived a young man and his brother. Their names were Gideon and Marnik. They lived with their father, Gregor, halfway up the foothills of the mountains on the west side of the kingdom, where they helped their father fell trees and prepare them for shipment down to the keep, there to go into the local Lord's cookhouses and fireplaces to keep him and his people warm and fed.

It was long, hard work, taking up all of the daylight and beyond every day except for the seventh of the week. God's Day as decreed by the church and the King.

On God's Day, the three of them would shed their many-patched work clothes and don their fanciest attire: homespun wool that was dyed blue for Gideon, green for Marnik, and red for Gregor. Feeling like men at the top of their station, they paddled in a canoe down the stream that Marnik liked to call the Redflow, because of how it reflected the sunset and sunrise, to the town surrounding the Lord's keep.

There they attended God's Day services and enjoyed a feast with the other people of their little part of the kingdom, and heard the

Lord announce the latest tidings, whether new proclamations from the King or local news, both joyous and sorrowful.

Then as the sun was nearing the rooftops in the town, they would get into their little canoe, feeling a bit less high in station compared with the townsfolk and especially the Lord but nonetheless happy and refreshed from the experience, and paddle their way home.

They kept up this routine for many years, and Marnik and Gideon grew to be fully men in their own right, strong and taller even than their father. When they came to the Keep for God's Day services, Gregor smiled with pride as the eyes of the maidens among the townfolk all zeroed in on his sons, and he knew they would soon start families of their own.

But thoughts of grandchildren reminded him that the boys'—the young men now—mother would never meet those younglings, and Gregor found the joy of the services and the feast much reduced.

Then came the day when that joy fled completely.

At the conclusion of the God's Day feast, instead of the Lord taking the stage at the head of the lined-up tables that were laid out in the town green for the day, the Lord's Chancellor stood up to speak.

A murmur of surprise went through the crowd, and Marnik, Gideon, and Gregor traded surprised looks. The Chancellor had never spoken to the people before; in all of memory only the Lord ever took the stage.

If not for the golden chain that marked his station, Gregor and his sons would not have known who the Chancellor even was.

"Lord Kendrick has taken ill," said the Chancellor. His voice was higher-pitched than the Lord's and didn't carry as well, but those words of ill spread throughout the gathered people as if amplified by magic. If there were such a thing.

"The healers and priests have examined him," continued the Chancellor, "and they have determined that the only thing that can cure his disease is a leaf from the Greenhorn Tree."

Murmurs of concern had begun circulating through the crowd after the Chancellor's initial proclamation. This added fact brought gasps of shock and fear, as mothers clutched children close and men's expressions slackened.

For the Greenhorn Tree was one of a kind, and grew up at the top of the highest peak in the mountain range. No one had gone to the Tree and returned in living memory, for the path to the tree was said to be guarded by ogres and giants that could squash a man between their fingers. And then even if one somehow won through, the tree itself was guarded by a great serpent which lived coiled around the Greenhorn Tree's trunk and that spewed venom that would burn a man's skin away at the merest contact.

Gregor got a feeling of deep dread in his gut, but the brothers grew exited as they realized what the Chancellor was going to say next.

"Magister Crowley has volunteered to head an expedition to the Greenhorn Tree. Two members of the Lord's Guard will accompany him. But," he paused to draw a breath, "the mountain passes are diffi-cult, and few know the way through them. Magister Crowley will need a guide."

The Chancellor's gaze had been sweeping the crowd, but now it came to rest on the table where Gregor and his sons sat And the dread became an icicle in Gregor's belly.

They alone of the townsfolk knew the ways through the foothills to the mountains. They alone had ventured into the peaks and learned their ways.

They alone could guide the expedition.

Marnik and Gideon's eyes lit with excitement, and they turned to regard their father with eager grins on their faces.

But Gregor could not feel their youthful excitement; their lust for adventure. The years lay heavily upon him, and he felt them in his joints more and more each winter. This was not something he wished to undertake; not something he thought possible to undertake.

Neither was it a request they could turn down, though.

Sighing, Gregor nodded, and the brothers stood as one.

"We will lead the party," Marnik said. Of the two brothers, his was the more powerful, more true voice when it came to speaking and singing, and he always took the lead.

Gideon nodded agreement and, with another sigh, Gregor stood to join them.

"Aye," he said.

But the Chancellor shook his head. "Winter draws nigh, and our wood stores are not yet filled. The town cannot afford to have all of our woodsmen go on this quest." Eyes narrowing, focusing in on Gregor in particular, he said, "Gregor, you must remain to complete winter preparations."

Neither Gregor nor his sons had ever suspected that the Lord or his Chancellor knew of them at all, let alone knew them by name. A flush of pride fought against chagrin at being excluded and sudden fear for the danger his sons would be taking without him, and Gregor opened his mouth to object.

But found he couldn't. The Chancellor was correct. Their work was not yet done, to prepare for winter. And if the wood cutting wasn't completed before the snows came, many of the townsfolk would likely freeze.

Feeling like he was doing nothing but sighing lately, Gregor closed his mouth, lowered his head, and nodded. Then he sat back down.

"It is agreed," the Chancellor said. "You leave on the morrow. Go swiftly, and safely, and retrieve the Lord's remedy."

Gregor bid his sons farewell, and paddled home in his canoe, his heart filled with trepidation over the perils they would soon face. But also with pride over their willingness to face them head-on, and in the people's trust in them. But the worry overcame the pride, and he could not sleep that night. He imagined it would be that way every night until they returned.

The brothers, though, thought little of the dangers ahead. They spent a heady evening basking in the townsfolk's adoration and well wishes—particularly of the maidens among the townsfolk—and then stayed the night in the Lord's Guard's barracks.

It was the first time they'd slept anywhere except for their father's cabin, or in a campsite up in the mountains. So although a soldier's barracks does not list up among the most luxurious of lodgings, to them it was like being in a whole new world. A good new world.

They awoke early, as was their norm, but found the soldiers already up and about, getting ready for the morning's exercises, followed by the day's routine.

Magister Crowley was tall, taller than either of the brothers, but skinny, like a man who had never had to lift anything heavier than a book. Or maybe two. He wore the flowing crimson robes of his office in the Healer's Guild and he had a small pack on his back, and sure enough a book tucked into his belt. His hair was grey, but long, flowing down his shoulders and halfway down his back, and braided on the sides to run down his chest. His beard was as long as his hair, and braided to match those of his hair. He had a little red headpiece perched right atop his head, and his eyes squinted like he was trying to focus on something directly in front of his nose.

The Magister met them out front of the soldier's barracks when Gideon and Marnik emerged in company with the two soldiers assigned to the quest. They were Damson and Korald, and they could not have been any more different from the Magister.

Lean with corded muscle, Damson of a height with the brothers and Korald a hand shorter than them, they had the bearing of men who had seen rough business all their lives and would not hesitate to meet it out. Their breastplates were polished to a mirror sheen and the leathers of their greaves and bracers stained purple to match the Lord's heraldry. Their helmets were open-faced except for a bit of steel that came down in front of their noses, and they each bore a broadsword on his left hip, a long dagger on his right, and a round shield slung on his back.

Gideon and Marnik were not fighting men, but they each had their long knives, and they knew how to use a bow from hunting game for food at home. So the barracks had issued each of them a bow and a quiver of arrows. But next to the two soldiers, both brothers felt naked, when it came to weapons.

The Magister looked over the four of them and nodded, then

without a word turned and set out for the western gate out of the town.

There had been talk of taking horses. But Gideon and Marnik didn't know how to ride. And anyway, a horse would be useless after a couple days when the mountain passes began to grow steep. So instead they walked, each man carrying his own pack and rations, and Gideon and Marnik still in their God's Day best woolens.

The passage was easy at first, and familiar for the brothers as thy ascended the foothills not too far from where they lived and worked with their father. The forest had begun the change into autumn colors, and everywhere was yellow and red and orange as oaks and maples prepared to shed their leaves for the winter. Pines and cedars mixed in here and there as well, islands of green in the ocean of color.

As the ascent grew more steep and their elevation increased, the evergreens began to dominate over the seasonal trees, and soon the party was walking over a blanket of old fallen needles instead of newly fallen leaves, and the underbrush grew more thin to match.

By the third day, even those trees had begun to thin, bare rock replacing more developed soil more often than not as the winds grew more intense.

It only promised to get worse ahead, as the Magister's intended track would bring them up through Charlton's Pass.

Marnik and Gideon had only been up Charlton's Pass once, but it was not a pleasant memory. Biting, harsh winds and no shelter to speak of. Just a long crawl up a steep rocky ravine that seemed to cut straight through the flanks of two monstrous peaks that still felt the agony of that strike; the shrieking of the wind sounded like screams to the brothers' ears.

But this time it was less harsh.

The wind still blew, and it whistled loudly. But it was warmer, and the whistling was more like a bad attempt at a melody than a soul-rendering scream that never ended.

Still, by the time they were halfway up the pass, there was not a member of the party who wasn't more than ready to be done with it, and may they never set eye on the cursed place again.

No one wanted to think about the fact that they were certain to see it again in some days, when they returned with the Greenhorn leaf. It was the only way back down that wouldn't take them weeks out of their way.

Of course, as Gideon remarked to Marnik when they finally reached the top of the pass, that assumed the ogres and giants didn't squash them, or the serpent burn the flesh from their bones.

He only partially sounded like he didn't believe the old stories.

Only partially.

Two more days into the journey, though, they still had not seen a single ogre. Or a giant. No even a trace of anything living except for elk and goats, and spore from a roaming wolf pack.

"Maybe there really isn't anything to those stories at all," Markin ventured at the campfire that night.

The two soldiers looked at him for a moment, then Damson sniffed. "Old stories always have some wild creature or other in 'em. Just exaggeration, to make the tellers seem like they weave a better yarn than they do, or to make the hero look better. Weren't never any ogres or giants up here. Just a barbarian clan, or a team of bandits."

Korald nodded agreement. "Nothing we can't handle, anyway."

But the Magister seemed unconvinced. "Even if you are right, we are small in number. It wouldn't do to be overconfident. According to the sources I read," he patted the book that he kept tucked into his belt all day and was now lying on his lap, "questors for the Tree didn't start encountering trouble until the second week of their journey."

"So two days from now," Gideon said.

The Magister nodded.

Neither he nor his brother got good sleep that night. Or the two nights after.

As the second week of their quest began, the brothers expected some dramatic change, like there ought to have been a great signal fire lit saying, "Now begins the PERIL," or somesuch.

But the terrain kept on as before: steep, rocky, with few growing things besides the occasional pine and little sign of animal life at all. The wind whistled continuously, and the temperature had dropped. And they could feel the thinning of the air as well, as each step seemed to weigh more than it had just a day or two ago, and it became harder to catch their breathe on the more and more frequent breaks that the party had to take.

But still no ogres or giants.

Three more days passed before anything happened to break the monotony. They rounded a bend in the path. Though path wasn't the right term. More like a semi-flat mound of rocks that was the closest thing to walkable that could been seen anywhere, and that backed up to a sheer rock face on once side, and as nearly as sheer a drop-off on the other.

It was precarious footing atimes, and more than once Gideon had to grab Marnik to keep him from falling a long way down. Or vice versa.

But finally, the cliff face bent to the left, rounding the flank of the mountain they were ascending. Korald had the lead, and he stopped shortly after rounding the bend. Gideon nearly ran into him, and the soldier shuffled forward a few more steps to let the others through.

Then they all stopped, having seen what brought Korald up short.

"Well," Marnik said, "I think that's it."

There could be no doubt in the matter.

The peak lay directly ahead, shooting off of the mountain they were climbing like an arm that had decided to grow out from the mountain's body of its own accord, to point an accusation toward the heavens.

It was tall, dwarfing the peak they were on, but thin, seeming more like a needle than a mountain. At first glance its sides almost looked sheer, but upon closer inspection there was a path, of course, that seemed to spiral its way around the spire, ascending resolutely toward its peak.

And at the top...

It was too distant to make out details. Probably five to ten miles as the bird flies. But there was something at the very top. Something stretching further up toward the sky in a way that didn't look like it was made of rock.

And, wouldn't you know it, just at that moment there was a break in the overcast that had dominated the sky the last two days, and that break allowed a single beam of sunlight to shine down on that thing at the top of the peak.

"Like God saying, here it is, boys," Gideon quipped.

Damson snorted out a chuckle, but the Magister nodded more gravely. "It could be that very thing, young man. The Greenhorn Tree is special. I won't say magic, because there is no such thing. But there is...something about it." He gave a little shrug. "Perhaps God touched it in some way." A second's pause, then he added. "Or perhaps not. It could all be a perfectly natural thing entirely. Just one we don't fully understand."

The brothers exchanged glances. Marnik preferred Gideon's take on it. But he didn't voice it; there was no point in debating the matter, and anyway it was getting on in the afternoon and they needed to push on if they were going to find a suitable campsite for the night.

That night saw them encamped below the path leading up the Greenhorn Tree's peak.

It was immediately obvious that the path was unusual, if not mysterious. It wasn't a staircase; just stones arranged haphazardly in a way that almost but not quite resembled a pattern that almost but not quite looked like it might be a set of spiraling stairs if you looked at it in exactly the right light and after a tankard or two of ale.

Clearly not stairs.

And yet...neither brother could shake the resemblance from their minds, and from the way the other party members eyed the trail as they set up camp and cooked dinner, and the way everyone resolutely did not talk about it around the campfire, everyone else saw it as well.

Saw it, and wondered.

How could such a structure have occurred in nature? And if it hadn't been naturally made, who made it, and why?

And if someone made it, had someone planted the Greenhorn Tree there intentionally? Maybe created the Greenhorn Tree as well?

Who? And why?

Gideon went back to God in his musings. Why would the divine interject to put such a remedy on the world, and make it difficult to attain?

But Marnik was not so sure. He couldn't rule God out. But did it have to be Him? Wizards were not real, at least not now. But what if they had been real some time in the past?

Or perhaps there was a more mundane explanation. Someone had discovered the Tree and set about building a path to make it easier to reach, not harder.

Any of those were possibly true, or none of them. And there was no way their little party was going to figure it out either way. So after a brief discussion amongst themselves, the brothers put it out of their minds, then hunkered down for a long and exhausting climb the next day.

And exhausting it was. Past exhausting, to grueling and then torturous into something demon-inspired. The path of rocks that weren't stairs but were scattered at usually about the comfortable stepping height for a staircase kept spiraling up and up and up and up until it seemed there would be no end.

They must have climbed two thousand feet straight up. Or more.

But at least there still weren't any ogres.

That was something.

Finally, the little party reached the top, and came to a halt, gasping in the thin air to catch their breaths and knowing it would be futile to do so. But gasping all the same.

The summit was round. Not completely perfectly round. Of course not. But close. It was flat granite, and featureless except for the Tree growing straight out of the center of the rock.

The Greenhorn Tree stretched upward at least another hundred feet, its limbs pointing almost directly skyward. Despite the chill of autumn becoming winter quickly at this altitude, its leaves were fully green: long, tubular green leaves that also pointed upward. Its bark was light brown, almost reflective, and smooth, except for in one area that twisted around It from somewhere high up where it was obscured by the limbs and leaves, until it ended where the trunk entered the stone.

The spiraling feature reminded Marnik of the not-stairs they had just ascended, and where it was the bark was coarse, almost scale-like. And down at the bottom, just above where it contacted the stone...

"Is it just me," said Korald, "Or does that look like a serpent's head?"

It did. But only vaguely, and probably only because...

"It only looks that way because we heard the legends," Magister Crowley said in his most annoying lecturing tone. "The mind sees patterns even when there really isn't one."

"Whatever you say, Magister," said Damson. "Looks like a serpent's head to me. And I ain't going near it."

Magister Crowley looked at the two soldiers and sniffed. Then he stepped closer to the tree and bent forward to look at the spiraling feature of the bark.

After a moment, he hummed softly. "Interesting. It appears that in the raised area, the sap is running, and has forced its way out from the tree's innards, for some reason."

"The sap?" Marnik said, and he began to get a crawling sensation of dread. What had the legend said about the serpent? "Magister - "

"I wonder," said Crowley, as he reached forward to touch the raised section.

He began howling the second his left hand contacted the raised bark. He recoiled immediately, but his scream only intensified as vapor of some kind began rising from his hand, the fingers of which began to curl and blacken.

"The sap!" said Gideon, "It's burning him!"

He rushed forward, in time with Damson, who was reaching to unstopper his waterskin.

Gideon reached him first and, seeing Damson's plan, held the Magister by the shoulders to keep his hand outstretched.

The Magister's howls continued, but his eyes widened when he saw the soldier approaching with the water.

"No!" he began.

Then Damson upended the waterskin over the stricken hand and squeezed.

Marnik only thought Crowley had been screaming before. The instant the water contacted his hand, the vapor began rising all the quicker, and the Magister's screams seemed to be the only sound in the entire world.

"God!" Damson said, and pulled back, dropping the waterskin to the ground.

"No water," Crowley managed to get out between screams. "Blot it! Blot it!"

Marnik wasn't sure what he meant, but the soldiers did. In moments they had cloths from their medical kits out and were dabbing at the stricken hand, removing the water and what of the sap they could without smearing it.

Finally, after what seemed forever, and after many scraps of cloth being eaten away by whatever that sap was, they got the worst of it under control, and they set to wrapping the Magister's hand in a bandage.

Marnik couldn't look away; the hand wasn't charred like it had been burned with fire. It was more melted.

He felt a sympathetic pang in his lower belly and groaned as he saw the wound, and imagined the agony of it.

But Crowley held through better than either Marnik or Gideon would have suspected. After the initial shock of the assault wore off, he was able to keep his wits about him and instruct the soldiers in the proper way to apply the bandage so it would do its job correctly.

Then, after they had seen to him as best they could, the party looked back at the tree, now far more menacing than it had been at first.

"Cutting a leaf off is going to be tricky," Gideon said.

No one expressed disagreement.

The sap was a big part of the problem. But it wasn't the entirety.

The fact that the lowest limbs on the Tree were high out of reach for even the tallest of the party was at least as big a hurdle to overcome.

Eventually, they went with the old fashioned technique of having Gideon squat down and having Marnik get on his shoulders, then the rest helping Gideon back up to his full height. With the added reach, Marnik was just able to grab onto the lowest limb and haul himself up. Then the others cleared out of the way as he took his long knife to two of the leaves and let them drop to the rock below.

His knife followed, leaving the same trail of vapor as the Magister's hand as the sap melted its metal away.

The others waited while he squirmed down the limb away from where he'd cut the leaves, then he lowered himself down to his fingertips and dropped to the rock below.

"Easy day," he said with a grin.

Twenty minutes later, after wrapping the leaves as thickly as they could, they were making their way back down the not-staircase that spiraled the peak.

They made town a week and a half later, to a fanfare of happiness and excitement. After several days of work analyzing the leaves and developing a treatment, the healers gave the Lord a dose that everyone prayed would cure his ailment.

Their prayer's came true, though Magister Crowley never regained the use of his left hand.

The brothers remained in town for a week, and received accolades from the Chancellor as well as the other members of the party. When they finally left to head back to their father's house, they each had no less than four maidens waiting breathlessly for them to return and call on them. And, almost as good, large sacks full of silver as reward for their deeds.

But all that was nothing compared to the warmth of their father's greeting, and the mixture of pleasure at seeing them and utter pride in their endeavors on his face when he embraced each of them in turn.

38

A CABIN IN THE WOODS

The wind rushed past, making the thin wooden sides of the tiny cabin Nancy huddled in shudder. A high-pitched whistling advertised its penetration through the cracks around the cabin's latched door, and she shivered as what warmth there was fled before its incursion.

She wrapped the threadbare wool blanket that she had found tucked beneath the cabin's clearly handmade cot, hewn from roughly cut logs, around herself, burrowing in as deeply as she could and wishing the unstained planks that made up the cabin's floor could open up and take her in, to help preserve the heat.

The room was dimly lit from flickering flames within the cabin's only other piece of furniture: a tiny wood-burning stove nestled into the rear corner opposite the door.

The flames bravely strove against the encroaching cold, nibbling at the lone log inside the stove. She longed to throw more on, but a glance at the piled fuel in the other corner, minuscule when she'd first found the shelter and even smaller now, told the futility of that idea.

There probably would not be enough to last the night even at this slow pace; if she used it all now there would be no more defense against the blizzard outside.

The wind howled past again, and Nancy barely held back a sob of misery, her breath misting in the air in front of her face despite the fire's best efforts at sending heat.

Nancy looked away from the stove toward the cabin's lone window, hoping against hope to see some glimmer of dawn, but she saw only blackness turned grey from the condensed fog of her many breaths turning to ice as it congealed on the warped glass.

Thinking back to her last meal, the granola bar she had crunched down hours ago when she was halfway up the mountain, and before she realized she would not be able to outrun the weather, Nancy felt her stomach growl and she cursed herself for not bringing more supplies.

But it was just supposed to be a day hike; no need to pack a full pack.

Lord, please let it be morning soon.

As if in mockery of her desperate prayer, the wind howled again. Nancy wanted to scream in protest against its mockery, but she dared not use the energy. She needed every little bit to keep herself warm.

Scrunching closer to the stove, as close as she dared without actually touching it, helped a little. Very little. But it helped.

But there was only so much good that would do, and it was like both she and the stove knew it. The log within popped, sending a little shower of embers into the confines of the stove's interior along with a briefly-increased flash of heat.

Two of the orange-glowing bits escaped the stove's open door, floating upward in the air of the cabin's room like little fireflies for a moment before turning from yellow-orange to red and then black as the residual heat in the embers fled and they fell, lifeless, to the floor beside her.

That would be her before the night was done, unless she did something. She had no doubt of it.

Again, Nancy looked toward the little stack of fuel for the stove, and she racked her brain for some way, any way, to increase it.

Her eyes dropped to the floor boards that she sat upon. They were unstained but well-sanded, carefully prepared and laid down. Held in place by nails at intervals, pounded into the joists below by the builder.

If she could maybe pry one up and break it into smaller pieces...

But how? If she had her full pack that she used for multi-day excursions, she'd have a hatchet and a collapsable saw. But in her day pack, she only had the granola bar she'd already eaten, a small knife, a flashlight, and some water in a camelback-style bladder.

Nothing that was up to the task she was contemplating.

Another pop from inside the stove, and Nancy swore. What kind of a dolt builds a cabin in the woods and doesn't stock it with tools?

Same kind of dolt who doesn't check the weather before going hiking, her mind answered back.

She snarled at that voice inside her, but the snarl lacked heat, like everything else around her, because she knew it was right.

She'd been dumb, and now she was paying the price. And if she didn't figure something out, and soon, she was going to pay the ultimate price.

Pulling the little blanket closer around herself, she hunched her head closer to the stove. After a few minutes, she realized she was no longer thinking; she was praying. Calling out to a God she wasn't sure she even believed in for help, for a way to make it through the night.

She found herself promising Him things that she never would have even considered before, and she tried to chide herself for fleeing rationality in her growing panic.

But again that voice pushed back. Because when there was no other option, why not try God, if only to comfort herself?

Nancy really was beginning to not like that voice at all.

The flames within the stove were growing more dim now, the log reduced to more glowing coals than anything else, and she realized she needed to add more fuel or the fire would go out completely. And who knew if she'd be able to get it started again.

She had to hold back her eagerness for more heat, moving deliberately to the wood pile. She picked up one piece. Then, after a moment, selected a second. She couldn't afford to use it up too soon, but the greatly diminished fire had taken its toll on the temperature in the cabin; it was noticeably colder than it had been just a few minutes ago.

No sense saving fuel if saving it just meant she'd freeze to death anyway.

So she put both pieces in the stove. She watched as the first and then the second caught, then she swung the door shut, recalling finally something she'd read about how closing a stove up with slow the rate of burn for each piece of fuel. Couldn't hurt.

And it seemed to help. Almost at once, it seemed like the cabin was warmer. And was the wind less fierce, or was it her -

The entire cabin shook, and there was a thump and a crash, like something had struck the building's side. The wind shrieked anew, as if calling out a challenge, or mocking her weak attempt at fighting the inevitable. Then another thump, and Nancy looked to the right, toward the side of the cabin where the noise was coming from.

The right hand wall, when looking at the door. Something had struck the wall twice. What - ?

Scratching from overheard, like something dragging down the roof, and then a third thump, but not on the wall itself. Like whatever it was had landed on the ground—in the snowbank—next to the cabin.

"What in the hell was that?"

Nancy almost didn't recognize her own voice as she spoke, but she could practically see the words in the air as the puffs of breath misted in front of her face.

She racked her mind to recall the surrounding area around the cabin, what she could see of it when she found it. The light was almost gone at the time, but the cabin had been in a little clearing, backed up against a rock face. But off to the left had been a couple tall pine trees.

She thought back to the scraping sound, and hope flared within her.

The trees hadn't fallen; if that had occurred they would have taken the cabin's roof down, and maybe the walls as well. And right now she'd be covered in an ever growing pile of snow as she shivered out her last minutes.

But perhaps the tree had lost a limb, and that was what had scraped down the roof?

The surge of hope grew brighter as she considered how fallen pine needles burned. Dry ones, at least. But something told her even the needles on a freshly felled limb would still work well. Not to mention the wood in the branch itself.

But there was still the problem of getting the wood without tools.

The voice popped up again, and this time Nancy found herself liking what it had to say: don't declare defeat before you've even looked at the situation.

She had a flashlight in her pack. She could go outside, around the cabin's corner, and see if her suspicion was correct. If it was, she could try to get some of that limb, as much as she could.

Even some small brambles would be a welcome addition to her tiny fuel supply.

But...

"Go outside?" She heard dread in her voice, and it about eclipsed the sudden hope.

Cold as it was inside the cabin now, it would be infinitely worse outside. Without the walls' protection from the biting wind... Could she even last long enough to really check out the situation, ill equipped as she was?

"Well you're not going to last here, doing nothing," she said to herself. And that was the truth.

Better to make an attempt and fail while daring than to sit idly and watch as the end crept in slowly, like a coward.

So she forced herself to her feet. It only took a moment fish the flashlight out of her pack, then she pulled the blanket as tightly around herself as she could, flipping it up over her head to form at least a semblance of a hood.

It seemed a mile, walking over to the cabin's door, though in truth it was only a few feet. But every part of Nancy's being wanted to not go there, to stay close to the stove and what heat it gave off, temporary and fleeting as that heat promised to be.

The doorknob seemed to resist her turning for the longest moment.

Then the wind gusted again, and the door swung inward of its own accord, propelled by the wind to try and smack her in the face.

She stumbled backward, the suddenly frigid air pummeling her even as a million little daggers plunged into every bit of exposed skin: snowflakes or ice shards driven by the wind and turned into cutting knives.

Nancy heard herself crying out, but over the redoubled noise of the wind she couldn't hear it.

It was like cold and darkness had engulfed her completely, and in a panic she looked back, fearing the fire had gone out.

But the dim glow of the fire inside the stove, protected at least for now from the elements since she'd shut the door, showed that bit of heat, at least, still existed. For now.

But for how long?

Longer than she could last, now that she was exposed. She was already shivering through the blanket at winter's renewed onslaught, and the weakness within her screamed at her to shut the door, get back to the stove.

And die. Just later.

Fine, but it won't be now.

Nancy tried to grit her teeth, but they were already chattering. So she contented herself by switching on her flashlight. Then, leaning forward against the wind, she stepped outside.

She only thought it had been cold before. Now, outside of any shelter...Her body went instantly numb, and Nancy felt the strength leaving her limbs.

Not far to go. Just around the corner, and see what happened.

She was praying again. That she was right, and the thumps had been a falling limb. That it was usable, and that she could manage to haul at least part of it inside before she gave out completely.

As she rounded the cabin's corner, her meager little light barely penetrated the darkness of the night, and the blizzard. But there was something up against the side of the cabin. Something...

Squinting, she shuffled forward, not daring to believe what she saw but unable to deny it.

In spite of her shivering, she found herself smiling in triumph.

She was right.

A fallen limb from the pine tree. And several bits of it had broken off in its fall from on high.

Bits that she knew without having to think on it that she could move by herself. Break with her weight once she had them inside. And create extra warmth within the stove.

Perhaps enough to get through the night. Perhaps not.

But more than before.

With the renewed strength that comes from hope, she hurried forward and grabbed hold of the largest of the limb fragments, then she hauled on it.

For a second, it didn't want to budge beneath the growing snowdrift. Then it came loose.

When she got it inside and forced the door shut again, she wasted no time in breaking off several smaller pieces, complete with needles, and shoving them into the stove.

The answering pops, and the immediate brilliance of the expanded flame within the stove, lifted her spirits almost as much as the greater heat soothed her body.

And for the first time in what seemed forever, she felt certain she would make it through this night.

Later, as she nodded off beneath the warmth that seemed almost tropical compared with what she had endured earlier, that voice in the back of her head quipped that maybe her prayer had been answered.

Or maybe it was just random luck that the pine tree had weakened when it did, giving part of itself so she could live.

She wasn't sure what to think.

But she'd have tomorrow to figure it out, one way or the other.

39

REVELATOR

Barnam licked his lips and bent forward. Squinting in the darkness, he could just make out the lock at the bottom of the window in front of him. It looked simple; an easy pick that should just take a minute or two.

Too simple.

He turned his head to the right where Luca squatted next to him on the slate tiles of the Museum Of History's rooftop. Half a hand taller than Barnam and five years older, Luca's dark brown hair normally danced just above his eyes. But tonight, he had his hair pulled back beneath a black skullcap and mask that concealed everything but his eyes and lips. Like Barnam's, his clothing was black and fitted for ease of movement. He had a rope coiled around his chest and his belt held pouches of various tools and components.

Luca's eyes met Barnam's, and Barnam could see the question there. What was he waiting for?

"You sure there's nothing?"

A slight eye roll betrayed Luca's annoyance, despite the calmness of his reply. "I checked it twice. No enchantments or wardings. It's clean."

Which didn't make Barnam feel much better. He glanced away

from his partner toward the roof's edge, just a couple feet behind them and below the window. From there it was a thirty foot drop to the cobblestone of the Museum's rear courtyard. He'd heard of security enchantments that would hurl a would-be burglar backwards just so he could make such a fall.

And the Museum was home to some of the Crown's greatest historical treasures. Surely they'd put the highest of security enhancements in place.

He knew for a fact they had; he and Luca had cased the place thoroughly over the last two weeks, noting the locations of every item on exhibit, every locked door, every security enchantment, every physical alarm...everything and anything that could make this night's job go wrong.

But they hadn't made it up here before, both because it was a very difficult climb and for fear of somehow alerting the security staff during an exploratory probe. They had decided to rely on Luca's own skill at enchantments to find any dangers.

But now, finding nothing, and with summer's nighttime wind beginning to pick up, its whistle combining with the scent of salt and rot from the city's waterfront a quarter of a mile away, Barnam wondered how the Crown could have been so careless?

Or maybe it was Luca being careless?

"You said that in Tanis, too."

Silence, then Luca replied in slow, cold words, "Are you never going to stop bringing that up? That was three years ago!"

Which was a fair point. And in the three years since then, the two of them had done many successful jobs, earned a lot of money together.

Still, that one mess-up had cost them dearly. Almost cost them everything.

He looked back at Luca and shrugged.

Luca moved forward. "Fine, I'll do it if you're so scared. Move over."

That earned him a snort from Barnam. "You couldn't pick your nose." Luca made an attempt at an affronted expression, but Barnam paid it no mind. They both know the truth of Luca's manual dexterity. With a soft sigh, Barnam turned back to the lock. "Ok. Here goes nothing."

Leaning forward again, he pulled his picks out and set to work.

He had to force his hands to hold steady when he first inserted the implements into the keyhole, but after a few seconds his nervous tension faded beneath years of practice as he sank into the task. Feeling the location of the tumblers, probing out the actuators.

And then slowly, carefully...

The lock clicked, and the window cracked open slightly.

No alarm. No magical shove off the roof. No other nasty surprises.

It really had been that easy.

Letting out a sigh of relief, Barnam gave Luca an apologetic grin, and got a wry, "See, I told you so," in reply.

Couldn't blame him for that.

Pushing the window the rest of the way open—thankfully it opened inward—Barnam slowly slipped inside.

It was a dark night, and even darker still inside the attic. He could barely see his hand in front of his face, but he moved deeper inside anyway, clearing the way beneath the window for Luca's entrance.

The floor felt like wood planks, as opposed to the polished marble of the Museum's public areas. But that was to be expected, he supposed, especially in an attic or storage space like this surely must be. No need to be fancy in spaces like this; no one who needed impressing would see it.

It smelled musty, like no one had been in here to clean in years, and it was a bit cooler than outside; a testament to the building's stone structure and its ability to insulate.

Barnam was just pressing another foot cautiously in front of himself when he heard Luca's voice making a low-pitched chant. Then all at once the room sprang into view, like someone had lit a lamp.

Barnam froze for a second, momentary fright that they had been caught changing to chagrin over the fact that, despite how many times he had experienced this particular bit of enchantment, it still caught him unawares.

He had no idea where Luca had learned it, and he'd never met another enchanter who could do it. But it did something to make light for them and them alone. At first, Barnam thought sure Luca was telling tall tales when he described its effects. It must cast light in the entire room, and would be useless for their kinds of work. But then he'd watched as four other men in a dark room with him and Luca kept on running into walls and furniture after Luca cast the enchantment on the two of them but left the other four out of it. And he was convinced.

Quite a clever spell, this one.

"There," Luca said, behind him. "That's better."

"No lie there."

And not just for being able to see again. Also for the confirmation that they were exactly where Barnam had hoped the window would bring them.

It was a storage room. It was filled with crates and shelves filled with dusty wooden boxes, all of which had been labelled in plain block letters with a series of letters and numbers that Barnam supposed meant something to the museum keepers.

The shelves made a passage of sorts from the window deeper into the room, and there toward the rear was a single door, which was latched shut. The door had frosted glass in its upper half, and the same blocky text that marked the boxes was painted onto the glass, on the opposite side from them.

The text was backwards from Barnam's perspective, but he could make it out clearly. "Archives."

Through that door would be a corridor made of wood planking that would take him and Luca past several other similarly marked "Archives" doors until it reached a single, narrow stairwell of stone that eventually would transition into one of polished marble that would intersect with one of the many halls in the Museum proper that led between various exhibits.

The Archives in the attic were not unique. Barnam had learned that during his research in the capital city's architectural publications registry a month before. The Museum had no less that a dozen such spaces, set aside for items that were deemed no longer worthy of exhibit, or that were still being studied and had not had their suitability determined yet.

But these attic Archives were well laid out in the plans he had found, which were accessible by any citizen who had the desire to know.

And how's that for a thumb in the eye toward the Crown's security men, eh?

Barnam had to restrain a cynical smile as he beheld the truth of his research's hypothesis. Then he advanced toward the marked door, Luca at his heels.

Sure enough, the door opened into a narrow corridor heading back towards the center of the Museum. They passed several pairs of doors, also marked as "Archives", before the corridor ended at a descending staircase.

Barnam took a moment to look behind himself toward Luca and grin, which Luca returned in kind.

Then he set off down the stairs toward the display galleries.

It was like transitioning into another world. Where above it was all wood panelling, most of it unstained, and hardwood floors, here it was polished marble floors and fluted columns leading from gallery to gallery. Long, wide corridors where entire crowds could walk from one exhibit to another, all chattering away mindlessly as they passed by priceless pieces beyond number. Vaulted ceilings that could have housed a dozen families under their roofs, if only the families had been given leave to try.

Barnam felt both awe and disgust at the opulence on display as he and Luca descended to the exhibition levels, both feelings tugging on his innards with its own strength as he fought to determine which should triumph.

In the end, Barnam decided on his own determination. Both were twisted. Both evil in their own rights.

But that was the world he lived in. The world he had to do his best to navigate.

Only the discipline of years of research, struggle, and training kept him from being overwhelmed by the sheer opulent beauty of it all. The utterly un-fightable extravagance of the Crown's imperial power, and how it had dominated man's consciousness for centuries.

"That is not enough," he found himself saying between clenched teeth.

And indeed it wasn't. Which was why we was here. He and Luca, both.

After all, without coin, a man could not eat. And it all came down to that.

But still, as he entered the exhibit hall, Barnam stopped at a marble balcony overlooking a sweeping gallery below, filled with trinkets from battles and sieges of years past, and he couldn't help feeling entranced by it all. Almost without realizing it, he placed his hands atop the stone mantelpiece and looked down, soaking it all in.

The shield of the Centurion who had guarded the crown prince from death during the siege of Alantis. The bust of Ingraham, the philosopher king who had single-handedly convinced the Tulteks to place themselves under the yoke of Imperial dominance through the force of his philosophical insight.

Revelator, the sword of King Ranulf, which he had used to drive away the forces of darkness, and with which he had perished at the battle of Normald Bay, in single combat with the conduit of the Dark Lord himself.

The sword hung there in the gallery, suspended point down by twin cables that were attached to its crosspiece and illuminated by sconces on either side, which Barnam knew from experience illuminated the finely honed steel of its blade and the gold inlay of its crosspiece as though it still glowed of its own light, which legend proclaimed it once had.

The scones were dark now, their coals extinguished by the museum keepers as they concluded their shift for the public at large. And Barnam knew their lack. For now, if legends were true, the sword would still glow of its own inner glory, shining forth with the light of Truth and Beauty that came from the divine.

But Barnam could not see it. The enchantment that Luca had wrought brought its own light to his eyes, and he saw the entire exhibit hall without blemish, and disregarding any other implement that might interfere with its illumination.

So he only saw the sword hanging there, suspended by its cross-piece. Like any other artifact that mattered not in the grand scheme of things.

Barnam knew what he was looking at. Wanted to feel the awe that he'd always felt as a youth upon hearing the ode to King Ranulf, the stirring in his loins that wanted him to rise and take up arms against the enemies of his people, so he could finally be a man worth remembering.

But he couldn't anymore. Those days were past him. And though he felt the same stirring in his soul when he looked upon the great sword Revelator, it was only a fraction of the primal joy he had felt in his youth.

"Come on, Barnam," said Luca, and he felt a tugging on his arm as his partner pulled at him.

And then the tugging was gone, as he turned away from the hanging sword and followed Luca toward their objective for the night.

It lay down a spiraling staircase and to the right, in an anteroom that few tourists even entered anymore, from what Barnam had seen during their scouting activities. But it was lavishly laid out, with multicolored tapestries lining the walls and multitudes of artifacts laid out under display cases all around the room.

The relics of the city of Hitopa, which the Empire had conquered five hundred years ago. Before any of the great kings whose relics were displayed in the great hall, before the Empire really could be called such. Just one city-state vanquishing and conquering another in the days of antiquity.

And yet their employer wanted one of these relics of yore, for whatever reason Barnam could not say and wouldn't venture to ask. It wasn't his business, and it didn't matter.

What mattered was that the relic in question laid in a glass-enclosed display case in front of Luca right this moment. The relic wasn't particularly beautiful. Oh, it had gems and was made of gold. But Barnam had seen multitudes more precious.

That didn't matter either.

Luca bent over, looking at the glass enclosure even as he chanted out the words of a different spell. Barnam didn't expect to see or feel the results of his enchantment; the sorts of detections Luca used only revealed things to himself. But still, he felt a bit of a chill when his partner rose from his crouch and turned to give him a smile.

"There was a splice on, but I lifted it. Should be clear now."

There was no lock on the enclosure; it appeared the thing could just be lifted up by main strength alone. Barnam considered that if he had constructed the security device for such a thing, he certainly would have made something more robust.

But before he could say that, Luca reached out, took hold of the enclosure, and lifted it.

Barnam half expected a whining alarm from some enchantment that Luca had broken. But there was nothing. Just the soft scraping of glass against stone as Luca lifted the enclosure off, then the tap as he set the glass down on the floor.

A moment later, Luca had the relic in his hands and he held it up studying it.

"Doesn't really look like much, does it?"

"No," Barnam agreed. He glanced around, then added. "Just get it and let's get out of here."

Luca looked sidelong at him, then nodded. He took a moment to slip the relic into one of his belt pouches, then he bent over, hefted the enclosure, and set it back into place where he had found it.

Then the two of them turned and headed toward the exit.

They had gone three steps when, all at once, all light blinked out.

Barnam cursed softly, then came to a quick halt, his stomach going to ice as he felt his heartbeat accelerate. Luca would not have messed around with his enchantment. Not at a time and place like this. Which only left -

Yellow-orange light flared from ahead, then from left and right, driving the irises of Barnam's eyes nearly completely shut. He stumbled backward a step, dazzled, and felt the impact in his back as he ran into Luca. His partner let out the same curse that Barnam was beginning to voice even as he blinked up a storm.

A moment later, some of his vision returned, and he saw they were surrounded by a dozen men, holding torches. They wore the black and silver livery of the Crown's guards, and they were armed with sword and daggers, though none had weapons drawn. Directly in front of him was a man with the epaulettes of a Captain, about ten years older than the others. He stood proudly erect and looked at Barnam and Luca with open disdain.

"Did you really think you could steal from the Crown so easily?" said the Captain. His voice was a smooth baritone, and it bore neither respect nor contempt, just a businesslike curiosity as he addressed them.

Barnam looked left and right and saw more of the Captain's guardsmen. Probably a dozen total. Then he looked back at Luca.

His partner had not yet fully recovered, but Luca had a look of defiance on his face. His eyes met Barnam's, and he lifted his left eyebrow.

"Blackout?" Luca said, soto voce, so only Barnam could hear it.

Barnam wasn't so sure that was the right play, but when he looked forward, the Captain spoke again.

"Obviously you were mistaken," the Captain said, as though whatever answer Barnam or Luca was going to give didn't matter. He waved the guardsman at his side forward, and the man stepped forward, reaching behind his belt to produce a pair of shackles.

Off to the right, a second guardsman did the same.

"You are arrested in the name of the Crown for burglary and theft," said the Captain, to repeat the obvious, apparently.

So. There was no way out expect straight ahead, it seemed.

Barnam didn't look back at Luca. He just said, "On five," under his breath, in a tone he knew would reach Luca's ears and his alone. He heard a grunt in response.

That was five.

The two guardsmen continued forward, and Barnam felt a tugging on his belt.

Four.

The guardsman in front of him pulled the shackles tight, and said, "Hands where I can see them."

Three.

Barnam complied, raising his hands. He couldn't see, but he felt stirring in the air behind him that said Luca was doing the same.

Two.

The guardsman let go of one side of his shackles and reached out to take Barnam's left hand. Barnam heard Luca beginning a chant.

One.

Barnam pivoted, drawing his left hand away from the guardsman, then drove a hook punch with his right into the guardsman's side.

The man lost his breath with a loud, "OOF!"

Then the lights went out again. All of them, Lucas' enchantment extinguishing the illumination from the guardsmen's torches simultaneously.

Pandemonium erupted. All around, men's voices raised in shouts.

Barnam heard the Captain exclaim, "Gets the light back on, you fool!" to what could only be the guardsmen's' enchanter.

Behind him, he heard Luca chanting again, more rapidly and with greater zeal. Barnam had heard that before; when Luca had been engaged in duels with other enchanters.

They needed to get out of there, fast. Luca was skilled, but whomever the guardsmen had with them would be, as well. And he had the advantage of not being stressed with the prospect of being imprisoned for many years.

Barnam surged forward, trusting in his recall of the many days he and Luca had spent casing the Museum.

From here it should be twenty-five paces ahead, then fifteen paces to the left, then forty paces ahead to the main gallery...

He felt a tug on his back, as the hook that Luca slipped into his belt pulled the rope connecting them taught for a moment. Then the tension lifted as either Luca moved to follow him or the rope was cut.

Hopefully the former.

Barnam heard a curse in front of him and to his right, and jigged left, then he continued his forward charge.

Should be time to turn...

He ran into a wall, and cursed, his nose feeling the impact like he had just been punched in the face. He reeled backward, and almost fell. But the cacophony of shouts and curses all around was all the enticement he needed to keep going, so instead he veered left, counting out his paces more carefully.

Somewhere between twenty-three and twenty-five, Barnam realized he could see. But it was only after he had begun running forward again that it registered.

And it wasn't just that he had left the boundaries of Luca's darkness spell. There was actual light.

A white-blue radiance glowed from up ahead, and Barnam found himself slowing as he neared it. Then he strode between a vaulted archway flanked between two fluted stone pillars and he came to a complete halt.

Revelator hung there before him, suspended in the center of the viewing gallery.

And it was glowing.

The blade shone with a blue-white light, illuminating the entire gallery in a glow that was at once eerie and warmly comforting. All of the relics of days past were perfectly visible, all of the scrollwork of the archways. All of the engravings on the pillars and in the ceiling.

But Barnam could not take his eyes from the sword itself.

The blade was a miniature sun, glowing with a brilliance that should have been painful to look at but was instead warming. He took it in, and again felt the stirring in his soul that he had felt as a boy.

But now it was twisted, tainted with guilt over the path he had taken; the life he had chosen to live. Instead of valor and truth, theft and deception.

It was like his soul was being laid bare for judgment, but he could not look away. The light emanating from the sword entranced him so. He needed to go to it.

To reach out and touch it. Become one with it.

He felt himself taking a step forward.

And then the back of his belt tugged at him, and he stumbled backward. He looked behind to see Luca gesturing frantically for him to follow as he ducked down a passageway to the side of the gallery, the rope between them completely paid out.

"Come on!" Luca said.

From the other direction, Barnam heard anew the shouts of the guardsmen, their voices raised in anger, their words promising vengeance.

Barnam spared one last glance at the sword, glowing with the same righteous power that the stories of King Ranulf had attributed to it.

Then he turned and sprinted off after his partner.

The boat rocked beneath Barnam's feet. Three pairs of raggedly-dressed rowers took to their oars, driving the vessel forward under the watchful eye of the boatswain sitting at their rear and pounding out the beat on his drum, and of the Captain manning the tiller at the rear of the launch.

Behind the Captain, to the east, the sun was coming up over the silhouettes of the city's buildings. The red-orange color of the sunrise usually was a comfort for Barnam, when he'd seen it before. But now, it seemed almost like the sky was bleeding, rent by some great wound that he could only guess at.

He stood in the bow of the boat, and he would normally be looking forward, toward the jutting headland across the bay, on the other side of which lay the ship he and Luca had commissioned to bring them across the Sea of Storms to Caliope, where their client waited to collect the relic they had acquired this night.

But today, he couldn't look forward. Only back, toward the Museum, and the blade hanging there on its cabled supports.

He saw the brilliance of the sunrise, but only registered the blue-white light that Revelator had given off. And he wondered at the meaning of it. Or if there was one at all.

The boat rocked again, and Luca popped up from belowdecks. He looked to the rear of the boat, then to the front, then sauntered up to where Barnam stood, wearing a satisfied grin.

"Well, that turned out alright, didn't it?" Luca said, gaily.

Barnam nodded. It was difficult to argue with that. They had obtained their prize and gotten away cleanly. No one hurt or killed, no one in jail.

Great results, all things considered.

Still...

"Did you see it, Luca?" he said, and was surprised to find his voice was still hushed, like it was inappropriate to speak loudly about this particular subject. "The sword was glowing."

Luca looked sidelong at him, then nodded. "And a good thing it was, too, or we probably wouldn't have gotten out of there. Don't know about you, but I lost track of my steps during all the ruckus. No way I could have found the exit without a light."

Barnam felt Luca's eyes on him, and after a moment he nodded agreement. Because it was true. The sword's light had been the thing that showed them the way to escape.

But that wasn't they sword's purpose in glowing, was it?

Or did it even have a purpose?

Luca clapped him on the shoulder and grinned companionably. "Don't overthink it. Come on below. Captain's got a cask of ale down there, and I could use a drink." He grinned. "You?"

Barnam nodded again, and Luca grinned more broadly. He went below, but Barnam didn't follow for a long moment. He just watched the sun creep upward over the city's buildings, and he wondered.

40

CUPID'S ARROW

"**Y**ou know Cupid?"

The young fairy who asked the question beamed at me through eyes grown wide with amazement. Her cheeks seemed to sink as her jaw dropped open in time with the expanding of her eyelids, and the cute little dimple just above her jaw vanished before the sudden tension in her skin.

She was the typical fairy. Slender, but curved. Dressed in a skin-tight leotard; this one of blue trimmed with white. Gossamer wings extruding from the back of her shoulders; hers were tinged blue to match her leotard...of course. Tussled hair that had to have been styled that way to be so appealing in a "Oh I just came out of bed and didn't bother to do anything with it" kind of way. Except that I'd never seen or heard of a fairy spending any time on it at all to get that effect.

Hers was, of course, black, fading to blue at the fringes.

And of course her eyes were blue as well.

She exuded a fragrance that reminded me of mint chocolate chip ice cream, though that didn't quite do it justice. It was more subtly appealing, but not in the way that would make your mouth water. More like the feeling of having just finished a splendid meal, and wouldn't it be great to kick back with a nice desert, followed by brandy and cigars?

The effect was ruined by the way she completely didn't look at me. Just at the doorway behind me, where Cupid had a few minutes ago shoved through into his own private locker room.

I sighed. For the millionth time.

Seemed I had to answer this question for every newly-matured fairy who came to work here at Valentine Hall.

"Yes, I'm Cupid's assistant," I said, keeping my tone level and polite, if slightly cool. "And no, you can't meet him. He's a very busy man."

"But - "

"No exceptions," I said. I watched as her awed expression faded, turning to one of chagrin, then petulance. I knew what would come next, so I cut her off at the pass. "Good day, miss."

Then I pushed my chair backwards, away from her, and slid shut the white and pink-painted panel that separated my desk, and the rest of Cupid's antechamber, from the remainder of Valentine Hall.

It wasn't part of the initial design. But after the first six months of being harassed by the young and hormonal fairies working here, I'd put in a request to management, and they'd consented to enclosing my desk behind a closable boundary, both for my and for Cupid's privacy.

And sanity.

Not that it did him that much good.

"But - " the young fairy's voice was crunched out by the solid clack of the privacy panel sliding home, and I pushed back from my desk, the casters on the bottom of my chair squeaking slightly as they carried me away from the panel; and the consternation beyond.

I breathed out an exhausted sigh, then pressed my hands onto the arms of my chair and pushed myself upwards.

My knees popped, and I winced in anticipation of the usual ache as they came to accept my full weight. But wonder of wonders, today my joints were lubed enough that I only felt a momentary twinge.

I didn't pause to wonder at my good fortune today. I just pulled the scarlet doublet I was wearing down over my hips, Picard style, and pushed the door open to Cupid's locker room.

My office space was small. Tiny, in fact. Barely enough to stand up and turn around in. But that's what an assistant rates in Valentine Hall, and I didn't begrudge it.

My wings never fully formed; all I had were lumps on the backs of my shoulders where they should have been. I was full-blooded fairy, but one of the occasional few who didn't manifest with all of the fey traits. It was a good thing I grew up with Cupid, and we'd been fast friends since we could only just walk; decades before puberty, when our wings were supposed to grow in.

When my disability became clear, he shielded me. Insisted that I be made his assistant.

He made sure I never had to worry about being kicked out of the faerealm for lack of manifestation. And I would never be able to repay that act of loyalty.

Still, the last few years....had been trying.

The door swung shut behind me, and all I heard from him was a grunt. A grumpy grunt.

Which was par for the course. But something about today's utterance made it seem especially unpleasant.

The locker room was well more than twice the size of my little work area. More like three or four times as big. The floors were polished white marble, and the walls were the same. Cupid had a private shower at the rear of the space with twin nozzles on either side of the enclosure that were specifically measured to meet at the exact correct angle so as to moisten the entirety of his body without having to move an inch away from the drain at its center.

He had a private sauna to the left of the shower area. And a quartet of large lockers to store his personal possessions, as well as his work attire, to the right.

Toward the front, where I came in, was his desk, carved from mahogany, where he had a state of the art computer and, above it, a huge flatscreen that management kept scrolling with feeds about the romance quotients in all of the various regions of the world. If he liked, he could scroll down to display stats down to the neighborhood.

But he almost never did that. That was my job.

Off to the left was a grey-white leather upholstered couch behind a black steel coffee table topped by a clear piece of glass. A darkly-stained humidor sat atop the coffee table, with a double-bladed guillotine cutter and a three-burner torch lying next to it, along with a black-stained porcelain ashtray.

Along with everything else, it was my job to make sure the ashtray was empty, the torch fully fueled, and the humidor fully stocked. And I was happy to do it.

But damn if I didn't wish he would share more often.

As I walked in, Cupid was emerging from the shower, a white towel wrapped around his waist. His wings, seemingly wilted from the water impacting their feathers, were tucked in tight to his back and his round face was red from the warmth of the shower.

But he wore a scowl, nonetheless.

"How'd it go, C?" He had preferred I use the diminutive since we were little.

Cupid grunted and made a little shrug of his shoulders, then moved over to the couch and settled down. The towel parted, but thankfully this time not enough for me to see what I didn't want to see.

"A wedding on Valentine's Day," he said, shaking his head. "Only humans could be so stupid."

He opened the humidor and pulled out a long, thick cigar. I recognized the wrapper. La Gloria Cubana, Serie R, No 7. His favorite.

As he clipped the end and lit it, sending the fragrant smoke into the space around us, I cleared my throat. "It didn't go well?"

Cupid sucked on the stick, and the end flared red, then he settled back into the couch, blowing the grey-black smoke out from his mouth. He shook his head.

"Went fine. I shot up the third groomsmen and the second bridesmaid. They're boning as we speak." He shook his head, an expression of near disgust on his face. "But the married couple will be divorced in two years. Tops."

"How do you know that?"

Cupid raised an eyebrow at me, then snorted. "Long as I've been doing this? I know." He sucked on his cigar again, then as he was blowing out, he said, "Do yourself a favor, Lorian. Never get married."

I wasn't sure what to say to that, so I didn't say anything. When he was in a mood like this, there was nothing really to say.

Cupid looked to his right, where I had, at his insistence, installed a shelf holding a myriad of alcoholic beverages.

"Get The Macallan 18," he said. Then he gestured toward the humidor. "And grab yourself a smoke."

It was going to be a long, long night.

My head hurt.

A lot.

But that was the price to be paid for such a night.

I'd had many of them with Cupid, going way back to before he landed his current gig. Lots of booze and cigars and extravagance... but no women.

Not for him anyway.

I'd met a few girls, and had a couple relationships. One lasted almost a year. But in the end they all faded, because Cupid was always on the move, always working, and I had to be there to support his endeavors. Otherwise humankind would lose romance forever, and then cease to exist.

There were plenty of fairies breeding, every day. Too many, in fact, based on the FaeRealm's recent decrees about family size. So I didn't feel like I was shirking on my responsibilities or anything. Still, it would have been nice to settle down.

Someday.

But C? He relished not having a wife, or kids. And never mind the conflict with his job for the humans.

Or maybe it was because of his job.

Regardless, we both were bachelors. But he got all the propositions from the fairy women at large.

So I wasn't at all surprised when I heard a gentle clearing of a throat behind me as I made my way to work, my head feeling like it was going to explode while I secretly prayed it would do so, to spare me the misery of my hangover.

I knew immediately what the girl wanted, before I saw her. And I really didn't want to deal with this crap. But it was part of my job, so I squared my shoulders and turned around.

"Look, miss," I said, "Cupid is - "

I lost my words when I beheld the fairy behind me. The same one who had come by my desk the previous day, blue leotard and all.

Please, Lord, let them have more than one pair of clothes.

I wasn't sure who I was praying to, but it was a valid, true prayer, and -

"I'm not here for me," the fairy said, and the prayer halted in my mind.

I raised an eyebrow at her.

She smiled, and that cute dimple I'd seen yesterday renewed with a deepening flare that I would have sworn was impossible before it just happened.

"Oh, Cupid's cute enough, I suppose," she said, "and certainly he is rich and famous. But he's not my type." She gestured to her left. "My friend, though..."

She left the rest unsaid, her words trailing into silence as the leaves of a nearby orchid parted and a second fairy came into view.

She looked embarrassed, like the orchid had revealed her without her wanting it to. And it may have, at that. Orchids were notoriously mischievous.

But whether it had or not was immaterial. I could not take my eyes off her.

All fairies are slender and shapely. But she was long, lean, and powerful. But also feminine, with an expansive bust and curvy thighs, and wings that held her aloft with only a beat every three or four seconds, so powerful were the muscles driving them. Her leotard, hair, and eyes were green, and her lips were rose red, with a hint of orange at the edges.

I didn't want to stare, but I couldn't help it. My eyes grew wide with astonishment at her beauty for a moment, then the shiver going down my spine brought me to my senses, and I shook my head.

Looking back at the fairy from the day before, she had a knowing expression on her face. Her lips turned upward slightly.

"Most men have that reaction," she said. Then she pursed her lips. "But not Cupid. Madeline has a heart only for him, but he's never looked at her twice. Never said more than a word to her."

I glanced back at Madeline, and had to look away for fear of being embarrassed by my body's reaction. "She's a grown woman. Can she not let her feelings be known?"

"She has tried," said the blue fairy, drawing my eyes back to her. "Many times. But Cupid will not hear her."

I shrugged. This was nothing new, and she and Madeline should have seen it already, and moved on.

"Cupid is an avowed bachelor. He's seen too much strife and pain from marriage and the like. He's vowed to take no part in it."

The blue fairy gasped and recoiled slightly, pressing a hand to her mouth. Her eyes were widened in disbelief.

Before she could ask, I nodded. "It's true; I do not jest. Tell Madeline she will be better off looking elsewhere."

Blue looked over my shoulder toward her friend, and it seemed to me they were communicating, though I couldn't hear a word being said.

I glanced behind to see Madeline returning blue's stare. And it seemed she was not blinking.

I was just swallowing down a sudden case of nerves when Blue spoke again.

"She cannot."

I raised an eyebrow at her.

"Madeline has pledged her heart to Cupid. If he will not return it, she will die."

Oh for the love of.... Not this tripe again.

"Look, blue - "

"My name is Holympa."

I drew a breath. "Look here, Holympa. I've heard that a dozen times in the last two years. Know how many really meant it?"

Holympa shook her head.

"None. And I don't believe Madeline does either. So don't try to play me."

She recoiled, and I saw her jaw working. Her eyes danced from side to side, as she obviously was trying to work out her next move on behalf of her friend. Clearly she hadn't expected that obvious bit of manipulation to fail.

Rolling my eyes at the pathetic plight of amateurs, I took a half-step toward her.

"Look. I think C's in a bad place too, and I want him to get better. Find someone, and be happy. But I'm not going to sell him out or play games with him. If that's what you and she are looking for, piss off." I glanced between the two of them, then raised my finger to my brow in a half salute. "Good day."

I'd gone three paces when a different voice, deeper and more powerful but still female, called out to me. "Wait."

I stopped and turned around, and found Madeline hovering in the air not ten feet in front of me. She was flushed, but her expression was hard, determined. Though her eyes betrayed a trace of tenderness, a silent fear of rejection.

And seeing that, I knew her intentions were true.

If Cupid is out on a mission, I stay until he gets back, and then we have a debriefing. Most times formal, with Management. Sometimes, just the two of us, and that's when I get to have a stogie. Depends on the rank of his targets for that particular mission.

But on the days that he doesn't have a mission, our routine is far less structured. There are days when he kicks me out right after lunch. And there are others when he insists I stay with him until well after sundown, to the kind of hour where, if I were married, I would have to object and perhaps bring a complaint to management.

I never did though. And I never will, since we've been friends so long.

But on this particular evening, I felt the lack of his permission to withdraw like a spike through my belly.

Not that I wanted to go home.

No, quite the opposite. Holympa and I had planned this evening's events out to the T, and I didn't want to mess them up. But they required me to be here, at work, after C went home for the night.

And it looked like he was never going to.

As I sat at my desk, doing meaningless paperwork that I'd been blowing off for weeks—because what was Management going to do to Cupid if he didn't turn in the stupid forms, fire him? Please.—I counted down the minutes in my mind, and prayed with each minute's passing that Cupid would finally get done with his work for the day, and get gone.

So I could do my own work for the night.

But the hours stretched on, and still he didn't leave, and I began to despair that he never would, and our window of opportunity would close.

Then I felt a hand on my shoulder, and a gentle squeeze.

I recognized the squeeze as coming from Cupid, but still I gave a little jerk of surprise, so engrossed was I in the fake, useless document in front of me, that still somehow managed to be compelling despite its utter triviality.

"Whoa," said Cupid. "You ok, L?"

I looked back at him and nodded, adding the best little grin I could manage. "Yeah. You just startled me, is all."

Which was completely true. And yet not entirely.

He looked at me for a couple seconds, then returned my grin and nodded as well. "Well, I'm heading out." His grin broadened a bit. "Don't stay here too late, ok?"

We shared a chuckle, and he exited through the back door—the better to avoid groupies—and headed home.

I waited for ten minutes, to be sure he was gone. Then I shut down my office equipment and turned around. As I expected, he'd left his doorway into his private locker room unlocked.

Of course he did. He trusted me to lock up, and not mess around with anything, or do him wrong.

For a second, I felt a flare of almost-guilt. I shoved it down. I wasn't out to do him wrong tonight.

I was hoping to do him some good, actually.

So I slipped into his locker room, then padded across to the lockers on the right side of the room from the shower.

The two closest the shower held his personal and professional clothing. Then came two more, in which he stored his on-the-job equipment.

And one piece of equipment, in particular, that I needed.

I knew the combination, so I set about dialing it into the locker's lock.

Cupid's condo is on the far side of a pretty large park from Valentine Hall. He didn't own a car because he hated to drive, so he always walked through the park to get home. Depending on the day—his pace, and how many people were in the park—the walk took anywhere from 25 to 45 minutes.

When I finished with the locker room, I figured I was about fifteen minutes behind him.

Plenty of time to get to the opposite side of the park via cab, and get in position. All things being equal, that is.

Unfortunately, all things are almost never equal. But this time, as a once in a lifetime turn, the winds of fate were actually with me.

So instead of getting there in 10 minutes, I got there in 5. So just within the minimum window for Cupid to pass through the park.

In fact, I ended up waiting ten minutes for Madeline to make her move.

The sun had long since set, and the moon was a crescent sitting a third of the way up in the sky. Its faint light combined with the stars to offer only a dim illumination of the park's hedges and flowerbeds, but it was enough to see Cupid trudging down the dirt path he usually took on his way to his home.

He could have flown, of course. His wings, though small, were strong enough to carry him. But as long as I'd known him, if he wasn't on the job, he preferred to walk.

So he trudged along, in his civilian attire. Gone was the white toga, and the silly sandals. He wore a collared shirt and slacks, and he walked with his hands tucked into the pockets of his slacks and his eyes cast down onto the path in front of him.

Madeline waited for him near the edge of a rosebush, and monkish though he was, Cupid was still male. No man could miss a female presence such as hers; and even if he determinedly didn't see her, the gently-subtle perfume of her presence would have been enough to halt a man in his tracks.

Cupid, of course, stopped, and raised his head to look at her.

From my position, a good thirty feet away, I could see the annoyance on his face. She was a lovely woman, but he had sworn off that particular passion long ago. And anyway, it was late.

Still, when she spoke, he halted to listen to her.

I couldn't make out her words, but I could see his features relax a tad. But only a tad. He made a shake of his head, then he spoke a quick reply that again didn't reach my ears.

Her charms alone weren't cutting it; not with his armor up.

Which was why I brought a bit of backup.

I'd seen the bow, of course. Helped oil and clean it in between missions. Replaced the bowstring when the old one was worn or frayed.

I'd helped him procure the materials for the arrows, and kept them well fletched and ready to go.

But I'd never drawn the bow myself.

As I drew the string back, I was reminded of the Odyssey, how Odysseus' wife used his bow as a means to keep suitors away, because no one was strong enough to draw it.

Now I'm no little guy. But I could not get the bow to its full draw. I'm told a good archer brings the string back to his ear. I could barely get it back to my nose. And even then, my arm shook.

I looked down the length of the white arrow with its pinkish-red, heart-shaped head, and watched as the missile bounced around against the silhouette of my friend.

I didn't have to hit the heart; I knew that. But I also knew it would be more potent if I did. So I held on, trying to aim.

And trying...

I lost my grip, and the string snapped to, sending the arrow flying.

It flew long and high, well to the right of both Cupid and Madeline, landing somewhere off in the dark, its magic spent uselessly.

I cursed myself, because Cupid was turning away from her, clearly done with the conversation, and with her.

She had a look of frustration and despondence on her face, and I knew the window would close in just a few seconds.

So I drew again. With more determination, I drew. And this time, I got the string back a more respectable distance.

My arm still shook, but I knew the pattern of it now, so I watched carefully as Cupid finished his turn and began to walk away.

Madeline lowered her head and began to leave as well.

And I loosed.

The arrow rose as it left the bow. I heard it make a soft whistle as it passed through the air. For a second I thought I'd missed again.

But then Cupid gave a little jerk. His eyes went wide, and he froze in place.

Then he spun around on his heel until he was once again facing the lovely fairy maiden.

He said something. Her name, I have to believe, and she stopped her own turn.

Her expression when she looked back at him was curious, then confused.

Then joyous, as he closed the distance between them and took her by the hand.

When Holympa came to see me, I was closing up Cupid's shop. He'd taken off early for the day, the better to meet Madeline for an early dinner.

He'd been doing that almost daily since their meeting in the park, and my little assist. And I have to say I'd never seen him happier. He had a renewed spring in his step, and when he went out on missions...

Well, the romance stats that management recorded and reported for the human populace hadn't looked that positive in as long as I could remember.

More people everywhere were falling in love. And I got an inkling of what it must have felt like to be Cupid, as he watched the fruits of his own labors.

Holympa looked happy as well when she reached the boundary that separate our office space from the rest of Valentine Hall. She gave me a grin, and as usual that cute dimple sprang to full life. "How you doing, Lorian?"

I returned her smile. "I can't remember when things have been so good around here."

"Glad to hear it." She looked down for a second. "I just wanted to thank you. Madeline is so happy, and..." She trailed off, then looked back up and gave me a little shrug.

I understood what she meant. It was great to see your friend thriving, and knowing you had a little something to do with it. "You don't have to thank me."

She opened her mouth. To protest, I was sure. So I beat her to the punch.

"But you're welcome, all the same."

She stopped, cocked her head at me, then shut her mouth again, grinning all the broader. Then she gave a little fairy curtsy and turned away.

Before I realized what I was doing, I said on an impulse, "Do you want to get dinner tonight?"

She stopped mid-turn, then looked back at me. I could feel her gaze as her eyes swept down my body and back up, and was tempted to cringe as I felt my lack of fully-formed wings. But then her grin broadened into a full-on smile, and she nodded.

"I'd love to."

And just when I thought the day couldn't get any better, it did.

41

HEAVEN'S GATE

The central marketplace in Theomor, the capital city of Heaven's Gate, extended for a kilometer in every direction, and housed merchants of all kinds, and without much in the way of rhyme or reason that Manolo could figure out. A sparkling clean, brightly lit, three-story store decorated in the latest modern flash and style and selling the latest network equipment to come off automated manufacturing plants three systems away could have, sitting right out front, a butcher stand from a local ranch, complete with recently-slaughter pig's haunches hanging from its display rack.

A hot—because it was always hot on Heaven's Gate, even in what passed for winter—and disorganized mess of every type of product, every type of person, and every possible scent from all over the Qorathi Empire. And no one seemed to mind or think it odd at all.

Manolo loved it.

And not just because of its vibrant energy, order seemingly on the very brink of chaos, ready to fall over at a feather's touch but somehow always remaining upright.

More important by far, for this day's business at least, it was just about custom-made for covert meetings, even wide out in the open.

Impossible for wide-area surveillance to zero in on one particular meeting, one particular conversation. There was too much constant hustle and bustle, too many moving bodies. And too many conversations all tumbling overtop one another in any particular space.

That wouldn't save him if his cover had been blown and surveillance had been focused on him alone. If that happened, Manolo knew well how difficult—nigh on impossible—it would be to not have his every act recorded and sent to data jockeys for scrubbing and analysis.

He'd done that to enough targets himself to know how that worked.

But he had no reason to think his contacts and their group had made him. None of the network spiders he'd set up had queued on any activity that might indicate someone was hunting the real him digitally. And his counter-surveillance drones, barely above nano-size and strategically placed at varying distances around his base of operations and his person, showed nothing that even resembled a targeted surveillance effort pointed his way.

So he was in the clear, at least for now. But that was to be expected; up to this point had been the easy part of his mission. The seeking and laying of groundwork, the sewing of trust from afar before the first face-to-face.

Even a nub just out of training could manage that. And Manolo had been doing this a long, long time.

As an operative for the Empire's Interior Security Service, he'd run missions and infiltrated threats from one side of the Empire's thirty-six systems to the other. He'd taken down threats that the civilian populace never even heard of, threats by the dozen.

Now it was time to take down another one.

Several month's back, confidential sources had reported rumblings of a plot against the wife of Count Poterick, the liege lord of Heaven's Gate. Since she was also sister to Emperor Lucien, this of course received high level attention, and demands for action.

Hence the reason Manolo had been assigned to root it out. As Magden, the head of covert ops, had said, it required the best, and Manolo was it.

Which was nice to hear. Though perhaps a bit overstated.

Regardless, he'd spent a lot of time and effort getting a false identity set up to run a real business here on Heaven's Gate, and then more effort using legitimate contacts to slowly worm his way toward illegitimate ones until now, after weeks of effort, he believed he was getting close to the group behind the plot.

This meet would tell the tale, one way or another.

Up ahead and on the left. A narrow alleyway between a haberdashery and a visual art gallery, mostly oil paintings from the look of it, that bore closer looking at after his business was done. Down there was The Millhouse, the tavern where his contact was waiting with the next link in the chain.

Manolo took a moment to adjust the olive green business jacket he wore overtop a plain white, stiff-collared shirt, and looked at his reflection in the glass windows fronting the gallery. Even to his trained eye, the pistol he kept on his hip was barely visible as the slightest of lumps under his jacket. And of course no one would be able to detect that the jacket itself had a very special inner lining made of high-tensile nanoweave that could halt most pistol caliber projectiles, or that the thin-rimmed spectacles he wore had not one but two microminiature recording devices built into them.

Tip top. He was good to go.

He strode into the alleyway.

———

The interior of The Millhouse was bright and cheerful. The wall above the bar was one big bas relief of an old-school waterwheel-turned mill, situated alongside a swiftly-flowing river with tall evergreens growing beside and behind the mill.

It was a very well-done piece. Manolo could almost see the water splashing as it flowing over rocks in the foreground, and it seemed as though the waterwheel actually was on the cusp of turning.

Extremely well done.

The rest of the room was dominated by red leather-backed chairs around tables set for four, and a trio of booths at the rear. Swinging doors with transparent windows in their upper half off to the right side led to a kitchen, presumably, and restrooms, segregated by the two genders with subtle engravings that still were easy to make out even across the room, were to the rear, on the left.

The place smelled slightly of polished hardwood and disinfectant, like the proprietor had just finished cleaning. And an acoustic guitar was playing solo over speakers in the ceiling, melodic arpeggios at a slow tempo that made Manolo just want to relax and take his ease from the moment he stepped inside.

He liked the place immediately, but he wasn't here for pleasure. He swept his gaze over the half dozen patrons in the place until he spied his contact.

Damian was fifteen or twenty kilos overweight, though he carried it well with broad shoulders and a burly chest that spoke of lots of exercise in his youth. His close-cropped hair was more grey than brown, though his mustache retained its youthful coloration, and he was dressed in casual but quality slacks and a blue open collared shirt that was the style here on Heaven's Gate. He was seated at the center of the three booths in the rear, across from a woman Manolo didn't know.

Presumably she was the next link in the chain of conspiracy. As Manolo approached, he took her measure. Relatively young: early thirties. With coal-black hair and deeply tanned skin that spoke of ancestry from a more tropical environment. She wore a loose-fitting red blouse with the first two buttons undone for ventilation, and distraction and manipulation as well, no doubt. He pants were white, and appeared tight-fitting, and she had her hair back in a ponytail.

Damian noticed Manolo's approach and nodded in his direction, and the woman turned her head toward him. He dark eyes flicked up and down, taking his measure, and Manolo thought he saw a wisp of an approving smile on her lips for a second. But it was gone as soon as it came, and when he stopped at their table all that remained was an assessing stare.

"You must be Victor," the woman said, her tone as flat as her stare.

Though there was a lilting melodious quality to her voice; Manolo would bet good money she was a hell of a singer.

Damian cut in. "Vic, this is Sefi," he said, and slid further into the booth to make room for him.

Manolo nodded in greeting to Sefi as he positioned into the, wall-warmed, position Damian had just occupied. "Nice to meet you."

She sniffed slightly, and glanced from him to Damian and back. Then she reached inside the open front of her blouse and pulled out a small silver disk. She must have been hiding it in her bra, and Manolo found he envied it that hiding place. She really was well-proportioned, in that way.

Sefi plopped the disk down on the table between them and pressed her fingers onto three places around its edge. It made a soft click, then the briefest of low-pitched beeps.

Manolo kept his face calm, but inwardly he scowled. It was a bug-sniffer. If he had brought any of his surveillance drones with him, it would scramble any signal they tried to send out. As it was, it would play havoc with the recording elements in his spectacles. Though, the ISS was pretty good. There was an excellent chance his tech jockeys would be able to retrieve the recording. But still, that would take time.

Time that he might not have.

Sefi flashed another almost smile at him. "So we can talk private-ly," she said, by way of explanation for the sniffer.

"Ok..." Manolo let the word draw out, as though unsure about her meaning. His cover was not a guy who would know much about such things. After a second, he cleared his throat, then looked between her and Damian, putting on his best curious but also slightly confused look. "Damian said you needed help."

Sefi nodded. "I need an item transported off-world, without attracting attention from...certain authorities." She raised an eyebrow, then her eyes flicked toward Damian. "I'm told you have a knack for that."

And it was true. Manolo's cover was as the owner of an import/export company. And after he had met Damian he had proved his bona fides by helping him smuggle a trio of small shipments of illicit goods off-world, and eventually to the Tsago Dominance.

He had, of course, verified that none of the goods would actually pose any sort of threat to Imperial Security. And they had been relatively harmless; the sorts of things that he personally could not understand being on the prohibited list.

But he didn't make the laws; he just enforced them. And he had made careful notes of exactly what was shipped and when and sent them to Magden, the better to wrap everyone involved up when the time came.

"Shipping is my business, this is true," he said, leaning back against the cushions of the booth's seat. "What sort of item are we talking about?"

"None of your business, that's what kind. But it's about two meters by one by half a meter tall, and about eighty kilos mass." Her second eyebrow rose to join the first, as if to say, "Can you handle that?"

Manolo did some quick math, and that sounded awful coffin-sized to him. Which in a way confirmed the rumors that HQ had sniffed out. But if they were going to kill the Countess, why bother shipping her off-world?

That just left kidnapping for ransom. A very distasteful sort of caper, that.

Manolo found he relished the thought of taking these people down. And soon.

"Getting such a small bit of cargo up out of the well is child's play," he said. "But I need to know if it's volatile, or dangerous in some way. There's safety of the ship to consider. Not to mention," he leaned forward, clasping his hands together on the tabletop. "I'd be the one taking the risk of actually shipping it. That means I need to know what the hell it is."

Sefi kept her eyes locked on his, and after a moment that wisp of an approving smile returned. But this time it remained. She sniffed again and made a little gesture with her jaw toward Damian. "He said you were no fool. Glad to see he wasn't wrong. But..." She paused for a moment then gave a shrug that Manolo thought was supposed to be apologetic. "In this case, believe me when I say you're better off not knowing."

Manolo put on a genuine frown, then shook his head. "It'll cost extra."

"I can pay it."

"I haven't said how much extra. I ain't cheap."

Her lips turned fully upward into a genuine grin then, and Manolo knew two things. One, she was very well financed.

And two, he was in.

Manolo's ship wasn't his own, of course. It was owned by the ISS under the front company that he used as his cover for this mission. But it was a fully-capable bulk cargo carrier, able to haul several tens of thousands of metric tons of cargo—he didn't really know exactly how much, and now that he thought on it that was a tremendous oversight in his preparation—out of a standard gravity well, and then transport it through half a dozen interstellar jumps before needing to refuel.

But damn, was it ugly.

Blocky and squat, with large engine nacelles and a big ass that opened up so standardized rectagonal cargo containers could be rolled inside and secured in the hold, the easier to transfer them later for rail or shipborne transport on their destination planets. The crewed section up forward was tiny, compared with the cargo space, the bunk rooms positively cramped.

Manolo was thankful he didn't actually have to go up in the bloody thing.

He had arranged with Sefi to meet at his landing pad at the Sunset Docks, imaginatively named such because they lay on Theomor's western outskirts, at 0200, a week after their meeting in The Millhouse.

And so he stood there, cargo ramp lowered with the ship's crew chief at the top of the ramp ready to help secure the Countess' prison and the ship's Captain at his side. Waiting.

Of course the Crew Chief and the Captain were both also ISS operatives. And there was a short platoon of other operatives waiting in the darkness surrounding the pad for his signal to come in and secure the miscreants. Manolo had overseen their briefing personally, and they were kitted out with both lethal and non-lethal weapons, along with the latest in protective gear.

The objective was, of course, to take the criminals alive for trial, and everyone knew that.

But if Sefi and her crew decided they didn't want that...

Manolo's lips compressed as he considered how that might go down, and he felt the telltale tingling in his belly that told him he would have a full-on heartburn attack in the next hour or so. And he wished he'd thought to bring his antacid tablets.

Oh well, nothing to be done about that. He went back to watching and waiting, and did his best to ignore the oncoming discomfort.

The pad was circular in shape, and raised a meter or so above the surrounding tarmac. Loading ramps led from warehouses on either side toward the rear of the pad, to facilitate cargo loading, and there was a personnel ramp at the forward section where crew or other people could come and go with more ease. A computer terminal and keypad stood at the bottom of the ramp, where customs agents or the Dockmaster could log their inspections and clearances. Past that was a chain-link fence topped with razor wire, which had a gate large enough to admit a small vehicle and which currently stood wide open to admit Sefi's people.

When they arrived.

It never really got cold on Heaven's Gate, but at night the temperatures did become more temperate, and natives to the planet tended to wear jackets even though it was still t-shirt weather just about anywhere else. The Captain and Crew Chief were natives, and they had theirs on.

Manolo just stuck with his specially-lined suit coat.

A light breeze had been blowing from the north, bringing the scent of exhaust from the fuel processing facility that lay in that direction, but thankfully it seemed to be shifting around to the east, and instead of a cough-inducing stench it had become more of a minor annoyance when headlights shown through the gap in the gate and a small truck pulled up to the pad.

It was painted white, and was the kind of truck that a workman would own as his personal transportation. Nothing super heavy duty or fancy, just functional and non-flashy. It was a good choice for the night's excursion, with a covered cargo bed in the rear so onlookers couldn't get a notion of what was there.

Manolo found himself nodding in approval as it slowed to a crawl and then ascended the ramp, then followed the Captain's waved directions to come around the ship's forward landing struts toward the cargo ramp at its rear.

There the truck stopped and a quartet of men, and Sefi, got out. Sefi walked over to Manolo as the men got about opening the cargo bed.

"All set?" she asked, all about business.

Manolo nodded to her. "The ship can be off as soon as you're loaded."

Which was true. The bay was filled almost to capacity with legitimate cargo containers; in fact they had held off launching for two days to make this meeting. But she didn't need to know that.

Sefi nodded, then reached into her back pocket and pulled out a small rectangular tab with a universal plug adapter on own end. Handing it to Manolo, she said, "Money's all there."

He accepted the credit chip and pulled his own device out: a black chip reader and wallet the size of his palm with a universal port on its side and a display that took up most of its face. Inserting the credit chip, he tapped the display and saw the number he expected.

Impressed that she actually had been able to come up with such a sum, he looked up from the screen to the Captain and nodded.

He whistled and made a "saddle up" wave of his index finger to the Crew Chief, who hurried down the loading ramp to assist Sefi's men, who now were busy hauling a grey metallic box that did indeed look like a coffin out of the rear of the truck and up the ramp.

Manolo waited until the cargo was down inside the ship, then he gave the pre-determined signal. He coughed. Loudly.

Floodlights illuminated on all sides of the ship and the platoon advanced as one.

Almost instantly, the pad was flooded with armed and armored men, and almost before Sefi or her men could even register what was happening, they were down and covered by rifles and Manolo's men placed handcuffs on them.

Sefi looked up at him, her eyes wide with fury. "Victor, what the hell are you doing?"

"What's it look like?" he said. "I'm ISS. And you're under arrest for kidnapping and attempted murder of a member of the royal family."

Sefi's eyes went even wider as the import of his words struck her. The penalty for the crimes he had laid out were...large.

"Wait. Victor, you don't understand, I - "

He gave a jerk of his thumb to the officer who had charge of her and turned away. As he ascended the cargo ramp, he heard the officer drag her to her feet.

"Victor!" she called out as he dragged her away, but Manolo shut the rest of her words out of his mind as he came up next to the Crew Chief, who now was crouched next to the cargo they had just hauled aboard and working at a control pad on the side of it.

"How's it look?" Manolo asked.

The Crew Chief shrugged. "Not too difficult. I - "

The cargo container made a clicking noise, and the lid popped slightly ajar. The Crew Chief shot Manolo a quick grin, then he raised it the rest of the way open.

Manolo had never met Countess Poterick, of course. But he had seen her on the vids plenty of times. There was no mistaking the long, thick, curly black hair, the high cheekbones and sharp nose that so resembled her father, the later Emperor Archibald. That was definitely Emilia Bandemyr lying inside the cargo container, dressed in a grey jumpsuit without emblem and fast asleep, with a number of IVs and monitoring devices hooked up to her.

The Crew Chief leaned over her and whistled, looking at the equipment that she was hooked up to.

"They've got enough sedative and IV nutrients here to keep her asleep and well for over a month, looks like," he said.

Manolo grunted. That figured. It would be enough time to get her just about anywhere in the Empire, and several places outside of the Empire, if that were the abductors' goal.

"Can you revive her?"

The Crew Chief considered for a moment, then nodded. "Looks pretty simple, actually. Let me just..." He trailed off as he got to work, and a few moments later, the Countess began to stir.

A minute or two after that, she opened her eyes, and blinked at the overhead illumination in the cargo bay.

"Wh - " she said. "Where am - ?"

Manolo leaned over the container so she could see him more clearly. "I'm Officer Manolo Garces with ISS, Countess. You're here on Heaven's Gate, and perfectly safe."

"Heaven's Gate?" The Countess' eyes widened, and she moved to sit up, but the various tubes and monitoring cables stopped her more or less in place. "What about Sefi and - "

"We have them in custody," Manolo said, as gently as he could. "Like I said, you're safe."

"No." She shook her head, as though to clear it. Then blinked three times. Then she looked back at him with firm, focused eyes. "You must release them, Officer Garces."

Manolo blinked, then shook his head. "You don't understand, Countess. We - "

"No, *you* don't understand. Sefi works for me, and you will release her. Immediately."

What in the - ?

Manolo saw the Crew Chief look up at him with an expression of utter confusion, and knew that was nothing compared to how he must look, right that moment.

Manolo always preferred clean, well-lit, and comfortable interrogation rooms. It was easier to set the subject's mind at ease in that kind of setting, which in turn made it easy to convince him—or in this case, her—to start talking, like they were friends.

The interrogation room on the fifth floor of the ISS Branch Office in Theomor was everything he could have wanted and more. Clean off-white walls. Stuffed chairs for interrogator and subject both. A nice black-framed coffee table between them. Even a coffee machine in the corner.

But he never thought he'd be interrogating a member of the royal family in a room like this. Never in a million years.

Emilia Bandemyr was still dressed in her jumpsuit, but she had the regal bearing of a woman dressed to the nines in the finest ball gown, and she sat upon her chair as though it was a throne as she sipped at the coffee he had made for her.

Not sure even where to begin, he just sat back in his own chair, his own mug of coffee still sitting on the table in front of him where he had placed it five minutes ago, and said nothing, waiting for her to start.

Finally, she lowered her mug and looked at him with frank eyes.

"You are aware of the circumstances of my marriage to Count Poterick."

Manolo shrugged. "As much as any member of the public, I suppose, my lady."

"It was my father's arranging. The lynchpin that ensured Heaven's Gate and her associated systems would enter the Empire without bloodshed." She sipped from her mug again. "A political alliance, to the benefit of both."

Manolo nodded. Not exactly a new story. Political marriages had been going on since marriage first became a thing, way back in the mists of antiquity.

"I agreed to it, of course. Count Poterick is not a bad looking man, and he seemed reasonably charming. And, I was eager to do my duty for the Empire." Was that a faint hint of irony there in her voice at the end? "I like to think my father would not have forced me, had I refused it." She looked away from Manolo, toward the closed door to her left, the room's only exit. "I'm certain he would never have consented himself if he truly knew what kind of man Count Poterick is."

A pause, where she drank another gulp. Then she shook her head again. "Or maybe he would have went ahead with it anyway." She half-smiled, half-smirked and looked back at Manolo. "You know how ruthless he could be."

In point of fact, Manolo didn't. Not personally. But he had heard the stories, and some of them were ugly.

But then again, you couldn't argue with results, and utterly ruthless or no, Archibald Bandemyr had grown the Empire from a collection of a few allied star systems to the three dozen system behemoth it now was. There was a lot to say for that accomplishment.

But something told Manolo that Emilia wouldn't want to hear that right this moment, so instead he kept quiet and just nodded.

"Anyway, I agreed. And at first it was alright. Good, even. But after the first year..." She shook her head. "He drinks, you know."

That Manolo did know. Poterick was well known as a lush with a fondness for brandy.

"The last couple years, when he drinks, he..." She trailed off, but her left hand moved from her coffee mug to her side, where she rubbed at herself, and just barely didn't hold back a wince. She inhaled quickly, probably to cover the lapse, for all the good it would do. "Anyway, I tried to make it work, but it got to the point where I grew certain he was going to - " She lowered her eyes, looking at the coffee table instead of Manolo now. "Well, I became afraid something bad was going to happen."

Which meant she had grown to be in fear of her life. Manolo had seen it many times before over the years, from both sexes. But the women were more willing to admit the problem than the men who suffered similarly. For obvious reasons.

"Did you tell the Emperor? He surely would have granted you a divorce, under the circumstances."

Emilia shook her head. "Before father died, it hadn't become that bad. But since then..." She shook her head again, more vigorously as she straightened back up to her previous regal demeanor. "You know of the reforms my brother has sought to implement since he took the throne."

"I don't follow politics, my lady," Manolo said, truthfully. It wasn't his place to look into or comment on the machinations of the nobility. Though of course he had seen some word of Emperor's Lucien's policy changes on the vids. He just didn't obsess over them, like some did.

Emilia raised an eyebrow at that, as though she didn't really believe him. "Many of the great houses oppose his policies. He is literally fighting for his life, and Poterick is one of his few vocal allies. If I - " She looked away again, and spoke more quietly. "He would probably kill Poterick if I told him. Challenge him to a duel and kill him. Veritas Morte, just like with Minister Ymmersen."

Manolo had heard of that. Of the former Minister of Diplomacy's treachery, and the plot to poison both Emperor Archibald and then Crown Prince Lucien, and how the Minister had challenged the Prince to a duel to the death to avoid facing the legal repercussions of his deeds.

Ymmersen had killed a dozen men in duels before, and was confident in his ability to win through again.

But Prince Lucien surprised them all, and won. And now he was Emperor and Ymmersen didn't even get a traitor's grave; they jettisoned his corpse, nude, from the airlock of the Imperial flagship.

"Lucien can't afford to lose Poterick's support. So, to answer your question, no I haven't told him. And I will not."

It wasn't hard to figure out the rest of the story. "So you decided to run away."

She nodded. "Whether from a duel or an Imperial Decree of Divorce, Lucien would lose a key ally. But if I just disappeared..."

She didn't say the rest, but she didn't need to. It wasn't a bad plan, per say. But -

"But where were you going?"

"Capestra. Princess Ophelia made arrangements for me. A new identity, a place to live, income."

Manolo recoiled, shock making his mouth drop open and his eyes grow wide. "The Capestrani Republic? We came within a hair's breadth of outright war with them over the Corellis incident, when your brother took the throne. And you were going to engineer a plot that made it look like they kidnapped the Emperor's sister?!"

Emilia gave him a flat, disapproving stare that faltered after a second. She looked down. "I thought you said you don't follow politics."

He didn't bother gracing that statement with a reply.

Emilia drew a breath, and continued. "It's not commonly known, but Ophelia and Lucien are close." She gave a little chuckle. "I think he may ask for her hand some day, actually. She was going to get in touch with him through back channels to let him know what happened. Once I got there safely and there was nothing Poterick could do about it. Lucien would know the truth, but to everyone else it would be like I just vanished without a trace."

"With all due respect, my lady, that is a terrible plan, and we're all lucky it didn't work."

She gave him a little scowl that didn't quite reach her eyes. "And how did it fail, exactly?"

Manolo looked at her for a long moment, mulling over how much to tell her of the full operation that her plotting had put into motion. Finally, he just shrugged. "Some of our informers sent word of some sort of plot against you. Protection of the royal family is one of ISS' primary duties, so they sent me to see to investigate."

"You came to protect me."

Manolo nodded.

"Then protect me." Her eyes flicked to the north, in the general direction of the Count's palace. "From him." She leaned forward. "Send me on to Capestra, and away from here."

Manolo shook his head. "My lady, I cannot do that. I cannot send the Emperor's sister into the clutches of a foreign power, especially one that, when all the chips are down, may end up being our enemy."

"Well I'm not going back to him, so where does that leave us?"

Where indeed? Manolo had been pondering that since before the interview started, and was racking his brain all the more now. He only saw one route that avoided complete disaster, both for her, for the Empire, and for his own career.

"You must go to Qora," he said, finally. "To tell your brother everything."

"No, I told you. If he loses Poterick - "

"And if Poterick had done something...permanent? Wouldn't His Majesty have lost him then, as well?"

Emilia's mouth abruptly closed, her teeth making an audible clacking sound it closed quickly, and so hard. Her regal calm wavered, and her lips compressed. She looked away from him again, and Manolo saw her eyes begin to water up.

Then she inhaled forcefully through her nose, blinked, and gave her head a little toss. When she looked back at him, the royal demeanor was back again, like it had never fled.

Manolo found he admired her, for that.

"What about my people?"

"Sefi and her lot?"

She nodded.

"They will remain in custody pending His Majesty's decision on this matter."

She was silent for a long time, then she looked down and nodded.

And that settled the matter.

The order to release Sefi, Damian, and their associates came through six weeks after the Countess left for Qora, as well as an Imperial Decree of Divorce ending her marriage to Count Poterick.

Manolo didn't see it, but he heard through the rumor mill that the Count received a personal summons to the Emperor, to discuss the matter. But, he knew the Count left on a ship that rumor said was packed full of brandy bottles.

He never heard what came of Poterick's meeting with the Emperor, however, because by then Manolo had departed Heaven's Gate. New orders came for him to investigate the apparent taking of a cargo ship under the flag of the Tsago Dominance by pirates based out of the Cordant System.

That promised to be interesting. He had investigated all manner of crimes in the past, but never an outright act of piracy.

So when he boarded his ship for Cordant, Manolo put all curiosity about the Count's fate out of his mind and focused solely on the new mission before him.

It wasn't his place to question the machinations of the nobility, anyway.

42

DRILLING FOR GOLD

Autonomous Drilling Unit Seven detected an overspeed condition on one of its drill motor drivetrains. Motor number six was approaching the upper limit of its allowed operational speed band, and the monitoring speed sensor flashed an alert.

This prompted a series of diagnostic algorithms, which ADU-7 performed in the background while it continued to monitor the status of the rest of its systems.

Drill motors one through five and seven through ten were operating normally. Speed, lube oil return temperature, current draw, and bearing temperature readings all in the normal band.

Primary drive engine output was at sixty-four percent, and forward velocity 2.4 meters per minute. Below optimal speed to reach the objective on time, but to be expected as external mineral analyzers located in ten locations around ADU-7's drilling cone had tasted iron starting 45 minutes earlier. It previously had been passing through limestone, which was a much easier material to penetrate, and had gained significant time on its schedule. So there was little risk of violating mission parameters.

The diagnostic algorithms completed, and the results appeared in ADU-7's primary access memory for review.

Prediction of drive shaft sheer on drill motor number six within 0.36 hours. Probability seventy-two percent.

Drive motor number six was located just below the center of ADU-7's drill cone. Additional algorithms activated, computing anticipated reduction in drilling rate from loss of capacity on drive motor number six. Results came back in microseconds.

Predicted loss of 0.4 meters per minute.

Odds of reaching programmed destination of schedule reduced by 27.8 percent.

ADU-7 checked mission parameters, and found the new results outside of acceptable criteria, so it sent a message to its customer interface unit, four and a half kilometers behind at the beginning of the tunnel ADU-7 had been drilling.

"What's up ADU?"

The human—Yanish, who was the one on watch at this time—pronounced it AHDOO instead of the proper pronunciation of A-D-U. Not for the first time, ADU-7 restrained itself from issuing a correction. It had tried—and failed—to impress upon its current customers the importance of etiquette many times already.

"Predicted failure of number 6 drill motor, resulting in failure to meet mission schedule. Initiating shutdown and drill retraction. Estimated repair time: twenty-six minutes."

The human took a small eternity to process this, 0.78 seconds.

"Shit. Do you have the spare parts onboard for the job?"

ADU-7 had run a check of internal stores as part of the diagnostic algorithm check. "Affirmative. No customer assistance required."

"How will that affect the schedule?"

"Probability of meeting schedule post-repair is within acceptable mission parameters."

"Ok..." The long pause suggested Yanish didn't know all of the parameters in question. Unsurprising. "Let us know if you need anything."

"Affirmative."

ADU-7 secured the conversation with its customer and focused on completing the drill shutdown procedure, while a subroutine fetched the needed parts from its onboard storage units.

After ADU-7's drill motors came to a stop, it reversed its primary drive engine, retreating 6.28 meters back down the drilled-out tunnel to ensure the drill heads pulled free of debris. Then it deployed two repair drones, their sensors and operating systems slaved to ADU-7's repair procedures sub-processor.

The drones were designed to be maneuverable in tight clearances, crab-like with collapsible legs and two deployable manipulator arms, one on either side of their forward sensor clusters.

It required a significant reallocation of processing resources, and a reprioritization of which parameters to monitor continuously and which to update periodically, to collate new sensor data from the drones. ADU-7 had protocols in memory for predicted optimal processing and collation arrangement, but it had to evaluate those protocols against actual operating conditions.

This took a fair amount of time, 0.012 seconds, after which ADU-7 determined the default protocols would perform acceptably.

By then the drones had obtained the needed repair parts, so ADU-7 deployed them to their required repair positions and got to work.

Jordan chewed his menthol tobacco-flavored gum and severely wished it was the real thing. He hadn't chewed the real stuff in ten years, since his older brother had come down with mouth cancer that took his tongue and most of his lower jaw. They hadn't had the money to grow replacements, so he lived with electromechanical prosthetics now.

Nowhere near the real thing, and life sucked for him as a result.

Soon as that happened, Jordan had given up on chew completely. But he still felt the need for something in his mouth, and he missed the taste of it.

Hence the gum. But some days, it really was a poor substitute.

As he bent over the plastic and metal fold-out table he had set up in the outer room of his crew's little headquarters, in the bottom of a narrow canyon three and a half miles southwest of Miller's Crossing, the center of commerce and government on this part of New Aukland, he felt a hefty craving for some real no kidding nicotine.

His grand plan was all starting to come together, but there were so many variables. So many things that could still go wrong...

"Damn," he said, and closed his eyes for a second, willing himself to focus, and be calm.

The printout on the table hadn't changed in any of the hundred or more times he'd studied it. But now as it was approaching go time, he felt the need to stare at it, hunt for that one wrinkle he missed that could get them all locked away for a good chunk of the rest of their lives.

The printout contained the blueprints for the New Aukland Savings Bank depository. And not the fake ones on file in the city records office, the real construction blueprints that only a select few got access to.

He'd paid good money for a copy, through some very dangerous contacts. But this job needed precision planning, and he needed to know exactly where everything in that building was.

And in particular, the location and dimensions of the vault in their sub basement, four stories below the main building.

He bent close, until his nose was practically touching the paper, and traced out each individual line.

It was still the same. But he could swear he had missed something.

"Just nerves," he said, and straightened, but not before a drop of sweat fell onto the blueprint and sat there like a little immovable lens, distorting the white line drawn onto blue background that showed the edge of the vault's wall.

Chuckling, Jordan thought for the hundredth time that they really should have installed an air conditioner in here. It was summertime in the middle of the desert, and it got hot in this little wood-walled cabin he and his crew had built.

Oh well, too late now.

He turned away from the table just as the bare wooden door to the back room opened and Yanish stepped through. He was taller than Jordan by an inch, and darker of skin, but he was beanpole skinny so Jordan was pretty sure he had a good ten or fifteen pounds on him.

Yanish's thick black hair spilled down his head almost to his shoulders, and his brown eyes normally sparkled with good humor. Right now, though...

"We've had a development with ADU," Yanish said, wiping his palms on his jeans. He was sweating; the underarms of his t-shirt were noticeably damp. Which was weird considering the back room really was just the entrance to the cave where they'd set up the drilling unit, and caves never got hot. "It had to stop to repair a bad drive motor."

"Dammit."

Jordan turned away from him and stepped over to the front room's lone window, which looked out toward the canyon's entrance, a third of a mile distant around a bend that was obscured by boulders and scrub brush.

"How long?" Jordan asked.

"About a half hour to fix. It says we're still within acceptable mission parameters, though."

Jordan nodded. "Well, that's good. Had me worried for a minute there." He'd had Gregor program the drill to stick to a 98% chance of making schedule or better. If it said they were still there...no disaster.

Yet.

"Sorry, but I thought you'd want to know."

"Thanks." He looked back at Yanish and raised an eyebrow at him. "Holler if anything else happens. If it gets there too late, or if it breaks through before Gregor takes down the security..." He didn't say the rest; he didn't need to.

"Sure thing, boss."

With the repairs completed, ADU-7 found itself making better progress than it had projected before stopping. A quick analysis of motor current draw versus forward speed showed that Drive Motor Number Six's degradation had affected progress more than ADU-7 had initially detected.

Now, it revised its schedule performance predictions and found it would reach programmed end of drilling slightly early. It reduced primary engine power to compensate, then went back to monitoring its various system parameters.

An alert popped up from ADU-7's customer preference program; it was to report when twenty minutes away from destination. So it sent another message to the customer interface unit.

A different human responded. ADU-7 recognized its vocal patterns as Shen.

"Report."

"Unit approached programmed destination. Estimated time of arrival 20.37 minutes."

"Standby."

ADU-7 had noted that Shen was much less talkative than Yanish. It preferred that; more efficient.

"ADU, proceed to destination."

"Acknowledged." Then it cut contact with the customer interface unit.

20.24 minutes later, the tip of ADU-7s drill cone penetrated a new material that the mineral analyzers registered as manmade concrete. Then the cone emerged into open space.

ADU-7 halted, and again consulted its customer preferences. It ordered ADU-7 to proceed completely out of its drilled tunnel, and turn on its forward-mounted spotlights.

It complied.

Jordan and his team hurried down the tunnel as soon as Shen relayed the message from ADU. Six men, pushing three antigrav loading pallets between them, making time down the rough, unpaved tunnel with only the illumination provided by the head-lamps each wore.

The antigrav loading pallets he'd chosen for this job were industrial strength. Painted black and yellow, they looked like normal wheeled dollies, with a metal handle and push-bar on one end, a couple feet above the dolly itself. Except that instead of wheels, they used antigrav plates to support the weight loaded onto them, and had a control pad mounted on the push-bar.

Much better choice for navigating that tunnel than wheeled units.

Still, now that he thought about it, this was an incredibly dangerous and dumb way to handle this part.

They should have strung up lights behind ADU as it went, or something.

"I knew I forgot something," he said to himself, and chuckled.

If that's all it ended up being, they were home free.

It was a bit more than five kilometers to the end of the tunnel. If Jordan had been running in the open, he could cover that distance in about 25 minutes. Going down this tunnel, it took more like 40. Which meant ADU would be sitting in the vault for 10-20 minutes before his team got there.

But Gregor had successfully killed the bank's security feeds, so he had no fear of that gap in time giving the caper away.

Still, it pressed him on to greater speed.

When they finally emerged from the tunnel into the vault, Jordan's legs were wobbly from exertion and he was breathing heavily. Sweat streamed down his torso, making his shirt cling to his skin.

But none of that mattered, because stepping around the rear of the drill brought the rest of the vault into view.

The vault floor, ceiling, and walls were made of poured concrete on three sides, and steel on the fourth. The main vault door was round and, from this side, just looked like a circle of steel set into the rest of the steel of the wall.

It was closed up tight. Good. Except that it kept all the dust from

ADU's final push through contained; it still lingered in the air, smelling of damp and dirt, and making Jordan want to sneeze.

But so what?

The trio of pallets sitting against the vault wall adjacent to the door, directly in front of the wall ADU had breached, brought a joyous smile to Jordan's face.

Or more specifically, the 300 gold ingots sitting on those pallets did.

Jordan turned to look at the rest of his crew, all of them except Shen, who was keeping watch back in the cabin, and Gregor, who was still making his way back from Miller's Crossing.

"Let's get it done," Jordan said, and the others nodded.

Yanish pushed a cardboard box off of his pallet before pushing it over to the gold. Three of Jordan's men broke the box open and took charges out, which they began planting in the mouth of the tunnel ADU had just dug.

By the time Jordan, Yanish, and Tom, a deceptively soft-spoken guy Jordan had known since grade school, had the antigrav pallets fully loaded, the charges were in place and it was time to go.

Tom pushed the first of the pallets into the tunnel, and the charge-layers followed him. Then Yanish. That just left Jordan, and the three last charges. He'd wanted to place them himself.

He picked them up off the floor where his guy had left them and made a circuit of ADU. He placed one of the charges on either side of its main engine block, and the third at the top of its drill cone, just behind the grinding teeth.

Then he stepped back and looked at the drill for a second.

He wasn't sure why, but he said, 'Thanks ADU."

Then he turned and pushed his pallet of gold into the tunnel, and started jogging.

When he got halfway down the tunnel, he'd call Shen and have him order ADU to return. Then after they were all out they'd blow the charges and take out both ends of the tunnel and ADU, burn their cabin, and head to a distant beach on another planet, with pretty much all the evidence destroyed.

It was all coming together.

ADU-7 received the order to return to origin from the customer interface unit, and maneuvered to comply.

It wasn't hard to retrace its route, as it had simply driven straight once its drill cone emerged into air, and then stopped. But when it re-entered the tunnel its mineral sensors signaled an alert to ADU-7's primary access memory.

Volatile compound detected.

Volatiles were potentially dangerous to workers, and could potentially compromise ADU-7's ability to properly complete its assigned mission. Protocol required stopping when they were detected, and investigation to determine the extent of the danger.

Acting in accordance with protocol, ADU-7 stopped halfway into the tunnel entrance and dispatched its two repair drones.

They skittered up to the top of ADU-7's drill cone and located five distinct volatile locations. Investigation with their thermal and visual imagers showed that they were flat disks stuck in place on the tunnel's upper half, and that each of the objects had a red light on it.

ADU-7 processed this and could not come up with a known correlation, so it directed the repair drones to attempt to remove them. They were able to succeed with little difficulty, using their manipulator arms, and ADU-7 directed them to deposit the unknown objects into its part storage units for later analysis.

But as one of the drones proceeded to do so, it detected another of the objects, on ADU-7 itself, just behind the cutting portion of its drill cone.

This continuing anomaly required several consecutive processing cycles to analyze, but ADU-7 could not come to a satisfactory determination. After an additional cycle, it directed that drone to take the latest anomalous object to one of its mineral analysis sensors.

When the drone placed the object directly onto the mineral

analysis sensor, the sensor immediately flagged a more detailed alert to the primary access memory.

Direct contact allowed a much more thorough analysis than proximity alone, and the material was identified as a manmade explosive.

ADU-7 had to spend more cycles, more than it had ever spent on any single task before, processing this new data.

It had already completed drilling the programmed tunnel. Why would explosives be needed?

It had no explanation, so ADU-7 went back through all its data again, from the moment it had emerged from the tunnel, and immediately found information it had not processed.

In addition to floodlights, ADU-7 had forward looking cameras, and they were activated by the same breakers and commands that activated the lights. Mission parameters did not require ADU-7 to utilize or transmit images from the cameras so it had not processed them. But the cameras still recorded imagery.

Now ADU-7 analyzed those recordings, and immediately several alerts were placed into primary access memory, from half a dozen different subsystems and processes.

Jordan emerged from the tunnel to find the rest of his crew all smiles. They were clapping each other on the back, and he immediately felt a flash of chagrin.

"Save the celebration til we're out of here," he said.

One and all his crew looked at him and their smiles faded. Yanish's did more than that. His smile fled, replaced by a look of shock, then he actually went pale.

"Boss," he said, his voice sounding ragged, like he was being strangled.

"You ok - " Jordan started to say, but a shout from out front interrupted him.

The door flung open and Shen dashed in, looking grave.

"There are lights out by the canyon entrance, and I think I heard a helicopter."

What in the hell? "Gregor's on the way back. He's - "

"BOSS!"

Jordan looked back at Yanish, and he was pointing at the drill's customer interface unit.

Jordan turned around to look at it, and the bottom dropped out of his stomach.

The customer interface unit had a text message written on its screen in a clear, bold font.

YOU ARE IN VIOLATION OF DEVISON ROBOTICS COMPANY END USER LICENSE AGREEMENT FOR AUTOMATED DRILL UNIT MODEL 18362

Section 4.2.5.5

"You may not use this product for any purpose that violates any law, custom, or moral standard on New Aukland or any other planetary system, anywhere in the universe. Failure to comply with this clause may incur civil and/or criminal penalties."

THIS UNIT HAS INFORMED THE APPROPRIATE AUTHORITIES OF THIS VIOLATION

Have A Nice Day

It was like being smacked across the face with a cricket bat.

After all his planning, meticulous to the T, here it was. The thing Jordan had missed. The thing that was going to get them all locked away for a good chunk of the rest of their lives.

"Wha- " Yanish swallowed, then tried to speak again. "What do we do?"

Just then came a crash from the front room, and a shout of "Police!"

Jordan closed his eyes, hoping for a second that this was all just a bad dream. But the shout came again, from more than one voice this time.

He opened his eyes back up and looked at Yanish, and he shook his head in apology.

"I guess we go to prison."

43

DROPS IN THE STORM

The lighting in the overhead seemed to swirl, making little multicolored kaleidoscope patterns in the air over Grant's head. Twist and swirl, swirl and twist.

He felt like his entire body was swirling along with the lights, like he was moving in time with them, and more. Like he was about to float up, way up there to be with them, in the warmth of their glow.

Only the top of his head was holding him down on the ground.

Only the top.

He threw up his hands, grasping toward the spiraling lights above him. Maybe if he could reach high enough, he could overcome that resistance and he could go where he was meant to.

Up.

Up, up and away.

There was sound all around him, murmurs and rumblings, something that seemed almost like speech, or maybe a musical note here and there. But nothing that he could put his finger on.

Not that it mattered. Nothing mattered, really.

But damn, he couldn't get past that resistance.

Slumping back down, he felt his arms fall to his sides, but that only registered faintly beneath the frustration bordering on anger that swept through him.

He needed to go up. HAD to go up.

But his Damn. Head. Wouldn't. LET. HIM!

There was a wall somewhere; he vaguely remembered that. Like the memory of a dream from when he was two years old. He knew the fact of the wall, but he couldn't grasp the reality.

But there was one nearby. Somewhere.

Maybe...

He stumbled forward, only remembering he even had feet in the split second it took between when he started to fall and when he reflexively adjusted his stance to keep himself upright.

The stutter-step drew his gaze down from the mesmerizing spirals, and he became aware of shapes in the world around him. Blobs, not amorphous so much as blurred out, washed beneath the sheen from above. But he could just tell the blobs were multi-colored.

And they moved.

Off to the left—or was it right—they moved in unison, like an external force was directing them. And for a second, he almost could feel that force; rhythmic, pulsing. But then it faded back into the general murmur all around.

To the right—left?—their movement was more random; some remained still.

Part of Grant's mind screamed at him that he should be wary, lest the blobs get him. Another, louder part chided that as paranoia. They were here to have a good time, just like Grant was.

No enemies in a good time.

He inhaled through his nose, and found that the odors around him weren't washed out by the glorious spiral above. Not at all. A musky, almost sweet, scent overtop moist sourness that triggered another of those almost-memories, and he flashed to a locker room, way back in High School.

Just as quickly as it came, the flash went, and Grant was looking back up at the spirals again.

He gaped at their beauty, and he longed for them.

It was warm enough here, but there would be even warmer, the bliss even more sublime.

He tried jumping, and for a second he thought he'd done it.

Then his feet struck the unyielding surface beneath him, and that frustration flared up even higher.

Damn this stupid head, keeping him down!

He pushed forward, driving his heels into the floor, and two of the blobs directly ahead parted so he could pass. He heard the general murmuring grow more distinct, chagrined.

Then he was past, and he moved on until his outstretched hand contacted something hard.

Hard, and angled. Like a wall.

A wall rounding a corner.

He knew it was there. And here was his answer.

He couldn't get up with his head holding him back.

So he stepped back, lowered his head, and charged forward.

The flash of light and searing pain when the top of his head struck the corner was hot, almost scalding. For a second, the world and the lights and the blobs all congealed and slowed, then stopped, and he caught a glimpse of a nightclub, with multicolored spotlights shining down from the ceiling. People in party attire scattered all around, those off to the right dancing to the DJ's beat.

And shrieks of shock from people nearby to him, as they all looked at him with mouths agape.

Then the flash flew away and it was all murmuring and blobs again.

And Grant was light below the pain in his crown.

But not light enough. Still the top of his head held him down, down away from where he needed to go.

Up, and up. Up, and up.

He stepped back and charged the corner again.

And again.

And again.

At some point, he stopped feeling the pain.

And then he stopped feeling anything at all.

The club was awash in pandemonium. Panicked party-goers, all decked out in club attire and most at least a couple sheets to the wind from booze, drugs, or both, were pushing back from the countertop below which Piotr's target now lay limply in a slowly expanding pool of blood and grey matter.

He had been in the prime of life, and was dressed to the nines, enjoying what he didn't know was to be his last night in this world.

Considering what he had done, it was fitting that Grant now was cast aside like so many rags. In disgrace and filth.

Alone among the people in the vicinity of the place where Grant had shattered his own skull and poured his grey matter out onto the floor, Piotr did not flee. He just stood in his navy blue suit and unbuttoned white collared shirt, arms crossed over his chest, with his back against the red-painted wall of the nightclub, and watched.

Watched, and felt neither pity nor revulsion nor remorse. Just satisfaction.

And excitement for the future.

The compound had worked better than he ever could have imagined. Just one drop into Grant's glass, during a carefully choreographed pass by the waiter who was bringing it to Grant's table.

One drop had set him off enough to do...that.

Impressive.

Piotr hadn't believed the scientist's claim. How it had driven a test subject to blow the top of his own head off with a .45. He assumed it was just braggadocio.

Apparently not.

Amazing.

The DJ's music turned off, the news of the event having finally reached him. Gone was the pounding bass and the electronic semi-melody, and now the only sounds were women's shrieks and men's expressions of shock as the crowd continued to back away.

Then, in the distance, sirens.

Paramedics. And Police, for certain.

They would have no reason to suspect Piotr. No way to connect him to Grant at all. And they wouldn't be able to detect the compound in Grant's bloodstream, let alone identify it. Piotr still carried the compound on his person in a small vial in the inner pocket of his suit coat, but it would appear just as a vial of cologne; even had a nice manly musk to it if sniffed.

Fortunately it had no effect unless swallowed; for whatever reason the scent receptors in a person's nose couldn't carry it.

That was another of the scientist's claims that Piotr hadn't bought. Until the scientist demonstrated by sniffing it himself.

Crazy egghead.

It all added up to there being no reason the authorities would detain him, or pay him any mind at all.

All the same, there was nothing to be gained by waiting for them to arrive.

So he pushed himself off the wall and turned to his left, toward the hallway that housed the bathrooms at the rear of the club and, in the same hallway, the rear stairwell down to the ground floor, and then the exit.

For whatever reason, the herd of people had all pressed toward the front exit, so Piotr had an easy time of it, and he stepped outside into the rear parking lot just as he heard the squeal of brakes as the authorities pulled to a halt around the front of the brick-faced former warehouse that now was down-town Toledo's most exclusive...and soon to be most infamous...nightclub.

Piotr sniffed, smiling ever so slightly as he slipped his sunglasses on despite the night's dark and zigzagged his way through the lot, three quarters full of parked cars that cost more than most people earned in two years of work.

The kinds of people who bought cars like that had no idea the storm about to swoop down upon them.

Yes, this had been a very successful night, indeed. It had taken a serial rapist—uncharged, but guilty nonetheless—off the grid and sent him straight to hell.

And it had provided a test run and proof of concept for the opening salvos in the war to come.

A war of liberation, one far too long in coming.

Oh, there was a storm coming indeed.

As he stepped out of the lot and turned left, walking down the sidewalk along a four-lane street that was still busy despite the late hour, he pulled a flip phone out of his coat pocket.

It was a burner, purchased by a guy he'd met outside the convenience store that sold them in exchange for a twenty. Untraceable, to Piotr or to anyone he knew.

Except for one person. But there was no danger in talking with her; she had no ties that mattered. He had made certain to keep her far away from his plans, and his compatriots.

What was not known could not cause her harm. Nor could she betray it, even unintentionally.

He hit Susan's number and pressed DIAL. A moment later, her voice came on the line.

"Da?"

"It is done," Piotr said, simply and without inflection.

She would know it was him; know his voice. He would not have tried to conceal his identity from her even if he didn't have such joyous news to bring to her.

Her breath caught, and he could envision her mouth opening slightly from surprise. She knew his intent; knew he would not rest until the man who had violated his sister paid for what he had done. But she could not have brought herself to believe he actually would —could—do it.

She always had refused to see that her little brother was not a little boy anymore.

"You are certain?"

"Certain."

Her voice broke then, and he heard a sob, quickly pulled back. In his mind's eye, she was blinking away tears, wiping her cheeks with the back of her free hand as she struggled to keep her composure, even there in the privacy of her bedroom.

"I don't - " She stopped talking, clearly unsure what to say.

"Say nothing. I will talk with you again in a few days. I love you, Susachka."

Then Piotr hung up and closed the phone.

He thought for a moment, then tossed the phone into a nearby trash can. Probably excessively cautious, but was there really any such thing? Burners were easy to obtain, and cheap. And he decided he could not take even the slightest risk Susan could get dragged into this thing he was beginning.

He continued down the street, picking up his pace as he went, to where he had parked his car—used and economical, unlike the monstrosities in the parking lot he had just exited—half a mile from the club.

The heels of his mirror-polished shoes made soft, rhythmic clopping noises, like the ticking of a clock. His smile, unbidden, grew until he felt the skin of his cheeks stretch.

It all had gone according to plan, without even the slightest difficulty.

He was ready. It was time to start preparations in earnest. And then...then comes the storm.

Soon, now.

Soon.

44

MISS MELODY AND THE SPRUCE TRAIL

I t wasn't every day that you rounded a bend in a hiking trail and found a cafe there, waiting for you.

At first, Jeff thought he was seeing things. He blinked, then rubbed his eyes. But when he opened them it was still there.

Right there at the side of the creek that was meandering its way down from the ridge Jeff had been scaling for most of the morning, on a patch of relatively level ground that was remarkably clear of trees.

The rest of the trail had been shaded by oaks...or were they elms? Hell, Jeff never could tell one tree from the next except that they looked different; he didn't know their names.

And he didn't figure he had to, to enjoy being out among them.

But whatever their names, he had been in the shade of their limbs and leaves for the last three and a half hours, meandering his way along the trail from the little pull-off by the side of the road that acted as the trail head. He had been the only person in the pull-off when he arrived, and he hadn't seen a soul the entire time he'd been making the slow but steady ascent up the mountain.

And that was just the way he wanted it. Just him and nature, nothing to listen to except the wind rustling the tree limbs, his Kresta

Hikers digging into the dirt of the trail, and the occasional scurrying of a small critters scampering away through the underbrush.

Nothing to smell except dirt and growing things, and nature, and life.

He always came out hiking when he needed to clear his head, and after last night he needed that more than he ever had. He'd found the listing for this trail—it was called Red Spruce Summit, though that wasn't the name of the ridge, so what the hell—and he'd never done it before, so he'd packed his day pack, filled two water bottles, donned his hiking boots, and headed out at first light.

It had been cool at first, but now as it was approaching noon the early summer heat was swelling, and his red t-shirt was nearly soaked with his sweat. At least it was good wicking material. His cargo shorts were getting wet too. Despite the relatively small grade, the trail hadn't exactly been easy, meandering up over the occasional boulder patch. And despite being simple to follow—he almost didn't need the trail blazes on the trees, the path was so worn from years of footsteps—it had been far from smooth walking even without the rocks.

So he was feeling it in his thighs, and he had been thinking to sit down a take a rest.

And then the cafe appeared as he rounded yet another wall of rocks, and he stopped, cold.

It could have been on Main Street in a Norman Rockwell painting. One story. Brick front with big wide display windows. A swinging glass door allowing entrance, with a sign overhead the display window. In a font that somehow seemed to exude cheer and well-being through just the shape of the letters alone, he read, "Miss Melody's Cafe. Food for the Body. Healing for the Soul."

Jeff looked left, then right, still convinced he was seeing things.

Was he that dehydrated already? It was warm, bordering on hot, and humid, but he'd brought two 1-liter bottles of water and he'd been making sure to drink.

He checked his bottles real quick, tucked into pouches on either side of his day pack.

The left one was almost empty; he could tell from the weight. The right one full.

So yeah, he'd been drinking.

And he'd stopped to pee fifteen minutes or so ago. He definitely wasn't dehydrated.

So what the hell?

There were lights on inside Miss Melody's Cafe, but he didn't see any power cables running into it. Hell, there were no power cables anywhere here. He was way the hell out in the middle of the woods.

Nonetheless, a cheery light illuminated pink and green and yellow and blue on the walls inside. And there were white-backed chairs around white tables, just screaming at him to come in a take a load off.

Before he realized he was doing it, he was at the front door, palm pressed against the door's glass, and about ready to push it open.

He stopped, and looked behind himself.

Just the woods, the way he had left them. Peaceful and still. Green and growing. Not a sign of man anywhere.

The door pushed open beneath his palm, and Jeff spun back to face it, taking a step back, suddenly tense as fight or flight welled up with a surge of adrenalin.

Just as quickly as his fright came, it fled when he saw the person who had opened the door from inside.

She was elderly, but not old. Plump, she had a round face and a gentle smile, and her silver-grey hair was done up on a bun atop her head. She wore a pastel green apron over a white blouse and khakis, and pink-rimmed glasses that made her eyes seem a little too big.

"Hello dear," she said in a warm, welcoming tone. "I'm Miss Melody. Would you like to come in?"

"I - " Jeff swallowed, glancing back at the woods again. "I'm not sure. I'm rather surprised to find you here."

"I get that a lot," she said, her smile somehow growing more broad. "You look hot and tired. Come have some iced tea."

Jeff had to admit, that sounded good. Real good. So good that he decided it wasn't so incredibly weird that someone had set up a business along a well-used hiking trail. Sure, he hadn't seen anyone today, but the way the trail had been worn down said tons of people used it other days.

She probably had a generator or something in the back for her lights. Probably made a decent profit, and it got her out into the country away from town every day.

Not a bad idea, now that he thought of it.

Jeff returned her smile. "Sure," he said, then he followed her in.

It was blessedly cool inside, air conditioning working like magic, and Jeff let out a sigh of relief, only now realizing how hot it truly had become outside, how uncomfortable.

He followed Miss Melody across the cafe floor toward a glass-fronted display case in the rear, and felt his worries drip away like the sweat that was still flowing; though flowing less by the second as the coolness of the air refreshed him.

The place smelled of chocolate chip cookies in the oven and chicken noodle soup on the simmer, and there was some kind of classical guitar music playing from hidden speakers, slow strumming and fingerpicking that combined with the scents and the coolness to put Jeff completely at his ease.

He was smiling freely when he stopped in front of the display case, where Miss Melody had taken up station behind.

"Now then," she said, and turned to his left. She opened something, Jeff couldn't see what but it sounded like a cooler case, and lifted a pitcher full of yellow-brown liquid with lemons cut into eighths floating in it. She waggled her eyebrows at him, and he laughed.

"Yes, please."

Miss Melody set the pitcher down and turned around to a white-painted cupboard behind the display case. Opening up one of the cupboard doors, she withdrew a glass, so clear that Jeff wondered for a second if it was crystal. Then she bent over and he heard a crunching sound. When she straightened, it was halfway full of ice cubes, which she proceeded to drown in the tea.

"Do you want sugar, dear?"

Jeff shook his head. No need to ruin perfectly good tea that way.

With an approving nod, Miss Melody set the glass on top of the display case and slid it across to him.

"Thanks," he said and lifted it up. He inhaled the vapors for a second, appreciating the tea's slightly earthy odor. Then he took a long, refreshing drink.

The cold seeped down his throat and into his stomach, and it felt like the coolness of it spread through his entire body without any effort at all.

He closed his eyes, just enjoying, for a moment. When he opened them again, Miss Melody was looking at him, not un-kindly, with with a direct stare.

"What brings you out on such a hot day, dear?"

Last night's news, and the fight, came back to Jeff's mind, and some of the calm that he had been seeking all morning, but had stubbornly refused to come until he followed Miss Melody into the cafe, fled.

He looked away from her gaze. "I just needed to get away. Get my thoughts in order."

From the corner of his eye, he saw Miss Melody nod in understanding. "Bad news is never easy to receive."

He looked back at her, the tension he had felt when she first opened the door returning, though it was a shadow of its initial self.

"Who said anything about bad news?"

Miss Melody didn't retreat, didn't show any sign of reacting at all to the accusation that Jeff had put into his tone without realizing it. She merely shrugged. "It's my job to know what people are feeling, and what they need." She reached down behind the display case and a moment later came up with a long, thin piece of paper, printed front and back in flowing script. Jeff didn't need to read it to know it was the menu.

"Thanks, Ma'am, but I think I'd better be going after this." He lifted the iced tea, then took another drink.

It really was pretty damn good.

"Are you sure? I make the best chicken and dumplings."

Chicken and dumplings.

Jeff flashed back to all the times over the years that Mom had made that for him and his brother, Keith. On every special occasion and holiday, to be sure, but also sometimes just whenever, because she thought one of them might need or want it.

No one had ever made it as well as she did. It was like love rolled out in a rolling pin and dropped into rich broth, with pieces of hope for his and Keith's incredible futures floating alongside in a whole that was as completely restorative as it was delicious.

No one ever made chicken and dumplings for him like Mom did.

And now no one ever would. Not now that Keith had sent her off to that -

Jeff felt one of his knuckles pop, and looked down to see his fingers gripping the glass of iced tea so tightly they had turned white.

If it wasn't for the fact the glass was circular, and thus very strong, he might had broken it, as tightly as he was gripping it.

He placed the glass down atop the display case and stepped back. He couldn't take his eyes from the glass; it was like he was afraid he had hurt it. And never mind that glass has no feelings, and that the thing was completely intact.

Jeff shook his head. "Thanks," he found himself saying, woodenly. "I'm just gonna go." He took another step back. "What do I owe you?"

Miss Melody gave a little shake of her head, drawing Jeff's gaze back to her face. Her smile, though still kindly, was sad, like she could feel some measure of the heartache that he had been trying to drive away all morning with exertion.

Trying, and failing.

"First visit is on the house, dear," she said. Then she turned to her right.

Sitting there atop the display case was one of those year-long calendars that you can tear off day by day.

Jeff hadn't noticed it before.

Miss Melody tour off the top calendar page, and for a second Jeff thought he saw a little group of golden lights puffing out around it, like fairy dust in those old kids movies.

She held the calendar page out to him and put some more cheer back into her gentle smile. "Take this to remember us by?"

Jeff nodded.

He reached out and took hold of the little page. As his fingers made contact, he felt a soft trill of energy, almost like the page had a small little static electric charge on it.

Of course, that was ridiculous.

The paper was thicker than he thought it would be. More coarse. He looked down at it and saw it was divided in two. On the right was the day and date, in large, easy to read lettering. On the left was another picture out of a Norman Rockwell collection. Two boys sitting on either side of a dining table, with their mother, clad in a blue dress and white apron, standing between them, holding a pot in one hand and ladling out soup into one of the boys' bowls with the other.

It struck close to home, so close to what he had just been thinking, that he almost didn't see the script at the bottom of the calendar page: Miss Melody's Cafe. Red Spruce Summit Trail.

He blinked, and those were not tears that he blinked away, and looked back at Miss Melody.

He wasn't sure what to say so he just said, "Good bye."

"Good bye, dear," she replied as he turned toward the door.

He pulled the door open, and he heard the tinkling of a bell over his head. He was just thinking that he hadn't heard a bell when he came in, and wasn't that odd, when a brilliant flash of yellow-white light tore through his vision.

The instant of the flash stretched out into a small eternity, and then he could see again.

He had just walked in the door. It had been a long, hard day at work, and he wanted nothing more than to kiss Nina, have some dinner, then take her to bed and just sleep—that's it, just sleep—for a year.

Somewhere in the back of his mind, a voice said he wasn't married to anyone named Nina. His brother was.

But he walked in the house anyway, kicking off his shoes inside the doorway like always. He felt the familiar thread of the carpet between his toes as he walked down the entranceway hall, past pictures of him and Nina and their son Jordan—I don't have a son named Jordan either, what the—to the living room.

And already he could hear the voices. The argument.

Mom was acting up again, and Nina sounded like she was at her wits' end.

Biting back a curse, and trying not to feel the anger turning toward hatred that always tried to rise within him when Mom got this way, he rushed forward, passing the living room toward the hall to Mom's room, to help.

Yellow-white light flashed again, and he was on the back porch. Sitting in his wicker chair looking out at the lawn where Jordan was practicing his kata.

It was amazing how grown up he looked. How strong, as he took a low stance, practically brushing the ground with his hand as he made a rising blocking movement and then stretched up to his full height and punched forward.

Eleven years old. Had it already been eleven years?

Eleven years old, and almost as tall as he was, already muscular and handsome. Jordan was going to be a lady-killer. He made a note to start having the talks about women with his son. Give him Rollo's books, so Jordan could avoid some of the mistakes he had made. Some of the pain.

If Jordan -

"She needs her bedpan changed again." It was Nina's voice, from inside the house. Flat, unamused. "She won't let me near her."

He sighed and pushed himself up out of his chair, nodding. "I'll take care of if."

He spared one last look at his son, sweaty and vibrant in the sunlight, then stepped into the shadows on his home.

It was dark inside. Even with all the lights on, it was dark. Dark, and joyless.

He wanted to wonder where they joy had went, but as he turned toward the bedroom and heard the complaining voice coming from within, he knew.

God help him, he knew.

He pushed the door open and stepped inside.

The scent of the bedpan struck him first. Then the wide-eyed, accusing eyes from the women lying on the bed. Accusing, and mixed with fear and anger.

"Who are you?" she demanded, her voice harsh in its lack of recognition for the son who had been caring for her, along with the rest of his family. "Where's my son? I want my son!"

"Mom, it's - " He meant to say, "It's me, Keith."

But she interrupted him, saying, "Where is Jeffrey?"

Another flash of yellow-white light, and he was bent over the kitchen counter, his elbows resting on the formica and his head in his hands.

He wanted to shut his eyes, not look at the papers on the countertop in front of him. But he couldn't.

It was necessary. God knew it was necessary. He couldn't care for her any more. She was driving him insane, and Nina too. And Jordan...

All the same, the guilt felt like it was going to gobble him up. Gobble him up and leave nothing behind except excrement.

And deservedly so.

He looked at his signature on the page that committed his mother to the nursing home, and he cursed himself for a coward and a weakling. A terrible son, and a horrible father, to set such a bad example for Jordan.

It was so selfish of him...

He felt Nina's arms around him as she came to his side and hugged him close. Felt her warmth, but it didn't help fill the hole where his heart used to be.

"You're doing the right thing," she said.

And he wanted to believe it. But...

"Jeff's never going to forgive me." He didn't know why he said it. After all, he wasn't sure he would ever be able to forgive himself.

Why was his big brother's approval the thing that came to his lips, right then?

Nina squeezed harder. "He's on the other side of the country, Keith. He doesn't know how it is with her."

He nodded. That was true. All the same...

"I have to call him, and tell him."

"You want me to do it?"

"No. I will."

The yellow-white flash came again, and then Jeff was stumbling forward.

He was facing toward the back of the cafe, and Miss Melody behind her glass-fronted display case. He managed to catch himself before falling completely, but it took him a couple steps.

He looked up at the kindly old woman, his jaw dropping. "What.... What was - ?"

He couldn't finish the words.

"Just what you needed, dear." She gestured toward the wall to her left. Jeff followed her hand with his eyes and saw the same thing as had been on the sign out front.

"Food for the Body. Healing for the Soul."

He retreated, confusion competing with fear battling with revulsion and anger.

"You stay away from me, witch," he said.

Then he turned and ran.

He flung himself through the door, then across the trail. He didn't register the water getting into his boots as he splashed across the creek through calf-deep water.

Then he was on the other side fo the creek, running. Except he lost his footing and stumbled again.

Pinwheeling his arms, he turned partway, and then landed against a tree trunk, curling his arms around it to stop himself from falling completely.

Jeff stood there—more like he hung there—for a long time. He wasn't sure how long, because his mind was racing so.

What was it that he had seen?

It had been so real. He had felt every second of it. Ever touch, every scent. All the frustration, all the guilt, the anguish...

At some point he pushed himself up off the trunk and fully back onto his feet. His vision was blurry. He blinked away tears that had been flowing freely, then brushed them away with the back of his right hand.

He brought his left hand up -

And it was still holding the calendar page from inside Miss Melody's.

Anger flared up within him and he grasped it between both of his hands, meaning to tear it asunder.

He stopped, as he saw the Norman Rockwell picture on the left hand side more closely.

That wasn't just any mother ladling out soup for the boys at the table. That was his mother. Vibrant and smiling, like when he was a boy. He could practically smell the chicken and dumplings in the ladle she was pouring out into the bowl -

That was his bowl. It was him in the picture. And Keith on the other side of the table.

What the - ?

He spun around, looking back at the cafe.

It was gone.

Gone like it had never existed. There was just the creek and the trail leading uphill on the other side. There were even trees growing right through the spot where the cafe had just been.

A shiver went down Jeff's spine, and he looked back down at the calendar page that he still held clutched between his two hands.

At the bottom, beneath the picture and the date, was the area where it had listed the cafe's location as being on Red Spruce Summit Trail.

Now, it said, "Wherever Needy Souls Are Located."

Jeff released the page with his right hand, then used that same hand to smooth the wrinkles out of the paper that he had inadvertently put into it.

Then he splashed back across the creek and went back to the trail. But this time, he turned downhill.

It took an hour before he got a good cellphone signal. As soon as he saw a bar, he called up Keith's number.

It rang three times before Keith answered.

"Keith, it's Jeff."

"Hey." Jeff could hear the trepidation, the hurt, the uncertainty in his brother's voice.

He paused, just now realizing he had no idea what he had intended to say. So he said the first thing that came to mind.

"Brother, I'm sorry."

The sudden hitch in Keith's breath told Jeff that was exactly the right thing to say.

45

THE BRIEFCASE

The slide of Jack's Glock locked to the rear, his magazine empty. He reached for another one, only to find his pouches of spare magazines empty.

He was plum out of ammo.

There were at least two men left of the team that had come after him; the sounds of their movements gave them away, and right before he had shot off his last two rounds he'd heard one call out to the other.

There was no chance his final shots had hit anything; he had fired them blindly, around the corner of the marble column he was crouched behind. Just suppressing fire, to keep their heads down so he could move again. Except that now he was flesh out of ammo, and just as pinned down as he had been a moment ago.

And how did he let that become a surprise?

Jack had undergone extensive training over the years, and he'd learned early to keep track of his rounds fired so he'd know exactly what he had left.

But this op had gone so badly, so quickly...

It was supposed to be simple. Bring a bundle of cash to the drop off and swap it for the merchandise. What merchandise, Jack didn't know and didn't care. He was a courier, nothing more, working on a contractual basis, and he never asked what was in the package he had been hired to pick up and deliver.

He often had to do exchanges like this, though. And that carried a bit of risk for things to go wrong, which is why a guy with his former military and intelligence experience was the right man for the job. Most of the relatively few other professional couriers he had met had similar backgrounds to his.

But he had never had a job go this completely wrong, and without warning.

The cash had been left in a black canvas duffle bag stashed in a locker at the bus terminal three blocks from Jack's hotel. His employer had given him the key along with his down payment for the job the night before.

This morning at 1000 he had donned charcoal grey slacks and a matching suit jacket, with a light blue collared shirt that he left open at the collar and his Glock in a shoulder holster beneath his left armpit, and black leather gloves. And he'd gone and retrieved the bag. As expected, no issue there, and he went to a charming streetside cafe, with yellow awnings overhanging the aging flagstone sidewalk out front and bare metal framed chairs set alongside round tables for two with white tablecloths and yellow placemats.

There he sat and enjoyed a light lunch and coffee, while he watched the Paris street traffic stream past.

He'd always hated this town; tried to avoid it whenever he could. But his last several contracts had sent him here, and this particular one had a nice paycheck associated with it. So he sucked it up.

Still, he couldn't wait to get back to a place that didn't have pretension so seemingly baked into its very soul.

After an hour of replaying the plan for the exchange in his head, he grabbed a cab and made his way over to the appointed place for the exchange.

It was a commercial building that looked like it could have been a museum, it was so extravagantly constructed. With a wide stone archway leading into a front courtyard, about forty feet on a side. It was paved with grey-white marble and ringed by square white marble columns that surrounded an eight-lobed fountain with a grey stone statue of a fish riding a wave up toward the sky in its center.

Naturally, water spurted out of the fish's mouth, leaving a soft trickling sound that echoed off the stones of the courtyard.

Jack arrived at just after 1300, and found the courtyard empty except for a lone man, who stood across the fountain from the arched entrance.

He was older, approaching fifty from the look of him. Lean, with curly dark brown hair, nearly black, that was going grey at the temples, and a small nub of a nose that was crooked as though it had been broken a few times in the past. He wore a black leather jacket over a red shirt that buttoned halfway down his chest and was collarless, and slacks that were just grey of black, and black leather shoes. His eyes were concealed behind round-rimmed sunglasses, and he gave the impression of continually scanning the area, checking all the angles.

When Jack stepped into the courtyard, the man stiffened slightly, then stepped back from the lip of the fountain. He was carrying a black leather briefcase in his left hand; his right was free, and lingering close to hem of his jacket.

There was no noticeable printing, but he was almost certainly carrying at four o'clock on his belt.

Jack raised the duffle bag, so his contact could see it, then slowly maneuvered clockwise around the fountain.

All was silent except for the trickling of the water. There was not even a breeze, and Jack was beginning to sweat from the early autumn warmth combined with the tension that he always felt when a job neared its pinnacle.

As he approached the man, he detected, alongside the odor of dampness from the fountain, the faint smell of lingering cigarette smoke. No surprise the man was a smoker; many in France were.

The man's head turned to follow him as Jack approached, and when Jack stopped a dozen feet away from him, he gave a little nod.

"Manchester United sucks." The man's voice had, of all things, an Austrian accent. It was more high-pitched than Jack would have thought to look at him, and slightly raspy.

Too many cigarettes.

Jack replied with the response phrase his employer had given to him. "Not as bad as Liverpool."

The man's lips quirked ever so slightly. Then he set the briefcase down on the marble tiles, right up against the fountain's lip.

Jack dropped the duffel bag and kicked it over toward the man.

He was just beginning to squat down to open it and check the contents when all hell broke loose.

At first Jack thought his contact had decided to pull a fast one, as four men in black fatigues and wearing black balaclavas sprang into view from between the rear columns just as the man was reaching for the bag.

They had rifles; in a glance he identified them as Steyr AUG bullpups.

As they raised the weapons, he cursed inwardly and began to raise his hands above his head.

But then Jack's contact noticed his motion and froze, then turned. He shouted an oath when he saw the men and moved to draw his pistol.

One of the men's rifles barked twice, and Jack's contact went down, blood spurting from his back where the two rounds punctured the center of his chest and passed through.

Jack didn't wait for them to decide to take him out, too. He dove toward the nearest column behind him, striking the marble tiles on his shoulder and rolling.

Another rifle fired, and he felt as much as heard the bullet zip over his body as he completed his roll. Then he slid around the column and got up into a crouch, drawing his pistol.

His ears were ringing from the percussion of the rifle shots, amplified and reverberated by the stone of the courtyard, and he went through the situation in the split second it took for him to reach his feet.

Someone had sold them both out; him and his contact. And he was alone, with a handgun, against four men who moved like they had training and who had rifles.

He was screwed.

It went through his head that they might be cops. He put that aside as quickly as it came. Their equipment was devoid of organizational logo, and if they had been cops they would have identified themselves as such immediately.

So, mercs. They wouldn't take prisoners.

Totally screwed.

But if that's how it was, he could at least go down fighting.

He heard their boots on the stones of the courtyard, as they spread out to either side to envelop him. If he stayed here, he was dead; if he was to have any chance, he needed to move. Make for the courtyard entrance. Although...

There had to be more than one way into this place. The men had to have come from somewhere.

Something to worry about later. He raised his weapon and edged around the corner of the column, muzzle first.

He immediately saw a black figure moving to his right. Reacting with instinct, Jack leveled the sights on him and made a trio of shots before pulling back to cover.

Multiple rifle shots from ahead, past the column, and to his left, and he heard the ricochets as the bullets struck the stone on the right hand side of the column, where he had just exposed himself.

He ducked left, and fired several more times at the first black figure he saw.

Then he drew a deep breath and sprinted back to the right.

It was about fifteen feet from his column to the next, and he would be exposed the whole way. But he was hoping they would have tracked with his last exposure and looking to the left side, while he went right.

A phrase went through his mind as he heard more rifle shots from behind him. "Kansas City Shuffle. They look left you go right."

Then he dove as he heard the hiss-snap of a bullet passing close by.

So much for the Kansas City Shuffle.

He struck the marble and slid, and felt something tug at his right calf just before he reached the next bit of cover.

Pain followed a second later, and he looked down to see his slacks torn and red welling up from his leg. But a slow stream, not a flood, and he was able to move his foot freely.

A grazing wound then. Could be a lot worse.

Jack forced himself to his feet and looked to his right toward the next column, and saw an expanding pool of red.

He blinked, and risked a quick look around the corner, to be sure.

Son of a gun. The guy he'd shot at first was down, flat on his face. And the blood looked to be coming from his neck.

That was one hell of a lucky hit.

There were still three more of the bad guys, though, and they were firing again.

He fired as well, multiple shots from each side of the column, stopping to snap in a fresh magazine before doing it again.

The whole way his thoughts were racing. They wouldn't fall for the Kansas City Shuffle again.

Hell, they hadn't fallen for it the first time. Whatever, it had let him get this far.

He glanced right again, and got off a few more shots toward another of the figures before ducking back.

Three more columns, then he could make a dash for the archway...

More rifle shots, enough that he couldn't hear anything else. But...he thought he only heard two distinct weapons. What had happened to the third guy? Had he hit him with his wild shots?

Duck left. He saw one of the mercs approaching the column he had just left, and he fired at him, then pulled back.

Just seconds left, and they'd have him flanked. Cover would be useless.

He swapped magazines again, then went right and fired. But this time he kept right on going, sprinting for the next column.

It wasn't a grazing shot this time. He felt the impact in his left side, and about crumpled into the column, just barely making his way around to cover again.

The columns ringed the fountain. So he would have cover from the merc by the first column. For a few seconds.

But he was hurt badly now. He felt the burning just above his left hip, and his hip and thigh were already wet from the bleeding.

Even if he escaped, he wasn't going anywhere bleeding like a stuck pig. The cops -

There was a lull in the rifle fire, and he heard, distant but louder by the second, the wailing sirens of the police.

The mercs must hear it too, and they wouldn't want to get caught either. Maybe they would pull back.

Maybe he could get them to do it.

"Hear that? Not much time." He shouted the words, trying to sound strong, confident. Defiant. He wasn't sure how well he did.

The mercs didn't respond verbally.

They did shoot again.

He went to return fire, and then realized he was out of ammo.

Completely out.

Son of a bitch.

Jack cast about, looking for something—anything—that could help him get out of this situation.

The wall of the courtyard behind his column was sheer, and even if it wasn't, it's not like he could climb it. Not injured as he was, and not without getting shot again.

More rifle shots. And the police sirens were getting louder.

Jack ducked his head around, and saw one of the men in black crouched behind the fountain, near where he had dropped the duffel and his contact had left the briefcase.

He pulled back just before another shot, then he heard one of men say something in a language he didn't know. Though it sounded familiar; he had heard it before, though he didn't understand it.

He couldn't say when, just then.

The men fired again, then there were rapid boot steps.

Jack risked another look, and saw the three men, two moving quickly the other more slowly, with a limp. They were heading back toward the gap in the columns they had entered through. And one of them carried the duffel bag.

Son of a bitch.

Without thinking, Jack stepped out from the cover of his column and swore at them. The man at the rear stopped and looked back at him.

He didn't bother raising his rifle, just his middle finger.

Then he followed his fellows past the columns, toward whatever exit they had used before.

Jack tucked his Glock back into its holster and moved as quickly as he could toward the far side of the fountain. It was slow, labored, the pain in his side becoming more intense with the second.

By the time he got to the place where his contact lay dead, he was almost doubled over, his left hand clutching his side.

He was beginning to get dizzy, and when he looked down at himself he saw why. His pants leg was completely slick with blood, and he had left bloody footprints across the marble of the courtyard.

If he didn't stem the bleeding soon, he would be in big, big trouble.

The sirens were very loud now; he was in big trouble no matter what.

But then he saw the briefcase. Still sitting there, where the contact had put it. Unopened.

Unbelieving, Jack picked it up and tried to flip the golden latches —certainly not real gold, but who knows?—that held it shut.

Locked. Locked with a pair of combination locks, and he didn't have the combo.

Apparently the bad guys didn't either.

Or they were only after the money.

Either way, Jack wasn't going to question his luck.

If he could somehow slip out of here and get back to his employer with the briefcase, he would have been successful with his part of the exchange, at least. And he could get paid.

More importantly, his employer wouldn't think he had tried to screw him. Couriers had found themselves with contracts on their heads from former employers who they tried to shaft.

Jack certainly didn't want that.

He stripped off his suit coat. Or tried to; his pained side didn't make it easy. But he managed.

The he shrugged off his shoulder rig and dropped it into the fountain. The gun couldn't be traced back to him; he had bought it from the local black market, and he had never handled it with his bare hands.

Then he balled up the coat and pressed it against his side to try to help staunch the flow of blood, and he picked up the briefcase.

The sirens were an overwhelming scream as he followed the mercs through the exit they had used.

Sure enough, there was a side entrance to the courtyard: a black wrought-iron gate that was hidden from side from the fountain by the positioning of the columns and the short alcove where the gate was tucked into. It was standing ajar from the mercs' passage, and Jack wasted no time pushing his way through.

It opened into an alleyway that ran along the side of the court-yard and the building it was attached to. To the right, toward the main drag where he had come in, the sirens had stopped but he saw lots of activity as the police most likely were setting up a cordon.

They knew the city's layout better than Jack did. If they didn't already know about this alley, they would shortly, and they'd move to block the other end, wherever it came out.

Jack couldn't tell, because the alley bent to the left a few tens of yards down in the other direction from the main street, following the building's wall.

The alley was paved, but also dirt-crusted and unclean. There were 10-Gallon sized trash cans and other debris strewn about outside of closed red or blue or brown doors that led to the surrounding buildings. It was narrow enough it would be very difficult to drive down, except maybe in a Mini or one of those tiny Fiats. But even then...

Looking around quickly, Jack didn't see any sign of tire marks in the dirt on the alley's floor. That wasn't definitive, but it suggested the mercs hadn't driven away.

Regardless, he wasn't going to. And he needed to get out of there rapido, or face the French prison system. And he didn't want that.

He considered for a moment going back into the courtyard and playing possum; the innocent bystander who had been in the wrong place at the wrong time. He just as quickly threw that idea aside. He had gunshot residue all over his gloves and the sleeves of his coat and shirt, and there was probably an Interpol notice on him. At the very least his fingerprints were on file in the DOD database.

Also, he really could not let the briefcase out of his sight; and it would get confiscated as evidence for certain.

And he had no idea what was in it. Getting caught with it might make matters even worse.

So he set off down the alley as quick as his feet could carry him.

Thirty paces on, he knew he wasn't going to make it out of there. He could barely walk, and he was getting more and more dizzy. Worse, despite the heat he began to feel cold.

He was swaying on his feet; but he had to keep going.

Couldn't. Be. Caught.

He staggered against one of the alley walls. He hadn't even realized he was going to do it until the stone of the wall smacked him in the chest.

He gasped as the impact made his wound flare up in a new pain. But he tried to force himself off the wall, to go on.

If he could just. Make. It.

He could get a doctor, square things with his employer.

Must. Go...

He thumped into something else hard, and it moved.

His vision had darkened, but he thought it was a door? And it swung open under his weight.

Then there were hands on his shoulders, and he thought he saw wide eyes, looking at him with surprise and fright.

Something spoken in French, but he couldn't make it out.

He tried to pull away, and found himself on the pavement...or he thought it was pavement.

The whoever it was who had caught him stood over him, and Jack thought he recognized him. Was that his employer?

He'd made it.

"Here it is," he said, feebly. He hefted the briefcase. Or he tried to. He could only raise it an inch. "Take it."

The person seemed to look at it, and he saw a shadow moving toward the briefcase's handle. A hand?

Jack smiled in satisfaction. Or he thought he did. "Call doctor," he said.

It sounded loud to his ears, but it came out just as a whisper. The young man, Gaston, who had followed him out of the door when he fell, bent over, taking hold of the briefcase as bid. But he couldn't make out what the stricken man was saying. It was too faint to hear.

He could make out the rattle in the man's throat a few seconds after, though. He had heard it on the streets many times, and before then from his own father as he breathed his last.

Gaston straightened and looked both ways down the alley. To the right, the way was clear; no one in the alley at all. To the left...the cops were out in the street there. And they would be coming down the alley soon.

Looking for this man.

He lifted the suitcase and looked at it. It was nice; made of good black leather, with gold clasps. Probably cost more than he had managed to make in the last month of begging and stealing whatever he could.

Gaston swallowed. Whatever was in the case, the man had been killed for it. And the cops would want it.

Which meant it was probably even more valuable than the case looked.

He glanced around; still no one.

Then he backed into the hallway he had just been coming out of and closed the door to the alley. He locked it, then hurried up to the seedy little flat he had managed to rent for the fortnight.

There to count his loot. And plan his certain to be much improved future.

46

LEGACY

The sky was burning crimson on the eastern horizon. The sun's disk was a third of the way gone, down into her nighttime abode, and rays of red-orange streamed down through gaps in the partial cloud cover like spotlights, illuminating here and there bits of the rolling grassland before the ridge where Selam stood just a little bit brighter than the others. Some last remnants of light against the encroaching blackness, hanging on just a little bit longer than their fellows, despite the fell cast to that illumination.

He shuddered, drawing his fine blue silk-cotton cloak tighter around his body despite a lack of physical chill. He watched the orb lower further past the hill lands east of his home, and couldn't help but consider that he could relate to those little swaths of land, seemingly desperately clinging to whatever light they could.

The swish of grass behind him brought Selam out of his reverie, and his hand went to the well-worn leather that wrapped the grip of his sword, master crafted by Farelio himself and handed down to him from his father as had been done for generations in his family.

Without thinking about it, he bent his legs slightly, his muscles bundling as they tensed, ready to spring into action.

But then the smell of horse and pipe tobacco reached his nose, along with a sweet-sour that he would recognize anywhere.

"Good evening, brother," Selam said, as he relaxed in his stance.

The movement from behind him stopped, and Selam could imagine the look on Hafi's face. He was Selam's senior, but not as skilled in the martial ways as Selam. He always was surprised when Selam saw the obvious traces and signs that he himself missed.

A rueful chuckle, and then Hafi stepped up beside him on his left. Hafi shook his head, his long, black hair swaying in time with his movement and his lips drawing upward into a wry grin, white teeth flashing stark contrast with the blackness of his beard.

He was of a height with Selam, but plump about the middle. He wore his robes loosely, white and brown cotton that hung down to his ankles and would restrict his movement if it came down to a fight.

But Hafi had never been one for the great contest. That's why he had inherited their father's business, and Selam the sword.

"How do you always know it is me?" Hafi asked.

Selam sniffed. "The cologne you wear. Its southern spices are... unique, here." And more than a little excessive, he didn't say.

Hafi half-chuckled again, and raised a meaningful eyebrow Selam's way. "The ladies of Tyrash certainly appreciate it."

"One wife is not sufficient for you? Would you seek two more? Three?" Selam had lost track of how many mistresses Hafi had these days. And really didn't want to know.

The humor went out of Hafi's eyes, and his lips compressed into a scowl for a moment. But instead of replying, he looked away from Selam toward the setting sun, now barely visible as the last rim of glow against the increasing darkness of the night all around.

Hafi drew a breath. "I met with Farooq today."

The name sent a little tremor down Selam's spine. As the man holding the lion's share of the debt the family business owed, he would have more than a slight influence on their future.

If there was to be any future.

"Not good news, I'm afraid." Hafi rolled his shoulders slightly, then crossed his arms over his chest. "He wants twenty thousand, by next month."

"Twenty thousand? But we only owe fifteen."

Hafi shrugged. "Late fees, and unpaid interest. And...other matters."

Selam looked sidelong at his brother, and Hafi did not meet his gaze. Had Hafi taken to the gambling dens again? Not that it mattered. They couldn't have paid the sum if it had been five thousand.

They were ruined.

Selam looked down, toward the hilt of his father's sword. Still bright, despite the swiftly departing daylight, the pommel seemed to almost glow of its own accord.

More than a dozen generations had born this sword, in wartime and in peace. In wealth and in poverty, but always with honor. Their father had said that as long as it remained in their family, they had a future to be envied, no matter how dark the days might look at the time.

But now, as the first of the stars became clearly visible overhead and the breeze seemed to already have become more cool as night crept over the land, Selam wasn't sure he could believe that.

They were going to lose father's business. Because Hafi was too—

No. He would not pass judgment on his elder brother. Hafi had inherited the business, and the right to direct it as he chose. And in truth he had often asked Selam's input, and he had not objected to Hafi's decisions. For the most part.

But somehow, still here they were. About to lose it all.

He ran the fingers of his left hand over the sword's pommel, and felt a bit of comfort.

Not all.

Selam felt Hafi's gaze on him, and he looked fully at his brother. Hafi's eyes flicked downward quickly, as though he were ashamed to meet his younger brother eye to eye. Then he visibly steeled himself and looked up.

There was no defeat in Hafi's gaze. Unexpected, and when Selam saw that, his heart leapt.

He reached out and clapped Hafi on the shoulder. "We shall overcome this, my brother," he said. "Our family will emerge stronger than ever."

Hafi placed his hand overtop Selam's, where it still rested on the meat of his shoulder, and nodded. "Yes, we will. I have a plan."

Selam raised a questioning eyebrow.

"Meet me at The Red Phoenix at midnight." His lips turned upward again, into an eager grin. "Tonight, we shall save our family."

Selam knew of The Red Phoenix, and had been inside a handful of times. But never for long, and never so late as this.

He had long ago forsook the call of late night debauchery; a true acolyte of the way of the sword did not go down that path. It was destructive to body and spirit, ruining discipline and eating far too much into the day's work.

He was not surprised Hafi frequented the place, and at late hours, however.

Again, the reason Selam had inherited the sword.

The blocky stone of the tavern's building was unadorned. Just a small sign posted above the dark wood of the double doors allowing entrance. In the daylight, it would show a broad-winged bird, wreathed in red flames, rising from a pile of ash, with the tavern's name written in script above the bird's beak.

Now, a few minutes before midnight, the sign was barely visible in the flickering light of the twin burning torches that rested in sconces on either side of the doors. But the sign was unnecessary, to those who knew Tyrash well.

Having grown up here, that included Selam.

Two thick-armed men in plain tunics stood on either side of the entrance doors. The one on the right looked Selam up and down appraisingly, and for a moment he thought the bouncer would try to make trouble. But then he just grunted and jerked his head toward the interior.

It was more well-lit inside by oil lamps hanging from the bare wooden rafters and mounted in holders along the walls. Tobacco smoke wafted over the long, broad common room that made up most of the tavern's first floor, and there was seating for easily a hundred patrons. Ranging from bare-wood benches alongside equally unadorned tables at the front to satin-cushioned divans at the rear, the tavern was equipped to cater to clientele of all levels of wealth.

The central bar was circular, with stations at three positions where serving wenches could sidle up to fill orders, and casks and more delicate flasks containing everything from the most rude ale from the savage wastes to the northeast to the finest wines from the western kingdoms were tended by a trio of bartenders in grey tunics who wore seemingly eternal smiles on their faces.

A trio of dark-haired dancing wenches in sheer silks that barely concealed their charms swayed on a stage off to the left, moving to the beat of a pair of drummers, a flutist, and a pair of men playing stringed instruments Selam had seen before but didn't know the name of. They produced a fine melody was all he knew; all he cared to know.

A stairway to the upper level was off to the right, and at a round table not far from the base of the stairs Selam spied Hafi.

His brother was standing there, in the same robes he had worn earlier in the night, with a tall, dark-haired youth. He was lean and muscled, and wore more tightly-fitting clothing than his father; the better to move efficiently in.

Selam found his lips turning downward into a scowl as he saw his nephew, lifting a goblet of what could only be wine to his lips. He had been training the lad—barely thirteen now—in the ways of the sword, as was fitting the men of their family.

This was not part of the way.

"Ah, brother," Hafi said as Selam approached, and reached out to grasp him on the shoulder in greeting. "Will you take wine? This is will be a great night."

Selam kept his eyes on his nephew, who swallowed and slowly lowered his cup to the table. He met Selam's eyes for a moment, but only a moment, instead looking down at the tabletop, abashed.

"No," Selam said, finally looking at Hafi, who had noted his son's embarrassment and had lost some of his enthusiastic expression. "We have business, you said?"

Hafi let go of Selam's shoulder and nodded. Gesturing toward the stairs, he said, "They are waiting for us."

"Who?"

Instead of answering, Hafi turned toward his son. "Misra, your uncle and I have business to attend to. Wait for us here."

Misra nodded, still not meeting Selam's eyes.

Then Hafi turned and ascended the stairs. Selam didn't follow for a moment, just looking at his pupil and unsure what, if anything, to say. Instead, he turned and followed his brother upstairs.

It was more quiet, and less smokey, in the upper level. The stairs emerged into a broad hallway, walled in stone like the rest of the building and floored in the same unpolished material, though covered in red rugs with golden fringes that looked like they were worth a small fortune each.

The hallway took them past a pair of doors stained the same shade as the double doors leading into the tavern proper, then stopped at a third door that looked somehow more ornate than the other two, though Selam could not have said what exactly it was that gave that impression.

Hafi knocked twice, and a moment later the door opened, and Selam followed him inside.

The man sitting on the divan in the center of the room beyond was the largest Selam had ever seen; but not in a righteous way. His fat rolled lasciviously beneath the loose silk of his silver-blue robes, and his jowls swayed grotesquely with every movement of his head. He was bald, his cheeks rouged to make his pale skin seem more pink, and he had small, pig-like eyes that flashed blue in the lamplight.

But despite his slothful, indolent appearance, there was a sharpness in his gaze and an aura of danger about him.

Selam knew him by description, though he had never met the man before, and immediately he felt the hair on the back of his neck stand up.

What sort of deal was Hafi getting them into here?

"Hafi," the man on the divan said. "Good of you to come." He made a vague sort of waving gesture that almost seemed too lazy to be a dismissal.

But the two girls who were lounging on the divan next to him in silks that were even more sheer than the dancers' below, leaning their lithe, young bodies up against his bulk on either side of his frame, immediately sprang to their feet and scampered off through a small doorway to the left.

The door they exited through was pulled closed by a muscular man in a fighter's tunic, who wore a broad, curved blade on his right hip and who looked at Selam with a frankly assessing gaze.

This was not the only fighting man in the room. Now that he was over his initial surprise at seeing the fat man they were dealing with, Selam noted no less than half a dozen guards standing unobtrusively but alertly in all corners of the square, tapestry-bedecked room.

He was liking this situation less and less, and was just about to pull Hafi by the shoulder to make him leave when Hafi instead stepped directly in front of the fat man and made a half-bow to him.

"Acharo," he said, "thank you for seeing us at this late hour."

The name confirmed Selam's suspicions, and he wanted to leave even more strongly. Acharo had a reputation in Tyrash. Seemly men did not do business with him.

Whatever this was, Selam was certain he wanted no part of it.

"I was about to ask whether you brought it, but I see you have," Acharo said, his gaze leaving Hafi to rest fully upon Selam. And in particular on his left hip. "Farelio's work, you say? If that holds up, you'll get every penny."

Selam froze, and his left hand went to his sword, his thumb wrapping around the metal of the crosspiece to keep it firmly in place within its scabbard.

"Hafi, what is this?" he said, but he already knew, and he turned accusing eyes on his brother.

He didn't even have the grace to look embarrassed. He met Selam's gaze, and said nothing.

"You would sell our father's sword, our family legacy, to this...this - ?" Selam gestured with his right hand toward the grotesque man lounging before them, unable to give words to his thoughts about the merchant.

"I would *save* our family legacy," Hafi said, moving a step closer to Selam. "There are less than twenty weapons from Farelio's forge left in the world. That sword is worth ten times what we owe to Farooq, and Acharo will pay it. With that much, we can secure our family's future forever!"

"This sword is our family's future," Selam spat back. "Father said—"

"I know what father said," Hafi said with a heat and a spitefulness that Selam had never heard from him before. Then he snorted. "Meaningless words. I'm talking about gold, in our hands. We can buy another sword."

Selam shook his head, and stepped back from his brother. He lowered into a crouch and his right hand found the grip of his sword, baring the first two inches as he twisted his torso slightly.

Acharo sighed, rolling his little eyes toward the ceiling. "Hafi said you might object," he said, "but it hardly matters. The arrangements are already made." He raised his left hand and made a swirling little gesture with it.

The subtlest of sounds from behind announced the movement of a guard that Selam hadn't seen yet.

Moving from instinct, he twisted to his right, drawing and cutting downward even as he got out of reach of the grasping hand that had been reaching for him.

Selam's sword met the guard's arm at the elbow. Blood and forearm both went flying, and the guard stumbled backward against the wall, screaming in sudden anguish as his one remaining hand clamped against the suddenly gushing wound.

Movement erupted all around him.

Guards moved toward him from both sides, drawing steel as they advanced.

Acharo bounded up from his divan with surprising speed and grace for one of his bulk, and headed toward the same door the two girls had vanished through.

And then Selam could spare attention to nothing but the approaching guards.

These first two were clumsy, half trained, and unused to coordinating with each other. Selam easily sidestepped a thrust from the one, and watched as the miss sent the guard stumbling forward into the path of his comrade's cut.

A chagrined shout from the second guardsman mirrored the first's cry of anguish as the blow struck him where the neck meets the shoulder.

Then Selam was dancing around the still-falling man and slipping the tip of his blade into the other's armpit, puncturing lung and heart before moving past him.

Both guardsmen fell behind Selam, and he saw there were only two remaining.

The muscular man who had been eyeing him before was closing the door off to the side, where Acharo had fled, and there were just this pair to face him.

From the looks on their faces, they wished to be just about anywhere else but right there.

Five seconds later, they were off to the next world, and whatever lay in store for them. Hopefully a good reward; despite their fear they were brave men and had met their fate standing up, with all the skill they had.

The fact that their skill was insufficient was not a blemish on their souls; there was always someone better out there.

Breathing deeply but with controlled, steady breaths, Selam turned back around to see Hafi standing where he had been when the confrontation first began.

His eyes were wide, but not from fright or surprise. He had sparred with Selam many times when they were growing up, seen him fight in actual battle before.

Hafi knew Selam's skill.

No, they were wide with chagrin, anger even.

"You fool!" Hafi spat. "You have ruined us!"

"I? It was not eye who buried himself in debt."

Hafi shook his head. "No, that was father. I tried to tell you, but you wouldn't hear it. He could do no wrong, in your eyes. The gallant swordsman, the noble warrior." Hafi's mouth twisted in disgust. "The spendthrift and the gambler, the whoremonger!"

"The devil you say." Selam found himself advancing on his brother, fiery anger flaring within his soul.

"It's true, brother." Hafi moved to his left, keeping the distance between himself and Selam constant. "He left the business in debt, and it's been all I can do to stop it from going under, for years. Well I can't stop it anymore." His eyes flickered from Selam's face to the sword, then back. "I could have, though. I am the firstborn. The sword should have been mine by right."

"You chose a different path. The sword is—"

"I know what the sword is!" Hafi's shout practically shook the walls. "That's all I ever heard of growing up, all father ever focused on. And what good did it do?" He shook his head, stopping beside one of the fallen guards. "He focused on it so much, he's destined us, destined his grandson, to be paupers."

"Our family has been poor before. We—"

"No," Hafi said. In one quick, smooth motion he crouched down and grasped the fallen guard's sword. "You can delude your-self If you like, but I will not live as a pauper. And neither will Misra."

Then he launched himself at Selam.

He was taken aback, both at the ferocity of his brother's attack and by the fact that he was making the attack at all. For a heartbeat, Selam stood still in stunned disbelief.

Then he spun to the side, leaving Hafi's blade to sing through the air where he had been moments before.

Selam backpedalled, keeping his sword up at a guard but no more. "Brother, stop," he said. "We can—"

Hafi's feral growl overwhelmed Selam's words, and again Selam had to dodge aside to avoid being skewered.

But Hafi kept on coming, and Selam kept falling back. From somewhere beneath the sounds of their fight, below the moans of the lone living guard, still clutching at the stump of his right arm, Selam heard shouts and screams from down below in the tavern's front room.

Word on what had happened up here was spreading. Soon, someone would come up to check what was going on and then—

Selam's thigh struck something hard, and he glanced down.

He had hit the side of the divan.

He looked back up to see Hafi's sword coming in again. Without thinking, Selam executed a spiraling parry that ended with Hafi's sword skittering across the floor off to the left and a bloody gash across his right cheek.

Hafi took a half-step back, his left hand rising to his cheek. He had a look of surprise on his face, like he had never conceived that such a thing could happen.

No less than Selam felt. He lowered his sword. "I'm sorry, brother. I—"

Hafi's sudden surge forward caught him unaware, and Selam froze again. This time for too long.

Hafi's hands clamped down around Selam's on the grip of the sword, and began twisting.

Selam was the stronger of the two of them. It had been thus for years. But now, this night, he found he could not resist the power of his brother's arms.

Slowly, inexorably, the point of Selam's sword moved. Twisting and rising until it was pointing upward between them.

Hafi grinned in sudden, mad triumph.

Then he hurled himself onto the point of the sword.

It was like the world went into slow motion. Selam heard himself cry out a denial, but it was from far away, in a distant country.

Hafi's body slid further down onto his blade, and he saw the pain in his brother's eyes. But also resolve.

And spite.

"What will you do now, my brother?" asked Hafi in a hoarse whisper.

Then his eyes glazed over, his breath rattled, and he went limp.

The world returned to normal speed and Selam pushed backwards, pulled the sword from his bother's body even as his mind screamed at him that this could not really be happening.

The door burst open to the side, and Selam heard Misra's voice.

"Fath—"

The youth broke off when he took in the scene. Selam turned to see his nephew's eyes grow wide with shock, then grief.

"Misra—" Selam began, then the youth's eyes met his, and grief turned to terrible anger.

Selam knew the young man would have a sword and be on him in a heartbeat. He also knew he could easily defeat Misra; he was good, but he had far too much still to learn.

But Selam had seen more than enough blood for one night. Precious blood that he never thought to spill.

He saw a second door off to the left, between a pair of tapestries that had been knocked askew.

He charged through it, then down the passage beyond toward the back of the tavern.

"Coward!" he heard Misra cry from behind him.

He found a set of stairs leading downward, and he followed them.

Selam was still running when dawn began to glimmer, bright and pure, in the sky to the west.

He had been running that direction ever since he emerged from the tavern's back door, ever since exiting one of Tyrash's half dozen gates, somehow getting there ahead of the news of the events at The Red Phoenix.

He ran until he had no strength left, but still he continued on.

Now, as the light of the new day bit into his eyes, eyes that could barely see from the tears still flowing from them, Selam finally slowed to a jog, then a walk.

Then he collapsed onto his knees and yelled. He yelled out the anger, the anguish of the night at that glowing orb that was slowly pushing its way up from where it had gone to bed a seeming lifetime ago.

He yelled until his throat was hoarse, then he sank down onto his haunches, and lowered his eyes.

The glint of steel drew his gaze, and he realized with a start that he was still carrying his father's sword, unsheathed in his right hand.

Sunlight glinted off the grey-blue of the curved, finely honed blade. Off the intricate engraving on the flat of the blade: game animals and constellations and weapons and men and horses all twisted into one mass of art that would have been garish, should have been garish, but somehow was instead sublime.

He looked at all that, and at the red stain of blood still coating the cutting edge in some places.

His brother's blood, along with others.

Selam raised his hand and drew back his arm, intending to just throw the sword away.

Except at the last second, the newly-dawned sunlight flashed against the pommel, the rounded metal that his father had made him trace with his fingertips countless times when he was a boy.

This was his family's legacy. His family's future.

Hafi had not seen that, not believed it. He had strayed from the path, and it had driven him, if not mad, at least to his end.

If Selam were to cast aside his legacy now, after all this. What would he be? And could he ever face his father without shame when they met again in the next world?

He lowered his arm again, letting the sword drop into the grass next to his knee, then he drew a deep breath.

Selam looked over his shoulder, to the east. Toward Tyrash, and the home he had always known.

He could never go back there. Maybe if he had not run, he could have explained. But running as he had...Misra would be past all convincing, and the authorities would have come to the same conclusion his nephew had.

Back was impossible. So it must be forward.

Selam looked back to the west, to the strange lands and unfamiliar kingdoms that lay toward the direction of the sunrise.

Then, slowly and deliberately, he cleaned the blood from his family's sword and sheathed it.

And he rose, and took his first steps toward those distant lands.

47

SEA LEGS

The light from the brass oil lamp hanging from the ceiling above me swirled, sending shadows careening around the room as the lamp swung and twisted about on its chain. The corners of my little room flashed in and out of view as the shadows swam, and I imagined I was somehow not resting in a tiny locked, oak-walled cabin in a ship at sea but already down below in the depths, the whirling eddies sucking me down to the Locker, and my ultimate doom.

I swallowed as the ship lurched again, sending the cabin heaving to the side, and the lamp with it, the chain holding it to the ceiling sending forth a clatter of protest as its links relaxed from their embrace with each other and then snapped to again.

My stomach heaved and I tasted bile, and I pulled the threadbare wool blanket that was my only protection against the chill of the late-autumn passage up around my neck and swallowed hard, willing myself not to give in to the motion again, and feed still more dry heaves into the already almost-overflowing chamber pot that was just now sliding across the deck out of my reach, slopping some of the fluids from my previous heaves onto the floorboards behind it.

Vomit and salt and smoke and piss and salt and water and salt filled my nostrils, overpowering the small scent of the hardtack and dried meat dinner that my captors had placed in a tin bowl at the foot of my bunk when they'd last come in an eternity ago.

I stared at it without hunger; in fact the entire notion of eating set my stomach to heaving again.

But yet I must eat, if I had any hope of surviving this ordeal.

The ship heaved upward, then down as the bow crested a wave and then plunged into a trough, and I slid down toward the foot of the bunk, where my unwanted meal sat.

I tried to move my feet aside, but too slowly, and the bowl overturned, spilling its contents onto the deck a second before the chamberpot slid up next to them, sloshing a bit more of its contents.

My heart sank as I watched the food ruined, despite my lack of appetite, and despair settled over me.

Twelve days of this cursed passage. Twelve days since they had taken me, snug from my bedroll, and hauled me onto this God-forsaken scow. Locked me in this cabin, and showed me not a soul except for twice a day for meals, and once to empty the pot.

And why?

I racked my brain, but could not come up with any answer to that question.

The ship groaned, the timbers straining as it heeled to port now, and I heard the lines in the rigging on the weatherdeck above my little prison snapping. Then men's voices raised in shouts of mixed chagrin and command.

I strained to pick out voices from amidst the din; anything to keep my mind off my roiling belly and the misery of my confines.

I had only seen two of the crew, who attended to my needs throughout the day. Neither had said so much as a word to me aside from a grunt, despite my attempts to strike up conversation.

The elder of the two, a man with a bulging belly, thinning grey hair, and an eyepatch over his left eye, had backhanded me last time he came in, to accentuate the point that he would not engage.

But I'd head more voices than that, and over the nearly two weeks since I'd come aboard I had sifted through them so I recognized a few.

The bosun was easy to pick out: a hard, raised voice, always speaking with command or threat. And a few of the mates. But the rest of the crew were merely disembodied voices, at least two dozen of them.

I didn't know ships very well, but it seemed there had to be that many or more to handle a vessel this size.

Unless it was a ship of war.

But I couldn't imagine a warship under a nation's flag would treat a prisoner the way I had been treated. There was the etiquette of war to be followed; certainly I would have at least been told why I was aboard?

Or not. I was grasping for meaning, for an answer to my predicament, and I knew it.

But now, when I listened to the voices, straining to make out any of the voices I recognized, there was an undercurrent of alarm in the men's shouts. I heard feet pounding on the deck above, then more shouts, and I thought I made out the bosun.

The ship heaved to starboard, and I fell out of my bunk, the blanket coming with me as I clung to it. I slammed into the oak frames of the cabin's bulkhead.

My tongue erupted in hot pain and I tasted iron as my teeth came down, and I cried out.

A hard something struck my back, then wetness, and odiferous stink.

The damn chamberpot.

I was just righting myself, unsure whether to swear or scream or weep, when from the upper deck came new sounds. Ripping and snapping, and then a dreadful creaking that became a deafening crack.

And then the ship lurched back upright, and I rolled back to the bunk, striking it on my side.

Shouts from above became more fervent, fearful, and more groaning and cracking.

Then a dreadful crash to starboard, and the ship lurched again.

I managed to push myself to my feet, and my head struck the oil lamp.

The ship rocked more, and more erratically now, but it was different. More random, like the ship was no longer shoving through the waves but just being tossed.

I heard a voice from nearby, somewhere past the door to my cabin. " - the lifeboats!"

A cold dread went up my spine, and the nausea from the ship's tossing fled before my reason as I placed the change in the ship's motion with that call.

Had the mainmast given way? Was that what the crash was about?

If that was the case, the ship's rigging would be dragging in the water, and she would not be able to make way. She would be at the mercy of the waves until the crew could cut it free. If they -

A new crash, from port, sent me stumbling again, but this time the scent of water was joined with water itself, which streamed through the seam at the bottom of my cabin door.

"Oh God," I said.

Or tried to say. My tongue was still screaming, and would not move as I wished it, so the words came out garbled.

But so what? The ship was taking on water.

I hurled myself at the door, shoulder striking the center of the sturdy oak.

It was sound, the lock solid. The door didn't budge, only struck back at my shoulder with a bludgeon that sent me reeling back a step.

I ignored the new pain from my shoulder, and surged forward at the door again. It didn't matter if I was hurt or not; if I didn't get out of there and the ship went down...

Still the door held, but I thought I felt it move just a smidgeon against the locking mechanism.

"Help!" I shouted, and struck the door again.

More shouting from abovedecks, but now what professionalism

there had been in the orders and reports was fading. I heard panic in the disembodied voices, and that chill in my spine grew colder.

Almost as cold as the water sloshing around my bare feet on the planking of the deck.

It was up to my ankles now, and I didn't kid myself that it was going to lower any time soon. If anything, it was going up.

"Help!"

I struck the door again, and this time heard a crack of wood.

The door still looked firm, but the crack was distinct. And had the wood given way a little bit more?

I redoubled my effort, lowering my left shoulder and stepping back, then charging.

The crack this time was loud, and the door definitely gave. I could see a gap of about an inch around the seal where the latch and lock were holding it shut. One more good hit...

I would have kicked it, had I my boots. But when they'd taken me I had only a nightshirt and my undergarments on, and they had given me no other coverings except for the blanket.

So I tucked my shoulder again...and then I was through.

The door popped free, and I stumbled forward into the passageway beyond.

The water was deeper here. The seam of my door had kept some of the fluid from seeping in as quickly as it had been filling the rest of the ship. There were no lights except for the lamp in my cabin. I could only see a few feet to either side before darkness enveloped everything; a mixture of being belowdecks and the dark of night.

I hadn't even realized it was night time. Though I supposed I should have. The meal that now was ruined and soggy, floating in the water and filth behind me, was the second of the day. But I hadn't seen daylight in nigh on two weeks, so my internal clock was weird.

No time to worry over the hour now, though.

I vaguely recalled turning left from the ladderwell they had dragged me down when I first came aboard. If that were the case, the ladderwell to the weatherdeck should be to my left now.

I peered in that direction, bracing myself against another roll of the ship, and could see nothing.

Voices were still shouting from above, though they were fewer now.

Had the crew already begun abandoning ship? If so, I had little time.

I glanced behind me, considering the lamp. Any light would be helpful. But I quickly gave up on the notion; it was securely bolted to the ceiling and the chain was strong.

I'd have to go by feel.

Taking a moment to gather up the blanket, I moved forward, feeling my way with my feet and hands.

Blackness engulfed me, the feeble light from my cabin only a memory to my rear. The sound of waves pounding on the hull and wind whipping through the tatters of the rigging topside was more plain now, as was a more ominous tone: the flow of water.

She was going down, and despite the hypnotic call of those swirling shadows earlier, I had no desire to explore the Locker.

So I forced my halting feet forward, dragging my hand on the bulkhead to my right as I followed the passageway.

A fresh gust of wind and a lessening of the gloom foretold the ladderwell before I reached it. Renewed hope gave me greater speed, and I grasped the twine ropes on either side of the ladderwell and hauled myself up into the blowing wind and rain of a stormy night at sea.

The weatherdeck was even worse a scene than I had imagined.

I was correct; the mainmast had gone over. But so had the mizzen. Fouled lines and shattered pieces of wood that used to be deck fittings littered the entire scene, and I saw in the dim light from two lamps that somehow remained lit amidships a pair of bodies pinned beneath a pile of debris.

Up forward, a group of men were clambering toward the starboard side rail.

The wind was blowing from port, so I supposed the lifeboats

would be launched from starboard to keep them close until all the men were aboard. But why would they be up forward…?

I turned after and saw my answer. The entire starboard side from midships aft was fouled, full of debris and lines. If the scene beyond was like that, no boat could hope to navigate that area of the ship.

The group up forward was small. Three, maybe four men.

All of whom had kept me prisoner below.

For a moment, I considered not joining them. Then I shook my head at my own idiocy.

Survive now. Worry about that later.

I hurried forward, dodging past the wreckage of the mainmast and its ropes and gear.

The deck was slick beneath my bare feet, and the ship was taking on a distinct list to starboard, and tilting downward by the stern.

Not much time left.

As I reached the bow the last of the men from the group I had seen was climbing over the ship's rail.

He dropped out of sight, and I heard a voice from below say, "Pull for your lives, boys."

The voice wasn't one that I recognized from the inventory of voices I had made during my captivity. But I knew its meaning plain. They were commencing rowing, so they wouldn't be near to the ship when she finally went down.

I picked up the pace, running across the more steeply leaning deck now.

"Wait!" I shouted.

I slipped as I neared the rail and slid the rest of the way. The wood of the rail struck my chest, and I coughed out a curse.

It hurt. But I couldn't stop to consider that.

Below, the boat was already pushing away. The men were just dim shapes in the darkness, but I thought there were five of them. And they were moving, like they were pulling at the oars for all they were worth.

"Wait!" I said again, and pulled myself erect.

"What the—?" came the voice I had heard. Then he cursed as I supposed he saw me.

A loud snapping from the stern turned my gaze that way, and I saw in the dim light of the remaining ship's lamps a portion of the rail back there break, and then peel away,

The angle of the deck abruptly grew more steep, and I couldn't wait any longer.

The boat was already a good ten or fifteen feet away, but I jumped anyway.

Water, cold and salty and dark as pitch, closed around me, and for a moment I hung there, unable to tell down from up.

Then I bobbed to the surface and took a quick breath.

"Wait!" I said, again, and began trying to crawl my way through the water toward the retreating boat.

But I had never been a seagoing man, never really spent much time learning the ways of water and how to swim. I could bob in a pond and pull my way across a shallow. But this...

The waves were choppy, the wind blowing, and the water so cold I felt the strength leaving my limbs more quickly than I ever imagined it could. And the blanket had tangled around my legs when I jumped, and was pulling me backward and down.

I kicked and squirmed, but that seemed to just make matters worse.

It seemed like the boat was getting farther away, not closer, and fear, lingering at the edge of my consciousness for as long as I could remember this night, clawed its way to the forefront.

I didn't want to explore the Locker, but I was going to regardless.

My head went under, and I forced myself to the surface, but I could only get a quick breath and let out an even quicker, "Help!" before I went under again.

I managed to get up again. But I could barely get even a portion of a breath.

Then I was under, and all my strength was going. I couldn't reach the surface no matter how I tried.

Darkness was all around, and I felt it reaching out to engulf me. The Locker calling to me.

I felt myself going to it...

Then powerful hands grasped me beneath my shoulders, and I felt myself hauled up to air once again.

I gasped in a great lungful as I flopped down onto hard wooden planking.

I lay there, coughing and heaving, for a short eternity. Then, at some point, I passed out.

I awoke to the sun shining down through scattered, puffy-white clouds overhead and air that was almost, but not quite warm. It wasn't as chilly as the last several days onboard the ship had made it seem. But it was still far from comfortable.

I was lying in the bottom of the rowboat, between the feet of two men who were sitting on the raised planks of the rower's positions, facing each other. They were dressed alike in sailors ankle-cut leggings, and each wore a woolen jacket cinched tight around his body. They were also alike in that they were both bearded, and wore their hair long and braided.

There their similarities faded, because one was blond and pale, the other dark of hair and skin, with a distrusting, squinty gaze.

Squinty snorted and nudged me with his boot. "He's up," he said, looking toward the stern of the boat.

At his nudge, I pushed myself up to a sitting position, though lower down than the two men since I was not up on a plank like they were. Still, I could see my initial thought from the night before—I presumed it was the night before—was incorrect. Instead of five men on the boat there were only four.

The other two were positioned at the bow and the stern, and also wore sailor attire. The man at the bow was noticeably younger than the others, and clean shaven with red-brown hair. The man at the stern, whom squinty had addressed, was broad of shoulder and only slightly lighter than squinty, with black hair that flowed loosely about his shoulders and dark, intelligent eyes.

He looked at me and scowled. "Who the hell are you?"

I blinked, surprised at the question. Then, glancing back at the other three men and seeing equal curiosity on their faces, I shrugged. "James Havlock," I said. "Of Moreton."

Not a bit of recognition at my name, but I saw one head nod slightly when I mentioned my home. Still, the men exchanged glances, and I saw a distinct lack of comfort in their demeanor.

Finally, the man at the bow said, "The cargo," in a resigned tone of voice.

That wasn't exactly the most comforting way to put it, though it did seem at least slightly more polite than prisoner.

Then again, it also had some other, more dire, implications.

"I was not on your ship by choice, if that's what you mean," I said, and raised an eyebrow at the man in the bow, who looked away.

Everyone was silent for a few seconds, the sailors just looking at me and me looking back. Finally, I shrugged my shoulders. "I don't suppose you know why I was brought aboard any more than I do?"

Again glances between the four of them. Then the man in the stern shrugged in response. "We don't get paid to ask questions, Havlock. Just sail the ship where Captain says to sail her."

"And where was that?"

More silence, and I sighed. Then, with a bit of effort that became pained as my shoulder protested the movement, I boosted myself up onto one of the rower's benches.

Squinty grunted and shifted to the side to give me room. After I got situated, I looked around.

And saw nothing but waves and sky as far as the eye could see in any direction.

My spirits weren't exactly soaring. But now they sank like a stone.

"So do we know where we are?"

From behind me, the man in the stern said, "Near as I can tell, about fifty miles west of Point Lemas." He paused, then cleared his throat. "But that's just from a glance at the sailing master's chart before I went up for watch last. Gods only know how far the storm blew us."

I nodded, trying to remember my geography and not coming up with any encouraging. If memory served, the sea west of Point Lemas was broad, and though frequently traveled the sheer size of it would make coming across another ship difficult, if not impossible.

On the bright side, it did give me an idea of where the ship had been headed. Point Lemas was a goodly ways west and south of Moreton. In the direction of the Chalene Kingdom. I'd been there once, a long time ago, and it was enough to make me not want to go back. But I didn't have any connections there. So why in the hell would someone want to kidnap me to take me there?

Shaking my head, I looked down and saw the rest of the bottom of the little craft empty now that I had left it.

Spirits hit rock bottom.

"No food or water," I said.

Grunts and shaken heads all around.

"Wonderful. Do we have a plan?"

The man in the stern snorted out a resigned-sounding laugh.

I closed my eyes and hung my head. I got the distinct idea that it would have been better to have drowned.

Two days later, I decided that idea was correct.

We bobbed on the sea without any propulsion but the boat's two oars. But though I thought it might be worthwhile to at least pull to the east toward where we thought land lay, even to my unseamanly mind the futility of that became apparent.

Rowing made for hard exertion, and slow going. That just meant a quicker death from thirst, with very nearly no hope of getting any return from the effort.

So why bother?

So we sat. And bobbed. Each of us in his own thoughts, at least at first.

I got the distinct impression the other men would have been more freely talkative if I hadn't been there. And no wonder. I was a stranger, and an illicit one at that. They couldn't have been eager to explain what had gone on with me on their ship if we happened upon some manner of authority or other.

For that matter, I was rather surprised when I awoke after that first night to find I was still in the boat. It surely must have crossed at least one of their minds to just toss me overboard, and rid themselves of the potential trouble.

Later on in the morning, I got up the nerve to ask why they hadn't done that.

Squinty just grunted. "No seaman leaves another to drown."

Which, I supposed, made sense. In a way.

The next morning, though, it seemed a moot point.

As I looked out at the barren horizon and licked lips that were cracked from salt and lack of water with a tongue that felt rough as a grinding stone in my mouth and that pained me with every move-ment, it seemed there would be no one for these men to have to explain me to after all.

And then as the day wore on, even that ironic thought fled, and my thoughts became nothing but a catalogue of miseries.

My companions were no better off.

We sat there like the living dead. Not moving. Not talking. Hardly even breathing. Each man of us slowly thirsting away in his own little place of despair.

I racked my brain for any reason I would have been selected for this fate. Had I offended someone way back when I had been in Chalene and didn't know it, and they had only just tracked me down?

I didn't think so, and anyway I didn't hobnob with the kinds of people who had the resources to fund such a manhunt even if I had.

Someone closer to home, or in Moreton itself? But if that, why send me hundreds of miles across the sea to Moreton's rival? Why not deal with me there?

Or maybe it was some god, just feeling frisky and deciding to tweak some random man's destiny and I was the poor sod who caught his—more likely her—attention.

No answer was coming from the waves, the wind, or the sun, though. And as the day wore on and I felt my strength ebb, I became more certain those answers would ever elude me.

When I fell asleep the next night, I did not expect to see the morning.

I was so weak, so racked with pain and thirst, so sluggish in mind and body, that I welcomed that thought. Looked forward to oblivion, or whatever it was that came in the next world. It could not have been worse than the slow misery we were all enduring.

So when I cracked my eyes open in the morning, it was with a groan that was as much frustration as pain and despair.

Just let it end already!

But it didn't. It kept on going, each moment worse than the last, without hope or respite.

At some point I managed to raise my head, and I looked out at the waves. I recall seeing the sunlight sparkling off of them, and that it looked to me like the reflections were in fact a little man made of light who was dancing from wavetop to wavetop, giggling with glee as his toes barely alighted before setting off again.

He was having such a fun time of it. I began to become jealous of him; why should he get to enjoy himself so, and we not partake in it also.

I reached out to try to grab him as he sped past, but my hand caught nothing but air.

"Bastard," I said, just barely above a whisper, and let my hand fall into the water alongside the boat.

The cool wetness only made my thirst all the worse, but I couldn't bring myself to pull my hand out. I just watched as the little light man danced, and trailed my fingers in the water, and became bemused when the little man struck into something dark and blocky-looking, then vanish.

I blinked, puzzled. What—?

The dark thing, out on the waves, was still there. But I couldn't make it out; it was blurry, indistinct.

It was like a dark block, with something white above it, more curved. Was that—

"Sail!" said one of the other men. I couldn't tell who, didn't have the strength to look.

But the word filled me with joy, for a reason I couldn't fathom at first. Until its meaning registered, and I grinned a cracked-lipped grin and let out a rasping approximation of a laugh.

Sail. Sail meant ship.

Which meant we were saved.

Somewhere in the back of my thirst-addled mind, I also registered that I just might be able to find out the answers to those questions after all.

And that made me laugh just a little bit louder.

48

CANDLEMASS

Ray knew he was in trouble the instant the lights came on.

It wasn't the two grim faces staring at him, round cheeks and narrowed eyes so similar the two men had to be brothers.

No, it was what Ray saw past them that clinched it. A broad window through which he could see nothing but the starscape of deep space. And the blocky, dull-grey form of a heavy lift starship, the kind that carried cargo and passengers; not a ship of war.

And it was receding fast; very fast like it was thrusting away from Ray's vantage point. Except that he was looking at it from amidships, not bow or stern-on.

So he was the one zooming away. In this little grey-blue walled space with the window, and him sunk into a surprisingly comfy black faux-leather upholstered crash couch with the two bulky brothers in brown suits staring down at him. The matching brown curls atop their heads going well with their matching eyes and scowls.

Ray didn't need to ask which ship that was. It was the SV CANDLEMASS, on which he had hoped to make his getaway from Icarus before the Syndicate could catch up with him.

So much for that grand plan.

Ray's throat was scratchy, like with the beginnings of a cold, and his head ached. Whatever tranq the two men had hit him with seemed like it was going to leave him with one heck of a hangover in a short while.

He turned his head to look at the rest of the compartment where he sat. Plain walls, and a single sliding door—hatch—off to the right, with a plain black touch pad next to it. The operating panel.

Recessed lighting overhead that was tuned to a warm light that, unless he missed his guess, simulated a G5 star like the one Icarus orbited. White floor tiles, not shiny like brand new but still obviously well maintained. And from the feel of his body in the crash couch, the grav plates were tuned to Icaran local, 1.02g. Or close enough, anyway.

To the left, the bulkhead was dominated by a built-in vidscreen, which was black from inactivity. But it was big, and Ray could see speakers mounted in various places in the ceiling; a surround sound setup.

The air was dry and cool, and smelled ever so slightly of lemon, and Ray pursed his lips.

This wasn't a prison room or holding cell. Not a store room. It was more like a sitting room or entertainment center. He could almost be comfortable here, except...

Turning his gaze back on the two brothers, Ray found their expressions unchanged, their stance still quietly menacing.

He swallowed, which helped the sourness in his mouth but not his throat, then tried a grin at the two men.

"So boys," he said, and raised his hands in a placating gesture. "Where are we going?"

The guy on the left just grunted. His brother's scowl turned into a vicious semi-grin.

"Fryberg wants to see you."

Fryberg. That was a surprise. Ray hadn't interacted with him or any part of his organization before, at least not that he knew of. Of course, in Ray's line it was entirely possible to have done so without knowing it.

Still...

Ray felt his spirits lifting. Fryberg wasn't out for his head, nor did Ray owe him any money. So though his carefully laid plans had been foiled, he wasn't completely screwed.

Hopefully.

"Well I am at his disposal," Ray said, grinning with all his might. "When will we be arriving?"

"Now," said the brother who had spoken before.

The quiet one stepped forward and reached out to grab Ray's upper arm, saying, "Get up, pretty boy," as he did so.

Ray tried to pull away, but the guy's fingers were like vices, and he could only obey the sudden tug as the thug shifted his weight back, pulling Ray up onto his feet.

"I can do it mysel—" Ray's protest died in his throat as he reached his full height. His head immediately began swimming, and he saw double for a second.

Which was unfortunate because that meant he saw two of the scowling thug's face spinning around in front of himself, and one was enough.

Ray felt himself swaying on his feet, and for a second it was only the thug's grip on his arm that kept him from falling.

Yeah, that tranq the brothers had used must have been a doozy.

He shook his head, and slowly regained his equilibrium, blinking to make the images of the brothers settle down.

The guy holding him looked stern as ever. The other—the one who had spoken first—looked, if anything, amused for a second. Then he turned toward the door and tapped the control pad.

"Come on, tough guy," he said.

The door slid open, and Ray half-stumbled, half-walked, half-got-dragged through into a space that was simply too large to be on a starship, unless it was a hangar bay or a cargo compartment. But even then...

It had to have been twenty meters across and thirty deep. The doorway to the little entertainment room, or whatever it was, lay at the left-hand corner of the room, from Ray's perspective.

The entire place was covered in thick greyish-white rugs that Ray would be willing to bet had been hand-sewn. Heavily-cushioned divans colored red and blue and black were strewn about apparently at random, the kind of intentional randomness that only a master designer could obtain. Toward the rear of the room was a long table that looked to be carved from real wood, and was flanked by a dozen chairs that also looked wooden. To the right from the table was a short dais on top of which sat a single simple, though still wooden so decidedly expensive, chair.

The entire place was illuminated by the same recessed lighting as in the entertainment room, though looking around Ray supposed this place was where the real entertainment happened. But here the lighting was a bit more muted, and closer to the red end of the spectrum.

The air was warmer as well, a bit more humid, and Ray scented incense on the nearly imperceptible breeze that the ship's ventilation created. And sure enough, turning his head further to the right, he saw a pair of brass braziers dangling from chains in the ceiling, each emitting a slow stream of fragrant smoke.

That alone, more than anything else in the room, screamed the wealth of the ship's owner. To allow open flames onboard, even the tiny ones an incense burner required, and apparently without concern...

The thug gripping Ray's arm yanked him forward, and Ray stumbled for a second before catching himself.

They threaded their way through the sea of divans toward the dais at the back, and Ray noticed there was a woman reclining on one of the divans at the foot of the dais.

He had overlooked her when he first looked around, but as he got closer he questioned how that could have been possible.

She was striking. Long, muscular legs and a torso boasting every curve a man could want. With long, wavy black hair that flowed over her shoulders onto her chest, and skin that was healthily tanned, but just enough. Her eyes were slightly angular, like she had descended from Han or Nihon who had fled the Tsago Dominance.

She wore a loose-fitting, black and silver silken skirt that clung to her thighs enticingly, and a blue silk blouse that was equally loose, and equally enticing without being revealing. She held a crystal goblet in her left hand that was filled with a deep burgandy-colored wine, and silver chain earrings dangled from her ears, making little tings that almost seemed to be tuned to specific notes as she turned her head to regard him when he approached.

"Ray Tanaga," she said, and rose to her feet in a smooth, languid motion. "Welcome aboard."

Ray put on his best smile and quickly looked her up and down, making it obvious since she so clearly wanted him—and everyone else—to do so. "Glad to be here. And who might you be?"

She raised an eyebrow, and her lips twitched slightly. "I am Fryberg." With that, she ascended the dais and turned back around to face him, then slowly, gracefully, she settled herself down onto the chair waiting for her.

Ray's smile slipped, and he found himself gaping before he could catch himself. "You— *You're* Fryberg?"

She nodded slowly, amusement twinkling in her eyes.

"But..." Ray shut his mouth, swallowed, then tried again. "I thought—"

"You thought I was a man." Her lips turned up fully now, and she took a sip from her wine. "Most men do."

Ray had no response to that which could in any way come off as witty. So he just shrugged. "Well, what can I do for you?"

Fryberg took another sip of wine and leaned back in her chair. From this close up, Ray could see that the chair was slightly padded, with blue-upholstered cushions inlaid into the wood frame. But they couldn't have been very thick, those cushions. Still, Fryberg's body language said it was a comfortable sit.

Go figure.

She lowered her glass and regarded him with frank, piercing eyes, which he suddenly realized were green.

"Ray Tanaga. Small time con artist and petty thief. But somehow you managed to catch the attention of both the Martucci and Jenkins families. And," that eyebrow lifted again, "get the Jenkins family to put out a contract on you."

Ray didn't reply, he just watched her. His initial reaction to her beauty was fading into wariness, and as she laid out his situation so plainly, he began to feel a smidgeon of fear.

But just a smidgeon.

"Why?"

He blinked. "Why what?"

"Why did they put out a contract on you?"

Ray looked left, then right, and saw the burly brothers still flanking him. Though they had backed off a couple feet. For now.

"You already know the answer to that." He met Fryberg's eyes again, and raised his own eyebrow.

She chuckled ever so softly, then shrugged and took another sip. "Better than you, I expect," she said, after swallowing. "Shall I tell you?"

Ray shrugged. "I'd rather you just get to the point."

Fryberg's eyes narrowed, her lips compressing slightly. Then she said, "You scammed a thousand credits off of a witless coed. And," she raised her glass toward him almost in salute, "took her virginity as well."

Ray blinked. He remembered that scam. It was about five months back, and he hadn't thought about it since. But that wasn't why the Jenkins family wanted him dead. They wanted him dead because he had—

"You didn't know this, but that coed was the daughter of Kevin Jenkins' brother in law."

Ray's train of thought skidded to a halt. "Wha—?" He shook his head.

Fryberg nodded. "Oh yes. And of course, they are Catholic, so an abortion was out of the question."

Ray's knees felt wobbly again, but this time his vision didn't swirl. He just felt light-headed and he tasted bile.

Totally not the tranqs.

"A—" He coughed, to clear the sudden clenching of his throat. "Abortion?"

Another nod. "Thanks to you, the Jenkins clan will be welcoming a bastard soon. And their niece is now quite unmarriagable." Fryberg paused. "By their standards anyway."

Ray shook his head. "No, that's not right. They want me because I—"

"Because you helped the Martuccis steal the Amestenol they so recently smuggled past customs."

Ray couldn't do anything but nod.

"That did anger the Jenkins', to be sure," Fryberg said. "But when they found your DNA at the scene of the theft and ran it, they discovered, quite by accident, that it was a parental match for the baby." She smiled wickedly at him. "Pre-natal care at its finest."

She drank from her goblet again, then said, "They probably wouldn't have killed you for the theft. Just made you work off the debt. But the violation..." She shook her head, and made a tsking sound.

That lifting of spirits that Ray had begun to feel earlier faded completely. He swallowed a sudden lump in his throat, then tried grinning at her again. "I don't suppose you brought me here to congratulate me on my prowess."

Fryberg actually laughed out loud, and shook her head. "No, I'm afraid not."

"And you're not looking for a baby daddy as well, I take it?"

Her lips pursed and her eyes tracked up and down Ray's body. For a second, he thought she almost might take him up on it.

Then she shook her head. "Definitely not. No," she leaned forward in her chair, all amusement lost from her face as she regarded him with eyes that seemed to stab straight through him, "I'm going to collect the bounty on your head."

"Well, hang on now. We can—"

"Vasili," she said to the brother on Ray's left. Then to the one on his right, "Liev."

As though taking their names as orders, the two men sprang on Ray, and grabbed him by the arms.

He tried to squirm out of their grasp, but they were too strong, and anyway he was still a bit loopy from the tranq. Or maybe they were just too strong.

Either way, he found himself being dragged away from Fryberg's little throne.

He cried out again; surely he and her could come to some other arrangement. He could do some jobs for her. Something. Anything.

But she just watched him go, sipping at her wine with a strangely satisfied expression on her face.

The trip back to Icarus was a lot shorter than Ray thought it should have been. After all, the CANDLEMASS had been halfway to the closest of the system's jump points went Fryberg's goons jumped him. And it had seemed to take forever to get that far.

But, before Ray really had time to get used to the idea that he was being taken back to his doom, the door to the little room where he had been stashed—quite a bit less comfy than the entertainment room he'd first met when he came aboard—opened, and the two brothers dragged him out.

Ray considered trying to fight. Actually began the attempt.

And then gave up on the idea as soon as it came. He was a talker, not a fighter. And these two fellows were the opposite. And each of them outweighed him by at least twenty kilos.

So after just a short struggle that didn't even count as such, he found himself dragged down a relatively short passageway and then down a ramp through which sunlight streamed.

On the tarmac beneath the ship, he blinked in the glare, so much brighter than the shipboard lights he had grown used to. But glare or no, Ray recognized the features of the man Vasili and Liev brought him to stand before.

Head and shoulders taller than both of them, lean and powerful despite the weight of many years, which had dug deep trenches into the lines of his face. With silver-grey hair cut short on the sides and back but left to grown long on top, and a thin, pristinely manicured mustache.

Ray had only met him once before, but he would never forget him.

Vincent Jenkins. The Jenkins family patriarch, and the head of all their enterprises, both criminal and not.

The old gangster looked Ray up and down when the toughs brought him to a halt, and a trace of a smile appeared on Jenkins' face.

"Ray," he said, his voice a silky-smooth baritone that almost seemed to purr as it issued from his lips. "How nice to see you again."

Liev poked something into the left side of Ray's neck, then the world went black.

Ray didn't wake as easily this time.

On Fryberg's ship, it was like going from lights out to lights on, like a switch had been thrown. The tranq Liev hit him with this time was both more gentle...and less.

The transition back to consciousness was easier, more gradual. But damn the headache was like someone taking a ball-peen hammer to his temples. Add in nausea and a taste like rancid meat on a tongue that felt like sandstone in his mouth, and it was worse than the worst hangover Ray had ever experienced.

Which is why he just lay there on something cold and hard, squinting his eyes shut against bright light that seemed to want to tunnel through his eye sockets and fry his brain, and groaned.

Loud.

His limbs felt like lead, and his stomach was twisting in his belly like a serpent coiling itself around a victim. But he heard the voice that said, "He's awake."

Heard it, recognized it, and then groaned even louder when the recognition registered in Ray's beleaguered brain.

It hadn't been a nightmare. That had been Vincent Jenkins he'd seen before. And that voice belonged to his son, Kevin.

Kevin, of the uncle-in-law to the girl Ray had taken five months ago variety.

"Get him up."

Ray felt hands grasp him beneath the armpits, and he found himself hauled to his feet.

The light was still bright, but his eyes had adjusted. A bit. So he was able to see the room around him, mostly.

He rather wished he could not.

It was smaller than Fryberg's reception room, or whatever it had been, despite being in a building on a planet instead of within a starship. It was the back room in a warehouse, unless Ray missed his guess. Metal shelving that showed surface rust in numerous places lined the walls in front of him and to his right, and harsh LED lights hanging from the ceiling provided illumination. The floor was tiled in black and white squares, and the place smelled like dust and sweat.

But Ray didn't pay mind to much else except the man in front of him.

Kevin Jenkins had similar facial bone structure to his father, but aside from that they were opposites. Where his father was tall and lanky, Kevin was short. Short and built like a brick shithouse. His shoulders were almost half as broad as he was tall, and his muscles strained the long-sleeved, collarless, navy blue shirt he was wearing until Ray could swear he heard the threads in the shirt's seams screaming in agony.

His hair was dark brown, not silver like his father, and he wore a closely-trimmed beard. His eyes were hazel, and hard as they burrowed into Ray's face. But he wore an expression of satisfaction.

"Good old Ray Tanaga," Kevin Jenkins said, and it sounded like he was talking familiarly with someone he wasn't about to have killed. "How you been, Ray?"

"Never better, Kevin," Ray managed to say, though the words came out jumbled and he could barely recognize his own voice, scratchy as it was. "Nice seeing you again."

Kevin snorted, then gestured to his right, where a second man stood. He was muscular, though nowhere near to Kevin's level, and a couple years younger than Kevin, which still put him at least ten years older than Ray. His hair was reddish blond, and he wore a light grey business suit, without tie; the collar of his light blue shirt was undone.

His eyes were green, but not as green as Fryberg's, and they looked at Ray with hate that should have set him on fire, it was so intense.

It had been five months, but Ray remembered the girl in question, and he saw reflection of her pretty face in this man's.

He was so screwed.

"This is Stephen O'Donnel," Kevin said. "He's been wanting to meet you for a long time now."

Ray nodded companionably at Stephen and tried putting on a pleasant grin. "Nice to meet you."

The right cross took him in the cheek, and Ray's head snapped to the side. His ears rang and he saw stars. He tasted blood, and thought he might have bit his tongue. Or maybe the punch had taken out a couple of his teeth. He couldn't tell; the entire side of his face ached and his cheek was already swelling, and he couldn't pick out what part was broken, what was just hurt, and what was screaming out in sympathy for its neighbors.

He spat out a mouthful of blood and turned groggy eyes back toward Stephen, who shook his hand out in front of his chest, letting his fingers loosen and the sting of his punch leave a bit.

Stephen did look a bit less hate-filled right that second; he even returned Ray's nod. "The pleasure is all mine."

Then he grinned, and the smile contained promises of long, long days of many unpleasant things in Ray's future, and that Stephen was going to enjoy every minute of it.

Ray would have swallowed, but his jaw didn't seem to be working right then. He glanced back at Kevin, who had a look of impassive almost-amusement on his face. The sort of expression that said he didn't much care about what was happening, though it was interesting to watch.

"Look," Ray said, and the word came out like, "Wook."

Great.

"Look," he said more slowly, turning back to Stephen. "I didn't know, ok? I'm sorry. You don't need to kill me."

"Kill you?" Stephen's eyes widened slightly, then that grin came back. "I'm not going to kill you. Just cut on you a little bit." He reached behind his back and pulled out a long, broad-bladed steel knife. The blade gleamed almost like silver in the LED light, and Stephen made a little gesture with it toward Ray's crotch. "Only a little."

Ray felt his eyes widening, and he tried to take a reflexive step back, but the hands holding him up, belonging to some nameless goon who had picked him up and was still standing behind him, gripped him tightly, and forced him to remain still. "Is that really necessary? I mean—"

Stephen stepped closer, so there was barely a foot between them, and Ray felt as much as saw the knife move downward.

"There's has to be another way we can work this out."

Stephen's eyes narrowed. "We can work it out, all right. Your choice as to how."

"What do you mean?"

"You're gonna to do right by my girl. Or you're gonna be a eunuch. Up to you."

Do right. He didn't mean... Did he?

Stephen nodded. "Yer gonna marry her, take care of her, and stay true to her. I learn she's not happy with you in any way..."

Ray flinched as he felt the blade—the flat of the blade, thank God —tap his nether regions.

"Of course, if you prefer to stay a single man..."

"No! No, I can do that. Be a good husband. Always wanted to be a

Dad." He really hadn't, but right then, he didn't see a whole lot of choice.

"Thought you'd see it that way." Stephen's smile was satisfied, but also more than a little sadistic.

***

And so, a week later, Ray found himself in a cathedral, in a tuxedo, exchanging vows with the lovely Miss Loretta O'Donnel. Stephen gave her away, then stood behind them as they said the vows, and Kevin was his best man.

As Ray slipped the ring onto his young bride's finger, he remembered a picture he had seen from old Terra, centuries before man had expanded to the stars. Of a young couple in a church, getting married, with the girl's father standing behind them, shotgun in hand.

He never thought it possible that a shotgun wedding could still take place. But he had no doubt what would happen if he didn't go through with it.

Then again, when he looked up from Loretta's hand to her face after he put the ring on her, he saw the simple beauty of her, augmented by the glow that all pregnant women seem to get. He thought of his son—they had found out it was a boy—growing within her. And as he saw the thing that almost was happiness—and the promise that it could perhaps truly grow into that over time—in her eyes, he figured it could be worse.

A whole lot worse.

49

BRIDGE MENDING

I'm not a super sentimental guy, but there are times when even I look back on past events through the lens of nostalgia and pine for those long-gone, supposedly simpler times.

Never thought an elf would do the same.

When they gave the Big Guy the finger over working conditions and left the Pole, they left for good. Or so they said.

Turns out, even a pointy can end up pining for the good old days.

I'm Dustin Cofield, and I'm an elfsterminator.

I was sitting behind my old, beat up wooden desk and typing out a report on an equally old but very well-maintained relic from the 30s, a mechanical typewriter, when a knock came on my door.

I looked up from the cursed machine, torn between being thankful that I could give my fingers and wrists a rest and being shocked over the sound.

I'd been stationed in Lockwood, and working out of this same eight foot square office in the back of a Wells Fargo branch, for years. And no one had ever knocked on my office door before.

See, I don't really work for the bank. I work for a non-existent Agency that helps the Big Guy with his production up at the Pole since the elves bailed on him, and helps contain the elf menace in the rest of the world. My line is more the later than the former.

The Agency had some sort of arrangement with the bank. I have a title: Senior Financial Analyst. I attend staff meetings and social events. But I don't work for the bank and I never receive tasking from the President or anyone else. The only real professional interaction I had with them was turning in my reports to Higher. Those went to the bank President, in double-sealed envelopes of course, who then dutifully forwarded them on via corporate mail accounts.

How much the Agency paid for my use of this space, or that one service the President performed, I have no idea and don't care. But the bank had been plenty accommodating over the years, leaving me with complete autonomy and never disturbing my space at all.

Not even the cleaning lady.

Which got annoying because it meant I had to clean up myself. But we all have our crosses to bear.

Now the knock had me stopping in surprise for a moment. Then I did a quick once-over around my office.

It was nothing fancy. Four beige-painted walls and a door, and a small slit of a window that allowed a bit of sunlight in to augment the recessed lighting in the ceiling. I put the potted plant—don't ask me what kind it is, I just know it's green and occasionally produces white-pink flower buds—that Nora, my girlfriend, gave me a while back in front of the window, and there was a single wood-framed chair for visitors next to it.

I rarely got those.

On my desk I just had a heavily coffee-stained mug that was painted round with holly, candy canes, and mistletoe, the cussed typewriter on top of a leather-backed calendar blotter, an old rotary-style telephone, and a small stack of finished report pages, typed in triplicate from carbon paper inserts. Nothing truly incriminating there.

To the left on the wall next to the door was a cork board on which I had posted mimeographed memos from Higher that I thought I would need: safety regulations, upcoming events, and a couple wanted posters of particularly infamous elfin conspirators.

Beside the board I had a few pictures hanging up. One of me and the Big Guy himself at an awards gala up at the Pole stood out.

That would be hard to explain, but it wouldn't be visible from the door so I didn't bother to take it down or hide it.

The only other things in the room were the lockers behind my desk where I stored files and my tactical gear, and the old weight-driven clock on the wall opposite the door, which made a soft tick-tocking sound that I sometimes found myself typing in cadence with if I wasn't careful.

The place smelled of carbon paper and old coffee, and I had gotten very comfortable with it over the years.

I stood, the casters on the bottom of my black leather-upholstered office chair making slight squeaking sounds as it pushed back.

"Just a moment," I said as I squeezed past the desk.

I gave one last look around the place, then I pulled the door halfway open.

There was a woman standing out there. Slightly plump, in her early thirties, she had long black hair that she kept pulled back from her face with a blue hairband that matched the pants suit she was wearing. Her green-hazel eyes were bright and intelligent, and she wore the slightest hint of a smile.

But then, she always did.

I knew her. Cindy, the bank receptionist on duty this morning.

"Hi Cindy," I said, returning her smile with one of my own. I noticed she smelled faintly of lavender; that helped.

"Mr. Cofield," she said, then gestured toward the front of the bank, "there's a man here to see you."

I blinked, surprise making me wary. I didn't have any appointments until later this afternoon, but that was a meeting with Colleen, the Agency's local forensic analyst, over at her office.

"Did he give a name?"

Cindy shook her head. "No, just said to give you this." She held out a business card. "He said you'd understand."

I took the card and looked at it. It was printed only on one side, and there was no name. Just a pair of candy canes going diagonally across the card and crossing in the middle.

My eyebrows rose involuntarily and I looked back up at her.

She must have seen the question on my face, because she again gestured toward the front of the bank. "He's in the customer seating area."

I nodded. "Thanks."

As she walked away back to her station, I pondered for a second what this could mean.

I'd worked a case a while back, an interstate candy cane smuggling ring. Some of the equipment they'd used had been marked with twin candy canes like that. I thought sure I'd mopped up all the pointies involved in the case.

Maybe not?

Or maybe this was another person from the Agency, just playing a little game with me.

Either way, I needed to see what was going on.

I walked across the polished faux-marble of the bank branch, and as always the sheer fakeness of the faux-wood veneer, the polished grins on the tellers and the loan officers back in their glass-fronted offices, the almost antiseptic non-scent in the air, and the soft hum of conversations all struck me at once and reminded me how false all of it was. Just a facade of polish over a sea of iniquity.

If the Agency hadn't stashed me here, there might not have been a single bit of societal good done in this place all year.

The customer seating area was to my right as I approached the slightly-raised faux wood desk where Cindy sat ensconced. The customer chairs were comfy enough, upholstered in smooth red-beige cushions, and positioned around a darkly-stained coffee table.

The seating area was empty except for one man. When I saw him, my hackles rose immediately, and I felt the tingle of adrenaline running through my system.

He was short; maybe he would have come to my waist when he stood. He wore a black double-breasted business suit not too terribly different from my own, except that mine was navy blue and pinstriped, and about two dozen sizes larger than his. His tie was just slightly blue of green, and his shirt seemed to glow it was so white. He wore round black-rimmed spectacles, and he wore his dark brown hair long, its loose curls flowing down his head to his shoulders.

He had a black leather briefcase sitting on the chair next to him, and he watched me come with dark eyes that were narrowed slightly.

He could have been a well-to-do, successful little person. Except I saw the slight bulges in his curls near the top of his temples on either side of his head.

Elf ears, concealed by the flowing curls of his mane.

I stalked forward, falling into a more ready stance without thought as I immediately began scanning the room around me. Where there was one pointy, often times there were others. And if this was some sort of trap, I—

The little guy raised his hands, palms out and fingers splayed as I drew near. "I come in peace," he said, his tone a rich baritone and not the squeaky noise that someone who'd only ever seen bad Christmas movies, or the Wizard of Oz, would expect from a person of his stature. "Just want to talk."

I stopped a couple paces away from him and planted my hands on my hips. "So talk."

He made a gesture with his left hand toward the rear of the bank, where I'd just come from. "Maybe in your office? Some things I have to say aren't for public ears."

I scowled at him. I really didn't want an elf coming into my private space. Never let one in there before.

But then again, I'd never had dealings with any of the pointies on the bank grounds. Always before it had been out on a case, or in a holding facility for interrogation. Once a pointy named Loomy had called me here in my office, when he kidnapped Nora for ransom. So I knew they knew where I was based.

Never thought to have a conversation with one of them in here, though.

Well, first time for everything, I supposed.

I drew a breath, held it for a second, then let it out slowly, and nodded. "Fine. Follow me."

Back in my office, I quickly dropped down into my chair while the elf closed the door, and scooted in so I had a good portion of its bulk between me and him...and so I could open the drawer where I kept a piece ready. Just in case.

Turning away from the door, the elf's eyes flicked toward my right hand, hidden from his view, and he raised a knowing eyebrow.

No fool, this one. He had to know what I had close at hand.

But if it bothered him, he didn't show it. He crossed his arms over his chest and peered around the rest of my office, taking in the decor and the furnishings with pursed lips for a moment.

"Figured you for fancier digs, Cofield," he said.

"Yeah, well. I used to be in a penthouse. But budget cuts. You know how it is."

He snorted softly, and his eyes flicked to my left, toward the cork board and the pictures. His eyebrow rose again.

"So you've actually met him. Most guys in your line haven't."

I followed his gaze to my awards gala photo. The Big Guy, smiling that big smile of his that never struck me as completely genuine. I recalled the twinkling intelligence in his eyes and the slight bit of inflection in his voice, the little feeling that he wasn't completely everything he made himself out to be. That maybe there was more to his operation than just magnanimity toward the kids.

I put that from my mind and looked back at the elf. "How would you know?"

"I've been around a long time, Cofield. Lots longer than you. I've seen things you wouldn't believe."

And he was probably right about that. Elves were remarkably long-lived. Came from their time with the Big Guy, as I understood it.

He had rubbed off on them, and they had rubbed off on him, but in different ways. This guy was probably at least a few hundred years old, if he was twenty.

"I see you're still doing it the old-fashioned way." The elf nodded at the typewriter. "He's still stuck on that, is he?"

That made me frown, but not because of the typewriter itself.

The typewriter, and the mimeographed memos, and the rest of the low tech, was a necessity of working for the Big Guy. Him and electronics don't mix. Not even for correspondence. Something about the residual field left by electronics meant he couldn't even touch a paper printed out from a modern device. It messed with his magic somehow.

So the Agency did everything old school, at least when it came to things that might come anywhere near the Big Guy.

I had electronic equipment. Just not in here, where the reports got written.

That was just a fact of life in this job. And though it sometimes was annoying, and painful on the wrists, it didn't really bother me right then.

What bothered me was the tone of voice the elf had used when he said that. Like we were silly for doing it, behind the eight ball. There had been several cases lately where it appeared the pointies were figuring out how to use electronics without it messing with their own use of whatever magic it was that powered everything associated with the Big Guy and the Pole. We hadn't come across anything truly definitive, though.

Here was another hint, and it irked me.

"You want to get to the point? Who are you, anyway?" I let some irritation through into my tone of voice.

It had the desired effect. The elf gave a little jerk, and some of the poise he had been exuding faded.

"Sorry," he said with an apologetic titling of his head. "Name's Willie." He gestured back toward the picture of me and the Big Guy. "Used to work for him."

"Didn't you all?"

"No, I mean really work for him. I was one of his secretaries." His tone turned, if anything, wistful as he looked more fully at the picture again. "I can't admit it to any of the others, but looking back, those were good times. I miss those days."

He inhaled, drew himself up, and looked at me square. "That's why I'm here, Cofield. To turn myself in. Defect. I want to go back."

I'm pretty sure I felt my jaw bouncing off my breastbone, it dropped so far, and so quickly.

"You what?"

"Want to go back." Willie threw up his hands. "Yeah, he's an asshole, and sometimes working for him sucked. But I'm sick of this shit, Cofield. Sick of running around in the shadows, always having to look over my shoulder in case guys like you are coming to nab me up just for trying to make a living. It gets to a guy, you know?"

"Nothing says you have to make a living screwing with Christmas. Lots of other things you could do, Willie."

"You think I haven't tried?" He clenched his fists and stepped toward the desk, and I took hold of the piece. There was a light in his eyes that I wasn't comfortable with at all.

"Take it easy."

He snarled for a second. But then he took a deep breath and slowly got himself back under control. Finally, he said, "Some of the other guys have managed to go legit. I tried to. But..." He shook his head, looking back at the photo again. "Maybe it's how long I worked directly for him. Christmas is in my blood. I can't do anything else. Can't think of anything else." When he looked back at me there were tears in the corners of his eyes. "And I'm tired of doing it like a criminal."

I eased my grip on the piece and nodded slowly. I understood what he was getting at. A bit. But...

"I don't know if he'll *let* you back, Willie. There's been bad blood there for a long time."

"Don't I know it." He looked down at his mirror-polished shoes and sighed. Then he sniffed and looked back up at me. "But there were good times before. There could be again." He smiled slightly. "Just asking you to try. Put in a good word for me."

"You know I can't do that, Willie." He opened his mouth to retort but I raised my left hand to cut him off, and kept going. "Not that I wouldn't want to. But I don't have that kind of access to him. I wouldn't even know how to do something like that."

Which was not completely true. There was a hotline. It wouldn't get me straight to the Big Guy's office, but it would get me to the Agency's Field Office at the Pole, and the Duty Officer there. The DO could get a message to him quickly, if necessary.

But Willie probably didn't know that. And anyway, I wasn't sure he was on the up and up, and I had no intention of getting played for a sucker.

"Of course you can't," Willie said. "You're just a lowly field agent. But you know people who can."

I shrugged. "Could be."

He looked at me for a long moment, then nodded, his shoulders sagging slightly. "But you don't believe me."

"Would you, if you were me?"

Willie shook his head ruefully. "Guess not." Again his eyes fell to the floor, and he sighed. Twice. Then he drew another breath and raised his head, squaring his shoulders. He had a determined look on his face, but also a resigned one. Like he was about to do something he didn't want to, but that was necessary.

He gestured toward the typewriter. "What if I told you there was a way to bring your operation up to civilized times?"

The words hit me like a prize fighter's jab. My mind whirled back to my earlier recollections of the recent cases, and the tantalizing hints.

If the pointies had cracked the electronics problem, that was a game changer. It meant their capability was about to take a quantum leap upward, and their threat toward Christmas as well. It was a thought that had the strategic planning office at Headquarters up nights with worry.

But if it was true, and Willie was willing to divulge the secret...

His lips turned upward into a broad grin. "Caught your interest now, didn't I?"

I tried to put on a bland expression, but he saw right through it.

"Why don't you get on that phone, and call someone who can make this happen." He paused. "Or I can just walk out of here. If I'm not wanted..." He trailed off, and there was satisfaction in his tone.

He had me. Or he thought he did.

No. He had me.

If there was a chance to leapfrog the pointies' potential electronics advancement, I had to take it.

I picked up the phone.

The call brought another field agent in from Pittsfield, about two hours away, and together we put Willie up in a safe house on the other side of the metropolitan area where Lockwood lies.

The safehouse was a no-tell motel not far from our forensics office. Not fancy, by any stretch of the imagination. But it did the job.

In the morning, more agents arrived, and they all took Willie off to Higher, for debriefing and evaluation.

Never saw him again, but a couple weeks later word filtered down from Higher that they were in talks with the Big Guy about getting him back to the Pole and on payroll.

No one said a damn thing to me about electronics, though.

Could be he was full of it, after all, but he gave something else up that made the high-ups want to go to bat for him. Or could be the electronics thing would take a while to crack, and they were keeping it on the down low for now.

Either way, I was the low man on the totem pole, and I knew it. I'd find out when they wanted me to find out. If ever.

But that's ok. I had my cases to work, and my nights and weekends to spend with Nora. A job I dig, and a girl I dig. Not a bad combination. Pretty good, if you ask me.

Still, as I turned out the light in my office and closed up for the day, I couldn't help but wonder if Willie would be content when he finally got back to the Pole. Or would he find out that his good old days weren't really all that good, after all?

For his sake, I hoped the former.

But I wasn't so sure.

50

THE SHRINE OF TULOK

Hot wind blew past Thurim, bringing with it the scent of impending rain overtop the other, more earthy odors that seemed to permeate the grasslands he was traversing. It whipped his cloak around behind him as he peered down from the hilltop where he stood.

The garment was once bright scarlet but now it was closer to burgundy from weeks of dust and grime as he made his trek into the wild. The rest of his clothing was equally soiled, and stiff from accumulated salt deposited by the near constant sweat that his exertions had generated during that time.

The weight of the sword on his belt, or the black lacquered breastplate he wore overtop his tunic, didn't help with that. But he did not dare leave them behind, though he lose all else on this journey.

As he just about had.

He had long since gone through the last of his food, which was nice since it made his pack light. But he felt it in the pit of his belly now, which was growing steadily more empty, like a growing maw that was opening wide to engulf the entire world. He had managed to keep his waterskin full, though. The many streams and occasional lakes that crisscrossed this endless, rolling prairie made that easy.

Though right then it felt like scant blessing.

Thurim looked over his shoulder, in the direction where the late afternoon sun was seeming to race toward its resting place on the horizon, barely staying ahead of the clouds that appeared to be rushing to catch it and keep it from reaching that haven.

Still no sign of pursuit; no obvious sign anyway. All the same, he could not help feeling certain Basmin was back there, somewhere. Seeking after him, but more than that, after the shrine that Thurim sought.

That they both sought, though only Thurim knew how to get there.

At least, so he hoped.

Thurim faced back to the east, squinting his eyes against the blow of the wind, and scanned the horizon again. It was becoming more difficult by the minute. Already the swiftly darkening clouds in that direction were casting a shadow over the land, so that the rolling hills seemed to merge with the boiling clouds overhead until the horizon was swiftly becoming jumbled, indiscernible in the mix of the elements.

Somewhere in that direction. Somewhere there lay they Shrine of Tulok, where legend stated the ancients had hidden their greatest treasure, the source of the wondrous power that had birthed an age of wealth and prosperity that had never been seen in the world since.

And Thurim meant to claim it, before Basmin did.

The first drops of rainfall splattered onto Thurim's cheeks, driven by the wind in front of him, and he realized it wasn't just the growing gloom that was obscuring the terrain ahead. It was the torrential rain that was approaching. Rapidly.

He didn't waste time looking around for a place of shelter. There would be none, not on these accursed and seemingly eternal plains. He'd seen nothing more than a few isolated trees scattered here and there for a week or more, and only one cluster that might strain to be called a copse.

Just long, thigh-high grass that had been growing yellow in the heat but now might grow green again after the coming deluge.

Not nearly enough to make Thurim even think about trying to stay dry.

Instead, he hunched his shoulders, flipped the cowl of his cloak up and drew the rest of the once proud garment tightly down about his body. Then, head lowered against the now steady downpour, he trudged down the hilltop in the direction of his quest.

The ground was still firm for the first few hundred paces, but soon Thurim's boots began to sink into the growing mud, making his steps more difficult with each passing moment.

Rivulets of water were now running freely, cutting swaths narrow and deep through the grassy knolls as the rainfall cut into the terrain, digging new furrows into the side of each little hill he passed.

And creating new streams in between them. Streams that were swiftly growing until Thurim thought they would soon become rivers in their own right.

And him caught in the middle of it all. If he wasn't careful, he would get swept away in the onrush.

This was beyond what he had encountered before. In the forest-land of Kadiz, where he had spent most of his youth and the first few years of his manhood, rain was plentiful but the tree growth even in the mountains kept the land mostly stable. It was becoming clear, rapidly, that the grass covering this land was not enough to do the same.

The entire region was going to flood out.

Thurim was beginning to regret departing that last hilltop, as the runoff from the rainfall was approaching ankle-deep now. He chanced a look back, and was surprised to see how far he had come from that little peak. No way he could make it back there now.

He would just have to continue, and get to as high a ground as he could in the land ahead.

The darkened sky flashed, and a few breaths later the rumble of thunder sounded. Thurim's spirits, already low, lowered further. Lightning and thunder meant this was not some passing rain shower that would speed past and be done. It was going to be a long evening, and a longer night.

The land sloped upward again to Thurim's right, and he hurried in that direction. At first the climb was relatively easy, the slope shallow. But after a few tens of yards the angle of the hill grew more steep, and Thurim found himself stymied.

He could have easily climbed it on a dry day. But with the downfall continuing, the entire hill was turning to mud, and he found himself sliding with each step so that he barely maintained his position on the hill's side.

It was difficult to see to the hilltop, as heavy as the rain was now, but it couldn't be that far. And the water was accumulating all the more the in little valley he had just been in. He had no choice but to make it.

So he began climbing on all fours, more a crawl than anything else. He grabbed at the tufts of grass that were still clinging to the side of the incline, using them for purchase as he pulled himself higher.

Everywhere water ran, and he was soaked to the bone. Covered in mud. The earlier heat of the day had gone, leaving Thurim cool, moving toward chilled, as the deluge continued to bombard him.

But he carried on, crawling truly now, using elbows and knees to dig into the ever more loosely bound-together mud to get that one more foot. One more inch. All the more closer to the top, to be safe from the increasing flood that covered the land beneath and below him.

Thurim lost track of time, could see nothing aside from the mud in front of his face. Feel nothing but the trembling of limbs grown numb from wetness and chill and exertion. He had to move his head to the side to breath, so strong was the flow of water—and mud— from the top of the hill, trying to push him down.

But he couldn't stop. One glance behind and down showed that.

The light was fading; the sun must have reached the horizon, so dark was it getting. But he could see the torrent flowing between the grass-covered hills below him.

He was not a strong swimmer, and anyway that current was looking strong. There was no respite below, only more difficulty, maybe a swift trip to his death. So he had to go on.

Go on he did. As the light faded and he could see less and less. Feel nothing but cold and the urge to just lie still. For surely he could not stand to go even another foot higher up this god-cursed slope.

He needed to stop. Had to stop...

And then the slope was gone. There was only the downpour of rain atop his prone body and at least something approaching level ground. Thurim could barely lift his head, but he forced himself to take a look about, and was shocked to see, in the all but completely faded light, that he had somehow reached the top of the hill.

Water fell down all around him, flowed down the inclines on either side toward the little valleys on all sides of his perch. But right here, where he was, was stability and at least a smidgeon of calm in this tumult.

No comfort, but that wasn't needed. Right then, all Thurim needed was a respite; any respite.

He slumped down, resting his forehead on the meat of his left forearm. And drifted away into the deepest sleep he could remember.

When he awoke, sunlight, warm and sweet, was streaming down onto him. The air was damp but warm; on any other day he would have considered the sopping heat an exercise in misery. But now as he pushed himself up onto his knees and looked around, still feeling the deep chill he had experienced during the rainfall in the marrow of his bones, the sauna-like warmth felt like heaven.

He was a mess. Clumps of partially-dried mud fell off him as he moved, and his clothing was one big mess of grime, uniformly brown, almost without exception.

But whatever. He wasn't going to complain. It could have been much worse.

Thurim inhaled deeply and looked around.

There was barely any grass remaining on his little hill, and the others nearby were the same. As far as he could see, what had been lush grasslands with growing plants to mid-thigh was now stripped bare. Brown sludgy mud and detritus from the deluge was everywhere.

Down in the valleys between the rolling hills, some of the mud still flowed, albeit slowly, carrying with it strands of grass as tightly-packed as logs being floated down-river from a woodcutter's camp.

He wouldn't trust the footing down there. Not yet. It looked exactly the kind of muck that a man could get caught up in and find himself stuck in, or worse, sucked down and smothered by.

"Going to have to stay up here for a time," he said, surprising himself with the sound of his own voice.

He was rested, sure, but he still felt the exertions of the previous night. His arms and legs were sore from use of muscles he hadn't had cause to use very often before, if at all. His throat felt scratchy, and his head was slightly sore, almost like the first inklings of an upcoming cold. And no wonder, from that chill he'd gotten.

But despite that, his voice sounded strong to his own ears, confident and determined.

And after a moment's consideration, Thurim decided that was indeed how he felt, physical discomforts aside. Which his mind said was odd, considering how bleak the landscape was, to match the bleakness of the prospects for his quest at this point.

No food, and no prospects toward finding any. No way to proceed forward for who knows how long until the valleys dried up.

And Basmin no doubt still dogging his heels.

Though, Thurim considered if he truly had been, Basmin would have been waylaid by the rainfall just as he had. So there was that.

Thurim's thoughts turned toward his erstwhile friend, and not for the first time he said a prayer that Basmin would have given up on this petty rivalry, this competition that never had to be.

They had together discovered the texts shedding light on the Shrine's reality; the proof that it was more than a mere legend. It should have been them working together to uncover its secrets. But Basmin had betrayed Thurim. He had resolved that he alone would be the one to find the Shrine. Find it, and control it. So he had stabbed Thurim in the back, set the local magistrates on him on a trumped up charge.

Or tried to.

Thurim had managed to evade his friend's duplicity, and fled with the texts, determined to get to the shrine first. It was a source of unbelievable power. Such a thing was not meant to serve the vanity of a single man, but to serve all.

He had to get to the shrine first, or he feared all would be lost.

But that wasn't going to happen right now. Now, there was nothing for it but to sit and wait for the mud to dry. Which could take days.

With a resigned sigh, Thurim shifted his weight, maneuvering to sit down fully, into the old meditation position his teachers had taught him, back when he was a boy being tutored and readied for a man's burdens.

It seemed so long ago...

His thoughts were just turning toward those days when he settled fully into the meditation position, his weight coming to rest fully onto his buttocks and the hilltop.

And the ground gave way beneath him.

That was the thought that went through his head in that first instant; but he quickly cast that away, as the sun was still just as bright and he could see.

No, the ground hadn't given way. The bit of not-fully congealed mud that he had shifted onto had slid, and now he was sliding as well, down the hill toward the slowly-moving mud and grass mix that he had just resolved not to go near.

He was gathering speed. The sludge at the bottom of the hill approaching rapidly.

Frantically, Thurim flung his hands out, digging his fingers into the earth on either side. But it was still mostly wet, and he found he couldn't get much purchase at all.

He was making his own little river of mud and water and debris as he slid down, and the pool that he now felt certain would lead solely to his death was looming. Thurim cried out, and his hand came down on the pommel of his sword.

He hated to lose it, but given the alternative...

Thurim twisted his body, pulling the sword free, and with all his might plunged the blade into the earth.

His momentum carried him on even as the steel dug deep into the soft earth, and Thurim took hold of the weapon with both hands on its grip.

He swayed there for a long moment, and the blade began slipping. It had only driven in halfway, so a good foot of steel was visible out of the earth. The mud on the downhill side of the weapon began to slip, the blade combined with the weight of Thurim's body compressing the mud and threatening to drag the weapon out completely.

Then, it stopped its slipping. The blade held firm, and Thurim stopped his downward slide.

He kicked with his feet, digging his toes into the mud to get a bit more purchase and take the strain off his arms, which were already beginning to tremble from holding him up from continuing his slide down the treacherous slope.

There wasn't much purchase, but there was enough to relax his grip, at least a little bit.

Virtually collapsing against the mud of the hillside, Thurim breathed in and out deeply for a long minute or so. Then he looked down.

The river of mud and grass was only a few feet beneath his feet now. If the sword hadn't—

But it had. And he didn't dare to pull it out.

Though he couldn't just perch here forever, either.

Thurim twisted his body, looking down at the mud river then up at the facing hill on its other side. Quite a lot more close-by than Thurim had at first thought. It looked as though the other hill's slope, less steep than his own and apparently mostly solid, was only ten feet or so from him.

Too far to jump. But maybe...

Thurim let go of his sword with his left hand and ran it down to the lacquered breastplate he wore. Once finely painted, plain and elegant while also being functional, it was now battered and mud-covered. Resembling nothing so much as a cast-off from a defeated soldier.

Nothing a good cleaning couldn't cure. But that wan't going to happen any time soon, and anyway...

He couldn't make the jump to the other side. And if he landed in that mud river, the weight of the breastplate would only aid in dragging him down.

Thurim hated it, didn't want to even consider doing it. But there was no choice. It had to go.

He ran his fingers to the clasp that held his cloak around his shoulders, then removed it, stuffing the fabric between his thigh and the mud of the hill so it wouldn't be lost. Then he got to work on the buckles that held the breastplate snug around his torso, slowly loosening and then undoing them completely.

Moving slowly and carefully, he shrugged his left shoulder, then his right, switching hands on the grip of his sword to keep his position as he slowly got the breastplate off...

And then it was off, sliding down the hill next to him for a foot or two before stopping.

Thankfully, it didn't slide all the way into the muck. Maybe he'd be able to retrieve it later on.

First things first, though.

His red cloak was a ruin, and he would need to ruin it more.

The sword was mostly stuck into the earth, but a portion of its blade was still accessible, and still sharp.

A few moments of ginger, careful movement later, and Thurim had his cloak cut into thirds, lengthwise. He tied the three strips together, end to end, then tied one end of the makeshift rope around the grip of his sword.

Then, slowly, he began easing himself down the slope toward the mud river, grasping onto the cloak rope to slow his descent and alternating his gaze from the mud river below to the earthbound sword above.

It was only the passage of a few feet. But it seemed to take forever before he felt the soles of his boots sink into that treacherous flow.

Thurim swallowed. Moment of truth.

Though the sword, driven as it was into the earth, had been able to support his weight so far, when he made his way across the mud flow he'd be tugging at a different angle. Would it hold then, as well?

No way to know except to try. One thing was certain; he couldn't remain where he was.

Thurim pushed himself out from the hillside, keeping his feet perched on the earth just above the mud river, until he was standing upright instead of lying against the slope, like he had been a moment ago.

Slowly, ever so slowly, he turned around, facing the mud river with his back to the slope. Working quickly to coil the rest of his makeshift rope loosely in his grasp, he took a long, deep breath, said a quick prayer.

And jumped.

He jumped as far as he could, straight across the mud river toward the other side.

It would not be far enough, not by half. But it would be better than just stepping in. And with the cloak rope to hang on to...

He splashed into the mud river with more of a slurp than a splash. The cool, slippery muck seemed to grab at him, caressing almost like a lover as it engulfed the lower half of his body and began sucking him further down.

The river was moving, too, and he found himself being drawn, however slowly, downstream, at the same time he was being drawn under.

Pulling strongly at the cloak rope to keep himself up and at least somewhat close to his desired destination, he moved slowly and deliberately, crawling forward through the swirling muck toward the other side.

He fed the cloak rope out as he went. It was difficult going. Very difficult. But it was working, and he was making progress. Just a few feet more...

Then he felt a tug in the cloak rope, and he looked back to see there was no more. He was at the literal end of the rope, and he still had a good three or four feet to go. He couldn't feel anything remotely like solid ground beneath his feet, nor could his grasping hand as he swept it out toward what passed for the far shore.

Had he misjudged? Was the other bank further than he had thought?

He had known the cloak wouldn't get him all the way, but it seemed he should have had some sign of surety by now, anyway...

Fear, fear that he had been working very hard not to pay attention to, welled up within him, and Thurim considered that if he let go of the cloak and set out without that anchor to breathable air, he would be slowly and inexorably drawn down. If he didn't reach the far bank, and quickly...

Fear almost became panic as he considered the horror of sinking beneath the surface. Tasting the mud as it filled his mouth and nostrils.

Suffocating beneath its slimy weight.

Thurim's belly heaved at the thought and he tasted bile for a second, so strong was the surge of panic that gripped him.

He had to go back. Haul himself out using the cloak rope and get back to safety. Yes, that perch on the side of the hill wasn't ideal. Far from it. But it was safe, relatively, and he could wait there until the mud river dried up.

It was tempting.

But it was also folly. For one, he wasn't sure he'd be able to haul himself back through all that mud, even with the cloak rope to assist; hell, it might give way at any time. For another, he would just be trading one relatively quick, though hideous, death for another, slower one.

Because now that he'd experienced this mud river, he doubted it would be dried up enough for him to cross in a week. Certainly not in a day or two. And he was now without gear; his waterskin was still slung around his waist, but it was mud logged now. Who knows if it would be drinkable or not.

Death by suffocation, or death by thirst.

Or a possible chance for life. And the continuance of his quest.

That thought roused him, and he shoved the panic down with all his might.

Then he stretched his free hand forward as far as he could, while inching his fingertips to the end of his cloak rope.

Get as far across as possible before...

He let go, and threw that hand forward, like a man swimming a forward crawl in a pond.

Immediately, he began to sink. His chin touched the mud, his cheeks.

He kicked, trying to drive himself upward, but to no avail.

Desperate, he threw his arms forward again, kicking all the harder.

His mouth went under, and then his nostrils. The mud was up to his eyes...

And his fingertips sank into something almost solid.

Still soft and slimy, but compared with the muck he had been traipsing through, it felt like granite.

Thurim kicked and, forcing himself forward, now he got a full hand into that firmer earth.

Then a second hand. Then his boot got more purchase, and through the fire coming from his lungs Thurim had the presence of mind to chide himself for a fool—leaving his boots on???

He was desperate for a breath, but he dared not open his mouth. He could just barely see; the mud river was just below his eyes now, but he felt he was making progress, faster progress now.

His heart pounded in his ears. Every fiber of his body screamed at him to take a breath.

Now.

NOW!

Then his face was clear fo the mud river, and he did just that, an explosive inhalation that felt like all the pleasures of heaven rolled into one.

He couldn't stop though. His immediate breath need fulfilled, he pulled himself higher, and higher.

Until, after what seemed like hours, he was clear of the mud river, and he lay there gasping, his entire body shivering from the coolness he had just crawled through, but more from the terror that had so nearly claimed him.

He just laid there, breathing. For a long time.

When Thurim finally pushed himself up onto his feet, it was all he could do to sway there for a moment, a mud-covered apparition that probably would have struck fear into the village boys back home, so far away in a different, wooded, world. He was thoroughly miserable, and completely strengthless.

But something within him told Thurim that he could not afford to rest here.

He couldn't have said why, but the certainty that he had to continue onward. Now. Filled him.

Almost like a physical force, tugging at his insides.

That was impossible, of course. But it was also real. And Thurim could no more resist it than the rising of the moon and the sun, not the way he was feeling right then.

So he put one trembling foot down in front of the other, and took a halting step forward, and up the slope ahead of him.

Then another.

It was a more gradual slope than he had come down, as it had appeared from afar. But the way was still slick with mud, the footing treacherous, and he was still exhausted from exertion and fright.

It was slow going.

Gradually, though, the footing became more sure, and his pace improved. After a time, the single slope he was ascending changed, to become more steep to his right and left, while still continuing its shallow climb in the middle directly ahead. It was like he was climbing up through a pass between two hills, which pass was gradually becoming more steep until the slopes to either side were practically sheer, and he was walking up into a canyon, more like a crevasse.

Part of Thurim's mind rebelled at what he was seeing, what he was doing.

There was no canyon anywhere in the area. No crevasse like this that he was now walking through. The hills of these grasslands were rolling and many, but most were not particularly high and if there had been a formation such as this Thurim would have seen it yesterday or the day before.

Hell, this morning.

Still he was ascending a path, and it was taking him through a crevasse. And he was breathing, his heart was pounding, his mouth was dry from thirst and every muscle in his body was trembling and aching from exertion and fatigue.

So he wasn't dead.

Maybe he was dreaming?

But he cast that thought from his head as quickly as it came. No dream had ever been this vivid, this real.

No, he was awake, and miserable.

And suddenly filled with awe.

Because the path through the crevasse took a sudden turn to the right, and when he rounded that bend brown mud and dirt gave way to polished white marble underneath his feet. Fluted columns of the same material stood ahead of him, flanking a high archway that looking to have been carved yesterday, it was so smooth and so highly polished.

The sunlight streaming down from almost directly above the crevasse struck the top of the archway, and reflected toward Thurim, every color of the rainbow springing in and out of his vision depending on how he turned his head.

The oppressive heat and humidity that had been plaguing his steps faded as well, becoming dry coolness that seemed to immediately offer comfort. But more than that, a trickling sound from past the archway brought a surge of hope and relief to him.

A fountain. That was the sound of a fountain ahead.

And God, was he thirsty.

Stumbling steps became a shuffling half-run, and Thurim stepped beneath the archway. As he did so, he felt a joy and satisfaction that he had not experienced in a long, long time.

Because as he looked around the marble-paved courtyard past the archway, and at the circular marble fountain at its center, which somehow had water splashing upward from its very center to shoot its sparkling droplets high into the air before plunging back into the pure water in the fountain's basin, he knew for certain exactly where he was, even if he had no idea how he had actually come there.

It was the Shrine of Tulok. He had found it.

Somehow, some way, he had found it.

And Basmin was nowhere to be seen.

His laughter of joy and triumph echoed for what seemed an eternity.

51

O'BANNON'S TALISMAN

Humidity made Carl O'Bannon's shirt cling to his torso, almost completely soaked despite not being out and about all that long. He felt like he was sweating a river, though in reality it wasn't all that hot out. It was like an ocean itself was condensing on top of him, and he helpless against its spread.

For a moment there, he almost felt that for real and a surge of dread filled him. He didn't know how to swim, so what would he do if an ocean...

"Dummy," he muttered to himself, and forced that foolishness down deep.

It was still bloody uncomfortable out.

He'd left his little cottage on the outskirts of Riverwood and set off even further away from what amounted to civilization maybe half an hour ago, clumping upslope in his old, well broken-in boots and brand new jeans and blue, long-sleeved collared shirt, with a Red Sox baseball cap on his head. And very quickly regretted being so heavily dressed.

The thought crossed his mind now, as he stopped to lean against a maple tree to catch his breath and instead had his drowning fit, that he ought to go back home and change. Or just bag this entire idea altogether.

He looked down the gentle slope he had been ascending, his vision quickly obscured by tree trunks and undergrowth so he couldn't see more than a hundred yards. But all the same, he felt the presence of his home; like a beacon calling to him. He was certain he was looking straight at it.

Or rather, at the talisman overtop his mantle. The relic passed down from father to son for generations, or so his grandfather had told him. It was bound to his line, and they would never be without it. Would know its lack, if ever it went missing.

And that had turned out to be literally true, for Carl at least. It was like a lodestone to his spirit; he could always turn and point straight at it. Feel how far away from it he was.

Remarkable, considering the thing looked like a competent but not overly impressive oil painting of a jagged mountain peak thrusting up out of rolling hill country, with the sun climbing up over the mountain's right flank.

He felt it now, knew how far away it was. And realized it would take less time to just get up to where he was going and finish his chore than it would to go home and change.

So screw it. He could deal with a little extra sweat and discomfort.

Wouldn't be the first time.

He pushed himself off the rough hardness of the maple's trunk and squared his shoulders, then resolutely turned back uphill and commenced climbing again.

The glade he was heading toward was another half mile away and probably a hundred fifty feet above where he had stopped. The ground leveled out here, forming a little bowl where the hill continued to slope up on either side but the flatness pushed back into the hill itself so that the back of the bowl was almost a sheer cliff.

The trees grew more closely here, the trunks more thick, so from a distance a person wouldn't know the little glade even existed. But after rounding and sliding his way past the seemingly impassible press of ever-growing wood, Carl stepped out into streaming sunlight.

It had been overcast when he left his cottage. For most of his hike uphill it had remained overcast through the breaks in the trees that he could see. But here the sun shone down without blemish of cloud, illuminating the crystalline pool at the center of the little bowl.

Grey-brown rocks lined the edge of the pool, natural yet also somehow not. Like someone or some thing had placed their uneven bulks there intentionally to separate the water from the land, which was covered with fine grass from the rocks to the edge of the treeline. No bare earth here at all, except on the cliff face at the rear of the bowl.

The place was quiet. A feeling of utmost calm permeated it, and the temperature and humidity had changed from the oppressive soup-air that Carl had trudged his way through to crisp and just pleasantly on the cool side of warm. It smelled of something semi-sweet that he could never quite put his finger on. Nor could he find any source, any of the times he had come here.

The ever-pleasant and calming odor just lingered, like the place itself exuded it.

Carl wasn't going to complain.

This little glade was special. Sacred, Carl's grandfather had said. Not just anyone could find it, and even those who could would not always be able to access its greatest secrets.

But his family could. Grandfather never explained why, just speculated that maybe there was some link between the glade and the talisman. That because their family was the keeper of the talisman they could—

Carl froze, his thoughts coming to a halt as quickly as his body when a jolt went through his spirit to the very core of his essence. And then he realized it.

The talisman was gone. The awareness that he had always lived with—that he had learned to live with but had never been able to ignore completely—winked out between one breath and the next, leaving him feeling like a vessel adrift, with no anchor and no engine, just bobbing along without direction or meaning.

Even as the realization of his sudden loss swept over him, Carl saw the light fading in the glade. He looked up and saw clouds encroaching. Looked back down and saw the pool drying.

The talisman was gone, and he was losing access to the power here. Perhaps for all time.

Biting back a curse, Carl turned and shoved his way through the tree trunks, now seeming closer than they ever had before, as though they were in fact merely one tree split into dozens and were now twisting back together into a single, solid whole.

It felt like he was going to get stuck between the last pair of silent guardians...but then he was through. Through and sprinting downhill toward his house.

He had to see what had happened.

Carl was huffing and puffing, and he only thought he had been soaked with sweat before, by the time he reached the cottage. He couldn't remember ever running that far so fast; it was only about a mile and a half total, but it seemed he emerged from the tree line to see his red vinyl-sided, one-story abode mere moments after he started off.

The front door was leaning open, the white-painted jamb surrounding it shattered where the deadbolt should have kept intruders out.

But apparently not determined intruders.

Carl dashed inside, and immediately his eyes swept to the back-fronted fireplace at the back of his small living room. And more in particular, to the bit of wall above the polished oak mantlepiece.

The painting was still there.

For a second, relief swept through him, but then he realized the feeling of the talisman was still gone. What was—?

He approached the mantle, stepping around his stuffed chair, which sat almost directly in front of the fireplace, its matched ottoman teasingly close to the transparent glass doors that separated the burning wood from the rest of the house. As he did so, he saw that the painting was there. But not all there.

A piece of the canvas had been cut out. Two thirds of the way down from the upper right corner. A section maybe an inch square.

Cut out and gone. And with it, any feel of the talisman's presence.

A car engine outside drew his attention back to the front of the house before he could fully consider the implications of that. Carl surged out the door in time to see an orange Dodge Charger zip out from behind his place to the left, fishtail in a sliding right-hand turn that tore up a sizable chunk of the grass in his front lawn, then tear off down the gravel path that made up his driveway, the one link from his house to the town not so very far away.

There were two men in the car. As it sped past, Carl locked eyes with the fellow in the passenger seat. Bright, dangerous green eyes tracked to follow his, then the car turned and swept out of sight.

"Son of a bitch," Carl said.

Then he dashed back inside, to the closet in his bedroom where he kept his shotgun and shells.

Still there.

Two minutes later, he was in his own car. Wasn't much, a late-90s model Explorer whose once-blue paint job was now turning to rust in the rear wheel wells and whose headlight lenses were so UV-degraded they looked more milky than transparent.

Still ran like a champ, though.

As he sped down his gravel driveway, he racked his brain. Why would someone come for the talisman, and more in particular....how?

It was a family heirloom, never talked about with outsiders. Or really among the family, because all this time, Carl thought the talisman was the painting. But apparently, it was actually something hidden within the painting.

But it didn't seem to do much except point the way home for him and his family members. And somehow, someway give them access to the glade and its pool. Which, again, seemed to have only subtle effects.

Why steal that, even if someone else had learned of it somehow?

He was still pondering when he came to the end of his very long driveway. The two-lane country road that the driveway T-ed into would take him back into Riverwood if he turned left. Or on to the interstate, fifteen miles away to the right.

No one in Riverwood had a car like that Dodge; it would stand out like a sore thumb. If the thieves had gone that way, they would be easy to find...probably. But it would take time, and if he was wrong...

Once they reached the Interstate, he would lose them forever. Them, and the talisman.

Just let it go.

The thought was hard to ignore. So he lost the thing. Not like it had ever really done him any good. And with grandpa dead now there was no one left in the family but Carl. Grandpa had had to watch both his sons die. Carl's dad to cancer when Carl was still a teenager. And Uncle Ted to the Gulf War.

Carl only had vague memories of Uncle Ted; images and impressions. But Dad he remembered well, even after all these years. And Grandpa all the more, since he had only passed three years earlier.

Seemingly useless or not, the talisman was their family heritage. Both men had impressed that on Carl his entire life.

He couldn't just let it go.

Fine, but call the Cops, at least.

And tell them what? That a magical talisman that didn't really seem to do much had been stolen by random strangers who he didn't know where they were from or who they were?

Fat lot of good that would do.

So he turned right onto the country road, and gunned the engine.

The speed limit far exceeded behind him, Carl kept his eyes locked on the road ahead. In his mind, the minutes ticked by slowly, inexorably, and with them, the miles. There were two crossroads between his house and the Interstate, and as he drew near the first one, he considered that the thieves may have turned off on one of the two.

He cast that thought aside as he began slowing toward the intersection ahead, and the yellow light turned to red.

It wasn't that they couldn't have turned off. But he had to think they'd head toward their avenue of quickest return to wherever they came from.

And anyway, if they had turned off, they were lost to him already. And with them, his family heritage.

So when the light turned, he gunned it again, and said a silent prayer that his assumption was correct, and all was not yet lost.

He passed through the second intersection without having to stop; he caught the timing of the light just right.

Then, a couple minutes later, he saw the overpass for the Interstate looming ahead. Still a few miles distant, but plain to see.

And there, approaching it but still with a ways to go...was that car orange?

He was already going faster than he ever had in his Explorer. The wheel vibrated beneath his fingers as high speed amplified every little glitch in the steering system, in the wheel assembly. Every tiny bump in the road.

Still, the engine was purring like always, but was that a faint hint of burning he smelled, like maybe some part of the exhaust plenum had parted, or had some wiring insulation begun to singe? And there was a rattle from somewhere in front of him and to his right that he'd never heard before.

But his quarry was in sight, so he depressed the accelerator again, and the Explorer strained forward to even more speed.

He was gaining, and at a more rapid clip than he would have thought. The car ahead was clearly visible now. Definitely the Charger.

For a second, he wondered at being able to catch up to such a more powerful car than his. Then reason wagged its finger at him. They wouldn't want to get pulled over. They would keep to the speed limit, and drive conservatively.

Which meant he had an advantage.

Until they realized he was pursuing.

He eased off the gas, letting his speed lower as he continued to gain on them. Maybe a mile and a half from the Interstate now, and the Charger was a quarter of a mile ahead.

Follow them. Wait for your time.

He nodded to himself and reduced his speed more, so that he was only a bit above theirs, closing very slowly. Carl glanced down at his gas tank. 2/3 full. He could go about 150, maybe 200 miles on that.

A satisfied smile made his cheeks feel like they were being compressed. Hard.

Ahead, the Charger's brake lights came on, and it shifted over into the exit lane for the Northbound onramp. Carl did the same. He lost sight of them as he rounded the long, circular ramp up onto the highway. But once he got firmly into the traffic flow on the Interstate, he quickly gained them again. A few hundred yards ahead, past a single intervening car. In the right-hand travel lane, going just slightly above the speed limit.

Carl hung back, watching them carefully as the minutes and miles ticked away again.

They passed exit after exit, and the shadows were beginning to shift. Carl glanced to the left, and saw that the afternoon sun had already begun dipping down toward the horizon. A glance at the clock on his console made his stomach twitch. Maybe a couple hours of daylight left.

Once the sun went down it would be next to impossible to keep track of the Charger unless he stuck directly behind them, and that probably wouldn't be a good idea.

Even Carl could pick out the same car behind him for a long time, at night. And he'd had no training in this sort of thing to speak of.

Of course, he'd have to stop for gas well before then at this rate. The needle was down to the halfway mark now.

How much gas do they have, and would they need to stop before him?

If not, he'd have to make a move before he ran out completely. But what kind of move? Run them off the road?

He snorted loudly to himself. Even if he wanted to do that, then what? What if he seriously injured them, or himself? Wouldn't do him much good to get the talisman back if he winded up in the hospital, or in jail. Not to mention if he wrecked his own car how would be get back home?

Really what was the plan here? He hadn't thought it through; he'd just pursued. But now, with time and opportunity winding down, Carl found he really had no idea what he was going to do.

One thing was certain, though. He couldn't just let his family's heritage drive away. Not without at least making an attempt to get it back.

Those thoughts were swirling around and around his head, going nowhere and generating no ideas at all, when up ahead, he saw the Charger's blinker turn on.

An exit ramp was coming up. The signs indicated gas stations and restaurants. Hope buoyed within Carl, and when the Charger shifted into the exit lane, expanded.

He followed them off the Interstate and then to the right, and found himself on a four-lane road. Ahead was an Exxon on the right, a 7-Eleven and a McDonald's on the left.

The charger was pulling into the McDonald's parking lot.

Awesome.

Carl pulled into the Exxon and stopped at the self service pumps. He got out and set the pump to fill his tank, then hurried inside, glancing to see the Charger stationary in the other parking lot and its two passengers heading inside before he did so.

A trip to the bathroom and a bag of potato chips later, he finished topping off his gas and got back behind the wheel.

The shotgun was propped up in the floorboard of his passenger seat. The shell box on the seat, next to his bag of Ruffles. He always kept the shotgun loaded, just in case, but not chambered. Now as he considered that he only had the 5 shells from the tube when he could have 6, he regretted that precaution.

"Idiot," he said, shaking his head. "You're not going into a gunfight. Not if you can help it."

He looked away from the weapon back toward the McDonald's.

The Charger was still there. And no sign of the men. They had parked on the side of the restaurant, away from its main entrance and opposite the 7-Eleven. There were only a few other cars in the parking lot.

Maybe they'd left the talisman in the car, and he could go snatch it—

"Idiot," he said again.

No way they'd be that dumb. A little scrap of painting, and whatever else was there, they would keep on their person. They wouldn't risk losing it by chance.

Still...

He started the engine and put the Explorer in gear, then eased out onto the road. A quick shift of the lanes and he was pulling into the McDonald's lot.

If he couldn't nip the talisman from the car, he could at least get their plate number. Might be able to use it, somehow, to track them down, if he lost them.

Though how exactly he could do that, he had no idea.

First things first.

He pulled into the parking lot and slowly maneuvered around the restaurant toward the Drive Thru entrance. That brought him past the Charger, and he craned his neck to get a view of it.

Yep, there was the plate. AGE 2182

Gotcha.

Then he was past and into the Drive Thru. There was one car ahead of him, and the driver was taking her—it was certainly a her—sweet time ordering.

In the rearview, Carl saw two men round the front of the McDonald's. He recognized their clothing—both had black leather jackets and wore dark cargo pants and boots—as being the same as the men who had gotten out of the car when it parked. And sure enough, they made a beeline for the charger, one of them carrying a McDonald's takeout bag in his hand and the other one sipping from a cup with a straw.

Carl looked back forward. The driver ahead still had not ordered.

The men got into the Charger and eased it back out of their parking spot. They drove out, around the front of the building, and a white minivan came into view where they had just left.

Damn.

Carl looked forward. Still not done up there.

Muttering to himself, he put the Explorer into reverse and looked back. To find the minivan stationary behind him, in the DriveThru lane.

"Son of a bitch!" Carl said.

The minivan wasn't moving. His reversing lights had to be clearly visible, but no, the driver, and older man with curly grey hair, didn't seem to care.

In fact, he was gesturing impatiently through his windshield for Carl to get moving froward.

Carl looked ahead and sighed with relief. The car ahead had finally moved up. He shifted back to drive and moved forward, ordered a strawberry milkshake, then sat impatiently while the people in front of him again took forever to take care of business.

Then he got his drink and was finally able to get the hell out of there.

The DriveThru window was located near the rear of the brick-fronted building. The exit lane passed about thirty feet of blank wall before emerging back into the parking lot after passing a dumpster enclosure on the right. Up ahead he saw three or four cars in the parking lot.

He hoped against hope that one of them would be Charger, but no.

Carl glanced toward the Exxon as he drew up alongside the dumpsters...

A flash of orange ahead and to the right, then he was surging forward in his seatbelt as the sound of metal meeting and then tearing reached his ears and the car shuddered.

The Charger had been parked right up next to the dumpsters.

Now it was halfway into the DriveThru exit lane, and his Cherokee's bumper had just impacted its right quarter panel.

"Oh shit."

Adrenalin surged through Carl as the two front doors of the Charger opened and the two men got out.

The passenger, blond haired and green eyed—Carl could still remember the near shine of those green orbs as they sped out from his property—stopped and put his hands on his hips, shaking his head as he looked at the impact zone.

The driver, darker of hair and skin—his hair was nearly black it was so brown—stepped all the way around the two cars until he was standing next to Carl's driver window.

He knocked on the window with his knuckles.

Swallowing, Carl hit the button to lower the glass.

The man had lighter eyes than Carl would have thought from the rest of him. Brown-orange, the tint of which Carl wasn't sure he'd ever seen on a man before.

"You suck at tailing people, O'Bannon," the man said in a smooth baritone that sounded, if anything amused.

Adrenalin surged again, and Carl fought to keep his face calm. He wasn't sure how well he succeeded, but he could feel the sweat beginning under his arms as his body began responding.

"I don't know what—"

"Can it," the guy said, his initial good humor leaving abruptly, replaced by icy steel. He met Carl's eyes with a gaze that was even harder than his tone, and shook his head slightly. "What I don't get is what you thought you were going to do? Jump us? Play," he gestured toward the shotgun, which had to be clearly visible from where he was standing, "some kind of half-assed Rambo routine?"

The man shook his head, making a tsking sound.

Carl didn't respond. Partly because the man's question so readily paralleled the questions he was asking himself not so many minutes ago. But also because he wasn't entirely sure his voice wouldn't break from nerves at this point. And he didn't want to give the guy the satisfaction.

For a second, he thought about just gunning it into reverse and getting away back how he'd came in the DriveThru lane. Then he recalled the minivan, and he lost that idea.

A glance in the rearview shelved that idea even further, as he saw the minivan right up on him, the grey-haired man staring hard at him.

But this wasn't a stare of annoyance. It was more serious. And Carl saw something black sitting atop the minivan's dashboard, no doubt intentionally so he could see it. A gun.

The minivan guy and the Charger guys were in cahoots.

Carl swallowed. Hard.

"So this is the part," the driver continued, drawing Carl's eyes back to him, "where we give each other our information." He flashed an ironic grin. "But I already know yours, O'Bannon. So this is your one chance." He leaned in slightly, and Carl could feel the hot breath on his face as the man spoke again, his tone gone past cold to entirely menacing. "Let. It. Go."

Then he retreated fully back out of the window again, and his tone returned to that almost playful amused voice he used at first. "No sense getting you or your family hurt over something you didn't really know what to do with in the first place, right?"

With that, the driver smacked his hands down onto the open window frame of the Explorer's door. Then he turned and walked back toward his car.

From the other side of the Explorer, Carl heard another knock. He turned to see the blond guy staring in at him earnestly, and Carl lowered that window as well.

"Hate to tell you, buddy, but your tire popped when you hit us." He was fidgeting with his hands, just high enough that Carl could see he was closing the blade of a pocket knife. Blondie grinned at him, amused mockery in the expression. "Hope you've got a spare."

Then he followed his buddy and got into the car. The engine started, and the damaged car pulled forward away from Carl's Explorer, then turned left and accelerated out of the parking lot.

It proceeded toward the Interstate onramps and Carl saw it switch on its blinker, indicating a left-hand turn.

Into the South-bound lanes of the Interstate.

"Son of a bitch," Carl said.

He pulled the Explorer out of the DriveThru exit lane and into a parking spot, then got out and watched as the minivan passed him. The driver gave him a mocking little salute with one finger, then followed his fellows out the parking lot.

Carl stepped out and watched the van go, and made note of its plate number. PYT 3145.

Then he opened his cargo compartment door. He did indeed have a spare, but it would take him a good half hour or so to get the flat off and the spare on. There was no way he'd ever find either of the vehicles with that long of a head start. Not today.

But he at least had something to go on for later.

Maybe the orange-eyed driver was right. Maybe Carl should just let it go. He didn't really know what the heck the talisman was or what it did. Near as he could tell, near as grandpa had ever said, it didn't do much at all except that beacon routine.

Was that really worth risking his neck over, even if he managed to find some way to use those plate numbers to his advantage?

The image of grandpa's eyes, so earnest, so proud as he told Carl the story of their family's legacy and the talisman they had been bequeathed by fate came to Carl's mind. And he put those questions aside.

O'Bannons may not be rich or powerful, but they were also not pushovers. And he wasn't going to just give up on his family's heritage. No sir.

So he changed the flat, then he drove back to the Interstate and then toward home. He was going to need a plan, and some help.

And more than a little luck.

52

STASIS TREATMENT

S ome folks call dead bodies stiffs. And boy, they ain't kidding.

Couldn't tell you what happened before then or how I got there. But when I opened my eyes on the cold stainless steel of the medical examiner's exam table and looked up at the bright fluorescent lights shining down on me, at first I couldn't move a muscle.

I could feel everything, just like normal. The subtle coarseness fo the blue cloth that was draped over the rest of my body. The slight movement of the ventilation-pushed air.

Smell the subtle aroma of decay beneath the more powerful scents of disinfectants.

Hear the talk of the coroner and his assistant from somewhere off to my left. Soft words that didn't quite register except that they both came from male baritone voices.

But I could not make myself move. Not even to blink.

I knew immediately I was dead. I wasn't breathing, my heart wasn't beating, and none of those small internal movements that we only register at the base of our consciousness were happening.

But if I was dead, why could I still see, and feel, and the rest? Why wasn't I chatting with Peter up at the Pearly Gates and seeing if I got First Class for eternity or got sent down to Steerage? Not that I expected First Class; Lord knew I was no saint. But to wake up here, of all places?

It's not like my name is Jesus. It's Bob. So how the hell was I back from the dead anyway?

It made no sense. If I could have moved a muscle, I would have thrown up my hands and screamed, "What the hell?!"

As it was, all I could do was lie there, staring up at that really, really bright light, and wish to God I could blink even because damn was that becoming painful to look at.

The voices grew louder, more distinct.

"...ought to see results in the next few hours. If—"

A face came into view overhead, the orb of the man's head blotting out two-thirds of the light above me, so all I could see of his face was shadow. But he was wearing a white lab coat, with a white shirt and an orange-brown tie underneath. His words cut off as he looked down at me, abruptly.

"Hot damn! Ken, check it out. I think it worked!"

Footsteps, then another face came into view above me, on the opposite side of the table from the first. The new head took out about half of the remaining light, so now I could see a little bit of their features.

The first one was older than me, in his mid fifties looked like. His hair was mostly grey, with a few streaks of gold remaining, and was long, pulled back from his face into a ponytail behind his neck. The other, Ken, was maybe thirty, darker of skin and eye, with short-cut black hair. He wore brown, round-rimmed glasses and also had a lab coat, but his was unbuttoned, revealing a Slayer t-shirt and jeans underneath.

Ken blinked, surprise showing on his face, and I envied him that ability. He bent over, looking at me carefully.

"His eyes are open, yeah, but are you sure? Could just be a reflex response, or..." He trailed off as he brought his face within a few inches of mine. His eyes squinted. Then he jerked upward and back, stepped back from the table a step so I could just barely see him, off to my right.

"Holy shit. His pupils just dilated a bit." Ken sounded a mix of surprised, excited, and scared, all at once.

"I knew it." The first man smiled, and leaned more directly overhead, so his face was all I could see, haloed by light from the overhead. "Mr. Shepherd, I'm Doctor Joseph Milar. You're in my laboratory. Can you hear me?"

I could, but damn if I could make myself say so. Couldn't even move my little finger, let alone nod my head. And I wasn't breathing, so talking was right out even if I thought I could move the muscles needed to do it. So I just laid there, listening.

Milar looked me up and down, then sniffed. "I imagine you can. And if my calculations are correct, you should regain muscle control over the next couple of hours." He grinned broadly. "You, my friend, are history in the making." He slapped me on the shoulder lightly, but the impact of it registered like a punch in the jaw. "We'll talk soon."

Milar looked up from me to Ken, then nodded toward something in the direction of my feet. The two men walked away, leaving my field of view quickly.

There was the sound of a door opening, then their footsteps going through and it closing behind them.

Then I was all alone, with just the light and the chill and the smell of antiseptic.

And a whole lot of questions.

Milar was right.

Within a few hours, I found I could move first my toes, then my foot, then my entire leg.

Some time later, I was sitting upright on that cold slab of stainless steel, the blue cloth pulled up around my waist to cover my nakedness as I finally took a look around and got my bearings.

I was wrong. This wasn't the medical examiner's offices. It had much the same equipment as I expected the coroner would have, but the room was too small. Just room for the one examination table, and then off to the left a laboratory bench and a small metal desk with a computer terminal on top.

The door to the room was painted grey-blue and appeared solid, and had a brushed nickel door nob. There was nothing else, just cream-painted walls and the bright light overhead.

I wasn't sure how long I sat there, not breathing but still awake and feeling. But some time later the door nob turned, and a moment later Milar and Ken walked into the room.

Milar didn't look at all surprised to see me sitting upright like a normal, non-dead person. But Ken's brows lifted slightly for a moment as they both stopped just inside the door.

"You're up," Milar said, and he grinned again. "Excellent. How do you feel, Mr. Shepherd?"

I surprised myself. I hadn't been sure if I'd be able to speak at all; I wasn't breathing, after all. The idea of that disability had frightened me, so I hadn't even tried talking to myself.

But I found I was able to make my diaphragm work, and bring air into my lungs. My voice sounded gravelly to my own ears, but it worked.

"What the hell is going on?"

The two men exchanged looks.

"What do you remember, Mr. Shepherd?" Ken asked.

I shook my head. I really couldn't remember much at all before I woke up on this exam table. Just flashes here and there. I knew who I was, but other than that...

"Not unexpected," Milar said. "The treatment is," he made a wave of his hand, "experimental. Side effects are unavoidable, I'm afraid."

I looked at him levelly, didn't say another word. He cleared his throat.

"An explanation is overdue, I suppose." Milar clasped his hands together in front of his belt. "Ken and I head a research project on life extension techniques. An immortality serum, if you will."

I blinked. Couldn't say I was completely surprised, but still... I'd heard of billionaires and such investing in silly things like that. And Walt Disney's frozen head, or whatever.

Well, maybe not so silly after all.

I gestured toward my chest, and its lack of motion. "You call this immortal?"

"You're awake and aware, aren't you?"

Hard to argue with that. "How?"

"That's a long and complicated, very technical explanation. Suffice it to say we were never able to get around the problem of cell decay from DNA replication errors. Stretch a creature's lifespan and eventually things will always...break. But what if we could find a way to suspend the cell functions. A sort of perpetual stasis. The initial results on animal tests were very promising. Except for...the side effects." He, too gestured at my chest.

I nodded slowly. What he was saying made a certain amount of sense. But I wasn't sure I entirely bought it. There had to be more to it than what he was letting on.

Not that it mattered. What mattered right then was how I ended up here, in this state?

He must have seen it on my face, as he nodded apologetically and continued, "We found you in a cancer support group. You had Stage IV pancreatic cancer. An extremely fast, and painful, way to die. When we approached you, you were eager to be a trial subject." He managed to look positively self-satisfied right then, as he gestured toward me again. "And now, here we are."

I winced. Something about what Milar said resonated within me, and I had a flash of a memory. Pain. Dreadful pain, and fear. But more than that, desperation and a desire to have it end.

But I must have had a family, friends. What about them? Did they know what I had volunteered for, or where I was now? How did this all come to be?

For that matter... "Where is this place?"

"Outside San Jose, California." ·

I nodded. "Funded by Silicon Valley tech billionaires, eh?" I shook my head and forced a snort. "That figures. So now what?"

"Well now we keep you under observation. See how your body responds to the treatment, whether there are any other side effects. The usual."

"You don't intend to keep me cooped up here, do you?" I waved my hand around at the exam room, or whatever it was. It was not exactly what I would call comfortable.

The two of them exchanged glances. "Well..."

To hell with that. I shook my head vigorously. "No way. A real bed and some real clothes, or I'm out."

Ken pursed his lips. "I doubt you'll need to sleep, Mr. Shepherd. But I understand what you mean." He raised a hand as Milar drew in a breath, to object I assumed. "He's right, Joe. Can't hurt to put him up in one of the rooms."

Milar frowned, then nodded. "Very well. But I must stress the necessity that you remain in this facility, Mr. Shepherd. We don't know what all the side effects may be, and we'll need to have you close to record them, and help you deal with them. Plus," he paused, then cleared his throat. "There's no other way to say it, but I don't think your being out in public would be a very good idea at all. People might react poorly to a walking, talking man who is apparently dead."

That made sense, after I considered it for a minute. "Yeah. A zombie roaming through Silicon Valley might get awkward."

Milar winced. "I wouldn't use that word, but....yes."

Nodding, I pushed myself off the exam table. The sheet fell away, and I felt a bit more of the room's chill. A thought occurred to me, and I looked down. "No heartbeat. Guess that's not going to work any more, is it?" I gestured downward.

The two men blanched, then Ken shook his head. "We don't know. But it's doubtful." He sniffed and looked away. "One of the many things we need to study and record for future changes in the treatment."

That sucked. I guess. But it beat being dead. Even though I kind of was dead. In stasis. Whatever.

"Well," I said, grinning at them and feeling at least a little bit like I had my bearings, for the first time since I woke up. "How about those clothes?"

They gave me medical scrubs for the time being, then brought me upstairs.

The room they put me in was one hell of a lot nicer than the exam room. It was four levels above the exam room, which turned out was in the basement of their building. An elevator ran all the way up, and my room was in the corner of the square-shaped structure, with windows that faced north and west, giving me a view of a commercial block filled with parking lots and other business buildings fronted in glass or brick, ranging from five to seven or eight stories high.

I saw business signs and logos that made me think most of the businesses in those buildings were tech firms of some sort of other. No big surprise there.

The surprise was that this room was set up more as a living suite than an office space. A queen sized bed with silky-smooth white cotton sheets beneath a thick, red duvet. Black leather couch and love seat positioned around a glass-topped coffee table facing a flat screen on the wall opposite the bed. A small kitchen with dark grey granite countertops and white shaker cabinets. A metal-framed, class-topped dining table with seating for six. A black corner-style office desk off in the corner opposite the windows, complete with a computer tower and an all-in-one HP Officejet printer. Speakers in the ceiling adjacent to the recessed lighting played a light, cheerful melody that I couldn't quite place, and the temperature was a lot more pleasant than it had been in the basement.

Overall, it didn't suck at all.

"Not too shabby." I glanced back at Ken and Milar from where I stopped by the windows after completing my survey. "You guys stay here a lot?"

Ken chuckled softly. "No, these rooms are for our clients. Or they will be, anyway. For now, our investors use them when they come to visit."

"Got it."

"How are you feeling now that you've moved around a bit, Mr. Shepherd? Any fatigue, or...?" Milar made a vague gesture. I was pretty sure he had as little idea what he was asking for as I did in how to answer.

The simple fact was that I felt fine. Not a complaint at all, except for the still vague unease I felt over the lack of internal movement and sound from within my body. But I felt fit and energetic, not tired at all. And moving around had gotten the last of the kinks out. What little of the initial stiffness that had remained when we left the exam room was gone completely.

I felt better than I had in twenty years.

Though how I knew that, I couldn't say. Something washing up from the disjointed memories in my head.

I shrugged and turned to fully face them again. "Call me Bob. I feel great. Excellent, in fact. Can you do me a favor?"

"Certainly."

"You got a file on me? Vital statistics, name, rank, serial number, things like that? I'd like to call Mom or my wife, if I can."

"No wife," Ken said, "and your mother passed away five years ago. But yes, we'll have records send up everything we have on you. The first thing we'll want to do is work to recover your memories." He made another of those semi-apologetic shrugs. "Last thing we'll want is future clients not knowing who they are."

But it was fine for me to? Intellectually, I knew that wasn't what he meant. But still, it rubbed me the wrong way. I shoved my annoyance down, though. After all, I was here to help them with their research. Wouldn't do any of us any good to get in a tizzy about things.

So I just nodded and said, "Thanks."

"I'd like you to keep a log of your daily routine," Milar said. "If you sleep. For how long. Sensations. When memories begin to come back. If you feel hunger or thirst or fatigue. Anything and everything of your biological and psychological functions. We'll be monitoring you, but getting the inside story, if you will, is essential if we are to get this right."

Made sense, so I nodded again.

"Excellent. I didn't say it earlier, Bob, but thank you very much for your assistance. With your help, we are going to change history, even life itself, for every human being on the planet."

Well, the rich ones anyway. But I appreciated the thought.

It's weird researching yourself, and feeling like you're learning about a completely different person.

Ken and Milar gave me the biographic information they had on met, and the internet connection on my suite's computer was apparently unimpeded. So before too long I had an idea of who I was, if not a feeling or a true memory.

I had a degree in Finance from the University of Minnesota. I'd grown up in St. Paul and never moved away until now, apparently. Ken wasn't entirely correct; I had an ex-wife and an eleven year old daughter named Kelly, but they had relocated to South Carolina four years back. No idea why I didn't follow.

I worked in an investment bank as an analyst. Owned a condo in downtown St. Paul. My credit score was 753 and I had a good chunk of change squirreled away in a 401k and Roth IRA.

I played the trombone and was a hockey and football fan, more hockey.

And I was, apparently, dead.

Actually dead. I found the death certificate on file. Looked like my estate was still in probate. I imagine I left it all to the kid.

Finding out that bit of reality came as a blow. And it pissed me off. Milar's explanation should have helped.

But it didn't.

"You have to understand how sensitive this research is, Bob," he said, looking up at me from behind his darkly stained wooden monstrosity of a desk two floors below my suite. "We can't just take someone and subject them to potentially lethal effects if they're otherwise healthy. Ethical issues aside, the liability alone would crush us." He shook his head. "No, we picked you because you were on your way out. Only weeks to live at most. So when the time came..."

He trailed off, and I finished for him. "You faked my death and brought me here."

Milar shook his head. "No faking about it, Bob. You died in the University of Minnesota Hospital. We injected you with the treatment and you flatlined. As far as your family and friends know, that's where you stayed. We flew you here as soon as arrangements for your cremation had been carried out."

"Well I'm back now, so—"

He shook his head vigorously. "There can be no contact with anyone outside this facility, Bob. You know the reasons why."

I did. And he was right.

It still pissed me off.

But that was how I learned my internet functionality wasn't 100% after all. Something in the computer system's setup, or the network architecture, disabled email and internet phone calls.

Oh sure, there was undoubtably any number of websites or applications I could find and use to get around those blocks. And after I stormed out of Milar's office following that discussion I determined to do just that. But I quickly calmed down. And I realized he was right.

Until we knew exactly how this new state of being for me worked, getting in touch was a bad idea. For all we knew I might drop dead... again...tomorrow, or in five minutes. Would it be worth subjecting Kelly to the confusion and fright of me being back just to put her through the pain of losing me all over again?

Until I knew more, the answer was no.

So I kept on keeping on, and learning more about what this new life, or whatever, was, and how it worked.

Ken was wrong, but also right. Kind of.

I don't need to sleep. I never get the physical fatigue that I assume I'd grown used to in regular life, the inability to keep going past a certain point, and the necessity of lying down for a time.

But I've found that after a certain amount of time, my thoughts become sluggish and I have trouble focusing. It gets worse and worse until I simply can't do even simple things anymore. But it's weird because I never get physically tired during this process, so I found that it really can sneak up on me and I become useless before I even realize it.

Amusingly enough, the effects start after about eighteen to twenty hours of activity, and I become unless after about forty-eight hours if I don't rest.

But it's not sleep. I lie down and shut my eyes, but I don't go unconscious. I'm awake the entire time, but it's like a switch flips and I get into this funky awake but dreaming state. I get some seriously weird dreams now. But the cool thing is one REM cycle and I'm good. Up and running, able to kick it on for another day.

So about ninety minutes instead of six to eight hours. I'll take that trade.

So that was one important question answered. Another was hunger and thirst, and other bodily functions.

My body isn't functioning, but it is. My bowels and bladder voided when I died, and near as Milar could tell there is no peristalsis in my gut at all.

Gotta get energy from something, though. So it stood to reason I would need to eat. Or something.

And I did get hungry. Though hungry isn't the right word. It's not the hole in your stomach feeling from normal life. More like a general feeling of lethargy. Like I'm sensing my energy level, and know when I'm getting toward the end of the tank. I start moving slower, enough that I notice, and things become more difficult to do.

Cool thing is this takes longer than getting hungry did when I was living a normal life. A few days as opposed to few hours.

The problem came in figuring out what I could eat, and how. Because if the gut ain't rolling it's not like I can swallow and digest solid food. So we very quickly figured out it would have to be liquid.

That brought a sinking suspicion to my mind, and I found myself confronting a horrible possibility.

"Tell me I don't have to drink blood," I said to Milar.

He looked at me, then shook his head and chuckled. "I highly doubt you're a vampire, Bob."

"How do you know?"

He shrugged. "I really don't. But blood isn't just liquid; there are cells throughout it. If you can't digest solids you can't digest them either. Plus, there's not really a lot of nutrition there." He shook his head. "No, I'm thinking liquid energy drinks, protein shakes, things like that."

That was a big of a comfort, but I still had that nagging, lingering dread. Until it turned out he was right. Those athletic supplement drinks and mixes seem to do the trick nicely. And it turns out I can taste still, so that's nice.

The down side is the liquid literally runs straight through me. It takes a little while, and apparently I absorb what I need from osmosis or something. But when it comes time to go...it's time to go and there's no holding it back.

On the bright side, the timeframe for the flowthrough is almost always the same. About four hours from when I drink something down, it's leaving. And because it's not digested it's not as messily nasty as bowel movements used to be. Still...

The other down side? I tried a shot of Jameson.

Doesn't work. No buzz from alcohol. Dang it.

Neither does Mr. Happy. No blood flow, so no way to make things happen down there. Unless I can make like a Ninja master and learn how to control my heart and make it pump, the way I can control my other muscles somehow.

No idea how to do that, though.

Super dang it.

Oh well, not too many girls probably want to date a dead guy anyway.

Still...

The other thing we wondered about was injuries. It's impossible to go through life without getting hurt. And if a body can't heal, that would make immortality, or stasis, or whatever you want to call it, really sucky.

Turns out, I can heal. After a fashion. And with a bit of effort.

I don't bleed, because no heartbeat. But I still need to put pressure on a wound, because I also don't clot and form a scab either. Put pressure on and use that cool skin glue that doctors use now. Then wait, and drink a bunch of protein shakes.

Not sure what happens or how, but the wound knits itself back together.

Takes a long time, though. Probably twice as long as a cut would have back in normal life.

Doesn't hurt as much as it used to, though. Not completely pain-free, but it's a duller feeling, more easily tolerated.

So that's nice

It took us weeks, going into months, to figure all this out. And I was starting to get a little stir crazy. Nice as my suite was, there was only so much being cooped up in the same place I was prepared to take. Especially since my "waking", functional, days were so much longer than normal people's, I had a lot of time without company.

Yeah, yeah. The internet.

People on the internet get old fast.

Yeah, yeah. Movies and books.

They don't take the place of people.

So I became more and more determined to get out and stretch my legs in the world again.

We'd ordered me a fairly nice, if small, wardrobe, so it wasn't like I was going to go running around in scrubs. And despite being dead, or in stasis, or whatever, I still looked ok. My hair had stopped growing, which was fine. And I was a little pale because of no blood flow. But I wasn't any more hideous to look at than I ever had been.

No reason I couldn't go mingle with normal people, except for the secrecy of the research.

Which was, of course, the rub.

Secrecy.

Near as I could figure, the project wasn't doing anything strictly speaking illegal. As long as the subjects truly were volunteers, anyway. But Ken, and especially Milar, were adamant about secrecy, to the point where every door in or out of the building required a magnetic keycard to open. Except for the emergency fire exits. They couldn't legally lock those from the inside.

But those were all alarmed and monitored by cameras, and there were cameras all throughout and surrounding the building grounds.

No one was coming in our getting out without the security team knowing about it, and allowing it.

But after several months in this place, I was getting to the point where I didn't care.

I knew how to navigate life in this new state of being now, and had given Ken and Milar a ton of data to use for the project. I bore them no ill will, but I also didn't feel obliged to be their serving man forever, either. It was quickly nearing the point where I was going to go, whether they liked it or not.

What were the going to do, shoot me?

First of all, they wouldn't do that.

Second of all, yeah it would hurt getting shot. But that's all it would do. Near as we could tell from our findings, short of actually burning me to ash, not much was going to kill me besides starvation.

It would suck healing from it, but getting shot wouldn't stop me from leaving if I really wanted to. Might not even slow me down.

But again, they wouldn't do that.

Or so I thought.

They day I learned the falsehood of that assumption was the day I decided I was out, never to return.

It was late, almost midnight, and I was taking my normal evening stroll through the building. It was something I had gotten into the habit of doing when everyone but security was gone and I had nothing to do. A relic of my normal life, and the need to keep myself and my muscles in shape.

I'd grown to love evening walks back in the day. Or I assume I did, considering how quickly I picked up the habit.

Regardless, as I was strolling down the second floor hallway, I saw a light on just before where the corridor turned left up ahead.

Milar's office. At first I wondered if he'd just forgotten to turn it off, but then I heard voices as I got closer and I realized no, he hadn't yet left for the night.

It was Wednesday, and he had an early morning teleconference on Thursdays. He was going to be a hurting unit in the morning.

I thought to stick my head in and tell him to get lost for home, but as I neared the ajar door leading to his office, I recognized the other voice and realized Milar was on the phone, and he had it on speaker while he was typing away on this computer.

I'd heard the voice before. It belonged to one of the money men who managed the contributions from the patrons of Milar's work here. Mr. Okuba, Milar had called him once in my hearing. Sounded like a Japanese name to me, but his deep bass voice didn't have even a hint of an accent.

Okuba was speaking now, and I came to a halt as I heard his words, a shiver going up my spine.

"If you've learned all you can from him, when will you proceed to the next subject?"

"I don't think we're ready to go there yet, sir. The subject still is learning and we are gaining great data. And we haven't finished collating what we have taken so far."

"At this point, is there anything he can give that wouldn't be redundant with what you already have?"

I could practically hear Milar's shrug. "Probably not."

"Again, after you dispose of this subject, when will you be ready to move on to the next?"

That shiver became a shard of alarm. When Milar answered without hesitation, alarm became outright fear, and outrage.

"Probably three to four months. We'll need time to reformulate the treatment to account for the—"

"Unacceptable. Time is of the essence, Dr. Milar. You know this."

"Yes sir, I do. But you can't—"

"Then I suggest you proceed to the next stage. Immediately."

A long paused, the MIlar said, "Yes, sir." I could hear in his voice that he did not like the order he had just been given.

But he also was going to carry it out.

He was going to order the disposal of their test subject. Me. Throw me out like a piece of garbage. Except worse, because they'd be killing me.

They'd justify it in their minds by thinking I was dead already anyway, and only "living" on borrowed time due to the work they were doing. And I was legally dead, to boot. So would it really be murder?

And if it was, did one murder really matter when weighed against the benefit that could accrue to countless other human beings down the line?

It struck me then that there had likely been other test subjects before me. Maybe many others. The utterly implacable insistence on secrecy took on a whole new meaning right then.

I about rushed in and smashed Milar's head in.

But no, I was not made of the same stuff he and Ken were. I wasn't going to harm them just because they meant to harm me.

I simply walked away from his office to the elevator, then went to my suite and threw as many of my things as I could carry into a bag.

Then I left.

The alarm wailed as I smashed open the fire exit at the rear of the building. I could picture in my mind's eye the security guy, drowsy from the lateness of the hour, jerking upright and flailing around as he struggled to figure out was was going on for a second.

It wouldn't take him long to zero in on my departure, so I ran. I sprinted full out across the parking lot toward the line of trees separating this lot from the next.

Unlike when I'd run cross country in High School, my heart didn't pound and my lungs didn't burn, my legs didn't wobble and my sweat didn't pour out of me like a faucet left to run.

I just ran, mechanically pumping my legs and arms and I'm pretty sure moving faster than I ever had, even back in my prime.

It was only after the building had vanished from site behind the tree line and I turned left toward the actual woods on the far side of this next lot that I realized I had just uncovered another memory; I hadn't discovered the Cross Country things on my Bob Shepherd research assignment. That came from within.

I smiled as I passed out of the light in the parking lot and into the shadows of the woods.

I'd uncovered more truth about myself. More would come as I continued to live this new life.

And I would uncover other truths as well. The truth of who the shadowy men who had commissioned this program were. Those men who would casually condemn me and others like me to advance their cause.

I'd find them. And I'd let the world know who—and what—they were.

Contemplating that, my smile became more grim.

And I passed on into the shadows.

CROWDFUNDING HEROES

It would not have been possible to put this collection together without the support of the following people, who backed my Indiegogo campaign. Thank you all! Your generosity and trust made this a reality. I hope you enjoy the final product as much I enjoyed creating it. You rock!

Amy Davis
Angie Oakley
Allen Lakner
Dr. Michel S Pawlowski
Arkie Bear
Gavin Hawk
Nancy Husanu
Jan Thomas
Lance Christensen
Stonecold Steve
James Nealon
James Joswick
Grady Houger
Mortiz Kraemer

M J Rabe
Cate Henry
Forrest Bishop
Philip Smith
Catherine White
Kimberly Riano
Nathaniel Story
Jed Anglin
Jeffrey Oxman
Timothy Clark
David Talley
Joe Katzman
Ole Sandok
Pierre Auger
William Finlay

MESSAGE FROM THE AUTHOR

Thank you for reading my book. I hope you enjoyed reading it as much as I enjoyed writing it.

Every review helps an author out, so whether you loved this book, hated it, or something in between, please take a minute to tell other readers what you thought. All of the online retailers make it very easy to do, and I would really appreciate it.

Feel free to come say hi at my website, on Twitter, or on Gab. I always enjoy hearing from readers, especially since you all are, collectively, my boss.

I also have a weekly podcast, Story Time With Michael Kingswood, where I read stories and talk through some of the latest goings on in my world. I'd love to see you there.

Thanks again. My best to you and yours.

Warm Regards,
Michael Kingswood

MAILING LIST

If you enjoyed this book and would like word on new releases and special deals from Michael Kingswood, sign up for his newsletter on his website. Guaranteed to be spam-free, you can opt out at any time. And you can rest assured he will not share your information with anyone, for any reason.

https://michaelkingswood.com/newsletter-signup/

ABOUT THE AUTHOR

Michael Kingswood has published more than 80 short stories, novellas, and novels. He has appeared in anthologies from WMG Publishing, Stark Press, and Knotted Road Press. A twenty year veteran of the US Navy's submarine force, he has four children and currently resides in San Diego.

Fans can contact him through his website, on Twitter, or on Gab.

Michael has a weekly podcast, Story Time With Michael Kingswood, where he reads his work and discusses writing, philosophy, and history. Subscribers are always welcome!

Listen on: YouTube Rumble Bitchute Odysee Podcast

MORE BOOKS BY MICHAEL KINGSWOOD

Glimmer Vale Chronicles

Glimmer Vale

Out-Dweller

Tollard's Peak

Robbed Blind

The Falconer's Stairs

Campaign Season

Glimmer Vale Chronicles Books 1-3

Stories From Glimmer Vale

Legacy

Hidden Magic

Captive Hearts

Wedding Gifts

Lost Credit

The Pericles Conspiracy

Passing In The Night

The Pericles Conspiracy

52 Stories In 2023

Volume One

Dawn Of Enlightenment

Masters Of The Sun

Novellas

What Lurks Between

The Necromancer's Lair

The Champion

Veritas Morte

Story Collections

Tales Of Adventure #1

Tales Of Adventure #2

Short Story 10-Pack

A Jar Of Mixed Treats

Short Mystery 10-Pack

Stories From Glimmer Vale, Volume 1

Stories From The Great Challenge

Short Fiction

Michael has also published a number of shorter works, which can be found at michaelkingswood.com/store.